THE COMPLETE DINERO DE SANGRE TRILOGY

BLOOD MONEY, BLOOD TIES, & BLOOD BOUND

LANA SKY

ACKNOWLEDGMENTS

Thanks so much to everyone who supported this draft along the way, including the many beta readers who provided encouragement! Please keep in mind that this story includes dark, graphic and explicit content matter that is not suitable for readers under the age of 18—or for readers who are uncomfortable with the following subject matter: explicit sex, mentions of sexual abuse, mentions of child abuse, mentions of eating disorders, graphic depictions of violence, and mentions of self-harm.

BLOOD MONEY

Blood Money

Blood Money By Lana Sky

Cover Design and Interior Formatting by Charity Chimni
Editing and Proofreading by Charity Chimni

People always laughed when they heard his name, Domino. Paired with his unique attire and penchant for straw cowboy hats, the moniker attributed to his unique allure as a bodyguard. As a result, people rarely took him seriously upon their first meeting.

Who does this motherfucker think he is? Skeptical men would sometimes ask that very question while strolling from my father's office—all while Domino himself would watch quietly from the sidelines of the sprawling boardroom they'd been summoned to.

The next time they were ever seen again would be in pieces, grimly documented by a medical examiner called to investigate the cause of death. Most determinations were just guesses, of course—*wood chipper accident, bear attack,* and the average *sky diving mishap.*

My father controlled the police commissioner, so the official reason didn't really matter. It could be as outlandish as "tiger mauling," and no one ever batted an eye. So was the hold the Pavalos family had over Terra Rodea—at least until the day my family was upended and Domino, that faithful soldier, set his sights on *me*.

Killing me would have been merciful on his end. Even a supposed wild bear attack would have been a better ending than the one he had in mind.

I never knew the extent of the hatred such a man could harbor.

I never knew the violence one human soul could be capable of.

I never realized that, when it came to destroying my father and toppling his million-dollar empire, Domino's price would have been relatively low in the grand scheme.

To betray my family, Domino Valenciaga requested only one thing.

Me.

CHAPTER ONE

He's late.

I try not to dwell on the potential explanations, or the fact that every passing second he delays risks us losing the reservation it took months to secure. It's just ten minutes past our scheduled meeting time of six. So what if he hasn't been answering his phone since then, either?

I know what—he has his dick in someone else.

Though, I shouldn't dwell on that. *Utilize your coping mechanisms more*, my therapist liked to harp. The main one she touted was counting to five whenever the anxiety started to build. *Ground yourself, Ada. Think of one positive to go along with every breath.*

One.

I'm wearing the new Alexander Marenti summer design from his exclusive collection, and it shows off my body well.

Two.

I hate this stupid dress.

Three.

Daddy got it only as a pity offering for missing my birthday dinner—and only on the say-so of that cunt bitch secretary of his who handled all of his afterthought social obligations these days.

Four.

Tristan's fucking Alexi again.

Five.

He's balls deep within that whore, and that's why he's late. If he shows up now, it will only prove me right. Again. The bastard can only last exactly six-point-seven minutes with an extra wasted to button-up his shitty chinos—

"Hey, baby!"

Someone grabs me from behind, sliding their hands along my hips, and I smother a hiss of disgust. Tristan. His cloying cologne gives him away, and I force my lips into a smile. "Hey, baby."

My nostrils flare as I spin to face him, and I nearly choke. He reeks of that signature cologne—more so than usual. As if he dumped half the bottle over himself to disguise the stench of Alexi's shitty perfume and their eight-minute sex session.

I note that his pink lips are unusually wet as well, his dark hair playfully tousled.

Fuck him.

He's smiling, but it's strained around the edges. Alexi was always a biter from what I've heard, prone to leaving marks that made him wince for days whenever we kissed. It was one of his telltale signs.

I promised not to take him back after the first time.

It's the tenth. Maybe eleventh, but I'm still here, letting him plant a chaste peck on my lips. The way he kisses me when Alexi's taste is on his tongue, and he hasn't popped a breath mint yet.

Fuck. I cross over to the bubbling fountain near the restaurant's entrance. Overall, the courtyard attached to the venue is beautiful enough to justify its long waitlist and hefty prices, with a Spanish design and a manicured garden. The fountain itself is large enough to swim in, sporting a statue of an angel in the center. Briefly, I consider what might happen if I sank to my knees and dunked my head beneath the water's surface. Perhaps for "five minutes" of calm.

Then I imagine how better it would feel to hold Tristan's head down instead.

Objectively, I know how it looks from the outside. For the daughter of Roy Pavalos to chase after some bottom-feeding lawyer who can't keep his dick in his pants where the town whore is concerned.

It's pathetic.

It's strategic. Said bottom-feeding lawyer just so happens to be the one pawn standing in between my father and a potential federal indictment.

I don't love Tristan. He's merely an assignment. My duty to the family.

Fucking me gives him a reason to drag his heels, greasing up the wheels of justice just long enough for Roy Pavalos to find a way out of the mess he created for himself. As thanks, Daddy keeps my debit cards well-funded and pays my car note. Though hell, it's not like I have a choice.

I'm not allowed to seek out my own employment.

I'm not even allowed to book a gyno appointment without his say-so.

Why? Because we are *Pavalos. Pavalos. Pavalos…*

From the day I was born with that goddamn last name, I've been cursed. My life has never been my own. Everything I do, down to the clothing I wear, is with my father's approval. So is the responsibility of being born a Pavalos. At least with a mother like mine who lacked the will to divorce my father for the sake of her children like his prior two wives did. We're both no better than dolls, placed beautifully on a shelf for the world to admire.

"Ada? You okay, baby?"

Tristan slides his hands around my ribcage, ghosting my breasts. It takes everything I have not to cringe from him.

"I'm sorry I'm late," he says, flashing a smile that displays the mouth of beautiful teeth he bought last year with one of my father's bribe payments. "I got held up by work. You ready for dinner? I know this is important to you."

Important. As if he would ever know what truly matters in my world. I don't even have that privilege.

Still, I smile and preen the way I've been taught my whole life. If I'm a marionette on strings, my mother, Lia Pavalos, is the expert porcelain doll. By the time she married my father, the woman had refined how to present a vision of perfection to the public. How to lie. How to sleep with a man who regularly fucks another and how to look amazing while doing so.

"I'm fine," I say. In fact, I never stopped smiling. "Let's go eat," I add, linking my arm through his. "I'm starving."

In reality, I haven't eaten a solid meal since Monday. It's Friday. That's nearly a full week, but nowhere near close to my record. The hunger gnawing at my stomach is a constant distraction, battling with everything else fighting for my attention at the present—and ignoring it might be the one damn thing I'm allowed to do without input from anyone else. I can pick when to silence my twisting, growling stomach, and when not to.

Tonight, I'll make myself try some crackers, at least. Maybe some fish.

I'm fine.

In a place so beautiful, how could I not be?

The restaurant's interior is lavishly furnished with walls an emerald-green and black marble floors. I forget the establishment's name, but it's something gloriously Spanish, and it's a perfect setting to serve as the stage upon which I'll play my role in the Pavalos family tonight.

That as the perfect daughter with the perfect boyfriend, on a perfect evening without a care in the world; it doesn't matter that every damn aspect of it is a lie.

"You've barely eaten your food," Tristan says once we've been seated and served. It all passed in a blur; I don't even remember what I ordered.

Soup, it seems, a nice contrast to Tristan's perfectly seared steak.

"What do you mean? It's delicious!" I make a show of prodding at the dish before me, composed of chunks of carrots and potato—Porrusalda, I think it's called—but I'm too preoccupied to even put on a convincing act. The press and the paparazzi are watching. After all, tonight's guest list has been coincidentally tailored so that everyone in this city who matters happens to be dining right here and right now. My father planned it this way, I'm sure. Even something as simple as a date has been carefully crafted to his benefit.

And that's the catch.

By tomorrow he will be arrested for murder, and no fancy dinner will be able to change that narrative. What a way for it all to end. For decades he spent his life playing the city as a chessboard, but this is one game that he won't dominate. We're already in checkmate.

"I know I haven't been the best lately," Tristan declares, reaching over to grab my hand. "I can tell you're upset."

I force a laugh. "I'm fine, really." Inside, I'm shaking, wondering what gave me away. I've spent six months of this relationship faking and faking and *faking*. I don't think he's ever caught on once, or maybe I've just been too wrapped up in myself to notice.

Now, he's eyeing me in a way he hasn't before, with his blue eyes narrowed over my face. Ironically, he looks like a lawyer, and I guess he must be a damn good one considering how badly my father wanted to extend his influence over him.

"I know I fucked up." The intensity in his voice catches me off guard. "I know I did. I promise that next time I'll be better. I won't let it happen again."

"You mean you won't fall into Alexi's bed again," I say, snatching a piece of bread from the customary basket resting between us. It's some fancy, flaky artisan style, and it tastes like ashes as I choke down a bite.

"Ada…" Tristan's cheeks flush, eyes widening with guilt, but I don't feel like having this conversation right now. In the grand scheme, I'm not even that upset. I was never invested in this relationship. Tristan isn't my type, but there's still the principle of the matter. The man is lucky enough to date the daughter of Roy Pavalos, and yet he still can't stop sleeping with a trailer trash whore.

"You should eat," I say, smiling wider. "I'm sure you can't stay long, what with your busy schedule."

"You always do this," Tristan says, setting his silverware down noisily.

I raise an eyebrow, and he continues, "Shut me down. You never talk about anything, not even yourself. Sometimes it's like dating the wall."

A wall or maybe a doll? It's simply the way I was raised to be. To always perform my pretty perfect role.

Until now. I could blame the wine, or the fact that I'm drinking on an empty stomach. Regardless, words bubble up before I can hold them at bay. "I'm not quite as stupid as I look, you do realize." I don't recognize the hard tone—or maybe I do, just in a very different pitch. My father speaks this way. Bluntly and cold. "I know you've been fucking her. Frankly, I haven't cared, but if you could be a little more discreet about it, I'd appreciate that."

He blinks. "Baby, I—"

"I think I want the flan for dessert," I say with my best smile, snatching a leather-bound menu. "We can pose for a picture of you feeding me a bite—"

"This is something we should talk about, Ada. You know, like a real couple?"

He has the nerve to sound so earnest. As if he doesn't know damn well what this really is. Not a relationship, but a business transaction.

"You were promoted to partner a month after dating me," I point out absently. "Don't tell me you believe that was solely on your merits as an amazing lawyer."

He frowns. I've insulted him. Good.

Wadding up my napkin, I set it aside and make eye contact with a passing waiter. "More wine," I tell him.

"Baby, I think you've had enough."

"I'll tell you when I've had enough," I say, grabbing my near-empty glass. I drain it with one hard pull and relish the liquid dripping down my throat.

My father enjoys the same vices. In reality, we're far more alike than either of us would care to admit. It's why he kept me close, long after he's shoved Pablo and Demelio—his two sons from a previous marriage—from his life. They challenged him. They took offense to his vicious actions and tyrannical ways with money. They had morals.

Souls.

They also had two different mothers from mine. Mine, Lia, is Roy's third wife and least impressive. The modest, religious daughter of a judge, she gave Roy a softer public edge than his previous debutante bride or the beauty queen with a penchant for charity he left her for.

Lia humbled me, he likes to say. Humbled him the way fire humbled the Devil. She merely gave credence to his more self-deprecating attributes. Before her, he blamed his problems on liquor and cocaine. Now? He blames God, disguising his viler acts behind a repentant sinner's façade.

"...don't know what's gotten into you," Tristan is murmuring, once I bother to pay attention to him again.

Into me. How would he know? He's never known the real me. I've always been a grinning puppet on his arm, or a perky sex doll.

The reality of who I am is a mash of far different descriptors. Liquor, cocaine, and laxatives. My vice arsenal.

In this moment, I crave all three. I'm not upset about Tristan—I'm not. It's how damn hot it is in this supposedly grand establishment. It's how bright the lights are. It's the fact that my arraignment outfit is already picked out.

The fact that I've been practicing my lines in the mirror for the moment I'm inevitably interviewed by the police. The fact that I've already programmed the state penitentiary number into my cell phone with the understanding that soon enough, calls from that building will dictate my entire life.

I might as well be imprisoned there, too, though the thought is far more appealing than I suppose it should be. Ironically, I'd have far more freedom behind bars.

"Ada? I think we really need to talk. There's something—"

"I need to use the bathroom," I say, rising to my feet. That piece of bread weighs on my stomach. I feel too heavy. Dirty. Unclean. My mother instructs the maids to clean the floors seven times a day.

Is this really so different?

"Ada, wait." He grabs my hand, and I just eye it, feeling detached from the slim, manicured fingers in his grasp. These hands have done things my mind can never comprehend. Vicious, vile, disgusting things.

All in the name of family.

"Ada? Fine, if you want to do this now, I'll come clean. I know about the indictment."

Blood rushes through my ears in a torrent of deafening noise. When I blink, Tristan's lips are still moving, forcing my brain to play catch up to understand.

"W-What?"

"I know, baby," he says gently. "Why do you think I was really late? I was busting my ass to make sure the goddamn reporters wouldn't try to catch you here alone. I know you're worried. And I could lose my job for this, but…it's been squashed. I don't know how, but according to my contacts at the precinct, the warrant to arrest your father has been put on indefinite hold. I can't get any answers as to why. Maybe they jumped the gun—"

"What do you mean?"

"Your father won't be arrested tomorrow, baby." He rises to his feet, pulling me into his arms. I think he's genuinely surprised when I wrench away. "What's wrong?"

My smile is gone, replaced by a look that haunts me in the polished reflective wall across from our table—one of abject horror.

Daddy won't be hauled off to jail tomorrow, plunging our family into international public scandal and turmoil.

I won't have to wear my chosen black dress or practice my "sad face" in the mirror for hours before facing the press.

I won't have to fear getting a call from the state pen every day.

Roy Pavalos will stay in my home. In my life.

Controlling my world with an iron fist.

"I need to use the bathroom." I twist out of Tristan's reach, staggering in the direction of the restrooms.

"Wait—" he grabs my arm, displaying a persistence he rarely has. "There's something else. I want you to come away with me. Tonight. I've already made the arrangements, and we can—"

"What?" I'm barely listening to him.

A flicker of movement catches my eye from across the room near the window. Or where the window once was. A hole is there now. Before it, a dance of swirling glass floats through the air, suspended for a second that seems frozen in time.

Then an explosion of noise sends everything moving again. *Boom!* People start screaming. Running. Dazed, I look back at Tristan, but he's not there anymore…

Or at least he's not on his feet.

My brain takes ages to connect the dots with the red liquid splattered all over the floor and the body lying nearby. Except it's not right. Can't be Tristan—the proportions are all wrong. There are two arms, two legs, a torso, but no head…

I'm aware that my mouth is open, but no words come out.

All I can do is stare.

Then run. It's an instinctive motion, pivoting on my heel, to join the press of people racing for the nearest exit. There's no rhyme or reason to it. No thinking.

I make it so easy for the man who must have been standing behind me all along, waiting to attack.

I see his fist come from nowhere and realize that nothing I can do will stop it from colliding with my skull.

The sickening thud that comes next, somehow sounds more violent than the previous noise that shattered the quiet atmosphere.

And the world goes black.

CHAPTER TWO

Some men wear their intentions so blatantly. You can look them in the eye and see every thought in their head rattling around, as legible as newspaper headlines.

In my world, the only things that matter are what could make a splashy news story, after all.

People love the sordid nature of my father's political career—a rags to riches fairy tale and a shining example of hard work. And ambition. Everyone ignores the darker side of his inspiring story, like the supposed cartel ties that catapulted him to power, or the origin of the money that funds his decade-long political run. They love the mystery of who he's fucking and what business move he might make next. The flashy stuff.

No one cares that he's a true monster. That he rules the lives of those around him with an iron fist. That he's cruel and volatile with a temper to match his ambition.

Frankly, those details are boring, the stuff everyone already knows. Men with power have secrets. They live double lives and aren't nearly as perfect as they want the world to believe.

My life certainly wasn't perfect. I think all of us knew that there was always a time limit ruthlessly ticking the seconds down until it all fell apart. You can only live on blood money for so long before the lies and secrets start to catch up.

Ours are plenty, locked away in a closet so full of skeletons it might as well be a crypt. My father had a way of justifying it all. For the sake of the family.

For my mother.

For me.

We were tethered to him beyond any familial ties.

He ensured as much. From the age of fifteen, I ceased to be his daughter, Ada-Maria Lucia Pavalos.

I became his accomplice. For years, every sick, sordid undertaking of his has stained my soul. I couldn't plead ignorance if I tried.

The day he went to federal prison, I wouldn't be far behind him.

But now, I don't have to worry about that possibility anymore—*I'm dead.*

As MY AWARENESS returns in bits and pieces, my first coherent thought is that I wish my head had been the one blown apart. Not Tristan's.

I know that for certain—his body was the one lying on the floor. Someone killed him.

Though, hell, maybe I've gotten my wish after all—they're just a poor shot and failed to kill me outright. My skull is on fire, every movement resonating like a kick to the head. I'd scream if I could, but my lips remain frozen, clamped together.

Am I paralyzed?

Or drugged?

I should know the difference…

"…she's a sexy piece of ass, ain't she?" The voice drips into my skull, uttered gruffly, but I don't recognize the speaker. A male. Fear drips through my veins, fighting to wake up my sleeping nerves and lifeless muscles.

Nausea rips through me, and I can feel the impulse to vomit. Purge. Reset.

But I can't.

"Don't touch her," another man replies. His voice is softer, and I strain to make it out more clearly. They sound close, but muffled, as if I'm hearing them from underwater. "Dom said she was his alone. No marks. No injuries. You better pray you didn't bruise her with that punch—"

"If he wanted her scot-free, then the bastard should have gotten her himself. We did all the fucking work and brought her out here, to the middle of fucking nowhere. Why not have a little taste? If he plans on doing to the little witch what he's done to the rest, it would be a damn shame to let this sexy bitch go to waste."

The rest…

"I've warned you, Trey," the second man replies. "He said we can't touch her."

My body is moved without any action on my part, and I land heavily on something solid and unyielding. A floor? It's colder than the tile in my bathroom. Marble?

Not the flooring of the restaurant, I suspect.

Where the hell am I?

Sensation is returning to the rest of my body, at least, in excruciatingly slow increments. The pain in my head is centered along my right temple—but that's the least of my worries.

Harsh, an unfamiliar touch grazes my thigh, inching beneath the hemline of my dress. Higher. Too high. Boldly, they shove my panties aside, prodding the flesh beneath the lace barrier. Horror rises up so fiercely I can taste it—but I'm paralyzed, unable to control my limbs, even to flinch. My eyelids are too heavy to lift. I can't even speak.

"Damn," the gruffer of the two men breathes, sounding sickeningly close. "She's like a goddamn little furnace—"

"Enough." That voice is unlike the others. Instantly, I recognize it. The guttural baritone shoots through me, triggering a sensation few men have ever inspired.

It takes a lot to scare the daughter of Roy Pavalos. My childhood was filled with inviting criminals and drug dealers over for dinner. My teenage years were spent in their beds, and all the while my father lorded over every single interaction like a tyrant king.

But it's rare to meet someone that truly sends a shiver through my core. In fact, I think only one man has ever fit the bill.

Domino Valenciaga.

He had an accent retained from a past no one knew anything about. Something from Latin America, maybe Portuguese, or Brazilian. The slight inflection turned every word he said into a double-edged sword, musical almost. Lethal in another sense. He was the only person I ever knew to make a death sentence sound beautiful.

For five years, he's been my father's righthand man, recruited from only God knows where, standing faithfully by his side ever since.

A funny thought comes to me now, despite the stench of blood in my nostrils and the fear pummeling through my chest like a barrage of blows—I've rarely spoken to him directly, apart from the typical greeting.

"Hello," I'd say.

His reply was always the same. *"Ada-Maria."*

It's a strange admission now, but I used to have nightmares, starring the very specific way he could say my name, mangling the two syllables into one unique utterance. "Nightmares" that left me so wet I had to relieve the ache with my own fingers.

It's his voice I'm hearing now, though he's speaking too quickly, and my head hurts too badly to follow. I only catch snippets.

"…blood. You killed him in front of her?" Domino asks. His speech is so flat that one can never get a read on his emotions. I've heard him praise my father and curse his enemies, all while sounding no different.

What is he doing here?

"Didn't have a choice," the second of the two men explains. "You wanted him dead. The bastard hired elite security. The restaurant was the only way."

Wanted him dead.

I keep seeing flashes of Tristan. His eyes. His face. His body lying prone on the ground, covered in blood.

A wave of panic drowns me in terror. I don't know how my body remains so still, each breath slow and heavy. Whatever drug they gave me, it's damn good.

So good, I almost give in to the mind-numbing calm that smothers most of my thoughts. Why fight? It feels better to be high…

"Still, you killed him in front of her," Domino says. "That might complicate matters. I aimed to use her ignorance to my advantage. Now she'll have an idea of the danger she's in."

Danger?

"You didn't say not to fucking kill no one in front of this bitch," the first speaker interjects, his brashness clashing harshly with Domino's suave monotone.

The drug in my system is strong—definitely a sedative—but it must be wearing off. All at once, sensation returns to my face, enough that I can flutter my eyelids, gleaning snatches of my surroundings snippets at a time.

I'm in a room, I think. Somewhere with dim lighting. Blinking is a struggle, turning my perception of the world into a disjointed slide show.

I see a shadow. A man? He moves quickly, growing larger by the second.

My heart races as a smell itches my nostrils, mingling with the stench of blood. Spice. Masculine musk. Lethality.

"No," Domino replies, his voice washing over me as that shadow becomes even larger. Him? "But do you know what I *did* ask you to do?"

My belly flips, picking up on the slow, subtle inflection that colors his usually emotionless voice.

"I asked you not to touch her."

"We had to carry her in here," the man argues. "Didn't we—"

"That's not what I meant. Two fingers. That's how many you shoved inside of her cunt just now, am I correct? Not to mention what you've done to her face."

A whoosh of air breezes past my head, triggering another wave of nausea. I can physically gag—and at the same time, I'm able to keep my eyes open for longer than a second.

The man standing before me is the devil, I'm sure of it. My mother spent enough of my childhood peppering my bedtimes with stories of the creature awaiting me if I dared to sin. The only problem?

I'd been born into sin, committing my first immoral act the second I'd been given the name Pavalos. This family is evil incarnate, my life an endless parade of sin after sin.

But if I ever felt the need to repent, it would be now.

The devil is a cold soul with dark eyes devoid of compassion or warmth. They stare at something beyond me, set in a face so beautiful it could only belong to a fallen angel who dared to forsake God himself.

Dazed, I realize that I've seen this face before—every day, in fact, for the past five years. He's certainly no angel, just a man with the beauty of a divine being.

Domino Valenciaga.

"Apologies, if I didn't make myself clear, before," he says, his voice so soft, his demeanor so casual—which makes the fact that he draws a blade from a sheath strapped to his belt all the more terrifying.

My father loved that gimmick of his. While his compatriots hired private guards armed with military-grade weapons, *his* man required only a blade, one that he displayed openly from a battered leather sheath he kept on his belt, no matter the outfit or occasion.

The unique weapon gave him an air of mystery, and made him unpredictable in a world based on surefire odds and getting one over on an opponent.

My father liked to call Domino his wildcard. His ace in the hole. His berserker.

As disoriented as I am, I can see why. He's riveting as the light reflects off his blade and highlights the lone glint in his eye that proves without a shadow of a doubt... He's soulless. An animal relying purely on instinct.

The will to kill comes as easy to him as breathing.

"I told you she was mine." His tone remains so level that the knife in his hand could be as trivial as a cigar. Something held merely to pass the time.

Until he crosses beyond my line of sight with a slow, easy stride.

A noise echoes next, so chilling that it snaps what remnants of the drug are still controlling my ability to move. I flinch, rolling onto my back with a better view of the ceiling above and the room's layout overall.

It's spacious, but I don't recognize the color scheme. Beige walls. A high, white ceiling.

And red liquid spraying in an arch as if by some new age fountain—or in this case, from a man clutching his right arm to his chest as he staggers into my line of view.

I've never heard someone scream like this.

Liar. But it's a sound I've tried my damned hardest to suppress.

The cry of a man in pain is so different from any other. So guttural, almost a howl—but it's the squeal you watch out for. That high-pitched inflection point that heralds true pain.

This man is nowhere near there. Yet. "What the fuck—"

"Raise your hand," Domino says.

My head lolls toward the sound of his voice and I find him, standing tall just a few steps away. He tosses his knife into the air, catching it by the handle easily. There's no mark on the blade, but it's the only weapon capable of causing so much blood…

"Do what he says," another man warns. He's too far back for me to see his face. I only catch a shadow from the corner of my eye.

"Your hand," Domino requests, snapping his fingers. "Lift it."

Still groaning, the other man complies, revealing fingers streaked in scarlet that tremble with agony. A gash slices into the flesh of his forearm, the source of the bleeding.

I am *so* high. The lighting plays off my vision, turning every drop of scarlet into a blazing, flickering trail like neon paint. It drips, drips, drips as Domino inspects the limb, his face unreadable from this angle.

Then he moves in a way that resembles some sick, beautiful dance. Without warning, he grabs the man's arm, ignoring how he whines as a result. Then he brandishes the knife.

The man sputters, "N-No—"

My eyelids fall, drenching me in darkness. I don't see the action that results in the horrific scream that echoes next, but I can guess. Something to do with the blade hitting a firm surface that gives with a crunching squelch.

The screaming takes on an almost musical quality, building to a high-pitched crescendo. Then, *bingo*. There it is. That note of true agony.

The one my father taught me how to play.

Disgust rips through my body, crawling up my throat. I gag so hard I lurch onto my stomach, forced to brace my hands against the floor as liquid issues from my lips. Over and over.

I'm still choking on bile when I sense a flicker of movement come from behind.

"Two fingers for the two you used to soil what is mine," Domino says. "Now get the fuck out. You—" his shift in tone makes me suspect he's speaking to the other man beyond my view. "Take his share and get him out of here. Now."

"Yes, sir."

Footsteps echo off the polished flooring—marble as I suspected, a tan color with white swirls interspersed within the mass—and the screaming grows distant, eventually silenced altogether.

My fear builds unchecked, and I turn my focus inward, fixating on every hair out of place and every throbbing inch of skin.

I think they hit me, whoever they were…

The same men who shot Tristan through the head. A whimpering cry escapes my throat, and I'm startled by the genuine pain in it.

Tristan…

He was a dick, but I've never seen someone shot before.

I've never smelled so much fresh blood.

I guess this means we won't be named the city's "Hottest New Young Couple" in the society pages…

"You're awake." That voice.

I didn't imagine it—or any of this for that matter. It's real. Even in my imagination, I couldn't fake the unique way that baritone deepens when it comes to me.

I focus on my breathing as more control of my limbs returns. I have enough strength to lift my head, viewing the strange room from a different angle.

It resembles a foyer of some sort. Large and circular with a high ceiling and a rounded archway leading off to a shadowed hall up ahead.

It's not the foyer of Casa De Mio, my father's estate. Neither do I recognize the space as belonging to one of his offices or associates. It doesn't even match the background of the restaurant.

Could this property belong to Domino?

"Look at me, Ada-Maria."

I shiver, feeling his voice vibrate through my bones. Somehow, I muster up the energy to crane my neck enough to see him standing over me. He retrieved a cloth from somewhere, using it to leisurely clean off his blade. This time it is streaked with red. Blood.

The color plays off the gold in his skin, enhancing the darkness of those piercing eyes that I've seen reduce men to quivering puddles in an instant.

Something's wrong. That inner voice tickles the back of my skull, growing louder as more realizations register on my tired brain. For one, I don't see my father. I don't hear his loud, booming voice, tinged with the playful accent that added to his charm.

Attempting to speak is a grueling exercise that seems to take hours to put into fruition. In reality, it must only be seconds. "W-Where…is Papa?"

His eyes cut to mine with a ruthless intensity, so sharp that it's like another dose of a far different drug. Fear? It seeps through my veins, ten times stronger than the previous times I shared a room with him.

He takes his time cleaning off his blade before re-sheathing it. "We weren't meant to speak like this," he says, gesturing with his free hand to the room around us. Then he snaps his fingers.

"Yes, sir?" a new voice calls out. A woman's, as foreign to me as the two men were.

"Help Ms. Pavalos get ready for dinner, Ines. The dining room, please. Ten minutes."

"Yes, sir."

Soft footsteps pad in my direction, and I turn toward the archway to find a woman entering through it. She's petite, wearing a gray dress, her hair slicked back. Barring the color of her attire, she could be one of the maids from my father's complex.

She approaches me, stooping to brace her hand against my shoulder. With a surprising amount of strength, she guides me to stand on legs that quiver like jelly.

It hurts to move, even enough to look over my shoulder, but I do, seeking out the figure with his back to me.

I try to speak. "Domino… Domino!"

He retreats through another doorway without a word.

"This way, Miss," Ines says, urging me forward.

Pain shoots up my spine with every step. My hip feels sore and bruised. Only God knows what happened after the restaurant.

Or how long I was unconscious. Between my legs feels damp, and an acrid stench reaches my nose with horrifying implications. Urine?

"This way." The woman guides me through a doorway, and I'm brought face to face with a woman so far from the image she spent thousands presenting to the world that I don't recognize her at first.

It's me.

It's funny that despite everything I've been through, nothing startles me more than seeing myself look like this. My hair is a rat's nest. My dress is torn, and blood streaks my thigh, visible through the slit. More dried blood is encrusted over my right temple, and my mascara is running.

My first impulse is to reach for my purse for my makeup pouch. Papa always prided appearance over all else. No matter what hell I'd been through, my foremost duty is to always look like I deserved to uphold the name Pavalos.

"We have ten minutes," Ines says, tugging at the sleeve of my dress. She has it undone, peeled down to my waist before I remember how to move.

The smell of urine grows stronger, definitely coming from me.

"S-Stop!" I bat her hand away and stagger to the counter, bracing my hands flat against the sturdy surface. "Tristan. I...we need to call the police. Call my father. We need to—"

"We have ten minutes," the woman insists, but there's an urgent edge to her voice that wasn't there before.

Her eyes meet mine over the mirror's surface, an intense shade of brown that gleams like gold.

When she tugs at my dress again, I just let her, sinking into the fog dulling my thoughts. It's been days since I've been on a high like this. The mind-numbing daze where you can just sit back and lose hours at a time. I used to compare the feeling to that of taking a warm bath as a child, with a caring mother to bathe your limbs and wrap you nice and warm in a towel.

But this high is harsher. A literal experience of being stripped naked and bathed by a stranger, doused in sickly sweet perfume, and dressed in an outfit I don't recognize.

Domino. I cling to his name like a raft in a flash flood, fighting to stay above the rushing waves. He's here... For a reason. He brought me here for a reason. But where is my father? And Tristan...

"We return to Mr. Domino now," Ines says.

I blink, faced with another stranger, the polar opposite to the creature I found in the mirror. It's a second before I even realize that this woman is also me. I'm as unrecognizable as before but in a very different way.

I don't dress like this—Papa would never allow it. The dress is too thin, a gauzy white material through which the dark flesh around my nipples is visible. The fabric sparkles, beaming in the harsh lighting until it hurts to stare at myself head-on.

I look away, feeling my stomach lurch as the room starts to sway beneath my feet. My eyes latch onto a nearby object that glows like a beacon, and I lurch for it. "I'm gonna be sick—"

This time I let the vomit flow freely. Before I know it, I have two of my own fingers jabbing down my tender throat to bring up more. Everything I have so that I can reset my body. Start over fresh.

Then purge again once it all feels too much.

No amount of vomit could ease the worries bearing down on me, one after the other, however. I know that. I'd have to claw out my insides to feel lighter. Rip them right out...

"Miss?" A warm hand taps my shoulder. "We return to Mr. Domino now—"

"Leave me alone!" I cling to the basin of the toilet, watching multi-colored liquid swirl in the bowl. Tan. Brown. Yellow.

I don't even know what the liquid is a remnant of. I haven't eaten. Maybe it's my soul coming up in vile-colored pieces, the last thing of value my body has left to expel.

My therapist tells me that I've been lying to myself when I claim that purging makes me feel better. Lighter, more grounded.

You're deluding yourself, Ada, she would quip. *You tell yourself that to justify the self-harm. You know what would make you feel better? Honesty. Trusting the process of therapy. Getting to the root of the issues between you and your parents. We can start with your father…*

One good thing to come out of this nightmare is that I finally have proof that all those expensive sessions were bullshit. I had the right idea all along. With emptiness comes clarity.

Finally, I can think, despite my pounding head and the fear waiting to descend the second the drug fully wears off.

Tristan is dead. My father isn't here.

I'm alone in a strange place with Domino Valenciaga.

He's protecting me, of course. From something. Those men? He hurt one of them for touching me. I remember that much, at least. But the harder I try to think, the less logical thoughts I can grasp. It's like my mind is a sieve, filtering out everything but panic and paranoia.

Something is wrong.

And my first impulse has been the one ingrained into me since childhood. Wait for orders. Papa will handle it.

He always has.

I don't know how much time passes before I finally manage to stand, leaning against the toilet for stability. For the first time, I take in my surroundings fully.

Wherever we are, it's beautiful. This bathroom is the peak of luxury with golden fixtures and the same tanned marble from the circular foyer. A long counter lines one wall, with a full-length mirror behind it, displaying my body in stark relief.

God, I look so…sickly. So weak. A shivering waif barely able to stand on her own. As I turn to inspect the rest of the room, I realize that Ines is gone. Her insistence on a particular timeline rings in my ears like an ominous warning.

Mr. Domino said ten minutes.

Mr. Domino… I never knew he had his own house, let alone his own staff. I don't even know how much he made working for my family. Could he afford a place like this on his salary? My father paid well, I'm sure. But I don't think he would pay *this* well, not even to a man whose job was to guard his secrets with his life.

More panic starts to creep in as my memories return in full. Those men brought me here for a reason. *Take his share,* Domino told one of them. His share of what?

I push those thoughts out of my head and focus on returning to the sink. I wet my fingers and work them through my hair, trying to scrub away the dry blood there. I discover a scratch, but nothing deep enough to scar—one small consolation.

I'm shallow enough to sigh in relief. For now, I'm still Ada Pavalos, blessed with the face my father staked his entire reputation on. How could a man with such a beautiful, loving family be capable of any of the atrocities the rumors circling around the city claimed?

He's an intelligent man, but his greatest asset was always his ability to subvert expectations. No one would ever expect that Roy Pavalos, with his genuine, charming grin, would ever be capable of any of the things he stood accused of.

An impending indictment would have robbed him of that trick for good. The world would have seen firsthand the evil a man like him could sow, murder being the least of his crimes. But does that make me any better?

Willing or not, I was still always an accomplice.

CHAPTER THREE

My hands are shaking when I finally finish smoothing my hair and step back from the counter. A sudden rational thought takes hold, but I gladly let it spur me into the hall, scanning wildly for Domino.

He's here to take me home, of course. Enemies of my father attacked the restaurant and killed Tristan, but Papa handled it. Domino rescued me—just as he has before. All is well.

"This way."

The voice comes from behind me, at the end of a darkened hallway. The light from the next room fills a round archway where Ines stands, her hands obediently clasped before her. She beckons me with a wave of her hand, and I find myself reentering that spacious foyer. At least four archways are leading off of it, though I can't even begin to guess to where.

It's cold in here, the kind of chill that seeps into your bones, turning every sensation into painful stimuli. The thin dress feels like weighted steel, with sharpened edges that bite at my thighs with every step I take. The neckline is far lower than I'm used to, displaying my body for whoever is near.

In this case, a pair of hungry dark eyes that take me in from across the room Ines leads me into next. It's a dining room, I think. One far larger than the one at my father's home, adorned with a rectangular glass table so long it nearly severs the room in two. The room itself is square in shape, with more round archways opening onto what looks like an open-air terrace enclosed by a wrought-iron balcony. The sky beyond it is dark, viewed from behind a row of potted palm trees that sway in a gentle breeze. Warm air blows in from outside, displacing some of that unsettling chill. I sniff, noting it's tinged with the hint of smoke. Barbecue?

I can't see any flames or a grill from here, at least.

Domino sits at the head of the table, his hands folded neatly over the glass surface. Or at least, this man sounds like my father's trusted bodyguard.

It could be my altered mental state, but he looks different. His hair is glossier than I remember, hanging loose around his shoulders, but slicked back. His skin gleams, and as I take in his outfit, I realize that it alone might be the cause for why he seems so strange.

The black silk button-up hugs the contours of his chest— and the fact that the first two are undone exposes more of him than I've ever been privy to. He doesn't ascribe to the same grueling waxing schedule as Tristan. Dark hair grows unbidden across his pecs, adding definition to the hard, rigid mounds of muscle that compose it.

For the past five years, I've only ever seen him in the same denim shirt with a collar that stretched to his neck, a straw cowboy hat, faded jeans, and the scarred leather sheath that housed his blade.

It was a memorable costume, so striking in contrast to my father's expensive tailored suits and coifed hairstyles. Roy Pavalos would never be caught dead in anything more casual than slacks. The clothing, in addition to the perfect family, only added to his persona as a seemingly honorable politician. Even his eccentric bodyguard didn't quite fit the narrative of the ruthless killers other men of power were known to keep on a leash.

I always wondered if my father was the one who insisted on the attire in the first place. It would have reinforced the illusion that this gruff, somewhat rugged foreigner must have been some cherished family friend or acquaintance that Roy Pavalos kept employed out of the goodness of his heart.

I don't get that image now. A simple change of clothing strips Domino Valenciaga of what little disarming charm he had. In its absence, the man is all darkness. Rippling muscle and terrifying strength.

My vision blurs, and I have to blink rapidly just to keep his face in focus. I don't know if I imagine the coldness in the way he looks at me, or if it's merely what his careful mask has obscured all along. Blatant, disinterest.

"Thank you, Ines," he says, waving one of his hands. "Please have Cook prepare to serve the meal we discussed. Then you can retire without any concern. *Gracias.*"

"Yes, sir." The woman nods and scurries off. My last glimpse of her expression unsettles me for reasons I can't name. She looks so…relieved.

"Where is Papa?" The question rips from me before I even fully turn back to him.

He gestures toward a chair on his left. "Have a seat, Ada."

I bristle at the authority lacing his tone. "I asked you a question—"

"You've already strained my goodwill once," he says over me. His smile is so disarming that it's nearly a full second before the ominous nature of his tone sinks in.

Strained my goodwill…

"Have a seat."

I'm too tired to argue. It's an embarrassing dance of wooden limbs and wavering balance as I stagger to the nearest chair, at least four down from the one he specified.

"Where is Papa? What… What is going on, Domino—"

"No longer will you have the right to use that name so flippantly."

My ears ring. I shake my head and blink to make sure I didn't imagine the startlingly deep baritone.

"What—"

"Your father is dead," he says. "As is your mother, though that was not my choice. Your boyfriend Tristan, as well. Your life was not spared by accident. Do you want to know my plans for you now, or after our meal?"

I rub my temples. My head is throbbing more than ever. This is all some strange hallucination. In reality, I hit my head back at the restaurant, and I'm still unconscious. A better explanation is that I never left the house. I'm in my bathroom, crouched in the corner by the sink with powder on my nose, partaking in the one act everyone always assumed was beneath me now. A year of therapy should have been the magic cure for any of my naughty habits.

But even the finest grade of coke couldn't produce a high this vivid. Gone is the manic euphoria I usually feel. Fear is a constant undercurrent, building and building at the back of my mind as if waiting for some grand moment to finally break loose.

Dead, he said. My parents. I try to process that in a dozen different ways, but none of them have the impact they should. I should be crying, I think. Gutted. Or horrified. Terrified.

It's like my body is too exhausted to go through the motions. The only coherent thought I have is that if they're truly gone…

Then no longer do I have to watch my mother waste away in silence. No longer do I have to submit myself to the will and tyranny of Roy Pavalos.

Not that the man currently in control of my life is any better.

Domino must say something else because he tilts his head expectantly. "Perhaps they gave you too strong a dose," he murmurs, and I shiver at the way his tone barely shifts. "I had them calculate the measurements with your drug history in mind."

Drug history. The way he says those two words sends my heart racing. My thoughts clear a little more as the fear grows into outright terror.

"Where am I? Where is Papa?"

"We can answer those questions all in good time," Domino says. "I will admit that I wanted to draw out this moment. Extend it for as long as possible before I told you everything. For my own selfish amusement, I wanted that. Alas, you saw more than I intended, so part of the mystery has been spoiled."

More than I intended...

"Tristan?" I croak. "What happened?"

Though I already know exactly what. He's dead.

Domino snaps his fingers, and another figure enters the room, someone taller than Ines. A man who sets a tray onto the table. It contains a bottle of wine and two glass flutes.

"My favorite vintage," Domino says once the man retreats. He grabs the bottle, reading the label. "The perfect drink to celebrate this occasion. Though, you may prefer water—" He snaps his fingers again, and the man returns with a glass pitcher of clear liquid. He pours some into one of the glasses and offers it to me. "Allow me to propose a toast. To the future, Ada-Maria. May we all receive that which we deserve."

A quiver shoots through my belly. I feel more dazed than ever. Like thinking at all requires the same effort as trudging through quicksand. Still, I try, straining to focus.

"Take it." He moved. Without my realizing it, he stood, glass in hand, and approached from my left, offering the water to me.

I reach for it and promptly spill half of the contents onto my lap. It's enormously heavy, like a lead weight in my grasp.

Unconcerned, Domino has already reclaimed his chair and began to pour himself a serving of wine.

"To new beginnings," he says, inclining his head toward me. He's drained half of his glass in a single swig by the time he cuts his gaze toward me. A glimpse of real emotion disrupts that blank, callous mask—anger. "You should drink," he warns, keeping the rim of his own glass near his mouth. "Otherwise, it's bad luck."

My hand jerks forward before I even process the motion, and more liquid spills down my front. It's ice-cold, each drop hitting my skin with a sensation reminiscent of stabbing needles—but that isn't what has me sitting straighter, every nerve on red alert.

His eyes find me, drinking in my body with an open curiosity he never displayed before.

I know I'm beautiful. Ten years after outgrowing an ugly duckling phase, it's an admission that no longer makes me feel like a conceited bitch to proudly state. I have my mother's oval face and slender body, paired with my father's large gray eyes. My body is the one attribution that I bring to the table when it comes to the Pavalos family arsenal.

My mother had her sweet, religious devotion and prominence in the local church.

My father had his political pull and the shadowy endeavors that bring in the bulk of our fortune.

I had my sex appeal. The ability to lure men into bed with only a smile and a nicely cut blouse. It was my sole thing of value. My sole purpose.

I've spent years training myself not to flinch when men of all shapes and sizes undress my body with disgusting, searching glances. After all, it was their privilege to stare.

All on Papa's say-so, how fucked up is that? The thought is one of the many dangerous ones that only creep in when I'm too high to keep them at bay. My therapist tried to insinuate that might have been one reason I found it so hard to stay clean.

Your entire life feels beyond your control. At least this way, some of that control is yours to harness.

I can't even control who I fuck and why—but I know, deep down in the part of me still tethered to some semblance of logic, that Domino never looked at me with anything remotely close to lust.

It was one of the reasons he unsettled me. One of the reasons why I'd obsess over him. When a man looked at my tits, I could gain his attention and use it to my advantage.

Domino only ever looked into my eyes with a deliberate focus. As if, to him, I was never worthy of anything more than a passing acquaintance. I always assumed it was a result of his loyalty to my father, that he didn't sexualize me out of respect.

Now, I realize just how damn naïve I'd been.

Without Papa here, those dark eyes dissect my body mercilessly, honing in on my tits and the hardened nipples protruding because of the cold. He inspects every inch of me he can without being hindered by the table. By the time I remember how to move, he's already taking another sip of his wine.

"We have much to discuss, Ada-Maria," he says. "I think our meal might be ready."

This time, he claps his hands together, summoning a train of four people who stream into the room from the direction of the terrace, each holding a different platter of food. The smells are dizzying, triggering another wave of nausea. The fact that my stomach is empty might be the only reason why I don't vomit again.

One by one, the different dishes adorn the table, each more complex than the last. Fresh rolls. A salad. An array of fruit. A plate of roasted meat appears to be the crowning dish.

My mother couldn't have done better.

The smells churn my stomach.

"This meal is in your honor, Ada-Maria. I hope everything is to your liking." Domino waves his hand, cueing one of the servers to cut the roast, while another sets about compiling two plates with equal helpings of the various dishes.

They place one in front of me.

"Eat," Domino says.

I've spent enough time around men in power to know an order when I hear one. Unfortunately for him, this is one realm in which I've always had control over. Not even my father could take that tiny shred of power from me. Aware of him watching, I clamp my lips together.

"I said *eat*."

His voice… It sounds like the man I've always known to cling to my father's coattails, but with subtle changes. Like a familiar song played backward, and the once unthreatening melody takes on an unsettling tempo.

"Did you hear me, Ada-Maria?"

I push the plate aside. Or I try to. I'm too weak to make it move more than a few inches, but the impression is the same regardless.

"Where is Papa?"

He cocks his head and swipes his thumb across his lower lip. "You should eat."

"I'm not hungry," I lie. My words slur, my pitch wavering. "What the hell is going on—"

"Eat."

"Who the hell do you think you are to speak to me like this?"

The latter half of that statement is still on my tongue—*I am a Pavalos!* The magic phrase that has been able to cow anyone from childhood bullies to government officials. The only worth my life seems to hold these days.

But his voice overpowers me before I can even utter it. "I've humored your disobedience once," he says. "You already owe repentance for being twenty-two minutes late—despite poor Ines' best efforts to remind you of our engagement. Don't make me add rudeness onto your impending punishment, Ada-Maria."

The air escapes my lungs, squeezed out by how violently my chest contracts.

Roy Pavalos had a beautiful, playful cadence that could turn any compliment into a song of the highest praise. At least when he wanted to.

Otherwise, he could stop the devil himself in his tracks with one word alone. My father, the power player. The admirable politician. The brutal crime lord.

I've never known anyone capable of rivaling the power he could command through his voice.

Until now.

I don't recognize this man. That familiar face takes on a newer entity—that of a dangerous figure I'm ill-equipped to face alone.

Where is Papa?

"For the last time, I'm telling you to eat."

I snatch a fork and stab it into the nearest item on my plate —a few leaves of a garden salad. I shove them into my mouth and chew, tasting nothing but salt. Blood.

A gag contorts my throat before I can help it, and green-colored liquid spills onto the table's polished surface.

"Try the au gratin potatoes," Domino says. I notice that he doesn't touch his own food.

I shake my head, my stomach heaving. "I'm not hungry—"

"I see you've made your choice." He smiles in a startling display of white teeth. Against his skin, they seem to glow. "Let's take a walk on the terrace, shall we?"

He stands. Three strides bring him to my side before I even finish processing his suggestion. His hand lands on my shoulder, and my entire body goes numb. I've had to endure so many different kinds of touch in my life. Wanted. Unwanted. Reviled.

He inspires so many reactions at once my body overloads on them.

"Join me, Ada-Maria." His voice sounds deeper than before, sinking into my muscle and bone like a wrench that physically yanks me to my feet. My head swims as I find myself staggering in his wake. Around the massive table. Through one of the archways into the warm night air that completely displaces any remaining chill, slicking my skin with a sheen of sweat.

The scent of barbecue grows stronger. Potent. Pork, I think…

Though it's been so damn long since I've imbibed anything more than lettuce and boiled eggs. And crusty restaurant bread.

"You didn't try the meat," Domino admonishes. His voice seems to carry further out here—a wide, circular balcony overlooking a bubbling fountain set within a square pool illuminated with delicate orange lanterns. A private garden, but not the one on my father's estate—or any that I know of for that matter.

"Where are we?"

"My cook will be insulted, Ada-Maria," he says as if I never spoke. Why? I struggle to follow the conversation. Something about the meat. "He prepared it just for you. It took him days to research the recipe best able to make such an exotic protein palatable. I'm disappointed."

We round the curve, and more of the terrace comes into view—an even wider section with white couches arranged around a fire pit. The stench of burning and smoke is suddenly stronger, irritating my eyes.

As they water, I spot the source of the smell—the meat is cooking here on a spit set above the flames. It's large. A cow? Or maybe a pig, set far enough back from the flames themselves that the meat blisters and crackles from the heat, but isn't burned. But wait…

"He hasn't come up with a name for this new dish yet," Domino continues. He releases me and approaches the spit, inspecting the cooking meat.

Something about it keeps drawing my notice. The shape isn't right… The proportions are far too slender to belong to any pig I've ever seen. Science was never my forte, and my education doesn't extend beyond high school. I'm no expert on biology—but I do know the human body. Men, to be exact.

The way they carry muscle. How their limbs can contort and how foreign they can appear when limp and flaccid.

Blood rushes to my head, deafening me to anything else he might say. Not only is the shape of this "animal" unusual, but the skin…

It's darker in places and nearly stark white in others. Like clothing?

Slowly, my gaze roves to Domino, and I find him watching me. The orange glow of the blaze reflects off his eyes. My suspicion wasn't wrong. He is the devil, gloating mercilessly as realization dawns over me with a horrifying certainty.

That is not a pig.

Domino's lips part, and I hear his voice again. *Only* him, as if this low, callous baritone is meant just for me. "I've suggested *Pollo de Roy*. It has a rather literal meaning, but I think it gets the point across."

Spanish was one of the few bits of study my father instilled in me, though I'm nowhere near fluent. I have to parse through the words as my eyes return to the spit. *Pollo*, chicken. Except this creature is far too large to be that of one small bird. *De*, means of. The last word I can't make sense of.

Roy…

A flicker of material catches my interest as the spit slowly turns. Fabric? It's slender, dancing in the breeze. At one point, it might have been a light blue despite parts of it blackening by the proximity to the flames.

My father's signature color. He always claimed it complemented his gray eyes, identical to mine. They were one of the few things we actually shared. Our eyes. Our tempers. Our penchant for sinning mercilessly to get what we wanted.

"I wish you could have sampled a taste, Ada-Maria," Domino says, his tone richer than ever, as if he's on the verge of laughter. "I've heard the flavor compared to chicken, but I'm inclined to describe this particular protein as tasting more like the finest fat, suckling pig."

Blackness. When my vision returns, I'm on my knees, tasting salt and earth. The once peaceful terrace is now ablaze with grating, loud noise. A keening cry-like sound that pierces my eardrums. I want it to stop.

It's only as my throat aches with my next intake of air that I realize the sound is coming from me.

Screaming.

Endless screaming.

CHAPTER FOUR

"Mr. Domino requests you in twenty minutes." The persistent, soft murmur draws me from a sleep too heavy to feel natural.

My body is a mass of varying aches and pains, each one blaring for attention the second I peel my eyes open to a mockingly bright ceiling.

Clara is my usual maid, but she knows better than to wake me up unceremoniously—unless Papa demands it, of course. Usually, by that point, I'm already late. What party or function am I doomed to be tardy for today?

Groaning, I roll onto my side, still processing her words. *Mr. Domino.* I stop dead, registering that name at the exact moment that I realize this room isn't my own.

The walls are white, the floor a familiar tan marble that seems to be the signature sight of this unending nightmare. The bed beneath me is larger than mine, the sheets the same shade as the walls.

The room itself is spacious, with a row of curved French-style windows—each one shrouded in lacy white curtains—letting in golden sunlight from the left.

At the foot of the bed stands a woman I vaguely recognize, her graying hair pulled tight into a bun.

"Mr. Domino requests you in twenty minutes," she insists. With a wave of her hand, she gestures to a metal clothing rack beside her. A single dress hangs from it—a frothy white wisp of lace and gauzy material that looks thin enough to rip should I attempt to put it on.

At the base of the rack is a pair of delicate white heels.

Neither garment is anything remotely close to what I own.

Because I'm not at home. My head is throbbing, filtering thoughts stupidly slow. The memories from last night are scattered snippets, but a part of me instinctively shies from inspecting them. *Not now.*

Instead, I focus on taking stock of my body as I sit upright and push the sheets aside.

The mattress is surprisingly soft—therefore not the source of the pain shooting through my lower back and my hip. Wincing, I crane my neck to inspect the area and find myself having to yank up the hem of another thin white dress.

It's similar to the one awaiting me, though shorter. The material, however, is fine enough to see the mottled bruising forming over my upper thigh, before I even yank the fabric away. That's not all. Small scrapes and cuts speckle my arms and legs, and my head feels so tender that even breathing hurts.

"Please, Miss," Ines calls. Something in her tone has me scooting to the edge of the mattress, despite the discomfort. Fear?

She doesn't meet my gaze long enough for me to be sure. Instead, she guides me into sitting on the edge of the mattress and tugs the dress I'm wearing over my head.

Within less than a minute, I'm wearing the fresh clothing, and she's urging me across the room to stand before a full-length mirror.

"Wait, please." She scurries off through a door while I face myself.

I feel so disconnected from the body before me. Only those familiar gray eyes trigger any semblance of recognition, though the whites surrounding them are bloodshot. A dark bruise paints the flesh above my right temple, centered around a scabbed-over gash.

Overall, it's the dress that I find the hardest to stomach. It's too pretty. Too sexy—a constant reminder of the dangerous reality lurking at the back of my mind. Something is wrong.

Domino.

He isn't in this room now, nor is he visible beyond the doorway as Ines returns, a silver tray in hand.

"Mr. Domino insists," she explains almost apologetically. I don't understand her hesitancy. At first glance, the tray holds nothing overly menacing, just a matching silver brush and comb, a small glass bottle of amber liquid, and…

"No—" The word slips from my throat as I step back, shaking my head. Panic is an animal clawing through my chest, threatening to unleash the full weight of all the memories I've kept at bay until now.

"Please, Miss. Mr. Domino insists," Ines warns. Again, something in her tone reaches through my building terror despite every cell in my body urging me to run.

If I had any hope that my recollections were all a nightmare, this new development alone proves me wrong.

No hero would insist on the woman he saved wearing what lies on that tray. Only a monster.

"Please, Miss. We have five minutes," Ines says, her voice wavering.

I don't move as she sets the tray on a nearby white dresser, carved with ornate reliefs of crawling vines and round fruit that resemble oranges. She lifts the brush and comb first, using them in tandem to tackle my hair. Then she dabs drops of the liquid over my neck. Perfume, I realize as the smell tickles my nostrils.

It's light and crisp, also reminiscent of oranges.

Finally, Ines lifts the final object and approaches me slowly, as if giving me ample time to resist. When I don't, she secures the item around my neck with a brisk familiarity that makes me suspect this isn't the first time she's done so.

On how many women? Did they all wake up in this same white room?

Were they all served pieces of their own father?

No. I squeeze my eyes shut, blocking out the images. I can't focus on them; I can't. Ironically, it's the same mindset my father himself taught me. Focus only on the present. What matters. Survival.

Ignore the rest. Don't dwell on what may or may not be—only the present.

You are a Pavalos.

"We have two minutes." The quiet voice intrudes on the monologue, but I welcome the distraction.

When I open my eyes again, I detach myself from the woman displayed on the glass before me and objectively inspect the item around her throat. It's well-crafted enough to pass as some beautiful fashion accessory—not a collar.

It's about an inch wide, formed of polished white leather, with a golden clasp responsible for the subtle weight I feel against my throat. One detail that separates it from an innocent necklace, however, is the distinct indent in the center of the golden clasp—a keyhole. A few inches down from it, is a golden ring embedded in the leather, protruding slightly. The perfect attachment for a leash.

I've seen dog collars more subtle.

My eyelids flutter helplessly as moisture forms beneath them, burning and searing, blurring my vision. I barely see Ines' face as she takes one of my hands, urging me after her. She's a blob of color against this otherwise stark white realm.

I follow her blindly, shocked when we appear in another room as if teleported there. I think I recognize it. A large circular foyer bathed in sunlight, with windows and doorways arching from it; the same place I woke up in last night.

"Morning, Ada-Maria." This iteration of Domino Valenciaga is still almost unrecognizable, dressed in black, the top buttons of his shirt undone. He sits before a small round table set for two and beckons me closer with a wave of his hand. "Thank you, Ines."

From the corner of my eye, I see the woman rush from the room, leaving us alone.

I'm tired enough to assume that the figure before me couldn't possibly be the man I've spent five years near. They don't even carry themselves the same. The Domino who served my father did so quietly in the background, his posture such that, even with his bulk, he could seamlessly blend into the scenery when necessary.

And, during the moments my father needed to make a point, the man could serve as a menacing, unmistakable presence.

"You…" My throat is so dry it hurts to speak louder than a whisper. Even then, I have to battle with the chirping of nearby birds and the rustling of the wind through the room's linen curtains to be heard. "You killed Papa—"

"Bygones," Domino says forcefully with another wave. His lips form an expression far too emotionless to be called a smile. It's merely the shadow of one. "I suggest you focus on preserving your own life, Ada-Maria."

Fear and exhaustion go to war over what little part of my mind is functional enough to think logically.

Focus, Papa would say. *Ignore the emotion. You are a Pavalos, not some sniveling whore. Act like it.*

"Have a seat." Again, Domino waves toward the chair across from him, but I don't move.

"Where am I?"

Not in Terra Rodea. I can't quite explain why, but the air tastes different than it does in the heart of the city. We must be somewhere beyond it. The countryside? Far from the city limits to justify the expansive gardens I remember from last night.

In the light of day, the architecture of this room alone is blatantly opulent. Though minimal, I can tell this property is expensive. A house perhaps, in the style of the older villas like the kind my uncle Rodrigo owns in Mexico. Regardless, it's somewhere that even the best-paid bodyguard would have trouble affording.

In fact, anyone who could purchase such an estate wouldn't need to work a menial job at all.

Seconds tick by as I realize he deliberately left my question unanswered. His eyes rake over my body, and I'm painfully reminded of how thin this dress is. I wasn't supplied any underwear, and the warm breeze blowing in ruffles the short hemline, snatching it from my body in a way that risks exposing what little the material does cover. All I can do is press it flat with both hands.

A rich, deep laugh rings out, startling me so badly I nearly lose my grip in shock.

"Please, Ada-Maria. The longer you delay with pointless questions, the more you prolong our much overdue discussion. You know where you are," he declares, his eyes narrowing. "The gist of it, anyway. Somewhere far beyond your father's influence. So, I suggest you drop the sheltered princess routine and act accordingly."

Something in his tone spurs me forward. I'm shaking, my knees knocking together with every step I take. When I grip the back of the chair to pull it out, I nearly tip it over.

A tanned hand shoots out, gripping the wooden frame just inches from where mine rests.

"Allow me." He stands, triggering a rush of cologne and musk to hit my nose in a battering wave. Did he always smell like this? Intoxicating, but in a bad way. Too many nuanced scents to make sense of all at once. My brain aches with the effort, and I'm caught off guard when he appears directly behind me.

"Sit." The heat of his breath is scalding, raising sweat that instantly glues the thin layer of fabric to my skin.

I obey—my knees bending to drop me on the edge of the chair—more out of a need to put any amount of distance between us that I can.

My heartbeat plays an unsettling melody as he lingers behind me. The murmuring nature isn't loud enough to drown out the ragged sound of his inhale. Alarm shoots through me, straightening my spine.

God only knows what he wants with me, and, for the first time, I toy with the more dangerous possibilities I haven't let myself consider before. Rape. Torture. Murder.

He's made you wear a goddamn collar, Ada—

"I will tell you when it's time to fear me," Domino says, his tone casual as he reclaims his chair. He could be referring to the weather if the words alone didn't contain a thinly veiled threat. "I suggest you save your energy for when that moment comes. In the meantime, relax. I've had Ines prepare some tea."

As he speaks, I notice the white porcelain teapot resting before him, pale enough to blend in with the table's ivory surface. An exotic scent emanates from it, tickling my nose. It's unlike any tea I've ever smelled.

Instantly, my suspicions run wild—especially considering one fact that occurs to me now. "You drugged me."

He laughs again, sitting back in his seat. While holding my gaze, he snaps his fingers, and a different woman appears from the direction of the terrace. Racing forward, she scrambles to pour the steaming liquid from the kettle into two delicate cups.

"The men I hired to apprehend you drugged you," Domino says, reaching for the nearest teacup. "Though, given your history, I'm sure it was nothing your system couldn't handle. Already, you're awake and alert. What a miracle. Another woman your size would still be unconscious."

I stiffen at the implied insult, swallowing hard. This very man must have sat across from my father all these years while he received every frantic phone call and wrote the check for every therapist or brief stint in rehab. My father didn't give a damn about my habit in general. Only to the extent that it might reflect poorly on him if I were stupid enough to be caught high in public.

But even my father wouldn't dare use my sobriety against me. The full extent of the danger facing me sinks in like a gut punch. This man is no stranger. He's seen me at my lowest throughout the years and watched my father navigate some of the most challenging moments in my life. He knows the Pavalos family in and out.

And he betrayed us.

"Drink, Ada-Maria," he says before sipping from his own cup.

I eye my hand, pale and limp, against the table's surface. In slow motion, I watch those fingers twitch to life, and every digit extend outward. Then I bat the teacup and send it flying, spraying boiling liquid in an arch.

It falls short, landing inches from my feet. Stray drops speckle my thigh, and I flinch at the searing pain.

And yet, the effect is clear—defiance.

"You will pay for that." Domino barely pauses before taking his next sip to utter the threat, but I feel it resonate down to my very core.

The way his voice vibrates through flesh and bone seems to shake a million different revelations loose all at once. Primarily one.

Run, Ada!

I jerk to my feet, pushing the chair over in my haste. I don't know which doorway leads to an exit. I pick the direction of the terrace, racing out into the blinding sun.

The beauty I find is such a stark contrast to the fear building in my veins. As every atrocity I've witnessed flashes through my mind, it's like my surroundings become even more dreamlike to counter the brutality.

It's as if the world itself is mocking me.

The morbid images of Tristan's death don't match with the beautiful blue sky visible from a swath of swaying palm trees and potted ferns. The horror of being drugged clashes with the bountiful gardens that seem to go on forever beyond this balcony.

The casual setting of white lounge chairs around a pristine fire pit doesn't seem capable of holding the smoldering remains of a human body.

My father…

I sway and trip, landing hard on my right knee, tasting blood on my tongue. The sunlight lances through my skull every time I blink, my brain on fire, the noise of birds and insects swelling to a buzzing drone that grows louder and louder…

I'm suffocating.

"I didn't want to use this unless absolutely necessary." Like ice, that voice banishes all else in its wake. The world goes dead silent as a shadow falls over me, dark enough to obscure all traces of sunlight.

The devil looms above, his eyes ablaze. They aren't completely dark, I realize. I've never been close enough to make out the subtle green lurking beneath the swaths of brown before. A hellish hazel.

Much like this property, he's too beautiful to seem capable of sowing the fear that breaks loose, constricting my chest and flooding my eyes with tears.

I can't breathe. Can't think.

I can only stare as he reaches for my throat and his thick fingers snag the thin leather of my collar.

He's choking me…

Abruptly, he lets go. Something swings between us as he steps back, and it takes my brain almost a full second to name it. A thin golden chain that feels surprisingly heavy. One end is looped around his fist, and the other…

He tugs, and my body jerks forward, forcing me to brace my weight over my hands. I gag as the pressure around my throat tightens. With one hand, I reach up, feeling along the leather until my fingers strike the once inexplicable ring of gold. Only now it's not empty—he's attached the other end of the chain to it.

Like a leash.

"On your feet," he demands.

The pressure returns, tight enough to crush my throat. My body moves automatically to lessen the discomfort, and I stagger to my feet, my eyes watering.

He's cruel, stalking ahead at a seemingly leisurely pace that I have to lurch to keep up with. I realize, horrified, that he isn't heading inside.

From my peripheral vision, I see other people lurking in the fields or passing beyond the archways inside the house. Servants? None seem alarmed by the man dragging me to the edge of the balcony.

"Take it in, Ada-Maria. Would you like to guess where we are?"

I sense that he doesn't require an answer.

Regardless, I blink, struggling to make sense of the fields in a different context from their sheer beauty. It's warmer here than it should be this time of year. The foreign scent in the air is more potent now.

I can't even begin to guess where we are.

"I wanted to draw out this moment, I will admit," Domino explains, winding the chain around his fist, forcing me closer. Closer. My feet wobble in these heels, threatening my precarious balance.

Suddenly, I'm thrown forward, forced to grapple for the railing to keep from flying over it. I taste my pulse as I eye the stone courtyard awaiting below.

"It is a beautiful view," Domino says. "This home has been in my family for generations. The land, at least. I'm surprised you don't remember it."

Remember?

He's insane—or worse, he's toying with me, playing with word games and riddles. Irritation combats the fear just long enough for me to choke out a reply.

"You were a guard."

He laughs at the insinuation.

"I was a *guard*," he echoes, his voice booming. "How the hell could I afford so much as a stone? It's how your father taught you to see the world. In numbers and worth. In your limited thinking, someone like me could never amass a fortune of his own. Only on the back of men like Don Roy."

I tremble at the title. How soon have I forgotten what he called my father day in and day out. *Don Roy.* Typically, he uttered it with a quiet reverence that always irritated me for reasons I can't explain.

Everyone spoke of my father the same way. Like he was God. A man so righteous he commanded respect from even his enemies.

I used to wonder if they were that desperate for a paycheck to grovel before him or just *that* blinded by money and power. They thought those fragile symbols of power made a man invincible.

Now, I sense it was all an act—at least where Domino Valenciaga is concerned. He never respected my father. Otherwise, he wouldn't be able to say his name with such disdain.

I don't know why that realization startles me so damn much.

My therapist claimed my drug use stemmed from a lack of control in my life. I would describe it more like exhaustion. I became so damn tired of playing my role like the perfect daughter worthy of the magnanimous Roy Pavalos. I always suspected that everyone around me was doing the same, merely going through the motions like automatons at one of those arcade-style restaurants my parents took me to as a child. We all sing and dance and play by the rules provided to us, knowing that everyone else is in on the show. It's all smoke and mirrors, but we'd die to keep the performance running smoothly.

It's another thing entirely to watch someone willfully drop the façade, exposing just how fake it all truly is, how false my life has always been.

A game. A lie. A twisted play.

A routine I have no idea how to survive outside of.

"H-How?" I croak, craning my neck to face him. His grip on the leash keeps me hunched over. From this angle, I can only see his profile, stern and emotionless.

"How could I afford this?" He gestures with a wave of his free hand to the gardens. They extend as far as the eye can see. "Or how could I slip under your father's radar for so long? Don't play coy, Ada-Maria. Ignorance doesn't suit you. In fact, I'll humor your questions, so ask them while you can."

I suck in a breath. I'm shivering, my teeth chattering despite the sweat I can feel beading over the back of my neck. It's swelteringly hot in the direct sun.

"Where are we?"

"That question I won't answer just yet," he says with a laugh.

The chain flashes in the light as he manipulates it so that I'm fully upright, no longer leaning over the railing.

"Try another."

"My father…" The rest of the words die in my throat. I don't expect the tears that fall, blinding me to everything else. Wracking sobs rip from my chest, and I welcome them. I don't care if it's a display of weakness. At least I can't hear. I can't think.

As long as I give into the fear, I'm unaware of anything else.

Until my windpipe is being crushed by the pressure of the collar. I'm on my knees, gasping for air. I'm choking…

I'm dying…

"Look at me."

I sputter as the pressure loosens enough for me to look up into the impassive face of the man before me. He's crouched on one knee, the chain wound almost entirely around his fist.

"I won't tolerate your fear," he tells me. "Your sniveling attempts at innocence. I am not one of your many, *many* paramours, Ada-Maria. When you speak to me, you speak with conviction. No games. Understood?"

The chain clatters as he loosens his grasp, letting nearly the entire length pool on the courtyard between us.

I flinch back, bracing my hands against the stone beneath me. This dress is too small, bunched around my thighs, the neckline gaping below my chest enough for him to see everything at a glance.

I bolt upright onto my knees, grappling to cover my exposed breasts.

He laughs in a way that makes me feel completely naked. Stripped. Every low chuckle creeps beneath this gauzy fabric in a way his eyes—or his hands—never could.

"What did you really mean to ask me?" he prods.

I rub my throat until I catch my breath again. "You killed my father." It feels so strange to admit. A part of me doesn't believe it.

Someone like Roy Pavalos can't just *die*. He can't wind up turning on a spit over an open fire.

He was larger than life, a creature I always assumed was too big to ever fall. Even a jail sentence wouldn't stop him for long.

"There now," Domino growls, his eyes gleaming. "Continue."

I lick my lips to gain enough traction to croak a single word. "Why?"

"Why gut your father like a pig?" He smiles, and I recoil, feeling my heart hammer against my ribcage. It's not the expression alone that inspires the reaction—objectively, it's a beautiful grin, enhancing the strange greenish hue to his eyes—but what alarms me is the fact that it's real. He's enjoying this. "I'm sure you can think of several reasons. I want you to pick one, Ada-Maria."

I manipulate my tongue to reply. "He trusted you."

And he did, allowing his virtual shadow to accompany him everywhere. At his office. Family gatherings. His political meetings. There wasn't a place Roy Pavalos went without his trusty protector Domino.

Part of the reason was that, as a man in his position, his life was always in danger. But there was another explanation, one my father would boast about on any occasion where he happened to drink too much wine. Smiling with pride, he'd discuss the origin of how he met his valuable friend and asset. Hell, I think he staked part of his political campaign on it.

Roy Pavalos, *el Salvador.*

The savior of all.

"He saved you—"

Stars explode to life before me, rivaling the intensity of the sun. My ears are ringing, my tongue flooded with the taste of salt. When I gasp in shock, I realize why. My mouth is on fire. Throbbing. Bleeding…

And Domino's fist is raised, his eyes so dark they suck all the warmth from the world itself, like smoldering coals feeding on anything remotely peaceful. He is hell incarnate.

"I knew you were a dumb cunt, Ada-Maria, but I didn't believe that you were ever *that* goddamn foolish."

He's already storming toward another part of the terrace. Belatedly, I realize that the chain is still in his grasp. I watch the pool of gold on the paving stones unravel, growing smaller and smaller until…

I'm tugged forward, forced to scramble to my feet to keep my airway clear. The ability to breathe is a luxury he makes me chase him for. Eyes streaming, throat burning, I nearly gasp in relief as he finally comes to a stop before an area I recognize with chilling familiarity.

"Your father didn't rescue me from some *barrio* with the promise of cash and freedom in America, Ada-Maria. Do you want to hear how we really met?"

His hand swings out, shoving me onto the nearest couch. I fall back, nearly sliding off the surface entirely. Panicked, I realize that my dress rode up my hips as a result, exposing everything from the waist down. I snatch at the hem, yanking it into place, not that he seems to notice.

Or care.

That piercing gaze is fixated in the distance. In the past, I suspect, far beyond me.

"That bastard got himself in deep with a particular cartel," he murmurs. "One of the many he toyed with. They sent an assassin to cut off his dick and return it to the boss on a silver platter. Until someone took the liberty of cutting off the bastard's head and rescuing dear old Don Roy from certain death."

He cuts his gaze to me expectantly, and the chain rattles against the stones like a drumroll to herald the question he deliberately left for me to answer.

"Y-You?"

He nods. "*Si*. I rescued that crooked motherfucker, and he welcomed me back with open arms. Hell, he practically begged me to ensure his safe passage back to his dear wife and loving daughter. I hadn't planned on that, you see. I didn't expect worming my way into his life would be that damn easy."

I flinch. It's such a callous admission. He sought out my father. Earned his trust. For five years, he worked for him diligently without a word of complaint, as far as I knew.

"Why?"

He laughs again, raising the hair on the back of my neck. "Why? Because the best revenge, dear Ada-Maria, is done slowly, over time, so that it ripens nice and sweet. Slowly enough so that when the time came, and I finally looked that bastard in the eye as my true self, all would become clear. How blind he was all along. How he trusted his wife and whore of a daughter to a snake. For a man who prided himself so damn much on his honor and his vigilance, he didn't even realize that the man he entrusted his life to had introduced his precious daughter to cocaine, and ensured that his wife found out about every little dalliance and indiscretion. Every cheap, desperate secretary or intern that he'd fuck in the cabana on the estate. Don't look so surprised, Ada-Maria," he scolds, eyeing me from over his shoulder. "Don't tell me you believed yourself the tragic little heroine of your own fucked-up fairy tale? No. God himself isn't anywhere near as malicious as I am."

The worst part is I don't even know if he's lying or not. My mind is a blur as the past and present meld. A million little things I never inspected in full, now seem woefully important.

I took drugs at the first party I snuck into on my own. Daddy had been too absorbed by his new campaign, and I convinced myself that a small act of rebellion would secure his attention. I only wanted him to hear me, for once. To truly consider my request to study abroad—everyone else with less money and even fewer brains than I had was already pledged to some prestigious university or the other.

No one else had been destined to die in Terra Rodea because their father thought they had more use as a prop to sell his political career than as a human being with an ounce of self-determination.

My way of reclaiming a shred of that control had been to find the most dangerous man I could and let him do whatever he wanted…

As long as he gave me a little sliver of freedom to hold onto, all I had to do was shove it up my nose.

"Did you think you were so unlucky?" Domino asks, his tone mocking once more. "You were always a pawn. Though I will give you some credit—you were never as easy to predict as your father. Don Roy was a smart motherfucker."

A genuine hint of admiration in his voice breaks through the hate.

"It took effort to outsmart him. Years of patience, and research, and waiting. But you? You were like a fucking rabbit born without an ounce of self-preservation. So desperate. So weak. At every turn, I found myself overestimating your sheer stupidity."

"What did you want?"

The way his eyes slice through me reveals a hint of irritation he usually conceals. As he clenches his jaw, I think I know why—I had the nerve to interrupt him.

Hiss. The sound of the chain plays like an ominous soundtrack—a constant reminder of the power he holds in this situation. The ability to choke me should he choose to.

To kill me.

And yet, I sense that I've contradicted his very statement. I've unnerved him.

So, I keep talking. "Why pretend? Why play the puppet master. Why kill…"

I still can't admit out loud what my eyes—and my nose— confirmed to be true. Papa is dead. And so much of the person I've strived to be dies with him. All of the secrets I've kept. All of the lies I told. Maybe Domino Valenciaga is my punishment for all of it…

"I'm rethinking my decision to spare you." His tone is so blunt. The sheer implications of his words land a second too late. I wince, clenching my teeth together so violently they clatter.

His decision to spare me…

At the expense of someone else.

"You killed Tristan."

His death isn't as easy to doubt. I saw him. I heard the impact of his body hitting the floor. I tasted his blood and felt the heat of it bathe my skin. I saw the bloodied socket where his head used to be.

"You're a monster. You're sick. You're—"

Cling! The musical chime echoes as he whips his arm through the air, gathering up another loop of the chain. Due to the shortened length, I'm pulled upright, forced to sit on the edge of the couch.

"There will be plenty of time for hysterics later," he says, his tone devoid of anything but ice. "You want to prolong your pathetic, worthless life, Ada-Maria? Then it's time for me to ask the questions. Just one, to make it easy for your little brain to handle—where is the file?"

I blink.

His eyes cut to slits, and the chain becomes taut between us. I gag, my eyes watering. Helpless, my hands fly to the base of the chain, tugging to lessen the pressure on my throat.

"Don't play dumb now." He takes a step, then another, winding the chain all the while until he's standing before me within arm's reach. "You may help him win the horny bachelor vote when it comes to political prospects, but you and I both know that he's kept you close all this time for more than that. Think, Ada-Maria. Where is the Inglecias file?"

Inglecias. I haven't heard that name in so long. Just that particular arrangement of syllables triggers a reaction in me —I gag, hunching over, in case there's anything left in my stomach to bring up.

There isn't.

I realize he's watching, but I'm not faking being the dumb blond for once. He's served my father long enough to know more about the Inglecias incident than I do. I barely remember it, let alone a file. Though honestly, I've spent the past decade trying to forget.

The past.

Pia.

Everything.

"Where is it?" Domino demands.

I look up, eyeing him through my tousled hair. He looks different, his head cocked expectantly, his eyes practically glowing with interest. This isn't a random request. He's desperate for it, this file on one of the vilest periods in my family's history.

My heart races with dread as to why he's interested in that particular incident, but—physical reaction aside—I don't hesitate to say, "I don't know anything about a file."

He frowns, his brows furrowing.

Cling! He jerks his fist, and I'm crashing onto the floor, dragged toward him by the force he easily applies to the collar. It hurts. Fire lances through my windpipe, and I fear that he's crushed it this way. I'll die slowly, suffocated by the damage.

Somehow, I manage to sputter down spurts of fresh air as he finally relents.

"You're lying." His voice is a chilling array of deep, resonating notes—but I'm beginning to pick up on the rare hints of emotion when they do peek through. It's easy, in a sense, given how flat he usually sounds. Anger adds color to the rich baritone. It will haunt my nightmares forever after this.

If I live…

"Pia, Navid, and Rosa Inglecias. Don't tell me your father didn't keep a record of what he did to them."

Because Roy Pavalos kept records on everything. From political rivals to the names of the lowest-ranked reporter who might be brazen enough to publish an obscure blog post about him. He knew everything about everyone.

Except, it seems, Domino Valenciaga.

"You would know," I whisper, and he raises an eyebrow, flexing his wrist.

I tense in anticipation of more pressure, but he merely tugs. Just a tease.

"One might think I would," he says softly. With his free hand, he captures his chin, stroking the dark stubble there.

Of all the times to have this thought, this is the least advantageous. It creeps in regardless, the biting, underlying truth that I always considered him attractive. Repressed, rebellious girls have repressed, rebellious thoughts. Like fantasies of seducing their father's trusted bodyguard and convincing him to steal her away. I've always consoled myself with the caveat that if I truly wanted him, I could have him. After all, I could land any man I wanted with a bat of my eyelashes and a wink.

It was a lie. No matter how many times I tried to meet his gaze in the past, Domino barely paid me any notice. And every taste of his indifference just fed my little private hunger more. There's something alluring in being ignored. Especially when the whole damn world seems to crave being inside your body. Or your head.

He never seemed to want either.

Now I know why.

"What did my father ever do to you?" I ask, my voice hoarse and broken.

"That is a tale for another day." Abruptly, he releases my chain and snaps his fingers. "Ines?"

The woman takes just seconds to appear. "Yes, sir?"

"Take Ms. Pavalos to her room. See that she bathes and rests —" His attention returns to me, his tone far more cutting. "You'll need it, Ada-Maria. Later tonight, we will discuss your transgression and how you may make amends. *Adios.*"

He walks away, leaving my chain untethered. Dazed, I stare after him, barely aware when a small figure stoops to grab the chain and gently winds it around her fingers.

"Here, Miss—" I jump as Ines appears by my side, pressing something cool against my hand. When glimpsed on my palm, it's unsettling just how small and delicate the golden chain appears. So light, I barely feel the pressure when held, and yet my throat is on fire. I can only take a few breaths at a time before needing to swallow just to relieve the burn, wincing at the sensation.

"This way," Ines calls, reaching for my hand.

I find that I can't tear my gaze from the man pacing the balcony with his back to me. I get the sense that I've confused him somehow. I've irritated him further.

Everything—from his behavior to the violence I've barely let myself relive—feels like I'm only seeing part of some elaborate puzzle. Or a game.

My father was known for them. When other men invited their guests to the strip club or lavish parties, my father hosted chest tournaments fueled by liquor and bets.

If one of you can beat me, he'd say to preface the event, *I'll give you whatever you fucking want. Anything. My house. My money. My ass.*

A harsh laugh would trigger everyone else to join in, lightening the mood despite the thrill of competition he loved to foster.

I'll let you have it all, he claimed. *You only need to beat me once.*

Suffice to say, no one ever could.

CHAPTER SIX

The second Ines leads me back to that white room; I fixate on the bed. I lunge for it. Crawling beneath the covers is a coping mechanism I've retained from childhood, but I indulge it, even now.

Buried beneath the fine, silken sheets, I feel invisible. Smothered. Silenced. If I close my eyes and slam my hands over my ears, I can almost pretend that I'm beyond this place, as insignificant as a snail buried in mud, unnoticed by all, wanted by no one.

That used to be my most fiercely wished-for dream —irrelevance.

Ines, however, is not my usual maid—who learned early on not to bother me when I'm in this state. Fearlessly, she flips back the blankets, her voice persistent enough to seep into my skull no matter how hard I press my hands against it.

"Please, Miss, Mr. Domino requested that you—"

"Please, leave me alone!" My voice echoes back to me, wild and hysterical. "Please. I just need a minute, please?" I sense her withdraw though I don't know if she ever leaves. I just burrow beneath the sheets again, wrestling with the part of me that wants to ignore, and the faint whisper of instinct warning me to get my bearings and find a way out.

The inner voice is harder to smother without drugs or alcohol. Combined, they're enough to silence that feeble thread of my conscience, but this time, it lives on, seeping through the chaos of my mind, presenting the reality I can't hide from.

Domino killed my father. He killed Tristan, and trapped me here. All for what?

Something to do with the Inglecias family.

It's funny how you can spend nearly every day in someone's orbit. For that fragment of time, they become the center of your universe. You know everything about them. You've tailored your entire life to reacting to their voice. Their smell. Their laughter.

And then one day, they're just gone, leaving no choice but to cope with their absence—but it's hard. Like adjusting to life with an amputated limb. Only you have no idea how or why it went missing in the first place.

Pia Inglecias was my best friend. We did everything together. We shared secrets, clothes, and even our beds, spending nearly every night in my room or hers. She was one of the few people my father ever allowed into his coveted world.

Until she vanished without a trace, and I went from talking to her every single day to not being allowed to mention her name.

Good, Catholic girls never question their parents. That's what my mother cautioned, anyway. Pia was suddenly taboo, and I was a cruel daughter to mention her around my father. Or any of the Ingleciases, for that matter.

Maybe it's a testament to how damn sheltered I was—or how selfish—that I never really questioned it after the first few days. I pushed all thoughts of her, my best friend, to the back of my mind, and I did what we Pavalos do best.

I wore my brightest smile and conveyed to the world that I had no real care or thought in my head. I was happy, innocent Ada-Maria. The only skeletons in my closet were those literally written in the Holy Bible. I was an upstanding girl who never feared that her father raped and murdered her best friend and disposed of her family the way one would plastic utensils after a barbecue.

Because Pia is still alive, of course—she *has* to be.

Even though I know full well that my father is capable of the worst.

Somehow, Domino is connected to everything... Is blackmail his aim? Though, who is left to extort if he's killed Papa and has me captive?

I dwell on the thought, and I let the fear consume me. I sob openly and loudly, rocking myself against the mattress as tears fall hot and fast from my eyes to wet the sheets. I shiver, feeling every bruise and scrape throb at full force.

And with every cry, I'm reminded of the danger lurking beyond my thin white shroud. The collar is a constant presence, and I'm aware of the length of chain dangling from it always. Especially when it's suddenly yanked by an unseen hand.

Mid-sob, I'm silenced, forced to crawl toward the source of the pulling. From beyond my realm of blankets looms Domino Valenciaga. He stands at the foot of the bed, the chain in hand.

Panic sets in as I take in the room's interior. It looks different. No longer is the sunlight a bright golden hue, but a sultry orange glow paints the man before me bronze.

He's changed as well, switching the all-black ensemble for one of all white. Wearing a loose dress shirt and a pair of white slacks, he embodies my prior religious comparison to a fallen angel. This man is Lucifer himself, here to condemn me to hell.

On second thought, the devil comparison is too easy. Too simple. This man is something far, far worse. He is vengeance incarnate, as elusive as his supposed motives.

"You are ungrateful, you know that?" He doesn't sound angry. Not even when he turns his back to me to stare from the nearest window.

I didn't notice before, but this room has a breathtaking view of the terrace gardens from another angle. Here, the sunlight bathes the fields and fountains in varying hues of soothing ochre. It would be a vacation spot most would die to inhabit during the summer months. Overall, a beautiful prison.

"Selfish. Spoiled. None too bright. I knew this all, of course, even after all the time I've spent watching you from afar. Still, Ada-Maria, your complete lack of self-preservation astounds."

He's insulting me. The worst part is that I don't truly understand about what.

"Ines was to prepare you a nice bath, feed you a filling lunch, and allow you ample time to sleep. But you've wasted it."

He shrugs, turning to face me. "I was going to issue your punishment now and deny you those little comforts, but luckily for you, I am not as punitive as your father. Unfortunately, however, Ines is off for the evening, so she will be unable to assist you."

He pauses. I sense that he wants me to parse over his meaning. That I'll have to wash myself? Objectively, I haven't bathed without a maid in years, but I'm more than willing to make an exception now.

But no… That would be too simple. The reality of what he intends sinks in with the impact of a stabbing blade, and I bolt upright, feeling along the sheets for anything I can use as a barrier between us.

"Stay the hell away from me—"

"I have no qualms in filling in for her," Domino says, confirming my worst suspicion. Heedless of my refusal, he advances, lowering his gaze toward the mattress—I didn't even realize that I've gathered the length of my chain, holding it loosely in a fist. When he takes another step, I brandish it, but my hand shakes so badly it sways, rattling against itself.

"D-Don't touch me!"

"I suggest you save your fight for later, Ada-Maria," Domino warns, taking yet another step. "Trust me, I am more than eager to experience firsthand how much the daughter of Roy Pavalos values her life, and I'd prefer you not to exhaust yourself before then. But—"

He lunges. One of his hands snatches my forearm, shoving me facedown against the mattress. My heartbeat surges through my ears as I feel the metal snatched from my grasp. Without warning, my throat is wrenched from behind, raising my head from the bed as I gasp at the air.

"I think I'll bathe you, first," Domino murmurs as he maneuvers to stand before me, chain in hand. "I want you clean and dressed before dinner."

I'm flashed back to our last "meal." Who could he serve to me next? My mother?

"No!" I sink my nails into the sheets beneath me, digging my heels into the mattress.

I barely see his arm move before I'm lurching forward, hitting the floor on my knees, my ears ringing.

"Come," he says, manipulating the leash so that I lurch another inch across the floor. "I won't enjoy having your skin covered in bruises by the time I can enjoy you, Ada-Maria. At least, any that aren't inflicted by *me*."

I choke, horrified by the insinuation. Rape?

No, a childish part of me whispers. He'd have to be interested in me sexually for that. My cheeks flame when I replay all the times I would prance before him, hoping to grab his notice. When each attempt failed, I consoled myself with a logical explanation for his lack of interest in addition to taking his job too seriously—he is homosexual.

That pathetic attempt to soothe my own pride might be my sole salvation now. I cling to it, finding the strength to crawl after him as he marches toward the door.

The length of chain is about ten feet long, meaning he's already left the room by the time I stagger to my feet and follow.

Again, this strange dwelling takes on a newer identity depending on the time of day. At night, it's a fortress. By day, it's an ethereal wonderland, and during this twilight hour...

It's hell. Ignited by the glow cast by the setting sun, the walls gleam orange like flames. Everything takes on the reddish sheen, and with his white clothing, Domino resembles a creature composed of shadow and fire.

Without warning, he turns into a room just before we'd enter that circular foyer. I recognize it the second I cross the threshold after him—the bathroom Ines brought me to the other night.

Beside her, I'd been able to appreciate the beauty of it.

Domino's presence transforms the sleek design into a torture chamber. The gold fixtures are potential posts he can wrap my leash around, the walk-in shower a likely death trap. My mind spins, envisioning all of the many ways he can hurt me here. He wants to.

When he turns to me, I take a step back, shuddering at the look I see in his eyes.

But I forget that he has the leash in his grasp. He winds a few more inches around his wrist—a warning. The chain is a rigid line between us. Any more pressure, and he'll be choking me.

"A bath or a shower, Ada-Maria," he proposes. "Your choice."

"Shower," I blurt, preferring the barrier of a glass stall to having him stand over me in the tub.

He nods. To my shock, he releases the chain, letting it clang to the floor. Then he maneuvers around the room, gathering various supplies as he goes. From a golden rack of cream-colored towels, he takes one and fetches a bottle from beneath the countertop. Bounty in hand, he walks right past the shower stall to the tub. He runs the water, adjusting the drain to let it fill. Eyeing me from over his shoulder, he says, "A bath it is."

I grit my teeth, irritated to have fallen into his trap so easily.

"You can wait as I prepare it," he adds. "I'll undress you myself."

My feet twitch against the floor. He's at least four feet from the end of the chain. If I can drag it toward me in time, I might be able to make it through the door before he could catch me.

"Try to run," he says above the roar of the water. "Ines may be off this evening, but Pedro and Miguel are not. They've been forewarned to merely apprehend you, should you try to escape, no matter how violent your attempt might be. Have no fear, Ada-Maria—only *I* can inflict punishment upon that beautiful body."

Chills. Despair grips me, so overwhelming that I croak out a sob before I can stifle it. My heart aches. Every breath is a struggle, and I almost wish he'd grab that chain and choke me now. End this.

Instead, he sits on the rim of the tub, watching me as though my terror is an amusing show. I feel my knees buckle, threatening to pitch me to the floor while I'd beg him to let me go. I might do it too.

If a part of my brain wasn't stuck on that one word. I'm sure he meant it as a threat, but it sticks out regardless, diminishing the overall malice.

"I'm not beautiful…t-to you," I add hastily. My self-esteem never hinged on his notice—but if it did, my vanity would be nonexistent. "You never wanted me before."

"And you sound so damn proud of that, Ada-Maria. Like you've solved some million-dollar puzzle." He laughs while reaching back with one hand, dipping his fingers beneath the rising water. The amount of steam issuing from it already has me on edge, but he doesn't react as though it's scalding. Finished, he flicks his fingers at me one by one, spraying droplets of water onto the floor. "Trust a Pavalos to take pride in whether or not her attacker wants to fuck her. Because you've wanted me to for a long time, haven't you?"

I feel my cheeks catch fire. "N-No!"

"Liar." He levels his gaze over mine with a piercing intensity.

Too intense. I look away, and he laughs again.

"Don't think I haven't noticed all the times you've pranced past me in some skimpy little dress, hoping to have me drooling like the other men in your father's employ. It was always a game to you, wasn't it? Seeing how many you could get to fuck you. Want to fuck you. It's the only thing you had to look forward to in your sheltered, pathetic life. Has no one told you that beauty doesn't last forever, Ada-Maria?"

If they did, it was some bitchy blogger or a jealous cunt from primary school. My mother is the perfect, shining example that beauty can get you anywhere and last as long as you damn well want it to. Even if you had to claw at it with Botox injections, fillers, and liposuction. Beauty is a construct, she liked to say. One that she perfected how to wield to her benefit—at least while in public. Pretty makeup can hide everything, even sickness and decay.

"You're right. I never thought you were beautiful," Domino says.

I'm pathetic enough that the admission stings. Despite everything, I'm not immune to that one form of insult.

Rejection based on my appearance alone.

"Beauty is too delicate a word to describe what you are." He nods toward me and inclines his head. "I've changed my mind. Undress. Now."

My heart plummets through my body, hitting the floor. I can taste my own fear, as potent as blood. I don't know what I'll do. *Run*, I think, as my toes twitch again.

Then it creeps in—that sick, twisted voice whispering from the back of my mind. Undressing myself would be better than having him do it. He'd most likely rip the dress from my skin. This way, I can keep some modicum of decency.

Besides…

The only way men use moments like this to regain control is by using lust as a cudgel to induce fear. In this case, I don't have to worry about that.

I have the upper hand.

"The water's almost ready, Ada-Maria," he scolds. He snaps his fingers, and it's a second before I realize that he didn't intend to summon anyone. He only meant to spur me on.

My hands shake so badly I can barely hook them beneath the thin straps of the dress. I'm sloppy and rough, refusing to take my time or give him a show. Instead, I jerk the material over my head and throw it toward his feet.

I don't know why, but it feels more liberating than humiliating to stand here, knowing that I've defied at least one of his sick games. I don't cower.

Until he stands. The way he looks at me…

My fragile assessment of him shatters. That gleam in his eye isn't disinterest.

It's predatory.

"Stop." His command sinks into my body, rooting me in place before I even register moving. I'd been poised to take a step back, my foot still hovering above the floor.

"*Ay, Dios mío.* I always want to remember you like this," he rasps.

My pulse turns painful, every beat of my heart registering like the blow from a fist. *Thump. Thump.* Belatedly, I can recognize that there was no real admiration in his voice. Not like the way I'm used to men admiring me. With covetous need and naked desire.

Domino speaks of me in this moment like I'm a toy on display. The way men boast about a piece of property they own. Or, the way my father sounded on the night of his first political victory. Like this small triumph was the first step toward his ultimate goal—utter domination of the city, its people. Everything.

"Pink tweed skirt and matching jacket. A cream-colored tank top that displayed your navel despite the conservative dress code your father enforced in his office. Or at least, he wanted everyone else to believe he disapproved. I know for a fact that he told you what to wear. How to wear it. The mayor was meeting with him that day to discuss him potentially becoming a deputy during his next term. You were to catch his eye, and of course, you did."

I swallow hard, swaying as the memory catches me off guard. I can still see that day so clearly, just as he described it. Like a good, doting daughter, I intruded on an important business meeting to make some menial request—using the credit card for shopping was my reason that day, I think—but my real aim was whatever my father wanted to achieve by flaunting me before his opponent like prey. It was a game to him.

I think he got off on it, far more than I did anyway.

That day stands out to me for one reason alone. As I sauntered through my father's office—an upscale building

I'd visited enough times to know inside and out—a new figure stood guard outside the boardroom where Papa was holding his meeting.

One look at him, and I felt tense and hot in a way I'd never felt before. Like my clothing was too tight, and the room was too small. Sex was a chore I'd grown bored of attempting sober, but I couldn't help but wonder how this man would feel inside me. He was so tall I had to strain on tiptoe to get a better look at the hard planes of his face. His eyes were dark, shrouded by the brim of a straw cowboy hat he somehow wore without looking as stupid as he should have. The shadow cast by it enhanced his chiseled features, deepening the mystery of who he was and why he was there.

Struck dumb, I'd inspected the rest of him, forgetting my purpose for being there at all. Tight faded jeans that clung to his muscular thighs, supporting a distinct bulge straining around the zipper where his cock would be, and a loose denim shirt that did little to disguise the bulk lurking beneath…

Overall, he was the most handsome man I'd ever seen. When I remembered how to move, I approached him, swishing my hips the way my old friend once taught me, my head held high.

As his eyes roved in my direction, I fixed him with my most charming smile. The one I'd spent hours practicing before a mirror to nail down that fragile line between sexy and coy.

I wanted him to look at me the way the lecherous mayor in the next room soon would. I wanted those dark eyes to drink me in with a raw precision that warned he was undressing me with them. I wanted him to look at me as though he wanted to take me then and there. *Strange,* I remember remarking. I never craved that kind of reaction so badly before.

He was a different sort of man. Perhaps that was part of the allure. He wasn't a bold, rich bastard accustomed to taking who or whatever he wanted.

No, he was someone who would look at me like a prize he could never attain. Unless I wanted him to.

"Hello," I addressed him in my lightest, flirtiest tone of voice. I even offered him a manicured hand—fully expecting that, like most men I encountered, he would brush his lips across the back of it rather than shake it. *"My name is Ada—"*

"I didn't know it was you," the present-day Domino admits. He's closer, stroking his chin as the fact that I'm naked grows more real by the second. His heat acts like a battering ram, rivaling the warmth emanating from the tub. "Not Ada-Maria, the chubby little ugly duckling I remembered, fully grown into a swan. I'd heard the rumors that you were quite the little whore. Still, I never imagined..."

He stops, snagging a lock of my hair between two fingers. Slowly, he grinds the strands together and sighs.

"That little pink skirt... I wanted to fuck you in it then and there, Ada-Maria. I'd never seen an ass so fucking round. Tits the spitting image of what every woman these days goes under the knife to achieve. Lips so pink I could imagine you biting them as I fucked you deep. Never in my life had I wanted a woman like that. I could feel my cock straining like a motherfucker. My careful plan would have been ruined in a heartbeat—"

I'm holding my breath, feeling my lungs strain for air. The worst part is that I can hear the truth. In every word. Every grudging bit of inflection. He wanted me.

Two days ago, I would have been elated by hearing those very words.

"But then," he continues, "I heard your name. Ada, you said. As in Ada-Maria Pavalos. Nothing has ever killed my hard-on faster than hearing that. Consider it a gift, Ada. The sick, twisted, disgusting soul you are inside is revolting enough to override a body designed by the Gods and a face so beautiful it's sin."

Shakily, I suck in air, hating just how deeply the insult wounds. I hear the words of my therapist, playing in a mocking loop. *You have low self-esteem, Ada. You seem to equate your sexuality and beauty directly to your self-worth. I'm sure that if you looked deep within yourself, you would find plenty of attributes worthy of being proud of. You are more than a pretty face...*

The bitch was wrong, of course. I knew that without having to hear Domino state it so bluntly. I'm empty inside. A shell over which my father would paint whatever he wanted me to be in that moment. Doting daughter. Dutiful doll.

A prize he could use to sway men to his side. Like the Mayor he met with that day. I spent that very night on my knees, choking down his cum with the same simpering smile on my face I'd attempted to charm Domino with. I think I would have fucked him even if Papa didn't tell me to; so fragile was my pride in the moments after I'd entered that boardroom.

"Hello," I told the man waiting by the door. *"I'm Ada."*

His dark eyes flickered, but not with lust or an ounce of interest. To my utter embarrassment, he looked away. Then he opened the door for me.

"Good morning, Ada-Maria."

Just that. Good morning in a flat, emotionless baritone. No innuendo. No flustered response. As shameful as it feels to admit in this present moment, I'd never felt uglier then. Not even during all those years as the "fat ugly duckling," so awkward my father had no use for me.

Wait…

"How did you know?" Returning to the present is like surfacing from minutes spent underwater. I'm breathless, panting after every word. "My weight… How?"

No one knew that. It was a time in my life when my father had no use for me. Overweight with braces, cystic acne, and poor grades, it was more beneficial to him to have me shipped off from boarding school to boarding school.

I had no one in those days. Just Pia and one other friend.

The three amigas.

"How did you know?" I ask, facing Domino. My father could have told him, but I doubt that. I personally went through our family photos and ripped up any that featured me in that state. I only kept one in a safe place no one else could find.

"Know what?" His tone shifts again. Did I catch him off guard? If so, his face stubbornly gives nothing away. "That you were a chubby, awkward teenager? It's not exactly an unusual origin story for a woman as superficial as you. Anyone could take one look at you and know that."

But they'd have to strip me to do so.

I remember crying into my pillow every night, praying that I could go through a growth spurt capable of adding inches to my height while subtracting double from my waist. Pia was so pretty in comparison to me. Standing beside her, was like being reduced to a piece of scenery. All eyes went to her. Men, women, adults, and children alike. Beautiful Pia, with her enchanting hazel eyes, slender frame, and dark hair, could light up a room with just a smile.

The same smile I stole from her years after her disappearance. I spent hours in the mirror trying to get it just right. But I never could.

For ten years, I've held a secret I wasn't brave enough to confess even to my therapist. That on my fifteenth birthday, I stood next to Pia, and I made a wish as I blew out my candles. Just one. No longer did I dream for another pony, or new clothes, or Daddy's affection.

I just wanted to be like *her*. As beautiful as her. As tall and as skinny.

As desirable.

A week later, she went missing, and six months after that, I shot up five inches and lost forty pounds almost overnight.

But no one tells you that Cinderella was the only bitch in the world to undergo a transformation without scars to show for it. Rapid weight loss leaves tiny little silvery stretch marks that speckle the skin like veins. No matter how much you scrub, buff, or pay for laser removal treatments, they never go away.

The men who fuck you years later might trace them with their fingers, sensing the slight flaws in your seemingly perfect skin. *Were you hurt?* One of them asked me once.

He didn't really care as to the answer.

My cunt worked, at least.

"Did you hear me?"

I shiver as thick, calloused fingers slip beneath my chin, gripping it tight until I face the man before me, my eyes streaming.

"I asked if you like it hot or cold."

I blink, confused. "W-What?"

"The water." He snatches my collar, sliding his finger beneath the thin leather. With a beckoning motion, he yanks me forward so suddenly I nearly trip into him.

At the last moment, he pivots, shoving me aside.

Whoosh! Water hits my skin, so hot, every ounce of air leaves my chest. A hard surface slams against my knee as I scramble to brace my hands against something firm, but curved, beneath me. The bottom of the tub? My head, however, is still above water, my mouth open. I'm trying to scream, but I can't even make a sound.

"Too hot?" Domino questions as he shuts the faucet off. "Don't," he warns when I grip the rim, ready to bolt from the basin. "I suggest you endure it, Ada-Maria. Think of it as practice for what else I have in store for you."

"You're sick." My reply is a wail, barely audible beneath the pain.

Everything hurts. My skin is raw, blistering wherever it contacts the water. I'm burning alive. More tears fall, and I'm helpless to stop them.

"You're a monster—"

"I'd advise you to save the insults," Domino suggests. He sits on the rim of the tub and plunges his hand beneath the water. Leisurely he feels down to the bottom, dipping between my legs.

I jump, bracing myself to feel his touch, but he evades my skin completely, retrieving something with a sigh. The chain. Deliberately, he loops it around and around his wrist, seemingly unbothered by the scalding heat.

"I have a lot more planned for you, Ada-Maria," he says once the majority of the chain is secured, leaving me just enough to breathe freely. "This is merely an act of mercy. Later, you'll thank me for seeing that you are fed and bathed. I will bet my life on that. This will be the last luxury your beautiful skin will feel for a long while. Now…" He bends, fiddling with something that must be on the floor by his feet. When he sits upright, he's holding a bottle of different colored liquid in either hand.

"Honey or Lavender?"

Body wash, I presume. Each one looks to be a golden liquid at the base, with one containing purple flowers, and the other simmering bits of pearlescent beads.

Eyeing them, I shiver so violently water sloshes over the rim. He couldn't know. Could he?

But those choices are so specific. So deliberately plotted. God, these memories hurt more than they should. It's been so damn long. Why can I still hear her so clearly, her laughter infectious?

Purple is the color of royalty, Adie. So is gold. They'll be our colors, the three queens…

"Pia," I croak, swiping at my cheek to banish whatever tears I can. "You knew Pia."

He looks away and makes a show of lifting each bottle for closer observation.

But I don't miss the satisfied tilt to his mouth. This test I passed with flying colors.

"Pia Inglecias," he murmurs. "I've heard the story. Who hasn't? What a damn shame for that poor girl and her family."

Her family.

"She only had her mother," I say. But the second the words leave my mouth, I realize I'm wrong. "And a brother, but he —" I break off, feeling my throat go dry at the possibility. Could he somehow be a living Inglecias? It could explain his grudge. Even as I think it, I recall a detail that renders that explanation impossible. "He was sick. With a terminal heart condition. It couldn't be cured."

Whenever Pia spoke of him, it was briefly, only to mention how precarious his health was. *My brother was the fastest runner in the neighborhood before he got sick. Could have gone to play ball in the big leagues, I bet. That's why I'm here,* she added, referring to our boarding school. It was an open secret that she was there on a scholarship as part of the school's community outreach toward promising students from poor families. *Mama is too busy with Nav to worry about me, too. I'm not jealous, though. He needs the help.*

As far as I knew, his life expectancy was months by the time we both turned fifteen. Even if he did manage to live, I doubt a boy who survived a congenital heart defect, so severe he could no longer run, would grow into a man sculpted from solid muscle.

He's been listening to me speak all this time, but I can't gauge a single hint of emotion.

"A brother," he says. "Funny. From what I remember, Pia Inglecias was an only child."

I shake my head. "No, I remember—"

"Lift your arms." When I don't comply fast enough, he snaps his fingers. "Now, Ada-Maria. As much as another man would enjoy the sight of your naked body, I find that the allure has worn off—" he inspects me with a ruthless sweep of his gaze, his eyes narrowing. "It's not quite as impressive as I imagined."

Because he *did* imagine me once. Five years ago, before he knew who I was, when I sauntered up to him wearing a pink ensemble with a cream top. He wanted me then.

But not now. No man can fake this level of disinterest. Like the vain creature I am, I cling to the same excuse I've used all these years to explain it. *He's gay.* There is nothing wrong with that.

It just means, in the grand scheme of his nefarious plans, I have nothing to fear when it comes to the realm of sexual violence. ...Right?

Slowly, I lift my arms without taking my eyes off his face.

He bends, grabbing something else from the materials at his feet—a cream-colored cloth. He makes a show of wetting it with the bathwater, barely grazing my knee with the fabric. Then he comes at me directly.

I stiffen, hating the way my body reacts to him. Part of it is instinctive. The rest is pure vanity. It's repulsive how his appearance can still have an effect on me.

He's handsome beneath the evil, and my brain struggles to separate the two. Why would it? I've spent my entire life in the shadow of a man who excelled at blending beauty with violence.

And therein lies the key to resisting him and dampening any attraction I may feel. Those in my father's orbit always joked that Domino was his shadow, damn near inseparable from his master. They were wrong, of course.

Domino is no better than my father, bred from the same stock all powerful, egotistical men are born from.

"What are you thinking behind those eyes, Ada-Maria?" His tone is so deceptively casual that a part of me is lulled by it. I respond to him without thinking.

"That you seem to hate my father, but you're just like him—"

I break off the second I see his arm move. My body braces for another slap, but when his finger does make contact with my face, it's gently, stroking along the corner of my mouth.

"You will never compare me to him again, do you understand?" His eyes hunt mine ruthlessly, reminding me of a stern father scolding a naughty child. "Do you?"

I'm terrified enough to nod—but as I do, my lips part. Curiosity is as addicting as any other vice when it comes to him.

"Why?" My eyes water, and blinking frees more tears despite how hard I try to keep them at bay. It's horrifying to think of all the ways he's been invited into the very heart of my family, becoming a regular fixture at my mother's perfunctory Sunday dinners. "You worked for him for five years," I add. "Why now?"

I think of all the times I snuck glances at him, imagining how that body would feel against mine. Was I so naïve as to not sense his true feelings? Was I just blind to the hate lurking beneath that stern façade?

Or just stupid enough to be easily fooled.

"Why?" He taps his thumb against my bottom lip, applying a bit more pressure with each pass. I hiss as he nears the throbbing mark from his slap. "You're right. For five years, I worked for the bastard. I hid his messes. Cleaned up his dirty work—"

"You killed for him." It's an accusation I've never made out loud, but one I know full well is the damn truth.

He doesn't try to deny it. "I did. I arranged hits on the political enemies he wanted out of the way. I sent covert threats to their families. I handled his contacts with the men who ran his drug mules in and out of the city. I covered up every illicit affair while your Mama's back was turned—"

I wrench away from him, eyeing the floor. Harshly, he snatches my chin, forcing me to face him.

"He had a type," he tells me, his voice gruffer. Guttural. "Some could say it was creepily specific. He liked them young with supple tanned skin, and big round eyes—bonus points if they were light blue, or even gray. He liked big tits, a tiny waist, and long, straight hair, preferably blond—"

"You're disgusting!"

He chuckles and dips the hand holding the cloth into the water just beyond my quivering belly.

"I'm not the man who liked fucking women who resemble his daughter, Ada-Maria."

Is he lying? Bile spills up my throat and I can't process the thought further. I squeeze my eyes shut instead, struggling to keep my breathing steady. I can't give in to the panic now. It's what he wants. He's trying to rattle me.

It's working.

"Don't tell me you didn't sense that his devotion to his only daughter verged on the unhealthy," Domino taunts.

When I open my eyes, he's smirking. He's gotten inside my head, and he knows it. Even if my father were screwing other women on the side, that has nothing to do with me. Nothing.

"I guess that means he molded you into the perfect woman according to him. Beauty. Obedient. No brains to speak of. The only downside was that he couldn't touch you, so he had to make do somehow." Withdrawing his hand from my chin, he uses both to wring the water from the cloth. Then he brings it to my chest as if daring me to react.

I do, flinching as the fabric makes contact. It's painful to subject myself to his touch. He swipes across the top of my breasts and dips the cloth into the water again.

"I'll spare you what the rumors have claimed about you and your dearest Don Roy. I hope, in that case, it was all merely talk—"

"You don't know anything!" My voice is a whisper, strained by how badly I'm shaking. Every secret I've kept at bay cloys on the tip of my tongue like a bad taste.

My father never abused me. Sexually.

But sex was always a game to me. A trivial act, neither overly fun or too boring to attempt every now and again. I never felt the rapture other women bragged about. I was damn good at faking it like I did, though. Sex never terrified me the way it did good, seemingly wholesome girls like Pia who openly fantasized about the man they would bestow their virginity upon.

I want a love like in the movies, she told me once. *Real tragic shit. I want to orgasm rainbows and live happily ever after...*

Deep down, I think I've always believed that there are other forms of violation far more degrading than sex. A body can heal.

The mind can't. I was never one to play the "my trauma was worse" card like some of the spoiled bitches from my boarding school, who equated credit card limits with child abuse, liked to. Still, I tend to believe that I'm smart enough to recognize that there are some lines a normal parent shouldn't cross. "Favors," they should never ask of their children.

Secrets they should never demand be kept.

"Your father never touched you," Domino declares, but when I look up...

He's scanning my face intently, and I get that niggling feeling again. He's telling me what he believes he knows. What he wants to hear. Anything otherwise goes against the narrative he's built.

"How did you kill him?" I don't think I really want to know the answer. Somehow, it feels important just to say it. To watch his expression shift as he mulls over his reply.

I think I'm hoping to catch him up. To prove that it's a lie. Papa is alive and well, and the nightmare that has ruled my life wouldn't end so easily.

Domino cocks his head. "It was slow," he tells me, his voice surprisingly expressive. He doesn't sound like someone recounting a traumatic event. He sounds like a man reliving a sweet, beautiful moment he wants to savor reminiscing. "Very slow, Ada-Maria. Over hours. He suffered, if that's what you really wanted to know. He suffered greatly."

I close my eyes again, inhaling raggedly. A wave of emotions crashes over me, but the worst part? I can't decide which one to feel; they all resonate with the same intensity. Horror. Grief. Pain. Relief…

"Turn around so I can finish," Domino demands, cutting my mourning short.

I comply in silence, too stunned to question.

"Wait—"

He grabs my arm, dragging me toward him, and I scream, reflexively trying to escape his grasp.

"No."

Something in his voice freezes me solid. I go still as he yanks me to my knees with my back to him.

The water drips from my body, playing an eerie melody as I brace myself for his assault. Will he hurt me now? I almost can't stifle another scream as cool air tickles my ass, warning of an impending touch.

Instead, he prods my lower back, and my confusion battles with the terror. Then I realize exactly what he's inspecting.

Oh, that.

"You were whipped," he says, his voice rough as he drags the pad of his finger over a long-healed scar. It's one of many. "Multiple times… By who?"

CHAPTER SEVEN

*Y*ou *were whipped…*

The anger in his voice seems alarmingly out of place. My breath catches as I weigh the possibility that my scars somehow offended him. They're so small, that I was assured surgery wouldn't be needed to erase them. In fact, few have ever pointed them out, at least not to me.

And not like this.

"I… I thought you knew everything there was to know about me?" I rasp. Especially since he spent more time with my father than anyone. He would know exactly what a man like Roy Pavalos is capable of.

"Apparently not," he replies. Hot like a poker, his finger traces one of the linear scars, triggering a memory I try to ignore.

Pain, sharp and stinging. The chilling hiss of leather snapping at the air. My own screams…

"Were you? Whipped?"

I flinch at the question, phrased so differently than the first time. Like he wants me to confirm it. This hint of violence clashes with the fictional version of Ada Pavalos he's formed in his head. I'm so sure of what he thinks of me—a dumb slut who never had to work a day in her life. No way could the scars on her back be anything more than a harmless accident.

"I fell into a cactus on a trip to the desert," I blurt tonelessly, shrugging his fingers aside.

It's funny how little I've said that lie in comparison to how many days I spent poring over every detail to make it believable. How much information to give. How much to withhold. How to make my tone the right mix of bored and embarrassed to sell it.

I've gotten so good that I've fooled myself.

I even fool him.

He withdraws, bored by the marks. No part of me holds his interest, I see when I sneak a glance at him from over my shoulder. Even naked, I might as well be a part of the wall.

Shame bites deep despite every ounce of logic in my brain warning me that this is a good thing. I don't *want* to appeal to him. Being seen as unattractive by a monster should be a blessing. It shouldn't sting.

"Get up." He's on his feet again, crossing over to the counter. From a drawer, he withdraws a silver brush similar to the one Ines used on me earlier. I shudder at the thought of how he might go about such a task.

When I climb from the tub, I spot the towel he procured, resting on the floor, just beyond my reach. I take a step toward it.

"No." Domino snaps his fingers. "Not yet. Come."

The floor is slick enough to make every step a struggle. I slide the second I try to move, flailing my arms to stay upright.

I don't know if he takes pity on me, or if it's a willingness to adhere to his "schedule" that makes him approach me himself, brush in hand.

"Look forward."

I cringe as he raises the brush, expecting the worst. As the first stroke runs through my hair, some of the tension in my muscles loosens. Some. He's as briskly efficient as Ines, and when he's smoothed every last strand, he grabs the towel himself.

I reach for it, hoping he'll let me dry myself. Ignoring my outstretched hand, he steps behind me, dragging the towel over my back. Then across my ass and down my thighs.

I think the fact that I'm waiting for the cruelty is why the softness of his touch catches me off guard. He's methodic, working just enough pressure into my skin as he goes to soothe the muscles underneath. As the cooler night air tickles my body in contrast to the heat of the water, his ministrations, paired with the quality of the towel's material, have me relaxing before I can help it.

Everyone knows how violent physical pain can be. How aching limbs can throb and sting. Few people ever recognize that the worst part can come afterward. When the very person responsible for inflicting those aches and pains is the same one who takes it upon themselves to soothe them. It does something to a person's mind, to have the source of brutality provide comfort.

My body is already conditioned to the dichotomy. That's why I arch into his next pass that travels from my lower back down to my thigh, raising goosebumps. I don't know exactly when it happens…

When I start to twist along with his movements as he dries off my legs. I have no control over how my nerves prickle with the awareness of him. How my breathing hitches the lower he goes.

My eyes are closing without permission from my brain. For a second, it's almost too easy to teleport myself somewhere else. But where? Clara would never touch me like this—swiftly but with a subtle, teasing intimacy that feels too hostile to match any prior lover of mine, either. No.

Those men worshiped me. Used me. Groped.

Domino…

He toys with me. Plays me the way my father would his old guitar when he felt the need to show off during a dinner party. Like any good entertainer, he knew how to create hype with every stroke of the strings. How to build anticipation by drawing out every second he spent tuning the instrument, well before he began performing in earnest.

I hate myself for how easily Domino can turn my own body against me. Conspiratorially, his heat eats through the towel, coaxing my limbs into submission. I'm suddenly aware of every breath expanding my lungs, filling my chest. I can feel each nipple tighten in the next breeze to blow in from the open windows. I can smell him. Taste his scent mingling with the aroma of the body wash he used on me —*lavender.*

It's like I'm drugged on the stench of it all. I forget the source responsible for the creeping pressure inching up my inner thigh. I forget that I should shy away from it.

I spread my thighs instead…

"Jesus Christ, Ada-Maria." The disgust in his voice hits me like a slap.

I wrench my eyes open as shame floods my cheeks.

"I knew you were a whore, but damn." He pushes past me, dropping the towel on the floor. Angry, fierce strides carrying him into the hall before the full weight of my embarrassment has a chance to sink in.

What the hell is wrong with me? I've become accustomed to training my body to react separately from my brain. To endure the touch of greedy, grasping old men, or drooling sycophants of my father. I've perfected how to smother every ounce of discomfort. How to turn pain into pleasure. I know how to fake and fake and *fake.*

But my heartbeat hammers out a mocking beat as if to taunt me with the truth.

Thump. You weren't faking. Thump.

"I said come."

The command lashes at the air, and a sense of foreboding erases all traces of his touch. I don't think I've ever heard that note in his voice before. That cold, detached hiss.

Run, Ada.

I stoop for the towel and drape it over my torso as I creep to the doorway and flick my eyes in the direction opposite the way he went. I should run now. Try to escape. A part of me knows deep down that to try at all would be a waste. Still, I can't shake the sense that I should, if only to prove to him that I can.

And to myself.

"Run," he calls to me as if reading my mind. I stiffen, puzzled by the prospect of him giving me permission to escape. "And you will sorely regret it. My patience is running thin Ada-Maria. *Come!*"

Left with no choice, I shuffle toward the voice, swallowing hard the closer I come. I finally find him in that white room, only now—considering the sun has fully set and darkness officially fallen—it's silvery in appearance, illuminated by a crystalline chandelier above.

It's been transformed in my absence—a pointed reminder that we aren't alone here. There are other servants in addition to Ines. During my bath, they stripped the bed and replaced the sheets with an identical set devoid of blood. A long, rectangular gift box, wrapped in white and topped with a matching bow, rests near the foot of the mattress. A present?

The floor has been polished to shine and in the center of the space now rests the same white table he offered me "tea" on earlier. Now, it's laden with a platter of white fish, a bowl of salad, and a basket of steaming rolls.

Rather than smirk at me from a seated position, Domino stands with his back to me, his gaze on the window.

"Eat," he snaps, and my unease grows. He's angry, but as I replay the incident from the bathroom in my mind, I don't think he should be. If anything, he should be gloating. I played into his narrative of a dumb, stupid whore.

The nerves contribute to how my stomach twists at the smell of the food. I can taste the freshness of the fish just from its aroma—but I don't dare trust it. Or him.

I quash the gnawing hunger pains, reclaiming my flimsy grasp on control. Meeting his gaze, I lie without an ounce of guilt, "I'm not hungry."

"I suggest you draw out your reprieve as long as you possibly can, Ada-Maria," he warns in a tone that stops my blood cold. "Now sit down and eat!"

I stagger to a chair and collapse onto it, reaching for a fork, only to fumble and send it—and the rest of the silverware by it—clattering to the floor.

My eyes cut to him, my lungs paralyzed. Seconds tick by, but he doesn't react.

Because he's dwelling on something, I suspect. Somehow, I offended him, more than just by responding to his touch. But how?

I bite my lip at the sensation washing through me. It's painfully familiar. Ironic, in a sense. Papa is supposedly dead, but this man can make me feel the same way only he could.

On pins and needles, dancing on eggshells around a mood as volatile as a summer storm.

"I don't hear you eating."

I grab the fork, as well as the knife and spoon. Hastily, I assemble a plate, noisily scraping each platter as I go to prove that I'm obeying.

Once my plate is full, however, I can no longer play pretend. Impulsively, I resort to my tried-and-true method for making it through one of my family's mandated dinners.

I stab at a piece of lettuce and drag it across the porcelain plate to a distant corner. Then I cut the fish into squares.

Quarters. Then those chunks into smaller slivers. Flakes. Mush. I spread it across my plate in random sections to make it look like I've picked through it. The bread I rip into three pieces and try to crumble them as small as possible.

It's a convincing effort when all is said and done—or at least it *would* be.

If I didn't look up a heartbeat later to find him watching me, his arms crossed, gaze unreadable. Gradually, his expression morphs from callous to interested. Then enraged.

He moves too quickly to muster a defense. All I can do is cringe into my seat as he snatches my plate from the table and hurls it against the wall. *Wham!* The porcelain shatters as the food speckles the floor in a colorful display.

"I've shown you mercy, Ada-Maria," he snarls that word as though it's the most coveted gift in all the world. Mercy from him. "I gave you time to heal from your journey here. I offer you nourishment. I bathe you. Give you clothing. I ask you nicely for what it is I'm after. And this is how you repay me?"

He's shouting, his voice booming. Brutally, he snatches the towel from me. A hard shove pushes me from the chair to the ground. I cry out, wincing as my sore thigh aches with the impact. Instinct takes priority, urging me to my knees. *Cower.* The way I have so many times before, I scurry from the threat, staring only at the floor before me.

Move, Ada. Move!

"You play fucking mind games," Domino snarls. "No more. I've decided that it's time for your punishment."

"D-Don't!" I cover my head as his steps resonate through the floor, but they blow past me. Through trembling fingers, I watch him approach the bed instead.

He grabs the "present," ripping off the lid. The box, he throws aside, revealing what it contained, brandished in his fist.

"N-No…" I've never heard my voice sound like this. This weak. Then again, I have—just in those memories I've pushed to the back of my mind, never to revisit. "Don't!"

I'm on my feet, racing toward the door with a single-minded focus.

I don't even see him coming.

Wham! I hit the floor on my side, unsure of what struck me. Or where. The air wheezes from my lungs as specks of light dot my vision. A shadow moves from the corner of my eye. His hand.

He grabs my hair, yanking me onto my stomach.

"I said, on your knees."

I rush to comply, toppling over twice in my attempt. When I look up, he's standing over me, that thing trailing from his hand to graze the floor.

It's a whip. Brand-new, made of braided black leather that fans into a tail of three separate points. They're naked—not tipped with metal, thank God—but I know that the pain is only *slightly* less. The wounds won't scar the same way. But God, will it hurt.

"Please, don't—"

"You were twenty-two minutes late the first night," he growls. With a flick of his wrist, he extends the whip. "You ignored Ines' request. For that, I will double your tally. And after the stunt you just pulled…"

His eyes glow, and I know there's no point in running.

I go numb, crying silent tears as he moves to stand behind me. His shadow paints the floor, illustrating exactly what he's doing—not that I need the visual.

Crack! He tests the whip against the air with a sound that draws a whimper from my chest.

"Please don't—"

"You try to run, and I'll add fifty more lashes for every attempt. You brought this upon yourself."

Fire. It's like being severed in two, this kind of pain. My brain disconnects from my body, and I'm just a bystander watching a pathetic, sniveling creature at the mercy of someone else.

One.

"Your father coddled you like a fucking child your entire life, and you obeyed him, didn't you? His perfect little girl?"

Two.

I groan as three individual lines catch the flesh clinging to my spine. It hurts. So badly…

I was wrong before. He is nothing like my father.

Roy drew out my punishments sadistically with an enviable sense of control. He rarely gave in to rage from the outset. It was a game with him. How long could he maintain restraint? Always right until I'd least expect it.

"You helped him!"

Three.

Seven.

Eleven.

"You helped him kill her, didn't you? Didn't you?"

On the one hand, I know that Domino's voice is in my ear, booming and gruff with rage. At the same time, another voice overlays him.

"You've made me do this, you understand? You aren't held to the same standard as those other little bastards. You are a Pavalos!"

"P-Please."

Another blow drowns out the plea.

Fifteen…

Or is it seventeen?

"Not a day goes by when I don't fucking regret letting your mother carry you to term. You are a disappointment, Ada. A fucking disgrace! Say that you deserve this. Say it!"

"I'm sorry." I go prone, pressing my forehead to the floor. I'm sobbing openly, snot mingling with the tears. It's what he wants, so I cry and rock back and forth with the pain. I put on a show; I give in to the fear. "I'm sorry. I'm sorry! I deserve it; I'm sorry. Please, Papa—"

"Jesus Christ."

I blink, confused. That voice isn't like Roy's. Never before would he relent this early. No. I'd need to repent for longer, and far more earnestly than that. I'd need to prove without a doubt that I deserved his forgiveness.

No matter how much blood he drew.

Thud!

I flinch, gritting my teeth against the next searing pain.

But it doesn't come. The only sound to follow is the slap of footsteps retreating from the room, into the hall.

When I finally contort myself to peek around my arm, I realize he's gone. Domino—because my father was never here. Nearby, the whip rests discarded on the floor, and I crawl in my rush to scurry as far from it as I can. My hip strikes the wall, and I finally take stock of the agony radiating up and down my back.

He lacked the cruel precision of Papa. He was ruthless. Reckless. My back feels sticky, my flesh so raw that it hurts to even attempt to stand or sit upright.

So, I curl into a ball and breathe through the agony.

He'll return soon enough.

He never finished counting.

CHAPTER EIGHT

"Good morning, Miss."

I peel my eyes open, alarmed when all I see is white. This iteration is a beautiful color, reflecting snippets of gold like rays of the sun. I must be dead. Only heaven could be this peaceful and this blindingly clean.

But then I feel the pain. It's dulled—which confuses me even more. Fiery, stinging lines throb all across my back, but it's as if an invisible hand is holding the worst at bay, allowing just a fraction of the discomfort to bother me. I recognize this dreamy, dazed mental state, where my brain feels like mush, and everything sparkles.

He drugged me again.

He drugged me *good*.

As a result, any fear I might feel is reduced to three tiny butterflies fluttering around in my belly, but I can still feel it, nonetheless; a prickling bit of instinct warning that I should be worried. I should question what he drugged me with and why. I should run.

"Mr. Domino requested that I treat your back again, Miss. Apologies."

Again?

I test my muscles experimentally and groan. My back is ablaze, but the rest of me isn't too far off. I hurt all over. The kind of pulsing discomfort I'd need an entire bottle of wine to dull completely.

The more I move, however, the more of my surroundings I'm able to take in. Heaven turns out to be the same white room I've been relegated to since arriving here. Beyond the bed, the picturesque illusion shatters.

My entire body goes cold the second I spot the white table a few feet away. It's in the same position as last night, though devoid of the food and only one chair remains. Someone took pains to clear the broken plate from the floor at least, though the wall still holds the multi-colored traces of where my meal shattered against it.

Domino isn't anywhere in sight—a fact that rips a sigh of relief from me.

But Ines stands on the opposite side of the bed, her hands folded before her. Within her reach is a white case placed on the edge of the mattress. Medical supplies?

"Miss?" She prompts. Apparently, she needs my permission this time.

I nod, jerking around to lie on my stomach again, facing the foot of the bed.

She moves gently, prodding my back to assess the damage. Only now do I realize that I'm still naked.

"Mr. Domino is away today," Ines explains while smoothing a cool liquid across my back. When it makes contact with the sorer areas, I flinch, but it's soothing, killing what little pain remains damn near instantly. Only when she's covered half of the affected area, do I fully register what she said.

And *how* she said it, phrased carefully as if inviting me to question.

"Where?" The second I speak, I'm reminded of the collar around my throat—and the chain neatly coiled a few inches from my head. The sight of it sends my heart plummeting, risking the peaceful mind state the drug is trying to set. No high could make this situation tenable.

"He will be gone until the evening," Ines adds. "Until then, he said that you are allowed to explore from the limits of the house, the terrace gardens, and the courtyard. You are to not go beyond the inner garden or the courtyard. Understood?"

I ignore her direct question the way she did mine. "Where are we? Why am I here?"

"Mr. Domino also requested that you enjoy lunch without him. He will require your presence at dinner. If you need anything, I am to assist you."

Her words all contain a monotone, practiced quality. I can't shake the sense that this is a speech she's rehearsed to death. Or one she's given many times before.

I twist my back as much as I dare and lift my head to face her. If she notices my staring, she goes out of her way to pretend not to. With careful, clinical precision, she dips what looks like a cotton swab into the mouth of a bottle of clear liquid, then applies that liquid to the remaining marks.

I hiss through my teeth at the sight of them—at least twenty lashes centered along my spine. Despite their angry, red appearance, I can tell that they aren't as deep as they look—only a few managed to rip through the deepest layers of skin, enough to bleed.

Ines doesn't bat an eyelash at the sight of them, cleaning each one with the same abject boredom I'd assume she scrubs the floor with.

"Your lunch will be ready in an hour," she says after swabbing the last open wound. "Until then, I recommend that you enjoy some sun. Though…" Her voice shifts, and something in me perks up to listen. For the first time, she meets my gaze directly, and all I see in her eyes is a desperate warning. "I would suggest you adhere to Mr. Domino's limits."

I swallow hard, blinking rapidly. I've already experienced the consequences of testing his "limits" once.

"Thank you," I croak.

Nodding, Ines returns the bottle of liquid to her white case. Then she gathers up the used cotton rounds in a plastic bag. "I will find you when lunch is ready to be served—"

"Wait!" I roll over to face her, scrambling to cover myself with most of the sheet. "Why am I here? What is he going to do with me? Help me…"

"Enjoy your day, Miss," Ines says, her head bowed respectfully. "I will find you when lunch is ready to be served."

Dejected, I watch her leave, feeling a sob build in my chest. When the tears fall, I marvel at their searing warmth. This is the most I've cried in…

Well, Pavalos aren't allowed to cry. Not in my father's presence, at least. We suffer in silence and endure any pain with bright smiles on our faces. *It's how we've survived for so long,* he used to say. No one could ever tell when we were wounded.

These days, wounds can heal into ugly marks easily lasered away or fixed with a simple surgery. Through it all, you just keep smiling.

"Oh, Mr. Domino requested one last thing." Ines scuttles back into the room, this time without her case.

I watch her cross over to the floor-length mirror she brushed my hair in front of the other day. She feels along the edge of it, revealing that the entire surface is really a door. It opens inward, into another room that she hurries inside.

Confused, I stand and follow her, limping with every step, though I still don't feel any real pain.

Perhaps, I'm far too distracted to. The doorway opens into a decent-sized walk-in closet.

And my throat goes dry.

He's had to have had many, many women here before—all of them the same stature as I am. There are so many dresses. Numerous shoes. The further I tiptoe into the closet, and the more I inspect each garment I pass, the more confused —and terrified—I become.

They're expensive. I note several distinct seasons from notable designers all within the past four years. Each one is the exact opposite of what my father would allow me to wear. Too edgy. Too dark, with most of the clothing falling into the range of black, cream, and white…

And one lone garment in red.

"He wants you to wear this one," Ines explains, holding up the delicate silk dress displayed on a golden hanger.

"What if I don't want to wear it?" I croak. Perhaps as an experiment to see how Ines will react.

All she does is meet my gaze and offer the dress to me. "Mr. Domino insists that you wear this one."

She must see the defeat in my face, because she finally advances and helps me pull the dress on. Gently, she smooths it over my hips, and I follow her from the closet to stare into the mirror.

It's objectively beautiful, but wearing it, the scarlet hue feels more like a death sentence. An ominous forewarning of what's to come. Domino Valenciaga plans on killing me. Perhaps in this very dress.

But intimidation wasn't his only reason for choosing it.

Ines motions for me to turn, and in the mirror, I glimpse the ensemble's unique features that make wearing it more prudent than threatening—it's backless. The material droops dramatically, falling down my hips and following the curve of my ass so that every mark from the whip is on display.

Like he planned each one as he went for the best effect. In his world, victims don't hide their scars. They wear them like some sick accessory for all to see.

"Lunch will be ready in an hour," Ines says, heading for the hallway again. "You can go."

I sense that the words convey permission and a subtle restraint in the same breath. Go, explore to my heart's content—but never forget that Mr. Domino wishes me to.

I eye the bed again, tempted to crawl beneath the covers and hide. Ignore his wishes and his plans. Let him come whip me.

Fear alone isn't what finally drives me from the room in the same direction Ines disappeared in. It's smart to take any opportunity I can to explore and plot an escape. I can't stay here.

I can't.

I've barely gone five feet from my room, however, before I realize that leaving this place might be easier said than done.

I'm already lost.

This section of the hall is long and winding with a row of windows overlooking the terrace but few doors that lead to spacious rooms and little else. I have to retrace my steps back to the bedroom and then retread the same ground Domino led me through last night to find my way back to that circular room.

So far, I know that one set of arches leads to the terrace. The other, to my room and the bathroom. A third takes me down a wide white hallway bathed in sunlight, and I stumble past the dining room. At the end of the corridor is a set of double doors, but they're locked. The entrance?

I don't think so.

I return to the archway and approach the remaining arch I haven't tested yet. It's a short entryway leading to a massive, ornately carved set of wooden double doors, curved at the top and nearly as tall as the ceiling. I reach for one of its two golden handles and tug half-heartedly, fully expecting it to be locked.

But it isn't.

It opens easily, revealing a different exit to the outdoors apart from the terrace. Tanned paved stones form a path around a bubbling fountain and through neatly trimmed hedges and tended beds of orange and red flowers in full bloom. It's as beautiful as the rest of the estate, but my heart lurches excitedly as I step beyond the house and realize that the path goes on until it abruptly meets a dirt road. A driveway?

My hands shake as I head in that direction on bare feet. There's no one in sight. No cars. No guards. Could escape truly be so easy?

I'm halfway down the path before Ines' warning echoes clearly in my mind. *The house. The terrace. The courtyard.*

My excitement dies, rendering me frozen mid-step, my eyes on that dirt road. This must be the last of those realms he's restricted me to. In a sense, I think it was his cruelest punishment, more so than the whip. Taunt me with the illusion of freedom and yank it just beyond my reach.

I could always test him, but I'm sure he has a trap ready to be sprung.

The despair that hits me next is so thick, I choke on it. Like always, my first impulse is to give in to fear. Run. Hide. Try to find a drug to dull it and a nice enough outfit to distract from the state of my life. Within Papa's rules, of course. Always within his rules. But he isn't here now…

Somehow, it sinks in at this moment that he's gone. For the first time in my life, Roy Pavalos isn't breathing down my neck or just a phone call away. He isn't here to tell me exactly what to do and how to do it. Though I think this would present a challenge, even for him.

Unless he was in on it.

Yes, my smart, calculating father would suspect from the start that his bodyguard was untrustworthy. He would have always been one step ahead, one move away from declaring checkmate. My kidnapping would only be a mere cog in his wheel, a necessary evil to reach his ultimate goal. I don't think he'd dare to risk my life, though. He needs me too much.

So he'd only put this plan into motion knowing from the outset that Domino would never kill me.

But as I try to cling to this imaginary Papa's scheming, my mind goes blank whenever I come to a motive. He always had a reason. He always let me in on his plan.

Like with Pia.

She's a dangerous little bitch, Ada. That girl is not your friend. What else does she have to do to prove that to you? If you love me, and if you love this family, you'll...

"Lunch is served, Miss."

I whirl around to find Ines standing framed in the doorway to the house. She doesn't look alarmed by how close I am to the limits of the property. With a wave of her hand, she beckons me inside.

I choke down any remaining tears and swipe at what little paint my cheeks.

When I finally return to the house, Ines is waiting for me in that circular room.

"You can eat in your bedroom, Miss," she explains. "Mr. Domino will be home for dinner later this evening. It will be served in the dining room."

With a respectful nod, she heads for the terrace entrance.

My stomach lurches as I creep toward the bedroom, sniffing the air. My "lunch" has been served on the same white table as dinner, this time with just enough for one. A creamy liquid in a glass bowl looks like some kind of soup, paired with another salad and fresh rolls.

I test a drop of the liquid on the tip of my finger and shiver. For all I know, it could be a purée of something far beyond the consistency of most soup ingredients. Like Mama?

I cringe at the thought and back away so suddenly I nearly trip. Turning on my heel, I re-enter the hall, this time venturing back down the end of the corridor opposite the circular foyer.

I assume it curves around the front of the house. There aren't as many windows to break up the pristine white walls. What few I pass reveal snippets of plain, manicured fields, the sky, and a sliver of demarcation in the distance where the lush landscape turns tan. Even so, it must sprawl for miles. Plenty of land to hold a woman captive for only God knows how long.

I think the only way I can still stay sane is to cling to the pathetic fantasy I dreamt up earlier. That Papa is alive, using Domino as a pawn, and my capture was all for a reason. Though what?

Focus, he would command were he here. I can picture him, his stern features set in a hard mask of determination, the eyes we share blazing with the full calculating intelligence that saw him rise from a poor boy living in a *barrio* in Mexico to the dominating force he's become.

Success isn't owed to any man, he told me once. It's bled for. Fought. Won. Those who hesitate wind up at the bottom of the heap. Or worse—they wind up dead.

Always keep your focus, Ada. What we've done, we've done for the family. For the name Pavalos. Never forget that.

As if I ever could. His sin is poison, haunting me for over a decade, consuming my life so that nothing I did could ever free me from his shadow. I think a smart, battered, traumatized woman like the cliché my therapist assumed I fit would see his death as a godsend. Despite how little I have left to live, at least—for once—I'm freed from Roy Pavalos, whatever that means. A part of me wants to believe that it should mean all of my past trauma is miraculously healed and I can proudly take the reins of my own life for the first time ever.

I'm not so naïve. In my father's absence, an even worse monster will rise to take his place. Could Domino Valenciaga be that man?

It kills me to admit that he could. To play the dutiful role of a bodyguard for so long… Five years of lying and scheming. In a twisted way, my father would have been proud.

As much as he seems to hate him, Domino must have picked up many tricks from his Don Roy. A preference of décor, at least, was not one of them.

This house is so plain. Most of the rooms I pass in this section are empty or barely furnished. I doubt this is where he lives. Though, I know for a fact that it isn't. At least not recently.

The Domino I knew dwelled on my father's estate in a converted guesthouse that faced the tennis courts, a good ten-minute walk from the main house—and if you went at night, you'd need a flashlight to cut through the rose gardens to get there. As I did, far too many times to count.

A sound in between a laugh and a sob rips from my throat as I sway, forced to brace my shoulder against the nearest wall to stay standing. Crippling shame washes over me as I recall every time I snuck out at night to see Domino—never with his knowledge or consent, of course. I'd hide behind one of the massive trees lining that section of the property, and I'd watch him.

For hours, I'd watch him.

He paced at night, usually in the small lawn outside his door in that sliver of time after midnight and before dawn once Papa went to bed. He'd pace and pace, with a cigarette in his mouth, and sometimes he'd pause mid-stride and tilt his head back to look up at the sky. He'd take off the hat, setting it at his feet, and rake his free hand through that thick mane of black hair.

I always found something beautiful in those brief, unguarded moments. A realness so different from the cultured façade of perfection I was used to. Curiosity alone kept driving me back there night after night, no matter the weather. Just to watch him.

Some nights, he'd sit in an old lawn chair Mama had relegated to the guesthouse, along with all of the old furniture she no longer deemed worthy of the mansion. He'd cradle a beer on his lap and stare out into the night with a look of such serious devotion on his face. As though whatever troubled his mind required his full focus and concentration. It worried him.

Back then, I assumed it was a woman. I used to seethe over the image of this fictional creature and what she must look like to entice a man like him. The opposite of me, I was sure. A brunette with dark eyes, quiet beauty, and a business degree, perhaps. Someone with her own life far beyond her father's empire. A woman I could never be.

Now I know what truly bothered him all those nights. Me—but not in the way I used to crave he would view me. No, he plotted on how to hurt me. How to hurt my father and my family.

Again, the why feels more pressing than ever to discover. What secrets has Domino Valenciaga been hiding all along? It's funny how, despite all that time I spent watching him, I barely know the first thing about the man.

Apart from my father's story about being rescued by a man from a barrio, I don't even know where he came from. He spent most of his time either by my father's side or in the guesthouse—apart from the few nights he had off when he'd leave the property in a battered blue truck that sputtered so badly I could hear it from my room in the mansion.

Blinking, I refocus on the present and keep moving, inspecting this winding hall with a different focus. He has to sleep somewhere.

Not this room a few paces from where I was standing. Further? I keep going, testing doors as I go. Near the very end of the corridor, I find a room with its door ajar. Cautiously I push it open, peering into what I can clearly recognize as a bedroom. Unlike the one I've woken in, this one sports dark wooden floors and an even larger four-poster bed in a matching shade. The sheets are gray, but overall, the layout of the room is the same. A bed. A mirror that I assume leads to another closet.

One step over the threshold, and I know instantly that I've found it. The place where Domino sleeps, at least while he's held me captive. His stench infects the walls, emanating from the bed itself. He slept here, I bet. Perhaps as recently as last night. He came here and climbed onto those sheets, sleeping soundly after brutalizing me.

The thought disgusts me. Though why am I edging forward? My steps are slow and hesitant. With every inch I gain, I lick my lips, tasting the blood still drying there from his blow. The man is a sick monster who claims to have killed my family.

I shouldn't be so fascinated by the sight of one space I've never glimpsed despite all my years of watching him. I've never been allowed into the guesthouse after he claimed it. I could only watch from afar, and the one corner of the structure where I suspect he slept always had the blinds drawn closed over the windows. Some nights I managed to see the hint of orange light peeking from beneath the barrier. A handful of times, I even caught his shadow moving. Pausing. Undressing in a blur of motion.

I've never glimpsed up close any space wherein he might have let down his guard and ceased being my father's dutiful bodyguard.

Though, perhaps I'm not being entirely truthful. I did see him drop his guard once before…

The memory is so fleeting on its face—a mere fragment of images and few snippets of dialogue. I'm ashamed to have clung to it so fiercely all along. Reliving it now just sows a wave of more confusion. My past admiration of him seems more like a violation in this context. He went out of his way to gain my trust.

And yet he always hated me, I think. He had to—because I would have willingly given him so much more. It sickens me to admit as much, but it's the truth. All he had to do was look at me. Ask. Snap his fingers.

I would have been his. Willingly, I would have been his. I wanted him in a way I've wanted few men in my life…

No. I wanted him more than anyone. I craved him so badly that I'd lie in my bed at night and imagine him, using my fingers to fill in where imagination alone couldn't. I could orgasm just thinking of his eyes. His voice. My only saving grace is that I wasn't enthralled by his looks alone. I had every reason in the world to obsess over Domino Valenciaga —no one could blame me.

Because he saved me once. Thinking back to that moment makes my head throb. I'm remembering it wrong, seeing care and concern in those broad features where none existed. But no...

I remember it clearly, despite how scattered those memories may be. Domino saved my life. He looked at me in a way no one ever had. Not my parents. Not Tristan. Not Pia.

I'd been so drunk, drunker than I'd ever been. Drunk enough to disobey my father and leave the property alone after nightfall.

I only remember walking. For miles and miles, with no real goal in mind. I'd been crying. Crying so hard, my eyes ached and felt swollen; my vision blurred. Eventually, I stumbled across the main road, and I just laid there, right in the middle of the asphalt. It felt so warm, baked by one of the hottest days on record. It was so dark on that stretch of the highway I could barely see my hand in front of my face.

As drunk—and high—as I was, I knew that no one could see me, and I waited. I waited for the pain to stop and the sound of a running engine, and the sight of headlights.

When an amber glow finally washed over me, I smiled. *Finally. Thank you, God,* I whispered to no one.

No longer would I be forced to play pretend. No longer would I have to live as Ada-Maria Lucia Pavalos.

But then I heard a sound I wasn't expecting.

"Ada-Maria!" His voice bellowed out like thunder, richer than I'd ever heard it. I'd been so high, I assumed it was God, at first, responding to my plea. Then I saw him in human form, kneeling over me, more beautiful than any natural-born man had a right to be. Domino…

"What the hell is wrong with you?" he demanded, wrenching me by my shoulders into a sitting position. He shook me, making my head loll back and forth, all while shouting. "You stupid spoiled little bitch! Have you lost your fucking mind? You trying to kill yourself?"

I think I still hadn't come to terms with the fact that he found me, assuming he was merely a specter conjured by my addled brain.

"Yes," I told him. "I want to die. Just let me go."

I asked him so nicely. As though it was a favor I needed him to do for me.

Then I saw the anger wash over his face. Looking back, I can clearly denote the fractures in his carefully constructed mask. I should have seen the truth then. But in that moment, I remember being startled from my daze as if struck by lightning.

He looked so furious at the thought of me dying. Furious and pained and so damn sexy, I would have done whatever he asked me to. Whatever he wanted.

All he did was drag me from the road and shove me into the back of his truck.

"You stupid little—" He broke off, clearing his throat. "I'm taking you home now, Ms. Ada-Maria," he added in his usual, cold tone.

I'd been so dazed by the whiplash that it wasn't until the following night—when my sober brain could piece together how I'd gotten home—that I realized it wasn't a dream. He saved me.

Then he ignored me the next morning as though nothing happened. He never told Papa either, from what I could garner without asking directly.

I never complained to Papa about the way he spoke to me, either. *You spoiled little bitch.* I used to replay those words to myself—usually when I had two fingers inside of me and needed one last hit to go over the edge. I'd think of him snarling those hateful words, and I'd orgasm, gasping his name softly enough that no one ever knew.

He treated me a way no one ever had. I'd been stupid enough to think that meant something. That I meant something to *someone.*

And now I know.

Domino saved my life that night because he had a more gruesome death in mind. Those things he said to me weren't the impassioned speech of someone afraid for my life. They were the frustrations of my would-be murderer.

And God, I wish he never found me, then. It's been two years since, and I've never gathered up the strength to try again. Maybe I stopped hating myself.

Or perhaps I knew, deep down, that Domino might not be there to stop me the next time.

CHAPTER NINE

My back hurts so goddamn much. I cry out, waking up to a darkened room, already on the verge of tears. At first, I assume I'm in that pretty white prison.

But wait…

This smell is different, so rich I audibly groan at the flavor, inhaling deeply to savor it. Then I remember. I'm in Domino's room, on his bed.

Alarmed, I bolt upright, disentangling myself from his sheets.

Because, sometime during my reminiscence of the past, I climbed onto the mattress beneath them. I lied in the same space as the man who tormented me, and, worst of all, I fell asleep breathing in the remnants of him.

I'd vomit if there were anything in my stomach left to bring up.

Instead, I lurch to my feet, scanning the room warily, expecting to find him stepping from the shadows. It's nearly evening now, I realize with a start. Beyond the windows, the sun has partially sunk beneath the horizon. I've lost hours.

And he'll be back soon.

Knowledge of that spurs me toward the doorway. I need to hide. Prepare. Do something other than wait for him patiently. I should devise a trap.

My father would. Usually, I would play a part in it. Domino mentioned the day I interrupted my father's meeting with the mayor—but I don't think he knew what happened after I entered that room. I sidled up to the man with a charming smile and playfully mentioned that I'd like a ride in the sports car he had parked outside. Of course, he gave me a ride hours later in that very car and fucked me in the back seat.

And while he wasn't looking, I slipped a vial of cocaine in the glove box.

What secrets does Domino have waiting to be found? Everyone has them, skeletons in their closet. Figuratively. Literally…

My heart pounds as I turn on the threshold and cross over to the full-length mirror directly opposite the bed. Copying Ines' motions, I feel along the edge until I find a concealed latch. Once I press it, the door easily swings inward, revealing a closet twice as large as the one in my room.

One look, and I realize that if Domino has any secrets hidden within his house, they might be within here. There's luggage, for one. I spy it lurking on a top shelf.

Another glaring sight is just how few items of clothing hang on the rails. I count maybe three suits, a handful of dress shirts, and even fewer slacks. A lone pair of leather shoes fills only one rung in a shelf that seems built to hold at least fifty. I only find one red tie.

But this closet contains one fixture mine didn't. In the center is a square, glass-topped counter. Beneath it, arranged neatly within separate wooden boxes lined with black silk, are watches. So many watches. I count at least forty different kinds. Most of them are stopwatches. Some gold, or silver. If I strain my ears, a strange ticking sound echoes faintly. They're all working, counting down the seconds.

I wonder if Ines' constant reminders about the time were more than just a devoted need to adhere to her boss' wishes. Of course, they weren't. She was being timed.

I was being timed.

Anger flares, as sharp as it is irrational. Perhaps he got a kick out of being the one to call the shots instead of the lackey taking orders. Though, come to think of it, I never saw my father order him outright the way he did everyone else—myself included. When it came to Domino, he seemed to adhere to a different code. I think it might have been respect.

And this is how he was betrayed.

I shake my head to clear it. *No.* I can't focus on the past any longer. The only hope I have of staying alive is to think, plot, plan.

I scan the room again with a different focus, hunting in the corners and behind the hanging clothing. There must be something. Some clue. Some bit of information he forgot to hide.

I'm nearing the back of the room when I finally spy something tucked behind a rack of shelves—a duffle bag made of black leather, like the kind someone might carry onto a plane. The main interior is empty, but when I open the zipper of one of the side compartments, a wealth of different materials spills out.

I crouch to retrieve them, feeling my hands shake as I realize what they are. Pictures. Some are grainy, like paparazzi shots taken from afar, barely in focus. Others are crystal clear, taken up close with the subject's full awareness.

I lift the nearest one, straining my eyes to make out the details.

"Son of a bitch."

It's Tristan. His back is to the camera, but I recognize his signature navy suit and the red imported sports car he loved to show off. That car was the only reason I gave him the time of day.

That and the fact that I had no choice.

I grapple for another picture that must have been taken soon after. It shows a passenger leaving the same vehicle, a woman in a tiny black dress. The one lying next to it shows her face, her bitchy grin visible even from the distance she stood from the photographer.

Alexi Rojas.

Is it fair to feel jealous over a man I truly never loved in the first place? *Yes,* I decide. Though, the fact that Tristan isn't here to bitch at helps temper my rage. I just feel hollow. Used. Lied to—a time stamp above each photo reveals the date of this particular meeting.

Just a week ago.

Another set of images were taken just a few days later, shot from a different angle inside the hallway of what looks like Tristan's apartment complex. In one, Alexi is visible sauntering up to his door at nine p.m. She doesn't leave until six a.m. the next morning.

At least five different instances are depicted in the photos altogether, spanning from a month ago up to just two days before our date at the restaurant. I'm sure he was with her that night as well.

And apparently, he wasn't the only one fucking her.

Four photos remain, each one a glossier, higher-quality shot from the others. These were taken up close and personal —*very* personal. If I didn't know Tristan's body so well, I'd assume it was him.

His hand, fondling the perky breast of a smirking blond. His fingers gripping her hair to expose her neck and the tiny heart tattoo on her collar bone.

Objectively, at least I know now why Tristan enjoyed fucking her so much that even the allure of dating Roy Pavalos' daughter wasn't enough to temper the lust. She's hot, with flawless skin and a taut little ass, and I hate her so goddamn much I could scream.

Tristan, she could have—the bastard could barely last seven minutes in the sack on a good day.

But I recognize those hands. That tanned, golden skin. The coiled, rigid muscle shaping his forearms…

For all of his taunts and superiority displayed toward me, Domino had no problem fucking a "worthless whore" like Alexi Rojas.

I think a part of me wants to laugh, almost as much as I want to seethe. For all intents and purposes, Alexi and I are one and the same—though hell, I think I have more than two brain cells to rub together, so maybe that's it. Domino likes his women flawless and stupid.

It fits.

Or maybe he just likes his women so easy they'd give it to anyone like a cat in heat?

Disgusted, I start to shove the photos back into the duffle only to jar something else loose. I almost missed it, hidden at the very bottom of the pocket. Two items, actually. One is a brown vial of liquid. It looks medical, like something taken from a hospital or doctor's office. Printed on a white label is the phrasing—*LORAZEPAM 2mg/ml injection solution.* Ativan, a drug I know well enough, thanks to my mother. She kept a pill bottle of it in the medicine cabinet. Her prescription was for one milligram as needed. She took three.

A chilling sensation washes over me as I realize that this might be what he drugged me with. How much? And for how long?

A shudder runs through me as I brush my hand across my sore thigh. Perhaps that's where they did it?

Beside the vial, is a syringe with a needle attached, still packaged for use.

A plan forms in my brain as reckless as it is desperate. It could work. I ignore the many cons and focus on the slim possibility of success.

Without thinking it through, I shove the pictures back into the pocket and return the duffle behind the shelf. Then I escape his room and return to mine.

My heart pounds as I glance over my shoulder with every noise to break the quiet. How soon before he comes back? What if he's already here?

I strain my ears, listening for any telltale sign. All I hear are chirping birds and murmuring insects. Apart from its purpose as my prison, more and more, the abject beauty of this landscape sticks out to me—as well as the fact that it's far from Terra Rodea.

There are none of the hallmarks of the city or its outskirts. The land beyond this lush estate looks dead. Like desert.

The nearest area with remotely similar terrain is hours from the city at least. I eye the vial in my hand and wonder how much he had shoved into my body just to bring me here. It was night at the restaurant and night by the time I came to in the foyer. I'd blurred them together, assuming they happened hours apart, but what if they were two different nights?

Which means that he was ready for me. The grill. The dress. He waited for my arrival and used every second since to torment me.

For what? Something tells me that there has to be a reason behind the madness. I guess I'm not insane enough to see it. My head aches again, the room spinning.

Then footsteps echo in the distance, advancing quickly in this direction.

Damn! I lunge for the closet. At the last minute, I pivot toward the bed and shove the vial and syringe beneath the top corner of the mattress.

I've barely stepped back from it when a shadow appears at the door.

"Mr. Domino is ready for you in the dining room, Miss," Ines calls.

My heart drops to the floor, and I almost can't disguise my alarm.

Domino is already here. For how long?

Long enough to see me creep through his belongings, laughing all the while in the background?

"He requests that you not change," Ines adds, and I jump to realize she's still here. "You can follow me."

A not-so-subtle warning not to delay.

"Y-Yes." I smooth my hand along the front of the dress. It's rumpled now, and I'm sure my hair is a rat's nest. I can't stop myself from combing my fingers through it as I hurry into the hall.

Again, the house transforms in the warm glow of sunset. This time, the fiery hue painting the walls resembles less of a figurative hell and more like a literal fire, threatening to consume me with greedy, grasping flames.

CHAPTER TEN

I smell him, even before we near the doorway to the dining room.

Domino.

He's seated at the head of the table again, his hands folded in front of him. He's switched the white shirt for one of gray, and somehow this color unnerves me the most. Perhaps because it acts as a neutral tone, softening the intensity of his eyes while enhancing the hardness of his features.

"Have a seat, Ada-Maria," he says, gesturing to the chair nearest him. "I promise that tonight, only chicken is on the menu."

I stiffen. "Not *Pollo d-de Roy?*" My voice breaks so badly I can barely get the words out. Tears fall, lashing down my cheeks but I don't dare wipe them away. I should crave any and every reminder of what he's done.

What he's claimed to have done, anyway.

"No, that is not on the menu tonight," Domino says, tilting his head to observe me. "I hope you enjoyed your full day to yourself. It will be the last you may have for a while."

I grit my teeth, alarmed by just how easily the threat creeps into his voice. I suspect he chooses now to deploy that bit of information for a reason. Most likely as a prompt to get me to ask, "Are… Are you going to kill me?"

He laughs. "Have a seat, Ada-Maria. This time, I'm afraid, the meal isn't entirely for your benefit. I'm starving."

Surprisingly, I sense a note of truthfulness in his voice. Maybe shock alone is what finally draws me closer to the table. I pick a chair halfway down the table from him, but as I pull it out, he shakes his head.

"No. No games tonight; you sit by me."

I bite back a sigh and approach him, still smoothing my hands down my front. God, it's as if every little thing I do might give away what I've done if I'm not careful. My hands shake. I don't know what to do with them. Can he somehow sense traces of the drug vial on them?

He says nothing as I sit. Here, his scent hits me full in the face, and another thought creeps in before I can help it, far beyond escape or my kidnapping.

I wonder how he smelled after fucking Alexi, drenched in her cheap perfume. The two-dollar hooker smell wouldn't mesh well with the spicy tinge of his aftershave. Though hell, they deserved each other. Why should it matter?

Still, sometimes I wonder if Tristan thought I really was as dumb as I looked, or if he just didn't care to hide it. He never tried to wash her smell off him. I was paranoid that I could taste her on his lips whenever he kissed me.

My only saving grace had been to remind myself that Tristan was too selfish a lover to go down on me, let alone her. But who knows? It kills me that I don't.

And now Domino…

"You seem distracted tonight, Ada-Maria."

He's touching me—a reality that doesn't sink in until I see his fingers moving from the corner of my eye, twisting a strand of my hair around a thick, calloused thumb.

"Tell me you've been a good girl while I was gone." His inflection dips in a way that makes me shiver. He wants an answer.

"I-I did what you said I could do." Belatedly, I realize how pathetic that sounded. Weak.

But as sick as it is to admit, I think I satisfied him. His tongue flits across his lower lip.

"*Only* what I said? You wouldn't lie to me, now would you, Ada-Maria?"

I jump, nearly choking on the nerves bouncing beneath my skin. The only way to distract from them is to speak, so I blurt the first thing that comes to mind. "You know a lot about lying, don't you?"

He sits back and claps his hands, ushering in another parade of servers who place a series of platters onto the table. At least he wasn't lying. The platters of baked meat look and smell like seasoned chicken, though I barely pay attention to them, or any of the other dishes.

For whatever reason, something makes me meet his gaze and hold it.

"I never lied to you," I say.

He sits forward again, leaning his face alarmingly close to mine. "Your father did plenty of lying for the both of us," he says. Reaching past me, he drags a plate so close to the table's edge it nearly falls into my lap. "Eat. Help yourself."

One of his servants fills his plate before scurrying out of sight.

I don't touch mine.

"I never lied to you." It feels important to repeat that. To ensure he can hear the honesty in my voice. And the hate.

"No..." He lifts a glass of wine I didn't notice until then. Bringing the rim to his mouth, he inspects me before taking a slow sip. "You just lied to everyone else, didn't you? Though considering the family you grew up in, do you even know what's the lie and what isn't?"

I hate how damn smug he sounds. I reach for my own drink only to stop short inches before bringing it to my lips, sloshing wine onto my lap.

"It's not poisoned," he admits—grudgingly, I suspect. His reluctance alone gives me the courage to take a sip.

It's divine. One of the finest vintages I've ever tasted, and I nearly choke in my rush to gulp it down.

"Didn't your Papa teach you, Ada-Maria? Never drink on an empty stomach."

Gasping for air, I sloppily set my glass aside, relishing the soothing burn of alcohol. It alone must give me the courage to spar verbally with him.

"My father taught me that all men are bastards who lie, and cheat, and steal. It's good to see that he, at least, didn't lie to me." It's a selective way of looking at it.

One he isn't amused by.

"Lie to you... Like your Tristan?"

I flinch, feeling fear flood my veins. Does he know that I found the pictures? Or was I so stupid as to give myself away? I can't tell.

Peeling his gaze from mine, he turns his focus to his food.

"You should eat." He picks up a fork and stabs at a piece of meat. Then he palms a knife and slowly severs it into pieces.

I swallow hard, flicking my gaze toward the selection of silverware lying beside my place setting. I wasn't given a knife, just a fork, and spoon.

"Miguel is a damn good cook who excels at preparing both impeccable entrees as well as corrupt politicians. Don't hold one experience against him. Eat."

"You make a joke out of it?" I croak hoarsely. "Cooking my father like some fucking animal?"

He inclines his head and samples a bite of meat. "You and I both know that he's done far worse to far more people, Ada-Maria."

Do I know that?

"N-No," I insist, pushing back from the table. "He could be ruthless, but even he wasn't that cruel—"

"Did he whip you?"

His tone startles me more than the question itself. I would never expect that low, gruff note. Like he cares. Does he?

No, I decide, looking at him. He merely wants another way to get inside my head.

"*You* did," I point out.

"Yes." He stabs at a green vegetable and brings it to his mouth. "I did. Which reminds me…" He pushes back from the table as well and motions with his hand. "Stand up."

My first impulse is to immediately sink into my chair.

His eyes take on that hard gleam again. He isn't asking. "I said stand up—"

I nearly knock over my chair in my haste to comply. When I do, he jerks his chin, and I step back from the table.

"Turn around."

My cheeks flame as I spin. When his low growl catches my ears, I go rigid.

"Goddamn," he rasps.

I don't know why I look. Something well beyond fear compels me to. When I glance over my shoulder, I find him stroking his jaw, his eyes on my sore, rent skin. Only by watching him do I catch his lips move and make sense of the rough grumble of syllables to leave his mouth next.

"So fucking beautiful."

Beautiful. Only a monster would find beauty in blood and pain. Whatever drug he gave me has long since worn off. I can feel every stinging, burning inch, and it hurts. But when I delve into that pain, my wounds don't seem to be the source of it. Just a selfish, vain realization.

He finds me beautiful only like this, bloodied and broken.

But he fucked Alexi with her perfect flawless skin. He didn't have to whip her.

"I always knew there was something wrong with you." The words are flying off my tongue, and it's too late to choke them back. I blame the wine.

From his amused glance, I assume he does as well.

"You did, did you?" He returns to the table and pours himself a serving of wine. Then he reaches for my glass and fills it as well. "Is that what you were thinking every time you pranced before me in one of those tight ass little skirts? That I was *wrong* for you?"

I grit my teeth. "I could have anyone in Terra Rodea," I snap.

He nods and takes a slow sip of wine. "Anyone but me."

He's right.

I think of him again with Alexi. Fucking that bitch.

Impulsively, I stagger to the table, snatching my glass of wine. I start to bring it to my mouth but sometime during the motion, I pivot and hurl it against the wall instead.

It shatters, and the liquid goes flying, staining the white wall like blood.

"You'll wish you hadn't done that," Domino warns.

Pride is a strong enough barrier against fear. "If I wanted you, I could have had you," I tell him. "You think you're better than any other sycophant to circle around my father like a vulture? You're all the same, with the same greedy cock and the same taste for a tiny waist and big tits. In fact, you were never worth my time—"

I don't even see him move.

My chin is in his grasp before I know it, wrenched back until I have no choice but to meet his gaze.

"And if I wanted you, I would have had you dripping wet any time of day and anywhere, wouldn't I, Ada-Maria? God, you couldn't hide it even if you tried. I only had to snap my fingers, and you'd suck my cock in a heartbeat, wouldn't you? Even in the bath…"

He trails off, but my brain picks up the sordid taunt for him. When he touched me, I reacted the exact opposite way a woman should respond to her captor. With insatiable need, like a shameless whore.

Stab. I want to stab him with the syringe, injecting every ounce of Ativan. God, I want to. My fingers twitch with the desire, and I wrench out of his grasp, contemplating running to my room and grabbing the vial now. Seizing my chance.

Wait. It takes effort to choke down the shame and rage and find the tendril of logic lurking beneath. I can't be stupid and waste my only chance at escape. A better route would be to milk him for whatever I can and lure him into relaxing his guard.

"You were always so transparent, Ada-Maria," Domino taunts, drawing my notice again. I wonder if he's been speaking to me all this time. "So desperate. So fucking pathetic—"

"Then what do you want with me, then?" I try not to let the pain in my voice show.

I fail.

Regardless, I turn to him, meeting those cold green eyes once more.

"Why kill my father but take me?"

"Why?" He laughs and snags my chin again. Using it as an anchor, he drags me toward him, bringing our faces within an inch of each other's. "I want something from you, Ada-Maria. Something that your father entrusted into your pathetic, weak little brain. I want you to be honest with me. Where is the Inglecias file?"

I rip out of his grasp. "Don't touch me—"

"Then answer me." He advances a step, his expression colder than ever. "Where is the fucking file?"

"I don't know what you're talking about!"

"God damnit..." He's closer in an instant, pressing his thumb against my bottom lip so hard it clips against my teeth. "You're stupid, Ada, but not that stupid. Though sometimes, I will admit. You have me fooled."

His voice... It's dangerous, rumbling through my belly. So deep. So hoarse.

The way I'd imagine him sounding during sex, too drunk on lust to give a damn about maintaining his ruse as a stoic bodyguard.

Enough! I shake my head to snap out of it. It's the damn wine addling my senses. Nothing more.

But then why is he frowning, still stroking my lip. Over and over again. "Give me what I want," he tells me, contorting his voice into a mockery of gentleness. The effect is more alarming than when he shouts. "Be a good girl, and I'll make this easier on you. Though admittedly, your fate is already far beyond my hands, Ada-Maria—"

"Get off me!"

I strike his chest with the flat of my hand and stagger away from him, crashing into the table as a result. Without looking, I feel along the polished surface for a weapon. Something. Anything. Then, as if by a miracle, my finger catches the edge of something sharp. Alarmingly sharp.

I find a dull surface to grab and brandish my weapon before me.

"Leave me alone."

Rather than cower in alarm, he laughs. "You couldn't use that on me even if you wanted to. Here, I'll help." In two strides, he's practically on top of me, snatching my wrist— but rather than wrench the knife away, he manipulates my grasp until I'm holding the tip against his throat.

"Go on and do it, Ada-Maria," he goads. "If you go straight into the artery, it's easy. There will be no resistance from any muscle or bone—at first. Until the full extent of the bleeding kicks in. I hope you like a nice, hot shower because that's what it will feel like—" his voice softens, damn near a whisper. "A warm, relaxing shower that tastes like salt and will stain that pretty little dress. So do it. I'll even get it started for you..."

Horrified, I watch as he tightens his grip, driving the tip of the blade into his skin. He bleeds in a fat bead of scarlet that wells up right over the edge of the knife.

"N-No!" I pull back, and he lets me go. Off-balance, I stagger back and trip, landing on my knees.

"Thought so." He shrugs, knife in hand, and brushes his thumb along the small nick on his neck. "A damn shame —" he brings that finger to his mouth and licks the tip. "I was looking forward to it. Your body covered in blood has always been a fantasy of mine."

I choke. At the back of my mind, I realize this is exactly what he wants—to push me to the brink. I'm playing right into his hands by shivering, gaping in fear.

My father operated the same way. Men like them rule by terror. The ability to sow confusion and doubt in their enemies so that they never see the knife poised to stab them in the back. I can't resist glancing over my shoulder just in case.

"I'll warn you, Ada-Maria," Domino says. "I'm almost bored of our game. Give me something useful if you want to play a little longer. Inglecias. Where did the bastard keep the file?"

I truly don't know, but I sense that now isn't the time to admit that. Instead, I ask the obvious question and pray it doesn't set him off. "Why do you care?"

He blinks, his eyes narrowing. "Information is money," he says, switching back to that disarming growl. "Let's just say I know someone willing to pay a damn lot for said information. Where is the Inglecias file—"

"It's personal to you, isn't it?" I ask, seeing through the lie. Still, I'm not completely sure I'm right until a muscle in his jaw lurches angrily.

"Where is it?"

"Did you know Pia?"

How could he, though?

We knew everything there was to know about each other. Or at least, we *did*. Weeks before she went missing, my charming, chatty friend grew quiet and evasive about what she did in her free time. And with whom.

I do have my own life, you realize? she sniped at me once, too busy eying a delicate silver ring on her left hand to even look at me.

Soon, she wasn't just keeping secrets. Our meetings after school became shorter and more infrequent, but she wasn't in any extracurriculars to explain all those consumed hours. I even asked her once, if she were seeing a boy.

Her response was a sly smirk and a wink. *I could be, though I wouldn't call him a boy. Why, Adie? Are you jealous?*

Of course, I was, and out of sheer pride, I never asked her again. Domino is in his early thirties now, meaning he would have been in his twenties back then. Too old? For a normal teenager, perhaps, but I soon learned that Pia's taste skewed far older than that.

Which makes Domino a fitting candidate, nonetheless.

"Congratulations, Ada-Maria," Domino says dryly. "You have managed to bore me—"

"Have I?" A dangerous stunt comes to mind. It's stupid, but I have nothing left to lose. He claims to not care? Then he can prove it. I wet my lips with the tip of my tongue and say, "Pia Inglecias was a stupid, dumb bitch, and she deserved whatever the hell she got."

He lunges, his eyes flashing. I don't think he even realizes what he's done until his hand is already around my throat, snatching the chain and pulling so tight my eyes bulge.

"How dare you even talk about her?"

"So you knew her," I croak, my eyes watering.

He lets me go as I grapple with the fact that I managed to pry some sliver of information loose from him. He couldn't fake that kind of anger. He knew Pia.

And that irrational sense of jealousy returns. I am ten times better than Alexi Rojas in every goddamn way. But Pia? She was always the brighter star of our trio, shining so fiercely I was all but invisible in her shadow.

But back then, I didn't mind being invisible. As the stereotypical ugly fat friend, I think I was at my happiest. I could live as Ada without being seen as my father's tool or a hot piece of ass. In so many ways, it was a better existence than having to stand on my own. Even forty pounds lighter, with a full face of makeup, I always knew at the back of my mind that if Pia were still here, I wouldn't come close.

Domino loving her...*that* I could understand.

"If you knew her," I croak, rubbing at my throat, "then you probably have a better idea of what happened to her than I do, or my father. She was barely talking to me when she left."

A fact that my father used to his advantage. *Why show loyalty to someone who only ever used you?* he demanded. *I am the only one who will ever protect you. Go do this for me...*

"And even now, you continue to play dumb," Domino hisses. The level of disgust in his voice stings. Almost as much as his anger confuses me. "Pia Inglecias is dead," he says. "Don't look so fucking surprised. I'm sure you know when, where, and have been dancing on her grave for the past ten years. Your father kept meticulous records concerning all of that, I'm sure. How he blackmailed the Inglecias family and tried to have them killed—"

"Pia... She's not dead." I can barely say those words out loud. I haven't, not once since she's been missing—even if I've suspected as much in the pit of my soul. She can't be dead. She ran away because she bit off more than she could chew. As for blackmail...

My father wouldn't waste time trying to threaten anyone to keep them silent. He'd cover his tracks too well to care.

"She ran away," I say slowly. I could laugh at the expression on his face. Or scream. "If you were fucking her back then, you'd know that—"

"Pia is dead." His voice rings out, chillingly final. "Stop with the little girl lost act. Your father killed her. You know that—"

"No." I shake my head. "No, he wouldn't."

"And how can you be so fucking sure of that? He's killed women before. Children—"

"No!" I stagger to my feet. "He wouldn't kill Pia, because I had to make *sure* he wouldn't. I'm sure he gave her some money and made her skip town—"

"What do you mean?" He sounds so hoarse. So desperate that I almost forget the monster I'm speaking to.

"Pia stole from us," I say, gutted by the admission years later.

My nearest and dearest friend turned out to be like everyone else in my shitty life—interested in me only as far as my last name went.

"She used me to break into my father's private office, and she took money from the safe. A lot of money. My father was so pissed…" I shiver at the thought, feeling the marks on my back prickle. Not the new ones—the older ones that may have superficially healed, but they always cut deeper than my skin. "He told me that he didn't want to press charges. He just wanted her to know how it felt to have someone steal something important. So, I snuck into her room and took her diary. He was going to use it as leverage to make her return the money."

In retrospect, it was just a stupid act, too petty to despair over. In reality, I was saving Pia from a hell of a lot worse. But still, I never felt dirtier than I did then.

Until I read said journal, of course, and felt even worse…

"I'm sure he gave her some of the money," I blurt, aware of Domino waiting. "And she skipped town, too ashamed to show her face."

"She's dead." Something in his voice makes me look at him again. His eyes are glazed, his lips set in a firm line that makes me suspect that he's moved beyond anger. He's suspicious. And confused.

"I wouldn't lie about something like that."

"No," he admits, and I'm startled by the sigh of relief that rips through me. "You spoiled little fool. Pia didn't steal money from that bastard. She stole—" He breaks off, stopping himself from revealing too much. "Now I know why Roy kept you so fucking close all this time. It wasn't because you were in on his schemes. You were just dumb enough to believe him at every turn. I'm sure that helped him sleep at night."

He isn't joking. He's dead serious.

"Stop talking like you know me! You don't know me!"

"Don't I?" His eyes flash, warning me to tread carefully. "I've known you from that very first day in Don Roy's office, Ada-Maria. I saw you then in crystal-clear focus. A woman with enough beauty to get a man hard in seconds. And the brains of a fucking bunny rabbit. You react to every man the same and prance around, noticing only those with a nice credit card or a sexy sports car—with your Papa's permission, of course. Am I too far off?"

"Yes. You're wrong," I snap.

But he's not.

Fully aware of that, he smirks, his eyes glittering. "How so? The brains part? Or your choice in men? Tell me, in between that lawyer you're fucking and the old man you let screw you a month before dating him, where am I off base?"

My cheeks heat with shame because he's right. I wait for him to grind my nose in my biggest fault of all—wanting him.

"I'm surprised you knew my name, Ada-Maria. At least beyond being your father's dutiful lackey."

And there I have it. It's stupid to cling to this one shred of triumph, but I do.

"I wanted you more than anyone," I blurt, sounding smug for once. "Always."

His smirk falls. "For a viper, bred from a family of liars, you sure are terrible at it."

Though I should be lying. I shouldn't want to prove him wrong. Obviously, this is bait to goad me into the trap of admitting my attraction to him. Still, I can't seem to resist tripping right into it.

"I always wanted you," I tell him, licking my lips as my mouth suddenly goes dry. He doesn't race to cut me off this time. He's watching, waiting. "Always. I watched you every night, in front of the guesthouse. I always tried to speak to you. And when I was in bed alone, I'd—"

I've said too much. My chest is heaving as every breath becomes a struggle. This dress feels too tight. My back is on fire, and beneath his gaze, I've never felt smaller, as fragile as the wine glass lying in pieces across the room.

Because in this moment, at least, all he wants to do is shatter me.

"I am not one of your old men, Ada-Maria," he warns. "Don't play your mind games on me."

A suggestion I am more than willing to heed. I'm so tired. I think of that bed in the room he's made my cell—but not the drugs hidden beneath my mattress. I just want to hide.

"Don't you dare run from me."

I'm spinning on my heel anyway, racing for the door. My thoughts are a blur. I don't even have a clear aim in mind but to run. When I finally make out a direction, I realize that I'm not heading toward that large, rounded door. I'm staggering into that white bedroom instead.

I can hear him behind me, his steps deliberately slow. *Thump. Thump.* They echo as steadily as the ticking of those clocks he has. As relentless and inescapable as time itself.

Think! I move to the bed, gripping the end of the mattress just as he appears in the doorway.

"I think I've grown tired enough of these games, Ada-Maria." He takes a step, and the harsh, pristine backdrop merely serves to illustrate how massive he truly is. So tall, with muscle straining against the sleeves of his shirt. The sliver of his chest visible ripples, his body tense with rage.

Viewing him now, I realize that there is no realistic way I could ever overpower him enough to deliver an injection. My only chance is to get him to relax his guard. To have him sit on the bed of his own accord, or sleep here, even…

One solution suddenly comes to mind—I could seduce him.

And I don't have any other choice.

Any shame or doubt, I push out of my brain as I meet his gaze again. "Why did you never come on to me?" I ask him, fighting to keep my breathing under control.

He laughs, but the question has the effect I want. He's distracted from his anger for now, at least.

He inclines his head, viewing me from behind dangerously thick lashes. Rather than soften his features, the attribute only serves to obscure what little emotion lurks within his gaze. "I thought I was clear enough on that point? No amount of beauty in the world can disguise a soulless interior—"

"I'm not talking about marriage, Domino," I say, sounding stronger than I feel. "I'm talking about sex. I'm sure you've fucked plenty of women with dirty little souls."

Alexi, for one. Knowing he's been with her reveals his high and mighty act for what it is. An act. Which means he had another reason for avoiding me.

"Was it because of my father?" I ask while gathering the nerve to take a step from my hiding place, toward the foot of the bed.

When I do, he narrows his eyes, those beautiful lips parting as if to order me to stop. He doesn't.

So, I creep forward another step. "He isn't here now."

Despite everything, I can't keep my voice from breaking. The reason for my father's absence is standing right here before me while I try to… What?

Seduce him?

If it were possible to, I would have at any other point during the last five years. Perhaps I wasn't desperate enough?

Because I think he likes this. Watching me tremble before him, toeing some invisible line. To cross it would mean debasing myself fully, forfeiting any ounce of self-worth I may have left. Then again, I am a Pavalos.

Nothing trumps survival.

I finger the neckline of my dress. His eyes track the motion, halting my next breath.

"You would fuck me now?" he asks gruffly. "Why? In hopes that I'd be so enamored by that magic pussy I'd let you go?"

I flinch as the jab strikes its target. "N-No. I'm just curious," I whisper. "You haven't tried to touch me."

Not outside of a brutal context, at least.

"If you wanted me, why not?"

"Because the world doesn't revolve around Ada-Maria Pavalos," he snarls, closing the distance between us. "I can die a happy man without fucking you. Trust me on that."

"But you don't have to." The air feels so heavy, every breath takes the utmost effort. Sweat dampens my skin, and I'm aware of how thin this dress is. How sore my back is. How insane it is to play with fire and consider fucking the man who kidnapped me and killed my father.

I've done far worse in my life.

But the flicker of excitement in my belly makes this time so different from the others. I shouldn't *want* this...

"Why not fuck me, if you could?" I ask, my voice heavy. "Especially if you don't plan on letting me go?"

"Because I don't want to be gentle, that's why." He grabs my throat, wrenching me closer before I can react.

I panic, struggling against his grasp before I realize that this is what I wanted. His nostrils flare with my scent as his gaze dips to my breasts.

Startled, I dare to assume that my seduction attempt is *working*.

"I wouldn't be," he says with the sincerity of a promise, still on the topic of gentleness. "I'd fuck you so hard, I'd—" He bites off the rest, but my brain takes up the task of imagining what he'd say. What he'd do to me. *Bite*, I think, given how his lower lip is skewered between his teeth, so hard the flesh is reddened.

Fear rises up, countering the fragile logic I've come up with. I couldn't willingly let someone like him have me. It would be insane. Dangerous.

"That fucking mouth," Domino growls, his eyes on the feature in question. "The things I've imagined those lips doing."

It's like my offer does something to him, unlocking the dangerous confessions I doubt he'd otherwise voice.

"If you want to play, then who am I to stop you?" He grabs my wrist, turning for the door.

To fuck me somewhere *else*, far from my only bit of leverage.

"W-Wait!" There isn't time to think or plan. I lunge for him, pressing my mouth to his, clawing at his shirt to feel the hard planes of his chest beneath.

For a second—just one—I forget. My brain overloads and melts with the sensation I've dreamt about for so long. Few men live up to the hype their good looks and stature imply. Tristan is a prime example. Sex with him was a chore I had to endure, moaning at the right times to keep him excited. I don't think anyone ever exceeded my expectations.

But this…

This is violent. He nips at my lips until they part, stealing his way inside. His taste, his scent, his heat. I'm drunk on all three, dizzy and breathless within seconds.

Abruptly, he pulls away, stepping back, his lips wet. He was toying with me, of course. Just as I think the thought, he snags a handful of my dress, lifting it.

The style forces me to raise my arms to assist him. I swallow in anticipation of his expression as the final piece of fabric is lifted away.

What I find is hunger. Raw open lust so scorching my skin feels seared in the face of it. The restraint he showed in the bath snaps. Boldly, he cups my breast against his palm, groaning at the feel.

I stop breathing at the sensation of his touch. Heavy and rough—yet soft and teasing. He is a wealth of contradictions as he strokes the peak of my nipple with his thumb.

I can't suppress a gasp.

At the sound, his eyes meet mine again, darkening as if he's battling some internal dilemma. Whatever conclusion he reaches makes him shrug.

"Fuck it." That gruff exhale is my only warning as he shoves me back onto the mattress. He rakes his gaze over me, settling between my legs.

At the same time, he's already ripping open the front of his slacks, and my eyes latch onto his movements, more curious than I'd ever admit out loud.

He's gorgeous. He's terrifying.

Already erect, he springs free, and I'm horrified to realize that I don't know what initially aroused him. My offer? Or seeing my back in the dining room?

Without revealing the answer, he steps forward, mounting the bed after me, and my attention returns to the task at hand. Not that he seems inclined to let me take the lead. He shoves my left thigh aside, making room for him to crouch between both. Harsh, his hands slide beneath my hips, yanking me closer.

A thrill shoots down my spine, mingling with a fiery burst of pain. It hurts, but the pain is like a welcome anchor to the grim reality. This isn't about lust, or even fucking.

This is war. To stay alive, I have to grit my teeth and bear the agony. I have to arch my hips into him, choking out a moan the way I have so many times before.

"Don't." A sharper sting overrides the various aches I feel. His nails, gripping the swell of my ass, biting deep. I gasp in shock.

And he pinches me again.

"No faking," he commands. "No pretending. I don't want that shit. I want…"

He doesn't tell me. Instead, he shoves his hand between my legs, sliding what feels like a thumb against my outer lips. I can't silence a cry of alarm. It feels…

Like I imagined it would. So damn good. His skin alone sows devious friction, and I can't stop my legs from drifting further apart, opening myself to more.

But his goal isn't to savor me. He rams a thick finger in deep without warning.

My eyelids flutter. *Holy shit.* He's rough, entering me swiftly without care. Like he's searching for something.

Gravely, his voice rumbles against my ear, revealing exactly what. "Wet." He says it with such disgust. Such awe. It's a marvelous discovery. A trap.

As if to prove the slickness he finds is real, he eases another finger alongside the first, stretching them both. Together. Apart. Further. *Too far!*

I cry out, gritting my teeth at the burn of being stretched. He doesn't take his time or rub like I'm some cheap wind-up toy. I get the sense that he's merely testing me instead. Satisfied, he wrenches his fingers free.

I hiss through my teeth at the loss. My legs are quivering, my heartbeat unsteady. I can't seem to catch enough air as he raises his palm to his mouth and spits. When he moves that same hand to his cock, I know that he doesn't need the lubrication. He's doing it to prove a point—this is what he thinks of me. A whore he can take selfishly without preparation. A slut.

Someone desperate enough not to care either way.

Selfishly, he guides himself forward while snatching a fistful of my hair with his free hand. He tugs, slamming his hips forward in the same swift motion.

There is no resistance. At first. It's like my body has become so accustomed to average men that his balls are striking against my ass by the time I register just how deep he truly is. How massive.

My lips fly apart, my voice a squeak. "You're so big."

He grunts in annoyance, pinching my inner thigh—but I'm not lying.

He's verging on the edge of painful, every thrust like being rubbed raw from the inside out. But when he eases himself nearly all the way out, the friction is like dropping a lit match over a trail of gasoline.

A strangled cry echoes back to me, and it's a second before I realize that it's me. It's been so long since I've felt something so intense. Nerves I'd forgotten existed come alive, begging for attention.

From him.

And he somehow manages to stimulate every last one as he shoves himself back in, slamming home with a grunt.

Even his sounds feed the tempests of sensation washing over me, addling my senses. I rock my hips into his next thrust. Groan when he slides out. Again. Again.

We're jerking across the mattress. Soon, my head slips off entirely, dangling over the floor as he grips me tighter, increasing his pace.

It's so damn good.

I'm whimpering beneath the onslaught, feeling my belly tighten like a rubber band stretched taut. Too taut. Snap!

My spine arches, fingers grappling for a fistful of the sheets. Orgasm, I realize. I can't remember the last time I had one like this. So intense I can feel every muscle clamping down over his cock. Every pulsating ridge of muscle ramming inside me, heedless of the way my entire body tenses.

My lips are open, but I'm too breathless to make a sound, my eyes on the opposite wall as my head lolls in time to his movements, slamming off the mattress.

"Fuck!" He lunges, sinking his teeth against my collar bone.

I can feel him coming inside me, and it's seemingly endless. I'll burst from the force of it, but he's already wrenching himself free.

Don't let him go.

The thought drives me to muster my aching limbs into motion. I grab him, finding his mouth, kissing him with all I have.

Tire him.

I don't think. I crawl onto my knees, shoving him back.

As his eyes meet mine, I freeze, waiting for him to shove me off. His gaze narrows instead. Impatient.

Without needing a prompt, I rake my fingers down his chest, tug at the remaining buttons holding his shirt together.

"Don't." He bats my hands away, but inclines his head lower.

Somehow, his cock is semi-hard, practically lurching into my hands. I ignore my hesitation and lower my head, taking him into my mouth as deeply as I can.

"Shit!" His fingers grapple for my hair, grabbing chunks so hard my eyes water.

I suck him like a starving woman, ignoring the taste. Until I can't, forced to acknowledge that it's nowhere near as repulsive as it should be. We taste like salt and sin together. Wrong and right. So damn good it makes my heart ache.

"Enough." He's thickening again, swelling over my tongue, but I don't stop. I can't. The desperate need to keep him here dulls me to everything else. Like common sense warning me to heed him. Like fear.

When he tugs on my collar, ripping my head free, I choke out a reply as his eyes flash dangerously.

"I've always wanted to taste you." My voice is so breathless, he can't tell if I'm lying. Am I?

Confused, he watches me, but he doesn't shove me off.

I return to sucking him, surprised by the pulsating ache between my legs. I'm so sore, overly sensitive from an orgasm.

And yet, I could take him again. God, some sick part of me wants to. Needs to. I'm writhing, rubbing my thighs together just to dull the ache.

"Jesus Christ," he says throatily. I can't tell if it's my mouth he's referring to or my arousal, tinging the air. My entire body betrays me. I couldn't hide my pleasure if I tried.

"Get on your knees." He pushes me back again, so abruptly that liquid sprays from my mouth, my lips still parted in an o-shape.

A smug gleam alights his eyes, setting my entire body on edge.

"Do it." He snatches my hair to make me comply faster, forcing me to spin, putting my back to him.

He doesn't waste time taunting me. He runs his finger down my spine before stroking directly over his new target.

I wince, real fear breaking through the lust.

Men have fondled my ass before, begging me to let them take me there. I heard that whores like Alexi preferred it, eliminating any risk of pregnancy, but I never was a fan.

When Domino nears that area, he doesn't beg for permission. He breaches me without warning, utilizing the hard tip of a thumb.

I shudder. "D-Don't." My act slips. I'm afraid.

He doesn't care, driving himself deeper as my muscles fight to keep him out. It's such a different violation than the other. My body can't make that part of me as ready. The only solution is to let myself relax into him and force my muscles to allow him in.

And the pleasure here is different, slow-burning and cautious.

"You'd let me take you here if I wanted?" he asks, his voice so thick I can barely make out the individual words. He thrusts in a little harder, venturing a fraction deeper, and my cry is too sharp to smother. "Hell yes, you would."

And that pleases him. Excites him.

He shoves me onto my hands, gripping my ass, and my teeth clatter as I try not to resist, bracing myself for the pain.

He enters my pussy instead, taking effort to go deep and hard.

This orgasm is harder to find. I have to reach between my legs, stroking my clit, finding it swollen and dripping as he thrusts in again. Lightning flashes with every stroke. Finally, release.

I groan, burying my mouth against the sheets to smother the noise.

He shouts, scratching me brutally as if in punishment.

He wanted to fuck me. Hurt me.

He didn't want to enjoy it so damn much.

CHAPTER ELEVEN

I get my wish. He pulls out of me but doesn't go far, lying on his back within the tangled sheets. My lungs burn as I try to catch my breath while dragging my legs together, feeling his seed drip freely between them.

If my life weren't already in question, I'd book an appointment at a clinic tomorrow—despite the implanted birth control I had placed in my arm just a few months ago. It's advertised to be good for four years at least, but this night alone will put that to the test.

I'm never this reckless. Even Tristan never took me raw, and I don't think he's filled a condom with half as much as what I feel inside me now.

Sex, in my experience, is normally such a boring, casual thing.

Neither term can even begin to apply to what just happened with Domino. That was something far different and far more violating. It was destruction. Being dipped into hellfire.

My overall body throbs badly enough to have been burned. I'm moaning with every breath, shaking as the high wears off and reality sets in. My back is wet with more than just sweat. The stench of blood intrudes on his masculine flavor. It's too much to handle all at once.

I just want to sleep.

But I can't.

Lifting my head, I look at him, only to realize that he's watching me. His eyes gleam, mockingly alert. I haven't even begun to tire him.

"Your little stunt won't get you anything from me," he says bluntly.

Concealing my disappointment, I lick my lips and wince as my tongue strikes an open wound. He bit me. "I… I don't want anything from you."

"Bullshit." He props himself on his elbows, an eyebrow raised with open suspicion. "You're so used to seducing men; I'm surprised your cunt doesn't have a credit card swipe. Did you think you could convince me to take you home if you fucked me? Be a good boy?"

I hate how he makes me sound.

"Then I'm sure I fit your standards," I bite back, picturing Alexi. Only as the words leave my mouth do I remember that I wasn't meant to see those photos.

And I might have just given away my entire fragile plan right on the verge of putting it into action.

"You don't know a damn thing about what I want," he counters, lying back, his eyes on the ceiling. As the seconds pass, I dare to hope that he missed my slip-up. "But if you thought to play your little mind games, it's too late. You should have tried to fuck me that first night. I still hadn't decided, then..."

"Decided to what?" I ask, falling right into the verbal trap he sprung.

"Sell you."

I wait for him to laugh or taunt, or otherwise reveal the joke for what it is. A joke. When he doesn't, I'm not surprised. Deep down, I think I already knew that his plans for me were far more nefarious than keeping me hostage.

And yet, even as my horror builds, all I can do is ask him, "Why?"

"Why else?" he replies, his tone as level as ever. We could be discussing the temperature of the room for all the emotion his voice conveys. "You are a Pavalos. You know better than anyone that the world runs on money."

He's right—and how much might he stand to gain by selling me? I don't want to know.

Instead, I just pray he goes to sleep while I visually measure the distance between me and the vial. No longer is this a long shot attempt—it has to work. I'm so close. I only have to shift over an inch and reach beneath the mattress to grab it.

But then comes the logistics of getting the medicine into the syringe and injecting him without drawing his notice.

Worry about that as you go, a part of me warns. I've come too far to back down now.

"You aren't curious," he points out, reinforcing that he's still very much awake. Fully in control. "I'll admit, selling you might not have been my original plan—" I shiver as palpable anger stretches his voice taut. If this is him holding back, I shudder to imagine what his original plan may have been. "But then I asked myself, why disrupt what was already in place?"

I catch that low note in his voice. It's a taunt, daring me to question.

"What do you mean?"

"Your boyfriend," he says. "Tristan, was that his name? He's been planning it for a while, Ada-Maria. To lure you somewhere far beyond your Daddy's control. Arrange for a violent 'kidnapping.' Have you whisked away right under his nose and profit from selling you to an underground trafficking ring. It was a pretty solid plan when all is said and done. One I'm sure he didn't devise on his own. All of it calculated to catapult him as the chosen media darling to speak out against the rampant violence against women crusade your father championed. Bravo—" he claps. "Sadly for him, he didn't plan everything as meticulously."

"You killed him," I rasp, but some of my initial horror is tempered by the grim reality that I don't believe he was lying.

My God…

I think back to how eager Tristan was to meet me, despite having blown off previous dates for important meetings or dinners with his father's influential contacts. I suspected he was planning his own political run.

One of the main reasons my father sent me in his direction in the first place.

But this… It's a level of ruthless, cruel calculation that has frankly become the norm in Terra Rodea. Everyone sees anyone else as either a prize to be won or a rung to step over on the ascent to power. Tristan, my father, Alexi. They're all one and the same.

Ironically, the only person I ever suspected to be any different lies beside me now, the most cut-throat and cynical of them all.

"His plan didn't go accordingly," Domino says, in response to my last accusation. He sounds so unbothered by it all. So cold.

Any remaining heat on my skin cools, and I'm freezing— and yet this moment feels too fragile that I don't dare slip beneath the covers.

"I always thought you were different from him," I say, though I'm not sure why I choose now to make this confession. Though, there's no better time than the present, especially if I can't find a way to escape, my destiny leaves no other chance to say these words to him. In a sense, it's cathartic to get them out. "My father. I used to think that you were too kind to belong in his orbit."

"Kind," he echoes with obvious skepticism at that word choice. "Was that before or after I performed hits on his enemies? Before or after I threatened his rivals and paid off the many women he fucked outside of his marriage? You have a warped perspective on kindness, Ada-Maria—"

"You were different," I insist tiredly. On paper, his actions are just as horrific as Roy Pavalos', but I always sensed an intangible quality to him that set him apart from the others. My father surrounded himself with cutthroats, cowards, and despots. None of them would drag me from a highway in the middle of the night without demanding something in return. None of them would make sure my mother always had her secret prescriptions filled while my father was too busy playing politician to care that she was dying.

I'm ashamed to admit it, but even I haven't been there for her. I love her, but from a distance, admiring her gentle calm and the grace I never inherited. The reality is we're virtual strangers. By the time I turned fifteen, she was already a specter in my father's shadow, meekly agreeing to send me away to a school rather than go against him. And yet Domino deferred to her with perhaps even more reverence that he displayed toward my father. No one else blended duty with humanity the way he did. I saw it myself.

"So naïve," he murmurs.

Something disrupts my matted, sweat-soaked hair—his hand, I realize, running over my scalp to smooth back the strands.

"So trusting. You hit the trifecta, Ada-Maria. Saint fucking Teresa herself."

"You don't have to mock me." I shift away from him before I remember how important it is that I remain close to the edge, focused on my ultimate goal. I can't let emotion distract me now. I'm so close.

"You're right." He starts to sit up, twisting toward the opposite end of the mattress.

"Wait!" I reach for him, desperate to keep him here any way I can. "Just tell me why. Just tell me, please!"

He pauses, reaching out to graze my jawline with the pad of his thumb. "I like you desperate," he admits. "So eager to please. Keep this up, and you'll fetch me a hefty penny at auction."

I flinch. *Auction?* That term was designed to throw me off even more than he already has. It's working.

"I just want to know," I say, marveling at the fact that he hasn't shrugged me off. "Were you planning to betray my family all this time? Please..."

"You seem very interested in initiating pillow talk," he says softly. "I assumed your Tristan wanted to sell you for the clout and money it would garner him. I think I had it all wrong."

It's a low blow that resonates more deeply than I'll ever admit. My eyes sting with the threat of tears. Suppressing them is my first impulse, but I can't. They fall freely, and Domino's eyes narrow.

He drags his thumb up to capture one, watching it break open against his skin.

"Fine," I say, pulling away to curl onto my side. I'm taking a risk by doing so. But it seems to be the only way to reach him. To provoke him outright. "Leave. Prove me wrong. You're just like him."

I don't turn to see how my words land. If anything, I almost hope he does leave. A million different realizations are waiting to descend the second he's gone. I'll have to face the aftermath of everything he's revealed and everything I've done…

For now, he stays.

"I want to hear you say it," he proposes, still in that unsettlingly deep tone. "You say you wanted me. Why? What gets little Ada-Maria's pussy so damn wet?"

I cringe at the crass language. My only rebuttal is that same childish statement. "You were different."

He's sexy enough, but deep down, I can admit to myself that his personality was what kept me watching—the mystery of who Domino Valenciaga might be at his core.

Someone different, I'd hoped, far from the norm of bastards I grew up around.

And yet, he's not satisfied. "How?" His fingers creep through my hair again, this time tugging as he goes, irritating my already sore scalp. "What about me was so damn special to you?"

"You could ignore me," I croak, hating how pathetic my voice sounds in comparison to his. Weak. Vulnerable. He doesn't scoff or deny me outright. No one could lie so tragically. "You didn't treat me like some trophy. You watched everything and everyone. You seemed fair."

Men in far lower positions of power than him lorded their influence greedily. As Roy Pavalos' righthand man, he could have commanded an entire slew of lackeys and women in his own right.

Though, apparently, he had.

I'm dying to ask him about Alexi. How long has he been fucking her, and why? It couldn't be for her thrilling intellect. It's aggravating how deeply the bitch managed to integrate herself into my life. First Pia. Now any man I take an interest in.

No one in my orbit is spared her insidious influence.

My assessment of him, however, only seems to amuse Domino. He laughs. "A fair man with an interest in being easily seduced—" a sharp reminder of my last slip-up. Thank God he can't see my face. "You watched me enough to categorize the women I fuck?"

There's another taunt lurking somewhere within that phrasing. More importantly, I sense a trap. *Damn.*

"I… I didn't have to," I say carefully. "I saw the closet. You must keep this place busy with a wardrobe as large as that—and expensive. I don't even think my wardrobe is as well stocked."

And considering that my only value to my father extended to how I dressed and how he could use my appearance to his advantage, that says a lot.

Domino continues to chuckle, and I stiffen at the sound. It's harsher. Angry? As if he didn't mean for me to see that part of this room.

"I'll make sure Ines is more careful when selecting your clothing from now on," he warns, and I shudder at the thought of getting the woman into trouble. Though, as he continues stroking my hair, I get the sense that the brunt of his irritation is directed toward me. "As for your little assumption, you're wrong. Four days ago, was the first time I ever set foot in this house. Not long enough to parade a stream of women through it, unfortunately."

I marvel at that. He supposedly came here the same day as my abduction, or close to it. Meaning he's been planning this for a while. Just how long? Perhaps since the day he was first hired…

"So you've killed my father. Then you sell me. And then what?" I ask, unsure if I even want to know the answer. "My father has enemies, but he has allies too. Men who will hunt you down like an animal."

"You forget that I know those men far better than you do," he points out. "I am always one step ahead, Ada-Maria. The police are still scanning the restaurant, hunting for clues of your disappearance."

I notice that he specifically doesn't mention my father. If he were really dead, all of Terra Rodea would be in an uproar, and any missing figure from my father's orbit would be a suspect. His face is probably plastered all over the city on notices stating he's wanted for questioning.

Which means wherever this place is, he's confident no one will find me here. At least not right away.

"We aren't near Terra Rodea," I say, risking taking my eyes from him long enough to glance from the window.

"No. We are far away from Terra. Far from the state. Far from the country."

And somehow, he managed all of this within hours, transporting me supposedly out of the country, all without catching the notice of the authorities.

"Why me?" I ask him, returning my gaze to his face. "I never did anything to you."

"You want to sleep, then sleep," he says. "The rumors were true—your mouth is much more bearable with a cock stuffed in it."

I cringe, my face heating. I hate the thought of him throwing those rumors in my face. Rumors I know for a fact were driven by Alexi.

But he's right. I want to sleep. I want *him* to sleep, and hopefully when he does…

I'll be ready to act.

I startle awake, blinking rapidly through the darkness. Within seconds I realize I'm still in that white room, though now it's bathed in shadow, the lights off. As I sense the mattress beneath me, my heart plummets with a mixture of dread and shame.

Damn it. I failed, letting down my guard long enough to drift off. Domino is gone, and I've blown my one shot at freedom. Numb with despair, I try to sit up and realize that my hair is tangled in something. In *someone*, their fingers, to be exact...

He hasn't left.

Slow and steady, his breath fills the air as a dangerous lullaby. I gather the nerve to look up, catching the chiseled line of his jaw, barely visible in the dark. He's actually asleep, and a terrifying question comes to mind. How long have we been like this?

Beyond the windows, the sky is pitch dark. Hope creeps up

my throat as I look back at Domino. I raise my hand, waving it through the air. He doesn't stir.

Slowly, I gather the nerve to roll unto my side next, lifting my head as high as I dare.

His hand falls free, but he doesn't move. His eyes are closed, his chest rising and falling steadily. He's asleep, and I nearly exhale in relief—only the fear that the sound might wake him keeps me silent.

What now?

My first thought is to scan the bed, searching for my dress, I find it slung over the end of the mattress, and I pull it on, ignoring my disgust at the stickiness coating my inner thighs. My lips…

Shaking my head, I try to focus. Carefully, I inch toward the end of the mattress, holding my breath as I feel along the seam between it and the bed frame. *No. No…*

Here! I clutch the smooth surface of the vial and wiggle it free. *Shit!* It slips from my grasp, rolling across the floor.

My heart falls along with it. There it is. I've blown my chance. I wait for Domino to wake up, but he doesn't move. I strain my ears to track the rhythm of his breathing. Slow and steady, still. He's asleep.

I don't waste any more effort on stealth. I lurch to my feet, racing on tiptoe for the vial. Then I grab the syringe, trying to remove the plastic casing without making too much noise. It's an eternity before I finally get it free and ease off the plastic cap covering the needle. It's so dark in this room. All I have are glimmers of a faint glow entering from the windows. Yard lights?

They barely illuminate the glass of the vial enough for me to find the rubbery top through which I can inject the needle.

Luckily, muscle memory takes over. Ironically, as far as drug use goes, my injecting phase didn't last long. It was too risky. Too ugly, leaving angry red marks that threatened my one defining attribute—beauty.

I switched to snorting and never looked back, but you never forget the intricacies of manipulating a syringe. Though, I don't think this needs a vein. Just muscle. Like an arm or a thigh.

Eyeing the bed, my gaze fixates on one of his outstretched legs, and I decide on my method.

For all my confidence, my hand shakes so badly that the needle goes into the vial crooked on my first attempt to fill the syringe. When I pull back on the plunger, liquid seeps through the rubber top, but I keep going. How much should I pull up? Is the whole vial too much?

I can't remember the dosage, so I just draw back until I can't anymore. The liquid glows amber in the faint orange light. It nearly fills the entire barrel, and for a second, I weigh the possibility that I could potentially give him an overdose. Kill him.

My finger jerks, spilling some of the liquid onto the floor, but there's still plenty left, and my conscience is a little lighter.

Though why the hell should I care at all? This man is a monster, and as I rise and pivot on my heel, I realize that if I do manage to hit a vein when I inject the needle, I could kill him with this. If not with the drug alone, then the infection he'll get from my sweaty, filthy hands, and the lack of sanitation.

But I don't have a choice.

Cautiously, I reach for his thigh, touching him as lightly as I can. Hard bone flexes beneath my fingertips. His knee? I go higher, until I find the thicker, sturdier feel of solid muscle.

Then I aim and stab, shoving the plunger down.

"What the fuck?" He comes alive swinging, easily snagging my hair in the dark—but not the chain.

I clutch the length of it in my palm and leverage my weight against him, ignoring the pain as strands of my hair are ripped clean from their roots.

"No!" I lunge for the door with everything I have.

Somehow, I break away, and I don't look back, staggering into the hall, racing for the circular room.

"You bitch!"

I can hear him raging behind me, crashing like a bull.

Don't look! I just move, despairing as I reach that round door, sure it will be locked. But when I throw my weight against it, it opens.

I race on bare feet down the stone path, meeting no one to stop me. It feels easy. Too easy, but the doubt isn't enough to make me second guess this plan.

I've come too damn far.

So I run, my lungs heaving, muscles aching. Still, I don't stop until the ground beneath my feet switches to dried, rough earth. It strikes me now that I have no idea of where to go or which direction civilization may be.

It's not like I have a choice to stop and plot.

All I can do is run.

CHAPTER THIRTEEN

I t isn't long before I realize that my "escape" is just an illusion.

This has always been a game from the start.

The sun rises, first as a faint glimmer of pink over the horizon, and then turns into a sweltering ball within hours, scorching my body from overhead. The illumination throws into stark contrast just how barren this landscape is. It's the middle of nowhere. In either direction, I only find cactus, dry earth, and scraggly brush.

I've gone far enough from the house that I can't even see it at least. Though, it's not much of a comfort when I compare being held captive there to dying of heat exhaustion.

Or exhaustion in general—my entire body is a throbbing mass of pain. The golden chain, wrapped around my wrist, is a boiling hot iron shackle weighing me down, but I can't stop moving. The second I do, I doubt I'll have the strength to get up again. Sheer desperation is the only thing keeping me going, even as the despair gets harder and harder to ignore.

No wonder he kept the doors unlocked, and the staff never stopped me from leaving. There's nowhere to go.

This place must be miles from any town or even a gas station.

And I don't have the strength to make it that far. My steps are sluggish and staggering as the heat drives out what little liquid remains in my body as sweat.

When I first see the approaching car in the distance, I'm stupid enough to feel a tendril of hope. I even turn to it, limping, my throat so dry it hurts to suck in the air needed to speak, let alone scream. *Help me...*

Then common sense descends once I note the speed of said vehicle—a pace vicious enough to kick up billows of swirling dust that engulf it like a storm cloud. *Run!*

I try, painfully aware of the roar of an engine easily eating up the distance between us. Every grueling, punishing step feels like it lasts an eternity, but it must be mere seconds before the car advances on my position, roaring like an animal. Veering around me, kicking up dirt and dust, it skids to a stop paces away. I've barely remarked that it's too expensive to belong to the average desert joyrider—some imported luxury sort, I bet—when the driver's side door flies open, and Domino climbs out.

Shock alone knocks me off balance. I fall on my side, crying out. My carefully wound chain comes undone, biting into the earth as a jagged mass.

One look at him, and I know my plan failed. He's standing upright, moving easily. Considering that same drug supposedly knocked me out for hours, I doubt a whole syringe wouldn't have any effect on him.

"Did you really think that would work, Ada-Maria?" he demands. Anger rips through each syllable, matching the ire flashing in his eyes. "That you could drug me and just prance away? That I would really make it that easy for you? Do you want to know what you really injected me with, Ada? The equivalent of vitamins."

I can't tell if he's lying or not. But nothing else could explain why he's here now, on his feet, obviously alert.

"I even had Ines prepare a wonderful breakfast in case you decided to come crawling back on your own," he adds, presumably his reasoning for why it took him so long to come after me. He wasn't drugged. He was gloating. "Shame you missed it. Though you can still run if you want." He forms a visor with his hand and comically scans the horizon. "Go ahead. Spend the day running to freedom. You wouldn't even get close. There is no one to save you here."

It's as if his words are the trigger for every ounce of pain, weakness, and exhaustion I've kept at bay until now. I break.

My sobs are dry and gasping with no real tears to show for them. Just teasing hints of moisture that blurs my vision and stings my eyes even more in the brutal sun.

"You're here until I tire with you," I hear him say over me. "After last night, that moment is drawing nearer, Ada. Look up."

He snaps his fingers, commanding me to.

But I can't. *So close...* My eyes downcast, I clench fistfuls of the brown dust beneath me and watch it filter away on a gust of wind.

I was so close.

The thought haunts me, regardless of if it were true or not. As long as I kept moving, I felt close. Brave. Strong. All of those things I never was.

Without my father, I was always nothing. Am nothing.

It was a mindset my mother instilled, abiding by that very creed until she was wasting away before him, and he didn't even notice. She let Roy Pavalos consume her and groomed me to sacrifice myself in the same way.

But I *can't...*

"Come here." I see his shadow as he lunges for me, but I don't move. Not even as he snatches the chain from the ground, unwinding the tangled mass. "You were quite convincing; I'll give you that," he says, letting the chain loosen as he returns to the car. "Spinning your little lies. Trying to get my guard down. Using the one talent you do have. I'll be sure to add that skillful mouth of yours to the listing. Those bastards at *La Guarida del Tigre* will have fun with that."

La Guarida…

I lose track of the thought as he braces his free hand against the car's sideview mirror and wraps his length of the chain around it.

"Think about how many other talents you might have to save yourself, Ada-Maria. Because when I get you back to the house…"

He lets the threat hang in the stifling air, conveying the same promise as a death sentence. I can't run anymore. I can't fight him. All I have to combat him with are three pathetic words.

"I hate you."

He scoffs and tugs on the chain, yanking me forward. I barely manage to brace my hands over the dirt to catch myself.

"Move."

He climbs into the car, slamming the door after him. I consider lying here, unmoving, letting the heat and exhaustion finish me off. I barely have the energy to stand. Slowly, I attempt to, groaning as I rise to my knees.

And the car begins to move.

As does his end of the chain. Unraveling, the coils of gold kick up dust as it extends with every inch of distance he gains, until…

Clink!

It's like being caught on a fishing line. I have no choice but to crawl in the direction of the pulling force. Stagger. Fall. Stand. Run.

Die.

He doesn't relent, no matter how many times I trip. The chain gets so tight I swear it will snap. Frantic, I grip it with both hands in a vain attempt to loosen the pressure. Then it becomes my only stabilizing force to find my balance.

The sun bears down, blindingly hot, until I can't see the car. I can't see anything. What a fitting metaphor for the hell my life has become—well before the kidnapping. Two years ago, I finally tried to take steps to end it.

And I failed.

If anything, this moment is the chance to finally make up for that regret.

So, I close my eyes as the chain grows tighter, cinching my throat.

And I just let go.

"Ada! You look at me! Ada!"

I can't breathe. It's just a relief. At the same time, it hurts. My lungs are on fire, my throat crushed. Even as I try to suck in air, I can't.

I'm dying.

"Shit—"

A metal clang sounds. Then air…

I suck in with faint, stingy breaths, but it's enough that my lungs fill. Too late do I realize that I've blown yet another chance.

Because of the same man who foiled my prior attempt.

"You look at me," he demands, his voice like sin, his eyes blazing like fire. "You look at me."

He's scowling, though his voice lacks any anger or rage. He just sounds bitter. A man too devoid of emotion to feel anything in this moment but aggravation.

He stands, but I feel myself being lifted as well. Into his arms, I realize. My vision blinks in and out of focus.

When I come to again, I'm shrouded from the sun, someplace darker. In a car? The engine roars beneath me as my head lulls with the force of the motion.

The driver's back is to me, but his scent is life-giving, sustaining my body when every inch feels broken and battered.

"I…" Trying to speak is excruciating.

He doesn't react, but it feels suddenly important to say it, if only for myself.

"I've loved you…since that day. On the road. I did. But you were just like them…"

And he just happened to join the long list of people I ever cared about.

My mother.

My father.

Pia.

Alexi…

In their own way, they all sold me, in the end. He just went about the most literal method of doing so.

CHAPTER FOURTEEN

The world is wonderfully quiet. And warm. And peaceful. And perfect.

Until noise crashes through my beautiful, white wonderland of unconsciousness. It's faint, as if heard from a radio, but I can't deny a sign of the real world rudely intruding upon my private sliver of heaven.

"…beginning to think you're reneging on our agreement, Dom."

"I told you," a man replies, his voice cold. "I got carried away. It's only been a week. She needs another one here at least. Unless you want her price cut to a third of what you could get for her. That's if she doesn't scar."

"If I didn't know better, I'd assume you played roughly with your toy on purpose," the first speaker scolds. "That way, you don't have to share. But you wouldn't be so sloppy as to do that, would you, Dom? She was your bargaining chip to bring me in. You change your terms, then I'm entitled to change mine. Take your week. Though, I might pay you a visit to ensure there are no more mishaps. You can play with your toy, but don't forget that technically, little brother, she belongs to me."

"You're more than welcome to take her from me. That is, if you have the balls, *big brother*."

"At least I *do* still have mine," the man counters. "Ada Pavalos already has yours in her manicured little hands, doesn't she? A week, Dom. No more."

Silence falls again, but it feels fragile, broken more frequently by various soft noises as if a veil is slowly being lifted…

Until everything is free to assault me all at once. Chirping insects. Muffling footsteps. More noise, noise, noise…

And a voice.

"Hold off on reinserting the tube," a man says, his tone resonating authority. "Her last dose should be wearing off. I'll see if she'll eat by mouth. Keep the equipment near, just in case."

Whoever he's referring to, he must hate. Utterly loath. Thinking of the negative emotions makes my head ache. Pain is cruel, creeping into my delicate realm of peace. My head. My skin. Everything, *everywhere*.

I just want to sleep, but with every passing second, I feel that oblivion slipping further and further away. Soon, the white haze around me turns brighter, pierced with bits of yellow. Sunlight. It's so vivid, like droplets of gold, shining so bright it hurts. I try squeezing my eyes shut and wind up blinking.

Gradually, my protective cocoon shatters, revealing the reality lurking beneath. I'm in a room, one decorated in shades of white and tan and a mockingly blue sky viewed beyond a row of windows. I think it's meant to be as beautiful and relaxing as my hazy dreamland.

But it isn't. My heart is already racing, my nerves prickling with an awareness that all isn't as it seems. This room is dangerous. So is this place…along with the scent seeping through my lungs with every frantic breath I take.

It's so spicy it burns with every exhale, conjuring memories that flicker at the back of my exhausted brain. A man. A terrifying man.

Domino.

His face fills my vision at the exact moment that name flashes across my consciousness. A sun-kissed gold, his skin gleams, his eyes shrouded by thick lashes, the rigid planes of his face set in a stern mask.

"You're awake," he says with no inflection. "Ines will be around in an hour with your meal. I suggest you eat it."

He stands, revealing that he was seated in a leather chair placed beside the bed. All black, it's glaringly out of place, as is the starkly metal structure looming behind him. It's something medical, I think. My head is throbbing too badly to properly identify it.

God, I just want to sleep.

I can barely process the words being spoken to me next. "…suggest you don't try to get up. Later, someone will come to change your bandages."

My brain sluggishly processes each syllable. *Bandages?*

That word spurs me to look down. Alarmed, I find that my body doesn't exist anymore. All I discover is just a seamless space of white where it should be. Until I move, and the whiteness moves with me. Blankets. Slowly, I strip them away. Beneath, my limbs are whiter than the fabric, damn-near blue, and pink and brown. I'm a patchwork of colors and textures. Tiny spots of dark purplish flesh. Jagged lines of scarlet. Splotches of raw, scabbed skin.

Then strips of white. Bandages. Like I've been ripped to pieces and put back together with glue. A Frankenstein monster of wounds and injuries.

The panic I feel is like a living thing, ripping through my insides, distracting from any other thought. I'm hideous, my one defining attribute gone.

Because he didn't kill me.

I look up and realize he's left the room. The harsher details I didn't notice before stand out. One of the windows is open, allowing in the warm air scented with flowers. I'm back at the mansion, even though I remember running. Confused, I scramble to view my feet and cry out in a mixture of pain and alarm.

They're both wrapped in bandages, but I can feel the raw skin beneath. Blisters and torn flesh ripped away by the dirt.

I walked on foot for only God knows how long.

And I was dragged back.

A hopelessness unlike any I've ever felt sucks my breath away. It's chilling and all-consuming. I just sink inside myself, knowing there is no way out.

No hope.

But I tried. I remember stabbing him with the medicine, and injecting him with some of it. From what I vaguely remember, he didn't seem drugged in the slightest when he approached me in the desert.

Did you really think that would work, Ada-Maria?

Somehow, he knew…

"Your meal, Miss."

I look up to find Ines at the doorway, a silver tray in hand. She advances toward the bed and places it on the rumpled sheets beside me. On it is a bowl of red liquid smelling faintly of tomatoes, a small dish of red berries in a gelatin mixture, and a piece of toast.

The color scheme of the meal seems deliberately designed to resemble my body's current state—burned and bloodied.

I'm not hungry. I try to voice my refusal, but my throat…

It's in agony, so sore even thinking of trying to speak triggers a sharp pain. Gingerly, I trace my fingers along it. The skin feels tender to the touch, scraped raw—but the collar is gone, I realize with a start.

So is the chain.

"Mr. Domino would like you to eat, Miss," Ines says, her soft voice conveying a clear warning.

Domino *commands*.

A wave of white-hot anger washes over me. I only register grabbing the edge of the tray, but it's like I'm watching a stranger throw it across the room. Or attempt to. It's too heavy for me to fully lift, and the tray and its contents merely land at the foot of the bed, spilling across the floor like blood.

If Ines reacts, I don't stay to watch. Instead, I crawl to the end of the mattress and attempt to stand. My legs are wooden, slow to respond to my brain's commands. I have to physically shove them over the edge of the bed. My bandaged feet drag across the floor, and I know standing isn't in the realm of possibility.

So I slide from the bed instead, landing on my knees. My hands smart as I brace them flat and try to crawl in the direction of the mirror. I nearly give up, but vanity gives me the strength where all else fails. I need to see myself. Driven by that goal, I drag myself inch by inch, my cracked nails scraping the marble surface.

By the time I've cleared the side of the bed, I've come far enough to watch myself advancing in the mirror's surface. I'm a broken creature. A desiccated demon, crawling out of hell. My hair hangs limp and lifeless down my shoulders. All I'm wearing is a plain black bra and underwear—neither looks like a brand I personally own, but that's the least of my worries.

My arms and legs are riddled with bandages, but what's been left exposed isn't entirely unmarred skin. I'm a monster. A woeful creation of scratches, bruises, and skeletal limbs.

I'm disgusting, every bit as repulsive as the man I see entering the room claims I am to him.

I expect rage as his dark eyes take in the mess on the floor. Ines stands behind him, her hands neatly folded, head bowed respectfully.

Finally, his gaze settles over me, and I stiffen, waiting for the impending assault I know is coming.

"Ada-Maria will take her lunch on the terrace instead," he says. "Have cook prepare a serving for me, as well. I would like her room cleaned in the meantime. Unless…" His eyes narrow. "She would prefer to continue receiving her meals via a feeding tube?"

Feeding tube. For some reason, his tone draws my notice to the tall, skinny medical device behind him. It looks like an IV pole, with a square box affixed to a long, metal rod with hooks at one end meant to hang bags of fluid from.

Or liquid nutrition.

I've been threatened with a feeding tube once before, five years ago when I had no choice but to see my first therapist —an overzealous woman my father quickly replaced when she took my "depressive state" too seriously. The next one only prescribed pills and smiles, a perfect remedy for the daughter of a man perpetually in the spotlight. Baggy sweaters and loose dresses were enough to disguise my "unusually thin" frame before I learned which number on the scale could garner the least amount of attention without making me look like a whale. It became a game of sorts, threading the needle of that delicate BMI range.

How far could I endure the hunger before it threatened to consume me? As it turns out, for a long damn time. It's sick to pride myself on something so self-destructive, I know that. But knowing that didn't make it any easier to loosen the reigns of control I'd mastered so obsessively.

But I will never forget the sight of one of those machines meant to scare me into eating "normally."

I cradle my throat in both hands, horrified by the thought of a tube being shoved down it, my body pumped full of only God knows what.

"I think you should help Ada-Maria get dressed and meet me on the veranda, Ines," Domino says, turning for the doorway. "Since she seems so inclined to stretch her legs. I'll inform cook as to the change in plans myself."

"Yes, sir."

I stare after him, too terrified to resist Ines' gentle touch as she eases me onto my feet. I lean on her so heavily I'm sure she'll topple over, but she's surprisingly strong, able to haul me back to the bed before entering the closet.

A moment later, she returns, holding a white sundress by its delicate straps. When she helps me into it, it's loose enough to avoid aggravating my injuries. Though, as I take stock of myself in the mirror, I think the fact that I'm able to move at all is due to being drugged again. It's wearing off, enough so that I'm conscious, but the pain is a mere echo of what it must be. Excruciating. In addition to the injuries, my skin is sunburned, my nose peeling, my eyes bloodshot and dry.

How long was I out there before he came for me?

The thought makes me shudder.

"This way, Miss." Ines, once again, is forced to bear most of my weight as she guides me into the hall. It must be late in the evening, just before that golden hour of sunset. It's stifling, with nearly every window we pass open to let in what little breeze exists.

The circular room is empty this time, but just beyond the archway leading to the terrace is a set of white loungers, centered around a low table stocked with platters of fresh fruit, cheese, and crackers.

Domino commands one, a glass of red liquid in hand. He meets my gaze as he takes a sip. Then he nods to the space across from him. "Sit."

I deliberate running. The fact that I'm entirely dependent on Ines to stand is the only reason why I comply with his suggestion—she hauls me there herself, lowering me as he directed.

The chaise is luxuriously comfortable, and this area is shaded by several massive palm trees in terra cotta pots. As a result, the wrath of the sun is diminished to a gentle warmth, and, again, I get that eerie sense of being in most people's version of an ideal vacation home.

Minus Domino Valenciaga.

I try not to look at him at first, but as his lounger creaks with movement, I glance over to find him hunched over the table, piling various items onto a small plate. Finished, he hands it to me.

"Eat." A low rumble, his voice alludes to an unspoken warning. *So, help me God.*

A shiver runs down my spine. Even so, I consider throwing the plate over the balcony.

But then he'd drag me into that room and shove the tube into me himself. He will. That much is all but promised in his gaze. In fact, I think he prefers I disobey him.

So, I grab the plate and snatch an item at random. A grape that looms large as I raise it to my lips with trembling fingers. My throat feels so raw that eating anything at all feels more unappealing than ever. Still, I ease the grape into my mouth and bite.

I chew and chew, cringing at the sharp flavor. When I finally choke it down, tears spring to my eyes. I'd scream if I could; it hurts so damn much.

Still, I embrace the pain a second time to croak, "You disgust me."

He sits back, a lazy grin playing over his mouth as he balances his own plate on one palm. "Try the berries," he suggests dryly. "They're ripe and sweet."

It's a taunt. I can almost see the invisible threat he wields behind the request. I find one of the aforementioned berries on my plate and grip it between two fingers. Sweat beads over the back of my neck as I attempt to bring it to my mouth.

Then I choke it down, squirming at the thought of it sliding down my throat, filling my stomach.

He's watching me, I realize. Sharp with avid interest, he tracks my every move.

"Why didn't you just let me die?" I ask. It's a thought that haunts me as I recall just how close I must have been to that reality. Another hour in the sun. A few more feet of being dragged behind his car…

It's as if the universe is conspiring to bring me just to the brink, over and over again.

"You're worth more to me alive," he says.

"Because you want to sell me," I rasp. "Was that always your plan? Is that why you saved me before? To bide your time for five years?"

He chuckles. "*You saved me. You saved me.* Your imagination gets away from you, Ada-Maria. So prone to exaggeration—"

"I was lying on the highway," I say. Did he really have such a low opinion of me? To think that all I wanted was attention.

But I didn't.

And, naively, I assumed he knew that. That he cared.

His expression hardens again, unreadable.

"Why not now?" I demand, setting the plate aside as the remnants of the berry churn in my stomach. "Sell me now."

He raises a single dark eyebrow. "You're that eager to be paraded on auction before a bunch of bastards willing to buy you? They won't intend to take you out to some fancy restaurant, Ada-Maria, I can assure you of that."

I cringe, but I see through the taunt to his real motive. He *wants* me afraid. He thinks the prospect of that scares me. It does.

But one factor outweighs any potential horror that might await me.

"I'd prefer anyone to you."

"No, you wouldn't." He sits forward, his jaw tense. "I can promise you that."

I try to ignore how earnestly he says that.

"I hate you." I've told him that before, I think. Shouted it.

He cocks his head, dropping his plate onto the edge of the table as if he means to lunge across it. "Good. Your hate means nothing outside of the walls of that fancy house of yours, Ada-Maria. Without your Papa here to wipe your ass and pay your bills, your only worth to anyone is as a body. A warm, wet hole. You'll learn soon enough."

He sounds so serious. As if he doesn't truly realize that he just described the only worth I've ever had from the very start.

I close my eyes, swaying as the air sticks in my lungs and my breathing feathers.

"I want you to sell me," I say hoarsely. God, it scares me how honest I sound. Genuinely ready. "Sell me now. Anyone and anything will be better than you."

And now I can say that truthfully, I realize in horror. I'm armed with the experience of what it's like to have him firsthand. I cringe from the memories, craving anything harsher to replace them. Old men with breath like stale cigars. Greedy lawyers with small dicks and no lasting power.

All of them never pretended to be more. I never expected more. Never wanted more.

"Do it," I hear myself beg in a whisper. "Just sell me. Get me far away from you—"

"You don't want that." His voice is deeper, radiating a warning. *Tread carefully.*

I open my eyes to find him standing before me, grasping my chin with one hand. He's careful this time, applying just enough pressure to force my head back, leaving me no choice but to meet his gaze.

"We can play this your way," he tells me, stroking along my jaw with his free hand. "I'll coddle you, Ada-Maria. I'll hold your hand and treat you like a goddamn princess. Then you give me what I want—" He leans in, brushing his lips against my earlobe. "And then, you can gladly take the hundreds of cocks awaiting you after me, and you can comfort yourself with the fact that I gave you the one thing they won't. It's mercy."

Mercy. My mouth is still wet from the berries, so when I spit, it comes out red like blood, splattering his forearm.

He eyes the liquid with a sigh, an eyebrow raised. I tense, waiting for him to strike me. He smooths a piece of hair behind my ear instead. Gently.

"When you heal enough, I'll make you wish you didn't do that, Ada-Maria," he says. "Count yourself lucky that I am a forgiving man."

He releases me, reclaiming his lounger.

"Forgiving? You are a monster."

He tilts his head as if he never heard the term applied to himself before. Then he nods and grabs a grape from the platter, popping it into his mouth. "I don't think you're in a position to judge the moral character of anyone."

The words sting. They're meant to, designed to keep me on the defense, reacting out of anger. And stop me from asking him the questions he doesn't want to answer.

"When are you going to sell me?" I ask.

He shrugs. "When I grow bored of you."

He's lying. A snippet of conversation returns to me, muddled like static and hard to parse through. *A week,* I remember someone saying.

"A week," I parrot out loud.

A hint of alarm flashes across his gaze, confirming the timeframe as correct.

But in his orbit, seven days might as well be seven years.

"Sell me now."

"Then tell me what I want to know," he counters, sitting forward. I've irritated him, but I don't think my talking is the sole cause.

"Sell me now," I repeat, watching him carefully. "Tonight… I'd take a thousand different cocks just to forget yours—"

There. He's more than angry; he's furious, looming larger, his muscles straining against the fabric of his shirt.

All because I dared to compare him to someone else.

"You'll get your wish soon enough," he growls. "And for the first few, I'll watch. I'll watch them brutalize you in ways you could never dream. This? You'll look back fondly on these days as heaven on earth."

He's not lying this time, which confuses me even more.

My eyes burn, they're so dry, but somehow tears manage to form regardless, sliding down my cheeks. "I don't think so, Domino. No matter how horrible they are, I will gladly forget you."

He's on his feet, and I'm sure he'll strike me this time. He lashes out, instead grabbing my plate.

"Eat—" He snatches an item seemingly at random and shoves it against my mouth.

Instinctively, I clamp my lips shut, turning away.

He hooks his fingers beneath my jaw, wrenching my head back around. Brutally, he continues to shove a piece of fruit against my lips so hard the flesh clips over my teeth.

I cry out, and he lets go, dropping the plate onto the stones.

"D-Don't!" I nearly fall off the chaise in my rush to get away from him. I'll jump off this balcony if I have to.

As if reading my mind, he raises a hand. "Ada—"

"Sir." Ines' monotone voice is like ice water dumped onto a raging fire. We both whirl around to find her standing in the archway of the house, a cell phone in her outstretched hand. "Mr. Jaguar is on the phone for you."

Domino blinks, raking a hand through his hair. "Tell him I'll call him back—"

"He says it's urgent," Ines replies. "Regarding your business back in Terra Rodea."

Domino's eyes widen. "I'll be there in a minute." He turns away, eyeing the mess of fruit scattered across the terrace. "Fuck! Can I get someone out here to clean up this mess?"

"Right away, sir," Ines replies. She rushes to gather up the spilled food herself as Domino storms inside. A second later, I catch his voice, uttered in a low tone, rapidly fading as if he's moving deeper into the house.

"You call me twice in one day? I'm not your fucking whipping boy."

The phone must be on speaker because I hear someone reply, though barely audible, their voice even gruffer than his. "Try ignoring my call again, and we'll test that theory, Dom. I may have let you keep your little toy, but that doesn't mean you get a vacation. I need you on the border. Tonight. A shipment is coming in, and I don't trust Vodello not to fuck us…"

"I will show you back to your room now, Miss." Ines stands before me, her hand outstretched, her expression as blank as ever. She's already cleaned up the food, piling everything neatly onto the platter.

I let her guide me back inside as my mind races. That man sounded familiar, the same figure he spoke to earlier. *Jaguar,* Ines said. A name? Or an alias?

It doesn't matter. What does is, for the first time since I've met him, I think I know a way inside Domino Valenciaga's brain. It turns out that he has the same weakness as any man—pride. A smart woman would be able to play on that. Play *him.*

But to be sure…

I startle to awareness as I'm lowered onto the mattress. We're already in my room, and Ines is swiftly retreating toward the hallway.

"Wait!" I call after her. "He's leaving, isn't he? Ask if I have to stay in here. Please."

She blinks, and I feel that I've caught her off guard. She has to remember which part of her script she needs to recite next. "You should get some rest," she says, her expression carefully blank.

"Please! Just ask him! Ask if I can leave the room. Please…"

She nods and scurries off, while I wait, so anxious I'm holding my breath. When footsteps return, I'm expecting Ines, but Domino is the one who appears, his brow furrowed with open suspicion.

"You want to take your chances in the desert at night this time, Ada?" he wonders. "Don't be fooled by the sun. The temperatures can plummet after nightfall, and I won't come after you quickly, should you try to run."

I lick my lips, contemplating my reply. I've toyed with enough men in my life that it should be easy to manipulate him. In a sense, I already have.

And then I wound up being dragged behind a moving car by my throat.

He's too dangerous to play with. I'll have to tread carefully, treating his ego like a loaded gun. But if he truly wants my admiration, he'll enjoy having me beg.

"Please," I shamelessly croak. "I… I just want to take a bath and stretch my legs. I won't leave the house."

He's advancing toward me in an instant, stroking his thumb from my lips, down to my jawline. It takes everything in me not to recoil.

"I warned you once not to treat me like one of your desperate little fucks," he says. "I'll let you roam to your heart's content, Ada. When I return, I better not find so much as a pretty little hair out of place. If so? I'll have you *begging* me to sell you—and it won't be some coy attempt to rile my pride, either."

He lets me go, marching into the hall as my heart pounds furiously enough to drown him out. I'm not as clever as I thought. He saw through even my little game on the terrace. And yet…

Did he play along out of pure amusement?

Or because he couldn't help himself…

A door slams, presumably the entrance to the mansion. I know he's gone without having to check. The entire atmosphere of the house shifts, and I can breathe somewhat easier.

But not by much.

Time is a constant adversary, but if I work quickly enough, I could use each passing minute to my benefit—or accidentally doom myself more than I already have.

All in all, I have a week to seduce Domino. To what aim? To convince him to let me go? To sell me sooner?

Either act feels preferable to submitting to his form of mercy. I need answers, no matter where my fate takes me. Who is Jaguar? The man he plans to sell me to? And for what purpose exactly?

Though I can guess.

My mind is buzzing as I try to stand on my own and wind up crawling to the closet. Groaning, I manage to open the door on my own and blink to take in the array of clothing.

When viewed the second time, this closet is overflowing in comparison to his. There's at least a full year's worth, and I figure that's without having to wear a single item twice. Obviously, he was lying. Maybe he hasn't dwelled in this particular house long, but he could have had the clothing shipped from somewhere else where he kept a steady stream of women wined and dined.

Or held captive.

Though in five years, I can admit that he wouldn't have much time to "play" with those toys, though. He barely left my father's side, let alone the estate, for longer than a few hours at a time. Once, I tried asking him about his family, during the holidays, I think.

He just nodded respectfully and ignored the question entirely. And all that time, he seethed in silence, hating my father, and hating me.

I can't dwell on that now.

I need to seduce him—*no*. I cringe at that word choice. It's too simple to describe manipulating a man like Domino. I need to get inside his head, whether he likes it or not.

I need to provoke him.

Of all these outfits, however, two modes of attack become clear. Aim for sex appeal with one of the skimpier, black ensembles, or try to claim innocence wearing one of the frothy white dresses like the one I am now.

No. I shake my head, irritated with my own thought process. It's too simple. No. No…

In fact, I've already tried both methods, and both have failed. But I did get him to fuck me using another route entirely—blatant honesty. Desperation.

And if I were desperate to screw him again, I wouldn't waste time on pretty dresses or makeup—none of that fluff has ever swayed him before. I can't resort to the same bag of tricks that I would use to confront a man like Tristan, who rarely thinks without his cock.

Domino uses his brain.

And mine is too damn sore to think. I'm exhausted enough to lie here unmoving and sink into the sleep waiting to descend.

But I can't.

Determined, I brace my hands against the wall and use the support to stand. Slowly, I limp into the room and then the hall, finding my way into the bathroom alone.

The spacious room looks surprisingly welcoming without Domino to taunt me from the clawfoot tub.

"Would you like to take a bath, Miss?"

I jump and nearly trip as I turn to see Ines standing behind me, hovering near the doorway.

"Y-Yes," I say.

Nodding, she starts forward and performs the same routine Domino did, running the water and gathering various materials.

She runs the water pleasantly warm, however.

"Your bandages are due to be changed," she explains before unraveling the ones on my feet. I wince as she helps me into the tub, but whatever she placed in the water feels soothing against the raw flesh.

I smother a groan as I lean my head back against the rim of the tub and let her work.

She washes my hair, combing through the damp strands, and supplies me with a rag to run between my legs. I'm frowning by the time the water finally turns cold, and she approaches me with a stack of towels.

"I will get a nightgown for you to wear, Miss." She starts for the door, but something makes me reach out, spraying water all over the floor.

"Wait! I… I'll find one on my own."

With the bath comes a renewed sense of clarity. I can think again.

And I know exactly the kind of stunt Domino can't ignore. Ironically, it's the same plan I thought of for five years. One I fantasized about, but never had the balls to implement. I had no problem approaching men—but his rejection was one I didn't think I could stomach.

So I never followed through on creeping into his guesthouse, finding his closet, and lying in his bed wearing one of his shirts as a blatant invitation.

This time, there is no thrill. Just a heavy sense of dread as I pad down the hall wearing only a towel. Perhaps she senses my intentions, because Ines vanishes as I creep past my room, toward that door near the end of this otherwise deserted hall.

The door is closed, and for a heartbeat, I'm sure he locked it, thwarting my attempt outright. When I twist the knob, it opens easily, but I have to feel along the wall for a light switch.

The bed has been left neatly made, the closet door closed as well—but the duffle is gone from its hiding place, this time resting in plain sight on top of the cabinet containing the watches. I'm sure the photos are gone, but I find them in the same pocket where I left them.

Like a dare.

Compared to how many times my past self may have envisioned this moment over and over, I don't take the time to agonize over which shirt of his to wear. There aren't many to choose from. In the end, I grab a white button-up and exchange it for my towel. Still dripping wet, I start for the bed.

But something makes me pause before I leave the closet entirely. I grab those pictures, flipping through them until I find the ones of Alexi. He's wearing a watch in one of them, visible on his wrist. Gold face with a scarred leather band.

I look for it among the selection in the case, but can't find the exact one. I grab a similar model, with a darker band instead of brown. It's large on my wrist as I slip it on.

When I reach his bed, I lie on my stomach across the very edge and inspect the pictures again.

Now that I've experienced his cock for myself, no wonder Alexi is smiling so damn hard, her blue eyes sparkling with the everlasting devotion of a dumb, blond bimbo.

We were friends once. I used to think her dumb expressions were endearing, her promiscuity inspiring. She was blessed with a body of a porn star that she didn't have to starve herself to maintain, always the bubbly one of our friend group.

Once, it was just the three of us, her, me, and Pia.

And Domino knew them both. How?

Immortalized in these photos, her sly smile doesn't give me any clues. I always assumed Pia was the one who turned her against me, at least a month before she went missing. One day, we three were as close as sisters, united by a shared, crippling sense of "rich daddy syndrome." Though, in Pia's case, minus the "rich" aspect.

Then one day, Pia was gone, and Alexi was too busy fucking anything that moved to seem to care. Years later, she went away to college, and when she returned, I was the bell of the town, and she went well out of her way to ensure that I couldn't ignore her.

Tristan was just the latest in a long line of men connected to me that Alexi made it her mission to conquer. She never told me why she hated me. She doesn't talk to me at all.

Not that I've sought her out. Some childhood memories deserve to be dead and buried.

Even old friends whom my entire world once revolved around.

CHAPTER FIFTEEN

He's here. I swear, it's like I close my eyes for one second, and open them to Domino Valenciaga bathed in the pinkish glow of dawn, his back to me, his chest bare. A part of me stirs, curious despite myself.

I've seen his cock, but little else of his body overall. And there is so much more to see. His back is ripped, straining with solid muscle that flexes in the faint sunlight streaming in through the windows. He has on a pair of jeans that look covered in dirt. Groaning, he reaches for the waistband and then kicks them down. Plain white briefs are the only thing shielding the full brunt of his ass from view.

I hate that he can still seem so damn beautiful after everything he's done. But I should know better than anyone that beauty is only skin deep.

Seemingly oblivious to the fact I'm awake, he enters the closet and snatches a white tee shirt from a hanger, wrenching it on over his head, along with a clean pair of black slacks. He must prefer this looser-fitting, less casual clothing to the uniform he wore while working for my father.

I watch him, content to believe that he hasn't realized I'm awake.

Until his voice rings out, rough with exhaustion. "This is the part where you get the fuck out." He turns to face me, hands at his sides, eyes narrowed over the sight of me, slumped on my side, hair shielding most of my face.

As I slept, I managed to scatter the photos all over the floor. One, however, seems stuck to my cheek as if I fell asleep eyeing it. I have to peel it off, ashamed as I realize which one I'm holding.

A shot depicting his hand, squeezing Alexi's breast as she arches into him, her eyes partially rolled into her head, her tongue between her teeth.

Disgust makes me angry. Bitter. Hateful.

But I have enough sense not to give in to it now. I already made it this far.

"This is the part where you reward me for being good," I say, not bothering to hide the pain and tiredness in my voice. Judging from the daylight, I probably slept hours, but it might as well have been seconds for the amount of good it did my body. "And you give me something. Anything."

He frowns, his gaze skeptical. He leaves the closet and stoops to snatch one of the pictures from the floor.

"You enjoy looking at these?" he asks, brandishing the photo in question—Alexi's legs spread wide, his hand on her inner thigh. He must have held the camera, straining to get just the right angle.

I want to hiss and make a crude, nasty remark about the rumors involving Alexi and herpes. Rumors I just made up.

Instead, I say, "Didn't you want me to? You left them for me for a reason."

I'm not sure until I see one of his eyebrows shoot up in amusement. Or perhaps it's admiration.

"You aren't as stupid as you pretend to be," he says, tossing the picture aside. "Ask your question."

He keeps coming toward the bed, and I lose track of what I should be focused on. Getting beneath his skin, trying to discover what he knows. Instead, I just gape at his body through my lashes and let the petty, jealous thoughts run wild.

Alexi had him first, and I have to wonder if he was any different with her than he was with me. Though, of course, he was—he wanted her, he merely humored me, knowing all along that I was plotting behind his back.

When it came to Alexi, he acted on his lust.

"How long have you been fucking her?" I ask, my throat still excruciatingly tender.

He frowns, running his hand along the dark stubble speckling his jaw. I doubt he's slept since he left. His yawn isn't for show, and I notice that his eyes are bloodshot as he continues to advance.

He snatches the picture I'm holding, eyeing it once before tossing it aside.

"Does it matter?" he demands.

It doesn't. Still, I can't resist prying. "She was fucking my boyfriend—all of them, actually. I'm not surprised she tried to climb you next. I'm more shocked that you let her."

He scoffs. "The high and mighty Ada-Maria Pavalos is sneering down her nose at me. How will I ever sleep?" He moves to the head of the bed and flicks the sheets back. "I thought I told you to get the fuck out—"

"We were friends once," I blurt, my gaze still glued to the image he threw. It landed upright within my reach, mocking me with its carefree, explicit depiction of raw lust and fun. Alexi's smiling in this one. The sex must have been good. I bet he teased her playfully and took her cowgirl style to watch her tits bounce.

He didn't pin her down like a conquest and grip the collar he had placed around her throat for leverage.

"I know," he says, surprising me. I look over to find him still standing, his gaze shrouded by a wayward lock of dark hair. "She told me all about you."

I stiffen, hating the implications of that. I may not have spoken to Alexi more than a fake greeting every now and again at some random social event throughout the past five years—but I know she hates me.

"All lies, I'm sure."

"Not lies," he counters, sounding surer of that than I like. "She told me all the things I could figure out for myself."

I look back at the floor as he moves. A heartbeat later, the mattress dips, presumably beneath his body weight.

"She told me that I didn't have a shot in hell with someone like you. That you would never know I existed if I didn't have a dollar sign beside my name."

That sounds like Alexi, the bitch.

"I'm surprised she wanted you, then," I snipe. "Especially if she thought I didn't."

The mattress moves again and his heat kissing my skin is the only warning I receive before my hair is drawn back from my face, gathered loosely in a fist.

"You want to know what I want?" He tugs, wrenching my head back until I'm forced to face him staring down from above. "I want you to get out of my bed."

A second ticks by, but he doesn't let go. Gradually, his gaze finds my mouth, narrowing further.

"You want to stay?" he asks. "Then prove it. Give me a reason to keep you."

His voice lowers in a way that makes me suspect exactly what he means, even before he snatches my wrist, dragging my hand toward him.

He doesn't stop until my fingers brush something warm, rigid, and firm bulging beneath the fabric of his slacks.

The right thing to do would be to run. Utter some coy quip about what else he can use to get himself off and save what little shreds of dignity I have left. I might do just that—if I had any pride at all. I'm too desperate for answers. Too desperate to feel like I'm doing something, even if it's playing a sick mind game at my own expense. I'll do whatever it takes to never feel as worthless as I did out in the desert.

"If I do it, what will you give me?" I ask him.

A new furrow appears in his brow—confusion. He didn't really believe I'd take him up on this offer. I can see him weighing the benefits of toying with me or maintaining the boundary between us. I can almost hear the question he must be proposing himself—*Can I really have my cake and eat it too?*

Or, in this case, abuse the mouth he loves to taunt. Before I know it, he has his thumb against the seam between my lips. He presses, ignoring how I wince as he aggravates the healing scrapes and marks left by his slap.

"If you do it… I'll give you exactly what you'd deserve," he says.

I shiver at the *double entendre*. Or maybe, in this case, there are a million different meanings, each one more biting than the last. *I deserve only his cum in my mouth. I deserve to suffer. I deserve to be sold. I deserve, I deserve...*

He pulls back as if expecting me to recoil now and do what he really wants—leave. He can't truly take the risk of letting me claw away another concession, another piece of him, no matter how small.

Alexi should have told him how selfish I am. How greedy, how stubborn. I'm the sort that even if I get hurt in the end, I'll still take the last cookie from the jar. No matter the overall cost, I'll still savor that brief taste of sugar. Or at least I would back when I still craved food at all. Hunger has been my constant companion long after my real friends vanished. It's the only thing I could trust, more satisfying than any cookie or piece of candy.

In this case, my "cookie" is more figurative. After years of craving him, a part of me can't resist experiencing what little I can, any way I can get it. At least then, I can square each session with that tiny bit of myself whispering that nothing is ever worth the effort. There's nothing worth fighting for. The world is shit; why not just starve until I fade away altogether.

That voice gets softer when I roll onto my aching side and press my cheek against his knee. One of his legs is outstretched, running parallel to me. The other he has braced against the floor.

Gradually, his expression shifts from wariness to a steely look I recognize. A dare. A demand.

My hands shake as I fumble with the latch of his slacks, folding down the fabric once I get it loose. That's about as much as I can do alone, I realize. He's too big to counter, and I don't have the strength to tug down his pants enough to have access to him.

Jaw clenched, he does it himself, working his cock free of his boxers. The state of him confirms my grim suspicion as to what aroused him to that extent before. It had to be my back. My blood.

This time, he only has my face to go off on, and he's barely firm, though still intimidating enough. It hurts to open my mouth wide enough to even consider taking him in. Then another consideration takes precedence—my throat is on fire, making the prospect of utilizing much beyond my tongue doubtful.

Not that he'll care. Still, I can't resist a desire to see his reaction if I dared to state as much out loud.

"My throat hurts," I rasp. "I don't think I can take you after all."

His eyes narrow, a smirk flitting across his mouth with breathtaking speed. One of his hands latches onto my skull, and there isn't even time to brace before he's guiding me lower.

The pain is worse than I could imagine. Burning and sharp as I stretch my jaw to accommodate him. I imagine healing bits of flesh being ripped open merely to satisfy his need for depth.

He groans the second he's enveloped in the heat of my mouth, my tongue cradling the underside. If I dull my senses and ignore the pain—and focus on the sheer act of taking him—there is a sick sense of pleasure a part of me gets out of feeling him stiffen. Harden. Swell.

He hates me, but he can't deny the simple pleasure even my battered mouth can provide. Soon, I feel his fingers flex, sinking into my hair, guiding my movements into a rhythm he likes. Slow. Steady. I can't tell if this is truly his preference, or if he's settling out of concern for me.

Then his nails scrape my skull as if to counter any chance of that second option. This is only about his pleasure, nothing more.

To prove it, he groans again, throatier than before, and I ignore the shame just to dissect the sounds he makes. Grunting boar is how I would describe most men—not him. He's nuanced, each groan or gasp conveying a different meaning.

Sharp and grated if I don't meet his expectations. Deep and rasping if I do. He praises me grudgingly with ragged, panting breaths that quicken as his grip on my head gets tighter and tighter.

I can almost track the ascent of his release through his shaft, but he surprises me by letting me go just as he nears that peak, allowing me to pull away if I wanted. And I should.

The first spurt catches me off guard, hot and molten. It feels like my throat is being boiled as I try to swallow. I can't. Coughing, I pull back, and his hand seizes another fistful of my hair to make me face him.

He continues to erupt, splattering the sheets and my chest. Satisfied, he shoves me away and turns to sit on the edge of the bed with his back to me.

"Alexi got one thing wrong," he admits gruffly. "She said you were shit in the sack. A doormat that lies there while it's being fucked." He parrots her voice, but he doesn't have to for me to know every word came from her.

I'm still swallowing him down, swiping my hand across my mouth. I'm shaking. Speaking is a daunting task, but it seems like he's waiting for me.

"Is…that…a compliment?"

He laughs. "No. It's an acknowledgment of your skill," he says, switching back to the mocking growl. "After all, you're the same girl who blew a banker to convince him to fund your father's fledgling campaign."

Ice. My entire body goes cold, and pain is an afterthought as I lurch upright.

"Where… Where did you hear that? Who told you that?"

He inclines his head, his eyes unfathomable again. "Who do you think?"

"Alexi couldn't," I rasp. She didn't know. No one did. No one but…

Domino levels me with a piercing glance. "*Who* do you think?"

"P-Pia?"

He doesn't answer. Standing, he adjusts his slacks and then nods to the doorway. "Get out."

I don't argue this time. I lurch to my feet and run—or, in this case, hobble. I don't stop until I'm back within that white room, crawling beneath the blankets.

Pia told him, he implied.

But how? Especially considering the fact that he seems convinced that she's dead.

Because he probably tracked her down, years later, and he killed her himself, at my father's behest.

I don't know how I fall asleep again—but a dream is the only reason to explain why I'm seeing her now.

Pia, her large upturned green eyes sparkling, a brown curl twisted around her finger. "Don't be so hard on yourself," she said. "If you bothered to wear something other than sweats, you'd have them eating out of the palm of your hand, too."

Them being the gaggle of older boys gathered on the tennis courts near the campus library. We were watching them from above, utilizing the last break before our final class of the day.

"Alexi's wearing sweats," I pointed out, nodding to her tight pink leggings and matching jacket, worn with the zipper pulled down to show her cleavage. Naturally. She wasn't wearing anything underneath it, or the pants for that matter.

"They've all already seen her naked, so she doesn't count,"

Pia remarked in that coy, cold way that could make her approval feel so damn valuable. Her shirt was worth a fraction of Alexi's entire outfit, and yet she wore it with a poise that made her the guiding star of our little trio. Alexi could have been naked right then, and most of the boys would have still snuck glances back at Pia, watching like a queen from our position atop the bleachers. "Alexi doesn't have what you do, and what you have is what men drool over."

"What's that?" I asked, still eyeing Alexi, who was in the middle of popping the round head of a red lollipop into her mouth.

"Innocence," Pia replied. "You have that look about you. That obsession factor. You're the kind of girl a man could spend his entire life chasing after. Alexi can have them panting after her now, but it's just a phase. It won't last. In ten years, she'll be lonely, still showing off her cleavage to get a date. But you? I bet you'll be married to the love of your life by then, happily ever after."

Pia was never wrong. At least while she was alive. It was part of her allure, that uncanny ability to seemingly know everything and everyone. Somehow, she even knew Domino.

What was his relationship with her like? Were they friends? Lovers? Who knew when it came to Pia...

There were so many things about her I'm still in the dark about. Her mystery was part of her charm. And her downfall.

"Mr. Domino requests you join him for lunch."

The soft voice intrudes on the memory, and it scatters. I open my eyes to the quiet darkness found beneath the blankets. When I lift them aside, I find Ines standing at the foot of my bed, displaying a sleek black dress on its hanger.

"Ten minutes," she warns, laying the dress over the foot of the bed. "I will assist—"

"I want to get dressed on my own," I stammer. "Please," I add, as Ines blinks, startled by the request.

She flits her gaze nervously toward the door. "I am not sure…"

"Ten minutes," I say, lurching to my feet. "I'll be there."

Finally, she nods and retreats, more than likely to find Domino and alert him of my insolence.

Which means I need to make this stunt even better than the last. This plan feels like crawling ten steps forward, only to be shoved back past the starting line—but I did get something. Whether intentionally or not, he revealed that he knew Pia personally, enough for her to tell him something about me.

I need to know more. At least something worth bartering my life for. There has to be something from me he truly wants, something worth tolerating me. I doubt it's sex. So what?

He thinks I know of an Inglecias file my father kept, but I suspect that's only part of it.

Confronting him directly has been the only way I've made any headway with him. With one last look at the dress Ines selected for me, I inspect the closet, keeping that time frame at the back of my mind. *Ten minutes.* I can almost hear a clock ticking down, but when I reach for the nearest dress, I realize that the sound isn't entirely in my imagination.

I'm still wearing his watch on my wrist.

With it as my guide, I try to decide which outfit would best impress someone like him. *No.* That's the wrong way of looking at it. A better question is—what would best provoke him? Which of these would best rattle a man like Domino Valenciaga?

Someone who swears I disgust him, but has no problem utilizing my body to his own ends…

With time to spare, my gaze lands on the only dress to fit the bill. I snatch it and head for the bathroom. I dress as quickly as my aching limbs allow, and I barely manage to rinse out my mouth and run a damp rag over my skin before I head for the dining room.

It's overcast, and the lack of sunlight robs the house of its warmth. It's a cold, gray landscape now, with the wind lashing at the windows. Each one is closed today, and the doorway to the terrace is sealed by a set of white lattice doors.

Domino sits bathed in the near darkness of the dining room at the head chair. White curtains shroud the windows and the sight of the storm brewing beyond the trees.

"I see you're well rested," he says as I approach. "So am I—" He sits up straighter, taking in my appearance with a swiping glance. I can practically smell his annoyance, heightening the strange spicy nature of his scent.

He doesn't call attention to my ensemble out loud, however.

"Sit," he demands, palming the table.

I do, inching toward the chair nearest to him. As I lower myself onto it, I know full well he's eyeing my clothing again, seething.

But it's a fragile victory.

This dress is the definition of dichotomy. Revealing and conservative at the same time. With a high, collared neckline and long, loose sleeves, it's damn near matronly compared to my usual outfits. Even Papa didn't specify such modesty with the style of clothing he picked for me.

But despite its form, the material of this dress is reminiscent of tissue paper. Thin enough to see through, catching glimpses of everything from the curls between my legs, to the darker colored flesh around my nipples.

As well as the scabbed, bloodied patches of skin.

I know the sight of it all bothers him. I chose well.

Sighing, he claps, summoning a single server who sets a platter of food in the center of the table. Much like yesterday, it contains an array of fruit and bite-sized pieces of bread and cheese.

Which isn't fair. I'm used to being plied with extravagant meals from my parents' dining table on plates so large it's child's play to make it look like I've eaten while resisting a single bite.

He changes the battlefield, picking food items that put the control in his hands. I can't fake my way out of it, and…

I'm so damn hungry it physically hurts. Gritting my teeth can't distract from it, and I realize that it's harder to resist him if the benefits aren't the same. He won't ignore my denial much longer, and for the first time I'm wary of just how long he'll let me deny him.

Another server appears with a bottle of blood-colored wine and two glasses.

Once we're alone, Domino gestures to the spread. "Eat. Though, since you're dressed as a nun, perhaps you aim to lead us in a prayer first? By all means. I assume you've been praying for bravery, because you've certainly become so brazen overnight. Attacking me. Crawling into my bed. And now you shamelessly brandish that which you've stolen from me—" he nods to my wrist and the watch I'm still wearing.

I swallow hard, knowing that my next words alone will convey the most impact. I can't threaten him, or ignore this slight, either. I have to provoke him.

"Since you plan on selling me, I didn't want you to be tempted any further," I say. Then I remember something I overheard. He'd been on the phone, I think?

I've let you keep your toy…

"I wouldn't want to cause another delay," I add, my throat so dry I swear I can feel it turn to dust and wither beneath the glare he shoots my way.

"Be careful before you get your wish," he warns. "Do you really think you're so sly that I don't see right through you?"

I shake my head. "I don't want you to see me at all."

It's a lie, of course. After five years of invisibility, I finally have his attention—and it's more addicting than I would have ever thought. The worst kind of drug, with a wider range of highs and lows than anything I've taken before.

To be fair, I've only experienced the lows—his anger, his rage, his loathing.

"You never told me what you wanted earlier," he says, his tone suddenly passive. He sits back in his chair while grabbing the wine bottle and an empty glass. Slowly, he nearly fills the entire goblet. Then he takes a sip.

"What I wanted?" I croak. His grin warns that I've stepped right into his trap.

"For being such a good girl and taking my cock like that."

I cringe, my face heating. With little effort, he's reset our dynamic, reinforcing that he's the only one with any real leverage to be had.

"They're going to love that, where you're going."

"Where, exactly?" I risk asking. A name floats through my thoughts, too faint to grab. Something about a tiger…

"A place where girls like you enter and never come out again."

It's the first time he's explicitly alluded to what being "sold" really means in the grand scheme, for me anyway—death. I should be terrified by the prospect. But I'm not. There are so many worse things than dying—all of which I might endure at this place, wherever it is. The unknown is more alarming than anything else. A pathetic thought gnaws away at my resolve. I want to go home.

"How far away is it?" I ask, resigned.

He takes another measured sip. "Far."

"When am I leaving?"

"You should have some wine." His deeper inflection warns that it wasn't a friendly request. He snatches the empty glass and fills it himself, placing it before me. "I think you'll find it's your favorite vintage."

I shiver at the bold claim, alarmed that he might be right. The bottle's label is deliberately turned, so I can't see it. Warily, I grab the glass, inhaling the liquid within. It doesn't smell poisoned. I take the smallest sip and wince.

He's right.

"A damn fine year. You have your father's taste to thank for that."

"You know me so well?"

His brows knit together, conveying suspicion. "There is a difference in knowing someone, and that someone being simplistic enough to understand, Ada-Maria."

The insult strikes true. He thinks I'm shallow enough to require the minimal effort to outsmart. Why not prove him right by responding with the most predictable answer.

"I know you," I say.

He laughs. "I'm sure you *think* you do." He takes another sip and washes it down with a grape fished from the platter. "Eat. Or not. I think I'll enjoy shoving the feeding tube down your throat when you're conscious."

I smother a gasp at the admission. "*You* did it?"

"You sound so surprised." He smirks, setting his wine aside. "And I thought you knew me so well."

"Were you medically trained?" I ask, taking a stab in the dark. "Or was that one of the torture skills you learned while working for my father?"

"No." His mouth falls into a rigid, hard line. "You could say I learned it indirectly as a result of the actions of Don Roy, though."

"Why do you still call him that?"

"Don?" He chuckles softly to himself, shaking his head. "I didn't realize you were never in on the joke."

"Enlighten me then," I dare him.

"It was a moniker his enemies cooked up to strengthen the rumors they spread about him working closely with the cartels. Mostly true rumors, mind you. Don is the title bestowed upon mob leaders, and your father proudly took up that name in a mocking salute to dispel the bad press and prove that he had nothing to hide. Perhaps I call him that out of respect."

"Why work so long for someone you hated? You lived with us. Ate with us. My mother gave you cufflinks for Christmas and invited you to sit at our bench during mass. My father trusted you."

"Trust means nothing to a man like Don Roy," Domino counters. "It's as fickle as currency. Mine was always too steep a price for a bastard like him to afford."

"So from the start, you were working against him," I deduce.

"And again, Ada-Maria, you prove that you are not as dumb as you look."

"No," I argue. "I'm far, far more stupid. I actually thought you were someone of integrity. The one man I could admire in a world of cutthroats and scoundrels. Thank you for proving to me that all men are the same—worthless bastards."

He should smirk, but that frown doesn't budge. "You didn't admire your father? Say it isn't so. You certainly had me fooled."

I look away. The wine glass is in my hand again, and I slosh some onto my dress in my haste to take a sip. A pull. Greedily, I drain the glass in one go.

"Careful," Domino spits. "You know that's no Kool-Aid you're drinking."

He sounds damn near disapproving. Still, as I set my empty glass down, I'm hungrily eyeing the bottle, wondering if I have the gall to pour more myself.

Get a grip, Ada! I shake my head, inhaling deeply. What did he say? A quip about my father.

"Maybe you don't know *me* so well after all," I counter. Too late do I realize from his fearsome grin that I've given him exactly what he wants—an opening to attack.

"Maybe I don't," he admits, appraising me with another searching glance. He lingers over my throat. Glancing down, I spot the scarlet stain there, gluing the fabric to my skin. "Those marks on your back. Were those from your father?"

I flinch and look away, biting my lip. *Shit!* I can't let him unnerve me like this. Belatedly, I get ahold of my senses enough to toss back, "I think they're from *you*."

"No. Before that. Don't play coy. Do you need a reminder?" I hear the quiet commotion as he stands. His presence disrupts the entire atmosphere of the room. Freed from his weight, the chair squeals in relief. The shadows stretching across the floor grow longer, with his bulk choking out what little light remains. When he comes up behind me, my entire body tenses—a reaction he is well aware of as he slides his hands around my shoulders, finding the button at the top of my collar.

"Let's refresh your memory, and mine. Get up."

He doesn't give me the chance to refuse or comply. He grips the dress' thin material and tugs until I have no choice but to stagger to my feet. Slowly, he undoes the next button. The next. The next...

I eye the wall as he exposes my breasts to the empty room. If a thousand men were here watching, I doubt I'd feel any more demeaned. They would lust after my body, at least, and be disgusted by my wounds.

He craves both. His low hum of appreciation sets my skin on fire with a crippling mixture of shame and...excitement? It's close to how he sounded on the verge of release, but this time he's merely peeling my dress down my arms, exposing my raw, ripped back.

He leaves the fabric hanging loosely from my hips and grips my shoulders, urging me down until I'm bending at the waist with my front pressed against the table's surface.

"I can tell the difference between old scars and new," he breathes out, ghosting his hand down my sides, grazing the bones of my ribcage as he goes. "These are very old. A few years at least."

Ten, to be exact. Newer ones were easier to have removed, but those were too deep. Too stubborn.

"These were made with more than just plain leather…" He runs the width of his thumb across my lower back as if reading the trauma simply by feel. "Metal tails. Or a spur."

"You sound impressed," I rasp, hating the quiver in my voice. I'm gazing up at the bottle of wine just beyond my reach, desperate for a sip.

"These weren't done to punish you," he continues as if I never spoke. "This was cruel. Harsh. If I were to whip you this way now, I could kill you."

He doesn't sound alarmed by that. My breathing feathers, and I squeeze my eyes shut, trying to ignore why my pulse quickens at that, my inner thighs shaking, my sore throat dampening…

"This hurt you," Domino surmises, withdrawing his touch, leaving me shivering in the aftermath. "Though I think you enjoy pain."

I bite my lip harder, remembering the way he whipped me. I didn't enjoy that.

"The right kind of pain," he corrects as if reading my mind. "Tell me who hurt you and why."

We both know the answer to at least one of those questions. But I forget my plan for manipulation in favor of giving in to the angry impulse to deny him.

"I will never tell you. Ever."

He growls. Or maybe that low series of notes was meant to resemble a laugh? His teeth are bared in a snarl fearsome enough to provide evidence for both theories.

Moving from my position, he grabs his half-empty wine glass and refills it. To my shock, he tops up mine as well.

"I'm sure we could come to an arrangement. I can think of several ways to coax an answer out of you." The malice in his voice sends ripples of alarm down my spine. "Oh, but what was that I promised?—" He inclines his glass toward me and sips from the rim. "To treat you sweetly, like a goddamn princess."

He slams his glass down, splashing liquid over his fingers and the table. The vivid splotches glimmer in the dim lighting, reminiscent of blood.

"I am to coddle you," he adds as a slow smile plays on his mouth. "So, what will it be? A bath by candlelight? A massage? Having me hand-feed you grapes as you lounge in bed?"

His guttural tone takes each suggestion and twists it to imply something nefarious. He'll hurt me, hurt me, or hurt me.

"I want you to give me answers," I suggest. "Why take me? Why now? What do you want? What do you think my father did to Pia? How do you know her—"

"I have a better suggestion."

He's behind me in a heartbeat, palming my lower back with both hands, grinding his touch into the marks beneath.

White-hot pain shoots through me. For a second, I see stars. Then blackness. It feels like ages before the world returns in full focus, though it must be mere seconds. He's still speaking. "I could fuck you senseless right here and now. You seem to respond well to that."

Panic grips me. I can't lose what little leverage I already have. So, I blurt, "A b-bath."

He stills, his breathing heavy. "Good choice. Ines," he calls, raising his voice. "Ada-Maria would like a candlelit bath. Run one in the jacuzzi. Bring out the rose petals. We'll make it fit for a queen."

He's mocking me again, and I suspect it's more than my impertinent questions that has him aggravated so. Something that's gnawing away at him, lurking behind those dark eyes. So he lashes out.

My only method to catch him off guard has been to play along. And make him break his own mold he's put me in.

"I...I want music," I say, a random request that gets his attention. He looks at me again, an eyebrow raised skeptically.

"Music it is," he says to my shock. "What kind?"

"I..."

"My choice, then," he declares, latching onto my hesitation. "Anything else?"

Yes, my instinct tells me. I need to keep him focused on me, anticipating my next action.

"Yes. I want wine. And…"

"And sweets, let's not forget the refreshments," he says, taking a step toward me to press his palm against my cheek. "I'll need you well rested and well fed for what I have planned for you. Despite what you may believe, cum is not fitting sustenance in the long-term, Ada."

Bastard. My cheeks flush with blood, but I hold his stare and nod.

"And… I w-want—"

"Such a greedy girl." He coaxes my chin higher, exposing my sore throat. Flashing dangerously, his eyes rake over the swollen flesh, and I realize my mistake—I've provoked him too much. "You want a more suitable item of clothing to wear," he adds softly. "Something more fitting than this matronly garb, *si*?"

I swallow hard and remain silent, having learned my lesson.

"Excellent," he murmurs. "Then what are we waiting for?"

CHAPTER SEVENTEEN

His room contains its own private balcony, through a door I missed on my earlier visits. Open to the night air, it's a wide space, shrouded by more trees and hedges—as well as an extension of the roof that protects us from the light rain beginning to fall.

Built into a raised platform near the balcony is a bubbling jacuzzi, arranged to his chilling specifications.

Rose petals coat the stone patio, tinging the air with the sickly-sweet scent. Soft music plays from unseen speakers, the tune light, featuring a male singer crooning in Spanish. Steam emanates from the bathwater, and along the rim, someone laid out a black, crushed velvet blanket strewn with red cushions. Placed in the center is a golden tray sporting various sweets, from cakes, to cookies, and pieces of chocolate.

It's terrifying how he can arrange something like this at a moment's notice. It shows the level of resources he has at his disposal. But how?

"So much fresh fruit," I say thickly. "But you said we're miles from any city."

Or any supermarket capable of supplying the amount he's paraded before me. I doubt he sends Ines on regular supply runs, either.

He's behind me, his breath hot on my neck. I rebuttoned my dress for the trip here, but he's already reaching around me to undo them, one by one.

"The estate is self-sustaining," he replies. "Most of the fruit and vegetables are grown here. The rest has been stocked well in advance, so if you're planning on seducing some charming delivery man into whisking you to safety, I would think again."

I smother my disappointment beneath a sigh. He already has me partially naked, tugging the dress down my hips.

"It's my turn to ask the questions." He palms my waist, guiding me forward. Only belatedly does he seem to remember my bandages. He fingers one along my forearm then withdraws his hand.

The second I hear the telltale hiss of leather on metal, I stiffen, already aware of what he's doing without having to look. I didn't even realize that he had his knife, dangling from that battered sheath affixed to his belt loop. He presses the flat side of the blade to my skin in a shockingly cool caress. Slowly, he guides it down, catching the edge of a section of bandages. It easily slices apart, falling away.

"You have such delicate skin," he remarks, cutting through a strip of bandages along my thigh next. "I have to take special care with you. I wouldn't want you to boil alive in the bath."

He keeps going, clearing the next wrapping around my left elbow before crouching down to clear away the ones on my feet.

The wounds beneath glisten, a pale pink. None of them are deeper than a few layers of skin, most resembling blisters formed after a bad sunburn.

"Don't worry," Domino says, rising to his feet. He smooths my hair down my shoulders, tucking a stray lock behind my ear. "I've taken precautions with the water's quality to ensure you won't risk an infection. I would never take the chance of you dying such an easy death, Ada."

A breath sticks inside my chest. It's several tries before I can suck in enough air.

"Is that why you went after me?"

I can almost hear the muscles in his jaw straining as he frowns. He doesn't like that insinuation. Roughly, he snatches my wrist, wrenching me around to face him. One of his fingers grazes my skin, settling against my throat.

"I went after you, because I own you."

He's lying. I can hear the subtle growl edging those words. Irritation.

"You don't, do you?" I rasp, recalling a name Ines said. The speaker on the telephone. "J-Jaguar? Does he own me?"

His eyes flash, and I have my answer. It's horrifying, proving that all along, his taunts have been true. He sold me. Maybe, deep down, a part of me refused to believe it. For five years, this man pretended to be willing to lay down his life to guard my father and me. Was it all truly a lie?

I don't want to think anymore. I don't want to fight or resist him. I'm too tired. I just want to sink inside myself and sleep. Burrow beneath the blankets in that white room and endure the remaining hours I have left.

"I've decided that a week and some change is not nearly enough to divulge from you all that I want, Ada-Maria," Domino warns.

The pure malice in his tone snaps me from my self-pity. I'm on edge again, painfully aware of his darker intentions. If I needed a reminder, he trails his hands down my back, carelessly running over the healing wounds.

"I want you to keep that in mind, no matter what you perceive to be happening at any given time. On your father's behalf, you owe me far more than could ever be paid in a lifetime, even with money. You owe me blood, Ada. I aim to take every last drop from you, in whichever way I choose."

The sheer weight of the promise in his voice is dizzying. He means every word—no matter how badly they contradict everything else he's stated up until now.

"How?" I demand. "You've already sold me. I'm not yours anymore… Not that I ever was."

He chuckles, urging me forward with a surprisingly gentle nudge.

"Your bath water is getting cold."

He makes me climb in by myself as he watches.

The water is hot, though nowhere near the searing heat he taunted me with last time. Still, I suck in a breath, hissing in agony as the water contacts the open sores on my feet and legs. I go rigid, anticipating the pain to last.

But it's brief, perhaps due to the gently swirling jets and whatever he must have added to the water. It smells faint but crisp like flowers. Soon, my torso is nearly submerged, leaving just my shoulders and up exposed.

I wait for Domino to squeeze into what little space remains. To my shock, he stretches out on the black blanket, picking at some of the items on the platter.

He's stripped his pants, wearing only a pair of black boxers, but his loose-fitting white shirt remains firmly in place, the top two buttons undone.

"You don't ever show your chest," I point out warily. Looking back, I realize that I can't name a single time I ever saw him in less than a buttoned shirt or the occasional wife beater. Could he have gruesome scars he's trying to hide? I doubt modesty is the reason.

Raising a grape to his lips, he takes a bite. "I would be more concerned with preserving your own beautiful skin than worrying about mine."

Point taken. I'm more than willing to stare down at the churning water or beyond the balcony than watch him. We're high up despite the house seemingly being all one level. This section of the property dips into a startlingly steep hill that puts into question any possibility of sneaking back here and trying to climb down.

Not that I would have to go to such lengths to escape, anyway. I've already walked out of the front door twice. Beyond this strange, lush realm is only desert.

The amount of water needed to sustain the gardens, let alone a supposed farm, must be astronomical.

"Were you able to buy this place with whatever you made by selling me?" I ask, daring to look at him again.

"I've always had my own means," he says. "Long before I toiled away for your father, doing his dirty work for scraps."

I say nothing, thinking back to the first day he arrived at the guesthouse. His truck had been a decade old, his clothing worn, all able to fit in a single suitcase. I remember being in awe of him for that, such a modest man from a humble background. I thought that made him different from my father, who prized his expensive possessions and expansive estate.

How wrong I was, especially if Domino owned this estate that entire time. It's larger than my father's, just in sheer size alone.

"Perhaps that explains your newfound obsession with my cock," he adds, fingering another lock of my hair. "You realized that I'm not some poor bastard living off your father's teat."

I cringe from his touch. "I always wanted you. Before," I clarify. "I didn't care that you had nothing."

And I didn't. Money to me was always an obscure concept, anyway. My father had it—not me.

"And now?" Domino asks. He sounds curious as to the answer, but I take my time devising one. How best to provoke him?

"I wanted to know if you were worth obsessing over for five years."

He scoffs. "And?"

I look down at the water, weighing my answer. Insulting him is the most obvious retort, but it's too easy—and exactly what he's expecting, I think. So I tell the truth instead.

"You aren't who I thought you were." And that saddens me deeply. I'm used to being disappointed in people, but Domino was admittedly my benchmark for so long…

It's a little like going to heaven and learning that Jesus snorts cocaine and has a gambling addiction, no different from the rest of us. Not that I ever thought Domino Valenciaga was quite on that level. But in a world of men populated by my father, he might as well have been.

"And who did you think I was?"

I shy from the real answer, but it isn't like I have anything left to lose. Meeting his gaze, I decide that this perhaps is the best way to keep provoking him. With the past.

"Someone I could love," I say. It sounds so juvenile out loud, though maybe it should. I'm utilizing Pia's logic and the future she always saw for me. Someone desired. Obsessed over. A woman who could dare to find true love.

"And what did I do to garner such an esteemed view in the eyes of Ada-Maria Pavalos?" His tone is disapproving. Skeptical. He doesn't believe me.

I sink deeper beneath the churning water until it sloshes at my chin. What did Domino do then that stuck out to me so? I ignore the man he is now, seeing past the cruel hard gaze for the vulnerable warmth I used to swear lurked beneath.

"You dragged me from the road in the middle of the night and never told my father. He would have beaten me senseless for that. Not because he cared, but because I might have been seen by someone else, and how would that look? He would have given you a handsome raise, I bet. Or you could have extorted what you wanted from me. I would have done anything to keep you quiet. And you knew that,"

I add before he tries to play dumb. "You knew him better than anyone. Don't pretend like you didn't."

"And if I did, I'd know that he wouldn't want to be bothered with tales of his drunk, coke-addicted daughter taking a nap on the freeway—"

"Don't minimize it!" I'm shouting, my throat on fire. When I look at him, he has the gall to appear shocked by the outburst. "You could have left me there if you really didn't give a damn."

"No." He leans forward, bracing his elbow on the edge of the jacuzzi to prop his chin on his hand. "That is where you are wrong, Ada. I see it now. You never understood your true worth, did you? How could I leave Roy Pavalos' daughter, drugged out of her mind, unaccompanied in the middle of the road? Any number of enemies would have taken you for their own."

Just like he has.

Anger plays on my common sense, making me think of the pettiest way to provoke him. He thinks he owns me, does he?

"Whenever I get to my *real* owner, I'll make him an offer— he can do whatever he wants to me. Just so long as he leaves me in the middle of the highway after—"

"Now it's my turn to warn you not to minimize." Domino snatches my chin, tilting it for his inspection. "You think this is a game? You have no idea what one of those men is capable of. Trust me, Ada-Maria. After one night, your entire time here will look like a trip to the spa."

I don't flinch. "You act as though this is new to me, Domino. But it's not. Cruel men and senseless brutality? You are just one in a long line of them. Trust me, I'm looking forward to this new place. I'll pray for a man who won't hit me on the face and feel I've won the lottery—"

Water splashes as he lunges into the tub, still wearing boxers and his shirt. Drenched, the fabric molds to his muscle-like armor as he yanks me to my feet.

"You want to know the kind of men you'll meet there? Men who will chop you into pieces—I'm talking literally, Ada. As they fuck you, knives stabbed right into your skin. They'll sic ten of them on you at once and gladly feed the pieces to the animals they keep there in cages, right next to the women. Still, sound preferable to me?"

I blink, startled by the tears that slip down my cheeks. The worst part is that I know he isn't lying. He's done this to me. He's condemned me to that fate.

And for what?

Growling with rage, he digs his nails into my jawline. "You didn't answer my question—"

"Yes! Yes, I'd prefer anyone to you! Because I hate you. I do. And even being eaten alive, I'll at least be comforted by the fact that I'll never have to see your face again."

Hearing that bothers him. I can see the rage boiling beneath his skin until he can't contain it. He shoves me back so fiercely I wind up sitting on the rim of the tub, bracing myself with both hands. As a result, I cannot defend myself as he advances, boldly nudging himself between my legs.

"You sneer down your nose at me, Ada, but I know who you are. A nasty, backstabbing little trollop-whore."

That word choice…

My eyes widen, my shock apparent. Only one person I knew ever spoke like that.

"P-Pia—"

"She told me all about you," Domino says coldly. He encircles both of his hands around my throat, forming a makeshift collar. "How sneaky you are. How untrustworthy. That you fed her to the wolves and made her life hell." He tightens his grip, pressing against my windpipe. "She told me everything I need to know about you, Ada-Maria Pavalos—that beneath that beautiful exterior, that haughty pout, and those limpid fucking eyes, you are a cunt, far more evil than even your father. Roy did what he did to protect his money. But you? You were a conniving bitch merely out of jealousy."

"Pia told you that?" I can barely get the words out.

He nods, stroking the falling tears from my cheeks. "Yes. She told me—"

"And did she tell you *why* I hated her?" I'm whispering. It's as if my own body is doing everything it can to resist unearthing these memories. I've spent so long ignoring them, smothering them, hating myself.

And yet Pia, wherever she is, has been laughing over it all, toying with the truth, turning men I barely know against me.

"Pia was a whore."

He moves to slap me, as if the impulse to protect even her name is that damn strong. But I don't cringe. I wait for the impact, so hard I see stars.

I cough, tasting blood as I stagger, forced to grip the bench hidden beneath the water just to keep my head above it. Meeting his gaze, I spit.

"She was… Pia was fucking my father. Did she tell you that? She was never my friend. I… I was only a tool to her. She used me. Just like everyone else did."

He blinks, his hand still raised as if he intends to strike me again. I recoil this time, holding my hands before my face in a pathetic attempt to protect it.

"You're lying."

It's my turn to laugh, frothing at the mouth as I do. He hit me hard enough to split my lip, and the blood drips freely. "How do you think she got access to steal from us in the first place? My bedroom wasn't where my father kept his accounts; it was in his office."

The same office where I would catch her scent on the days she told me she was too busy to hang out after school. The same office where my father would work late. I wasn't sure until she wore a ring she said her secret boyfriend had given her.

It was my mother's. I didn't realize that until later, of course, after things with Pia had already reached a boiling point.

"She was fucking him," I add tonelessly, "and she tried blackmailing my family when he grew bored of her. She was never my friend. She never loved me. It was always him."

For everyone, it's always *him*. Don Roy. Roy Pavalos. Until the day someone did something as simple as dragging me from a highway in the middle of the night without asking for a damn thing in return.

"You were the only person who didn't treat me like a way to get to him! I thought you were…"

And it guts me to realize how stupid a hope that was. How childish.

"All along, you were just like them. Like Pia. Like everyone!"

I shove him away and climb from the tub, tripping over my own feet. My eyes are on the balcony, and I lunge for it, leaning over the railing. I eye the darkened landscape below. I'm not afraid. I don't feel anything, and in this moment…

I know for sure I could jump.

Fall.

"Are you fucking crazy?" A masculine arm comes around my waist, wrenching me back.

"No!" Blindly, I lash out, striking whatever part of him I can reach. None of my blows do a damn thing. He's immovable. As impenetrable as a brick wall. "Let me go!"

He doesn't, gripping my entire body within a bear hug so that I can't fight. All I can do is scream, no matter how painful it is, until my voice breaks and I can't even make a sound.

But as I fall silent, I realize that he's still speaking to me. He always has been.

"…you walk around with your nose in the fucking air. How could I think you were any different?" The words are meant more for him than me, I realize. With my face pressed against his chest, I can hear how fiercely his heart is raging. A near-constant boom that rattles his ribcage.

"The dumb whore with a heart of gold—no one fits that fucking cliché. No one…"

He's trying to justify it, I think. Why it was so easy for him to believe Pia about someone he hadn't even met. All along, he's thought the worst of me, lies planted by my old best friend.

"How could I ever think any bastard who would work for my father could be any different?" My voice is so hoarse I'm sure he doesn't hear that.

Regardless, he looks down, his eyes sharp and mistrusting. He adjusts his grip, loosening his bear hug to grip me by both forearms, holding me captive inches from his chest. When he lunges, I go still, expecting another slap.

Not the feel of his mouth over mine.

He's brutal, gnashing with his teeth until I part my aching lips and let him in. He grunts, gripping me tighter, pressing me against the planes of his chest. Using his weight as a battering ram, he jolts me back, forcing me to step down into the tub.

I can see the intention written across his face as he pulls back, tugging at the front of his boxers.

I don't resist, letting him spin me around and manipulate my body until I'm standing in the tub, leaning over the edge with my hands braced before me.

One thrust, and he's deep, sending the water sloshing between us. I close my eyes, surrendering to each thrust. It's a brutal rhythm that's somehow gentler than the roughness of the other night.

His hand cinches my hair, his mouth against my ear. "For so fucking long, I've wanted you," he growls. "Always you…"

He's lying, I know he is. But that knowledge doesn't dull the effect those grated words have on my body. Nerves I didn't even know existed ignite and smolder. My breath quickens, my bones turning liquid beneath his touch.

He makes me chase after him, grinding against his hardness to salvage my own pleasure as he selfishly takes. Right when my breaths feather and eyelids flutter, his hand snakes down my front, dipping beneath the water, grinding against the sensitive flesh between my thighs.

He's ruthless, as if he studied how to touch me. Pleasure me.

Break me.

I never stood a damn chance.

WE WIND up on the blanket, the platter kicked aside, scattering the food all over the black material. He's on his back, his eyes on the overhang that shields this part of the terrace from a fresh bout of rain. I doubt it could protect us from lightning, but he doesn't seem worried.

I am.

Harsh, mindless sex I can stomach—not this. Whatever this is. Something more than physical, as foreign to me as it seems to be to him.

To break the silence, all I can think to say is, "Where is she?" Pia. He claimed she was dead, but obviously, she's not if she's able to feed him intel on me. Lies.

He tilts his head to shoot me a searching glance. Whatever he finds makes him frown and look away, turning his attention to the sky. "She's dead, Ada."

"Then how—"

"She never told me a damn thing herself."

So, he lied or made it up. It's cruel. But it doesn't match, unless he had another reason for hating me other than using a dead girl as his proxy.

"Your father killed her," he says tiredly. "I know he did."

"How?" I demand, slamming my hand against the stone tiles.

He stands, heading for the doorway. "I don't know how," he admits. "Or when. Or where..."

He enters the room but, just as I stand to follow, he reappears, holding a small object in his hands.

"But you are going to help me find the answers to those questions." He offers the object to me, and I sway.

It's a pink book, decorated in a multitude of stickers that were in fashion a decade ago. A name is written in a pink gel pen across a white label stuck to the front of it.

This diary belongs to: *Pia Alicia Inglecias.*

The last time I held this very book, I gave it to my father. "H-How?"

"That's not important. What matters is that Pia wrote about her 'favorite place' where she would hide her secrets. Where?"

I shrug. It's been so long, and Pia was known for her elusive word games. A favorite place could mean anything from the beach, to the ice cream parlor, to her favorite park bench.

"You know exactly what I'm talking about," Domino says, but it's not an accusation. He tosses the book onto the blanket before me. "You've read it, haven't you?"

How could I not? My father tasked me to steal it, but I needed to know why. And I needed to see exactly what my old friend thought of me.

And she hated me. I bored and annoyed her from the very start. I was an amusing pet to play with when she needed someone. The way she spoke about me...

It was vicious. Cruel. But still generally polite in Terra Rodea standards. After all these years, I think I should despise her. I still don't. She wasn't like me, and that was another layer of her appeal. She was poor, forced to navigate the world without a powerful last name.

But there was one person she did care about—enough to justify her stealing and backstabbing. Enough to justify her scheming ways.

Slowly, I look up to find Domino still watching me, his shirt even more out of place now that his bottom half is completely bare.

"Take it off," I rasp. "Take off your shirt."

His eyes narrow, and I expect him to refuse. Instead, he snatches the hem, balling it. By the time he drags the material over his head, I've already seen the glaring proof I needed to cement my suspicion.

"You're Navid." Pia's brother, stricken with a heart condition —only the harsh scar slicing in between his pecs reveals how he managed to circumvent that ailment. He must have had a transplant, years before he joined my father.

And so many things start to click.

Greed was never his motivation. Just revenge.

And that makes him far more dangerous.

"I imagined this," he says with a harsh scoff as he flicks his wadded shirt aside. "You, gaping up at me on your knees, whimpering my name like it's some fucking revelation."

My performance must not satisfy him. He climbs into the tub and sits, tilting his head back against the rim to watch me.

"You hated us all this time," I croak. "So what? By killing my parents and selling me, you get some sick, twisted enjoyment out of it?"

He raises an eyebrow. "This is about far more than a silly tit-for-tat, Ada-Maria," he says. "Far more than just revenge. You only factor in as a very small part. This was never about just *you.*"

"How?" I demand, drawing my knees up to my chest, feeling the exposed wounds smart and sting. No matter the discomfort, it feels important to shroud myself from him. It doesn't matter that he's already experienced nearly every inch of my body.

He doesn't own me.

"I'll tell you—the price you'll fetch is more than enough to square away some old debts of mine. Nothing more, nothing less."

It's a gut punch. He says it so casually. So callously. That's all I ever was to him. A bargaining chip.

"Debts," I whisper. "To Jaguar?"

"I wouldn't go around parroting names and terms I didn't understand, were I you. In the real world, Ada, a name is a man's most important possession. He'll do anything to protect it, even kill."

"Which is why you spent five years living under a false identity, *Domino*," I point out.

"I am Domino Valenciaga. Any prior name I may have had is no longer relevant. Disrespect it, and I'll teach you firsthand how these disputes are settled by those without a rich father to hide behind."

"My father taught me that respect is earned," I counter.

He leans back as if relishing the feel of the jets. "You only say that because you think I won't lunge from this tub and wrap my hands around that pretty throat. Respect is a term beyond any Pavalos."

I flinch, stung. Again, I want nothing more than to flee. Run. Hide. Jump off the balcony and end my suffering now. I can't take another moment with him. I can't.

"Come." As if reading my mind, he beckons me with a dripping finger. "Join me."

It's both a dare and a test.

His eyes gleam mischievously as I comply, sinking onto the submerged bench across from him. Our legs intertwine, and I cringe at the sensation. He's both firm and unmoving, like living metal, his limbs serving as makeshift bars to this newer prison.

"Tell me something," he demands. "You keep pouting every time I voice my assessment of you. You are what you are, Ada. But let's hear from the little princess why she may have some depth."

He can be so unbearably mean. His words, at times, cut deeper than even the leather of his whip.

"I loved you because I thought you were someone of integrity. Not perfect—" I add before he can interject.

No, Domino was never perfect.

"But someone who could think for himself. Who supported my father for his own reasons—" And in a way, I was right all along. "But a man who could determine on his own what was right and wrong. Someone with enough honor to ignore his attraction to any woman who might interfere with his duties. I especially loved that."

I'm not ashamed to reminisce over this fictional Domino. In a sense, it's freeing. Let him hear all the lofty standards he never lived up to. Though, I figure, no man could.

"I thought you were loyal and brave. I thought you were fair. Fair enough to save my life and ask for nothing in return. You could have extorted me a million times over, if all you wanted was money."

"This is about more than money, Ada," he finally says after letting me speak.

I fling open my eyes, exasperated. "Then why sell me?"

"Blood debts require a more nuanced currency to satisfy," he says, once again resorting to word games. "Even the Bible provides its own rough description. An eye for an eye. A tooth for a tooth. A heart for a heart…"

And a woman for a girl.

This is about Pia—but on whose behalf does he seek to satisfy this invisible debt? His eyes are so emotionless, I can't tell.

"This is more than merely personal, either. Try as you might, you will never understand it. What a pity to shatter the lofty image you've built up for me."

He sounds mocking enough, his sly grin firmly fixed on his face.

But he's angry. I can see it in his glinting eyes and how stiffly he holds himself. I've struck a nerve. If only I knew which one.

"I'm used to being disappointed," I say softly. "Another reason you are just like my father—"

"I am nothing like him!" He's on me before I can react, his hand around my throat, forcing my back to arch as he leans over me. One of his hands feels out along the rim of the tub, returning with an item that he presses against my lips.

"Open."

His commanding tone is too fierce to resist.

I pry my lips apart, steeling my body for a horrific taste. Instead, a richness floods my tongue, conveying a flavor I haven't tasted in years. Chocolate. Insanely good dark chocolate with some kind of fruit filling to balance the salty bitterness.

"I prefer your mouth stuffed full," Domino warns, reaching for another sweet. Some kind of truffle that he dangles between two fingers. "I could keep you forever like this."

My ears pick up at the word choice. Is that his way of hinting that he won't sell me after all? A hateful mixture of hope and dread washes over me. As much as I try to tell myself that any fate is preferable to him, I know better…

I can't focus on the *what-ifs*. So, I just fixate on the potentials. If I could manipulate him into keeping me, what else could I make him do? It could be a slow, painful process, but one I think I could decipher if I tried hard enough. A somewhat known entity is far better than the unknown.

With my eyes on the chocolate, I choke down any hesitation and stick out my tongue, allowing him to place the morsel onto it. I chew slowly, hating the feeling of the chocolate and sugar disintegrating.

He watches, his curiosity piqued. He doesn't know what I'll do next, and there's power in those heavy few seconds before I finally lick my lips and say, "I could be yours alone. Why share me?"

Share. That word makes his nostrils flare, and I have my answer—he doesn't really want to. Not out of concern but greed. Jealousy. He's right. There's more to this than I'm aware of, and the thought terrifies the hell out of me.

It makes me reckless. Reckless enough to eye him through my lashes and soften my voice.

"I could be good to you."

"Little Ada," he taunts, bringing his thumb to my mouth next. He rams the pad of it between my lips, chuckling when I wince. "So good at the sexy mind games. No wonder your father sent you to assist with all his dirty work."

I let the barb pass unchallenged, keeping my focus on what matters.

"When is Jaguar coming for me, then?" I make my voice as weak and feeble as possible, even as I'm forced to speak around his probing thumb. "I could show him how good I can be with my mouth. Maybe he'll keep me—"

"He will *never* fucking touch you." Anger explodes from him, and I recoil. Seconds pass before I realize he just withdrew his hand. He never struck me. "Not if I have any say in that. I'll rip you to pieces if you even let him look at your body. Don't think I won't."

He's shaking, his hands in fists, eyes blazing. Slowly, he deflates. That display wasn't for my benefit. For once, I slipped beneath those barriers to the man beneath. Seething and jealous of this Jaguar and what he may or may not have.

Me.

I dull myself to the little voice at the back of my mind warning me not to and place my hand on his forearm, sensing the coiling, lethal muscle.

"If you don't want to sell me," I whisper, utilizing the same purr I'd employ to charm any other man in my orbit. "Keep me then."

And I can spend every waking moment afterward plotting my escape. Even if I have to drive that knife into his throat myself, I'll defeat him. I will.

He strokes my cheek and for a second, I think his guard is lowered enough for my ruse to work. "So eager to please. I like you better this way…" He leans forward, brushing his lips along my earlobe. "You think you have power. It's sexy."

I wince, concealing the act behind a smirk of my own. It feels hollow and lopsided, but I hold it for all I'm worth.

"I can have whatever you want me to," I parrot. "I can be whoever you want me to be. As long as you have me…"

His eyes flash at the subtle taunt.

He himself stated that fact won't be for long.

Unless, of course, he changes his mind.

Or rips me to pieces.

"You know what I want from you?" he asks in a tone that warns he'd very much like to enact the latter of my mental options. His finger flexes against my jawline as if best deciding where to start if he is planning on ripping me to pieces. Near my lip? My ear? Down along my throat? "I'll tell you one day. Preferably when you're less inclined to stab me with a hypodermic needle."

I grow cold at the reminder. Did he really plant that vial, knowing I'd take the risk to inject him with its contents? Looking at him, I can't tell and that unnerves me more than if he'd gloat over his plan outright.

"Why leave that stuff for me? Those pictures?" I demand.

He curls his fingers against my cheek, tilting it so that his mouth has better access to my ear. "To test you."

I feel my lips curl into a frown and I pull away from his touch. "And what's the verdict?" I ask nastily.

His laugh catches me by surprise, low and amused. Abruptly, he stands from the water and walks, dripping wet, into the bedroom.

I wait for my cue to follow, but it never comes. Apparently, though, our rare ceasefire is over. I don't know how I feel about that as I climb out of the water on my own and creep into the darkness of the room. I head for the hallway blindly—I'd rather leave naked than run the risk of him turning a request for a towel into another mind game.

With every step, my head is abuzz with too many questions to keep track of. His identity. Pia. My fate…

When I finally reach the door, I only hesitate at the thought of leaving the diary behind. In his hands, that tome from the past is a goldmine of information he can use against me.

"Did I say you could leave?" The gruff question comes from the direction of the bed. I didn't even realize Domino is already lying there, unabashedly naked over the neatly made sheets. Only the glow of the lights from the direction of the balcony gives him any definition against the shadows. "Come here."

I choke down a refusal and inch a step toward him, against my better judgment. One way to spin my obedience is that I can use this rare moment when he isn't coming at me with a whip or a collar to my advantage. Lure him into a false sense of security.

Though, as he snatches my wrist the second I'm within his reach, I realize that if anyone has let down their guard, it's me. I gasp as he drags me down until I'm practically on top of him. One of his hands claims my thigh and the heat basting my shoulder tells me that we're lying face to face, my breasts against his chest.

"I like you plotting and scheming," he murmurs in a tone that makes me shiver. "It bodes well for how you'll react when you see what it is a I really have in store for you."

A probing response is on my tongue, ready to be voiced. At the last second, I grit my teeth and remain silent.

He wants me angry and helpless—and I'll give him that and more.

Just on my own terms and on my timeline.

Even as I relax against him, I can tell he doesn't expect the way I sink into his touch, resting my head against his shoulder. The second he falls asleep, I'll sneak onto that balcony and grab the diary.

And I'll be the one capable of turning the tables then.

CHAPTER NINETEEN

I'm on top of him, though I don't remember making the decision to sleep here. On his bed. On his body. Naked.

It should feel far worse than it does, wrapped in a cocoon of a stormy, overcast morning and the semi-darkness of his bedroom.

Peace is a strange concept here. Maybe calm is a better word. The calm before the storm comes in the form of soft footsteps, and a gentle voice that pierces the quiet.

"Sir?"

"Goddamn." Domino hisses his irritation though he doesn't move. *Because of me?*

"Ines… What the hell? It's barely seven." He's taking pains with her that he doesn't usually, straining to keep his voice level, avoiding the use of any curse words. He respects her.

"I am sorry, sir. But Mr. Jaguar—"

"Tell him I'll call him later," Domino snaps.

Ines sighs. "I am sorry, sir. But Mr. Jaguar is *here*."

BLOOD TIES

Blood Ties

Blood Ties By Lana Sky

Copyright © 2021 by Lana Sky
All rights reserved.

No part of this publication may be reproduced, distributed, or transmitted in any form or by any means, including photocopying, recording, or other electronic or mechanical methods, without the prior written permission of the author.

This is a work of fiction. Names, characters, businesses, places, events and incidents are either the products of the author's imagination or used in a fictitious manner. Any resemblance to actual persons, living or dead, or actual events is purely coincidental.

Cover Design and Interior Formatting by Charity Chimni
Editing and Proofreading by Charity Chimni

1

Mr. Jaguar is here.

Those four words have the effect of a seismic shift —though the destruction seems limited to Domino's once calm mood. Abruptly, he shrugs me off, lunging to his feet, and, within the blink of an eye, he's my cold captor once more.

"Where is he?" he demands of Ines.

She gestures helplessly toward the hall, just as the sound of distant footsteps advances in our direction—several sets to be exact. My breath catches as the first pair echoes off the walls, heavy and solid. Male? The second is softer, trailing behind.

Neither visitor, however, seems to have been invited here with Domino's permission.

Nervous energy flutters between him and Ines—but I don't know if I should be alarmed or relieved. *Finally*, I'll come face to face with this Boogey Man I've been supposedly sold to. A part of me should take some sick glee in seeing Domino so visibly rattled, at least.

But I don't.

"Ada-Maria." Domino cuts his eyes to me, but they're unreadable in the semi-darkness. Only his voice conveys a hint of emotion. "Cover yourself," he growls.

I grapple for a handful of the sheets, but I've barely shrouded my breasts when the footsteps grow louder. Each thud resonates like a morbid drumroll as a man finally appears in the doorway.

Fear pinches my spine, and I sit straighter. He's huge. I have to crane my neck to take him in fully and, if he is Jaguar, I'm disappointed. I expected someone who suits the callous, violent description I've gotten of him so far—someone physically ugly to match their brutal reputation.

Instead, he's as much of a twisted contradiction as my current captor is—beauty and brawn in one intimidating package.

In fact, he and Domino share so many similarities, I assume the latter lied to me when he denied they're brothers. They must be. Both sport dark hair, though this man has his cut short. Instead of a haunting green, his piercing eyes are a deep shade of brown that feeds on the shadows in the room.

Animal comparisons pop into my head. Domino is a tiger, quiet and reclusive, preferring to rely on stealth, but fully capable of making his stand with a fearsome roar when he has to.

This newcomer is a lion—or, perhaps more literally, a jaguar. Bold, his smile alone is dazzling, his gaze piercing, lingering over my chest. "Morning, little brother," he says. His booming voice betrays the hint of an accent. Mexican?

I can't decipher it by the time Domino replies. "Jaguar. You're five days early."

"What are you saying?" Jaguar raises an eyebrow. "*Family* can't just drop by to say hello?"

"You're here unannounced," Domino replies, lacking the same enthusiasm. "I'm sure you brought backup. Ines, why don't you go make sure they're comfortable while we have a chat?"

The woman scurries off, and Jaguar watches her go, his gaze indecipherable.

"You know," he says, returning his attention to Domino. "I thought I'd announce my little visit, but then I had a better idea. Why not come see what little Dom-Dom is hiding with my own two eyes? And now that I've gotten an eyeful of her myself, I'm impressed—" He winks, unconcerned by the way Domino moves to stand in front of me, further obscuring his view. "No wonder you didn't want to share her."

"I was to have a week," Domino snaps. I hate him, and yet his unease drives my own dread, sending my pulse racing as I grip the sheets tighter to myself.

Perhaps he hasn't been exaggerating about what he's hinted of Jaguar?

That he's no savior.

As the thought crosses my mind, the man enters the room fully. If I doubted his identity, he wears a short-sleeved black shirt that exposes his muscular arms—along with the full sleeve tattoo of a familiar feline predator crouching beneath carefully shaded leaves on his left bicep.

The rest of his outfit is simple. His plain dark wash jeans are marred with various spots of grease and grime that remind me of the mechanics my father hired to service the luxury vehicles he kept on his estate. His hands bolster the image, gnarled with scarred knuckles and fingernails sporting hints of dirt beneath them.

I carefully inspect every inch of him that I can, but the longer I put off one glaring realization, the more obvious it becomes. I hate myself for noticing, though why should I? I have no loyalty to the man beside me.

And if I were vain enough to care, Jaguar is just as handsome. His face is remarkably expressive, displaying every observation to cross his mind. Irritation. Amusement. Lust.

His eyes keep coming back to me, drinking in longer glances with each pass.

Until my captor steps forward, putting himself directly in front of me. "What do you want?" he demands.

Seconds pass before Jaguar replies. "Don't be so cranky, Dom-Dom. You can still have your week," he says, and I realize that his extended silence was for deliberate effect. He wanted Domino to watch him watch me.

And not say a damn thing.

Unlike those hours when he'd stand emotionlessly by my father's side, Domino is an array of twitching muscle now, practically lurching on the balls of his feet as if he's physically restraining himself from lunging.

"*But*," Jaguar continues, "I don't want you to get too comfy here, skirting your duties, ignoring your role in the *Guarida*."

Guarida. I file away that term, sure I've heard it uttered before.

"Is that a threat?" Domino asks softly.

Jaguar chuckles. "No. It's a… Let's call it a suggestion. I've decided you need a reminder as to what you're missing." Inclining his head toward the door, he raises his voice, "Baby, get in here."

"Coming!"

It's my turn to lurch forward, barely concealing my disgust at the sound of that low, feminine purr. *No…*

But yes—I smell her before she even saunters into the room, her hair perfectly coifed and styled in a blowout, her outfit pretty much nonexistent. Wrapped in a sheet, I'm dressed more conservatively.

Some things never change, not even after ten damn years. Alexi Rojas is just as beautiful, her perky breasts jiggling as she comes to stand beside Jaguar. Her heavily lined blue eyes sparkle, her glossy lips pursed in a forced grin. It's an act, of course. She's no better at hiding her real emotions than I am. Like a snake, her gaze slithers over Jaguar before darting in my direction.

That single glance conveys all the anger one might suspect from a woman who's made it her mission to fuck every man I interact with.

Even my captors.

The bitch. She's still smiling, seemingly unsurprised by the sight of me, battered and bruised. Considering that she's running her hand down Jaguar's chest, she's been in on their plan from the start.

The shock I feel is too dull to really make an impact, though. Unlike Domino, I never put betrayal past Alexi. I'm just surprised her smile isn't half as wide as I'd assume it would be.

"Hello, Domino," she says huskily. Her eyes lower to his hips, and considering I'm faced with his bare ass, she seems to be enjoying the view from her angle.

"You see?" Laughing, Jaguar pats her head before looping his arm around her tiny waist. He's so strong, that simple gesture nearly takes her off her feet. "Everyone's happy. We're all in for a good, fun time, eh, Dom? Little Lexi-Lex will stay here and party for a few days. You have my permission to wear her the fuck out. Give Ada here a rest, eh?" He winks, but Domino doesn't seem thankful.

"You think I need a babysitter, Jagger?" he asks, his tone dangerously soft.

"No." Jaguar's smile falls, and he shrugs Alexi aside. "I think you need a fucking reminder as to the price you agreed to pay, Domino. You roped me into this mess, and I gladly agreed to help you because that's what brothers do, *si*? But let's not pretend like I couldn't take her right now if I wanted to."

"Is that why you're here?" I can't see Domino's expression from here, but I sense the subtle challenge in his tone.

Jaguar laughs. "I haven't touched her, have I? Have your *week* if it's that important to you. Play your little games and fuck to your heart's content. Just don't forget our bargain, the one *you* initiated. You want out? You buy your 'freedom' with blood. *Adios*."

With a wave of his hand, he turns on his heel, storming from the room. "Have fun, Lexi-Lex. When you get dressed, Dom-Dom, come find me for a little chat. Don't take long."

I nearly collapse with the force of the sigh that leaves my chest. I must have been holding my breath all that time. Then I remember the woman watching from the doorway and stiffen, meeting her hateful stare.

The last time I saw her as anything other than an enemy was nearly a decade ago, in the aftermath of Pia's disappearance.

"She's missing, Ada! What the hell is wrong with you? Don't you even care?"

Aged ten years, she holds my gaze now for a split second before turning away. "Let's have fun, Domino," she murmurs, sauntering over to him with a familiarity that has me clenching my jaw so hard it aches. Her manicured fingers run down his arm in a gentle caress. "I'm yours until Tuesday—"

"Not now." He bats off the hand she tries to place on his chest. "Get out."

She blinks at his stern tone, but scampers obediently into the hall. I can't help but wonder if she also has had a taste of his temper. His collars. His whip. His cock.

"Don't forget what I told you," Domino warns, turning to face me. He must have snatched the pair of slacks in his hand from the closet. As he tugs them on, his eyes rake over my body, devoid of the hunger he displayed last night. He looks conquering instead. A general, surveying land he's already claimed as his. The way my father would look out at the city of Terra Rodea as he gave his political speeches.

"Nothing he said factors into my arrangement with you," he adds, his voice low and tight. "Don't assume that you leaving here negates what you owe me, Ada-Maria. You are mine until the moment I *choose* to release you."

For a second, I'm not sure if that was a promise. Or a request.

Then I see how his eyes blaze, and I know for sure—it was a threat.

"Why sell me, then?" I croak. "If you still think you own me?"

It's dangerous to play word games and semantics with him. A part of me can't resist anyway. I'm as genuinely curious of the answer as I am terrified by the implications of what he means.

I own you.

"Money and blood are two very different currencies, Ada-Maria." He steps forward, brushing his hand along my cheek. There's no warmth in the motion. It's as chillingly possessive as the way he held me last night, cock buried deep. "I recommend you not forget that. Now get dressed."

He turns for the hall, and I sigh, still clinging to the bedsheet. My stomach lurches at the thought of trying to make it to my room with just this thin slip of material to cover myself with.

Only as he crosses the threshold does Domino call back, "Pick your clothing from my closet. Not yours."

I remain rigid on the edge of the bed. From *his* closet. Does he mean for me to wear his clothing?

Warily, I stand, creeping toward the portion of the room in question. As I open the door, I realize the request wasn't intended to limit my options.

Hanging neatly beside his modest selection of masculine apparel is an array of dresses and other clothing items sized for a woman.

The strangest part is that I can't tell if they all were taken from my closet or newly purchased with my body specifically in mind. The general color scheme is familiar—white, black, and cream—but with a new, bold hue that catches the eye, the same color he made me wear after he whipped me.

Red.

He must have had these brought here recently. Perhaps Ines snuck them in during those twisted moments when he had me on the balcony, naked in the jacuzzi. I wouldn't be surprised if, while buried inside of me, he lorded over the knowledge that he'd soon deploy another method of control, just as damning as his collar.

Fuck him.

Anger seems irrational to feel in lieu of everything else—like terror—but I embrace it fully as I tear through the nearest selection of hangers. Deliberately, I overlook anything remotely feminine and focus only on what I know to be his —the shirts and pants and boxers folded neatly in a built-in chest of drawers.

At random, I pick a gray button-down and a pair of black boxers I have no chance in hell of fitting into properly. It's the principle of the matter.

Unwelcomed visitors aside, my original plan hasn't changed when it comes to Domino Valenciaga. My only means of defeating him lies in trying to seduce him. Unnerve him.

Then stab him.

Stab him.

Stab him—repeatedly with his own knife, all while gazing into his eyes so that he knows I was the one who twisted the blade. Me.

Ada-Maria Lucia Pavalos.

I will have the last laugh. God, I swear I will. Until then, he can lord over my body as he pleases. I won't break.

"You will use this bathroom."

I flinch as his voice drifts from the direction of the bedroom. I find him there, casually lifting our torn, damp clothing from the floor. A grunt of appreciation dies in my throat, and I hate myself for the way my gaze finds the firm curve of his ass.

With his back to me, it's easy to forget the sheer depths of evil this man is capable of. His body is sin, beauty, and strength melded into one glorious form. Flexing muscle dances beneath his skin in a mouth-watering display.

I almost forget I'm meant to despise him.

Then he turns to face me. "Over there." He inclines his head toward the direction of the balcony. "Follow the balcony around to the left."

I bite my lip before obeying, exiting into the warm morning air to find the full extent of the estate unfolding before me. In the dark, what looked like a sheer, endless drop turns out to be a small hill where the terrace gardens meet swaths of rolling, lush fields.

Standing here feels so surreal—bringing home just how isolated we are in this tiny sliver of the world. A man could easily hold a woman captive on a property like this one.

Forever.

Luckily, my stint at Domino's villa already has an end date —Tuesday. By the beginning of next week, I'll belong to Jaguar and be subsequently dragged off to only God knows where.

"I said to the *left*."

I flinch as the reminder is voiced directly against my ear, I didn't even notice him coming up behind me, gripping the railing on either side of my body, trapping me here.

"Don't let the arrival of prying eyes lull you into a false sense of security, Ada-Maria. They won't stop me from punishing your insolence in any way I see fit," he warns, his voice a fraction deeper. "Trust me, I'll very much enjoy having an audience to perform for, their gasps drowning out your screams…"

I shiver, sufficiently cowed. Still, I can't resist a parting jab of my own. "Shouldn't you be busy fucking *her* now?"

Alexi.

Her presence bends the rules of this hellscape prison, and I latch onto the distraction. It's petty to be jealous at a time like this, but fear is the only alternative. It was easier to suffer as a lone captive under a madman's purview. But as a third wheel, forced to inhabit the same dwelling as two of my enemies fuck like rabbits in the other room?

Or plot against me…?

"She can join us, if you'd like," Domino says in a tone so neutral I can't tell if he's joking. "I, however, am not fond of sharing my toys."

I cringe, noting yet another subtle warning. About Jaguar? He's sold me to him, and yet he seems irritated by the reality of what that means.

It's a dangerous theory to test. His possession isn't out of concern for me, of course—mere jealousy. But how strong?

Hopefully strong enough to buy me more time.

"I could ask her what positions my new owner might like." What I intend to sound mocking comes out far too hoarse. I'm horrified. Still, I can't stop. "If he likes anal or oral—"

"Enough." His grated rasp startles me silent as he grabs my arm, manually steering me toward the direction he first indicated. To the left. Just beyond the bedroom doorway is a narrow path leading to a sliding glass door, and inside is a space that might be classified as a bathroom.

Or a torture chamber.

Still, behind me, Domino cups the back of my throat. "This is where you will bathe from now on," he declares against my ear. "And where you will bathe *me*. You can start now. I think we both could use a shower, no?"

He's right. His seed is still drying between my thighs, his taste in my mouth, his sweat on my skin.

And yet, Alexi's presence is too glaring to ignore.

For whatever reason, amid the possibility of being sold and the arrival of Jaguar, *she* stands out as the most alarming factor in this twisted equation.

Why the hell is she here?

"Aren't you going to invite your guest?" I croak, still unable to pull off a playful tone.

He turns, stepping into me so that he's facing me directly, his jawline grazing mine. "Jealousy isn't becoming on you, Ada," he scolds, his tone low with warning. "Don't misunderstand me—you will never mean more to me than as a tool. A body. A hole. Whatever I desire in the given moment—" He cups my cheek, roughly smoothing a stray curl behind my ear as he pulls back to hold my gaze. "If I want another woman, or another man, or several to fuck you—or whatever the hell I want them to do, I will say so. Do you understand?"

My eyes brim with tears as I force a nod.

But I won't let him hurt me without a parting shot in return. Prying my dry lips apart, I croak, "I'll be ready for every last one of them. Jaguar seems like he might be promising in that aspect at least."

His eyes narrow, but he turns away before I can decipher what the reaction might mean. Instead, I shift my focus to examining the room in full, becoming more awed—and terrified—with every observation I make.

It's massive, everything gleaming with a shiny new aura that makes me suspect it's an addition that he had built specifically for this purpose.

To "bathe" together in torturous harmony.

At the back of my mind, that suspicion doesn't mesh with the fact that he plans on selling me by the beginning of next week. Why go through such trouble?

But this man is a mystery I don't have the energy to solve. I'm too damn tired to.

So rather than think, I stare and make a note of every alarming detail of this space. There is an enclosed walk-in shower large enough to constitute an adjacent room, lined with black marble and complete with large, built-in benches on either side. A computerized screen affixed near the entrance presumably controls the spray.

Across from it is an oval-shaped pristine tub, large enough to fit two people—and more. The sleek silver fixtures give it a more clinical design than the other bathroom. A look that implies it could be used for soaking, as well as the perfect vessel for a madman to boil his kidnapped lover alive just for the hell of it.

The thought makes my breath catch in my chest, though I'm not sure which detail unnerves me more. The fact of him actually doing that to me, or that I referred to myself as his lover.

I'm not.

The appraising look he sends my way next makes that more than crystal clear—I am his trophy. A toy. A minor inconvenience.

"Get in." He nods to the shower stall and reaches for his slacks, intending to remove them. I look away, my cheeks flaming.

Not that I have the right to any shred of modesty. I've already seen and experienced nearly every inch of him. What little I haven't lingers in my mind, and I can't resist sneaking another glance at it as he marches past me and fiddles with the shower's electronic screen, his ass bare.

That mark on his chest undermines everything I've come to believe about Domino Valenciaga—before the kidnapping, at least. More than anything he's said or done, the sight of that scarlet, surgical scar proves that the man I knew was a well-crafted lie.

The real man is a stranger. Domino isn't even his name.

He is Navid Inglecias, brother of Pia, the girl who was once my best friend—until she went missing—a disappearance Domino insists was because of my father. That's why he's done all of this, after all, betrayed us and killed my parents.

He thinks Roy Pavalos murdered his sister.

And that I know why.

CHAPTER TWO

"**I** said get in."

I snap to awareness at his hostile tone, but he doesn't seem inclined to follow up with violence. Yet. He's already gotten the water going and steps beneath the spray first.

Numbly, I set aside the clothing I procured for myself on a nearby row of pristine gray countertops. When I face him again, I'm still wrapped only in a sheet. As the seconds tick by, I take my time fiddling with the twisted fabric to study him in full.

Based on Jaguar's demand, I have until Tuesday. On its face, I'm not even sure what that date symbolizes, or what I plan to do in the meantime. It's not like I have a wealth of options—I could either escape, kill Domino outright, or convince him not to sell me. The sad part? I'm not sure which of those aims is even remotely achievable.

I already tried the first plan to no avail.

Killing him is a far more tempting option.

But seduction… It's the only method I've had even a modicum of success attempting—though, I assume that depends on what one might determine as success. I've gotten him to listen to me, anyway, and let his guard down long enough to sleep in the same bed.

Twice.

That must mean something.

"Don't make me tell you a third time." His voice, aided by the roar of rushing water, comes as a low rasp I know better than to challenge. Without fanfare, I yank the sheet away from my body and stagger toward him, wincing as I walk directly through a cloud of warm steam.

"Wait." He meets me as I cross the threshold, grabbing my wrist. I wince before I realize what he's doing—unhooking a brown watch from my wrist. I've forgotten I'm still wearing it, one of his, taken from his closet.

He throws it onto the counter, near my pile of clothing, and turns his back to me. "Sit—" He nods to indicate a long bench on the other end of the space. The surface is textured so that I have purchase on it, even while wet. Shuddering, I find myself fixated by the only sight in view—him, his naked body facing away from me, his hands braced over the stone wall.

The angle strains the coiled muscle along his back and upper thighs, conveying better than words how this morning's impromptu visit has affected him. He's pissed, though damn good at hiding it. For someone so solidly built, I marvel at the fact that he was once a sickly boy who needed a heart transplant just to have a shot at survival.

Or so he says.

Were he anyone else, I'd use his past as a delicate attempt to start a conversation and pry what little information from him I could. It would be so easy were we still in Terra Rodea, and I had the cloak of my father's power to hide behind. Why wouldn't it be? I've been bred to manipulate men and women alike, all with a coy grin.

This iteration of Domino Valenciaga makes me rethink my entire approach toward people—and my life as a whole. From day one, none of my attempts at friendliness—or otherwise—ever worked on him. Maybe I never was as charming or as pretty, or as sexy as I thought?

Or at least, not until he ensconced me in his private estate in the middle of only God knows where. Here, away from the city where I always believed I had influence, I could finally get him to fuck me.

And I hate myself for being proud of breaking down his barriers in such an insignificant way.

"Why don't you let me go now?" The question springs from my lips before I can rethink the pros and cons of asking it. "After all, if my father is dead—" I choke, barely able to spit out that word. "Then I'm of no danger to you. You have no worry of anyone seeking revenge."

"If?" He scoffs at the phrasing, his head lowered, hair hanging damply. "Don't be flattered by your presence here, Ada-Maria. I'll still give what's left of you to Jaguar when I'm done."

It's a horrifying threat that robs the air from my lungs, just as he intended it to.

And…

It's a lie. I'm not sure at first. Not until I parse over that subtle dip in his inflection. No, I don't think he intends for me to go to Jaguar.

Not anytime soon, at least.

And the confusion sowed by that thought is more than enough to dispel any exhaustion I may have felt. I sit forward, newly electrified with a desire to get a rise out of him. It seems to be the only way we communicate effectively.

Via taunts.

"You had no problem letting Alexi go to him," I point out, cringing at the feel of her name in my mouth. I hate the thought that he had his cock in her first. That he enjoyed her first.

That he did so without the excuse of hateful lust and that she had the nerve to smile after. She smiled like his attention was comparable to heaven itself—that elated fucking smirk porn stars spend years trying to emulate.

God, I hate her.

I hate him more. Enough that I don't take the tensing of his entire body as a warning sign like I should.

"Is that what this is about?" I continue stupidly. "Revenge? He stole your woman, and so you have penis envy—"

"*Finally.*" Pulling away from the wall, he whirls on me. "That mouth says something relevant for fucking once. Say it again."

Penis, I presume, because he grabs his, cupping his fingers along the engorged shaft. I feel my eyes bulge. How could I miss the extent of his erection until now?

Does the topic of Jaguar fucking his women get him so horny?

No, I realize as he stalks in my direction, spraying droplets of water as he goes. It's anger that arouses him. Rage. Disgust. All things inspired by *me* alone.

When he's close enough, he cups my chin, tilting it. I grit my teeth experimentally, wondering if I have the strength to resist the intention written in his gaze.

I don't. He merely flexes his fingers, and my lips fly apart.

"These lips," he murmurs, shocking me further by stroking the underside of my jaw with his thumb. "Some men would kill to have a mouth like this at their disposal."

Still holding me, he returns his opposite hand to his cock. In this position, I'd only have to lean forward to have access to him—and the way he tilts his hips in a silent demand makes it clear that's exactly what he wants. Me at his beck and call like a worthless whore. Like trash, as disposable as he claimed I am. My cheeks heat with shame.

Though why should I feel that way?

I'm not the man absently praising a woman he hates. He assumes there's power in degrading me. But I am a Pavalos.

We were born into power and taught from day one how to claim it. The catch is that I never had to do so without my father's commands, but there is no better time than now to start.

Meeting his gaze, I hold it, leaning forward of my own accord to graze the tip of him with my tongue. He lurches, and I savor the brief moment of triumph. He claims to own me, but he can't own *this*.

If I ignore the man, his cock is a beautiful specimen. He's circumcised, his arousal so thick already, he's practically pulsating. Were I the whore he claimed I am, his beauty alone would make his personality easy to overlook.

Warily, I cup him in the palm of my hand, testing the formidable weight. Aided by the warmth of the water, he's molten, and I feel a jolt shoot through my core.

"You look at my cock like it's a lollipop." His cool remark complicates my desire to ignore him. To thwart me further, he grips my chin, forcing me to meet his amused stare.

"Let's see what that beautiful little mouth can do. Open it."

I bristle at the command. *No.* This moment feels as fragile as he proved my body can be against his violence. If I let him dominate me in this arena, I might as well roll over and present my throat for the killing blow.

This brief power, and my sexuality…

They're all I have, and I own both by delivering a slow, savoring lick to the underside of his shaft despite his warning.

His shock is a thing of twisted beauty. He groans, his head shooting back while the hand on my chin slides down to my throat, almost in a grateful caress. Then he squeezes so tightly my eyes bulge.

"I told you to open," he grates.

Choking down any doubt, I lick him again, going slower, so slow the entire world seems to come to a screeching halt, hinging on the time it takes my tongue to clear the length of his shaft.

"*Dios mío…*" His voice is constricted with a grudging hint of something that could be pleasure, paired with his low grunt of annoyance. The hand around my throat sinks into my hair, cinching a fistful. "I told you to—"

I cup him again, curling my fingers around his impressive width. Then I stroke, up and down, each time with increasing amounts of pressure.

He breathes out roughly, his head still tilted back, eyes on the ceiling above. The shower spray continues to pelt us in that faint, fine mist, but the sensation acts like a cloud, obscuring us from the rest of the world.

In here, only the two of us exist, battling for control of this secluded realm. I aim to win. I have to—there isn't any other choice.

"Damn you." His anger is palpable in the vibrations running through me as he speaks. "Obey me. Open your fucking mouth—"

"I want you to make me come, instead," I gasp out, the first request that pops into my head. My aim is merely to test how far I can push him—nothing else.

And his soft, startled grunt shouldn't make my stomach flip. His brows shoot together, eyes like slits, and I nearly back down. Almost. But I'm genuinely curious of the answer to a question only he has ever made me bold enough to ask.

"Can you? Just with your cock, nothing else?" It's a fantasy I used to mull over in agony while in my old bed, forced to make do with my own fingers, while the Domino I thought I knew ignored me.

Here and now, the real man doesn't even try to disguise his interest. His expression shifts as he processes the challenge. When he grazes my windpipe with the tips of his fingers, I expect him to grip it, forcing my mouth open. Instead, he withdraws…

Only to snatch a length of my hair in the same breath. Viciously, he tugs, yanking me to my feet, wrenching me around so that my back is to him, my hands forced to brace against the wall of the stall.

He gives me no forewarning. No preparation. Only the water basting our bodies provides him any lubrication as he slams inside of me with a ferocity so intense, I cry out—that and the fact that I'm already wet for him. He hisses as my readiness drags him deep—so deep that his balls smack against my inner thighs, driving home the depth he's reached.

It should hurt, I think.

But it doesn't.

It stings, and it burns, and it's terrifying just how *good* it feels.

I should hate this man, vomit at his mere touch.

And yet, he has me moaning in a way I never have. Only as he abruptly withdraws do I realize he imparted that single thrust. Nothing more.

"You think you can command me," he murmurs against my throat. Then he bites, raking his teeth down to my shoulder. My startled cry nearly drowns out his next words. "I am the one in control here, Ada—" He jerks me around to face him, his eyes glowing, teeth bared. "Do you understand that?"

"Yes," I croak. But, before I can talk myself out of it, I run my hands down his chest, hoping to further distract him. I've already found the ridge of his surgical scar by the time he angles his gaze toward my rebellious fingers, his brows furrowing. "But I was just curious," I murmur, letting my voice meld with the hum of the shower spray.

He inclines his head, betraying the fact that he's listening to me at all. Yet, he has enough pride not to ask me the question my coy answer demands.

So, I give it to him anyway. "I was curious," I say, arching against his chest. This close, I can feel his breath catch, his muscles going rigid. Especially when I bring my mouth near his ear. "I wanted to know how quickly I could come on your cock. How good it could be... So that when you sell me, I can be confident I'll please my buyer—"

Snarling, he snatches my throat, bucking his hips at the same time. Fire. I'm suffocating and stuffed...and it's...

Incredible. A cry builds and sticks in my lungs as he tightens his grip, shoving me down onto the bench. He releases me, only to snatch my legs, one in each hand, and hike them against his hips as he pistons.

The harsh surface beneath me bites into my lower back like a brutal anchor as my thoughts become less coherent with every punishing thrust.

I've never been used like this. *Ridden* is the only term I can think of to describe it. Taken.

And thoroughly enjoyed by the bastard doing so.

Grunting, Domino throws his head back, his throat cording, nails piercing my flesh with every stroke. He couldn't hide his pleasure if he tried, and the more I watch him, the easier it is to forget. And hate.

And ignore how long I craved to have him inside me just like this.

Soon, it's too dizzying to look at him. I just close my eyes, surrendering to the pleasure ripping through my body, piece by piece. My impending orgasm is a death sentence and looms closer with every harsh stroke of his cock. Each brutal shove as he draws me into him.

But it isn't until I hear his voice, hoarse and grated, "Fuck… Ada—" that I finally feel it hit with the force of a crushing blow.

I hate that it feels as good as it does.

I hate that he's proved my little dare to be a reality—he can make me come like this, with only his cock, deployed as a weapon however he sees fit.

I'm still writhing when I feel him pull out, shoving me away. Boneless, I slump off the bench, landing on my knees against the damp floor as the water continues to pelt us both.

I hear him move, and I look up to find him snatch a rag from a built-in shelf and briskly wash himself off. Then he throws it aside and steps from the stall, storming into the bathroom, presumably to get a towel.

I don't know how much time passes before his voice finally reaches back to me. "We're done. Get out."

The water shuts off a heartbeat later, leaving me drenched, but still unclean. His seed mingles with the droplets of moisture dripping down my inner thighs.

A fact he is well aware of, I realize, as I look up to find him barring the entrance, a cream-colored towel slung around his waist. He doesn't offer me one of my own. Instead, he jerks his chin. "I said get out."

Rather than argue, I stand, surprised to find myself limping after him. I must have struck my hip when I fell, but I welcome the pain. Every fiery, throbbing jolt grounds me, reaching past the drunken haze of sex to reinforce the grim reality lurking beneath.

He's a bastard who sold me and killed my parents.

What the hell am I doing here?

I go still mid-step, pondering just that. I'm so lost in the daze that I miss the second he comes for me until it's too late. He already has a grip on my forearm, forcefully steering me back against the row of granite countertops.

Without a word of explanation, he snatches my hips, lifting me unceremoniously so that I'm sitting on the hard surface —with him standing in between my legs. I instinctively try to close them, but he doesn't budge, fixated on my left thigh. Already, a deep red mark is visible, stretching from my hip to my knee. I can tell merely from how it aches that it will bruise.

"At least I've proven I can ignore pain," I croak, hating how conditioned I sound already. Broken. "That will please my buyer, too. You might get a better price—"

He hisses through his teeth, silencing me mid-taunt. I just watch him instead, riveted by the slow, careful way he drags his finger along the mark, pressing down so hard I wince. It's as if he's remembering every mottled bit of flesh, noting how easily I bruise.

Not to denote on some fucked-up seller's manifest.

But so *he* can do it all over again.

And again, and again.

"Get dressed." He pulls away without remarking on the pile of clothing I've already selected for myself. I'm sure he can tell from the shape and color who they belong to.

He must be too distracted by his own thoughts to engage in another battle of wills so soon. Or, he's preoccupied with another matter entirely. His hand lands on the counter just beyond my reach, snatching up a familiar brown object as I flinch—his watch. Coiling his fingers over it, he cocks his head toward me. "By the way, Ada-Maria," he adds, his voice ragged. "At *La Guarida del Tigre,* they won't care how much pain you can endure. They'll only want to hear how loudly you can scream. I suggest you think about that as you process how little time you have left." Still sporting his towel, he strolls onto the balcony and disappears from view.

I collapse, landing hard on my knees, tasting blood as I bite my lower lip to smother the scream still building in my throat. I almost succeed, reducing the noise to just a pathetic gasp that echoes for a split-second before I scramble to my feet, drowning it out.

I eye my carefully selected outfit and consider just leaving this room naked. I feel trapped again. Like even if the thought felt like my own, wearing his shirt would only cement this strange hold he thinks he has over me. Ownership. The ability to decide whether I live or die.

And how.

But as my gaze flits to the doorway again, I realize that the second option is far less appealing, knowing that Alexi Rojas is lurking somewhere beyond this room as well, ready and waiting to gloat.

I snatch the shirt and pull it on, then scramble into the boxers. By the time I cross the balcony and re-enter his room, Domino is already dressed, buttoning a crisp black shirt all the way up to his neck.

I watch him, hating the glimmer of appreciation that hits my chest before I can help it. He can seem so graceful when he wants to.

And so cruel when he needs to.

He rakes his gaze over me before strolling into the hallway. Automatically, I start to follow, and I've barely reached the threshold when I find the door slammed in my face.

A harsh click warns that he locked it, though I test the doorknob anyway. It won't budge.

"Domino!" I slam my hand against the wooden surface, but the only response I hear is the sound of his steps retreating down the hall, away from me.

The bastard locked me in, but for whatever reason—in the grand scheme of everything he's done within the past twenty-four hours alone—this unnerves me the most. It heralds a different mode of operation apart from his usual indifference when it comes to my captivity.

This is possessive. Or selfish. Is he keeping me from Alexi on purpose, afraid of what she might say? Or of what I could learn…

Though, the most likely explanation is that he's gone to fuck her uninterrupted.

Of all the people in the world to trigger the crippling jealousy biting through my chest, it has to be them. A childhood enemy and a longtime hidden threat, both who hate my family and me for their own reasons.

The devil himself couldn't have picked a better pair. They belong together. I hope he fucks her raw in the shower and they both trip, earning lethal concussions that will make my escape a literal walk in the park.

I try not to imagine it—but it's too late; I already am. His body hunched over hers, that sly, stupid smile on her lips, her perky tits bouncing.

He wouldn't bite her, I bet.

He wouldn't fuck her hard enough to bruise.

He wouldn't swear one minute that she was his and sell her to a stranger the next.

The only man who should be on my mind is Jaguar, my supposed buyer—or at least the owner of the place Domino sold me to, *La Guarida del Tigre*. Despite my limited knowledge of the Spanish language, I can hazard a guess as to the meaning—The Tiger's den.

"The world is a zoo," my father told me once, his voice roughened by his nighttime cigar. It was the hour before he usually retreated to bed, when he'd exchanged his suit for a robe and slippers. That wasn't the most jarring change, though—that time of night was one of the rare few when his trusty Domino wasn't by his side, already having retired for the evening.

The lack of his "shadow" humbled him somehow. He could have been a normal man—if you ignored the gleam in his eye that warned he was always scheming, no matter who was in his orbit.

The world is a zoo, Ada-Maria. You can either be a warden or a beast. Do you understand that? He reached out, grazing my chin with the tips of his fingers. *Without me, all those bastards would be salivating to eat you alive. No matter what happens with this fucking indictment, you remember this—you are a Pavalos. Without me, you are nothing but a morsel they can't wait to devour. Together, we will always hang on to the keys to this kingdom. Loyalty, that's what matters. You fucking remember that...*

His voice fades beneath the squawk of a nearby bird, and I shiver despite the stifling heat.

If that memory serves a purpose, it's to remind me that Domino is no longer my main obstacle. In fact, I should ignore him entirely.

The world is a zoo, and I need to fend for myself, damn him and the cage he's designed around me. Shedding his shirt, I give in to the petty rage and step onto the balcony naked. The sun is just starting to rise, though hidden behind a swath of gray clouds. This section of the estate feels more secluded than the sprawling terrace. I can only see the tail end of the structure from here, as well as the shadow of two people strolling across the second level of it.

Alexi. I'd recognize her slender frame anywhere, her clothing so skimpy it just resembles lines of color across her torso and hips. She's standing beside someone taller, their bulky frame etched onto my psyche.

Domino.

He locked me in here just in time for a morning stroll. I don't know what feels worse—knowing that I'm just a hole to him? Or realizing that he doesn't even think highly enough of me to throw the fact that we've fucked in Alexi's face.

He's hiding me here out of shame.

How sweet.

The rush of anger blinds me to everything else—like the fact that another figure is standing within view of me, though from a different part of the property. On the far right, a section of circular, flat stone is visible—near the front of the house, I realize, though positioned diagonally from the terrace as a whole. Set within a section of hedges and tended flower beds, I assume it's a driveway, given the set of black cars parked there. Beside one, holding the driver's side door partially open, stands a man whose shape makes me go rigid. Him, I don't recognize as easily as Domino.

Not until I hear his voice.

He whistles, his laughter booming enough to echo across the property. "Well, good fucking morning," he calls to me.

My cheeks sear as I realize that he can see me—and my lack of clothing—clearly. Automatically, I raise my hands, attempting to shield myself.

Then I stop, my fingers raised just beneath my nipples.

From the corner of my eye, I see the distant shape of Domino go rigid, like a speck of darkness over the otherwise bright landscape. I know he's watching me. I can practically feel his eyes raking over my skin with that unspoken possession.

Don't. I can almost hear him voicing the warning in his signature unstable rasp. *Don't you fucking dare.*

I don't take my eyes off him, even as I lift my hand and wave toward the figure in the driveway. He chuckles, whistling even louder. Something in the sound sends a shiver of unease through me. It's primal, like the way one of my father's dogs would snarl when it had a bone it didn't want to share with the others.

A warning.

When I look back at Domino, however, he's gone. It's like he vanished, leaving Alexi standing alone.

At least until I hear a door open and slam with the force of a gunshot.

CHAPTER THREE

"What the hell are you doing?" His voice is softer than it should be, perfectly controlled to not be overheard by anyone beyond this room. "Come here—"

"Why?" I'm still watching Jaguar and his posse. They look dangerous, even from afar. The sort of men my father would meet miles from the city when he thought no one saw him. A reporter did once and threatened to blackmail him, using photographic evidence.

Until my father sent me to charm my way into his office and plant materials that he reported stolen from our house earlier that week, ensuring the man was jailed and unable to access his so-called evidence. At least until he was released on bail and found all of his electronics smashed to pieces. Such was the way my father handled any threat.

With vicious, underhanded tactics or outright bribery.

Whatever he wanted protected, he hid under lock and key, deploying them only when necessary. Whether he realizes it or not, Domino's been acting the same way—obscuring his hatred toward my family, then revealing Pia's diary...

And by taking me now?

Trying to decipher his motives hurts my brain. Banishing all thoughts of him, I relish the heat of the weakened sun on my body, counting down the seconds that pass without him dragging me inside.

Then, some harrowing moment between Jaguar's next whistle and my own heartbeat, I realize that he won't. He *can't.*

Because to do so would risk breaking his façade before the one person he seems determined to hide me from. Alexi or Jaguar?

That's the real question.

When I turn to face him, I can't glean an answer from his expression alone. All I find is pure, molten rage.

His teeth flash, the only break in the shadows that shroud most of his expression. "Get in."

I don't refuse him outright. I just brace my elbows against the balcony on either side of me and lean back, feeling my heart race like mad. I'm terrified. I'm also resigned.

Honestly, in this moment, I feel like I wouldn't have any problem at all with leaning back further. Too far. Falling over this balcony entirely and landing on the rugged terrain below.

He must realize that, but the prospect alarms him enough to stalk forward, coming into view of our audience below. I watch his eyes, waiting to see who they flicker toward first.

Unsettlingly, they remain fixated on me, a writhing mass of brown and flecks of green, promising a wrath unlike any I've experienced from him so far.

For a second, I rock on my heels, testing how much force it would truly require to actually hurl myself over the edge.

Too late.

He reaches me within a fraction of a second, palming the side of my face to pull me close.

"You have no idea what game you're playing, Ada-Maria," he murmurs, his tone so level and soft it's damn near gentle. His hands betray his malice, however, shaking against my skin as if it's requiring every ounce of restraint he has just to keep from ripping me apart.

"I think I *do*," I counter, shocked by how hard my voice sounds in comparison to his.

His eyes narrow—he's shocked as well.

Possessed by whatever boldness has taken hold of me, I keep talking. "I think I'm showing the man you sold me to what he can expect once he completes his purchase."

I wince at the intensity his eyes take on. Something beyond anger, beyond rage.

"Oh, how I will punish you for that," he growls, lowering his mouth against my ear. "You have no fucking idea of the danger you are in. The sheer *stupidity* of what you're doing—"

"Then tell me." I'm louder than he is, threatening to break the show he's putting on.

Touching me like this…

From the outside, I know what it will look like. Like I'm out here with his permission—that his relationship with me is cordial enough to permit him to stroke my cheek and stand so close.

But why? It's not the expected behavior a man would show toward a woman he's brutalized and kidnapped.

And relenting to his touch isn't the way one would expect such a woman to act toward her captor.

I must twitch or make some move to pull away because he's closer, using his body weight to practically crush me against the railing.

"Get the fuck inside." His tone loses any shred of control; it's rippling, verging on something too primal to be considered speech. "You dumb, stupid cunt. You have no idea what you've done. None!"

But said ignorance isn't any fault of my own. It strikes me now that, against his demands, I have one last card to play, however fragile it may be.

I raise my hand, cupping the back of his. As a result, his nails scrape against my cheek in a silent warning—but I'm playing along.

For now.

"Then tell me," I demand.

Finally, his eyes dart away from me, and I have my answer as to whose presence has him on edge—Jaguar's. Whatever he sees triggers a flicker of alarm across his expression.

The next thing I know, his mouth is on mine, his hands roughly cupping my hips, pulling me into him. From the outside, it must look like a sexy, heated kiss filled with lust and passion.

In reality, his teeth seize onto my lower lip, preventing any chance I could easily pull away. With his strength, he snatches me to him, maneuvering me from the balcony and within the room in seconds.

Once we're away from view, he shoves me so hard I go flying, barely managing to catch myself on the edge of the mattress.

"You will pay for this," he warns, his voice ice. "You—"

"Tell me why or I'll scream," I croak, still stunned by how quickly he moved.

The threat, however, must slip beneath his armor. He flinches, his eyes slits as I open my mouth and suck in air in preparation.

"Tell me—"

"You aren't supposed to know that I've sold you." He says it so tonelessly. As if he's referring to a pair of shoes and not a woman. Me. My body. My life.

Voice rasping, the only reply I can choke out is, "W-What?"

"Why *would* I tell you?" he adds, closing the door to the balcony with a thud. Arms crossed, he starts to pace, his back to me. Ironically, it's reminiscent of the times I would watch him in the dark, performing this very act in front of my family's guest house, seeming as though the weight of the world rested on his shoulders. "As far as Jaguar knows, you think I've rescued you from the attack that killed your boyfriend. You think you're safe under my protection here. It minimizes the risk to him for you to be in the dark."

He doesn't laugh or sneer. He's telling the truth.

In Jaguar's eyes, I'm his simpering little fool.

"You… You unimaginable bastard." My voice breaks. I almost can't fathom the cruelty—let alone the thought that he's telling the truth. That could have easily been my reality if I didn't regain consciousness to overhear his two goons discussing his ownership of me.

He even said it himself—*I aimed to use her ignorance to my advantage.*

The worst part that I find truly horrifying is that it could have worked. In a different world, I could have easily been lulled into a false sense of safety, believing he was my savior. In fact, that was my first hope soon after I awoke here.

And he took great pains to reveal that hope for what it was —fragile and pathetic.

"Why?" I demand. "Why tell me at all? Do you get off on my fear?"

Or maybe he truly hates me that much. He couldn't even endure a lie long enough to gain my trust and have me put my faith in him. I am *that* repulsive to him.

The thought stings, but he never takes the chance to drive the truth home, right when it will hurt me the most. When I look up, he's watching me, his expression devoid of any hint of emotion. He might as well be stone.

"You know what I want," he says.

And maybe I do.

"Pia," I rasp. Drawing my knees to my chest, I hunch over myself, suddenly aware of how naked I am in comparison to him. "You think she's dead, and you think I know where some file my father had is. Because you are her brother."

Navid.

Surprisingly, he doesn't deny it outright. He cocks his head as if weighing my word choice. Apparently, I got some details wrong.

"You *know* where she is," he says softly. "Maybe you think you don't, but somewhere in that vapid, fucking brain is the answer. I'm sure of that."

"You're wrong," I say. I don't think I've ever heard my voice sound so hollow. So hopeless.

Can I even blame him?

I could play the victim and ignore the things I've done to Pia. I may not have killed her, but I certainly betrayed her. I conspired against her, and I shunned her without hearing her side.

Though who could blame me?

She slept with my father and used me to get to him, just as Domino seems determined to use me. And my father…

That's all my life has been—being used, and used, and used.

"Where do you think you're going?" Domino demands.

I'm staggering to my feet, heading for the balcony despite him moving to stand in front of me.

"I'm going to see if Jaguar is still here and beg him to take me with him—"

"Don't!" He snatches my arm, yanking me back. "You have no fucking idea who he is. You think he'll be your knight in shining armor? You are dead wrong, Ada-Maria."

"I don't care."

And I don't.

"Wait—" He tightens his grip when I attempt to take another step.

"Why should I?" I pull back to see his face, but I'm not prepared for the expression I find. Not one of hate. Instead, his eyes are narrowed, his head tilted as though he's contemplating a puzzle he only has seconds to solve.

"I want to find Pia's body," he admits, pulling me even closer.

Not because he truly thinks I can break away, but because he's that worried about being overheard. Whatever he's saying, he does so while being fully cautious of Jaguar, despite the other man being yards away outside of the house.

"Help me, and you will have my protection. Trust me, it's a better offer than anything else you'll be presented with."

"I…" *Don't know* is my first impulsive reply. Truly I don't. If Pia is dead, she could be anywhere. Besides, Domino has worked with my father; if anyone would have an idea of where he'd bury the body of a dead girl over a decade ago, it would be him.

And yet, something makes me swallow those words before I can fully voice them.

He means what he said to me—*you will have my protection.* It could be a lie, or another mind game. In the grand scheme, he could just sell me to Jaguar once he's through with me and never look back.

But he's right.

I don't have a better option.

Why not get some leverage over him, no matter how fragile, and bide my time until a better opportunity comes along?

"Jaguar is a dangerous man, Ada-Maria," he warns, still speaking in an undertone, his jaw practically pressed against mine. "You have no idea what he's capable of, the things he will do to you if he gets the chance. I am your only hope of surviving with that pretty little body intact."

"Fine." It pains me to choke down a nasty retort and face him while keeping my expression blank.

He's wary, his eyes slits as they scan my gaze, hunting for any sign of deceit. I don't know if I aim to reassure him, or I merely have to hear myself say it out loud to believe it.

"I'll play your game if you promise to protect me. I'll do what I can to help you find Pia."

That phrasing makes it not an outright lie.

But he didn't miss it. "You lead me to Pia's body if you want a damn thing from me," he warns. "In the meantime, you prance around here like a happy little cum whore, and you let Jaguar and his spy believe that you are oblivious to everything. I am your hero who rescued you from a living nightmare after you watched your boyfriend be murdered right in front of you. Understand?"

I don't. My head is spinning, trying to juggle it all, and now I know why he locked me in here—to protect his lie.

And yet, it betrays a rare hint of vulnerability on his part that he's even revealed as much to me.

"I guess this means that you have no need to lock your naïve, captive bunny rabbit in a bedroom without her consent, then," I croak. His nostrils flare, his grip on my arm tightening—but the display alone reveals that I'm right. Therefore, I don't mind twisting the knife just a little more. "I guess that means no more collar, either."

"Don't forget that Jaguar knows I injured you badly enough to require an extra week for you to heal, Ada-Maria. This isn't some fairy tale fucking romance—"

"How *did* you explain it?" I ask, jutting my chin as I parse through what few possible explanations I can come up with. None make sense. "Why would any woman stay with you willingly after what you've done? Why would my 'hero' collar me and have me whipped?"

"Do you really want to know?" He smiles, but it's a grotesque distortion of his mouth, nothing more. "I told him you like it rough—" He releases me, retreating toward another corner of the room. A second later, a wad of fabric lands against my chest, thrown by him. "Get dressed. And if you want to extend your life beyond Tuesday, you'll do what I say—which is keep your mouth shut."

The clothing he gave me is his, I realize. His shirt, which I pull on without complaint, too distracted by his revelation to care that, in this context, my little stunt has lost all its meaning.

No longer am I toying with his boundaries, but playing right into his sick narrative. His loyal, love-struck captive would, of course, choose to wear an item of his.

Did Alexi?

Her presence here irritates me more the longer I ponder Domino's reaction to her. He kept pictures of him fondling her naked body in his closet. And yet, how did he refer to her?

Jaguar's spy…

"Ines will bring you your lunch here," Domino says.

I look over my shoulder to find him entering the hall. From the way he reaches for the doorknob, I can tell what he intends to do.

Lock me in.

"I thought you said I could leave?"

He scoffs. "I am not as dumb as I look, Ada-Maria, and you are not as convincing as you think you are. I've humored you this once, but if you want my trust, batting your eyelashes and showing off your tits isn't how you get it. You *earn* it. Or so help me God, I will get that collar you like so much, wrap it around your throat and tie you in the closet like an animal for the week. Jaguar be damned. Do you understand that?"

He doesn't give me the chance to answer.

He slams the door, and a definitive click that sounds after reveals that he wasn't bluffing.

I'm locked in.

Quickly, though, I realize that I'm not completely without a weapon of my own.

I almost miss it as I pace, tearing my fingers through my hair as I consider going back onto that balcony and screaming bloody murder for anyone to hear.

He left it on the glass case of watches in the middle of the closet, perhaps as his own twisted attempt at a peace offering.

Or a taunt.

The pink surface mocks me as I approach it and warily run my fingers across the cover. Apart from last night, I haven't touched this object in ten years. A decade.

Plenty of time for Pia's lies and schemes to come back to bite me.

You think you're so different from me? she screamed at me during one of the last times I ever saw her. *You're just a selfish, spoiled little bitch who can't see beyond her stupid life. The rest of us? We're not so lucky, Ada. I don't have a papa to snap his fingers and fix my problems!*

I'd been so angry; I could have exploded. Never, had I felt that kind of rage before, or since. *So that's why you had to fuck him, then?* I'd thrown back at her. *Who's the bitch now?*

She blinked, her green eyes blazing, glistening with unshed tears. I'll never forget the look she gave me. Almost one of pity. *You have no idea what the hell is going on, do you? God, you're pathetic, Ada. Just give me my fucking diary back, and we can forget this ever happened…*

But it was too late by then, of course.

I'd already given it to my father.

And I'd already read every word.

CHAPTER FOUR

This time, I don't read a single page of the diary.

Maybe I'm just not brave enough. Or the avoidance is more an act of defiance than anything else. As much as he pretends not to, Domino badly wants me to help him decipher whatever mysteries his sister left behind. He's desperate enough to hope that the answer to her supposed death lurks within those pages.

Though why should I help him? My own self-interest aside, trusting him would be foolish. If my father did kill Pia, and I lead him to her body, only God knows what he'd do to me in retaliation.

He's already claimed to have killed my parents as well as Tristan.

Using the past as a predictor of the future, he'll more than likely shoot me himself and bury me in Pia's grave.

If there even *is* a grave.

361

A part of me still can't buy it—which makes the revelation that Domino might be her brother even harder to stomach. He would know, wouldn't he? If his sister were alive. She would have tried to contact him at least once within the past ten years?

Or Pia turned out to be the same old Pia, as selfish and cruel as I remember.

Though, even as a part of me desperately wants to cling to that belief, I can't. Pia may have hated me, but she loved her brother. His name dominated the pages of that diary, from what I can recall. Her entire justification for stealing the amount of money she did was for him.

His surgery.

I have to wonder if, indirectly, Roy Pavalos paid for the transplant he inevitably received. That would make his betrayal far, far worse, I decide. To betray the man whose fortune saved your life, no matter his supposed crimes.

Only a monster would do that.

Though, to be fair, Domino doesn't seem to have any idea as to who his sister truly was. Can I blame him? For the longest time, she had me fooled as well.

I loved her like a sister.

But to her, I was nothing but an obstacle to overcome.

The painful thought spurs me as far away from the diary as possible. Thankfully, he didn't lock the door to the balcony. As I escape into the warm, mid-morning air, I find that

Jaguar—and his posse—is gone. So is Alexi from her position on the terrace. An image of her and Domino fucking somewhere else, in some distant room of the house, sneaks into my skull, and I don't have the strength to block it out.

I hate that I can't predict him. Despite five years of knowledge regarding the man he used to be, I'm forced to admit that I know nothing about who he is.

Apart from what turns him on, of course. I know that a smart mouth—literally and figuratively—gets him going. But nowhere near as much as the sight of blood can.

My blood.

Here, in the warm, humid air far from prying eyes, there's nothing to stop me from reliving those sordid moments. Over and over again.

His touch. His pleasured moans rippling through my eardrum. His breath, hot on my throat. His taste.

His chest.

I keep seeing the stark, surgical line that denotes a past I can't deny. Whether or not he truly is Navid Inglecias, he's suffered. Suffering that he seems to blame my father for—and, indirectly, me. It certainly puts an ironic twist on my past attraction to him, anyway.

To crave a man without a heart… His own, at least. It's why his body can fuck me despite the hatred he harbors inside.

And yet, he's the only man to truly make me feel…anything remotely close to pleasure during sex.

How goddamn sad is that?

INES COMES HOURS LATER, leaving a tray of food for me on the bed.

I ignore it, barely paying it a glance on my way into the bathroom. I strip his shirt, leaving it carelessly over the threshold, and approach the now empty shower stall.

It's an exercise in clicking through various options on the digital control panel before I manage to get the water running. Safe within this glass cocoon, I lean against the granite wall and force myself to think.

If my father did kill Pia all those years ago, where could she be?

In our backyard? It's an obvious guess, but one I can easily rule out—my mother would have long since found her during all of the many renovations she's had done to the property in the last decade. I'm sure during the tennis court reno, it might have gotten back to us if the workers stumbled upon the body of a fifteen-year-old girl.

It isn't long, however, before my thoughts turn away from Pia to the man who claims to be her long-lost older brother.

Because he's here.

His scent packs a physical punch despite the overall stealth of his entrance. He watches me for a while, from beyond this realm of glass. I can see him from the corner of my eye, a shadow over the gray color scheme.

Eventually, he grows bored of merely watching. Without bothering to disguise his entrance, he slides open the glass door—slowly enough for the cool air to battle with the wall of steam I've let build up.

I don't turn to see if he's naked or not. When I sense him claim the bench across from me, I move to a different corner of the stall, finding a hook where he left the washcloth from this morning.

He never let me clean myself, I realize. Even now, I can feel the remnants of him, stubbornly clinging to my innermost, sensitive parts. Snatching the rag, I find a bar of scented soap and work it into a lather. Then I take my time, scrubbing every last inch of my body.

I'm methodical, so intent on my work that I almost forget he's watching.

"You think you can ignore me?" he asks, his voice heavy, though I don't detect his usual anger.

A good fucking session could do that to a man, leaving him languid and relaxed after.

Enough! I shake my head to clear it and run the rag between my breasts, then over my stomach—all without paying him a single glance.

"I like you quiet, Ada-Maria," he continues, still sounding as if he's across the stall. He hasn't moved.

Yet.

"I don't think I like you bitter, though. Your lips aren't meant to be pursed so tightly. The expression ages you."

I scoff, giving him the attention he wants. "Don't tell me you're partial to my father's tastes. How did you put it? Young, dumb, blond—"

"I'm not talking about any other woman, am I?" he counters in a tone that makes me grip my washcloth tighter. "I'm talking about you."

"Me," I echo hoarsely. "The woman you hate. The woman you hurt and have brutalized. The woman who hates you."

"You couldn't fuck a man you hated the way you fuck me."

I feel my mouth fall open at his bluntness. The worst part? He sounds confident—too confident.

As if he's studied how I fuck in general, well enough to make an educated inference.

"I'm good at faking it, Domino," I counter. Finally, I gather the nerve to meet his gaze from over my shoulder.

There is no sly, mocking smile on his face. He's dead serious.

"That you are," he agrees, seated on the bench, leaning back against the wall. He's naked, I realize, my cheeks flaming. The water pelts him, glistening off his skin and erasing any traces of sweat or exertion that he might have sported beforehand. "You are a damn good faker, at least for a man who doesn't know any fucking better."

I shiver, turning away to face the wall as I continue to wash myself. "You seem sure of that."

"Because I am," he replies. "Your boyfriend videotaped nearly every time he fucked in that penthouse of his—you, along with the many other women he was toying with. If it makes you feel any better, you were by far the sexiest. The bastard came faster with you than any other."

I stiffen, horrified by how callously he can reveal such intimate acts. Is he telling the truth? Only God knows. Tristan, the bastard, wasn't known for his faithful nature. I'd suspected his affair with Alexi early on, but am I surprised if she wasn't the only one?

But therein lies another secret revealed by Domino's admission—*you were by far the sexiest.* Is he including Alexi in that assessment?

God, I shouldn't care…

"The second I heard you moan for real, I realized how damn good of an actress you are," he continues, his voice loud and booming. Gone is the gruff undertone he took on with Jaguar in earshot. He's shameless now, uncaring of who might overhear.

Perhaps, because he tired out Alexi well enough to know she's dead to the world.

"I am a good actress," I agree, dropping the washcloth. "So good I made you think you actually got me off, Domino—"

"Your fake moans are pretty," he continues as if I never spoke. "The real ones? Goddamn, Ada-Maria. You could drive a man insane with those cries. Whether you're in pain or in pleasure, it's the same damn tune."

My next breath sticks in my chest as my heart hammers like mad. Is he joking? I can't tell, and this time I'm not inclined to look for myself.

"Enjoy your shower." I start for the door, scrambling to slide it open.

"Tristan," he practically snarls the name, "never went down on you—at least not in any of the recordings. He never spread those legs and tasted that pussy for himself. I used to imagine how you'd taste."

The intensity of his voice takes my breath away. I hate that he almost sounds genuine, like he truly did just that—dwell on the taste of me.

"How did Alexi taste?" I demand, turning to face him.

He raises an eyebrow. "How do you think she tasted? Like fucking roses. Why don't you ask her?"

I flinch, gritting my teeth, desperate to disguise just how deeply that taunt cuts. So deep it hurts, outshining my general aches and pains. I hate the thought of him lying with her. Kissing her.

Tasting her with the same tongue I used to fantasize about tasting me.

Spotting my rag on the floor, I cross over to it, leaving the shower door partially ajar. Grabbing it, I turn to face him. "You want to know what I taste like, Domino?" My voice is a low, husky purr.

But I'm struck dumb by his reaction. He sits forward, his head cocked, eyes obscured by strands of black hair plastered to his forehead by the shower spray. They slice his face into slivers, each one more unreadable than the last.

His eyes track every step I take toward him, blazing and burning.

"Here—" I throw the rag at him so hard it rebounds off his chest and lands at his feet. "That's the only taste of me you'll ever get. Savor it."

My words ring hollow, of course. He's too strong to overpower on my own—and there's nothing stopping him from lurching to his feet and pinning me down, taking from me whatever he damn well pleases.

To my shock, he grabs the rag and brings it to his mouth. Slowly, he extends his tongue, dragging it across a section of the rag in a way that makes my cheeks flame, my body heating. Licking his lips, he sits back again.

"Like milk and honey," he says raggedly.

And I sway. He's tasting the flavor of the soap I used. Not me. Getting ahold of myself, I once again stagger for the exit.

"That shitty camera of his never showed your back in detail," he says with a certainty that makes me stop short, my horror returning in full. "I couldn't see your scars from the footage. Tell me who hurt you."

"Why? So you can get pointers?" I toss back, eyeing the sliver of the bathroom lurking beyond this fragile pane of glass. Freedom. All I have to do is take the necessary few steps to reach it.

One…

"No," he says so coldly I'm frozen again. "So, I can kill them."

It's a strange boast to come from a man who hates me so. He whips me. Collars me. Lies to me.

Then confesses that he mused about what I taste like and vows to kill the man he thinks hurt me.

Though, it's an empty threat.

We both know who whipped me and what happened to him.

"Luckily for you, he's already dead, Domino," I rasp, taking another step. I'm close enough to grip the edge of the sliding glass door—and I do, for dear life, rattling it on the metal rail keeping it in place.

The sound of him rising to his feet is loud enough to overpower that delicate clinging noise. There's the thud of the rag hitting the ground a second time, followed by the patter of water dripping from his body, and his slow, heavy footsteps as he advances toward me.

All I can do is watch as he grips the door above where my hand is, easily wrenching it shut. I barely manage to pull my fingers out of the way.

"I want you to tell me why he did it," he demands, his breath fanning the space between my shoulder blades, though I don't dare turn around to see him there behind me. "And you will, Ada-Maria. You'll tell me every fucking detail. Why? I'll do what I know you've been dreaming about since the day I first met you in your father's office."

"Leave?" I croak hopefully.

He laughs. At the same time, he takes his hand from the door and uses it to grip my chin, whirling me around to face him. The glass rattles again as he pins me against the cool surface.

I have no choice but to see his face—to see the eyes ruthlessly raking over my body as if he truly does own it. Every inch, long before he had me brought here.

"I'll taste you," he declares, his voice rippling with lust. "And I'll have you wishing that I put a bullet in that bastard's brain sooner."

Tristan? Or my father?

He doesn't clarify, and I'm too unnerved to ask. I don't want to know the answer.

"I'd rather die," I hiss, "than feel any part of you on me *anywhere!*"

"You should be dead." He traces my jawline with the pad of his thumb, roughly as if he's trying to memorize every inch by feel alone. When he nears my ear, he leans in, bringing his mouth against the lobe. "If it weren't for me, you would be. That bullet was meant for *you.*"

CHAPTER FIVE

That bullet was meant for you...

I gasp, overwhelmed by the implications of that statement. Then I recoil, shoving at his chest with both hands.

"You're sick! Get the fuck away from me—"

"Think, Ada-Maria," he demands, not budging an inch. "Ask yourself who had everything to gain if his daughter, keeper of his secrets, happened to die a horrific death the night before his impending arraignment."

His tone is different. Too persistent. Too cold. Too...believable.

"No!" I wrench away and yank the door open enough to squeeze from the stall. Tripping over the threshold, I stumble, losing my balance so that I wind up on my knees, gripping the edge of a counter for balance. "You're lying. Playing with my head. You're lying!"

"I'm not." God, he sounds so calm. So gentle?

No. No. No. I slap my hands over my ears and hum.

But nothing short of screaming could drown him out. "You were always a liability to him, but I wasn't sure until I saw those scars. A man who would beat his own daughter like that? He didn't give a damn whether you lived or died. He was only ever out for himself."

"That sounds like *you*." I whirl on him, hauling myself to my feet, utilizing the counter for balance.

He's still technically inside the shower stall, watching me from beyond the gap in the glass partition.

"You were the one who only ever gave a damn about himself. After what you claimed to have done to my father, don't you dare bring him into this."

"So he did whip you."

I groan in exasperation, feeling as though my brain is being manipulated and twisted, all for his amusement. "No. You did—"

"I didn't hurt you," he claims, still in that aggravatingly level tone.

"Oh really?" I hiss out a vicious excuse for a laugh. "You could have fooled me!"

"I merely punished you," he adds, taking a step to bridge the gap between the shower and the main bathroom. Behind him, the water continues to fall, creating steam that billows around him like smoke. He looks like a literal demon waltzing out of hell, and my pulse surges to a painful, pulsating rhythm.

"If I wanted to hurt you, Ada... Trust me, there are a million ways I could do so." He takes another step, exiting the shower completely, dripping water onto the floor. "And believe me when I say I've considered them all."

"You want to know something funny?" I rasp.

Though it isn't funny in the slightest. It's pathetic, a painful reality stabbing at the back of my mind, threatening to reduce me to tears if I think on it long enough.

"I'm used to men not living up to their hype. Tristan was a dick, but he never disappointed me. I never expected better from him. Not good sex, not real commitment, not even loyalty. I'm sure you know better than anyone that I only gave him the time of day because the relationship benefited my father. In fact, most of the men I've dated and fucked were just that—peons my father wanted to control, so he used me."

It sounds horrifying when said out loud; I can admit that. Internally, I've always processed it differently than I figure anyone outside of the family would. My father used me—but he *trusted* me, too. He relied on me. He needed me.

We had a bond forged by blood and family, strong enough to outlast everything.

Always.

But if one man ever came close to earning a glimmer of that same amount of loyalty from me, it certainly wasn't Tristan Lucas or any of my other conquests.

"Every man I ever met or interacted with, I never had any high hopes for," I admit hoarsely, staring down at the floor. "Why? I was always mentally comparing them to someone else. Someone who always won out. Always. And who was that?" My voice thickens as the threat of tears burns my eyes. I start to blink, hoping to keep them at bay.

It's too late. They fall, but in this instance, I jut my chin to brandish them like war paint. I'm not ashamed of them. They, better than anything I could say, prove how sincerely I mean the words leaving my throat. He can't deny them.

"It was you. Always, it was *you*. No one could ever measure up to the fictional version of Domino Valenciaga I built up in my head."

Not even the real man, as it turns out.

"Do you realize how pathetic that makes you? Tristan never had a chance in hell of measuring up, but you? You can't even match the man I *thought* you were."

That gets a rise out of him. His eyes darken, his head dipping low, and my heart stutters fearfully. With three heavy strides, he advances on me before I can even regain my balance fully.

His hand captures my chin, weighing it against his palm as though he's considering how easy it would be to crush it. I feel his fingers twitch excitedly—God, he wants to.

"I would watch you," he tells me. "Over and over, I'd watch those fucking videos of you with him."

Tristan?

"And not only that dumb son of a bitch." He brings his other hand up to stroke the damp hair from my face, dragging me closer until I'm straining on tiptoe. "Most of the men you've ever fucked within the past five years, I caught a glimpse, Ada. Of you, riding their dicks in the back of a fancy sports car or in that private cabana your father owns at the country club. I've heard you moan; I've seen that perky little ass bounce. I came up with the impression that you were a dumb slut, so easy that a fancy gift and a glass of wine could get you wet."

He trails off, giving me plenty of time to picture the twisted ways he's tried to emulate that. With his "gift" of a whip, and the imported vintage, he claimed to know I love.

"I see now that I was wrong, Ada. You failed to live up to even that rather generous impression of you. I thought you were too stupid to know better. That you enjoyed the lifeless sex and cheap affection. Why else subject yourself to man after man, after man who only saw you as an object? But now I see the truth about you."

He cradles my jaw in both hands, lowering his mouth enough to baste my lips in the warmth of his breath.

"You were never stupid, Ada-Maria. You were calculating, doing whatever your papa told you to, without even taking your own pleasure into account. I worked for the man to get close to him. To learn how best to overpower the sick bastard. But you? What did you get out of being his daughter other than shitty sex and learning how to best fake an orgasm? Oh, and don't let me forget—being beaten and whipped—"

Thwack! The unmistakable smack of flesh on flesh leaves me stunned. All I can do is brace myself for the pain I should feel—and I do, throbbing like hell, but not on my face or any other part of my body within his reach.

My hand hurts. I eye the reddening, trembling fingers and realize that I'm the one who struck him.

"I'll let you have that one hit," he says, running his hand across his mouth. He eyes his fingers, and even from here, I can see the streak of red painting them. He's bleeding from his bottom lip. "You can savor this, Ada," he adds. "I gave you one more thing that he couldn't."

And what might that be?

I'm not brave enough to ask.

"Stay away from me." I lunge toward the balcony and into the bedroom, entering it on my own, free from any assault on his part. With my eyes on the door to the hall, I keep moving.

"You never asked me why."

I glance back to find Domino still standing in the doorway, his hands braced against the wall on either side as if he's physically stopping himself from lunging for me.

"Why I watched you," he clarifies. "Why I know the most intimate details of your little rendezvouses. You could assume it was because I sought to satisfy my own twisted obsession—" He laughs, proving the folly of that suspicion. Ice cold, he cuts his eyes up to mine, drilling in the fact that everything he's about to say is the brutal, honest truth. "Or I was only doing my job. What my boss commanded of me. You see, he never trusted you. No matter how many times you fucked for him. Lied for him. It was never enough. He never saw you as anything more than a tool. You meant nothing to him."

I don't let myself process the hatefulness in those words. I just run, wrenching open the door and entering the hallway without another word from him. He doesn't follow me, either. I'm allowed to tear through the house, unbothered by anyone.

For the first time, I take notice of my surroundings beyond the confines of Domino's room. It's later in the evening, with the sunset visible beyond the windows, painting everything in a bloody red glow. If I were to run out of the front door and take my chances in the desert, at least I could do so without running the risk of getting heatstroke. Already, the air feels cooler, aided by the fact that I'm still naked, dripping wet.

Rather than forge ahead with another escape attempt, I find myself padding down the hallway before the white room I've subconsciously come to think of as my own—but when I throw open the door, I realize just how foolish I've been.

Nothing in this house is mine. He's already taken great pains to prove that.

By giving this room to someone else, he's merely reinforcing my status as his captive.

"Domino?" The voice identifies the blond woman lying sprawled across the white bed, her ass up, legs kicking at the air. She's wearing a black dress that I can tell was taken from the closet, her cleavage spilling out onto the sheets beneath her. Before her is a plate of ripe strawberries that she's picking at with her fingers.

"Took you long enough." She rolls over, her coy smile falling flat the second she sees me.

And I know instantly that I interrupted something. She was waiting for him.

"G-Get the fuck out," I rasp. It's all I can say. The thought of retreading my steps is too painful to bear. I can't leave this room. So I stumble across it, aiming for the only sanctuary I can spy at the moment—the closet.

"You look like you've been having fun," Alexi taunts, her tone just as bitchy as I remember. I can tell without having to look that she hasn't budged. She won't.

Not unless I give her a good enough reason to get her perky ass in motion.

"He's all warmed up for you," I tell her as I feel alongside the mirror for the latch to activate the door beneath. I can't even look at my reflection. I just close my eyes to everything, this room, this reality.

Even without the aid of drugs, I'm determined to float away. Refuse to exist in this space anymore.

"What the hell is your problem?" I hear Alexi snipe, her presence clashing with my attempts to fade. Zone out. Become numb.

The two of us were never as close to each other as we both were to Pia. She was the glue holding our impromptu group together, but looking back, I can't deny that I had fun moments with Alexi, too. She was the silly girl, always cracking jokes—the balancing force between Pia's aloof confidence and my shyness.

In her own way, she was a decent enough friend. She taught me how to wear lipstick, and tried to teach me how to flirt.

And, after Pia disappeared, she taught me what true loneliness could feel like.

"Are you just going to stand there?" Her voice startles me back to the present, as icy as ever.

"I told you I got his cock hard enough," I snap. "So why don't you do what you do best and go fuck my leftovers."

I don't wait to see if she heeds the offer this time. I peel my eyes open long enough to lunge inside the closet and slam the door behind me. Then I make my way into the furthest corner I can and curl into a ball small enough to wedge my body in between two shelves.

It's not my preferred hideout beneath the blankets, but it's close enough. Here, the world fades to a dull hum, only discernable if I choose to listen closely enough.

First, there's only silence. Endless, oppressive silence…

Then sobbing. Such loud, wracking, frantic cries as though the person voicing them is on the verge of utterly breaking apart. They can't be coming from me.

I've been through enough hurt and rejection by now that nothing should be able to break me down. No one should be able to reduce me to a sniveling, sobbing mess.

Especially if they've only voiced the truth I already know.

My father never loved me.

He needed me.

But in my world, those are the same damn thing.

CHAPTER SIX

"Have you ever been in love?" Pia asked me once. The question came from nowhere, uttered in her typical crisp, confident tone. But I could sense something lurking beneath her seemingly calm veneer.

We were in my room at St. Margarita's, pretending to pore over study materials for math class. In reality, we were gazing from the window at the small sliver of lawn belonging to St. Benedict's, the boys' boarding school next door. That time of day, the lacrosse team would practice, and Pia and I would rate the players by their fuzzy silhouettes.

"Have you?" she prodded, sitting cross-legged on my bed.

I was on the floor, my math textbook opened in front of me. Using the pretense of reading it, I tried to disguise how I blushed.

Love was such a mystical, foreign concept back then. Something we both fantasized about with starry eyes and grandiose delusions of our future lovers.

"I hate it," Pia declared, and I looked up to find her twisting a silver ring around her finger, her gaze on the window. "We're told that it's supposed to feel wonderful, like magic. But it just makes you feel crazy. Like everything you thought made sense doesn't matter anymore. The entire world revolves around this one person. And they can decide to make it stop spinning whenever they want to. However, they want to. It's like they own you."

"That sounds cryptic," I joked, utilizing one of our English vocabulary words. So badly did I want to ask her more, but I'd remembered how she'd brushed off my earlier attempts to pry about her mystery man and backed down.

All I did was clear my throat and whisper, "What if it's not really love?"

"What?" Pia inclined her head, her beautiful lips pursed thoughtfully. "You'll never understand, Ada. You just don't know what it's like."

She gathered up her books then and left, calling over her shoulder as she entered the hall, "I'm going to hang with Alexi."

And I spent the rest of the night crying into my pillow, seething with jealousy.

But now...

I have to wonder just what she meant. Was she referring to my father then? Or someone else?

Who knows. Damn Domino for dredging up these old memories.

I never think of her this often. Certainly not twice in a handful of days. I've spent years smothering her ghost beneath a heap of repressed thoughts and subsequent trauma.

I will never admit it out loud, but her betrayal hurt me the worst, before Domino's, anyway. Such a beautiful, rare gem of a girl she was. So strong, so confident. She could empower a stone to come to life and speak with one of her smiles. She could have had any boy in a ten-mile radius with merely a wink and a nod.

Pia Inglecias could have had anyone she wanted.

She didn't need my father. She didn't have to prance around in outfits that—while modest—showcased her body's subtle curves and her tiny waist. She didn't have to be so damn beautiful, with eyes a mossy green and curling dark hair that framed a delicate face. She didn't have to carry herself with a maturity well beyond her fifteen years.

She didn't have to want him.

But she did. She used me to get to my father, and it was child's play for her. She thought she could manipulate the great and powerful Roy Pavalos.

And her plan worked—as long as my father was amused by her. Pia couldn't see it then, but she was only ever a toy to him. A playful distraction. A sick conquest.

Eventually, he grew tired of everyone. My mother. His two prior wives. Any piece of ass he took on the side.

They never held his interest for longer than a handful of minutes at a time. Why? Because Roy Pavalos only ever truly loved one person.

Himself.

If my father *did* kill Pia, then her diary alone wouldn't hold the answer—he would. Her final resting place would be a clever twist, a way for him to prove that he was always in control. His sick, twisted version of declaring the ultimate checkmate.

I could never think like him. I never understood his plots or his ploys. I only knew enough to play my role.

When it came to Pia, I was to lure her away and steal her diary.

But what if I was just seeing what he wanted me to see? A small piece in a much bigger plan...

Frustrated, I finally open my eyes, forsaking the past for the grim reality of my present circumstances. I can't tell how long I've been sitting here without a view of the sky, though my body is protesting in enough various aches and pains that I suspect at least an hour has passed.

Groaning with the effort, I disentangle myself from between the shelves and set my sights on the numerous items of hanging clothing. Alexi's familiarity with the wardrobe makes me suspect that, once again, Domino lied to me. He's had her here before, fucked her here, perhaps on that very bed he's regulated me to.

The thought sickens me, though I don't know why. I'm not jealous. I can't be. Domino Valenciaga, as I knew him is dead, and the monster holding me captive is a creature I want nothing to do with.

Though, for once, I'm willing to take a page out of my father's book. I can use him.

When I grab a dress, I put no thought into it, just picking the nearest item. I pull it on over my head without bothering to find any underwear to put on beneath.

My head held high, I finally leave the closet, only to realize that Alexi is gone. The room is drenched in darkness, proving my suspicion correct—it's already past nightfall. If I had to guess where Alexi might be, it's in Domino's bed right now, doing the very thing I told her to.

I shrug off the thought and make my way into the hall, moving blindly. I try to push everything else from my brain but the need to survive. Endure.

Domino dangled a sliver of freedom above my head, and I'd be a fool not to take it—though I don't trust him one damn bit. He'll screw me over in the end, I know that.

But not if I can screw him first.

As I near the door to his room, some of my resolve wavers. It's closed, and I can't help but wonder if the fact is a warning not to enter. Because he's busy fucking his toy. By breaching this boundary on my own, I'll only be asking to have that rubbed in my face.

So be it. I don't care about either of them enough to be offended. I'll be the daughter my father always wanted and refuse to give a damn about anyone but myself.

And, when it comes to survival, I'll do whatever it takes.

No matter how many times I feed myself that mantra, my fingers still shake as I grip the doorknob and twist, pushing the door open to a darkened room. My nostrils flare with Domino's scent, but to my surprise, I don't smell sweat or the fresh traces of sex.

Neither do I smell Alexi.

Straining my eyes, I blink through the shadows, and realize that the bed is empty. I feel along the wall for a light switch, revealing that, at a glance, the room itself seems deserted.

But no. *His* scent grows stronger the further I travel. Eventually, I venture far enough to see that the door to the balcony is open, letting in a wave of warm night air.

I don't check to see if he's there. Instead, I enter the closet, searching with a single-minded focus until I find what I'm after—Pia's diary.

I flip it open to a specific page and read while leaning against the cabinet full of watches, hearing them tick ominously in the background. The noise can't disguise the sound of his approach, however.

He's slow, lingering in the doorway with only the rasp of his breathing to give him away.

"Did I give you permission to go through that?"

I flinch but don't look up. In reality, I haven't been able to read a damn thing. At the sight of Pia's neat, deliberate handwriting, my vision blurred with the unmistakable burn of fresh tears.

I've missed her; how pathetic is that? All this time, I've held out hope that one day she would come out of the woodwork and explain where she'd been the last decade. Somewhere glamorous, of course. She would have amassed her own wealth somehow, and jet back into the city in a flashy sports car, her smile as charming as ever. Always bold, she'd seek me out without giving a damn about the rift between us.

Then she'd cajole her way back into my life, and things would go on as they used to be. When I felt like I had an ally outside of the carefully constructed world of Roy Pavalos.

But our friendship, much like everything else in my life, was nothing more than a well-crafted lie.

"Did you hear me?" He advances a step that has me sucking in a breath and jumping back before I can help it.

"D-Do you want my help or not?" I demand.

But then I make the mistake of looking up.

He hasn't been fucking Alexi—or if he has, their session was light enough that his hair has maintained the same shape our impromptu shower left it in—gently tousled around his shoulders.

He's left his chest bare, opting to wear only a pair of black slacks that don't look as though they've been hastily rebuttoned.

Not that I take comfort in the realization. Whether he's fucking Alexi or not is neither here nor there. All that matters is getting the leverage required to make him act on his word.

"Help," he echoes, his eyes flashing. For a second, I fear that I've misunderstood him all this time. Or that he's already grown bored of pretending to see me as anything more than a toy. "I don't remember asking for your help, Ada-Maria. I asked for answers."

A subtle warning that he won't accept anything but a concrete location when it comes to finding Pia's body.

Luckily for me, I think I may have an idea.

With his presence serving as a reminder of the threat looming over my head, I return my attention to the diary pages, this time seeing them clearly.

I'm on the right month, but the wrong day. Absently I flip toward the back of the diary, only to find that the week abruptly ends.

But not where it should.

I keep searching, scanning the remaining pages over and over until I notice a faint strip of ragged edges lining the binding.

"Some of the pages are missing," I blurt, raising my head to find Domino staring.

Rather than smug, or defensive, he looks… Confused. "If this is your way of trying to manipulate the situation, I would warn you to rethink that plan."

"I'm not. Look—" I shove the open book across the cabinet's glass surface.

Warily, he approaches, inspecting the journal himself. He frowns.

"Where did you get this?" I ask, recalling his vague answer the first time I asked this very question.

"Let's just say I found it," he says, still tracing the ragged edges of the pages. I know just from his clouded expression that he didn't realize they were missing at all. Which means they were torn out before he received it.

"Did you take it from my father?" I prod.

It's the most likely choice. After all, I personally gave him this diary, and I can attest that those remaining pages were there, though I barely remember what exactly they said.

I just know how angry they made me. How furious— enough so that I gave the journal to my father with no guilt.

At least, not then.

"Did you?" I ask when Domino doesn't reply.

His frown has deepened, his expression more guarded than ever. Finally, he sighs. "I got that book years before I even started working for Don Roy."

Some of my excitement deflates, replaced by even more confusion. "I… I don't understand."

"It's the truth," he counters. "But don't expect me to go on a wild goose chase, either." He takes a step in my direction, reinforcing the dangerous boundary between us. Captor and captive. "You've already read it, haven't you? So what the hell are you looking for?"

I ignore the question to phrase one of my own. "Did you read it?"

But he already confessed that he has.

"Then you know damn well that I wasn't lying. She was sleeping with my father."

And he knew that all along. It's why he started this vendetta against my family in the first place. Revenge.

But, again, his expression doesn't match. Instead of smug, he just looks cold. Impassive. Stone.

"I knew she was fucking someone," he says. "But nowhere in that journal does she write the name Roy. You know whose name she does write? Over and over, and over again? Yours—" He palms the counter with both hands, leaning across it so that his face is mere inches from mine. "Ada-Maria Pavalos. She wrote about how sneaky you were. How conniving. How much time the two of you spent together, and that you followed her around like a lost puppy—"

"Because she was using me," I rasp. "Duplicity and deception must run in the family."

He raises an eyebrow. "Respect for her is the only reason why I haven't slapped the taste out of your mouth," he warns in a tone so harsh I'm left reeling. He pushes back from the cabinet, turning for the main room. "I'm thinking I might rescind my offer—"

"I might know where to look," I rasp.

He stops over the threshold, his back to me. "If you think this is a game, I'm warning you. You don't want to play with me."

"I'm serious," I say. But hell, for all I know, this guess could be a wild shot in the dark. It's all I have. I'm not putting myself in Pia's shoes, though.

I'm thinking like my father. If I were a man like him with a secret to hide, where would I bury it?

It's obvious. Perhaps, *too* obvious. The consequences of being wrong are too dangerous to fathom, so I push all thought of failure from my mind and meet his piercing stare without flinching.

"I'm sensing you have the balls to tack a 'but' onto that statement," he murmurs.

"Y-Yes," I croak. His gaze is too intense; I have to tear my gaze away to the wall instead. Eyeing it, I find the strength to make a demand of my own. "*But,* I want something."

"And what is that?"

"I want proof that my father is dead."

He's silent for so long I risk a glance in his direction just to make sure he's still there.

He is, watching me with an unreadable expression. Finally, he inclines his head, running his hand along his jaw. "His smoking body cooking over an open spit wasn't proof enough for you?"

"I want a news article," I say, cringing. It's been hard enough trying to get those images from my mind. "The coverage must be wall to wall. Let me see it for myself, and that's all I'm asking for. Then, anything that I may know is yours."

As the seconds tick by—audibly, given his watch collection —I'm sure he'll refuse outright. Instead, he turns on his heel and reenters the room without a word.

I'm forced to follow him, catching him on the balcony, leaning casually against the railing as if he's enjoying the view.

"And?" I demand, my voice shrill.

"Give me a day." His tone is flat, betraying no hint of inflection. It's reminiscent of the chilling monotone he utilized as my father's trusted soldier doing God knows what for him day in and day out. Still, his acquiescence in this matter is something.

I'll take it.

"Thank you," I whisper, preparing to bolt back into that white room, regardless of if Alexi is there or not.

Before I can take a step, he turns, leveling me with the full weight of his icy stare. "You would thank the man who has your life in his hands? Don't be so eager, Ada. Your good girl act won't work here. I never promised I still won't sell you, did I?"

The dread I feel is like being drenched in ice water—a million different variations of shame and betrayal washing over me, one after the other.

Then I remember that I haven't told him anything. Either he stupidly revealed his whole plan to be a lie, or he's merely trying to rile me.

"I'm not eager," I counter, remaining within his orbit for a second longer despite every cell in my body urging me to run. "I'm earnest. Unlike you or my father, I am not a heartless, cruel excuse for a person, and I refuse to let you make me that way."

Rather than seem insulted, he laughs.

"So says the woman who fucks men with the same discernment most use when picking a public bathroom stall to use. You have no integrity. No shame. No honor."

"I have more honor than you do," I whisper harshly. "You act so high and mighty when you fucked Alexi. You've killed. You lied to me. You dragged me here, and you've hurt me. More than my father has, mind you. So don't you dare stare down your nose at me, Domino. You? You're evil—"

"You shut your fucking mouth about things you don't understand," he warns, pulling back from the railing to return to his full height.

"Or what?" I counter. My voice shakes so badly the words lack any confidence, but that's beside the point. I'm still here, standing as he advances with slow, heavy footsteps that radiate malice.

"Or..." He runs his fingers through my hair and cups the back of my skull in the same brutal motion. Swiftly, he yanks me toward him, nearly taking me off my feet. With our faces inches apart, he meets my gaze and holds it. "I'll teach you what evil truly is, Ada-Maria. Your father came as close to fitting the definition of that word as anyone I've ever met—but even he would shy from the things I've imagined doing to you."

I tremble at the pure, vicious intent in his voice. He means every word, and the gleam in his eyes seconds that. Whoever this man is now, he's not my father's trusty lackey or Pia Inglecias' long-lost brother.

He is a monster...

And I am at his mercy.

CHAPTER SEVEN

"I'm not talking about sex, either," he clarifies, lowering his gaze to my mouth. "You seem to enjoy that. I'll take pleasure in learning what it is you *don't* enjoy, as soon as I grow tired of hearing those pretty little moans of yours."

My cheeks sear, and the despair I feel is enough to drown me—but not yet. This time, I won't go down without a fight. I'll drag him down with me.

"You can do them," I rasp, "Whatever vile things you can come up with in that sick brain of yours—and know that with every vile act, I'll hate you more and more. Not that you'll care about that. But then you'll have to wonder, Domino. You'll have to compare every scream and cry to every night I've spent with you, and you'll realize just how damn good of an actress I am. Because every 'pretty little moan?' I've been faking them all this time. Why?" I force a laugh that has his nostrils flaring. "You truly believed that a brute like you could ever really get me off? Keep dreaming."

The lies assuage my aching pride, and his darkening expression makes toying with him in this way worth it. No matter how violent he is, or how much he claims to hate me, he's still susceptible to the same weakness as any other man.

Male pride.

"Sell me if you want to, you bastard," I add, hissing through my teeth. "At least then I might experience what a true orgasm is before I die—"

He grabs me by the throat, and I swear I see my entire life flash before my eyes. And what a sad, pathetic excuse for a life it truly was. Who was Ada-Maria Pavalos in the grand scheme?

Just a memory, the daughter of Roy. No one special enough to make her own mark on the world. Merely a tiny blip on a much bigger picture.

Men like Domino and my father make lasting impressions without even trying. They destroy the lives of those weaker, leaving destruction in their wake.

I wait for the violence in his touch—for the suffocating ache of my throat being crushed in his fist. Instead, he strokes his thumb along my windpipe as a lethal, gentle reminder of the damage he's capable of.

"So bold without your papa's shadow to hide behind, Ada-Maria," he taunts, but I can tell that beneath the mocking amusement is genuine curiosity. "That smart mouth has many hidden talents, though I strongly suggest that you reconsider which attributes might help extend your life a little longer."

"Why?" I ask in a tone that resembles a wail more. A whine. "I have nothing left to live for."

Except trying to preserve what small shreds of freedom I can claw back from him.

"You've taken everything."

"Everything?" The shift in his inflection is my only warning before he spins me around, putting my back to the railing. With his gaze boring directly into my own, he uses his grip on my neck to steer me back.

Back…

The metal rung digs into my lower back, but he keeps going, forcing me to bend against it. My heart lurches as I scramble for purchase, gripping the barrier on either side of me with both hands. Already, a sheen of sweat disrupts my grip—it will be child's play for him to shove me over entirely.

Kill me.

But, at least for now, his eyes lack any murderous intent.

"Everything?" he wonders softly. Viewing him from below, the harsh lines of his face are even more starkly beautiful in contrast to the way the moonlight glints off his skin. Soft, overhead light bathes everything on the terrace in a gentle, orange glow. The hue reflects off his eyes—he's on fire.

"There are so many things I deliberately haven't taken from you, Ada-Maria," he tells me. "Yet."

He releases my throat, and I writhe to pull myself upright. But he doesn't fully withdraw, forcing me to balance awkwardly, practically sitting on the railing while he blocks me in with his sheer bulk.

"Do you want to know why I put that feeding tube down your throat myself?" His eyes trace the line of my throat, skimming over my breasts to fixate on my heaving stomach. "Do you?"

His tone is persistent, though I'm too stunned by the abrupt change in subject to come up with a fitting answer. "W-What?—"

"I wanted you to have meat on that ass so that when I take you there, I'll have something to grab onto."

I blink, shocked by the coarse, blunt word usage as much as I am by his tone. Real emotion breaks through the level baritone, rousing a fear I've never felt before. He isn't angry or trying to scare me. He is dead serious.

"I needed you stronger," he adds, sliding his fingers against my jaw before cupping my entire cheek against his palm. "The things I have planned for you, Ada… You'll need all the strength you can get."

My mind goes blank as my fear builds to the point that I can taste it—fire, salt, and blood.

"First, you offer to save me," I croak. "And now, you threaten to hurt me."

"Don't sound so surprised." He drags his gaze up to mine, and I find his eyes devoid of a hint of sympathy or guilt. "I am a man of many talents," he confesses. "However, I never said that you wouldn't enjoy what I plan to do you. Oh no, Ada, I think you'll enjoy them very, very much. So much so that we can put your little theory to the test. How good of an actress are you?"

He laughs, leaning in so that his face is directly beside mine, his eyes on my throat.

"One could say I've become a connoisseur of the sounds made by Ada-Maria Pavalos over the years, and I have to admit that if you were faking, your acting skills have grown remarkably from over a month ago."

Was that the last time he watched some sordid recording of me?

I don't feed into his narrative outright. Instead, I meet his gaze and choke down the crippling unease warning me not to tangle with him. I should keep my mouth shut, or better yet, run.

Instead, I say, "What you think you heard, you'll never hear again. At least not in person. If you're still planning on selling me after all, then maybe you'll get lucky while I'm with my buyer. He might even let you watch."

His eyes narrow, and a jolt of alarm shoots down my spine. *Careful, Ada. You're on fragile ground.* "I don't think you'll enjoy making the sounds he'll wring from you, Ada-Maria."

He. The way he voices that word carries such vitriol that I know he's not referring to some nameless man in general. No, he has someone specific in mind.

Licking my lips, I hazard a guess, "Jaguar?"

"You…" Voice rumbling, he lowers his head, and his hair falls forward, shrouding his expression from view. "I think you'll want to be very careful with what you say next…"

I shiver, but I'm too tired to fight. The longer I maintain this precarious balance, the less fearful I feel. Why not just let him push me over? At least I'll be in control of my life for those final few seconds. No one can manipulate me anymore.

And yet, I can't resist one last jab, aiming to get under his skin any way I can.

"I'll ask him to record it for you," I murmur, arching my back, so that my mouth is near his ear this time. "And I'll make whatever damn sounds he asks me to."

He lunges.

A scream builds in my throat, but I don't even have the chance to voice it before he withdraws his support from me completely. I slip as my fingers lose their grip on the railing. In a heart-stopping jolt, I pitch backward.

At the same time, his hands latch onto my hips, anchoring me down. Rather than push me over, he sinks to his knees, wrenching my thighs apart.

A new kind of fear has me croaking, "D-Don't!"

Not that he heeds the refusal.

Unconcerned, he snatches up the hemline of my dress, exposing me to the warm night air. I shudder, trying to clamp my knees together, but he's too strong, utilizing brute force to keep them spread. Then his head lowers…

I squeeze my eyes shut, praying that he won't do what his position implies he might. Every muscle in my body goes rigid in grim anticipation as I feel his breath graze the innermost parts of me.

He breathes in. Out.

In and out.

I think he's toying with me on purpose, heightening the tension until it's electric. Unbearable. The folds of my pussy burn, exposed to his heat. Nerves explode, even without the aid of his touch. It's a cruel, pulsating sensation.

"S-Stop—"

"I could have you begging me to fuck you." His voice is a grated rasp—as if every word is being torn from the darkest parts of his brain. Those fantasies he's barely even aware of. "I could. I could have you screaming for me, gushing like a fucking geyser. I'd make you choke on every last word you've said."

The warmth basting my pussy turns hotter. Sweltering. I can't stop myself from writhing, wanting to pull away.

Get closer…

"But I won't." All at once, he stands, wrenching me down from my perch. His grip on my shoulder is the only force keeping me upright. My knees are wobbling, my legs jelly. "You want to know why? The world doesn't revolve around Ada-Maria's pussy."

He lets me go, forcing me to grapple for the railing to find my balance.

Dazed, I watch him re-enter the bedroom as his voice reaches back to me. "Decide if you plan to waste my time or not. You only have one chance to earn my trust. If not, I'll drag you to *Guarida del Tigre* myself, and believe me when I say that I will watch, Ada-Maria. But I don't think you'll enjoy yourself half as much as you seem to think you will. Jaguar's world won't be as kind to you as mine has."

When he's gone, the impact of his words resonates like a gut punch. Dejected, I sink to my knees, still gripping the balcony, my eyes on the shadowed landscape below. I'm terrified of what might await me; I truly am.

I'm more terrified, however, by the prospect of what his "protection" entails. Something tells me that Domino Valenciaga has a warped concept of the phrase. The last thing on earth I should strive to gain is his trust.

And yet…

I don't have a choice.

It's either him or the unknown, and—at least for now—I'd rather take him.

If only to be the one to push him figuratively overboard in the near future.

CHAPTER EIGHT

I wake up in the white room, startled and disoriented. For one, I don't remember how I got here. I have no recollection of leaving Domino's room…

In fact, my last memory is huddling on the balcony, still stung from his taunt.

For now, I put the mystery out of my mind and sit upright, realizing that I'm lying on the bed, atop the neatly made sheets.

Alexi isn't anywhere in sight, at least. Golden sunlight bathes the room in warm shades of yellow that cast a chilling background to the tension still lingering in the air. Domino isn't around either, but he's close. I can sense him and his rage smoldering somewhere within the house, waiting to descend.

I'll make him wait a little longer, though.

I enter the closet and strip my black dress in favor of a new one. This style is lighter, made out of white cotton, and breathable in the heat. When I return to the bed, I find that someone must have come in without me realizing it, leaving a silver tray on the bed. Ines?

I barely pay the food a passing glance, but something catches my eye. A square, white envelope strategically placed upright against a plate of scrambled eggs and beautifully arranged fruit. My name is written across it in sloping handwriting.

Cautiously, I open it, finding just a plain white card with a message written on it. While Ines may have left this tray for me, I doubt she penned these two lines in menacing black script.

I suggest you eat. Or you will regret it.

A friendly morning missive from Domino.

I rip it in half, letting the pieces fall at my feet. Then I turn my back on the tray, fully intending not to eat so much as a damn bite. Let him make his demands and pose all the threats he wants.

But then I realize that I would only be giving him an opening to escalate his taunts. My stomach drops as I remember what happened on the balcony. Every time I try to meet him tit for tat, he turns the tables.

Ignoring him now would be a blatant invitation for him to impose yet another change to our dynamic. Perhaps try to do more than shove a feeding tube down my throat, for instance.

I shudder at the prospect and wind up sitting on the edge of the bed before I can rethink my options. I grab a fork, stab at a piece of egg and bite it, chewing mechanically.

The taste barely registers, but the sickening sensation of food filling my stomach is unbearable. I nearly spit it out. The need to purge is so damn overwhelming that it takes effort to swallow. Once I do, I drop the fork, lurching to my feet.

I've done enough.

But then I picture his expression as he said, "You'll need your strength." In reality, he likes me weak and powerless. He prefers having the utmost control over my body and my life.

He'd love having one more reason to rip away what fragile autonomy I have left.

So I force myself to pick up the fork and take another bite. And another.

The food feels like lead going down my throat, but with every subsequent bite, I can't ignore the selfish satisfaction I feel at denying him a victory in this arena. He'll have to look for something else to lord over me, another weakness to exploit. I won't let him play on my insecurities so recklessly.

Fuck him.

I surprise myself and nearly clear the entire plate. I even manage to consume most of the fruit, and when I finally step back from the tray, I'm grinning. For the first time in years, a full stomach doesn't make me feel disgusting and stuffed.

I feel ready to face him and whatever he might throw at me next.

But the second I step one foot beyond the doorway, that bravery fades. I'm on his turf again, forced to navigate his twisted, dark world without any sense of direction.

It's still morning, I think. When I head for the circular foyer that serves as the heart of the house, a rare sound reaches my ears, so disarming that I stop in my tracks and crane my head to listen.

Laughter. Sexy, raucous laughter—a female and a male's, his deep and melodic and unmistakably genuine.

I'm skeptical as I gather up the nerve to follow it, convinced that a different man must be out on the terrace where the sound resonates the strongest. Perhaps the mysterious Jaguar returned to see our dynamic in action for himself?

But no.

The figure chuckling shamelessly on a white lounger, his head thrown back to expose his throat, is Domino Valenciaga, Alexi seated across from him.

"I told you," she purrs, leaning toward him so that her ample breasts threaten to spill from her low-cut white tank top. "I am a woman of many talents."

"I believe you," Domino replies. "It takes a certain talent for attracting trouble to catch Jagger's attention."

"Oh no you don't," Alexi teases. "No prying, Dom. It's rude."

She doesn't see me, smirking at him, her blue eyes sparkling.

But he does. He goes silent mid-laugh, and even I can admit that the shift in him is terrifying to witness. His eyes lose what hint of warmth they had and go cold as his shoulders fall into a hard, rigid line. With a stern tilt of his chin, he levels his gaze in my direction.

God, he must truly hate me. It's the only explanation for why he can react to me so harshly within seconds.

And yet, while alone with Alexi, display a relaxed demeanor I don't think I've ever seen him embody. Not once during my captivity, not even during all the years he worked for my father. In fact…

I don't think I've ever heard him laugh like that.

"I need to speak to Ada-Maria in private," he says. His chilling tone spurs Alexi to lurch to her feet without argument. Swaying her hips, she heads inside, staring right past me, her nose in the air. I ignore the slight and focus on the man before me.

He's leaning forward, his hands braced on either knee like a soldier readying for battle. His outfit reinforces that comparison. He's swapped the dark attire for white today, opting for slacks and a loose shirt—but, for what I think is the first time, he's left the buttons completely undone.

Given the fact that Alexi didn't seem bothered by the sight of his scar, I realize that it wasn't modesty or shame that drove him to cover it all this time. It was me.

He didn't want me to see it, and I doubt that fear of my reaction was his motive. He wanted to make sure that he held all the cards at his disposal until the last possible second, shielding his supposed identity as Pia's brother.

Which means that he doesn't think I'm quite as stupid as he pretends.

"Morning. Did you enjoy your breakfast?" he asks, his tone flat in comparison to his laughter.

I force a smile in return. "It was marvelous. I was starving, thank you."

I see his eyebrow go up, and I get the sense that he's wrestling with storming into my room and seeing the tray for himself. Instead, he snaps his fingers, and a woman appears in the doorway, too short to be Alexi.

"Ada-Maria is done with her breakfast, Ines," Domino says, which I assume is her cue to go check.

In the meantime, he nods toward the lounger Alexi vacated.

"Have a seat."

I deliberately skip over the lounger he indicates, claiming the one slightly further apart, just beyond his reach.

His eyes narrow at the insolence. To my shock, though, he doesn't call me out directly. Instead, he sits back, crossing his arms to inspect me with a searching glance that has me squirming.

"I'll give you one last chance to rethink lying to me," he says, his voice soft and nonthreatening—which just makes me even more on edge. I don't trust this suddenly patient side of him. A threat lurks beneath it, I'm sure of that. "Admit now that you were playing a game, and when I whip you in punishment, I'll do so gently."

The genuine excitement in his voice chills me to the core—though it shouldn't. Hurting me is one of the few things that seems to arouse Domino Valenciaga.

That, and when I dare to step toe to toe with him and play devious mind games of my own.

"And if I'm not lying?" I counter, lifting my chin to hold his gaze unflinchingly. "What will I win?"

His teeth flash in a dangerous smile, his laughter coarse, echoing throughout this part of the terrace. "You'll earn time," he says. "Trust me, that's the most precious commodity you can attain at a moment like this."

Because he's the one who decided to leverage my "time" in the first place by selling me. He's the monster in this equation—I can't forget that.

Even if I have to pretend to make nice with him long enough to earn as many precious seconds as I can.

"I think I know where you can start looking," I say, phrasing my wording carefully. I'm not outright claiming to know where Pia's body is—or if she's really dead. But if he hopes to find something, I'm the best option he has.

All I have to do is see the world from Roy Pavalos' cruel, calculated viewpoint. Where most men would see a plain, featureless map, my father would see territory ripe for the taking and various features to exploit.

As long as he worked for him, I'm sure Domino knows exactly how his old boss used to operate. He wouldn't demand an answer from me if he didn't think I was capable of coming up with one, either because my father told me or because I happened to guess.

Aware of that, his sly grin falls.

"I'm the best chance you have," I say, risking provoking him by prodding his weakness outright. I can't help it. For once, I have some semblance of an upper hand.

For a heartbeat, of course.

A second later, he's on his feet, approaching me slowly. I shiver as he places one hand on my shoulder. His fingers flex, teasing me with a fraction of his strength, a mere reminder of the damage he's capable of.

"Don't think you can jerk me around, Ada-Maria," he warns, using that same hand to brush a stray curl from my cheek. "I could kill you right now, and never even have to justify why I changed my mind." He strokes a path up to sink his fingers through my hair, capturing a handful of it. Brutally, he yanks, so hard that tears spring to my eyes. "Understand?"

"Again, you keep hinting that you have no intention of honoring your own offer," I croak, blinking back unwanted tears. Gradually, he releases the pressure, still keeping his hand against my skull. "Why should I even trust you?"

His nostrils flare, his eyes darkening as if he's mulling over the prospect of humoring me at all. *Too far, Ada*, a part of me warns. *You can't push him too far.*

My only hope is to reel him back.

"I want to trust you," I force myself to whisper. The words fall flat, nowhere near convincing.

And yet, he laughs, amused all the same.

"I love the way you look when you try your mind games on me." He lets me go and moves to stand near the balcony, gazing at the gardens below. "You get this pathetic, hopeful glint in your eyes. It's fucking sexy. If I were a dumb cunt like the other men you've fucked." This time the warning in his voice rings out loud and clear. "Don't make the mistake of thinking I am. For your sake, Ada-Maria."

"I won't," I rasp, though I think I'm speaking to myself more than him. I can't keep getting caught up in his game. I need to stay one step ahead. "So what if I do know where she is, Pia? Do you have proof that my father is dead?"

With his back to me, I only have his posture from which to discern his reaction. But it's… Alarming. He stiffens in a way that has me bolting to my feet, readying for an assault from his end at any moment. I hate these volatile shifts in him. They're like a storm that comes on suddenly with no warning.

"Proof," he echoes in an unsettlingly deep tone. "Should I have his body dug up for you, Ada? The pieces, anyway. Or dissect the dogs I had the rest of his remains fed to? I'm sure you thought out exactly how you might be presented with such evidence?"

I'm winded by the grisly images. At the same time, I'm resigned, almost anxious to see them. Anything. It won't be real until I know for sure.

Only then can I truly grieve.

Or dread the possibility that he's been lying to me all along.

Without revealing an answer either way, he heads toward the archway leading inside the house. I start to panic, worried he's about to turn the tables yet again. Leave me waiting.

Instead, he cocks his head, my sole warning to follow.

Eagerly, I trail him through the foyer, past my room, and into his. In neither space do I find any sign of Alexi. Is she still here?

I don't have the strength to ask. He demands my sole focus, and every brain cell in my skull is consumed with him.

I hold my breath as he approaches the bed. Will sex be the next hurdle I'll have to jump through?

No. He reaches past the rumpled sheets for a nightstand made of dark wood. From it, he grabs a small, electronic device that I'm sure wasn't there before. He had it ready for this moment. Waiting.

"Here—" He hands the object to me—a small tablet with a video already pulled up on the screen. A white play button lurks over a still shot of what looks like a reporter in a newsroom. "Watch it."

My finger shakes as I tap the screen, triggering the video to play.

Within seconds, I get my answers as to my father's fate.

"Tragedy in Terra Rodea, as more details about a fatal crash involving mayoral candidate Roy Pavalos and his wife Lia, who was declared dead on the scene. Mr. Pavalos has been transferred to a local hospital where he's still listed in critical condition…"

Thud! My knees hit the floor as the tablet falls from my grasp, clattering across the polished marble. It all comes back to me. All of the fear, and the pain, and the uncertainty.

Like a punch, the revelations slam into me, and I sob louder with each one.

My mother is dead, beautiful and sweet and innocent in the grand scheme of my father's empire. I haven't let myself think of her until now—I couldn't. She wasn't perfect…

But the loss of her guts me. I'm hollowed by the thought of never seeing her again. Never having her presence as a buffer against my father's criticism.

Because he's still alive.

Roy Pavalos is still alive.

And I wish Domino would have killed me himself.

CHAPTER NINE

I don't know how long I lie here, screaming and screaming. Eventually, he must leave and return because everything goes cold all at once. Wet.

Sputtering, I realize that he threw something on me. Water? It's cold enough to suck the air from my lungs, rendering me silent in an instant. My mouth is still open though, making noises that scratch from my throat, robbed of all intensity.

"You will have plenty of time to mourn later," Domino warns in a voice so cold the liquid dripping off me feels scalding in comparison.

I watch, numb, as he sets an empty glass pitcher onto the same nightstand he took the tablet from. With his back to me, he rakes a hand through his hair, and I can sense the irritation prickling beneath his skin. This is restraint from him, I realize.

Because in reality, he wants to do a whole lot more than douse me with ice water.

The full extent of his cruelty—and his hate—feels dizzying to examine in full, now that I have video evidence. My father may not be dead, but in so many ways…

The truth is far worse.

"She loved you," I croak, once I find my voice again. It sounds like such a childish thing to say, but it's the truth. I think of my mother and how much she struggled over the past few months. A struggle I did everything in my power to ignore, from drinking myself into a daze to resorting to cocaine. I denied her when she needed me the most.

Selfishly, I think. Because I assumed she already had someone to help her through that pain, someone more reliable than I ever could be. As much as he may deny it, Domino ran errands for her when he thought no one was looking—but I always had my eyes on him and never missed the days he'd take her prescriptions to the pharmacy. The nights he'd escort her from dinner when the exhaustion became too much. I used his loyalty to her to justify my indifference.

And he killed her.

"Why?" Tears lash at my vision, blinding me to everything, even common sense. Somehow I'm on my feet, launching myself toward him—but I don't even touch him before he pivots, shoving me onto the bed.

"This shouldn't be a shock to you, Ada-Maria," he points out. "I've told you the truth from the start."

He has. Maybe, all this time, despite his taunts, I truly didn't believe it.

"Why Mama?" I rasp. "She was a good person. She never hurt anyone. She—"

"She left you at the mercy of a tyrant for your entire life, Ada. Don't make her out to be a saint," he scolds, but his tone falls flat. He's merely saying those words, but they lack the hatred of when he speaks of my father, or even me.

"Why?"

"Why do you think, Ada?" His tone turns cutting and harsh. "She had terminal cancer, was taking enough pain medication to fell a horse, and she suffered the trauma of a 'car crash.' A papercut could have killed her at this point. Crying changes nothing. It happened."

"But my father…"

That news report must be from days ago, I realize. Probably the same night I was abducted. If my father was in the hospital in critical condition, I doubt Domino would have been able to obtain his body in time to roast over an open spit.

"Still in critical condition," Domino says, now facing the windows that portray storm clouds moving across the horizon. "Last I heard, the bastard is still peeing out of a tube and breathing with the aid of some very expensive machinery. The DA is still hot on his ass, though. He'll be in for a rude awakening, dead or not—"

"So… You lied."

I'm on my feet again, and this time I feel my palm connect with his shoulder hard enough to sting.

"You bastard!"

He doesn't waste effort to restrain me this time. He merely turns, leveling me with the full brunt of a glare so chilling I stagger back in the face of it.

"Tell me, Ada, are you truly this gullible? Sometimes, I will admit that it is hard to tell."

"You're sick." I'm sobbing in earnest, barely able to get the words out completely. The full breadth of his lies is mind-numbing. Insane. And twisted. "Who was that?" I demand, swaying on my feet. I have to brace most of my weight against the nearest wall just to stay upright. "On the spit?"

"Oh, that?" he shrugs as if I asked him about the brand of clothing he's wearing. "That was a clever arrangement of pork. Very convincing if I say so myself."

Too convincing. It strikes me that I honestly don't know which is the lie.

My head is spinning, my throat constricting. The food from earlier jolts in my stomach, heavy and repulsive.

Purge.

The impulse is so strong that I'm already racing into the hall by the time he catches me, looping an arm around my waist. His strength imbibes that limb with the sturdiness of an iron bar, driving every ounce of air from my chest in one blow.

I wheeze, finding myself slung into the air, my legs kicking helplessly at nothing.

"Oh no, you don't," Domino growls, his voice emanating somewhere near my head.

I blink, finding that the floor is whizzing by below me, but I'm suspended against a firm, moving surface heading swiftly in the direction of his bedroom.

"No," he repeats, dropping me without warning.

I brace myself for a brutal impact and land on something soft instead. The bed. Scrambling for purchase, I watch him approach the door and slam it shut.

When he faces me…

It's like my brain flips some internal switch. Anger gives way to a terror unlike any I've ever felt. It's all-encompassing and draining, leaving me slumped on my side as he advances.

"I won't let you play the hysterical victim, Ada," he says coldly. "Scream. Cry. Commence with your fake mourning —*after* you give me what you promised."

Fake mourning.

"She was my mother," I croak, my face still damp with tears. Fresh ones continue to fall, dripping from my jaw onto my collar. If I close my eyes, I could imagine them to be droplets of blood.

Though in all honesty, this is no different. I'm bleeding in a way that feels as real as if I'd been stabbed through the chest. Some of it is shock, I think.

To really see her smiling photo paired with that tragic headline. That makes it so much more real than having him taunt me with her death.

It hurts.

But if I'm being honest with myself, I'd admit that some of this emotion stems from another source entirely, one more primal than pain and love.

It's fear.

My father is still alive, and yet Domino has kept me here for over a week without anyone coming for me. It doesn't make sense.

It feels so much more unsettling than being faced with what I presumed to be his body, turning on a spit. Roy Pavalos is never caught off guard, never. He is never without a plan or some kind of insurance policy to make sure that, no matter what, he comes out on top.

What the hell has Domino unleashed?

And why?

"Did you hear me, Ada-Maria?" His voice intrudes on my thoughts, and I blink to find him watching me with an intensity that puzzles me more than the fact that my father is still alive.

"W-What?"

"Where is the body?"

Whose body? is my initial response. Then I remember…

Pia.

I promised to give him a place to look.

"In hell," I snarl. "Where all of you belong!"

It's the wrong thing to say. I don't even see him move before my throat is between both of his hands, crushed like a stress ball.

I see stars. Death feels so imminent that I don't even have the chance to feel the full extent of the fear I should be experiencing. I just stare up at the ceiling, waiting for my vision to finally cut out once and for all.

But he merely intended the violence to serve as a warning. Barely a second passes before he releases some of the pressure, allowing me to choke down the minimum amount of air to stay conscious.

"Think carefully, Ada," he cautions. His voice shakes, betraying just how close he is to losing control. I've never heard him like this.

Unstable. Enraged. Unpolished.

"Give me what you promised, or I swear to God you will regret it. Your mother will soon become a distant memory, because I will put you through a living hell before sending you to meet her. Do you understand?"

I do. His voice alone conveys as much. He means every word he's saying; I can't deny that. Even as I pull back far enough to see his handsome face sculpted by rage, bathed in the gray overcast light filtering in from the windows.

I can see understanding dawn across those very features as I open my mouth and spit at him.

Wham! One moment I'm on the bed; the next, I'm on the cold, hard floor in a place that I sense isn't the main bedroom. The lighting is different here, the flooring polished enough to display my reflection in pitiful relief.

I'm shaking; my eyes resemble black holes; they're so swollen. But my appearance is nowhere near as frightening as that of the man looming over me.

He waits until I look at him before he moves, crossing over to an oval-shaped tub paces away. We're in the bathroom, I realize with a start.

Which means…

I see his arms strain as he wrenches on the faucet, sending the water streaming into the tub's basin. Somehow, I can easily read his intentions. It's like our minds are in sync, one and the same. I know exactly what he intends to do.

Kill me.

Kill me slowly.

Run! I scramble onto my hands and knees, my eyes on the door.

He's already gaining on my position before I can even make a move. Cruelly, his hand latches onto a chunk of my hair, using it to drag me across the room to the tub. Then he yanks me onto my knees, forcing me to bend over the rim as the water churns below.

I can't even suck in air before I'm submerged. The shock is more terrifying than the fact that I can't breathe. All I can do is fight with everything I have.

I feel my legs kick against the floor as my fingers claw at his hand, nails scraping against his flesh.

He's too strong. When my head is suddenly wrenched above the water's surface, it's entirely of his own will. I might as well be a gnat fighting against a mountain.

"Where is she?"

I sputter, more intent on breathing than compiling an answer.

With a growl, he shoves me down, and I'm under again.

Never, in my life, have I felt anything like this. My pulse is a thundering beat hammering through my eardrums, my lungs on fire, every nerve screaming, on red alert.

And yet, internally, somewhere in between his next vicious reprieve as he yanks me above the water, I realize that there's no point in fighting. Let him win this round.

So, I make myself so limp he doesn't seem prepared to resist.

"Shit!"

His voice echoes in tandem with a sickening *thunk!* Pain washes through my skull as pressure fills my nostrils. But this doesn't feel like drowning.

It hurts too damn much. But then a flood of warm, hot liquid spills over my face, filling my nose and seeping into my mouth. He must be pouring it onto me, I realize, because I'm staring up at the ceiling now, choking on the substance that my brain belatedly identifies. Something far too thick to be water…

Blood.

"Ada, shit—" He grabs me, hauling me upright. This time, his method of suffocation comes in the form of a delicate, white substance that he presses frantically against my nose. "Tilt your head! I said, tilt your fucking head up!"

I obey him solely on impulse, the need to breathe outweighing all else. My mouth is open, though, gulping at the air, despite the pressure on my nostrils. He's holding them both shut, forcing my head back against his shoulder.

Frantically, my gaze darts around him, trying to discern the source of the substance still dripping down my face. Blood.

So much blood. I'm covered in it, and droplets of red speckle the floor.

"Why the hell did you do that?" His voice echoes off the walls, losing its emotionless cadence. Rage and confusion add color to his tone, enhancing his mysterious accent and giving his baritone a threatening timbre it usually lacks. "You'll be lucky if you didn't break your fucking nose—"

"I hate you." It feels important to say that despite everything else.

He has me on his lap, I think, his legs sprawled over the floor beneath me. One of his hands loops around me from behind so that he can hold the tissue to my nose, while the other has both of my wrists in an iron grip.

To stop me from slapping him.

"I hate you."

"I know," he says, monotone once more. His chest rumbles against my back as he speaks, his breath on my ear, his grip unwavering.

"I will never forgive you for this." A sob edges my words. I sound like a child, wailing and desolate.

"You won't," he agrees, forcing my chin even higher.

My nose is the source of the bleeding; I can tell now. I must have hit it off the tub. It throbs, sending pain lancing through my skull with every beat of my heart. Is it broken?

How fitting if it is. He took my mother away, my family, my life.

Why not take my beauty, too? It's the only thing of value I ever had, and it's somehow managed to outlast the other bastions of my life as a Pavalos. What use am I without my father to control my every movement and my mother to lurk obliviously in the background, pretending that she doesn't realize the hell we're both living under?

"I hate you—"

"So hate me, then," Domino commands, sounding in control once more. Still, he applies even more pressure to my nose, forcing me further against his chest. "Hate me all you want, Ada… I can allow you that much."

More tears spill down my cheeks, mingling with the blood. This is his idea of mercy—doling out hate as though it's a cherished gift. The only thing he can and will ever offer me.

Hate and pain.

And lies.

CHAPTER TEN

He goes away. I'm so numbed by exhaustion that I don't even recall when or why. I'm still lying on the bathroom floor, facing the tub, surrounded by a graveyard of crumbled, blood-stained tissue.

It took several tries before the bleeding stopped completely. My nose feels like a swollen, painful lump that hurts to breathe through. I try running my finger along its bridge to assess the damage and wind up moaning, seeing stars that speckle my vision.

"You didn't break it."

I stiffen with the realization that Domino is still here, just somewhere beyond my line of sight, his voice effortlessly resonating throughout the entire room.

"You'll live."

It's a mean choice of words, and I can't help but laugh at them. However, the sound comes out resembling a sob more.

"You are nothing like Pia," I tell him. Considering everything Pia Inglecias put me through, that isn't a compliment. A teenage girl who used lies and manipulation to get her way, still possessed more tact and humanity than he has.

I think of them in comparison to each other, and I can't even discern a physical resemblance. Except for their eyes, maybe. Both have that same, murky hue of hazel, though the green in Pia's was more prominent.

She was so very beautiful. That beauty aided in her confidence and ability to win anyone over to her side. She had a way of making someone feel special, like the most important person in the world, just as long as they had her attention. She could be so sweet when she wanted to and so damn charming.

On the other hand, when the mood struck her, she could be so very mean.

"I'll keep that in mind," Domino replies, and his voice alone reinforces the divide between him and my childhood friend. Pia spoke musically, her emotions evident in her tone. When she was happy, she almost sounded as though she were singing. When she was angry, her words became honed like a whip, lashing out at whatever had sparked her ire.

"I don't think my father killed her," I admit, though I don't know if I'm speaking to myself more than Domino.

Why would he kill her? She was everything I could never be, a perfect missing key to his arsenal of manipulation and influence. He could have molded Pia under his wing, using her to do whatever he desired. Not just sexually, but politically.

She would have served him far better than I ever could.

Killing her would be messy. It would mean utilizing his precious resources and covering his tracks. Doable, but requiring far more effort than I think a schoolgirl with a crush would demand. Even if she went public about her relationship with my father, it would be her word against his.

And his word was law.

"But if he did," I add, my voice scratching at the silence. "He would need a reason..."

Something more egregious than her simply stealing money from him. She would have needed evidence of something far more damaging. So damaging, in fact, that nothing plausible comes to mind. This isn't some scripted crime drama. My father was a violent, egotistical, misogynistic man, but he wasn't pure evil.

Though, I guess I should use present tense, considering that he's still alive...

"I have reason to believe that Pia had something that would put his entire future into question," Domino admits. "More than money. Something that would cast a shadow on him not just politically, but make him a walking target of his most powerful enemies."

I frown, triggering a wave of pain that spreads from my nose and into my eye sockets. I let my eyelids lower and contemplate such a possibility in the darkness. If his reputation was on the line…

Well, that was something that Don Roy would kill to protect. He'd do anything to shield his image, no matter the cost.

Anything.

"What was it?" I ask.

Only silence comes in response. I start to question if he's still here, but I can sense his presence, as vibrant as the blood. He must be behind me, lurking by the door, blocking my potential exit should I gather the nerve to stand.

I'm too tired to move at all, and I contemplate drifting off here and now. Let him wallow in his hate and self-pity. Let him go on a wild goose chase after rumors and a ghost.

And yet, I can't deny a prickle of curiosity strong enough to make me peel my eyes open again.

"Do you even know?"

"I know," he says with a certainty that irritates my already frazzled nerves. He's not lying—and I hate that. It gives him some tiny semblance of a right to hate my family all this time. If my father really did kill Pia, he would deserve far worse than a car crash.

But what about me?

I'm guilty too, I decide, shying from those memories. Anything that happened to her would be squarely my fault.

"If he… She'll be in Terra Rodea," I say, voicing my fragile hunch.

"Damn it, *that's* all you have?" He scoffs. "If that's a guess, Ada, I would have expected something with more effort. Do you think if she were still in the city, she wouldn't have been found by now within the past ten years? I would assume he'd dump her in a swamp, or a lake, or on one of your family's vacation homes—"

"He'd keep her in Terra," I insist. With what little strength I can muster, I roll onto my side, groaning at the pain. I'm panting when I finally turn to face him. As I suspected, he's leaning against the closed door to the balcony, his arms crossed, eyes narrowed.

"So you were bullshitting me all along—"

"He would keep her in Terra," I say over him, surer of that than ever. I may not have learned much in my life, but I know my father. I've gotten a taste of the way he thinks and how he moves. How he likes to gloat and lord himself over the things he believes he owns, be them places, objects, or even people. "Why do you think I stayed there?" I demand when Domino's expression remains skeptical. "Why do you think he kept me in that house, by him always?"

It wasn't out of the devotion of a caring father, though I think Domino knows that already. A grudging expression crosses over his face. I have his attention. For now.

And I don't waste it.

"He would keep her somewhere close, but within plain view. A place he could always have access to but somewhere that couldn't be directly traced to him. Not a vacation house or one of our properties, either. That would be too obvious."

And I'm sure that there are no dead bodies buried on our property. My father could be cruel, but he was never sloppy.

"If I had to guess, I would narrow it down to a handful of places," I add, though I rationalize even telling him this by reminding myself that I don't believe it. Nothing—short of his own mortal soul—would be worth the risk. Pia wasn't some political rival or a lawless cartel leader. She was a fifteen-year-old girl with a family, and people who loved her enough to mount a search.

I remember seeing the flyers. I remember hearing word of her mother's anxious search. I remember that a broken heart was rumored to be the cause of death when Rosa Inglecias collapsed four months into her daughter's disappearance.

"Where?" Domino demands, letting his hands fall to his sides. His fingers twitch impatiently, and I suspect it's taking restraint on his part to keep from lunging at me and wringing out an answer. "If the bastard would be stupid enough to bury her in Terra, then where?"

"His office," I say, naming one of three potential locations.

"Where would he bury her?" Domino counters. "Under the elevator?"

He's right. I haven't had time to consider the logistics in full. They're just guesses of the places I know my father values and frequents.

"One of the parks he had dedicated around the city, then?"

"The earliest one wasn't erected until two years after Pia went missing," Domino says, proving that he's considered these options already. He's obsessed over them, I realize as he starts to pace, wearing a frown reminiscent of the one he'd sport all those nights when I'd watch him on my family's property. "Where else? Tell me you have a better guess than that."

The final one I've considered the least. It would be the most unlikely of all, I can admit that. And yet…

It would be the cruelest.

"The old Inglecias house," I croak.

Domino stops mid-stride, his foot still hovering in the air. I can tell from how his eyes widen that he hasn't considered that location for himself.

"No," he says, shaking his head. "That would be fucking stupid. Why would he…"

"Because it would be so obvious," I point out. A hollow laugh escapes me at the thought of how he would have gloated, were any of this true. "My father was… Is a selfish victor, Domino. Don't tell me you haven't realized that. He guards his prizes jealously."

My mother.

Me.

He wouldn't see Pia as a person, or even an innocent victim who got in his way. He would only see her as a prize to be won. Or conquered.

"He would keep her in Terra," I decide, ignoring his skeptical frown. "Not that I believe he did it in the first place."

I can't tell if Domino agrees with me or not. He's still pacing, raking his fingers viciously through his hair. He has to be hurting himself, ripping out stray strands with each frantic motion, but I don't think he notices. Or cares. Wherever he is mentally is somewhere beyond pain or discomfort.

"Fuck," he says finally, moving to brace his hands against the counter. He eyes himself in the mirror positioned above, and from this angle, I can see his expression clearly.

Angry. Bitter. Thoughtful.

As much as he may have challenged it, I think my hunch made sense.

Which sickens me to my very core.

"And this is the part where you laugh like a superhero villain," I croak, too drained to put any real effort into the taunt. My head lolls, and I find myself staring at the shower instead of him. "Then you tell me that it was all a trick. You'll leave me to die. I was an idiot to even think of trusting you—"

"I'll uphold my end of our agreement," he snarls, marching to cross my line of vision. "I'll *trust.*' But can you?"

I blink, puzzled by his statement.

His expression shifts before my eyes, becoming musing again, reminding me more than ever of those nights I would spy on him. He's thinking. Plotting. And this time, whatever he's planning most definitely involves me.

"I'll need to do this right," he grumbles, stroking his chin, fixated on his own internal thoughts. He's not speaking to me. And yet, as his eyes dart suspiciously around the room, I suspect that I'm not who he's wary of, either. At least now. "Get up."

He lowers his voice and inclines his head toward the shower stall.

But I don't move.

"I said get up!" He storms toward me, his nostrils flaring. One look at me, however, and he seems to realize that my rebellion isn't entirely out of a need to defy him.

I can't move. My head is floating, my body like lead.

Without a word, he crouches, yanking me into his arms. I barely have the chance to marvel at the sensation of being held by him—carried—before I'm unceremoniously placed on one of the benches in the shower stall.

He exits long enough to get the water running, but this time the spray is heavy, pelting us with lukewarm water that ricochets off the walls in a deafening roar.

"Trust is what you want, is it?" Domino questions, his voice low as he returns to my side, bringing his mouth near my ear. "Keep your mouth shut, follow my lead, and I'll do what I can to help you."

Help me?

It takes every ounce of strength I have left to find the energy to lift my head and see his face. He's leaning down, still wearing his shirt and slacks, and I realize that all of this is a way to disguise our conversation.

From who? Alexi?

But in comparison to him, even she no longer seems like my biggest enemy.

"You did this to me!" I'm on the verge of another sob, and he nods, tugging me from the bench and onto my feet. I sway, forced to submit to his strength just to stay upright. He hooks an arm around my waist, and I have no choice but to brace my hands against his chest for stability.

"I did this to you," he murmurs. "But do you want to learn why? Or would you rather wallow in your role as the victim?"

I recoil at his harsh tone, pushing against him. Belatedly, I realize just what he said—learn. It's the first time he's even hinted at giving me more than taunts and mind games. God help me; I'd do anything for answers. Clarity. Something.

Even if it means humoring him a second longer.

"What do you mean?"

"This was always bigger than you," he tells me. "Bigger than us. If you want any prayer of getting out of this alive, I'm the only shot you have. Do you understand that? Ines can't help you. Not Alexi, not your father. No one but me."

He's still speaking softly. But that does nothing to diminish the seriousness in his tone.

"Then tell me why."

He pulls back, forcing me to stand on my own. "I will," he says, turning to brace his hands against the hard, granite before him. "But if I do, you will no longer have the luxury of doubting me. This isn't a game, Ada-Maria. The stakes are higher than you could ever imagine."

"You keep dancing around the truth," I point out, approaching him only because I need the support of the wall just to stay upright. I lean against it, closing my eyes as the water continues to pelt us both. I can feel the steam rising, enclosing us in a false layer of privacy. We're in our own twisted realm now, just him and I.

And I should be busy finding a way out. Not listening to him.

"Speak, or I swear to God, Domino, I'll…"

"You have four more days." He says it with such malice that I shrink inside myself, picturing what lurks at the end of that timeframe.

I'll be sold to Jaguar, of course, and thrown into yet another hell.

But as the seconds pass, I realize that his statement wasn't a threat. It was a reminder.

"You want to learn more? Then follow my lead for now. I need you blissfully ignorant, and I need you to put on a damn good show. Prance around naked if you want, throw your ass in the face of any man to pass by. Give me that time, and I promise you, I will do whatever it takes to keep you alive."

"Alive and not sold," I prod, mistrustful of any way he might play the semantics to his benefit. "Alive and not your captive. Alive and—"

"Alive and with far more freedom than you entered this mess having. Don't pretend that you were living of your own free will before. You were already a prisoner before I took you."

I flinch, blinking my eyes open to find him still glowering at the wall, his head lowered, knuckles white with how hard he has his hands pressed against the stone.

I'm startled by how drastically rage can transform him. Consume.

Though, in a way, it makes sense, reinforcing just how expertly he's lived under his lies. I'm only seeing five years of the rage and hate he's been suppressing all along.

And God, is it terrifying.

"Be a good girl, and you'll have my balls in a vice, little Ada," he adds gruffly. "That's what you wanted from the start, isn't it?"

It is. Only now, I want his literal balls and a real metal vice to crush them with.

Still, I'm not stupid enough to stick my nose up at the only shred of honesty he's offered me. I'll worry about the details and the morality of it later. For now, I'm desperate for some shred of hope.

Something to fight for.

"Fine, Domino," I tell him softly. "I'll be a good girl and play my role. After all, I was born to play pretend, wasn't I?"

His nostrils flare, his expression guarded. "I suppose you were. Go—" He inclines his head to the balcony. "Get cleaned up. Incs will call you for dinner. I suggest you think long and hard about how exactly you plan on being a good girl and don't second-guess that decision. I'll only ever extend my trust to you once. Remember that."

His words haunt me as I lurch from the room on trembling legs, still dripping blood as I go.

CHAPTER ELEVEN

"Dinner will be served on the terrace soon, Miss," Ines calls from the doorway, jarring me awake.

I peel my eyes open with a groan, feeling more exhausted than I did when I finally rested my head on these pillows. I'm in my pretty white room, but this time I remember how I got here—I practically crawled, merely to escape Domino and his blood-stained bathroom.

This room isn't a much better prison, but at least he isn't here. Neither is Alexi, though I'm sure both are still on the property somewhere. Stupidly, I hope that Domino regulated her to her own virtual jail cell on the other end of the estate.

But no.

I can hear her, giggling uncontrollably somewhere beyond this room. Her voice alone isn't what sets every nerve in my body on edge—it's the deep, masculine tone that accompanies it.

Jealously is the last emotion I should feel at a time like this. If anything, I should be relieved that someone has his attention other than me.

Until I hear him speak. "You know I don't play fair," he says, sounding so prideful of that fact, his voice devoid of any of the rage he displayed earlier this morning.

Because it was all an act, of course, him claiming that he needed me to play along with his game. He was lying then, I realize with a sense of dread that guts me.

I was the idiot who fell for it. All along, he's been scheming with Alexi, manipulating me for their own gain. They're in this together.

"Just this once," Alexi taunts in that sexy little purr. "Make an exception for me."

I don't strain to listen to Domino's reply, if he answers her at all. Instead, I climb to my feet, groaning as pain shoots through my skull. Disoriented, I sway, forced to grab the edge of the mattress for balance, and I don't know how much time passes before I can stand without shaking.

Enough time, it seems, for Alexi to get her way, because a series of giggles taunts me next, sounding fainter, from the direction of the terrace.

Ignoring them, I stagger into the closet and grab the first item I can reach, pulling it on without inspecting it in full. Then I return to the mirror and brace myself for what I might find.

Nothing I imagined comes even close to the specter awaiting me from the glass' surface.

She's so pale, her eyes bloodshot, her arms and legs speckled with bruises. My nose is unmarked, at least, though sensitive to the touch.

If Domino wanted to pretend that I was here willingly, he'd have to have a damn good explanation for why I'd submit myself to this kind of abuse. What was that he mocked me with?

You like it rough…

For a second, I reconsider everything. Forget trusting him— I should run. Now. I even start toward the hall with every intention of racing for the front door, his ruse be damned.

But then I hear them, both laughing as though they don't have a care in the world. Domino's voice rings out, unabashedly booming in a cadence that sounds so damn…genuine.

Curiosity alone is what spurs me to turn around and creep past the circular foyer and out onto the terrace.

It's a blindingly bright day, with a beautiful blue sky above and a gentle warmth emanating from a blazing sun. Gone are the storm clouds from earlier. It's a perfect hour to lounge around the fire pit on the terrace's mid-level. Domino claims one of the seats facing me, his head inclined against the back of it.

Alexi sits across from him, practically spilling out of her own chair to face him, her laughter easily reaching across the terrace.

"My round," she taunts. "Think you can beat me at least once?"

Domino flashes a grin that has me stopping short. It's fleeting, but bright enough to transform his entire face into that of a stranger's, relaxing his afternoon away.

Until he sees me.

He sits forward, palming his knees with both hands, his eyes cutting to slits. It's as if he has some internal switch designed to instantly wipe all emotion from his face. Alexi says something to him though I can't make out exactly what it is.

His frown deepens, his jaw clenching as if he remembered his own rules. We're supposed to be here under slightly different roles. He's my rescuer, and I'm his very grateful victim.

It strikes me now how I could send his ruse toppling with very little effort on my part. I could scream. Demand he let me go. Cause a scene.

And he's afraid I'll do just that. I can see the lethality in how he tracks every step I take once I remember how to move again. He's hunting me, desperate for any excuse to lunge and drag me back into that room.

A strange feeling unfurls in my chest, and I don't know how to identify it at first. Not until I finally reach the lower level and draw even with the playful couple.

This feeling? It's power.

"Look who decided to join us," Alexi says, though I notice that most of the playfulness is gone from her voice, leaving it hollow. I sense her eyes trace me up and down, not that I pay her any notice.

My sole focus is Domino. He sizes me up with a cautious glance, trying to decipher just what I'll do next. Do I remember our flimsy excuse for a truce?

I do. And that's the frustrating part. As much as I hate him, I can't deny one awful truth—I *need* him. For now. At least until I can find enough leverage to escape him once and for all.

So, I make myself smile and sway my hips so that I'm sauntering toward him, just as playful as he appeared to be seconds ago.

The way he stiffens gives me immense satisfaction—but it's fleeting. Because playing my role in this instance means I have to touch him, and this moment is so different from the hundreds of other times I've toyed with men I wasn't attracted to.

He's wearing white today, a shirt buttoned as he usually wears it while being here at least—the top two undone. A loose pair of white slacks gives him a casual air that his rigid jawline contradicts. As serious as he looks now, no one could ever mistake this man for anything but a jailer on red alert.

Because of me. I rouse this dark nature in him. I saw it for myself—he wasn't like this with Alexi. Does that bother me?

I can't tell as I push down my revulsion and palm his chest, urging him back into the more relaxed posture he held before.

To my shock, he relents to the pressure, spreading his legs as if sensing my intentions before I even lower myself onto his right knee. His body is stone beneath me—he's wary. I think if it weren't for our audience, he'd shove me to the floor—and make it hurt.

So I draw out the motion, settling back against his chest while I seethe inside. Turning to him, I see his eyes cut to mine and flinch. I want nothing more than to run away. Hide.

But this is what he wanted, isn't it? For me to play pretend.

Well, luckily for him, I've perfected how to do just that. He accused me of being a whore and faking it, but he has no idea how good I can be. How real it can feel to have someone pretend to adore you.

Only to rip it away the second they've gotten what they wanted from you.

It's a feeling reminiscent of what Pia made me feel all those years ago. Like I truly had an ally in this world, someone I could rely on outside of my father's control.

When all the while, she was laughing behind my back.

I'm not laughing now. Forcing my lips into an even wider grin, I place my hand against Domino's cheek, urging him to face me.

"What's so funny?" I ask, and damn. I'm impressed with myself. I sound giddy enough to put Alexi's chirping to shame, and Domino's gaze becomes unreadable in response.

"We were just chatting about old times," Alexi pipes up, and I recognize the note in her voice. That of a bitch who already believes she has her claws sunken into her chosen prey.

The only problem for both of us is that Domino is no one's plaything.

"We'll catch up later," he says to Alexi without taking his eyes off me. I shudder inwardly at the challenge lurking within those haunting green irises—along with a clear warning. "Ada-Maria missed lunch. Could you inform Ines that she can bring her meal out here? I'll make sure she eats every bite."

"Okay."

Alexi doesn't sound too enthusiastic, but the second she disappears from view, I attempt to shift my weight from his lap entirely.

His hand latches onto my knee before I can, effectively riveting me in place.

"You seem cheerful this afternoon," he remarks in a voice like sin. It's a low, husky baritone that anyone who happened to overhear might mistake for warm, considering my position on his lap.

But as his nails graze my flesh in a teasing swipe, I know exactly what he intends—to have me shivering, choking down a hard swallow.

"I hope you slept well, Ada."

"I-I did," I counter, failing to keep my voice level. It shakes, and I know my fear leeches into my carefully constructed mask. So much for fighting him on an even playing field. I can barely keep my composure for longer than a few seconds at a time.

I keep equating his hand on my thigh to the same grip he had around my neck, plunging me beneath the water. If I hadn't hurt myself, would he have kept going?

I can't tell just by looking at him.

He's smug again, the corner of his mouth lifted in a subtle smirk.

I hate him. And that hate makes me petty enough to keep playing with fire.

"I thought of you," I tell him, lowering my mouth near his ear despite the tension his nearness inspires. I even manage to laugh, just once. "My hero. And I slept like a baby."

"Good," he growls in return.

I can't see his expression fully from this angle. All I have to go on is his hand, stroking higher to bridge the gap between my legs. Too high. He's boldly reaching beneath the hemline of my dress, and I can't stop him.

"It couldn't have been a very good dream," he remarks with faux concern. "You're not dripping wet like a cat in heat."

I clamp my thighs together, heedless of his hand between them. He's won. I try to wiggle from his lap again, and he shrugs as if to nonverbally dare me to.

But then I make the mistake of looking over into his eyes. Those smug, confident, incredible fucking eyes.

They make me reckless, and I recall the few times I managed to make those very eyes widen.

With provocation.

"If you're my hero, as they say, Domino… Shouldn't I *always* be dripping wet for you? Ready and willing. My hero."

He grunts, conveying a mixture of irritation and grudging amusement.

"My Ada." He works his other hand into my hair, tugging ruthlessly hard as he goes. "Such a good, happy girl this afternoon. I think I should come up with a reward for you being so cheerful."

My grin falls flat before I can even think to salvage it. Panic sends every coherent thought scrambling.

I want to run.

You can't give in, a part of me warns, even as my muscles twitch with every intention of me lurching to my feet. *You do that now, and he wins.*

And in spite of everything he's done, I can't let him dominate every interaction. Not again. Therefore, risks must be taken. My father called it "the fucking kamikaze" method, where a man puts all of his effort into one harebrained scheme with the hopes that even if it backfires, it takes out at least some of his enemies.

That method got him to the top of Terra Rodea's political scene.

But he didn't have to navigate a man like Domino Valenciaga in this manner. I'm at a loss of how to manipulate him. How to keep him on edge. How to keep up.

All I can do is meet his dare and not flinch. Instead, I lean in, grazing my lips against his chiseled jawline, ignoring the pain lancing through my nose as it's nudged by his.

"A grateful girl should want any reward her hero can give her," I say, letting my voice dip down to a hum that isn't quite as shameless as Alexi's.

I can feel a rumble through his chest as he exhales, even more suspicious than before.

"But when do I get what I really want?" I ask, inclining my head to face him directly.

His wicked smile steals my breath away as he runs his fingers through my hair. "After four days of being a good girl, you'll get what you deserve," he says softly. "In fact, here's your next chance to prove just how good you can be."

I stiffen with alarm as his gaze drifts to something behind me. When I turn, though, I only find Ines approaching from the direction of the house, a silver tray in hand.

She places her bounty on a low table set in the middle of the couches and respectfully nods.

"Thank you," Domino says, dismissing her. Once we're alone again, he palms my waist with both hands, settling me more firmly on his lap. I'm straddling him now. My knees are the only parts of me that have any contact with the couch at all, barely touching down on either side of him.

"Now it's time for you to continue being such a good girl." His voice contains a chilling hint of malice despite his blank expression. Leaning forward, he jostles me against him, and I realize that he picked an item of food from the platter. A piece of strawberry that he cradles between two fingers. "Eat."

My stomach churns. I want more than anything to deny him. On second thought, I want to preserve my pride more. The need for control and the desire for victory go to war within me. It only takes a second for one to win out.

I open my lips and smother any hesitation, allowing him to place the sliver of berry on my tongue. I think I see surprise cross his face for a split-second before his eyes narrow to convey another sentiment entirely. Challenge accepted.

He grabs another morsel of fruit and dangles it just beyond the reach of my mouth. I have to lean forward to take it, biting into the ripe berry dangerously close to his fingertips. At the last second, something makes me swipe my tongue along the pad of one, licking away any remaining juice.

His sly grin falls flat, his chest rumbling again.

The sound does something to me, working with the warm air and the hot sun to make my breathing quicken and my chest tighten. I'm painfully aware of how large he is, and how dangerously close I'm seated near the front of his slacks. The loose fabric conceals any telltale bulge or sign of arousal. I'd have to touch him to be sure.

"You are in a good mood, today," Domino remarks, though he doesn't sound as smug about that as he did just minutes ago. "I wonder just what my Ada-Maria is thinking to feel so damn happy."

I take my time swallowing down my berry. Then I lick my lips deliberately slow, and I don't miss the way his eyes dart down to track the motion.

"I'm thinking of all the ways I can show my hero how grateful I am for what he's done to me."

I've gone too far, failing to disguise the hate in my voice behind fake charm. Rather than dwell over the fact, I relish the wary way he eyes me while letting one of his hands slide from my hip.

"Such a bold girl today, as well." And yet, for the time being anyway, he seems content to grab another offering from the tray and shove it against my mouth.

I eat, and I eat, and I eat, ignoring any discomfort or anxiety building at the back of my mind. This is war, and as such, I have to fight just as dirty as he seems willing to.

"You seem happy today as well," I remark after taking a blueberry from his hand. "I'm sorry if I interrupted your fun and games." I soften my voice, posing my lips in a playful pout.

He scoffs. "Simpering isn't a good look on you, Ada," he scolds. "I like you better when you run that smart fucking mouth."

Challenge accepted.

"How do I know I'm not the game being played?" I demand, raising an eyebrow of my own. Our expressions must mirror each other's now, equally guarded and mistrustful. "You seem to be having so much fun with Alexi. How do I know you're not setting me up?"

"You don't," he replies, snatching a piece of what looks like cheese from the tray next. "Though, believe me, it wouldn't take nearly half as much effort as you seem to think. Eat."

I open my mouth, still mulling over his words. He wouldn't waste the effort to play me, but he seemed unwilling to outright deny that his interactions with Alexi were part of a mind game.

"Don't tell me that you're taking advantage of her, Domino," I murmur after chewing.

It would serve the bitch right. And yet…

I can't be jealous, so that can't possibly be the reasoning behind the pang I feel in my chest. Even during his entire tenure as my father's trusted bodyguard, he never tried so hard with me. He never played "games," or reminisced about the past or lounged so visibly relaxed in my presence. Most notable of all, I never once heard him laugh.

Never like that.

"Don't tell me you're jealous, Ada-Maria," Domino counters. The amount of genuine disgust in his voice warns that he would disapprove of that scenario.

Rather than take the bait, I shrug and dutifully sample the food he's holding before me. "Why would I be? You cared for me enough to bring me here, and protect me from the big bad men who tried to kill me. I'm the fool who would willingly stay here, gladly accepting whatever lies you told me to explain my parents' supposed deaths and everything else going on. Damn. I know you think so little of me, but I must be known for being quite the dumb bimbo for even your accomplices to buy that."

His eyes flash in a subtle warning. "I don't think you should go around pontificating on what those big, bad men might want to do to you, Ada. You'll give yourself nightmares. I suggest you continue to be so damn accommodating and keep your mouth shut."

"Unless I have a cock stuffed in it, right?" I can't resist the taunt, and for whatever reason, it seems to rile him beautifully.

His nostrils flare, and both of his hands return to my hips, gripping tightly to readjust my weight against him.

"Right," he murmurs, his eyes staring dead into my own. "Maybe we should test that theory; what with you being so damn agreeable all of a sudden?"

I swallow hard at the threat, fighting to keep my breathing steady. I can feel his muscle flexing beneath me, his thighs drifting further apart as if to accommodate a growing body part he can't ignore. He's gritting his teeth, a muscle in his jaw lurching.

As foolish as it is to admit, even to myself, I'm not sure what could be getting him hard in this scenario. Our banter? Or the mention of Alexi?

"I would gladly let you utilize my mouth however you see fit," I say, wrenching my gaze down to his mouth, a safer territory than his eyes. Or so I think until he seizes the flesh of his lower lip between his teeth and a growl rumbles through his chest. "If only you didn't have another willing mouth at the ready close by. I'm sure you already got up to plenty of fun and games while I was out. Why let me ruin your fun?"

I'm done with this game. I brace my hand against his chest to pull back and stand. He tightens his grip, easily keeping me locked in place.

"I haven't had fun since the last time your pretty little lips were occupied with me," he warns, and I suck in a breath, suddenly dizzy. The heat in his voice is far too dangerous. As if he means every word. "You would know if you were interrupting anything I didn't intend for you to see."

I flinch. It's a blatant hint that he's been toying with me all this time, with or without Alexi's consent. I don't know what to make of that. Then it strikes me that's exactly what he wants—to confuse me of his motives and leave me constantly second-guessing my own instincts.

I only let myself consider my following actions for a split second. Then I lean forward, deliberately rocking my hips into his. As much as I hate him…

He's all rigid muscle, and I gasp when I feel the firmness of his thighs against my ass. He stiffens, digging his fingers into my waist, only his hands slip, and he's palming my ass instead. I smother any urge to pull away, letting his hands linger, fingers spread apart over both cheeks.

"Don't tell me you've been faking your fun all this time, Domino," I taunt.

He laughs. Then he drives his nails into my flesh—harshly —and I can't smother a cry.

"As it turns out, I am *very* good at faking, Ada," he tells me, nudging my earlobe with his mouth. Then something warmer brushes the lobe with a teasing swipe. His tongue?

I can't let myself get distracted. I just focus on his words and realize what they imply. He's still playing with my head, trying to keep me off balance.

"So am I," I say, palming his cheek so that he's forced to face me again. He's frowning, and a prickle of alarm nips at my spine, warning me to tread carefully. Even if he seems to want information from me—badly enough to agree to a hostile cease-fire—I know better than to push him too far.

So I consider my next course of action the equivalent of a friendly tap.

"I am very good at faking, remember?"

"I remember." His eyes glint with a dangerous gleam. "I've personally watched you 'fake it' many, many, many times."

I cringe at the insinuation—that his claims to have spied on me were all true. And yet, there is one way to use this to my advantage.

"So then you know that even if you do sell me, I'll have no problem faking it then. I'll fake it for whoever can give me a lifeline, no matter how flimsy, and you can lounge around this big, empty house knowing that I'll be comparing them all to you."

It's a boast that riles him like no other. He jolts forward, nearly knocking me backward, if his hands didn't happen to clench against my ass, snatching me to him. Our pelvises collide, my breasts pressed against his collar as though it's a platter.

And I'm the only meal he has any interest in devouring.

CHAPTER TWELVE

I've angered him. His eyes latch onto my mouth, and when he yanks me forward again, I'm sure he'll bite me outright, like a true beast.

He kisses me instead. What my brain processes as a kiss anyway, the act of two mouths meeting for longer than a peck.

But Domino doesn't suck at my mouth sweetly to compel me to silence. He brutalizes. His tongue lashes at mine like a whip, demanding submission. Nothing more, nothing less.

But it shouldn't feel so damn good.

He makes me fight to keep up with him or risk being consumed. I have to meet every prodding jab of his tongue with one of my own. Open my mouth further to let him in. Take him in.

In so many ways, this feels more intimate than even sucking his cock. I can hear him more clearly—feel him in my head. His grunts of pleasure when he nips me with his teeth. His startled hiss when I bite him back.

His heartbeat rages, hammering through my breasts as the scrape of my dress' fragile material irritates my nipples into sharp, stabbing peaks.

He grips me tighter, practically kneading the flesh of my ass until I'm arching my back to escape the pressure. Then leaning into it...

God, he makes me hate myself. My body turns against me, and my brain struggles to keep up. I hate him. Hate him...

And yet, I shiver in anticipation as he slips his fingers beneath the hem of my dress, finding the bare skin of my ass.

And the delicate, sensitive valley in between.

I jump, unable to silence a cry of alarm—one he greedily swallows before letting me withdraw.

My lips sting, my heart racing as I realize how close we are —practically skin on skin. If it weren't for the fabric of his pants...

We'd practically be fucking. A pang shoots through me, joining a pulsing pressure building in between my legs. Gritting my teeth, I ignore it.

"Not entirely a good girl after all," Domino remarks, leaning back, his posture casual once more. To any onlooker, at least. I can feel the tension ripping through him, and I have a terrifying suspicion that I'm not the only one smothering an ache.

Though, as if to counter the mere possibility of him being unable to resist me, he brings his hand to his mouth, taking the pad of his thumb between his lips.

My throat goes dry as I realize where that finger has been.

"One day, you'll beg me to take you there." He says it so casually I'd laugh were he any other man. But his tone lacks the pleading desperation theirs would carry. He's so confident of the inevitable he doesn't even bother to put effort into stating as much.

He'll take me there.

"Ticktock," I manage to croak. "I only have four days to prove how good I can be after all."

His eyes narrow. Sensing his thinning patience, I'll take this as my cue to leave.

When I ease myself off of him, he doesn't react, letting me stand on my own. I'm bold enough to turn toward the house and take a step, though who knows where I'll go once I'm inside. Somewhere far from him to regroup and think. I need to stay focused on my goal—finding a way to get out of this alive. I should be hunting down any information, not humoring him.

Though I can't escape the feeling that anything worth learning wouldn't be kept in the house. He must have another hiding spot somewhere, in a place he thinks I won't reach.

"Wait." His voice rings out when I've barely gone beyond the ring of white couches.

"Yes?" I stop, though I don't dare look back.

"I think it's time we take a swim. Somewhere where we can discuss the duties of a good girl in private."

My heart aches; it's pounding so hard. I have to physically make myself breathe. In and out…

"I don't have a bathing suit," I wheeze in a ragged exhale.

"Good. I don't intend for you to wear one. After all, my good, grateful girl would hide nothing from her hero."

The bastard.

My eyes burn with frustration at how easily he can yank my chain—literally and figuratively. My only consolation is that he hasn't retrieved that despised collar from wherever he's hidden it since my escape attempt.

I want to deny him. I even start to, my lips parting.

Then I recall the tidbit he snuck within the mocking banter —*discuss in private.*

Apparently, he wants to talk to me outside of Alexi's earshot. Recalling this morning, how he ran the shower before making his offer, I have to admit that it's a convincing stunt.

So I'll play one more round of his sick game.

Still, I can't resist a desperate attempt to turn the tables, no matter how small a move it might be. As I spin to face him, I run my hands along my hips, bunching up the material of my dress as I go. Slowly, I wind it up, up, eventually lifting it over my head entirely. Wadding the fabric in a fist, I throw it onto his lap with a final dare. "Lead the way."

His idea of "a swim" occurs in a section of the property I have yet to discover, just past the terrace gardens. There are three levels of the feature in total, each one graded downward to the next until finally the paved path reaches the ground. The amount of landscaping, let alone water, required to maintain such a property astounds me.

Domino lurks just a few steps ahead, his face angled away, shoulders tensing with every step we go. He's paranoid, though he's very good at hiding it. I suspect Alexi isn't the only one he's second-guessing the motives of.

He's wary of me.

"You said once that you owned this land before you started working for my family," I point out.

"I did, and you've been here before." His voice reaches back to me, barely audible above the chirping of insects and bubbling waters of a small fountain we pass. "You don't remember?"

"I think I would remember if Pia owned a place like this," I counter.

If the Ingleciases owned even a fraction of this amount of land—and were able to afford to maintain it like this—I think Pia's life would have been very, very different. She wouldn't have needed to pry her way into my world at all. I could have grown up alone, without her friendship.

The thought stings, and I shy away from it.

"I think we established that your memory can be faulty at times," Domino says, leading me around a bend that coils against the outside of the house. Perched on the hillside above, the structure of it is breathtaking, made of tanned stone and a beautiful array of Spanish architecture mixed with that of an Italian-style villa.

I'm so distracted by the sight, that I almost miss the carefully concealed dig hidden within Domino's reply. Was he referring to my recollections of Pia?

Or of him?

I haven't decided by the time we finally reach our presumed destination.

It's a square-shaped naturalistic pool sunken into the earth, placed close to the hillside. A fake waterfall extends, nearly as tall as the height of the entire terrace itself, compiled of tan stones built into the earth and gently trickling streams of water that enter the pool from three different locations.

Now I'm sure of it—Pia Inglecias definitely didn't possess a property like this a decade ago.

Still, I hold my tongue as Domino approaches the water's edge and strips his shirt before tugging off his slacks. "Get in."

My nakedness feels more heightened here than during the entire walk across the property. This place is shrouded by a row of planted palm trees, not visible from the house itself. I don't spy any hint of the servants who I know lurk throughout the rest of the property.

We feel more alone here than even locked inside his room or in a shower stall.

If I were to scream, I doubt anyone would hear me or even care enough to come running.

"Don't tell me Ada-Maria Pavalos is afraid of a little swim," Domino remarks as he steps down into the water himself. It's so deep that only his head and shoulders are visible once he's waded toward the center. Cold, his eyes meet mine, chilling enough to have me shivering despite the persistent heat. "I know for a fact you're not that shy. Get in."

I choke down my unease and dip my foot beneath the water. It's cool, but refreshing when paired with the full brunt of the sun. I keep going, realizing that a set of broad, stone steps beneath the water's surface help me gradually adjust to the various depths. By the time I join him near the waterfall, I have to kick my legs to keep my head above the water.

He watches me, able to remain standing with his height advantage.

"You seem to know me so well," I rasp, stopping as close to him as I dare.

"I know that you've spent enough time on the yachts of rich men to lose the right to feign caution when it comes to the water," he snipes.

My cheeks flame. I hate how readily he can throw these snippets of my past in my face. Even if I want to deny his insinuations and cruel assertions—I can't. He has five years of information on me stored away, but I have nothing on him. Just snippets and details he may have intentionally left for me to find.

Still, I sense that he's ready for me to start asking some questions of my own. His eyes glitter, electric in contrast to the turquoise water. On second thought, I think he's impatient for me to start asking, like I'm taking longer than he thought.

Maybe because a part of me is rightfully terrified by the potential answers.

"Why lie?" I demand, my voice breaking. "Why pretend that you killed him?"

And then serve his "body" to me in well-cooked pieces.

He inclines an eyebrow as if this wasn't the question he had in mind. Still, he humors me, lifting his shoulder in a shrug that disrupts the water between us. "I will kill him," he clarifies with a finality that leaves me reeling. "But I needed to know if you were just another pawn in his game."

I don't like how his tone shifted over that last statement.

"What do you mean?"

He inclines his head, eyeing me for so long that my legs start to ache from the effort it takes to paddle in place. "I mean, I needed to know if once again Ada was merely playing her role in a larger game on her daddy's say-so."

I blink as his meaning strikes me all at once. "You thought I knew."

It sounds so ridiculous in retrospect. And at the same time, so damn cruel. He wasn't sure if I knew my father's fate, so he decided to test me in the worst way.

Even now, a part of me recognizes that he could still be lying. If he claims to have faked a cooking body, a fake news broadcast would be child's play in comparison.

"I thought your father valued your life more than he apparently does. I was skeptical of how things looked on their face. I'm finding myself warming up to the idea that they are as they look, after all."

More word games and subtle insinuations.

"If you want to turn me against my father, it isn't working," I croak.

Mainly because I'm still in whiplash over the various disruptions in my view of him over the past few days. First, he was on the verge of being indicted. Then he was dead. And now…

"I'm not as stupid as you think I am," I snap, meeting his gaze as he remains rigidly in place while I start to drift, exhausted by the effort of swimming. I drift back to the shallower end, where I can stand with my feet touching the pool's bottom. As a result, there's a good ten feet of distance between us, and I consider climbing from the water altogether. "I know what you're trying to imply."

"What? That your father conspired with your uninspired, politically ambitious, philandering asshole of a boyfriend to use your presumed kidnapping and death to take pressure off of his impending legal battles? Could a man truly be so cruel, Ada-Maria?"

I cringe at the picture he paints, even as I rail against it. "Don't mock me. I know firsthand what my father is capable of."

So does he.

Yet, he raises an eyebrow. "That doesn't sound like a denial."

"He wouldn't," I insist but, for whatever reason, the words sound flat, easily overpowered by the roar of the water surging between the rocks above.

"Come here." He extends his hands behind him, propelling his body toward the largest waterfall, positioned at the very back of the pool. At the same time, the tilt of his chin makes my belly quiver. It conveys a dare he voices in a gruff rasp, "Unless you aren't as confident of your beliefs as you think you are."

I swallow hard before lunging toward him. "I'm *confident* that I don't trust you—"

"You should." When I come within his reach, he grabs my wrist, easily tugging me closer. "I suggest you not take offense to the series of events that have prolonged your life, Ada," he warns, his tone unusually deep.

I stiffen as he drags me toward him, gripping my waist beneath the water. With his strength supporting me, I don't have to fight to stay suspended. Warm, his lips graze my ear, his voice a grated murmur that resonates through flesh and bone, into my belly.

"The possibility that you may be innocent in this scheme of your father's at least, is the only reason why you've kept my attention for as long as you have."

Before I can counter that, he starts to drift, carrying me into an even deeper section of the pool while my thoughts reel. Only our heads are above water now, and I find myself bracing my hands over his shoulders, unnerved by the loss of control. In his grasp, I'm at his mercy. If he decides to pull me under here, I won't be able to fight him.

Satisfied by that very fact, he positions me so that our faces are inches apart, our mouths so close I feel each brush of his lips as he speaks.

"This is the part where I give you permission to run that smart ass mouth of yours," he murmurs.

It's the best chance I've had to question him. So I'll take it.

"Tell me what you want? Who is Jaguar? Why were you fucking Alexi? Why is she even here? How—"

"So greedy," he scolds, flexing his hands against my waist in punishment. Beneath the water, his heat is neutralized by the colder temperature, meaning that I'm forced to contend with the texture of his touch in a way I haven't before. He's strong, every finger resonating a subtle pressure that warns he could easily hurt me if the mood strikes him.

And it already has more than once.

His eyes are unreadable, shrouded by heavy lids that cast shadows over those imperceptible green irises. I can't tell if he's annoyed by my barrage of questions or amused.

"One at a time like the good girl you've been so eager to be."

His tone makes his meaning clear—choose wisely. Piss him off or push too far, and he'll stop.

I lick my lips only to realize that his eyes drift down to track the movement of my tongue from one end of my mouth to the other. His throat lurches, betraying a hard swallow, and I nearly lose track of what it is I'm supposed to be doing.

Right. Learning whatever he's willing to give.

"Tell me about Jaguar."

"*Julian*," he corrects, putting a harsh emphasis on the name. "Tell me something, have you ever heard of Carlos Domingas?"

I frown, recalling the many acquaintances my father had circling around his orbit at any given time. There are too many to keep track of, their names a blur.

"No—"

"You should have," Domino cautions in a way that recalls a disapproving teacher during a complex lecture. "Though I wouldn't be surprised if you haven't. Carlos Domingas was a man your papa knew very well indeed. They were partners, long before Don Roy slipped across the border and became the polished, savvy politician he presents to the world."

I'm curious despite myself. He could be lying, but I don't have the privilege of ignoring him. To his credit, I don't know enough about my father's past to challenge anything he might assert. It was a time in his life he rarely spoke about, not even among family. In fact, he only ever referenced himself as a boy when boasting about his scrappy instincts and cunning that led him to crawl from poverty to where he is today.

My father, the ultimate survivor, fashioning himself as the city's savior.

"Carlos Domingas was a tough son of a bitch. He ran a whole series of enterprises that your daddy would swear now never to have been a part of. That doesn't erase the fact that when Don Roy first entered Terra Rodea all those years ago, he did it hand in hand with Carlos Domingas and the full backing of his cartel."

It's a blunter retelling of the same rumors that have plagued my father's entire career from its inception. That he was a puppet for drug trafficking and used his cozy position with those in power to force the authorities to look the other way or outright ignore corruption.

He's always denied as much, publicly, anyway.

If I had to be honest with myself, the man whispered about in those rumors sounded closer to who I knew my father to be than the way he portrayed himself during his campaign speeches.

"When Roy got too big for his britches, he tried to turn on Carlos Domingas, arranging a hit on him. It was clever, of course, and he covered his tracks. But Carlos Domingas was a man who thrived on revenge. Before Roy ever got the thought in his head of betraying him, Domingas already had ten plots of retaliation set in motion."

"You?" I ask, hazarding a guess.

He grunts out a sound that might pass for a laugh were he anyone else. "In addition to a wealth of cutthroat allies and 'associates,' Carlos Domingas had two sons that he started training to replace him before they were even out of diapers."

His tone prompts me to take another guess.

"Jaguar?" I ask.

He nods. "Julian and a younger brother named Juan. Under the alias, Jaguar, Julian has been amassing his own realm of influence over the ashes of what his father left behind."

"And his brother? What about him?"

His eyes cut away from me, darker than ever. "Dead. Jaguar runs his little kingdom alone."

"But what about you?" I recall a fragment of their conversation I overheard. "He called you little brother—"

"A sick attempt at a joke on his part," Domino says, swatting away the insinuation. "He meant nothing by it."

"So why me?"

He smiles, but there's no warmth in it. With his teeth bared, the expression resembles a snarl. "You, Ada-Maria, are here only by the grace of God. That 'car crash' hit on your father was never intended to kill him, merely distract. It seems, however, that even Roy Pavalos can't walk away from such serious trauma without a scratch. When it seemed like he might die after all, Jaguar had no use for you."

It sounds so cold to hear him state it so bluntly, reducing my worth to my mere designation as the daughter of Roy Pavalos.

"He was tempted, you see, to let Tristan Lucas put his little plan in action to hog the glory of your apparent abduction and claim the vacuum left by the impending death of Roy Pavalos. He would have been a very useful pawn to have under Julian's thumb. However, I managed to convince him to sever such sloppy loose ends."

His tone deepens, devoid of all emotion. It's how he sounded while conversing with my father, accepting any and every task he would hand down. I used to marvel at how one man could seem so detached from the world. From emotions. From everything.

And yet, I hoarded over every brief glimpse I managed to catch of the real creature lurking beneath that mask. Perhaps I fantasized so much about that hypothetical Domino that I lost sight of the stark reality of who he was. Who he's always been.

A soldier following orders, with no moral compass of his own.

"He's let me keep you merely to placate me for the time being," Domino adds, bringing his mouth near my ear again.

We're still floating through the water, my thighs resting against his hips, his hands still on my waist to hold me steady. I think this is the longest we've been so close.

Apart from during sex.

"Why?" I ask him hoarsely.

His brows furrow as he returns his gaze to mine. "Your father's condition, though critical, is rapidly improving," he says, ignoring that I've spoken. "Which means that your usefulness to Jaguar has just skyrocketed. He's let me keep you for now because I'm shouldering the logistics of keeping you hidden from the manhunt searching for you, and he doesn't have to take the risk. Yet. But trust me, Ada, he'll come for you, and he won't be your knight in shining armor."

"And you are?"

He frowns at the slight, but seems to let it slide without comment. Instead, he shifts so that my back is to the outcroppings of rock. I can feel stray droplets of moisture speckle me from above, and the gentle hum of the water is even louder here.

"I have my own uses for you," he admits.

Suddenly, he lifts me from the water, and I scramble for purchase, gripping a firm surface in return. With a start, I realize that he's set me down on a rocky ledge while remaining in the water, in between my legs.

Through his lashes, his eyes seem even more intense than usual. He's like some fucked up, masculine version of a merman, his damp hair clinging to his shoulders, body bare.

Without warning, he grabs my chin, balancing it against the palm of his hand.

When seconds tick by without him expounding on his statement, I once again get the feeling that he's waiting for me to prod him for more. In this instance, he wants me to.

"What do you want?"

A dangerous smirk flits across his lips before a sterner expression replaces it. He's scrutinizing me carefully, sizing me up by the time he's done. And yet he's not nice enough to voice his impression of me, out loud.

I have to guess from the way his fingers flex against my skin, startlingly soft... Until his nails tease my flesh to give me a taste of the pain he's capable of inflicting.

"You once claimed that everyone wants to use you to get to your father. Well, you've gotten your wish. I want *you*—fuck Roy Pavalos. But unfortunately, Ada-Maria, I won't just tell you why. I want you to guess."

My eyes sting, and the moisture falling from them catches me off guard. Tears. As they lash down my cheeks, I realize why they've sprung forth now.

It's so very cruel, the way he's toying with me. Days ago, I would have died to hear those very words. I'd have done anything.

But now I know that beneath them lurks a million secrets and lies. They mean nothing on their face.

I want *you.*

I wish he'd claim to use me against my father instead.

"You hate him," I point out, craving more than anything that I had the strength to shove him aside and swim away. I need to get away—because I can't hide it. Not my pain or the grim reality that these tears are real and I'm not faking anymore. "Everything you've done to me has been retaliation against him. For Pia. For whatever you think he did—"

"This was never just about him," Domino interjects, his tone cutting. "I warned you of that fact once. I suggest you listen to me, and that you never underestimate Julian."

His eyes blaze. He means every word, displaying a hostility that I don't think I've ever seen him exhibit, not even toward me.

"What about Alexi? How is she involved in all of this?"

Some of the bitterness leaves his gaze, and I hate that I react to that, my chest tightening. "She is a pawn of Julian's, nothing more. I don't feel strongly about her either way," he adds, conveying a hint of mercy toward her that he's never shown me. "But she works for him. Do not forget that, and I would advise against thinking of her as an ally."

I let the jab pass unchallenged, fixated on the way he said that—*she works for him.* In his cold baritone, he might as well have said—*she belongs to him.*

"How did she meet him? How did you meet her?"

He strokes the length of my jawline as he withdraws his hand from my chin, returning it to my unclaimed thigh. "I'll let you ask her those questions, if you're truly that curious."

I hiss in exasperation. "First, you warn me not to talk to her. Then you dare me to—"

"I don't want you to forget…" His voice softens, and I have to strain to hear him. "I'm the only one you can trust."

I recoil as far as I dare without risking my balance, crossing my arms over my exposed breasts. "My father said that," I reply.

He laughs, but it's a sharp, vengeful sound. "I think we both know for a fact that I am not your daddy, Ada-Maria. At least not in that context."

My breath catches, my cheeks flaming. It's suddenly hard to suck in enough air to breathe.

"I… You… You were fucking Alexi," I say, latching onto the next topic demanding an explanation. "I saw the pictures."

Pictures that he alluded to leaving for me to find in the first place.

His smile returns in full, ripening as his eyes take on a playful, wicked gleam. "You know better than anyone, Ada-Maria. A picture is worth a thousand words. Fake, useless words meant to spin a narrative. You yourself have starred in dozens of photos that might portray a reality that differed from the truth. Videos as well."

I hate how easily he wields my own past against me. The worst part is that I can't accuse him of lying. If anyone would know, he would. He was right when he claimed my father would want confirmation that I followed his orders. And, like a good dog, he gladly followed after me, gathering evidence as he went.

"Tell me, Ada, were your simpering smiles and moans genuine then?"

I flinch. He knows precisely where to prod to slip beneath my defenses. I can't resist wondering if anything else he hinted at was true. Like that my father was indifferent to my impending kidnapping all along…

And my death.

No. He was lying, of course. Besides, I have to stay focused. Meeting his gaze, I look past my own fear and try to find a weakness of his to exploit.

"Whatever your relationship with Alexi is, you were with her," I point out. "And yet, you don't seem to have a problem with her 'belonging' to Jaguar now. But…"

His nostrils flare, conveying a warning I fail to heed.

"You don't seem too willing to share me with him. Why is that?"

He spreads his fingers out along my inner thighs, and I suck in a breath, grappling for a better grip on the rock beneath me.

"Because I never wanted Alexi." He lowers his head, leaning forward so that his mouth comes dangerously close to my breasts, his gaze fixated below my waist.

I gasp as he nudges my legs apart, easily claiming the space between them.

"I never claimed Alexi. I never spent five fucking years wondering what she tasted like. I never cultivated a kill list of all the men she casually fucked—" His nails dig in as he spreads my legs further, fully opening me to him. The heat of his breath lashes me in searing waves, and my eyelids flutter, my brain paralyzed by the sensation. He's growling, real anger seeping into every single syllable. "I never wanted her so badly I could get hard at just the sight of her smile. I'll let you parse over those words, Ada-Maria. I'll let you decide what that means."

He lunges downward, and I barely manage to throw my hands in between us, feeling his mouth brush my trembling fingers.

"W-Wait," I croak.

Not stop.

He looks up, eyeing me through a fringe of black hair, his eyes so vibrant they practically glow.

"I know you're just toying with me," I rasp, but it should be the least of my concerns at the moment, his approval. His lust.

Besides, my sloppy phrasing was a pathetic way of avoiding what I really mean—*I know you're lying to me.*

"Good," he says, his voice gruff. "I want you to think of that while I have my tongue buried inside of you. I want you to tell yourself that over, and over until it hurts, Ada. That pouty face you make when you doubt me… It's sexy as hell."

CHAPTER THIRTEEN

I can't stop him this time. My hands are easily batted aside, and I wind up grasping for the nearest source of stability I can find as his heat sears the flesh between my legs. It's so soft, whatever it is, like I'm grasping at silk—his hair, I realize.

It's my turn to rake my nails over his skull and pull as he does exactly what he warned he would.

He buries his tongue inside of me.

In this instance, I have no frame of reference to compare him to. As it turns out, most of the men I've slept with were only interested in their own pleasure, never mine. I was just a smiling, warm sex doll. The closest anyone came to attempting to get me off manually was Tristan, and only with his fingers, sloppily with no real effort put into the act.

But Domino…

Eat is such a dangerous word—so vulgar to describe simply putting your mouth on someone. When a woman sucks a cock, it's not described so viciously.

But the feeling assaulting me now can only be described by terms that should never apply to something like sex. Devoured. Swallowed. Choked down. Worshiped...

He turns my body into his altar, and then he douses me in sin. After sin. After sin.

I scream, writhing as his lips press against my inner flesh, while his fingers come to spread me open. Ruthlessly expose every inch and fold. Then his tongue lashes, hot and violent, irritating every single nerve to a painful degree.

His teeth graze me next, and I jerk, trying to push his head again. Then gripping him for dear life as my eyes roll back.

It would be one thing, if he could abuse me in this way, and I'd have to endure it. Suffer through each slow, savoring lick. Keep my senses. Hate him and hate him.

He turns my body inside out instead. Every bit of twitching muscle and heated flesh becomes my enemy, rebelling against the faint sliver of my brain fighting for control.

I whimper, realizing it's too late to shut him out. His tongue easily slips inside of me, molten hot. My body welcomes him, each drop of moisture flooding like gasoline toward the lips and tongue working in tandem like a match and tinder.

I'm on fire. Too hot. Burning alive. Melting. Ashes.

Then, just when my stomach stops flipping, and I can breathe again, he keeps going…

Shame is a concept that feels harder to grasp with every brutal, gut-wrenching orgasm he wrings from me. My spine is his toy, my limbs jelly, my voice so hoarse and broken I can't speak.

Hurting him is the only language I have left to communicate with him. Raking nails and tugging fingers.

But he's impervious, no matter how hard on his scalp I pull.

"…faking." I feel his voice vibrate through me; it's so guttural, overpowering every other sound to ripple through my skull. "So good at faking. My Ada. *Keep* faking."

He's taunting me, and I don't even have the sense of mind to counter him.

My moans are shameless, reduced to whispered gasps as my voice breaks. I see stars by the time I start to believe he'll finally take mercy on me. He's stopped, his head resting heavily on my thighs, his pants basting the drenched skin between my legs.

"I imagined roses," he rasps, tilting his head so that his eyes find me.

I'm too sensitive. Too raw. With one look, a pulse shoots down my spine, and I flinch; it's damn near painful. One look, and it's like he's touching me all over again.

"Or bubblegum, or some shit," he adds, his eyes narrowing. Slowly, he trails his tongue across his wet lips, tasting whatever moisture is there. The flavor must anger him. Infuriate. He glowers at me, through damp strands of black hair that frame his face like scorch marks. My devil, enraged by my taste. "How is it possible that you taste better than that?" he demands.

"Please," I croak as he lowers his gaze, crouching between my legs again.

I'm panting, my back on fire, ass scraped raw by the stone beneath me. "Please... Enough."

As if he would ever show me mercy.

Ruthlessly, his mouth engulfs me again. Torments me again.

The pleasure is so sharp and intense it borders on painful. It *is* pain, every hungry, groping touch from him. Every slow, relishing lick.

Eating is the only word that comes close to describing what it feels like. With nibbling, greedy tastes, he devours me whole.

I lose track of time and space. I just know that when the pressure finally relents, I'm leaning against a sturdy surface, softer than stone, but just as impenetrable.

"I've got you," he says in a voice so rough my toes curl. "I've got you, Ada... Always, I've got you."

Something in his tone reaches through my dazed, dizzying thoughts to some part of me beneath that stirs in alarm. It's hard to remember why I should be. Why I shouldn't relent to the grip of the man holding me against his chest, cradling my head against his shoulder, as he propels us both through the water. Why I should hate…

It's like being amid the throes of the wildest, reckless, dangerous high. The rules of reality start to blend and blur, and my giddy brain tells me that anything is possible. Even the prospect of Domino Valenciaga craving me in a way that roughens his voice like I've never heard it.

But somewhere in the process of him lifting me from the water and carrying me across the property toward the terrace, my common sense starts to return. I wake up.

With the house looming above, there's no denying who I am or the identity of the man holding me in his arms. I stiffen, scrambling to regain control of my limbs.

"L-Let me go," I demand.

Either he doesn't hear me, or he doesn't care, swiftly mounting the bottom level of the terrace even as my palm lands harmlessly against his chest. I can't see his face fully from this angle. Just a curtain of dark hair and the edge of his jaw, clenched so tightly it's a firm, solid line.

He's facing straight ahead, as though I don't exist, even as he adjusts his grip on my body to keep me contained.

We must have been in the pool for hours. The sun is lower over the horizon, marking the hottest part of the late afternoon, not long before sundown. Bathed in the golden glow, the house looks majestic.

And more inescapable than ever, my beautiful paradise of a prison. Two figures lurk on the topmost part of the terrace, watching our approach.

One is short and diminutive in stature. Ines.

The other is tall and lithe, her blond hair swaying in a light breeze as she leans over the railing.

"Boo! No fair," Alexi calls. "If you were going for a swim, I would have come! We could have played chicken."

I can sense her barely concealed innuendo from here, even without having to see the simpering smile on her face.

Then I realize, that to know we went swimming, she can tell that Domino and I are dripping wet, our hair plastered to our heads. A quick glance down reveals that he donned his slacks at least before heading here.

But I'm still naked. Still raw and overly sensitive, too exhausted to even stand on my own, let alone cover myself.

The knowledge of people watching has me shrinking against him, forced to submit to the width of his arms to cover any exposed parts of me.

And the bastard is enjoying this. He has enough tact not to laugh outright, but I can feel the subtle tremors ripple through his chest. He loves having me unnerved, left with no choice but to rely on him.

A fact that I should always keep at the back of my mind.

I stay alert as he follows the gradual incline of the terrace, eventually winding his way to the top where Alexi and Ines wait, the latter poised for instruction.

"We'll have dinner in the dining room," he says to the maid who dutifully scurries off. Then, Domino inclines his head toward Alexi. "We'll change and meet you there."

I can't look at her directly. Not when my face is on fire, every insecurity I physically possess screaming out in the open for her enjoyment. I'm sure she can see the marks and bruises on my body in stark detail. The slight trembling in my legs.

The wetness leaving Domino's lips glistening.

I'm sure she can connect the dots—but that's not what has me on edge. It's the fear that in her eyes, I'll find a conspiratorial gleam that warns she's not the least bit surprised to see me like this, with him.

Because, every step of the way, she's been in on his plan from the very beginning.

"Can't wait," she says finally, in a flat tone that doesn't reveal her impression of the situation either way.

As Domino heads inside, crossing the threshold of the circular foyer, I can't stop myself from looking back.

She's watching us, one hand casually braced on the railing behind her, her head tilted so that the sunlight hits her from the best possible angle. She's so effortlessly pretty that it hurts, her eyes the same big, endless blue that I remember, her face perfection, perky tits on full display by her lowcut top.

Her smile is cheerful, stretching eagerly across her face.

But in her gaze lurks open suspicion and a quiet hostility that she doesn't bother to disguise. Domino isn't the source of her annoyance, either.

Just me.

As Domino crosses the foyer, she disappears from my line of sight, and I find myself being carried into his room seconds later.

He sets me on the edge of the mattress and strolls for the closet, tugging his slacks down as he goes.

There is a shameless pride in how he stands utterly naked and scans the items hanging from the rails. At first, I assume that he's putting so much scrutiny into picking an outfit for himself. One that will impress a certain blond, perhaps?

Then he fingers the hem of a black skirt, and I realize what he's doing. He's picking out an outfit for me.

I'd forgotten that sometime during the chaos of Jaguar's arrival, he had women's clothing brought here. He scans them all with a familiarity that makes my breath quicken. Like he already has the exact white A-line style dress in mind for me to wear. It's just a matter of finding it.

When he finally approaches, chosen dress in hand, he eyes me with a ruthless sweep of his gaze.

"I'll need to wash you."

I shiver, my head swimming. It's unnerving how he can shift from emotionless to bristling with intensity on a dime.

"I can wash myself." I try to stand, and I barely flex my feet against the floor when I'm assaulted by a million different, conflicting sensations. My various scrapes and injuries are on fire, each one throbbing at full force. Between my legs feels sore, rubbed raw. Even the slightly cooler air inside feels like stabbing knives against that sensitive skin. Forget washing myself; I don't even know if I'm brave enough to risk standing up.

"So damn stubborn." Domino hauls me to my feet by my wrist, making the decision for me.

I'm biting my lip so hard I taste blood as he makes me follow him into the bathroom and lean against the counter. He retrieves a clean cloth from somewhere, wets it beneath the faucet, and then wipes me with a rigorous, clinical focus.

The same way my father maintained his luxury vehicles. It was one of the few tasks he preferred to do himself, waxing them to perfection, ensuring they made the best possible impact.

I'm as much a possession to him as those cars were to my father. I can see the same cold focus in his eyes as he drags the cloth over my belly and between my legs. He's making a note of every scrape and scratch. Every time I flinch and jump when he grazes a barely healed injury.

He's making a mental map of every inch of me.

A man who planned on selling you wouldn't be this obsessive, a part of me warns. I ignore it.

His motives aside, I try to reassemble my logical thought process as I come down from that sexual high. The things he said come rushing back to me, mainly about Jaguar and Alexi.

"Why was she after Tristan?" Is he implying that she was doing so on Jaguar's say-so?

She works for him, he said.

"Why is she here now? What do you—"

He presses a finger to my lips, sealing them with just enough pressure to cut me off.

"You'll get your answers," he says, dropping his rag into the sink. He retreats into the room and returns with the dress bunched in both hands. He motions for me to raise my arms, and when I do, he dresses me, tugging the material down to fall over my hips.

With an appreciative glance, he surveys his work in the mirror. Hunched behind me, he can't disguise the way his eyes dip over the V-shaped neckline. "I knew this one would suit you," he remarks in a voice so subdued I almost miss what he says.

He knew...

I inspect myself, noting that the white dress—like pretty much everything he's had me wear since my arrival—is far beyond the usual norm I'd stick to. It's too bold, and at the same time, too minimal. The demur shade of white makes my eyes look even larger than they are.

In comparison to his bulk, I'm as delicate as a porcelain doll.

A contrast that I think he enjoys.

"Come." He crosses the balcony, reenters the closet, and grabs a shirt and dry slacks, pulling them on with little fanfare. Then he leads the way into the dining room, where Alexi lounges shamelessly against the back of the chair placed at the table's head.

At the sight of Domino, her mouth quirks into a sly smirk as she arches her back so high her nipples threaten to pop out from the neckline of her top. "I'm *starving*," she purrs. "I'm just about ready to stick anything I can get ahold of into my mouth."

The bitch.

She looks past me, her eyes tracking Domino as he claims a seat beside her. His hand latches onto my wrist, forcing me to take the one next to him.

"It's about time we got to catch up, Adie," Alexi says, flicking her attention to me. "Gosh, how long has it been?"

Not long enough, in a sense. For so long, Alexi has so doggedly pursued any man I've had any hint of interest in.

Am I surprised that she managed to dig her claws into Domino?

No. I'm more alarmed by the fact that she succeeded.

She's mastered his talent for poker faces, it seems, her blue eyes unreadable as I meet her gaze. She sits forward, letting her breasts press against the table while she curls a bit of blond hair around her finger.

"Little Adie, all grown up. It's so weird, you know I almost didn't recognize you when I came back."

Two years ago, Alexi Rojas returned from obscurity to make my life hell any way she could. But before then, we were as close as sisters. Not to the same extent Pia and I were, but close enough.

I used to know all of her secrets, and she knew mine. Like the bad little habits we both indulged in, and one she taught me to perfect.

You should keep a toothbrush in your purse, she told me once, as we huddled in the bathroom of a classroom building on the campus of our boarding school. *You can stick it down your throat, and it helps make everything easier. I bet we'll both lose ten pounds by next month, and then no one will dare make fun of you the next time we wear bikinis.*

I thought that was so kind of her. Sweet, actually. It's funny how, despite the world in which I grew up, I could still be so goddamn naïve. To me, back then anyway, Pia and Alexi were the best friends any girl could ever ask for.

I was sure we'd be close forever.

"You look the same," I tell her. "I guess some people keep their baby fat forever. It looks cute on you, though."

Her smile falls flat, and I'm pathetic enough to take a grim sense of satisfaction in that. It's so surreal to see her head, uninjured, her skin unblemished, giggling with Domino like they're old friends. Even now, she keeps herself angled toward him, cleavage on display. It's as if she's become so accustomed to seeking out male attention, she's compelled to do so, even when the male in question seems to have no interest in looking her way.

He's fixated on the windows instead, eyeing the rapidly darkening sky.

"I'm going to check on our meal." He rises to his feet and heads for the hallway. When I start to follow him out of habit, I swear I see him jerk his chin in a silent command. *Stay.* "I'll be back in a moment."

Confused, I stare after him as my heart pounds unsteadily. Given that—in my entire time here—he's preferred to summon servants who appear on a dime, rather than fetch our meals himself, I'm on edge. I'm flashed back to the night he had what he claimed to be my father served on a silver dish. Does he have a similar meal in mind for Alexi's benefit?

Or... I realize as I turn my focus back to the woman in question, he left purposefully. So that we could "catch up" in private.

And what a lackluster reunion it's shaping up to be. Without her required dose of testosterone nearby, Alexi slumps back in her seat, her eyes openly displaying disinterest. Sighing, she inspects a manicured hand, watching the light glint off her pink nails.

It's a convincing show—because that's exactly what I sense it really is. An act.

As the seconds tick by, she grows visibly impatient, waiting for me to make the first move.

Because she's unsure of what I know, a part of me suspects. As much as she seems to hate me, she doesn't want to say the wrong thing. Some sick, twisted corner of my brain gets immense pleasure out of watching her squirm.

But something tells me that Domino won't give us long to reconnect. Is this impromptu opportunity for an interrogation done for her benefit? Or mine.

"So," I say, flattening my hands against the table's glass surface. "How long have you been fucking him?"

Alexi's smile returns in full as her eyes narrow. "You know, I spent a long time trying to imagine how this would feel. To see the high and mighty Ada-Maria Pavalos sniveling in fear for once, cowering in the shadow of a plot she has no damn clue of. I thought I'd feel bad for you. Pity, maybe? In all honesty, I'm enjoying every minute of it. Humility looks good on you, Ada. You should try to embody it more often."

I flinch, and I almost forget Domino's warning from the pool. *She works for him.* And, their apparent relationship aside, it's evident from the lengths he's gone to conceal our conversations that he doesn't trust her.

I have to tread carefully.

Hopefully, I can do so while knocking her down a peg or two.

"Why don't you give me some pointers on humility?" I say. "In between fucking Tristan and Domino, I'm surprised you had room for anyone else."

Her brows furrow for a split second before she disguises the expression behind another forced smile. Still, I know that I confused her. How?

"How has Dom been?" she asks in that husky purr, leaning back against her chair. "Poor man. To have spent so much time under the thumb of the mighty Pavalos family. I bet it was like being in prison. Who knows how much sexual frustration he's built up over those long, hard years? No wonder you look like you've been dragged to hell and back. I think I would have trouble keeping up with that kind of virility, and I've heard that you're the sort of girl who doesn't like to break a sweat."

"Haven't you heard," I croak, desperate to appear unrattled. "I like it rough."

She purses her lips, crossing her arms over her chest. "You know, I never took you for the type to wind up in a situation like this," she says, but I know a taunt when I hear one. "Alone in a big-ass manor with your father's bodyguard and no connection to the outside world. I would have thought that someone who brands herself as a socialite would be a little concerned about what might be happening in Terra Rodea."

I sit straighter, trying to disguise as much of my interest as I can. She's hinting at something, dancing around it. But what?

I'm tempted to ask her outright and drop the caution. Damn Domino and his mind games, I need answers. The only thing holding me back is the knowledge that Alexi would never give me something I wanted. I'd have to trick her into revealing it.

"Why should I care about the big bad world?" I ask with a shrug. "I'm safe here with Domino. If there's something I need to know, he'll tell me."

She smirks, an eyebrow raised. "You really are that fucking gullible."

I get the sense that statement slipped out unbidden, though she does her best to cover the break in composure with a forced laugh.

"I think I'd feel a bit differently. Then again, I always was a bit less self-centered than you."

It's my turn to smirk. "Oh? I agree. You've been so selfless you've been fucking anyone who so much as looks at me. Like Tristan."

She scoffs. "Oh, come off it, Ada. Like you actually gave a damn about Two-second Tristan. For what it's worth, I couldn't stand him. Not only was he bad in the sack, but he had horrible taste in women. I had to practically drool, or he'd lose interest. No wonder he liked you so much. I'll let you in on a little secret, Adie—" She leans across the table, and the breeze carries the scent of her cheap perfume to my nose. "He didn't even tell me he had a girlfriend when he started fucking me—though I already knew, of course. When I finally asked about you, do you know what he said? That he was humoring you out of respect for your powerful daddy. Fancy that."

My brain goes blank. I don't know how to process her nasty digs all at once. Instead, I try to ignore them, looking past the hateful rhetoric to the truth lurking beneath.

"If you didn't like him so much, why fuck him at all? At least I actually had some interest in him." I nearly choke on the lie, not that Alexi seems to notice it.

She's practically lunging across the table, blue eyes blazing. "Why? Don't be such a dumb cunt, Ada. You know. I'm sure Domino told you all about his little scheme. To have me get close to Tristan and suss out all of his bad-boy plots. I know you've made a name for yourself based on being a dumb, blond bitch, but Jesus Christ, you can't even drop the act here?"

"D-Domino had you get close to Tristan?" I croak.

Her raised eyebrow quirks even higher. "He didn't tell you." A shadow falls over her expression as her beautiful features rearrange into a blank mask. She sits back, putting space between us that feels less like a retreat and more like she's hiding something. Or she said too much. "Maybe Domino hasn't been quite as talkative as I thought; what in between all those hot and heavy rounds of screwing."

I don't miss the note of jealousy in her voice then, but I'm too distracted to pounce on it like I should.

Domino manipulated Alexi into sleeping with Tristan. Though, of course, he did. It makes so much sense it should have been evident from the start. He took those pictures of them. He had Tristan's home outfitted with a camera to make secret recordings. He even threw as much in my face, leaving me to put the pieces together on my own.

And yet, it somehow feels ten times more violating to hear it straight from the horse's mouth. Not only was Alexi in on his scheme, toying with Tristan for a reason beyond just getting back at me. She was doing it for Domino.

And he trusted her enough to have her enact his scheming for him.

Suddenly, I don't want to play this game anymore. I don't want to know what else I've been so fucking oblivious to. More and more, it's starting to feel like, once again, I'm the butt of a joke everyone else is in on but me. I'm the pawn being manipulated across the gameboard.

Alexi alluded to the chaos unfolding in Terra Rodea. With my mother dead and my father in the hospital, I can only imagine. What the hell has Domino unleashed?

And what does he really have in mind for me?

I start to push back from the table, too overwhelmed to stay on task. I've barely moved when I sense a presence approach me from behind, bringing with them a scent of cooked meat.

"Dinner will be more informal tonight," Domino explains. His muscular arms reach past me, placing a platter of what looks like meat and vegetable skewers on the center of the table. Ines appears at the other end and sets down a dish of rice and a platter of fruit.

"Can you please bring us some wine," Domino tells her before reclaiming his seat.

Within the blink of an eye, Alexi is back to her smirking, overly extended self. Boldly, she reaches out, placing her hand on Domino's shoulder.

"You didn't have to go through so much trouble," she chirps, but her gaze is on me, narrowed and searching. "I didn't even know Ada loved this kind of food."

Domino turns to me, and I stiffen, unprepared for the intensity I find reflected in his gaze. He cradles my chin against his hand, stroking along my jaw. "She's surprisingly adventurous," he murmurs. "So willing to try different things."

I grit my teeth so hard my jaw cracks. I hate not knowing. I can't tell if they're both allied conspiratorially, playing mind games at my expense.

But this time, I don't suppress the urge to run. I wrench out of Domino's grasp and push back from the table.

"I'm not hungry—"

"You will eat." He somehow manages to sound more charming than threatening. Perhaps it's the grin he flashes that robs the bite from his words. Or the fact that his hand slides against my lower back, unseen from Alexi's position. "We wouldn't want to offend our guest?"

He grabs a skewer of something that looks like seasoned chicken and bites off the top most chunk. Then he hands it to me.

I feel Alexi's gaze on me, itching like a nasty rash. Domino, however, forces eye contact, and I can see the dare written clearly across those green irises. *Eat. Or so help me God, I will shove this stick down your goddamn throat.*

I grab it and take a bite, chewing without tasting. As I swallow, Domino sits back while Ines appears with the bottle of wine. She dutifully pours three glasses, and Domino grabs the one nearest him.

"A toast," he says, lifting his glass to the air. "To old friends."

"And to new ones," Alexi chimes in, taking a drink of her own.

I claim the final serving and bring it to my lips without waiting for him to solidify the toast.

Chuckling, he follows my lead, but I keep going long after he and Alexi set their glasses down again. Until I've drained every last drop.

"You should eat first, Ada-Maria." Domino's tone is swift and cutting. "I wouldn't recommend drinking on an empty stomach."

"You know what I wouldn't recommend?" I toss back.

God, his expression transforms so quickly it's terrifying. He's a beast, teeth bared and ready to bite. I know I'm going too far—every ounce of common sense in my body is warning me to stop. Play along. Trust his promise, even though he's lied, and abused, and brutalized.

By the time I reconsider provoking him now, it's already too late.

"I wouldn't recommend fucking a man who fucks the trailer trash—" Looking Alexi dead in the eye, I add, "Twice."

Then I scramble to my feet, knocking over my chair in my haste to move.

But I'm nowhere near quick enough.

Domino snatches my wrist. "I suggest you sit down, Ada, and return to our meal." He's audibly angry now, unable to carry on his playful ruse.

Good.

I'm done being his little toy.

"I *suggest* you don't kidnap women from the family you work for. That you don't claim to have killed their father or orchestrated an attack that caused the death of their boyfriend." I rip my hand away, but—to my shock and growing alarm—he lets me. "I would also suggest that you don't fuck the town whore, Domino. And maybe next time? Try not to sell me, either."

I run, and surprisingly no one chases after me or throws me down. I make it all the way into the white room, slamming the door in my wake. Then I lock it. Heart pounding, I search for the heaviest thing I can find—a white dresser against the wall near the closet entrance—and I throw my weight against it, pushing it before the door as a makeshift barricade.

I have no delusions that it will hold him. For good measure. I strip the bed of blankets and drag the mattress to the door as well, propping it upright against the dresser for added reinforcement.

Then, like a coward, I race into the closet, close the door and wedge myself behind the back shelf.

CHAPTER FOURTEEN

Sound travels in this house. I can hear the clinking of silverware and muttered voices. Apparently, Domino and Alexi have carried on with their meal without me.

Somehow, I find that more unnerving than if he had hunted me down the hall and was banging on the door. It means that he's willing to make me wait, stewing in his anger and devising a crueler punishment.

The full extent of what I've done doesn't sink in until I parse over what I said to him—all within Alexi's earshot. If I truly wasn't supposed to know about his role in masterminding the twisted plot that got me here, well, then I'm about to find out.

Though, I can't feel too guilty for tarnishing his little ruse when I realize that Alexi let a secret of her own slip. Domino had her sleep with Tristan and was ready and waiting to take pictures.

Did he convince her during those sexy sessions between the

two of them that he also documented? All she had to do was "play her role."

It stings to think of him working with her—of the two of them plotting against my family and me. Even if I did cause a rift between him and Jaguar over his apparent deceit, I shouldn't care. Right?

I can't ignore the way he looked at me in the bathroom as blood dripped down my face. He seemed unguarded then, as though he had nothing to hide. Nothing left to lose.

What will he do if he thinks I've put a wrench in his carefully crafted plan?

I don't have to speculate for long.

I hear footsteps first, light initially, then firmer. Heavier. They advance slowly in this direction, as though the source of them has all the time in the world.

But the closer they come, the more anger becomes apparent in every steady, resonating footfall.

My heart starts to race as they grow nearer, eventually stopping where I assume the door to be. I hear a distinctive jangle as if they tested the doorknob, finding it locked.

I tense, expecting banging. A threat. Promises of violence.

Instead…

The steps retreat.

My confusion spurs me to creep from my hiding place, straining my ears for any other sound that might give me a clue of his next course of action. All I hear is silence, and the chirping of insects encroaching from outside. I must have left the window open.

But despite how hard I listen, I can't discern any noises that might be coming from inside the house. No footsteps. No voices, either Domino's or Alexi's.

No noise at all, except for my rapidly beating heart and the frantic sound of my own breathing.

Warily, I creep to the closet door and push it open—only to have it wrenched out of my grasp, flung from the outside.

Domino lurks behind it, though I don't believe my eyes at first. Behind him, the mattress and wardrobe are still positioned before the closed door. There's no way he could have gotten in.

Then I feel him—the heat of his breath against my temple as he exhales harshly. With one hand, he grips the doorway, blocking me in. His fingers shake, the knuckles stark white, his entire body resonating with tension.

"You have no fucking clue what you've done," he tells me, but his voice is worlds apart from the restrained growl he displayed in the dining room. It's nowhere close to his bellowed shouts or the angriest snarl I've heard him utilize. It's different. Colder. Softer. Like a whisper ripped from his chest, against his will. Something so hard for him to voice he can't believe he's actually doing so. "Do you?"

He releases the door and snags my chin, dragging me toward him. "You stupid, foolish…" He breaks off as if I'm not even worth the effort of insulting. "You've just fucked up everything I've spent five fucking years putting into motion. Again."

I flinch at that. It sounds like such an overreaction to one petty outburst. Alexi Rojas has the power to unravel the schemes of the great and powerful Domino Valenciaga? I wouldn't believe it if it weren't for his words that choose now to haunt me.

She works for him.

His eyes narrow, nostrils flaring. "Goddamn, I should just let him have you. You're not even worth the fucking effort of—"

"Maybe if you would stop lying to me," I croak, trying to wrench away. "I could actually *trust* you."

He tightens his grip, tugging me even closer. My breasts graze his chest, and through the heated skin, I swear I can feel his heart pounding. Pulsating. Raging.

He's so angry, and I can't resist this pathetic need to defend myself, even though I damn well shouldn't have to.

"You sent Alexi after Tristan."

He blinks, and I take advantage of the brief moment of distraction to pull away and stagger further into the closet, putting as much distance between us that I can.

"You told that whore to fuck my boyfriend, and then you took photo evidence as proof. For what? So you could get off on having both of us as your little pawns?"

"No." He shrugs the insinuation off, his expression cold. "I sent Alexi to Tristan to find out what he knew. Your father had been coy on his role in their little scheme. As it turns out, I had a damn good reason to be suspicious."

"My… My father?"

It doesn't make sense. There are too many strings composing this twisted web. I can't make heads or tails of it.

Domino advances a step, clenching his hands into fists at his sides. I can practically feel his restraint, causing a shift in the atmosphere like a building storm cloud just before the rain breaks loose.

"He was growing paranoid, Ada. Restless. A wild beast is always the most dangerous when it's cornered. When it feels its life is on the line. By that point, it will resort to any option it can to free itself. Like using its daughter as a pawn to throw off suspicion for its connection to a potential crime spree."

It's my turn to blink, caught off guard by the word choice.

"What are you even talking about?"

He scoffs. "Silly little Ada. Of course, you wouldn't take time from your shopping to educate yourself on something as trivial as your father being openly linked by the media to a sex trafficking ring."

I swallow hard, bristling at the disgust in his tone. "My father was about to be indicted for some silly hit and run," I say. "They didn't even have strong evidence against him. He was just being set up to take the fall so his enemies could run roughshod over his reputation."

I'm parroting exactly what my father told me—what he ranted and raved about for the last month before this mess even began. He needed me to use Tristan as a way into the prosecutor's case, though he wasn't assigned to it. Somehow, he still knew enough information to make those shitty, unmemorable nights with him worth it to my father. Enough that he kept pushing me to meet with him.

And maybe, I liked the attention. I liked knowing that, despite having someone as beautiful as Alexi to screw around with, he still desired me—even if it was because of my proximity to my father. I still won.

It's so silly now to think about that. I feel my cheeks flame, and I almost miss Domino's reaction to that statement. Rather than look shocked or satisfied that I at least knew something about the case, he frowns.

"What was the man's name?"

"What?"

"The man who died, what was his name?" He makes his tone flat, speaking deliberately slow.

"I don't know. Some jogger, I think—"

"Some jogger." He laughs, raking a hand through his dark hair. "Try some businessman that authorities had been trailing for six months as part of a sting operation to catch the ringleader of a sex trafficking ring that stretches from

Terra Rodea to halfway across the country. That man dies and so does the investigation and the only link they had to finding a mastermind. Unless they could put pressure on the suspect who might have wanted that man dead, even if they had flimsy fucking evidence."

"My father?"

"*Bingo*, as they say, Ada-Maria. I know you rarely left that mansion of yours, but I would think you'd have access to the internet, at least."

"What does that have to do with me?"

"Think." He takes another step, and I hit my shoulder on a shelf in my haste to retreat. As the wall meets my back, I realize that I'm trapped. There's nowhere left to go. "Who stands to benefit if you happened to be kidnapped —let alone murdered—in a violent raid on some fancy restaurant? Maybe the man desperate to prove to the police and the world that he isn't connected to the same ring that might have stolen his only daughter? It's a sloppy plan, but desperate times call for desperate measures, Ada. Tell me that I don't have to spell it out for you."

"You're lying," I snap. And I have plenty of reason to doubt him, stemming from his own cruel attempts at manipulating me. Besides, I remember something else from the night I was taken. "The indictment was being called off. Tristan told me. They weren't going to make an arrest."

Domino's brows knit together with a swiftness that makes me suspect he didn't know that tidbit of information. Just when I start to believe that might be true, he shrugs.

"I wonder what else did Tristan tell you? That he was fucking multiple other women? That he was working with your father behind your back? That you were just a steppingstone on his own ambitious career path?"

"And maybe I should have appreciated him more," I croak. "Because he at least pretended to give a damn about me. Which is more than I can say for you. You want me to be worried that I ruined your little plan, Domino? Well, I'm not. You've yet to prove that you're any better than the hell you claim awaits me. A hell you sold me to—"

"Sir?" The quiet voice, paired with a delicate series of knocks on the door, seems so out of place amid this tension that I lose my train of thought.

Raising his voice, Domino heads into the bedroom. "Yes, Ines?"

"Mr. Jaguar will arrive tomorrow afternoon," she says. "I will make the necessary arrangements."

"Thank you." Domino waits until her soft steps retreat down the hall before he turns to me, snatching my wrist.

"You doubt me? Well, now you'll get to see firsthand if you've made the right choice or not. Don't you realize?" He yanks me to him, staring me down with eyes like fire. "I can't protect you this time, Ada-Maria."

"This time?" I echo hoarsely. "When have you ever protected me? Even once?"

He slams his free hand against my jaw with barely enough restraint to keep from hurting me. He merely forces my head to the side, inspecting me from this newer angle. It provides him the chance to lower his mouth to my ear without breaking eye contact.

"When have I protected you? From the second I set foot in that fucking house, my only focus *was* you."

He shoves me aside, and I trip, landing on my knee. As I scramble to regain my balance, I realize exactly how he got in.

One of the large, French-style windows is open, letting in the warm night air. He must have come through it. But why?

The easiest explanation is that he wanted to catch me off guard, but I think it's more than that, lurking in the reality that a man like him would have no problem breaking through my barriers. Easily.

The only reason he'd circumvent the more violent action is if he wanted to avoid making a scene—and exposing Alexi to his more ferocious nature.

God, I don't know why the thought stings. It's so stupid to take offense to his apparent awareness of her. She's his accomplice, after all.

"You never cared about me," I say, eyeing one of the many scrapes on my legs that prove that point. "I was an idiot to believe you'd ever keep your word."

"No," he growls, advancing toward me. "It's your turn to keep your word."

A rustling sound catches the air, and I brace for a blow. Instead, something lands against the floor within my reach. I have to blink just to make sure it's really here.

He must have had it on him all this time, at least during dinner. Pia's diary.

If Jaguar's impending visit has him on edge, then why choose now to bring up the past again?

Because he believes this will be his only chance, a concern that should definitely add strength to the "jaguar is no better than he is," column.

"You think Pia's at the house. Her house. Why?"

"It was a guess—"

"You're not that naïve, Ada," he snarls. "Neither am I."

He appears before me, crouched on one knee, his expression like ice, each rugged feature etched in stone. "Give me a reason to believe there might be something in that empty skull of yours worth salvaging."

I can't escape the feeling that he's proposing the dare like a test. Make him value me. Give him something worth saving. Cower and beg.

"You never knew her very well," I say, matching his soft tone. "Your sister. Because if you did, you wouldn't seem so puzzled by the breadcrumb trail she left behind. That's what she did, Domino. She kept secrets. She fed on lies."

"And you seemed to have learned plenty from her." He stands, crossing his arms, staring down at me with a glare so piercing I go numb in the face of it. "You're more selfish than I gave you credit for. Too fucking spoiled to even consider what might be for your own fucking good."

"So tell me, then," I counter, jutting my chin. "Stop dancing around in circles and just tell me what kind of danger I'm in. Tell me the truth about everything—"

"The truth?" He inclines his head sharply, his eyes narrowing to slits. "The truth, Ada-Maria, is that Jaguar doesn't see you as some worthless pawn through which he can control your father. That's just a bonus. He sees you as…"

"What?" I demand, unnerved by how his voice deepens and his eyes take on a faraway gleam. It's as if he's staring a million years into the past, rooted here by sheer force of will.

"Jaguar sees you as a way to get to me," he says. "And he'll do that however he can. He'll hurt you. Violate you. Anything he can think of to keep me in line."

He doesn't sound like he's lying, but I can't square that description of me with a man who's done all those things to me himself. Hurt. Violate. Anything he can think of. A part of me questions if it's just jealousy that has him so on edge. Even so, I'm not sure if I'm brave enough to be at the mercy of someone else.

"Who is he to you?"

He stiffens, his teeth gritted. Again, he tears his hand through his hair, turning his back to me as he starts to pace. "He is… No one," he declares, looking down on me from over his shoulder. "No one that will interest you, anyway. But congratulations, Ada-Maria, you've gotten your wish—someone seeks to use you beyond just getting to your father. Congratulations. I can't save you this time."

CHAPTER FIFTEEN

"You have a funny definition of that word. Saving," I point out, too exhausted to take offense. In so many ways, this man is a stranger in comparison to the steady, comforting presence I've known him as for the past five years—at the same time, he's terrifyingly familiar. His secretive, manipulative ways and penchant for brutality remind me of someone I knew better than anyone else on the planet.

My father. Domino picked up way more from his time with "Don Roy" than he seems to realize. They're utterly the same.

"It seems like *you've* gotten your wish," I counter, bracing my hand against the floor in an attempt to rise to my feet. "Jaguar gets to hurt me, torture me. Whether with you or with him, it looks like I only have agony to look forward to—"

"I am nothing like him," he growls, his voice rippling like thunder, and yet still low enough that I doubt he penetrates the walls of this room, even with the window open. He turns on his heel and yanks me to my feet, capturing my chin with one hand. "I'll give you something he never would, Ada. Mercy—" Roughly, he scrapes the hair back from my face, leaving nothing in the way of his gaze meeting mine. "You want my protection now? Then beg me for it."

I'd laugh if he didn't sound and look so damn serious. There's no hint of amusement glinting in those disarming eyes, no mocking in his tone.

"I'd rather die."

"That can be arranged," he says without an ounce of hesitation. His fingers twitch as if to reinforce the dark intent glinting in his eyes. He'd have no problem at all "arranging" that ending for me—but only on his terms. "Fortunately for you, I still need you before then, and Jaguar won't be so accommodating. Beg me to help you like a good girl," he coaxes in a gritty baritone. Using his grip on my chin, he manipulates my head so that his mouth is near my ear again. "Use those sweet words and that sexy little pout. Tell me that I'm all you ever wanted. Spin those little lies about how I earned your gratitude forever just by dragging you off a fucking highway. Make me believe it, little Ada. Lie sweetly about how much you need me, and maybe I'll be convinced."

I can't even put into words how much it hurts to have him mock me like this. It's comparable to having a rusty, filthy nail puncture wound that never fully healed over and over again.

I could deny I ever gave a damn about him. Spit in his face. Lie.

Instead, I strain his grasp until I'm staring directly into his eyes. "I wanted the person I thought you were; I have no shame in admitting that," I confess, feeling my upper lip pull back from my teeth. I'll get nothing out of sinking down to his level, but I don't care. It feels strangely good to speak this openly to him. Damn mind games and verbal tricks. "I wanted the Domino I considered brave and honorable. I would have given that man anything. My body. My heart. My soul. You can laugh at me for that if you want. Joke and make taunts. That doesn't matter. The truth is still this—you never had to brutalize me, Domino. You could have told me anything, and I would have believed you. You didn't need Alexi to get to Tristan. I would have told you whatever you wanted to know. I could have been yours with so much less effort, and if you played your cards right, you would have never needed to spin a lie for Jaguar or anyone else. Wholeheartedly, I would have trusted you. That makes *you* the fool, not me."

His eyes darken as he processes that speech, and I expect him to scoff in disbelief. Deny it. Make another low dig at my expense.

Instead, he tilts his head thoughtfully as if giving serious consideration to every alleged claim. It's so surreal being on the receiving end of one of these appraising glances. Usually, he'd look at my father this way while trying to figure out how to best implement one of his many orders.

"Maybe you think you're telling the truth," he deduces finally, in a voice like sin. Hell itself. "Maybe... But it's my turn to let you know something, Ada-Maria." He strokes down to my throat and toys with my windpipe, applying varying amounts of pressure. Soft at first. Then harder. Harder... "Maybe I didn't want to be put on a pedestal based on your childish, unrealistic expectations. What if I wanted more than that? What if I needed to shatter your fantasy of me and make you squirm, see how you react under pressure, get to run that smart fucking mouth with no regard for the paparazzi or your daddy's wishes. What if I wanted to see you despair at your rock bottom to know if you were even wort—" He bites off the rest, and I can sense the tension in what he doesn't want to say.

"Worthy of what?" I demand.

He shoves me back so hard I go flying. Only the wall can break the momentum, and breathless, I brace my hands against it, struggling to get my bearings.

He advances on me slowly, sizing me up with a ruthless, raking glance. He comes toe to toe with me, palming the wall on either side of my body, using his weight as effectively as prison bars to keep me boxed in.

When his mouth finds my ear again, he bites down on the lobe. Hard.

"That you were worthy of being the only woman on my fucking mind for the past five years."

My throat goes dry, thoughts utterly blank. This man doesn't sound like Domino, or even the monster I've been faced with since coming here. No, he is a new creature entirely, one who radiates possession in every single word ripped from his throat.

"That you were worthy of having me wonder what you taste like. What you fucking smell like. I've obsessed over this body, Ada-Maria. What I would have you wear when you were mine. How I would bathe you. Fuck you. Command you. I've imagined a million goddamn times how that ass would feel in the palms of my hands. The look on your face when you finally realized you were mine. Always mine, meant to be claimed since the moment I first saw you in Don Roy's office. Or maybe I just like toying with you," he adds in a guttural rasp, bringing one of his hands to my throat. Cold, his eyes spear through me, as violently as that blade he carries. "Maybe I like seeing that fragile, pathetic hope bubble in your eyes that you might be something more than the warm, wet hole Roy Pavalos could pimp out to further his own aims. You make it so fucking easy."

I gasp. Or maybe it's a sob? By now, I should be so accustomed to his mind games that nothing he said could ever hurt me. But it does.

He does. And his nostrils flare as if savoring the scent of that pain.

"In fact, I could just tell you everything," he adds. "You wouldn't even know what to believe or not. Like maybe I do remember that night on the road, Ada-Maria. I remember how fucking angry I was to see you there. I could have wrapped my hands around your throat then and there, and your papa would be none the wiser. What if I always sensed you beyond the trees at night? I could smell you on the wind even if I never saw you… Or hell, maybe I was the one watching *you*, following Don Roy's orders to an extent, but everything beyond that was of my own volition. I'd see you with those men, hunt you down while you were alone with them. Sneak a glimpse of you in any way that I could and memorize every inch of that body. You'd never know the fucking difference."

He's right, and my head is spinning, trying to keep up with his many twisted narratives. The only way to salvage what little sanity I have left is to close my eyes, blocking him out.

The second I do, he applies more pressure to the hand he has around my neck. Enough to make my eyes bulge, my lids springing open again.

"You were always mine, Ada-Maria. You just never realized it. You still don't—not the lengths I will go through to keep you mine. The harm I will do to any man who dares to defile you. Take you. Harm you. You looked at your fantasy Domino with childish love once, but frankly, Ada, you have no idea what that concept means. None. Love is agony, you see. It is cruel obsession. It leaves no choice in whether you want it or not. It is all-consuming. So when I tell you to beg me to keep you, I want you to realize that you already have. Just by listening to me now with that hungry look on your face. Just by humoring the feel of my body next to yours and letting me shove my tongue inside of that greedy pussy. From day one, you've been begging."

He strokes my cheek in a motion that feels cruelly gentle. Then he tilts my head and lowers his mouth to mine.

The kiss catches me off guard, firm and possessive.

My thoughts scatter, common sense far beyond my reach—so it's entirely out of reflex that I sink my teeth into his tongue. Rather than recoil, he grunts, leaning into the motion, making it a part of the kiss itself. I taste blood as he sucks at me. Devours me.

Somehow, I release him, knowing I need to break away. Push him off. Run.

His hands are already gliding down my hips, drawing me into him. I'm breathless when our lips finally pull apart, but he's the one in control of the action, blood smeared across his lower lip.

"I don't need to hear it," he reiterates gruffly, in between heavy pants. "But I want to—beg me to protect you."

I use both hands to push against his chest, but he doesn't budge. "Go to hell."

"Gladly." He pushes back, forcing my hands aside as he brings his mouth within inches of my own. "I'll meet you there. Because what we are, Ada? It sure ain't heavenly." He runs his thumb across my mouth, thrusting it between my lips without warning. "It's sinful."

I spit him out and contemplate slapping him again. Instead, I say, "We aren't anything, and I'll never beg you for a damn thing. Except to let me go."

"And you might get your wish." His expression shifts, becoming even more indecipherable than I'm used to. He is all shadow and gold. "You are an expensive woman to keep, far more than you know."

He lets that cryptic phrase hang in the air as he turns away, his shoulders rigid. "It would be easier to let him have you. Far better in the long run. And you…" He looks back at me, his eyes dark and shadowed. "You're so good at fucking pretending, you wouldn't even notice, would you? If he were touching you instead of me—" He's back, dragging me against him no matter how violently I resist. My nails dig into his forearms, and I kick, wincing as the sores on my feet throb at full force. He's unmovable, easily able to maneuver me away from the wall, across the room. "You wouldn't care if he were fucking you. You'd make those little noises, and bite your lip and ride him as though he were a fucking king—" He shoves me back, and I land on the box spring, gaping up at him as he looms above. "Can you even tell the difference, Ada-Maria? Between the cock of a bastard you despise, and the one of the man who worships this little body from the inside out?"

His hands land on my thighs, applying enough force to flatten them against the box spring. My heart starts to race, my throat suddenly dry. His shift in tone is giving me whiplash. Emotionless one minute, dark and gritted the next…

"Can you even tell the difference between pleasure and pain?" He crouches, running one of his hands along my thigh.

I kick at him, attempting to clamp my knees together. He drags them apart, pulling me to the edge of the bed so that my legs are on either side of him, perched against his hips.

"Can you tell the difference between fucking a man who doesn't give a damn about you and one who craves every fucking inch of your body?"

Yes, a part of me whispers, pairing the way Tristan would touch me to…

"I used to imagine it," he tells me, holding my legs captive. "Having you at my mercy like this. Mine alone."

My only mode to attack him is to rear up and lash at his chest, nails drawn. Every blow, he withstands without flinching. When I aim for his face next, he hooks his fingers around the back of my skull, wrenching me toward him. As a result, I'm forced almost onto my knees, chest pressed against him as he claims my mouth again.

This time, I don't go down without a fight. I bite, scratching at any inch of exposed skin. He groans, swallowing each attempt at aggression. Like he's getting off on it all. My fight. My hate. The fact that there's nowhere I can go.

He has me, body and soul. Not by choice.

He's too strong, his lips like fire, lashing me open and igniting any flesh he comes in contact with. Against my will, I groan for him, letting him eagerly drink down the sound.

Then I remember my senses and bite him again, so hard he pulls back.

"I will never be yours," I hiss, startled by the intensity in my own voice. "So sell me if you want to. You can't hurt me."

No more than he already has, at least.

He makes a low sound in the back of his throat as he shoves me down. This time, he mounts me after, pinning my limbs to the bed, all while distributing his weight so as to not hurt me. A part of me marvels at that, though I can't tell if it's actual concern on his part.

Or merely so he has easy access to snatch a fistful of my skirt and drag it up over my waist.

"I *can* hurt you," he clarifies, and the look in his eye bolsters that warning. "But I can also give you more pleasure than any other man. You know that. Just in case, I should refresh your memory..."

He lunges, using one hand to pry my legs apart for his mouth to assault me again. Somehow, I'm still sensitive from the first time, and the shock of his warm lips nudging me apart renders me senseless. For one pathetic, brutal, beautiful second, I forget how much I should hate him, and I merely relent to the overwhelming wave of sensation he arouses with just one brush of his tongue.

And a thrust.

And another.

Another…

My back arches as my nails scrape at the unyielding material beneath me. Even it isn't a sturdy enough anchor. Desperate, I reach for something stronger and find it in the form of silk attached to a firm surface.

A "surface" that growls when I flex my nails against it. Hurting him is my only form of retaliation as he torments me with every stroke of his tongue.

The orgasm I can feel building coils in my stomach, growing stronger and stronger until I'm swallowed by it.

"Jesus Christ," he hisses as I writhe, my body convulsing.

I think the whiplash is too much, even for him. He rises onto his knees, his lips glistening, gaze seeking out mine.

I'm still gasping for air when I realize what he's doing—not retreating, just wrenching his pants down his legs, freeing a cock that stabs proudly at the air, already fully erect.

I think I try to say something. Refuse. Mock him. Deny him.

Any sound dies in my throat as he guides my legs apart, entering me with one swift thrust.

I take him deeper than I can stand. So deep my head rears back, and I swear I can feel him forcing his way up my throat. There's nothing gentle about the way he takes me.

He grinds with his hips, forcing his cock into my furthest depths with a boldness no one has ever dared utilize before. Like he truly believes what he said—he owns me. He's studied me. He knows me.

And all I can do is take every inch he has to give.

CHAPTER SIXTEEN

I hate the feeling of his breath on my breasts. Even if I don't move to escape the punishing bursts of heat, I hate it. I hate how he holds me after, like he didn't just insult me moments ago. Like the feel of my body in his arms is enough to please a man like him.

Someone so violent, so vicious.

I despise the way he can lull me into a false sense of security before I even realize it. Only when his nostrils flare, and his brows furrow do I remember where we are. Who I am.

And what he's done.

"What are you doing?" I ask him in a whisper.

That simple question flips a switch in him. "My Ada," he growls, shoving me from his chest as he rolls onto his side, putting his back to me. "Still begging."

I don't bother to deny him. I'm too tired. I merely lie back, looking up at the ceiling and count the many ways I've let him regain the upper hand again.

On second thought, denying him is the only modicum of power I have left. Still, not in the outright sense of the word. It's more subtle than that, lurking in all the things he hasn't said just yet.

"Why *Domino?*" I ask of the darkness surrounding us, so thick I can only see the outline of his muscular back, ghosted by a hint of pale light coming in through the windows. "Why that name?"

It's so long before he so much as sighs in response. I think he won't reply at all.

"Because Navid Inglecias is dead," he says, startling me.

At first, I think literally—that he's revealing yet another twist to this wicked plot he's set into motion. Then I realize that he would sound far smugger if that were the case.

Not…exhausted.

"He died of a congenital heart condition," he adds. "The poor bastard."

"Why pick Domino?" I ask, though I'm not sure why I'm even curious. His origin means nothing as it relates to my ultimate fate. One he seems resigned to.

"If you were listening closely, Ada, I think you might be able to put the pieces together all by yourself."

I bristle at the brush-off. Then I remember a name he mentioned once. *Domin… Domingas.*

"Carlos Domingas," I say. "Did you pick the name as an homage to him?"

"Again, you prove that you are nowhere near as dumb as you pretend to be," he says.

A compliment? "I don't think even Don Roy made that connection."

I can see how the name would appeal to someone like him. He could rub his true allegiance in the face of his enemy from the start. Considering how long my father kept him around, maybe he never made the connection at all.

"What about Valenciaga?"

I expect that he won't answer directly or spin another riddle at my expense.

"My mother…"

Something in my chest gives way, startling me at the intensity of the emotion. Is this sympathy? When applied to him, I can't tell.

I don't remember Mrs. Inglecias much. Just that she was a kind, beautiful woman with dark hair and warm brown eyes. Pia spoke of her rarely, but I got the sense she respected her in a way I never would my own mother.

"Her mother's maiden name," he adds, his voice gruff. "An obscure enough distinction to hopefully go unnoticed by Roy Pavalos."

He put a lot of thought into this, I realize. He had to in order to go five years undetected. The level of depth is mind-blowing, especially when I consider the trajectory of my life during the same amount of time. I lived in my parents' home, on my father's dime, and I implicitly trusted any man he brought into our orbit. Before now, if I had been forced to guess which of my father's associates would have betrayed him, Domino would have been at the very bottom of the list. I would have never imagined he could be Navid, either. Namely for one reason.

"Your heart? How did you afford it?" I ask, rolling on my side. The box spring isn't as forgiving as the mattress would be, and the material protests in grating creaks with every movement.

He sighs. "I'll humor you, Ada-Maria. Would you like the long version or the short?"

I'm surprisingly curious to hear any ounce of information he'll give, but I'm not foolish enough to waste his amicable mood on one story.

"Short," I say, to play it safe and hope he hasn't grown bored of me yet.

"As a favor to my mother, a kind, mysterious benefactor gave it to me out of the goodness of his heart. How is that explanation?"

"A lie," I suspect. "No one does anything out of the goodness of their heart."

Not even him, apparently.

"I'll let you put the pieces together," he says, cryptic once again. "In the meantime, I suggest you shut that pretty mouth of yours, unless it's to beg."

Because Jaguar is coming tomorrow.

And I have no idea what that heralds for me.

I wake up to the sensation of warm sun on my back and the feeling of an empty bed, over which I'm lying lengthwise, my feet dangling off the edge. I know without having to open my eyes that Domino is gone.

Maybe I'm too fucking pathetic to check for myself. I don't need any confirmation to reinforce the coolness of the box spring beneath me or the lack of thick, brutal fingers raking through my hair.

And I can hear his voice…

Faint, it sounds like it's coming from beyond the room, but not in the direction of the hall. The closet?

"…be ready for me. I know it's earlier than we planned. Just be fucking ready. I have no idea what he'll do; just wait for my signal. *Gracias.*"

Curiosity alone spurs me to open my eyes, just in time to catch him storming from the closet, a cell phone in hand.

My gaze latches onto it for a second before my brain sleepily catches up, and I realize why the sight strikes me as so odd.

I've heard him on the phone, but I rarely see him with it. In fact, the last time Jaguar called, Ines brought the phone to *him*. He must be keeping it hidden somewhere beyond my reach.

Just in case, I decided to do the smart thing, like call for help or try to figure out where in the hell we actually are.

"Get up." He meets my gaze while stowing the phone in his pocket—a spot where I know for a fact that he doesn't keep the device regularly.

As if aware of me watching, he gathers the clothing scattered across the floor one item at a time.

"Go wash yourself and get dressed," he tells me, tugging at his collar. Today, it's buttoned all the way, the closest he's come to embodying the dress style he utilized while working for my family.

Is it merely coincidence that today happens to be the day Jaguar has made it known that he'll arrive? I'm not bold enough to jump to that conclusion. Yet.

Instead, I scramble to my feet, still naked. I catch his eyes raking over me, and I note that they gleam as coldly as his tone. It's a subtle, but disarming change from his relaxed mood last night. Once again, I have whiplash at how volatile he can be. Calm, like a sheet of ice one minute, and blazing the next to rival the most intense inferno.

Staggering to my feet, I slip past him, eagerly darting into the closet. I can't escape the tension weighing down the atmosphere. I can taste the unease. The dread.

In so many ways, it reminds me of those brief moments when my father would be away on business, right before his return. The faint smile my mother would sport in his absence would fade, and the servants would become frantic, ensuring every little detail was in place.

On second thought, it's not exactly the same. Jaguar inspires something in Domino that not even my father seemed to. In the presence of Roy, he was always the stoic bodyguard, despite his supposed hatred of us from the very beginning.

But when it comes to Jaguar, or Julian, there is no ounce of restraint that I can sense. He's shamelessly angry, uncaring of who sees it.

As hilarious as a comparison it might be, in my head, I'm bold enough to make it. When it comes to Jaguar, Domino reminds me of…

Well, me. Trapped in a world, he has no clue of how to escape. All he can do is go through the motions and loathe every minute of it.

But therein lies a murkier set of questions that I'm not even sure I want to toy with speculating on. My father had twenty-five years to break me down and mold me into the creature I've become. In essence, that time has numbed me to all of the vile things he's made me do. Some of them, anyway.

But what has Jaguar made Domino do to garner such hatred? For the past five years, he's spent nearly every waking moment in Terra Rodea? Does their feud stem from before that, maybe around the time he received his mysterious transplant?

I'll let you put the pieces together, he said last night. I thought it was a cruel jab at first, but now I can parse over all of the other little breadcrumbs he's let slip. Once, he told me that he owes a debt that can't be paid with paper money—only blood.

How did he put it? *An eye for an eye. A tooth for a tooth.*

A heart for a heart.

I brush my fingers along my chest and realize I'm shaking, even before my newest suspicion has fully taken hold. Could Jaguar's interest in me go beyond sex? He bought my "body," but in the literal sense…

"I told you to get dressed."

I turn, startled by the sight of him still here. His gaze flits over me, dark and unreadable. Any other moment, I don't think I'd be brave enough to provoke him so early.

But, as it turns out, I might not have much time left to find answers of my own.

"You sold me," I croak, hating the raw pain in my voice—and the fear. "Be honest. You didn't sell me to some sex dungeon, did you?"

"I don't follow," he replies.

"Did you sell my…b-body. You said you owed Jaguar more than money. Did he find your heart? And now you've promised him a new one."

He laughs, and I blink at the sound; it's rich. Almost as real as the one he displayed with Alexi. As he chuckles, he enters the closet again, and my own heart stutters.

"You think I've sold your body parts on some transplant black market? That's too creative, Ada-Maria, even for me."

"So then clarify it and stop dancing around the truth."

His eyes cut to slits. "I sold you to be fucked and tossed from buyer to buyer. Use your imagination to fill in the gaps." He might as well be referring to an animal. Or a bug. Something he deems beneath the need for empathy.

An object.

I don't know which ultimate ending would be worse, to be honest. To be used for sex or sliced to pieces. Either way, it's obvious that he doesn't give a damn.

"Maybe you should wrap me with a bow," I whisper, feeling so helpless… I could scream. "Then I'll be ready either way."

"I'd tie the bow around your neck," he suggests. "*Then* you would be ready either way. Now get dressed."

He stalks past me and snatches a dress from a hanger. Then he reenters the main room and approaches the makeshift barricade still blocking the door. With graceful ease, he shoves the mattress aside and pushes the wardrobe back to its usual spot.

Opening the door, he leads the way into the hall and into the bathroom. Then he runs the water in the tub, and when he reaches for me, I can tell from the set of his shoulders that he expects me to run or put up a fight.

I don't do either, letting him drag me into the water with no resistance.

I submit to the surprisingly warm—not scalding—bath and barely pay him any attention as he retreats to the other end of the room.

I'm too busy dwelling on the current state of my life. In retrospect, could I have ever expected to end up any differently? Still a pawn of my father's, despite what Domino claims. It's hate for Roy Pavalos that darkens his gaze every time he looks at me.

"You have that look," Domino scolds, reappearing with a towel that he places on the floor, a rag, and a bar of soap. Sinking into a crouch, he dips the rag into the water and works it into a lather. "That pining, kicked-puppy look that warns Ada-Maria hasn't gotten her way."

"I'm not in the mood for jokes," I say absently, staring straight ahead even as I feel the water swish as a result of his ministrations. "I'm thinking of how sad your life must be. Five years. All this effort, and my father is hooked up to a machine keeping him alive, and I'm 'at your mercy.' And yet, you don't seem very happy, Domino. You could have done so much more rather than gain so little. All in the name of revenge."

"How many times do I have to say it?"

A gasp catches in my throat as the warmth of the rag strokes over my chest, guided by his hand. He makes the motion brusque on purpose, I suspect. I've seen men wash a car with more care.

"This was always about more than just you or your father."

I finally look at him. He's hunched over the tub, seemingly intent on dragging the cloth down over my belly before moving to the part of my thigh exposed above the water's surface.

"Then why work so hard to infiltrate us?" I demand. I sound angrier than I have the energy to feel. If he did it all for no reason, then that makes him less dangerous mastermind and more… Callous, sloppily cruel for no reason. "Why arrange for my mother to be killed. Why—"

"I'll tell you a story, Ada-Maria." He tosses the rag aside and braces his hands against the rim of the tub. "A story about a stupid, poor boy with a broken heart who made a deal with the devil because he believed life was worth living, enough to fight for it, no matter the cost. Then he quickly realized what men like Roy Pavalos take for granted. Some bargains aren't worth the price you wind up paying. Life, as wonderful as it may be, isn't worth selling your soul to maintain, and sometimes the consequences for hunting down wealth and power, no matter the cost, can be heftier than anyone is willing to pay. You may sob for your father, all while forgetting the hell he put countless other people through. The dozens of papas and mamas he stole, the families and lives he ruined. And yet, as twisted as he may be, Ada-Maria, he is but a tiny cog in the wheel of evil men who keep this cruel world turning. I suggest you dry your tears, because this is only the beginning."

I am crying, though I didn't even realize. It's like my eyes have been so overworked these past few days; they drip without any warning or input from my brain, painting warm trails down my cheeks.

I try to garner any meaning that I can from his little story— that my father is just one in a long line of men he plans to ruin? A part of me doesn't care, and doesn't want to waste any more time trying to understand the complexities of Domino Valenciaga. It's the same impulse that used to drive me to drugs—a vicious need to ignore my life and current surroundings no matter the cost.

I embrace it now, putting everything else out of my mind but a desire for quiet. I ignore him, leaning back to wet my hair beneath the water. Then I submerge myself fully beneath the surface, drowning out the world. And him.

He's still speaking, I realize, as a rumble of syllables reaches me, distorted by the water. I contemplate ignoring him, using that as an excuse to stay under, long past the moment my lungs start screaming for air, and the blood rushes through my skull…

Finally, I sit up again, gulping for breath.

But he's still speaking, unperturbed by my interruption. "…and what if this boy made a bargain without knowing there was a price to pay at first," he says softly. "He merely wanted to live and cease being a burden to those who loved him. He lived his borrowed life like a good soldier, staying within the confines of his new identity. But then he realized that it's suffocating as hell being forced to live a life you never asked for. You start to believe that you'll do anything to escape it. Kill anyone. But everything in life comes with a price, one that must be paid."

I'm holding my breath again. He sounds different than before. I suspect this story is less hypothetical than he led me to believe, and I scramble to listen, inspecting every word and the picture they paint. Domino believes himself to be that boy, I think. He made a deal with the devil —Jaguar?

And now he's paying the price.

"So to cancel your debt, you sacrifice me?" I ask him, gathering the nerve to meet his gaze. I expect to find the same bold, mocking man I've been battling with all morning, poised to deliver an insult at my expense.

"No."

The figure I'm faced with now is a man I've almost forgotten he used to be these past few days. The stoic, cold Domino Valenciaga with a wealth of secrets hidden behind that searching stare. Even without the aid of his cowboy hat, his mystery returns in full force—and I can't escape the feeling that I'm only seeing a fraction of the real danger he's thrust me into. Only what he wants me to see.

"No, Ada-Maria." He plunges his hand beneath the water's surface, skirting my parted legs, to withdraw the rag. Deliberately, he takes time wringing out every drop of moisture from it. "You haven't been paying attention. If selling your cunt could save the world, Tristan Lucas would be a very happy, very alive, and very wealthy man. You have value only to the right people. The right kind of men."

I'm more frustrated than ever. It feels like he's spinning me around and around, taking immense satisfaction in watching me squirm and question. He loves keeping me blind and off-balance.

What's the point of even attempting to resist him? Why not give him exactly what he wants?

"I want you to protect me," I ask him directly. "I'm asking you to."

I expect him to grin evilly over the prospect of me pleading for help. Instead, he frowns, his eyes narrowing.

"I was wrong," he says, rising to his feet. "Begging doesn't look good on you. Get up."

I obey, letting him dry me off and dress me in the outfit he procured from the closet—a black dress with spaghetti straps and a neckline low enough to rival Alexi's.

I wonder where she is. Has she left now that Jaguar is arriving? Was she the one who called him in the first place?

"I'm sorry if I caused a rift between you and your little friend," I say, as he withdraws from me and heads for the hall.

"Don't be." The look he shoots over his shoulder is eerily calm. Composed. Too composed when paired with his rage from last night. "You did exactly what was expected of you."

He leaves without grunting out a command, and I don't race to follow him. Damn the smug bastard. He has my head spinning again. Just what was he hinting at? That he knew I would lose my cool around Alexi and blow up his little plan? Then why tell me to keep quiet in the first place?

Because he's lying, obviously. He didn't plan this, or he wouldn't have been on the phone earlier, confessing to a change in timeline. But that just brings up the bigger question of what exactly he is planning.

And why.

I must lose track of time, because the next time I startle to awareness, my hair is nearly dry, and Ines is standing in the doorway to the bathroom.

"Mr. Domino requests you join him for lunch," she says with a respectful nod. "He is on the terrace."

My heart pulses as I move to obey, entering the circular foyer to find that it's mid-morning already, if not the early afternoon. Domino is lounging alone this time, a platter of food on the table nearby.

I square my shoulders before stepping out from the archway, prepared to do battle yet again.

Instead, he gestures to the seat across from him. "Eat."

It's strange how he's broken down the one bastion of control I've ever maintained in my life. Hunger has always been a beast of my own making, always at my discretion for how gnawing it could become before I'd finally give into it.

Around him, hunger means nothing but a tool with which he can use to escalate any standoff to his advantage.

So I sit and snatch something from the tray at random, bringing it to my lips. I chew woodenly, holding his gaze for as long as I dare. When I finally look away, I hear the cushions of his lounger creak beneath his weight as if he shifted his position.

"Alexi was a pawn brought in by Jaguar to help me navigate the more delicate intricacies of the Terra Rodea social scene."

In other words, to fuck the men in my orbit.

"Why are you telling me this now?" I ask, glancing at him again.

He leans forward, staring past me, his expression harder than ever. "She fed me intel and kept me updated on the whereabouts of Tristan Lucas, but that was as far as our relationship extended. I never fucked her."

There's no inflection in his voice, and I can't tell if he's lying or telling the truth. All I can do is reiterate, "Why tell me this now?"

"Because Alexi belongs to Jaguar," he says coldly. "She always has. Everything she does, she reports back to him. I don't know what he has over her, so in some ways, I can't blame her. But you need to keep that in mind the next time you get the urge to run your mouth because I've pissed you off. Beyond your father's fancy mansion, everyone belongs to someone, Ada. The world is a patchwork of alliances and rivalries, and I suggest you think long and hard about who you align yourself with."

"How would someone like Alexi wind up with someone like Jaguar?" I ask.

He raises an eyebrow. I've surprised him, I think, but only because he seems to believe the question is too obvious to humor. "Why else?" He snatches a piece of fruit from the platter and takes a bite. Its juices paint his lips red as he declares, "People will do anything for love, or for revenge."

Is that his way of telling me that Alexi's motives stem back to what happened ten years ago? On the one hand, it sounds ridiculous. On the other...

After seeing the lengths Domino himself has gone through in the name of vengeance, I can't count out anything anymore.

"What does that mean? You alone can help me? Pardon me if I'm skeptical of that."

"You can be skeptical," he warns, taking another bite of fruit. "And still be smart. Tonight, you'll need to make a choice."

"You? So you can spin more riddles and torment me with even more mind games?"

"So I can find my sister's body," he counters in a tone so serious it catches me off guard. "And so you can tell me what really happened to her and stop using the missing pages of a diary as an excuse to feign ignorance. I want the truth from you. I'd prefer if you cooperate, but even if you decide to jump on Jaguar's cock tonight, know that I will still have you."

"Because you own me?" I ask softly, rephrasing the same claim he made against Alexi when it comes to Jaguar.

"No." Finished with his meal, he licks his fingertips clean. "Because you are not as stupid as you look. Sooner or later, you'll come crawling to me, and this time your begging won't be for show."

He thumbs my cheek and stands, wiping his hands on his pants.

"I'll be gone until tonight. Play nice, and I suggest you don't get tempted to go running into the desert again, either."

"Where are you going?" It's a bold question, one he humors with merely a raised eyebrow instead of an outburst of rage.

"A place where naughty girls, daughters of a monster like Roy Pavalos, can't follow. Ines will keep an eye on you, so don't get any ideas."

He strolls past me, entering the house, and I somehow can sense the exact moment he leaves. The tension in the air lessens, and I can breathe easier.

But in his absence, that ominous feeling from before only grows.

Jaguar is coming, and despite Domino's word games, I'm not sure what it means. Something bad, my intuition warns. I would be a fool to sit around and wait patiently for my impending doom to be handed to me on a silver platter.

I rise and enter the house, surprised to find no one wandering the spacious halls. Not Ines, or even Alexi. Is the blond still here? I can't sense her presence the way I can Domino's.

When I enter his room, however, I don't find her twisted in the sheets. His bed is still neatly made, which makes sense considering he slept with me. I'll parse over that glaring lack of judgment later. For now, I set my sights on the one task I should have been fixated on from the very start.

Finding answers.

I inspect the closet first, retracing my steps to the same duffle where I found the vial of Lorazepam and the explicit photos. Do I believe him when he claims to have never touched her? Of course not, though it doesn't matter now.

The side pocket is empty, the photos gone.

Of course, he wouldn't leave me with anything more than the breadcrumbs he deems worthy of taunting me with. I know this entire search is in vain, but I can't stop myself from scanning every shelf, inspecting them in more detail.

The clothing stands out to me, the more I inspect each garment. In fact, the female clothing outnumbers his. I'd be tempted to suspect he has some sort of secret fetish for wearing it himself, if the sizing wasn't skewed so small that I doubt he could fit a single thigh where the waist is meant to go.

Something I heard him say comes back to me, uttered in a tone so gruff and deep that I suck in a breath just reliving it.

I've obsessed over this body, Ada-Maria. What I would have you wear when you were mine.

I'd almost believe it… That he bought these with me in mind, my body, his tastes. If it weren't for the glaring fact that Alexi is the exact same size, along with most of the women in Terra Rodea. How many has he plied and captured before sending to Jaguar?

I let the resentment build, giving me the strength to keep searching, hunting for anything out of place, merely out of pure spite. I rummage sloppily through the hangers so that he'll know I was here, touching his clothing. His shirts. His pants. I toy with the material, noting its quality but also how new it all seems. Which makes sense—after dropping the Domino persona, he would need all new clothing with which to embody his freed self. A man who harbors more secrets than any man should have the right to.

And every step of the way, he'll only feed me pieces at a time, at his discretion. He must get off on my confusion, more than even my pain. I bet it makes him feel powerful to exert so much control over me, thinking he can anticipate my every move.

And if I were a smug bastard like him, I'd gloat over my captive's supposed innocence. I'd take joy in hiding snippets of information right under her nose, and I would relish in watching her squirm.

Whether by accident or subconsciously. I'm near that black duffle again. This time, I unzip the main compartment, even though it was empty initially when I first found the things he planted for me.

This time, it's not.

Inside is a neatly folded set of clothes. A passport. A wad of coiled cash. Underwear—*women's* underwear…

The clothing, too—a black sweater and light wash jeans—are far too small to fit Domino Valenciaga. Could they be Alexi's?

I bring the bag to the watch cabinet and remove each item one by one. The first observation that takes my breath away is, when I open the passport, Alexi's picture isn't the one I find inside.

Though, the name reads Alicia Garcia, I vaguely recognize the woman in the stern-faced passport photo. Her hair is a dark brown, the same length as mine, her eyes listed as gray, her height listed as five foot, five inches…

She looks like me. The photo could be one of me, in fact, though altered with darker hair. When I eye the clothing again, a dull sense of dread begins to build in my gut. While the right size to fit Alexi, they'd also fit me. The style is much more practical than a flimsy, revealing dress should I decide to go "wandering in the desert again," as Domino taunted. Or for another reason entirely.

Like maybe he plans to let me go. Take me back to Terra Rodea and refuse to sell me after all? Hope is an insidious impulse, flaring before I can counter it.

A more likely explanation is that this is what he plans on shipping me off to Jaguar wearing. Why not make his job easier?

Angrily, I tug my dress over my head and throw it to the floor before pulling on the sweater and jeans. I take the passport and stuff it into one pocket, sliding the wad of cash into the other.

Now I'm truly ready to play my role—a toy to be bought and sold.

I exit the closet and eye myself in the mirror, trying to use this act of disobedience to distract from the growing fear, warning that, despite all of Domino's taunts about Jaguar, I still have no idea what to expect. The only name I have to go on is *La Guarida Del Tigre*—a place filled with men even more despicable than he is, I assume. Hell.

By the time I finally leave and reenter the hall, my shoulders slump with the weight of the impending visit. Jaguar's arrival feels more like an execution date, when I'll finally find out my sentence. Death? Or something far worse?

In a daze, I make my way into the white room and stare from the windows watching the day slowly slip away as the sunlight darkens, turning golden. I don't know what causes it—this imperceptible tensing of my muscles and a quickening of my heartbeat. A part of me is on alert even before I hear the telltale thud of a door opening and closing and a raised, masculine voice ring out.

When soft, shuffling footsteps approach my door, I'm already lurching to my feet just as Ines appears in the doorway, her head bowed.

"Mr. Jaguar is here, Miss," she says softly. "He requests that you join him on the terrace."

I notice that she doesn't mention one other figure by name, and I can't suppress the urge to ask, "And... Domino?"

She shakes her head, but if I'm not mistaken, a hint of alarm flits across her brown eyes before disappearing just as quickly. "Mr. Domino is not back," she says.

But I sense there's so much more lurking behind those ominous words. That gnawing unease chills me to the core as I stand and make my way through the house, bathed in the ochre light of sunset.

I hear him before I see him, a man with a booming voice that echoes loudly from the direction of the terrace.

"...So I came a little early," he says, presumably into a phone given that I don't hear anyone reply. "Don't worry, I'm sure your little birdy tipped you off the second she saw me coming. Just take your time out on your little errand, Dom-Dom. I'm in no rush. In fact, it looks like I'll just have to find a way to entertain Ada-Maria all by myself. See ya when I see ya, little brother."

He's standing at the balcony, eyeing me with a wink from over his shoulder. When faced in the full light of day without the shadows of Domino's bedroom to obscure him, the man is imposingly tall, built seemingly from the same mold as his "little brother." Muscle strains against the back of his thin white tee shirt that he wears paired with jeans. The tattoo covering nearly the full length of his left arm is on stark display—a predatory feline with dark fur, crouched among jungle leaves. I can't help but notice that its hungry glare resembles that of the man spinning to face me, his lips parted in a sly, disarming grin.

"You must be, Ada-Maria." His brown eyes size me up with a sweeping glance, lingering over my breasts, barely visible beneath the sweater's relatively modest neckline. I'm already sweating, feeling the jeans cling to my legs uncomfortably. Perhaps it wasn't so smart to try provoking Domino while having to face the brunt of the sweltering sun.

At the same time, some vain part of me is grateful for the extra fabric as a barrier against Jaguar's scrutiny.

He has an aura so different from Domino's—an all-encompassing swagger that instantly transforms this remote domain from an isolated paradise into a realm firmly under his control. He holds himself as though he owns the place, snapping his fingers to command Ines, who appears on cue.

"Bring us some wine," he says, dismissing her with a wave of his hand. "The good stuff. I know little Dom-Dom wouldn't want to be stingy when it comes to serving his guests."

As she retreats, his piercing eyes return to me, his smile even wider. "Shall we?"

He inclines his head, beckoning me to follow him to the terrace's second level. There, a familiar blond lounges on one of the white couches wearing a black string bikini. Her gaze is unreadable as she watches our approach, but when she turns to face Jaguar, I note that the angle is far different from how she'd contort herself before Domino.

She's not letting her breasts spill out, but bearing her throat in a gesture of subtle submission. My mother looked at my father the same way. Like she'd die for him.

And at the same time…

Like he had a knife to her throat, ready to slice should her expression convey anything different. I learned in my early childhood that slender line between love and devotion. And oppression.

"Baby, why don't you take a walk around the property. I need to talk to Miss Ada-Maria alone."

Alexi's simpering smirk falls flat. "But you just got here—"

"What the hell did I say?" His inflection never changed; merely his expression did. A hardness set into his mouth, and his eyes seem even darker.

Without another word, Alexi lurches to her feet and takes off toward the gardens.

"Have a seat, Ada." Jaguar claims Alexi's former couch, sprawling out with his arms braced along the top of the chair on either side. He nods toward the space beside him.

Instead, I pivot and take the couch across from him. His eyes narrow to slits, but his smile doesn't budge, remaining a fixture on his face even as his gaze takes on a more calculating focus.

"I think I prefer you naked," he remarks with a bluntness that sets my cheeks on fire. He eyes my chest with open disapproval and sighs. "Dom-Dom must prefer to keep you covered while he's away. What a damn shame. When we get you to the *Guarida,* that will change, I can tell you that."

"The *Guarida.*" The word tastes heavy on my tongue, lacking the musical quality his accent gives it. "Is that where…"

I find that I can't finish that sentence out loud. *Where I've been sold to.*

"It seems our little Dom-Dom has been more forthcoming with you than he's led on." He leans forward, stroking his fingers through my hair without warning. It takes everything I have in me not to flinch, submitting to his coarse touch. "All for the better, though. I don't enjoy breaking in the new girls myself, but I'm up for a challenge. I'll give you a little crash course, even. The *Guarida* is my paradise, you see. A world where the trappings of society and the silly rules some stuffy men in suits decide for us cease to matter. It is freedom."

He runs his fingers along the underside of my chin, raising goosebumps. A part of me reacts to his touch in a way I've never responded to anyone—not even Domino. It's electric. The closest feeling I can compare it to is what I felt around my father's guard dogs. Rumor had it that he trained them with live animals, and they were always on a hair-trigger, taught to heed only his command.

Jaguar has that same look in his eye. Like all he wants to do is bite. Attack. Brutalize.

Only I doubt he'd heed any other man's commands to stop.

"You are very beautiful," he tells me. "I'll give Domino that much." He sits back and gestures toward his lap with a wave of his hand. "We should get to know each other more. Come sit with me."

It's not a request. Knowledge of that spurs me to my feet despite every warning blaring at the back of my mind to put as much distance between us as possible. I aim to play it safe, meaning to perch myself on the very edge of his couch.

He snags my wrist before I can, dragging me toward him. His smile remains as he wrenches me down, and he doesn't stop until I trip and land almost entirely on his lap.

"There. This is much better." He hooks his fingers around my ass, yanking me forward so that I'm straddling him, much like I did Domino not too long ago.

But this position feels nothing like that. There's no fragile familiarity, despite the animosity between us. With Jaguar, I'm on edge, painfully aware of the strength coiled in the muscle flexing against me.

"I can't wait until we become more acquainted," he murmurs, his gaze on my lips.

Maybe it's because I'm pathetic enough to admit that I wanted Domino for years before he took me. I fantasized about every inch of his body, and a part of me will always fight that attraction.

But with Jaguar…

My body can't get past the danger radiating off him in waves. It takes me a moment to identify it, but I stiffen the second I do—rage. It's far different from the lethal anger that explodes from Domino, barely restrained. Jaguar's hostility is far more nuanced, lurking beneath the planes of this handsome face, smoldering behind the dark irises.

"You have sexy fucking eyes," he says with an intensity that makes me jump. I've been so focused on observing him, that I didn't pay much notice to the fact that he's been doing the same to me. "Like you're thinking hard. I like that." He grazes my cheek with the pad of his thumb, brushing the hair from my face. "Plenty of men will pay extra to enjoy a girl who seems like she has a brain in her head while she's sucking his cock."

I grit my teeth, feeling my cheeks flame as I look away at the sun sinking into the horizon. Domino wasn't coy about this place and what would happen to me there, but still…

It's one thing to hear him taunt me like it's a game. It's another thing entirely to listen to a man state it so plainly. He's not exaggerating to manipulate me to conform to his twisted plans. He's being honest, and I think I should be grateful for that.

No more mind games to navigate.

Just a minefield.

"I'm surprised he told you," Jaguar muses, still petting me with the tips of his fingers. "Our little Dom-Dom never sent me a girl before."

He chuckles when I flinch and cups my jaw, guiding me to face him.

"Oh yes," he says, frowning. "You're his very first. Domino has always looked down on my little enterprise, you see. Acted as though he was too good to care for the girls, and guide them toward a better life. Until you, Ada-Maria Pavalos. Though it sure as hell seems that he got his money's worth out of you, first."

He strokes the edge of a scabbed cut on my forehead disapprovingly.

"Though if you could please a stuck-up, prudish motherfucker like little Dom-Dom, then you must be worth every fucking penny."

He slides his free hand beneath my sweater, ghosting the flat of my belly.

Given the number of unwanted touches I've had to endure from various men throughout my life, he should be no different. It should be easy to simper and smile and arch into his calloused palm the way I have so many times before.

I jerk back instead, nearly falling off his lap entirely. Domino's voice explodes in my head, grated and guttural—*I'll rip you to pieces if you even let him look at your body.*

It's instinctive. I can't help it.

But Jaguar's eyes gleam as he withdraws his hand, and I sense that I've made a terrible mistake. My first impulse is to relax against him, forcing my muscles to contort. Then speak, anything to distract him.

"H-How… How do you know Domino?"

His frown deepens. "He hasn't trained you," he remarks softly as if he's speaking to himself more than me. He strokes his hand along my cheek again, and I sense whatever irritation my reaction aroused in him diminish slightly. "At least the bastard did one thing right," he says. "He saved the best part for me. I should teach you the basics now, baby." His thumb finds my lips, grazing the seam between them. "You don't speak unless I give you permission. Understood?"

I swallow hard, but he must mistake the jerking motion for a nod because he chuckles and leans back, his posture softening.

"But if it's about our little Dom-Dom, I'm an open book. Ask me what you want."

I hesitate, sensing a loaded weapon more than a kind gesture. He's testing me, probing in his own, cautious way —so different from Domino's doublespeak and intimidation tactics. Jaguar is far more predatory, patiently setting a trap in plain sight.

If only I knew what might trigger it.

"Don't be shy now," he scolds, batting my cheek with his knuckles. "I won't bite. For now."

The ominous feeling grows, but it's not like I have a better option. It takes me just a split second to weigh the risk.

No matter what Jaguar does, I have nothing left to lose.

"Who is he to you?" I ask him, making my voice as soft and non-threatening as I can.

The demureness must please him because he tilts his head thoughtfully and shrugs. "Dom-Dom is my brother," he says. "Family is important to me, you see. There is no stronger loyalty than blood ties. Nothing."

I choke down the urge to ask the most obvious question. Instead, I take another tack.

"You seem so different," I croak in what I hope passes for an amicable purr.

He laughs, flashing a mouth full of blindingly white teeth. "You're smart as well as sexy. You don't need to share a womb or have the same sire to be brothers," he says cryptically. "Those bonds lurk in pieces of us you can never erase. If I were to fuck you here and now, plant my seed in that sexy little body. My child would make you mine in a way you could never escape. *Both* of you would be my family. Forever and always."

His voice is musical enough that even the most horrific imagery lacks the necessary impact. Only the intensity of his gaze gives the boast the edge of a threat. A promise.

My heart is pounding so hard I can taste blood reverberating through my tongue. I feel like my chest will explode, but rather than arrange for medical attention, he'd just fuck me in the gaping hole. I can see the intention in him, so clearly, my entire body goes cold. Paralyzed.

Then he blinks, and his smile widens, displacing any hint of malice.

"You know, Ada-Maria, I will admit that I had you all wrong. The way Dom-Dom spoke about you, I thought you were a dumb little cunt. He made you sound like a puppy on your daddy's tight leash—" he taps the tip of my nose playfully and chuckles. "I knew he always wanted to fuck you, though. Dom-Dom isn't subtle when he's being greedy. Selfish. I'm surprised he waited until recently. He *did*, didn't he?"

Whatever my expression must tell him makes him nod in agreement.

"He waited five long years to stick his cock in that tight little cunt. I think he's a… What's the word? Masochist? He gets off on control or some shit." He flattens his palm against my jawline, eyeing me more closely. "I was never as patient as he was. When I want something, I just take it. To be fair, most women want me just as quickly."

His grip tightens, urging me toward him, and I panic, blurting the first thing that comes to mind.

"Alexi. H-How do you know—"

I see stars and taste blood for real. When the world comes back into focus, I'm hunched over the cushions beside Jaguar, eyeing a strange series of red splotches speckling the white fabric. Then I press my hand to my lower lip and realize why.

He hit me.

"Remember, Ada," he says, almost gently. Like a teacher trying to enforce the rules of his classroom. "You speak only when I tell you to. I suggest you try to pick up on that rule quickly. We don't believe in second chances at the *Guarida*. You strive for excellence, but I see it now..." He grabs my chin, turning me back to him. I'm bleeding freely, not that he seems to care as the drops of scarlet drip down onto his shirt. "Those cucks are gonna bust a nut for a girl like you. Sassy and bold, but still obedient. None of that overly mouthy shit."

He means it, I realize with abject horror. To him, those vile terms are compliments. Virtues he prizes.

"I'm sure Dom-Dom has had plenty of fun with you. On second thought, I might keep you a little bit rougher around the edges than I typically like. I can see the appeal in it. And now I'm even more curious as to what other talents you might have. I heard from Lexi-Lex that Dom-Dom has a preference for bitches who give good head."

I fight to keep my expression clear. I honestly don't know if I fail or succeed, but somehow I manage not to hiss in disgust out loud. Does it hurt me that he lied so easily to my face—yet again?

Yes. God, yes, it does. It's a rusty knife stabbing through my chest, striking the one open wound on my psyche that Domino Valenciaga seems to enjoy poking. Vanity and jealousy.

He fucked Alexi. Or Jaguar seems to believe so.

"Hmmm." He makes the low sound in the back of his throat, drawing my attention to him. One look at his face, and I realize that once again, I've made a mistake.

If only I knew how.

"He's claimed you," Jaguar says, drawing out the word to convey a meaning that goes completely over my head. Something that surprises him. And irritates. His eyes gleam, turning inward as if he's processing some internal puzzle that's been on his mind for a while. Finally, he's able to solve it, but the resolution leaves him frowning, his brows furrowed. "He's told you that you were the only woman he's been fucking. Hasn't he?"

I blink, more confused than ever.

Somehow, Jaguar seems able to glean an answer, and he purses his lips, an eyebrow raised.

"Dom, Dom, Dom." His voice deepens with every iteration of the name, ending in a growl. "That's not very friendly, is it? Promising you to me and then wiping his dick all over you, marking his territory and planting dangerous lies inside that pretty little head. It makes me question his integrity, you see," he says, but his voice is raised, his anger palpable. "How can we have a fair trade if someone is already poisoning the merchandise? I've been good," he adds, stroking my cheek again, but he's rough, straining my tender lip until my eyes water. "I've upheld his little feud against Roy Pavalos. I've supplied him with my resources. I've kept our family business running in the background. By my fucking self, mind you, while Dom-Dom was off playing toy soldier and wiping your daddy's ass."

He grabs my throat, curling his fingers around my windpipe with just enough pressure so that I feel my flesh graze his palm with every breath I take.

"I always had his back," he continues, regaining his composure. Now he sounds eerily calm, almost monotone. The way Domino used to while carrying out my father's orders, no matter how heinous. "Always. Because family means something to me. Honor means something to me. Promises, Ada-Maria… They mean something to me. I wouldn't take for myself that which I already pledged to another man. It's just not fucking polite."

He's implying something. Something dealing with whatever issues lurk between him and Domino, but I can't keep up. Fear floods my veins slowly as the pain in my lip sets in. The cool casualness with which he uses violence shocks me, and I don't think part of my brain has still registered the blow. There's something impulsive and wild about his rage. He can smile while making someone bleed and never miss a beat.

"I always knew he had a soft spot for you, though," he muses, still smoothing back my hair, his expression contemplative. "The things we initially planned to do to you…" He chuckles darkly, and my breath catches in my throat. "But then little Dom-Dom kept changing his mind, always moving the goal post. I thought, at first, that he just wanted you for himself, but now I think I can see what he was really after. I can tell just by looking into your eyes, that you aren't like my Lexi-Lex—good for fucking, but not much else. No… I think you're a little smarter than that, Ada-Maria. Smart enough to know at least some of your daddy's secrets. And if I were a selfish bastard of a man, looking to betray his only family… I would desperately want to know those secrets." As he speaks, he lets his fingers crawl up to my scalp, sinking into my hair to graze the tender flesh beneath. Slowly, he starts to squeeze from both sides. "I have to wonder what lies our precious Dom-Dom has been putting into your head. Or what answers he's been trying to beat out of you—"

I think of Pia and his obsession with the past. Her body.

Jaguar grunts, letting his hands still. "You won't be a mean girl and try to keep anything from me, would you?" he wonders softly, his smile widening into a beautiful, chilling mask. "Because then we can't be friends if you deceive me, Ada-Maria. And that, you see, would be a damn fucking shame—" Abruptly, he cuts his eyes to something behind me, and his posture shifts, becoming defensive as he moves his hands to my waist, utilizing them like lead weights to keep me pinned against him. "It's about damn time," he snaps, and from the corner of my eye, I see Ines scramble to place a bottle of wine and two glasses on the low table behind me.

Jaguar snaps his fingers, his gaze cold. "Pour it." To me, he flashes another icy smile. "Ines here has served my family for decades. She practically raised my little brother and me modeling what I thought was the perfect example of loyalty and honor. But then, Ines made her choice. She chose against me, the man who saw her as family, the closest thing to a mother he ever knew." He speaks in such a level tone that the anger conveyed by those words is only visible in his eyes which glint more dangerously than before. "I suggest you think more carefully than dear Ines, Ada-Maria. I would very much like to be your friend—" Cutting his gaze back to the old woman, he snaps, "Leave us. Though, I'm sure you stalled long enough to ensure that your master is well on his way. I guess that doesn't leave myself and Miss Ada-Maria long to get acquainted, then."

He leans forward, jostling my body against his chest, to snatch a filled wine glass from the table. Rather than drink from it himself, he brings the rim to my mouth, and his expression loses all shred of feigned cheer. He's stern, inspecting me carefully. "Drink."

I don't hesitate, slurping right from the edge of the glass.

As I swallow, he stares me down so intently my heart races, my palms sweating. It's like he's waiting for something. A reaction?

When he's seemingly waited long enough, he sits back, satisfied.

"I hope you weren't fooled by Ines' subservient act. She's a wonderful actress, but she is no shrinking violet. In fact, I'm sure she's been filling our Dom-Dom's head with devious little ideas from the start. I wouldn't put poison past him —" He nods to the wine. "How he loves to spike drinks, I'm sure he's been drugging you while you've been here, dulling your senses to make you more susceptible to whatever he demands. We do the same at the *Guarida,* mind you," he adds, "but at least you'll be well accustomed to it."

It's getting harder to hide my disgust. The worst part is that he's right. All those times I woke up dazed, feeling high. I assumed he'd injected me somehow whenever I was asleep, but now I can see how he could have drugged my wine all along.

"Drink up," Jaguar commands, tilting the glass toward me again.

I have no choice but to take another sip, analyzing every drop that floods my tongue for a trace of anything out of the ordinary. All I taste is a damn fine vintage, and when he seems convinced that I'm not poisoned, Jaguar takes his own sip.

"Dom-Dom isn't like the rest of us," he continues, laughing softly. "He has a much higher tolerance to most benzos, opiates, and the like. It would take a hefty amount to down someone like him. I'm sure he told you all about his tragic backstory."

He waits as if prompting me to agree. When I don't, he laughs. "Well, it seems our little Dom-Dom is more shy than I would have thought. Especially with someone I would assume might be a kindred spirit."

Every muscle in my body goes rigid. Is this his way of hinting that he knows about my attempt to inject Domino with a taste of his own medicine? I can't tell if he's merely speaking to hear himself talk, or testing me purposefully to gauge my responses—and I don't dare ask him to clarify.

In the resulting silence, he takes another sip and sets the glass aside. Then he sighs.

"Alas, our private fun has been cut short," he says. "Though, now more than ever, I'm looking forward to seeing exactly what you have to offer. You'll make a fine addition to the club, isn't that right little brother?" He raises his voice, seemingly for the benefit of the figure who comes storming across the terrace from the direction of the house.

I turn just in time to see him reach our level of the terrace, dark hair flying out behind him, hands in fists.

CHAPTER NINETEEN

"Brother!" With a jovial laugh, Jaguar nudges me from his lap and raises his arms. "Nice of you to join us—"

"You show up unannounced, *twice*," Domino growls. His expression is iron, every single muscle rigid. Only his eyes reveal any emotion, flashing angrily. "I suggest you try not to make a habit of it. One might think that you didn't trust me, *brother*."

"And one might think that you've been having way too much fun with Miss Ada-Maria here."

As I scramble from the couch, Jaguar's hand flies up, smacking my ass. Hard.

I can't silence a gasp, but by the time it leaves my lips, my wrist is seized in an iron grip. Brutally, I'm wrenched to my feet and shoved behind Domino.

"Relax," Jaguar taunts, his smile unshaken. "We were just having a nice little conversation before you interrupted. About the rules of my *Guarida* and what will be expected of her there."

"You hit her." He must spy the blood on Jaguar's shirt, because he turns, grabbing my jaw, tilting it for his inspection. His nostrils flare as he eyes my lip, and I can't even begin to process the reaction flitting across his gaze.

"I was teaching her," Jaguar corrects, his tone playful. "And I can tell that, despite as much as you've been fucking her, you haven't been training her much. It's a good thing, then, that I'm more than willing to take over from here."

Domino's brows knit together as he releases me. "I have until Tuesday," he says. "That gives me three more days."

"If I were feeling generous, that is," Jaguar says. In the blink of an eye, he transforms. Gone is the mocking grin as he lurches to his feet. Practically toe to toe with Domino, it's apparent that they're similar in height and bulk, but each man carries his strength in drastically different ways. Jaguar is lean, light on his feet, reminding me of his feline namesake, while Domino resembles a wall of stone, immovable and rigid.

"I think I'm done giving you more playtime," Jaguar adds, stroking his chin as his smile returns. "Yes… I think I'll take her back with me tonight and get well acquainted with Ada-Maria myself. Maybe I'll learn if it's her pussy or her mouth that has you so whipped. I'm willing to try both."

"Are you going back on your word, Julian?" Domino demands, his voice colder than I've ever heard it. I find myself instinctively inching back a step, and for a good reason.

At the sound of that name, Jaguar inclines his head, his lip quirking downward. "Anything I promised you beforehand is invalid," he says. "Considering that you've been lying to my fucking face from the very start. What have you told her, huh? And why are you so damn fixated on keeping her? It couldn't be because you're planning on taking her for yourself, right from under my nose?"

These past few days, I've become so accustomed to reading Domino's every nuanced expression, that I think it's the only reason why I catch the flicker of alarm that crosses his features.

Apparently, so does Jaguar because he laughs. "Don't look so surprised, Dom-Dom." Turning on his heel, he strolls for the balcony. "You may have your own network of spies and allies, but so do I. Some of the people who you think are in your corner have always been squarely in mine. I've known for months that you've been planning and squirreling away your money and assets where you think I won't see it. You've been clever," he admits, gripping the railing. "Very, very clever. But not clever enough. You see, Dom-Dom, you can't outsmart me. I am always one step ahead, and the next time I catch wind of you plotting behind my back, I'll come back here and run a knife through Ines' throat and use her blood to water your pretty little flowers. I fucking dare you to try me."

"You're bluffing." Domino scoffs as he barks out a laugh of his own. "Always taking shots in the fucking dark. Your paranoia will be your downfall, Julian. So eager to find a hint of betrayal. If you thought I was dealing behind your back, you wouldn't come here with open arms to sunbathe on the fucking terrace."

"You're right." Suddenly serious, Jaguar turns around, his eyes glinting with a calculating gleam. "I'd set this place on fire with you inside that pretty little house, and I'd use the screams of you, and all of your traitor staff, as the soundtrack to a nice barbeque I'd hold right here on your so-called terrace."

He doesn't look relieved of his suspicions. If anything, his raised eyebrow conveys irritation, as if he'd been confident of a win only to have his power play foiled.

Because, in this game of verbal poker, Domino has an unshakable poker face. I can't get a read on him either way, and I realize that all those years playing toady for my father paid off to his benefit. He's mastered the art of deflection.

Deep down, some sick part of me might be impressed before I remember that neither of these men has my best interest at heart. If anything, I sense that I'm some kind of toy being yanked back and forth between the two of them in a twisted game of tug of war. Who will win? I honestly can't decide which victor I prefer.

"Fine." Jaguar throws his hands into the air, his grin firmly in place once more. "You win. Why don't you tell Ines to find us something to eat, and we can discuss our differences like men, over dinner."

"Ines!" Without taking his eyes from Jaguar, Domino waits until the woman appears dutifully near the entrance to the house.

"Yes, sir?"

"Have cook prepare us some tapas and serve them in the dining room."

Jaguar claps as she scurries away. "Wonderful! After you."

"As you wish." Domino snatches my wrist before heading inside. I scramble to keep up with him, noting the slight changes to his appearance that I missed. He's wearing jeans —the first time I think I've seen him in such casual attire since he brought me here. His hair is windswept and wild, his shirt a plain gray tee shirt that betrays the tension coiled in his muscles. He looks…

Tired. Like he raced here, not expecting Jaguar to arrive so soon—a surprise I think the other planned for that very reason. He wanted to both unnerve him and catch him off guard. And he primarily wanted to speak to me alone.

I shudder at the potential reasons why, and decide to fixate on the only damn thing worth contemplating now. How the hell can I escape both men? Despite all of Domino's taunts about what awaits me in Jaguar's domain, meeting the man firsthand has cemented that I don't want to find out. My throbbing lip is warning enough—Jaguar's *Guarida* will make my time here, with him, seem like paradise and the thought of that utterly hollows me.

I go numb, reduced to staring blankly at the surface of the glass dining table as Domino shoves me into a seat beside him. Surprisingly, Jaguar takes one directly across from us without comment. Though I sense his gaze on me continuously, noting every little thing down to how many breaths I take.

Within minutes, Ines scrambles in, carrying a tray of tapas that she places on the table's center along with a fresh bottle of wine and more glasses.

I reach for one, desperate for something to dull the fear I'm barely able to keep at bay. My fingers have just grazed the goblet when I see a shift of movement in my peripheral vision. Domino. If I'm not mistaken, he shook his head. *Don't.*

"I don't think I'm very thirsty," Jaguar declares as I withdraw my hand.

If his refusal foils some plan of Domino's, I can't tell. His expression is more guarded than I can recall, even from his days at my father's side.

"Where is Alexi?" he asks. "I would have thought you'd want to spend your time getting reacquainted with her."

"Lexi-Lex, is taking a walk," Jaguar says dismissively. "Let's talk about Ada-Maria instead, shall we? As smooth a talker as you may be, Dom, I don't think you need three extra days. In fact, given the state of her, who knows if you'll lose control and render her unconscious for another week. I want her in the *Guarida* safe and sound tonight. If money is what you want, I'll pay whatever you think she's worth. If it's the sex you'll miss, I'll leave Lex here to satisfy any need you may have—bondage included."

"I don't think she'll like that very much," Domino counters.

Jaguar chuckles, shaking his head. "She'll like whatever the fuck I tell her to. Unlike you, I know how to handle my women. If I tell my Lex to walk, talk, and act like Ada-Maria here, I doubt you'll be able to tell the difference. Unless her sexy little pout isn't the *only* thing you want her for."

"You promised me three days," Domino repeats. "I want what I'm owed."

"And you promised me that I could have Ada-Maria Pavalos in exchange for my assistance arranging a hit—albeit a sloppy one—on Don Roy. Do you realize how precarious a position it places me in? To go against a man so revered in our circle? Many, many of my enemies might assume I'm vulnerable and see it as a time to strike."

"You wouldn't have done it if you didn't like the *position* it left you in," Domino replies, his head cocked, brows furrowed. "Right at the top of the pecking order. If anyone dares go against you now, they risk getting the same treatment. No one will take that risk."

"Not even you?" When his question is met with only silence, Jaguar sighs. "I don't like fighting with you, Dom-

Dom. No two brothers should ever let something as trivial as pussy come in between them."

I stiffen when I realize he's referring to me. The sick part? I don't think he intends it as an insult. To him, that's all I am —a hole to be bought and sold.

But does Domino see me the same? God, I hate that I still can't get a read on him. I'm tempted to reach for the wine again and drain the whole bottle. My nerves are so scattered, my pulse racing. I feel my fingers twitch for my glass, but this time a firm, unmistakable pressure lands on my knee. His hand. The touch alone conveys his meaning —*do not drink.*

I let my hand fall to the table, and this time Jaguar tracks the movement, his eyes glittering with interest.

"I hate to pull the rank card on you, Dom-Dom," he says. "Really, I do. But I am the leader of the *Guarida*, and if I say I want her tonight, then I'm going to fucking take her tonight—"

"Fine." Domino pushes back from the table and shrugs. "Take her."

My blood runs cold at his tone, paired with his disinterested expression. He means it.

But Jaguar, on the other hand, doesn't seem satisfied. "I have to admit that I'm skeptical of your sudden change of heart," he admits, his voice grated with a rare hint of open annoyance. "You wouldn't be up to your old tricks, now would you."

"No. I just hate hearing my leader beg me for pussy," Domino replies. "Take the bitch. I think she'll like being put on display for the bastards at your little den."

Jaguar raises an eyebrow. "Who said anything about putting her on display? Oh no, Dom-Dom…" He strokes his chin, drinking me in with his gaze. "I think I might keep her for myself. At least until I discover what it is that has you so damn enamored."

The hand on my knee grips tighter. Too tight. Wincing, I try my best to smother the pain.

"I never thought you'd want my sloppy seconds," Domino says in a tone that's the polar opposite of the violence I feel in his clenching grasp. He sounds unbothered to the point of boredom, his eyebrow cocked to match Jaguar's open skepticism. "I always assumed that my tastes in women were far different than yours."

"Pussy is pussy," Jaguar snaps. "And what's 'sloppy' between brothers? Perhaps we can initiate little Ada-Maria into the family? Then I wouldn't have to worry about you always trying to slip away, so desperate to gain your… What do you call it? Your freedom?"

"We are *not* brothers," Domino says coldly, and his unfazed mask cracks—violently. His eyes flash, conveying raw, open hatred so intense that I stiffen in the face of it.

"Oh yes, we are," Jaguar counters, his smile equally feral. "In every way that matters, my friend. You belong to me. You are my family, and if some blond little bitch will make you act like it, then we both can take turns fucking her all you like. One big happy *familia*—"

"Enough." Abruptly, Domino lurches to his feet and slams both hands flat against the table. For a second, I truly think he'll lunge across it.

If he fears the same, Jaguar doesn't seem frightened. If anything, he looks… Excited. Like he'd love more than anything for the chance to fight. Destroy. Make someone else bleed.

"I…" My weak argument dies in my throat before I can even voice it, but the sound I make has both men turning to me.

Domino looks furious, his knuckles whitening as he clenches both of his hands into fists. Jaguar, however, laughs.

"Enough fighting," he says softly. "I think I have a better idea of how to end this. Let's let the little minx decide for herself where she would like to spend the next three days. Here, with you? Or with me?"

I'm not stupid. He's not asking as much as he's warning. All that talk of alliances and training. If I don't pick him now, as far as I know, I'm still destined to arrive at his *Guarida* within a few days. And I suspect that if I dared to choose against him, he'd make me utterly regret that decision.

In fact, he's such the obvious choice in terms of self-preservation that it's laughable to even consider choosing Domino. He's already sold me to Jaguar and made it clear that his interest in preserving my life extends only to finding Pia's body and whatever secrets regarding my father he thinks I know the answer to. Trusting him at all would be foolish. Stupid. I'd deserve the inevitable betrayal he'll commit against me, and I wouldn't even have the benefit of being surprised by it. The man has made it clear that he owes me no loyalty, and—after what he's done—I certainly don't owe him a damn thing.

Even his promise to protect me was coded in his trademark doublespeak.

But…

Therein lies the dilemma. Domino is a known evil. I have some experience, no matter how thin, navigating his moods. I've even learned how to manipulate him in my fragile, pathetic way, but it's more knowledge than I have against Jaguar.

He is an unknown entity and one that I suspect I won't be able to survive so easily.

CHAPTER TWENTY

"Since when do you let your women call the shots?" Domino remarks nastily, and I realize why—he knows the conclusion I've come to, and exactly who I'll pick. Hell, haven't I been taunting him with that very reality all this time? I'd gladly fuck any man who isn't him and beg for the pleasure.

"Now, now," Jaguar scolds. "There is a first time for everything. After all, it's rude to discuss business so openly in front of the merchandise. Let's let Ada-Maria choose for herself." He turns his gaze on me, softening his expression in a way that reminds me of a parent asking a naughty child which choice of punishment she'd prefer. A beating or a whipping?

It was a choice I was presented with often in my early life—and one I quickly learned to master. A beating left bruises and marks that could ache all over my body. A whipping, at least, would be regulated to my back, and the results of which would be far easier to hide.

"Would you like to come with me tonight, and meet your new friends at the *Guarida* three days early, or stay here with dear old Dom?"

Once I hear it stated out loud and so bluntly, I don't hesitate. "Domino."

The silence that falls is beyond unsettling. Like a bomb has gone off, ending one battle in a long-fought war decidedly. The losing side conceals his anger behind a cold grin, but even the victor looks shaken. Far from triumphant, Domino is left frowning, his confusion so blatant that I start to fear it can't be for show.

I chose wrong.

"Fine." Jaguar rises to his feet and snatches a cracker covered in some kind of sauce from the tray. "She's made her choice, and I am a man of my word after all. Let's shake on it." He pops the cracker into his mouth and extends his hand, but when Domino starts to reach for it, he shakes his head and nods to me. "This bargain was between Ada-Maria and me," he says. "I can swallow my pride and let bygones be bygones."

Warily, I place my palm in his, and his fingers latch onto my wrist as his eyes stare dead into mine.

"It's nice to see which sides we're all on."

He moves his hand as if he means to initiate a handshake, but the movement is too sharp. Lateral, not up and down.

I hear an unnatural crack first, and I start to incline my head for the source.

Then I feel it—*pain!* White-hot, it lances up my arm, and I'm screaming, doubling over with the force of it. My vision goes white. Everything sparkles, like some horrible, twisted high where my brain forgot to interpret the pleasure I should be feeling.

God, it hurts. Everything hurts.

And then, all at once, sensation returns to my fingertips. They're on fire, burning so intently I can't move them. They just flop onto the table as Jaguar releases me.

"Three days," he shouts, but the blood rushing through my ears distorts his voice, muting the ringing baritone as if I'm hearing him from underwater.

And someone else, who sounds louder, more insistent.

"Hold it to your chest," he commands. "Breathe in through your mouth. Breathe, Ada. I know it fucking hurts! Listen to me—"

"My wrist… My wrist…" It's all I can say over and over on a broken loop. I'm on the floor, sitting amid a pile of broken glass, clutching my right hand to my chest.

Jaguar broke my wrist.

Somehow I wind up in a different room, with a familiar marble floor pressed against my cheek and my right arm extended in the air, doused beneath a rush of cool liquid.

My brain can only process what happens beyond the agony in bits and pieces. One, someone is standing over me, holding my arm aloft, and at a slight angle so that it's extended over the tub, with my wrist beneath the faucet. My fingers hang limply, like a limb on a broken doll.

"That sick motherfucker." The voice is Domino's, and he repeats that assessment over and over, uttered with a different inflection each time.

That sick motherfucker, hissed with disgust.

That sick motherfucker... This time with an unsteady note in his voice I'm not used to hearing. Fear?

"When I get my hands on that sick motherfucker, I'll kill him." He means every word, voicing them with a clarity I haven't heard from him since I woke up on the floor of this damn mansion.

Gone is the mocking hate, and the twisted innuendo.

He wants to kill Jaguar with every fiber of his being. Very, very badly.

"Why?" I croak, though I'm not sure what exactly I'm referring to.

Why is he crouched beside me, holding my broken wrist beneath running cold water with a care that shocks what little sliver of my brain is still fully functioning?

Why would he sell me to a man like Jaguar in the first place?

Why does he hate me so much?

Why? Why?

"Ines!" His raised voice echoes off the walls, answered within a heartbeat.

"I'm here, sir."

"I think the bastard broke her whole damn arm. She needs something strong enough to get her through the night if we want to make it out of the valley in time."

The urgency he speaks with leaves me dazed. *The valley?*

"There is enough for a decent dose," Ines replies quietly. "But, you should know that this is the last of your supply."

"Are you sure?" The tension in Domino's voice calls to some part of me that stirs in response. He's worried. "Fuck. I was planning to get some more today, but that bastard came too early."

"Apart from whatever you have on you, this is it," Ines insists. "Do you really want to use it now? It could be hard to find more once you leave."

"Shit…" Domino clenches his jaw, and from this angle, he looks conflicted and so beautiful I hate him for it.

"Sir, you could go into withdrawal—"

"Give it to her," he snaps with a nod.

"Alright."

I sense someone approach me from the left, but when I try to turn to see who, Domino tugs on my arm, forcing me to lay on my side or risk aggravating my wrist. Only this position keeps the pain at bay enough for me to think.

And though I can't see Ines grab my left arm and wrench up the sleeve of my sweater, I certainly feel the needle she jabs into the muscle a second later.

I scream in shock, but the sting has already eased, and I recognize the throbbing ache working its way down my deltoid. She drugged me.

"Did you make the arrangements like we planned?" Domino asks next.

"Yes, sir," Ines replies, sounding more distant, as if she's speaking from the doorway. "But…"

"You've known me long enough not to play coy," Domino says in the closest tone to scolding I've heard him use with her. "Spit it out. What aren't you saying?"

"You should go tonight. He took the other one with him, but I know Julian. He'll be back. You should go now—"

"I haven't secured your passport yet," Domino says over her. "Mateo is fucking me on the timeline—"

"Don't worry about me." Ines' voice rings out with a strength I'd never expect. Jaguar alluded that she practically raised him, but that she chose Domino. What does that mean? "You go now. You won't get another chance. I know you prefer to stick to your plans, but Julian is like his father. They are unpredictable. That is what makes them so dangerous."

"You know what he'll do to you if he realizes beforehand," Domino says. He releases my arm, setting it beside me. Then he shuts the water off and pivots to face Ines. "I won't have your death on my conscience."

"So damn noble," Ines says disapprovingly. "That's why you were always at a disadvantage with him. You hesitate where he wouldn't. I know the risk after three decades of working with the Domingas family. Better than you, I think."

"I don't know how I can repay you—"

"Go," Ines says, but it sounds as though she's commanding him for once. "Find your answers. And I suggest you think long and hard about what it is you do value. Because Julian will take pleasure in destroying it before you can even admit to yourself that you wanted it in the first place." Her tone softens, returning to her dutiful murmur. "The arrangements are made. I'll have Miguel bring the car around."

"Luckily, Ada-Maria already made one part easier," Domino says, but his tone conveys more irritation than admiration.

Without warning, he lifts me into his arms, carrying me into the hall so swiftly I can't keep up. The next thing I'm aware of is that we're passing through the circular foyer. Then another door I've seldom traveled through.

Suddenly, we're in the dark night air, bathed in the sweltering heat. I strain to pay attention, noting the front of the house illuminated by windows flooded with golden light. The paved walkway. A car with its headlights blaring like the red eyes of a beast, eager to swallow me whole.

The drug is kicking in so damn quickly. Ines must have given me one hell of a dose. It's like I blink, and I'm seated, leaning against a pane of glass as the world rushes before me, dark and endless.

Domino sits beside me, bathed in the faint bluish glow of a dashboard, his hands on the steering wheel.

"Where?" I ask with the last amount of strength I have left.

His answer comes as my vision fades to black.

"I'm taking you back to Terra Rodea."

BLOOD BOUND

Blood Bound

Blood Bound By Lana Sky

Copyright © 2021 by Lana Sky
All rights reserved.

No part of this publication may be reproduced, distributed, or transmitted in any form or by any means, including photocopying, recording, or other electronic or mechanical methods, without the prior written permission of the author.

This is a work of fiction. Names, characters, businesses, places, events and incidents are either the products of the author's imagination or used in a fictitious manner. Any resemblance to actual persons, living or dead, or actual events is purely coincidental.

Cover Design and Interior Formatting by Charity Chimni
Editing and Proofreading by Charity Chimni

CHAPTER ONE

I've never felt hatred like this before—it devours me. My head pounds, my vision blurred by tears. At the back of my mind, I know I'm being irrational.

Insane...

But all I can do is approach her in a way I never have, snatching a slender arm the second I'm close enough.

"Ada? What the hell?" She turns, fixing those green eyes in my direction. They blaze irritation and that smug confidence she always possessed. Like nothing in the world could ever hurt her.

And no one.

"Finally come to show your face?" She wrenches her arm away from me, her teeth bared in a snarl. "I know what you did, you little bitch. Though should I be surprised? You're just like them. Evil..."

The memory fades as I startle to awareness, unsure of where I am. All I know for sure is that I'm lying on something soft. A bed?

The air is so heavy, scented with an acrid stench reminiscent of beer. I think… The harder I try to get my bearings, the dizzier I feel. It's like I'm underwater. Every sound echoes, muddled and distorted.

Except for one.

"You shouldn't have come here." The hostile tone sends alarm shooting down my spine.

Something's wrong. What, exactly? I'm not sure.

I think I should be with someone…

"She needed medical attention," another man replies as if answering my unspoken question. His name comes to me with chilling recognition. *Domino.*

"And you did too, I suppose," the first man replies.

We must be in a room. I think I hear the whirl of a fan, and cool air teases my skin every few seconds, lessening the overall heat that has sweat dripping down my forehead. The voices sound nearby, but I don't see a thing. Belatedly, I realize my eyes are closed, too heavy to lift.

"I see the way you're shaking like a fucking leaf, Dom," the first speaker continues. "How long has it been, huh? You think you can go toe to toe with Jaguar while you're fighting through withdrawal? Spit it out and ask what you really want."

"Her arm. How bad is it?" Domino demands. I shiver as his voice runs through me. For once, it contained some vague emotion. Concern?

Her arm.

A wave of memories washes over me. *My wrist. Pain…*

"I set it," the man replies with a sigh. "She'll heal up fine enough. I might even have an extra brace around here somewhere. Now, let's talk about *you*. How much longer do you think you can go on without a dose?"

"I need you to keep an eye on Inez while I'm gone," Domino continues. "I mean it, Luis. If anything happens to her—"

"She knows the risks of going against Jaguar better than anyone. Hell, she practically raised the bastard."

"You think that will stop him from killing her if he gets the chance?"

"Of course not," Luis replies gruffly. "I'll see what I can do. But like I said, she knew the risks. The same risks that come with going off painkillers cold turkey without a backup supply."

A low sigh teases the air before Domino finally bites out, "So do you have any?"

"Not much," Luis admits. "Enough to get you over the border, at least. Can I ask what your plan is from there? Fuck around and hope that you can traipse through the city unnoticed with Ada Pavalos in tow? What?" he scoffs. "You think I didn't recognize the face that's plastered all over the news reports? If you want to buy yourself more time, I suggest you cut her hair, at least."

Domino's reply is muffled, as if he moved further away. I find myself straining to hear him. My eyelids twitch, but even that amount of movement is a struggle. More sweat drips down my forehead by the time I manage to pry open one eye enough to see through.

It's blindingly bright. Only snatches of my surroundings register. White walls. Yellow sunlight. A sputtering ceiling fan, and…

A shadowy figure who looms just out of sight, his silhouette chillingly familiar.

"She should be good for some light travel at least," the other man, Luis, continues. "But I suggest you get her to a doctor soon. Only a crazy motherfucker could cause that kind of a break with his bare hands. You really want to go up against that alone?"

"I…" As he speaks, Domino finally comes into view. He's pacing, his back to me, shoulders rippling with tension, straining the black shirt he wears. With a tilt of his head, his eyes cut in my direction. It's like I've been holding my breath, instinctively waiting for his acknowledgment.

Once I have it, my mind goes blank, unsure of how to process him. Friend?

Or foe.

"She's awake," he says, frowning. "Give her another dose. Enough to buy me a few more hours, at least."

Another dose of what? I attempt to speak—say anything—but I can't. All I can do is frantically try to meet his gaze, but he looks away. Almost as if he's deliberately avoiding eye contact.

"Don't you think you've put her through enough?"

"Trust me." His lips twist into a grimace. "She'll enjoy the ride."

"You haven't said what you're even after?" Another man appears at his shoulder, fumbling with a small glass vial. He's relatively short, with graying brown hair and piercing eyes gazing from behind wire-rimmed glasses. I don't recognize him, but I assume he's Luis.

"Breaking your cover after so long. Taking on Jaguar directly," he harrumphs. "You must have friends in powerful places. Rumor has it you've been working with the feds to cover your ass when Pavalos' little empire falls. I shouldn't have to be the one to tell you how fucking bad of an idea that is if true."

"Just get her ready."

"I will… But I hope you haven't forgotten the only reason I'm risking my neck for you in the first place. Because of Lia—"

"I haven't," Domino replies, advancing closer to me. Still frowning, he palms the side of my face, radiating an addictive warmth. "But don't forget *your* end of the bargain either."

"I've already secured a truck you can use, and my contact is ready to ferret you across. The only catch is that you'll be on a tight deadline. You need to reach him within two days, not a second later. Understood?"

"I just need to make one detour. Then I'll be there."

"And where would that be? Plan to go sightseeing before you catch a bullet in your skull? Oh, don't give me that look, Dom. I could have called Jaguar by now if I wanted to turn you in."

"North," Domino says cryptically.

"Through Mateo's territory? He won't like that."

"Which is why you won't inform him," Domino warns.

Luis shrugs. "Mind if I ask exactly how you plan on traveling anywhere with an injured woman in tow? Besides, what I can spare regarding your little problem will last you only a few days, at most. Then you'll have to find your own supply."

"All you need to worry about is making sure your contact holds up. As for the rest… Once I return to Terra Rodea, not even Jaguar can stand in my way."

He steps closer, and I try to speak. Move—anything—but I'm paralyzed as a sudden wave of exhaustion washes over me.

Was I drugged already?

A violent high could certainly explain the last thing I see as my lids flutter shut—Domino Valenciaga, looming above, the devil, ripped right from my nightmares.

WHEN I REGAIN CONSCIOUSNESS, I'm still floating in that dreamy state of awareness. Not awake. Not asleep. I hate this feeling. The stupidest things come back to me—memories that should have died a long time ago.

Like Pia…

Her face haunts me, ripped right from the last night I ever saw her, her blazing eyes fixed in a hateful glare.

"You're just like them," she hissed. *"Evil!"*

She lunged for me next, nail drawn. All I could do was throw out both hands, pushing back as hard as I could. The move was impulsive. Instinctual.

But the sickening thud that followed was way too loud. Too heavy.

You're evil, Ada…

Perhaps, we are; everyone cursed with the last name Pavalos. An insidious nature infects my father's bloodline, doomed to corrupt all who follow in his path. A Pavalos will do anything to survive—a tenet I embodied in every way—

until Domino Valenciaga weaponized that tried-and-true creed against me.

I remember now. Everything responsible for the pulsing anxiety building in my gut, at least. When given a choice between Domino and another monster, I was stupid enough to trust that, even for a second, he had my best interests at heart.

Perhaps it's a blessing in disguise that I'm too exhausted to face what I've done—not that I find much reprieve in unconsciousness. Sleep continues to come in broken fragments as the noisy, violent world beyond fights for my attention. One persistent sound rises above the rest, giving me some clue of where I am. Near a radio or a television broadcasting a news report:

"...politician Roy Pavalos is still hospitalized in critical condition, while a search is underway for his daughter Ada-Maria. Arriving at the Terra Rodea international airport early yesterday morning, Rodrigo Pavalos declined to comment on the status of either his brother or his deceased sister-in-law..."

Rodrigo? It's seconds before I finally make the connection—Rodrigo Pavalos—my uncle. I haven't seen him in years, but any hope I feel is immediately swallowed by horror. If he's in Terra Rodea, then it's further proof that at least one of Domino's claims is true.

My father is alive...

And the broadcaster confirmed another horrifying claim of his—my mother is dead. The sick part is I haven't found the space to mourn her amid the chaos my life has become. Even now, someone else takes precedence—the owner of the masculine scent flooding my nostrils with every breath.

Domino.

No one so cruel should smell like he does. Like sin. One inhale, and some twisted part of me ignites, despite the million other ways the man repulses me. He's a liar for one, and a murderer…

More memories return by the second, reinforcing each menacing descriptor—but any real fear is kept at bay by a dreamy, warm cloud separating my brain from the rest of my body. I recognize this feeling. I'm high. But not high enough. What lurks beneath this dizzy euphoria is still recognizable, though dulled and distant. Pain. A lot of pain.

Along with that unshakable sense of unease.

For now, I ignore it all to reassemble more of my scattered thoughts. *Think.* The most pressing issue, of course, is where am I? My hazy memories provide a clue, uttered by Domino himself, *I'm taking you back…*

To Terra Rodea—but not in the hopes of a joyful Pavalos family reunion. No. He wants me to find Pia's body.

The low rumble of a vehicle's engine reinforces that very scenario. We must be in his car, jostling over an uneven road. Hell, for all I know, we could be in Terra right now.

The noise that first woke me—definitely a radio—continues, fragmented and disrupted by static.

"...no further news on the whereabouts of Ada-Maria Pavalos, but a nationwide search is currently underway. A press release by the office of Roy Pavalos stated that—" Suddenly, the sound cuts off, replaced by a guttural rasp.

"I know you're awake. Open your eyes."

His voice serves as the catalyst needed to jumpstart my exhausted brain. I can move again. Warily, I blink, wincing as my vision adjusts to the blinding hot sun spilling in through the windshield. My first observation is that we aren't in the car I remember. This vehicle is higher off the ground, sporting a narrower cabin and tan, fabric seats instead of leather. A truck?

The landscape visible beyond the windows differs slightly from the desolate fields surrounding his estate. Instead, tan grasses and cacti speckle the earth beyond a poorly maintained dirt road.

Domino doesn't seem alarmed by the remoteness. With a steely calm, he manipulates the wheel to navigate the rough terrain. His hair hangs loosely down his shoulders, his eyes narrowed with determination. A hot jolt of jealousy shoots through me. I hate how unfazed he always manages to seem.

"Where are we?" I croak, wincing as my throat aches. I'm thirsty.

The last thing I can coherently remember is him putting me in a car after nightfall. Then waking up, though in a room. He was speaking to a man, Luis, referring to my arm, and a "dose" of something I assume is responsible for my current high. Who knows how much time has passed since then?

"On schedule," Domino cryptically replies. "We only have time for one break, so make it count."

"On time for what?"

Abruptly, he pulls onto the side of the road and parks. As he wrenches open the door on his end, a burst of acrid air slams into me like a battering ram—followed by fear.

Weakly, I turn in his direction. "What are you doing?"

"I suggest you stretch your legs now," Domino continues, unconcerned by my discomfort. "That is, if you want to piss without getting bit by a rattlesnake. They come out in droves to sun themselves on the rocks this time of day."

I don't know what disarms me more. His uncharacteristic calm—or that his statement doubles as a thinly veiled threat.

"Where are we?" I demand a second time, testing my sore limbs. In the end, I manage to slump closer to the nearest window, but the low hills don't enlighten me on our location one damn bit. There isn't a house or building in sight.

"Luis," I rasp. A glance behind me reveals no one in the back seat, either. "Where is he?"

Appearing on my end, Domino raises an eyebrow. I've surprised him.

Without supplying an answer, he yanks my door open so suddenly I nearly pitch over, too weak to hold myself upright. His grip on my shoulder is the only thing keeping me from falling out of my seat—my *right* shoulder.

I gasp out, recalling at the same instant that my wrist is broken. Panic surges down my spine as I tense in anticipation of the agony that never comes. Looking down, I realize why—my arm is immobile, supported by a black brace made of sturdy material. It extends from my shoulder to my wrist, lessening some of the pain.

"Look at me." Domino grips my chin, impatience radiating through his fingertips. "You've had one hell of a ride," he murmurs, tilting my head for inspection.

"What do you mean?" I ask.

Only as his eyes narrow do I realize what he's doing. Checking how dilated my pupils are. Whatever he finds makes him purse his lips in disappointment. "It's a damn good thing we aren't trying to cross now. You'd get us flagged the second any agent takes one fucking look at you. I suggest you take my advice and try to piss while you have the chance. Hold onto me."

He offers his arm, and I blink.

"You're wearing your costume," I croak.

Gone are the casual loose shirts and slacks he sported around his estate. Both have been swapped for jeans and a denim shirt with the collar buttoned. All he's missing is the wide-brimmed cowboy hat, and he'd be the spitting image of my father's faithful bodyguard.

His scowl, however, disrupts the façade, proving what it was all along.

An act.

"What you call a costume, I call practical in the heat, Ada-Maria. Now move." He lunges for me, and I wince, too weak to push him off.

Pain is the only thing I've come to expect from him, but all he does is loop his hands around my waist, hauling me from the truck himself—gingerly. The second he sets me on my feet, my knees buckle.

"Lean back," he growls, shoving me against the vehicle itself. I was right to guess it was a truck. Painful nostalgia brings back bittersweet memories of watching him drive off in a battered pickup. Unlike his old navy model, this one is red.

I'm so caught up in observing it that I miss the moment he palms the front of my jeans.

"W-Wait!" My belly flips, my thighs tensing as I try to bat him off one-handed. Images flash through my brain of the last time he had me in this position, and all I can do is ask, "You'd fuck me now. Like this?"

He chuckles, but it's not malicious or mocking. Dare I say it even sounds genuine? His teeth flash, bared by a smile that lasts a heartbeat. Then he's scowling again, focused on the task at hand.

"I want you to *piss* like this." He kicks my legs apart, drawing my attention downward. I'm still wearing the black sweater and jeans I took from his closet—but someone added a new component to my outfit while I was unconscious—sturdy black hiking boots.

My first impulse is reckless—all I'd have to do is push past him and make a break for the scraggly hills surrounding us. With proper footwear, I'd probably last longer than my previous escape attempt.

The second feeling washing through me is just more confusion. Kindness is so unsettling from him.

In my experience, it's only ever followed by violence. A smart woman would run now—though there is the small dilemma that I can barely hold myself upright. My knees tremble, straining to support my weight.

"I need a hospital," I insist.

"You need to listen to me," Domino snaps back, shifting so that my shoulders are braced against the side of the truck. Then he crouches, continuing to drag my jeans down my legs.

"W-What are you doing?" My cheeks flush as hot air teases the skin of my thighs, melding with his body heat. The sensation reinforces the reality that I'm at his mercy, helpless against whatever he has in mind. When his fingers twitch over my hip, I suck in a breath. "S-Stop—"

"Relax." Anticlimactically, he stands and grips my shoulders so that if I did happen to pee, I wouldn't wet my pants or the shoes.

Or him, for that matter.

Rather than gratitude, his rare display of thoughtfulness spurs my unease. So I retaliate the only way I can. With spite. "Are you going to drag me all the way to Terra?"

"I could." He lets that statement hang menacingly in the air. "Or I could leave you here as a tempting decoy."

I don't miss the underlying threat—yet another reminder that, according to him, I have no one else to rely on.

But he's wrong.

"My uncle is looking for me," I blurt, merely to gauge his reaction. I so desperately want to see him flinch. Frown. *Something.*

His eyes narrow, but I can't tell if it's out of irritation or amusement. "I wouldn't go looking to Rodrigo as a savior."

A part of me quivers. I know my father is no hero, but is my uncle no better?

"If anything happens to your father, who do you think will be next in line?" he adds, feeding on my doubt without me voicing it. "Your uncle. Your brothers. They aren't your allies—merely claimants to the throne. Loyalty means nothing when power is up for grabs."

"You should know," I hiss.

"I *do* know. Which is why I suggest you don't take my protection for granted."

He sounds so damn smug—as if he's dancing around something unspoken, daring me to voice it. Rather than ask outright, I deflect, "Because you're the one who has my best interests at heart? Would that be before or after you had me kidnapped?"

"Because I'm the one with your life in his hands." He flexes said hands at his sides, cracking the thick knuckles one by one. "After all, you're the one who put it there."

"Not by choice," I bite back—but it's a lie.

Gradually, bits and pieces of that last night at his estate return, putting the truth into blinding focus. I *did* choose him over Jaguar—but Domino made a monumental choice of his own. He left the estate without Jaguar's permission, taking me to only God knows where for only God knows what.

Though, to be fair, he did give me a hint. He's aiming to get back to Terra Rodea, a task that involves a border crossing. Suddenly the fake passport I discovered in his closet makes more sense.

I wonder if that's how he smuggled me here in the first place.

"Who is Luis?" I demand a second time, changing the subject. "A friend of yours?"

"You have four seconds to piss before we need to move." As he angles his head toward the sun, I see a genuine hint of alarm cross his gaze. He's worried.

"I could always leave you here," he adds in the same breath. "Cutting the deadweight would keep Jaguar off my scent for a few more hours. At the rate you're going, he'll catch up by lunch, just in time to break more than your wrist."

As much as I try to suppress the fear, I can't. Neither can I ignore the pressure in my bladder and the million other pressing concerns my body chooses now to make known. I'm starving—but this hunger isn't the same bastion of control I've clung to for the past decade. It hurts. The gnawing ache in my belly makes it harder to think. Harder to reason. Harder to find the strength needed to resist the man before me.

Shame sears my cheeks, but I close my eyes and relieve the one discomfort I can on my own.

"It's about damn time."

I open my eyes again as Domino advances, withdrawing something from his pocket that he unceremoniously swipes between my legs. A dry rag. Satisfied, he yanks my pants back up and fastens them. Then he retreats, waltzing toward a thicker patch of grass—presumably to follow his own suggestion.

Alone, I inspect our surroundings more closely. This landscape varies from the region around his mansion in more ways than one. It's drier, the air liable to suck every ounce of moisture from my throat. Given the rugged terrain, I don't think Domino's quip about rattlesnakes was merely to unsettle me.

"Come on."

I jump as he reappears near the back of the truck, zipping his fly. My gaze tracks the motion, and I swallow hard as he draws close. Easily, he lifts me into my seat before returning to the driver's side. When he reclaims the wheel, he slams his foot on the gas, kicking up a swell of dirt as we go.

I inspect the truck's interior, noting that on the back bench is a black duffle I recognize from his estate, along with an unfamiliar burlap sack.

"What's in there?" I ask, eyeing him guardedly.

He doesn't even take his attention off the road. "I suggest you put your energy into preparing to walk." Apparently, he isn't in a mood to reveal any more secrets.

"Don't you think you owe me answers?" I ask, trying a different tack. "Something? After everything you've done—"

Abruptly, he flicks the dial for the radio, triggering a barrage of upbeat mariachi music. "It's at least a six-hour drive where we're headed. Then we'll need to move on foot. Focus on that. Here—"

He reaches across me, wrenching open the glove compartment. From it, he snatches what looks like an energy bar and tosses it onto my lap.

"Eat."

The question of how—with only one hand—crosses my mind. Rather than ask for help, I grab the bar with my good hand and bring it to my mouth. Thankfully, I manage to tear the package open with my teeth, but then I hesitate.

I wait for the disgust. The nausea. The desperate need to cling to this gnawing, aching hunger and seek that fragile grasp on control I've come to rely on.

Instead, my stomach growls, and in three bites, I consume half of the bar outright.

"Where are we going?" I demand after swallowing, raising my voice above the noise.

If he hears me, he doesn't bother to answer.

Good. He had a point—I should focus—like on what the snatches of the broadcast I heard as I woke up revealed. My uncle is in Terra. While he lacks the political pull of my father, Rodrigo has influence and money of his own. If I could find a way to contact him…

"There is a search for me," I say carefully, watching Domino's reaction from the corner of my eye. "My uncle. The police. How do you plan to get me into Terra without drawing notice?"

He makes a show of scanning the road, still silent, but I know he's listening.

"Either you talk to me, or I leave." To bolster the threat, I muster enough strength to swipe at the door handle.

"Stop." He shuts the music off, leaving only the hum of the engine to fill the quiet. Finally, he sighs. "Do you have any idea what I've done?"

He lets the silence resonate for a handful of seconds before answering his own question, "Jaguar claimed you. I took you anyway. He'll see that as a direct challenge. Do you have any idea what that means?"

His tone chills me to the core. I swallow hard, weighing my response before replying. "That you're a selfish bastard?"

"No," he says softly. "That I let five goddamn years of planning go down the shitter because of you. He won't stop. Not if he feels I need you—that I want you for some other purpose. *Fuck*—" he strikes the wheel so hard I jump. "If you'd waited another fucking day at least to have your petty little outburst…"

I must be more out of it than I thought—either that, or he's lost his damn mind. "So, this is my fault?"

Riling him is a dangerous game, but I'm too exhausted to dance on eggshells anymore.

"You did this," I remind him in a hiss. My eyes burn. I frantically blink, but there's no stopping the tears that fall. "You sold me to that sick bastard! What the hell did I ever do to deserve that?"

"You haven't been listening." Real emotion colors his tone; he's angry. Furious, in fact, though he's managed to disguise it until now. "I suggest you pay close attention, Ada-Maria.

Jaguar will kill you if he thinks your death will affect me. Congratulations. You did the one fucking thing sure to provoke him."

"What?" I demand.

"You chose me over him," Domino growls. "You might as well have wrapped a noose around your neck."

"What was I supposed to do?" I ask, genuinely curious. "Hop onto his cock?"

"You were supposed to shut your fucking mouth and do what I say."

"Oh really?" I watch him, but fury isn't what I find straining those handsome features into a frown. This is something far more unsettling. My pulse surges as if warning me to back down. I don't think I want to know the answer to this riddle.

"Maybe I should have stayed with Jaguar?" I suggest, choosing to play with fire. "At least he was upfront about what he wanted from me."

"Damn you."

The truck veers off the road in a cloud of dust, and we stop so suddenly I jolt forward, forced to brace my good hand against the dashboard. Any pain I feel vanishes in the face of his cold scoff.

And terror instantly replaces it.

"So fickle are your affections, Ada-Maria," he snarls. "I guess pain is what truly gets you off. Maybe I shouldn't stop myself the next time I feel the urge to wrap my hands around your fucking throat—"

"You've done that," I counter breathlessly. Reaching up with my good hand, I trace the flesh in question. It's still tender, smarting from his use of a collar. "You think you're so different from him?"

His eyes flash, and I recoil against my seat. The way he looks at me... It's an expression somewhere in between shock and hate.

"You don't know how many fucking times I've gone against my better judgment when it comes to you." Gone is the false calm. *This* is the Domino I remember.

The same twisted figure who held me captive for weeks.

"I could have let you die a million different ways by now, Ada-Maria. Don't think I haven't considered it. From that very first day your boyfriend offered your head to Jaguar on a silver platter, I could have let you go to him then, and I can tell you for a fact that more than your wrist would be in pieces by now."

"So why didn't you?" My heart pangs, betraying just how badly I crave an answer to that question. Why? Even if it's a cruel, selfish reason—which it must be—I still need to hear him say it.

"Why?" He lashes out, fisting his hand in my hair so hard stray hairs rip from my scalp. Pain isn't his motive.

Control is—he wrenches me toward him, bringing my face within inches of his.

"I told myself how easy it would be. To watch you die. To see him fuck you. Hurt you. Sell you." He ticks the horrors off one by one, his voice devoid of any emotion. But when he brings his free hand to my jaw, it trembles—and that rare hint of instability chills me to the bone.

"Some men have to commit horrific crimes to know they've crossed some moral line, Ada. Kill men. Women. Children. Not me. I'll let you in on a little secret. *You* were always my gauge—"

"What does that even mean?" I snap.

Irritation radiates from him so fiercely I can feel it on my skin, hear it bitten into every word.

"My pretty, Ada-Maria... As long as I didn't give a fuck as to what might happen to you, I could face Don Roy on even ground. No one could stand in my way. Not even his daughter with the perky ass and Bambi eyes. God, you make it so easy to hate you."

As if to prove it, he drags his fingers through my hair, tugging on random strands as he goes. Hard. Harder. I wince, and he changes tack, stroking my forehead with terrifying care.

"I knew that I could step aside and let Tristan play his little games at your expense. I could use your body to settle an old debt and never think twice. You meant nothing to me."

I hate the tears that spring to my eyes. It's one thing to experience his hatred firsthand—but it's torture to hear him state it so plainly.

"Then why not kill me?"

"Why? Five years," he says hoarsely. "Five damn years. That's an odd time to plot revenge, Ada. Have you asked yourself why I would act now? Or why *that* time frame? After everything I've done for Don Roy, what could make me finally act against him? Believe me or not, five years wasn't anywhere near long enough—" the look in his eye cements the conviction in his voice. He means every word. "I would have worked for that bastard for ten decades if that's what it took. Why ruin the life I built up, huh? I knew Jaguar's stupid ass stunt wouldn't kill him. I had to beg that bastard to help me in time. I had to scramble to get the resources in place to bring you to me. Why? What might force me to tip my hand? I'll tell you…"

He flicks his tongue across his bottom lip. Then, in a voice like sin, he grates out the answer, "*You.*"

He adjusts his grip, grazing his nails carelessly against my scalp, using the pain to reinforce his next words. "I wanted to spare your feelings before, but no more. That bastard ordered me to kill you. Not Tristan. Not some nameless cartel. *Me.* You were meant to die that night—but by *my* hand."

Ice-cold, his eyes don't hold a shred of remorse or pity. Just endless hate.

"Do I have to spell it out for you? Your own father wasn't just willing to sell you," he says gruffly. "He wanted you dead."

CHAPTER TWO

He wanted you dead…

No. I shake my head, refusing to process the rest of his claim—it's too insane. This is just another sick mind game at my expense.

"You're lying."

"Am I?" A muscle in his jaw twitches as he releases me, settling back into his seat. "He didn't think I'd question him," he adds. The lack of fire in his voice makes my blood run cold. Though he's lying. He must be…

"It wasn't the worst act he's ordered me to commit, by far," he continues, his expression contorting into the calculating frown I know so well. "Hell, I couldn't tell you everything he's done in the name of your family. But I never thought he could order the death of his own daughter over a cigar and a whiskey."

"You're lying—"

"You don't believe that." He doesn't even put effort into his voice. "You know it sounds like him."

He's right. I can easily picture my father as he claimed, standing on the balcony, glaring out over his estate. Cigar in hand, he'd blow out smoke rings while contemplating his next move.

He was always plotting and planning.

Ironically, Domino seems to share my doubt—even Roy Pavalos isn't capable of this.

"You said he was working with Tristan," I point out. "First he wanted me kidnapped, and now—"

"Ada…" His heavy sigh leaves me paralyzed, and it takes everything I have not to slap my hands over my ears and scream just to drown him out.

"You were an obstacle in his way," he explains. "At that moment, you ceased to be his daughter—"

"No!" I reach for the door handle, fumbling with the lock. "You're lying."

"I asked him why," he adds, and I watch my hand fall, landing helplessly on my lap. "Why you. Do you want to know what he said?"

So cruel, he lets the silence hang until I finally glance over my shoulder to find him staring back. "He said, 'You've never questioned me before, Domino. I suggest you don't start now.'"

Despite everything, a laugh rips from me. And a sob. *That* definitely sounds like the father I knew—a tiny sliver of my soul can admit that.

But…

"He wouldn't."

Domino rests his head against the top of his seat. For a long, long while, he observes the unmoving road, and I can't deny how twistedly beautiful he can seem like this. As unreachable as some mythical God, detached from emotional beings. To him, the only forces that matter are power and fear.

"I don't falter," he says finally.

I flinch. His tone resembles the stern baritone that was a hallmark of his dutiful soldier façade. The voice that would make me tremble every time I imagined him at night.

The same voice that will haunt the nightmares I'll undoubtedly have from here on out.

"I don't hesitate. If I want something, I take it. If I need something, I take it. And in the name of revenge, I will become the errand boy of a man I hate for a decade if I have to. No one will ever stand in my way, do you understand that?"

He soldiers ahead without waiting for a response.

"If your father orders me to put a bullet in the brain of his only daughter, then I'd do so without question. After all, who would mourn Ada-Maria Pavalos? Your mother, perhaps, but we both knew it was only a matter of time before she joined you in the afterlife. Beyond her, you were merely a symbol, and your death would make you a martyr. An albatross your father could wear around his neck for the rest of his political career. It doesn't matter that you've spent your entire life degrading yourself for him, pining for even a scrap of appreciation. Or that you sold your body and soul in the name of his ambition. Your life didn't matter as long as you stood in his way. More than anyone, I'm sure you understand that."

My vision blurs with unshed tears, but he remains unmoving—briefly. Upon closer inspection, even I can see how his hands shake over the steering wheel.

"So why didn't you?" I ask thickly. "You wanted your revenge first? To hurt me?"

"I'll ask again. Who would miss Ada Pavalos?" He inspects the endless blue sky expanding before us as though it holds the answer. Apparently not. He has to voice one of his own, "Who watched her, day in and day out? Who watched her play with countless men like toys? Who knew every hue of gray her eyes could touch on when she was frustrated? Or sad? The way she pursed her lips when angry... Who could see through that fake fucking smile to the pain lurking beneath? Who would crave the sight of that bouncing, perky little ass of hers—" he laughs, but it resonates more like a heavy sigh, devoid of inflection. "It would have been far, far easier, Ada-Maria, for both of us, if I took my gun like I planned to and blew out your fucking skull."

He says it so callously that I know he's not lying—and that's what is so terrifying. The way he described me, the raw craving in his voice… Those tiny little realizations serve to tip me over the edge.

I can actually *feel* something inside me rip apart. I can hear it as faint as tearing tissue paper, so fragile when all is said and done.

Who knew that a few careful words would utterly break my soul? And yet, the only sound I can make is a ragged intake of air. "Please stop lying to me—"

"No. You ruined my carefully plotted timeline, Ada," Domino soldiers on, unwilling to show me mercy, even now. "You ruined every fucking thing, and I knew then and there that your father was merely testing me. Of course, he saw the way I looked at you—how could he not? Don Roy realized I'd been working against him from the start. What better way to flush me out than by using the best tool at his disposal?"

He's thinking out loud, revealing a hint of the convoluted mindset I would have given my soul to understand just a few weeks ago.

"Still, I decided to play along," he continues. "I'd arrange a test of my own. I had to scramble to get everything in place months, years before I'd planned to. I needed Jaguar, and the bastard loved having me crawl to him on my hands and knees. He thinks he has me by the balls, but I knew that I could use this moment to my advantage and punish you, Roy, and Jagger in one fell swoop. Neither would ever see it coming—and as a bonus, I would have you. Even if you were a scheming little snake in on your father's grand plan, I'd fucking have you."

"You… You sound insane," I manage to rasp.

He doesn't even hesitate. "I am."

"Why?" It seems surreal for one man to crave having that kind of hold over another.

It's demented.

A cruel obsession.

And yet…he smiles, and it's the most wickedly beautiful expression I've ever seen.

"From that very first day when I saw you in Don Roy's office, Ada-Maria, I haven't been able to get those gray fucking eyes out of my head. That smile. Your voice. I wish for your sake that I could have been one of those poor bastards you're used to playing your games with. Someone who could fuck you once and forget you. If I only wanted your body… It would have been better for you in the end."

His earnest tone makes my heart feel liable to lurch right out of my chest. I sense that he's trying to tell me something. Something important.

And horrifying.

I try to ask, "W-What are you—"

"It should have been easy to overlook you. But you were never stupid," he continues, tapping his knuckles against the steering wheel for emphasis. "Never. You were always watching, always alert. Behind those empty fucking smiles was a little viper staring back, missing nothing. You didn't follow your father's orders because he hurt you, or because you were too much of a silly fool to question. No. You obeyed him because you love him."

Love. He makes it sound so different from the dreamy way Pia and I would reflect on that term as schoolgirls. In his grated inflection, that term becomes something lethal. A weapon.

"You loved him enough to stand by him no matter what he asked of you. You trusted that every time you went into hell for him, you were earning his love in return. A fool isn't capable of that sacrifice. Idiots have no honor, no integrity. A real fool would have turned on her father the second she got the chance, but not you. You valued your loyalty to him, even if the bastard never truly deserved it. Men like Jaguar pride themselves on trusting no one. They believe there is strength in that, but it's bullshit. If it's every man out for himself, then what's the point in fighting so damn hard?"

As if seeking out the answer, he eyes his hands, pulling them from the wheel.

"I saw it firsthand. The way you'd lie for him. Cheat for him. Sell your soul to the highest bidder. You'd die for him; he knew that too—don't think for one fucking second that he didn't. He thought that it was because he had you cowed enough. Because he whipped you hard enough. Because you were terrified enough to do whatever he said with no complaint. But that wasn't it. Fear doesn't make you loyal; it makes you seethe. It makes you desperate to escape the leash you can feel around your throat. You'd lie, cheat, and steal. You'd become the monster if you have to, anything to break those bonds. So no, you didn't serve your father out of fear. You did it out of love, and in so many ways, Ada-Maria, that's far, far worse. Your love blinded you, and it made you suspectable to hope, and that hope? It will kill you faster and more painfully than I ever could."

"I don't have any hope when it comes to you," I finally spit out—but I have to strain just to hear my own voice over the harsh sound of his breathing. "Not anymore. Over and over, you hurt me—"

"You play the part of a dumb woman well, Ada, but you are far from that, aren't you? Your father is one of the most calculating men I've ever met. Together, you two have taken down mayors, and journalists, and anyone who might even dream of threatening the Pavalos family legacy. If your father suspected me even once during my time working for your family, he would have told you. He would have used you to get close to me, and you tried. I managed to resist your every attempt."

Shock cuts through me like a knife as it hits me—this is his attempt at honesty. This is why he tortured me so cruelly.

I see myself in what feels like another lifetime, preening for him, smiling, desperate to cajole him into grinning back. Something. Anything. I wanted a fraction of attention from him, and who knows what I would have done if he'd given it to me.

But all he saw was manipulation. A lying little bitch he had to resist.

"You think this changes anything?" I ask, practically wailing at the insanity of it all. "That you hurt me out of doubt? Bullshit! So much for wanting my loyalty—"

"I'll earn more than just your loyalty." His confidence rattles me into silence, my mouth still open.

What truly unsettles me is the look in his eye. It's determined. "By the time this is over, you'll be willing to put a knife in Roy Pavalos yourself," he says. "I can promise you that."

I almost laugh again. At least now I have confirmation that whatever he feels for me, is far beyond compassion.

"Oh really?" I choke out. "I'm not as stupid as you think."

It's mind-blowing how conflicting his opinion of me seems to be. A dumb, senseless whore one minute. A thoughtful, loyal woman the next, someone worthy of his admiration— as twisted as the term is where he is concerned.

"I never thought you were stupid, at least in that context," he admits. "You're so damn stubborn. You'd deny yourself pleasure just to get a rise out of someone you hated. You'd starve yourself just to make me watch you die. Don't pretend like you wouldn't."

I look down at the energy bar crumbs on my lap. "Why tell me this now?" I ask, unsure which of his confessions I can even risk trying to believe. "So I can be your lovesick puppy again and lead you to Pia's body? Then you'll kill me, won't you? Or sell me, anyway—"

Abruptly, Domino grips the wheel, and we accelerate so quickly a cloud of rust-colored dirt billows up around us.

"I'm telling you this so that you can understand the choice you made," he says darkly. "Put your trust in me, and you'll have nothing to fear. Doubt me, and Jaguar will be the least of your worries. But don't take my word for it. You want it driven home just how little your father cares about you? Fine. I'll let someone else explain it better than I ever could. In their own words, you'll learn the truth."

I lick my lips, thrown off yet again. Someone else. "Who? Alexi?"

"I'll take you to them," he says evasively. "Right now. It's not like you have a better option."

"What about Jaguar," I whisper, shivering at the sound of his name. "You sold me to that monster. How can I even begin to trust you? What if he were always the 'better option'?"

He laughs, and I'm so startled by the rich cadence that I just gape.

"If you were paying attention, Ada-Maria, you would have known from the start that I never had any fucking intention of giving you to anyone. You were always mine. Always. Mine to take, and mine to destroy. I suggest you don't forget that."

The grit in his voice guts me. As tired as I am, I don't have a chance in hell of playing his mind game—not now. Everything he said was all lies, and I'm better off not believing a word of it.

I can't risk going off on my own now, either. Not yet.

Instead, I close my eyes again, letting the hum of the engine lull me into a flimsy excuse for sleep.

He doesn't speak again, and I savor every second of silence. Something tells me it will be the only reprieve from Domino Valenciaga I'll receive.

CHAPTER THREE

"Get up," a voice I know all too well drips into my ear, jarring me awake. Gone is the unrestrained possession. He's cold again.

"We need to walk the last leg," Domino adds gruffly, sounding further away. "Get ready to move."

The last leg…

Supposedly before we meet with someone who will offer proof as to my father's true intentions. That thought spurs me into motion. Reluctantly, I blink my eyes open, but all I see is black. Then silver…

Moonlight. Gradually, my vision adjusts to the faint glow of it seeping into the truck. It's dark. The absence of sunlight enhances the remoteness of the terrain as the moon itself shifts from behind a patchwork of purple clouds. A sobering mixture of awe and dread washes over me, shattering any remnants of sleep. I can't escape the thought that this sight would be beautiful if I had someone I cared about to share it with.

Someone other than the man eyeing me from beyond the open driver's side door of the truck. "It's a long walk," Domino warns, his gaze electric in the shadows. "I can only drive so close. It's risky to take a chance on this terrain in the dark, but it will be harder to track us than during the day."

"To where?" I demand. Another fragment of memory comes back to me. "I heard you speaking to someone before. A man. Luis. He said you were trying to cross the border—"

"Get out." He circles around to my end, muscling my door open for me. He grasps for my uninjured forearm, leaning in so close his breath sears my throat.

"I can move on my own." I try to shrug him off but, aided by only one hand, I'm no match.

For all my bravado, I sway, forced to rely on his strength for stability. I shudder as my fingers latch onto his forearm, sensing the thickness of the muscle twitching beneath.

"Where are you taking me?" I manage to croak, craning my neck to see his face. Better yet, "Who do you think will convince me you're telling the truth about my father?"

He inclines his head as if surprised I remembered that much.

Good. My thoughts are clearer now. The drug is wearing off, but in its absence lurks the pain lancing up and down my right arm. Thankfully, the makeshift brace is strong enough that I can hold it against my chest without much discomfort.

"Was he a doctor?" I ask again, trying a different tack. That occupation would explain the relatively stable condition of my right wrist, anyway. "Luis?"

Maybe it's my soft tone that wrings a frown out of him. "Something like that," he grunts, slamming the passenger-side door. "We'll need to move fast to make it before sunrise. Then it will be a game of trying to cross the border in time."

I don't miss the unofficial deadline he tacks onto that statement. He's hiding something, and his posture only bolsters that suspicion. He's edgy, his jaw clenched, eyes blazing through the darkness.

"I can't carry you," he adds, lifting an object that he must have taken from the truck without my noticing—the black duffle. He slings it over one shoulder, hefting the burlap sack with his other hand. "So you'll have to keep up. Come on."

He sets off into the rugged terrain at a pace that makes my legs throb in sympathy.

Despite the rapidly growing distance between us, I don't move, contemplating what he'd do if I climbed into the truck and made a break for it. Damn him and his secretive plots.

As if reading my mind, Domino cocks his head my way. "Jaguar's men will be watching the roads, if they aren't just hours behind us already. I don't think you'd enjoy what he'll do to you if you happen to fall into his hands again."

Sufficiently cowed, I take a step. Then another. As I start moving in earnest, I have to throw out my free hand for balance. This is harder than I'd thought. Every inch I advance takes twice the usual effort, and I'm panting by the time I draw even with him.

"Stay close," he tells me, moving assuredly—but slower than I think he would if I weren't here. "It's a little over a mile before we can stop."

"Where are we going?" I ask for the umpteenth time.

Predictably, he keeps walking.

His concept of a mile is as laughable as his concept of loyalty. I'm pouring sweat by the time he finally slows, shrugging the duffle from his shoulder.

"Sit," he commands, his expression unreadable in the low lighting. "We'll rest here."

Here being a roughly flat strip of earth, riddled with unseen rocks and scraggly grasses. I'm wary, picturing those rattlesnakes he hinted at. Who knows what else might be crawling in the shadows?

Not that Domino seems concerned by either possibility. The picture of confidence, he crouches, rummaging through the items in the burlap sack. As I crane my neck to get a better view, he shifts to block me.

"I suggest you don't waste time," he calls back. "We only have an hour before we need to be on the move again, and you won't be able to sleep."

The ominous edge to his tone prompts me to ask, "Why not?"

He inclines his head, and a fraction of moonlight illuminates his eyes long enough to catch the glimmer of interest that flits across them. "I think it would be better if you listen. You're about to get a crash course in the Domingas Cartel."

I hold my breath. For all I know, the promise of information could be his way of luring me into another trap. Another mind game. More lies.

But, fuck it. I'm desperate to learn any scrap of info, and he knows it. With a sigh of defeat, I start to sit, only to realize how hard it is to maneuver with my right arm in the brace. Losing balance, I nearly pitch over—but a firm grip on my left hand saves me from the impending impact.

The second I can steady myself, I wrench my hand away, my cheeks flaming. Then I sit down on the hard earth, heedless of whatever creatures might be slithering nearby. "Start talking," I snap.

He sits as well but counters me with a demand of his own, "Let's see how well you were paying attention. Do you remember that name I told you? Who used to run the cartel?"

I swallow hard, unnerved by this impromptu pop quiz. "Carlos," I say, recalling that name. "Jaguar's father?"

"Yes. And he was just one of many players you'll need to remember. Here—" He withdraws something from the sack that he hands to me. I recognize it from feel alone—a water bottle. Eagerly, I drink from it, aware of his gaze on my throat.

As I swallow, I risk choking out another question. "Is Luis another 'player,' too?"

He looks away, scanning our surroundings with an eagle-like focus. Finally, he says, "Consider him an old friend of your family's, but not someone important at the moment."

His tone contains a warning—I'm testing his patience.

"I-I'm listening," I say.

"I suggest you do," he warns. "This is the only shot you'll get to understand a small piece of the mess you've found yourself in. Carlos ran the *Guarida*. He operated on both sides of the border, using his clubs as a front for his true trade in cocaine. Jaguar's continued his tradition, but in a lesser capacity. Thanks to Roy Pavalos, another man now claims most of the old Domingas territory. His name is Mateo Morello."

"Mateo…" I recognize that name though I'm not sure how. I think he said it once, referring to a passport. *Mateo is fucking me on the timeline—.*

"He and Jaguar have something of a truce now, but it's only a matter of time before one goes for the other's throat. The main territory in dispute sits along the border, the perfect spot to transfer goods from either side."

Could that be his intended route to reenter Terra Rodea? I start to ask, but Domino continues, even as my lips part.

"Jaguar's expanded his father's business well beyond what Carlos ever intended. The old man never dabbled in anything beyond the drug trade, and perhaps illegal weapons. Blinded by ambition, Jaguar's been taking on whatever business can get him the most money the fastest, morals aside. The only problem was the border. Without a stable crossing point, he found it hard to keep up a regular supply while avoiding the authorities. That's where Mateo comes into play. Both Jaguar and your father used him as a middleman. Ironically, I could communicate with him, even after I worked for your father, without drawing notice."

"How convenient," I interject.

He nods. "Unfortunately, Mateo has taken to transporting more of his own merchandise than Jaguar likes, but tipping the scales without an insurance policy would risk closing off his access to the border completely."

"So, what are you saying?"

"What I'm saying is that whoever can take out Mateo controls the flow of trade in and out of Terra. That puts us in the middle of a powder keg I'd rather not see blow up in my face."

I note the way he phrases that. Carefully. As if to disguise that one key player in this mix has every reason to crave the same outcome.

"What's your gain in all of this?"

He grabs the water bottle from me and takes a drink. Beads of liquid drip down his chin as he eyes the sky, letting the moonlight bathe his face completely.

"I never planned on making my move quite this early," he admits. Rarely have I heard him use this tone. Deep and rasping, devoid of any anger or rage. He's speaking unguardedly for once. "I knew I would leverage a strike against Pavalos and Jaguar, preferably at the same time. But once again you, Ada-Maria, seem determined to accelerate my timeline."

His eyes find mine, but I don't see anything remotely close to gratitude in them.

"What do you want from me?" I demand, hating how soft my voice sounds in comparison to his.

He shuffles to face me directly, his legs outstretched. "I want answers. Answers about Pia. You can start with the night she went missing."

A heavy knot of dread settles in my stomach. Perhaps I'm too much of an optimist, but I never imagined I'd have to relive those memories in the middle of the desert, seated beside a madman.

It's not fair. Pia is one of the few secrets that has always remained mine, ignored at my discretion—and I liked it that way. I relished the control that relegating Pia Inglecias to the past gave me, no matter how pathetic it was. And were I to provide Domino even a fragment of those memories, I'd want it to be on my terms.

Only mine.

"Why?" I ask, evading a direct answer for now. "What are you looking for? Besides, what makes you think I'd even tell you a damn thing? You've already established that I'm doomed either way."

"Ada…"

I brace for the rage I've come to expect. For his nostrils to flare and for his eyes to narrow. Instead, he merely steals another sip of water, wiping his mouth with the back of his hand.

"You aren't the least bit curious?" he asks, switching his tone from cold to cautious. "You claim you know exactly why Pia did what she did, but then I tell you that you're wrong. That your father killed her, and that it was over something far more valuable than money. And yet, you aren't curious as to the truth behind it all?"

"Why should I be?" I counter, but hell, he has a point. Maybe the answer is simple—I don't want to know. "Nothing changes the fact that I'm here with you now. You've already taken me from Jaguar, and I suspect that puts you in just as much danger. It seems like you're all out of threats, Domino."

He laughs before taking another long swig. "My Ada and her smart fucking mouth. So let's say I release you right now, and you manage to make it to Terra Rodea on your own–assuming Jaguar doesn't drag your sweet ass off to the *Guarida,* and you manage to become a free woman. A happy ending with sparkles and roses. But then what?"

I haven't dared to envision such a scenario. When I do, one glaring reality sucks any hope from the prospect.

"Oh, that's right," Domino softly remarks. "I'll tell you what happens—you go right back to being the daughter of Roy Pavalos. A man out for blood. You claimed to know your father better than anyone, so you do the honors and tell me what he might do to *you.* Especially after you've been in the hands of his enemies for so long?"

"Go to hell," I spit.

"I'll see you there," he snaps back. "Because we both know exactly what he'll do. He'll lock you inside that beautiful familial estate and beat that precious sense of loyalty back into you. Piece by piece. Then he'd bandage together whatever was left, package them neatly with a little pink bow and send you back out into the world under his discretion. There is no escape from him, no matter what you delude yourself into thinking."

Damn him. I never realized how a few short weeks without my father's presence might change me—and ironically, not for the better. Three weeks ago, I had a sense of direction, even if that direction led toward hell.

Now? My perception of the future is in pieces. And the reality I never wanted to face is staring at me—literally—impossible to ignore.

In a sick twist of fate, I went from having my father pull my puppet strings, to watching Domino Valenciaga dangle them directly in front of me.

"And," he continues, "are you really so sure he didn't try to have you killed? I know you don't trust me, but you aren't that stupid. What I've told you sounds plausible enough. Admit it."

I close my eyes, wishing more than anything that I had the strength to just ignore him and surrender to whatever fate this desert has in store.

But there is a possibility that fate could lead me straight to Jaguar, and it doesn't seem so tempting anymore.

"I want you to tell me the truth," I say, opening my eyes again to his silhouette bathed in silvery moonlight. He can seem so beautiful it hurts, his eyes a dangerous green. The sad part is, if he could offer even a hint of real kindness, I'd swallow anything he told me.

"No more lies," I rasp. "No more mind games. Tell me what you're really after. It's not like I'm a threat to you—"

"Ah, but that's where you're wrong." Without warning, he cups my cheek against a calloused palm. The intensity in his eyes sends a shudder through me. It's more predatory than smug. "You are the single biggest threat to me there is, Ada-Maria. With one word, you can destroy everything I've spent the past decade working toward. I can't risk you doing that. Not until you've proven yourself."

To *him*. It stings how easily he's managed to turn the tables, making me the enemy—when he's the one who dragged me into this mess.

"I'm starting to question if you really are a better option than Jaguar."

His hand slides down my jaw only to grasp my uninjured wrist instead. Possessively, he runs his thumb over the protruding bones. It's a chilling caress—and an unmistakable warning.

"I haven't broken your wrist the last time I checked," he softly reminds me. "I haven't whipped you until you were on the verge of death, either—"

"But you still whipped me," I hiss, ripping my hand from his grasp. "You took pleasure in hurting me, and you enjoy having me squirm for your amusement, so pardon me, Domino, if I'm not willing to place you on a pedestal."

"So, don't," he counters with that infuriating calm back on display. "Everything I've done has been for my own reasons; I don't deny that. But…"

I swallow at his hesitation. Any perceived weakness on his end is only a trap, meant to lower my guard. Still, I can't help myself by playing right into it.

Voice rasping, I ask, "But what?"

"I would be lying if I didn't tell you that there was another reason why I intervened when I did."

I suck in a breath. Could what he said before be the truth? God, I'm such a fool for even wanting to believe it…

"Then why?"

"Because your mother asked me to," he says. "And I can prove it."

So many emotions strike me all at once, I can't process them. I just breathe…

Within minutes I'm sobbing, feeling fresh tears mercilessly lash down my cheeks.

"How dare you?" Though, am I truly surprised by the depths he seems willing to sink to? I shouldn't be. "I can understand you hating me, but my mother was nothing but kind to you—"

"You don't even know the half of it." The worst part is that he seems to be agreeing with me. "Which is why I did what she asked. I intervened, though I would have done so regardless—but I can prove it, and more. So, what will you do? Continue to pout or listen to me for once, and take what I'm telling you at face value."

Listen to him. It's not like I have any other choice.

"What are you talking about? What did my mother tell you?"

"Not yet." He shoves the water bottle into my hand again. "I'll reveal that tidbit of information in my own time. But I will educate you on another topic—you. Keeping you away from Jaguar relies on getting you across the border in time. Every second you doubt me, risks that. So, if you want to stay alive, then keep moving. Now drink."

I've barely taken a sip when he snatches the bottle back, stowing it into his bag. I expect him to move on, leaving me to catch up. Abruptly, he snags my uninjured wrist instead, hauling me to my feet.

"We're almost there," he bites into my ear. "And whether you're ready to hear them or not, you'll get your answers soon enough."

CHAPTER FOUR

Morning comes with a scorching heat that sears my skin before the sun fully rises. Only sheer pride keeps me moving. If I stop, I doubt I could get up again.

Infuriatingly, Domino hasn't even broken a sweat. His speed remains steady over the uneven ground, and I suspect that I've only kept up with him because he's tailored his pace. If he wanted to, he could easily leave me behind to rot.

Would such an end be so bad, all things considered?

I'm starting to fantasize that very scenario when I spy something up ahead glaringly different from the reddish landscape surrounding it. The closer we come, the clearer it is to make out—a square structure of wood with a rusted metal roof. It looks like it could have been a gas station or a store at one point, though long since falling into disrepair.

"This is it?" I ask in between pants at Domino's back. "This is your way over the border?"

"Keep moving," he replies, hiking his bags higher on his shoulder. "The sooner you make it, the sooner you can sleep. We can't move again until evening, at least."

The veiled offer of rest spurs on my tired limbs, though I should have learned my lesson about trusting him by now. For all I know, beyond the walls of that decrepit shack, Jaguar lies in wait, ready to cart me off while Domino watches on with that blank, unreadable expression.

Even so, I can't ignore the way his words replay in my brain. *I wanted you. I stayed for you. I was always there for you…*

"Stay close," he warns.

I startle to awareness and realize that not only have I found the strength to keep moving, but I've surpassed him by a few feet. I wish I were brave enough to pull ahead entirely. Run. Get inside that shack and barricade it against him, or —better yet—breeze past it. Leave Domino and his twisted world behind and hope to come across anything better.

Though who am I kidding? The happiest ending I have to look forward to is dying before he or Jaguar can desecrate my body for their own means.

"Don't get any cute ideas," Domino remarks, and his relaxed façade cracks, revealing the tension lurking beneath.

Damn him. Teeth gritted, I slow enough for him to pull ahead.

Despite seeming so close, it feels like hours pass before we finally reach the crumbling shelter. With the sun beating down relentlessly, every second scrapes by. I'm standing only by pure muscle memory. Sweat soaks through my sweater, dripping down my forehead in rivulets.

Domino must sense my exhaustion because he appears by my side, grabbing my left arm the second I start to sway. "Don't look up," he commands. "Breathe in through your nose. It's just a little further."

I marvel at the concern. Then I remember that Domino Valenciaga always has a motive. Craning my neck, I eye him through a haze of stinging sweat, searching for whatever his aim might be.

All I find is the same handsome face that's haunted me for so damn long. Like always, I'm unable to discern an ounce of emotion from it.

With renewed determination, I focus on walking, forcing one foot in front of the other.

Domino releases me as we finally approach the door. Shrugging off his sack, he seems to inspect the area. Up close, abandoned seems too kind a term for this structure. More like… Lost. A small sliver of the world passed over by time, leaving behind a weathered husk liable to collapse should the wind blow hard enough.

"It's going to storm," Domino remarks, casting a wary glance at the sky. I copy him, skeptical. To me, it seems like an endless blue with nothing to shield the sun.

"The rain will help cover our tracks," he adds. "But it will make it harder if it doesn't stop by tonight. Get in. We don't have long to prepare."

It's strange to hear him speak so openly. I'm exhausted enough to chalk it up to my brain hearing what it wants to hear. Seeing what it wants to see.

Like the searching look he sends my way before he reaches for the door. Rather than test the handle or retrieve a key from somewhere, he wrenches on a loose plank of wood that seems barely attached to the structure overall. It gives way in a cloud of reddish dirt, and I do a double take at what lies beneath it.

A pristine electronic keypad affixed to the wall doesn't seem possible in an area so remote. Even more shocking is how it comes to life as Domino taps a series of keys. With a subtle beeping sound, a decisive metallic *thud* echoes somewhere behind the door.

Domino finally tugs on the rusted door handle, and it opens, but the interior doesn't seem worthy of the heightened security. The wooden walls are so decrepit in places, slivers of the reddish landscape outside are visible—and yet it's stuffy, the air thick. So much for Domino's promise of rest as well. There doesn't seem to be any furniture to "rest" on, let alone supply a supposed desperate trek across the border.

Even so, Domino only hesitates to grab his bags before urging me inside with a jerk of his chin. Then he slams the door behind us both, and I half-expect it to fall off its hinges entirely.

"What is this place?" I ask.

"Move." He pushes past me and crouches, smoothing his hand along the dust-coated floor. Without warning, he curls his fingers around one of the floorboards and tugs.

In a cloud of dust, part of the floor gives way entirely—a trap door. Coughing, I peer into the gaping square space cut directly into the earth itself. Wooden steps lead deep underground—too far to even see where they end from here.

"Come on." Once again, Domino hefts both bags and descends the staircase first. An unsettling rattle issues from the wood every time his foot lands against it, and I hesitate, noting that the trapdoor at least seems capable of standing on its own.

Still, I take another glance at the rickety door we entered through. My foot twitches against the wood before I remember there is no way in hell I could outrun him.

As if catching wind of my rebellious thoughts, Domino calls from below. "If you want to eat, shower, and sleep, I suggest you follow me. Or hell, take your chances with sunburn and the rattlesnakes."

His relaxed tone is back again, and I think that—more than any other factor—is what finally spurs me into inching after him.

It's a long descent, extending for several yards into the earth. Devoid of any railing, I'm forced to trail my left hand against the wooden planks lining the stairwell, each one gritty and coated in dust. The deeper I go, the more my eyes adjust. In the absence of sunlight, faint illumination comes from up ahead—a lightbulb hanging from the ceiling at the base of the staircase.

Naked wiring snakes from it, crudely nailed to the wall, eventually leading to a haphazard arrangement of black devices that must be part of a generator. Presumably, it's also powering the electronic keypad outside.

"You must not be so eager to rest after all," Domino taunts from up ahead.

"What is this place?" I ask as I descend the bottommost step.

Here, the floors are concrete, and the artificial lighting casts a grayish glow. Like a crypt. Domino, lurking on the other side of another doorway, looks ghoulish, more zombie than man. He's already dropped his bags, approaching me with both hands at his sides.

"Lie down on the bed and wait for me," he commands before brusquely mounting the steps. To secure the trap door, I assume.

I hesitate, frozen mid-step, even as my muscles ache with exhaustion. "Bed" carries two drastically different connotations where he is concerned. A place to sleep—but also a tortuous arena where he can tie me down, drug me, or inflict a far worse torment.

I toy with the potential outcomes as his footsteps resonate from above. Apparently, he's doing way more than closing the trap door, and I try not to let myself imagine what. Instead, I finally inch forward, peering beyond the doorway he came from.

Shock blinds me to any previous apprehension I may have felt. At first, I assume I'm hallucinating. There's no way that all of this could fit beneath such a seemingly dilapidated shack.

This being a square room, sparsely furnished, but with a queen-sized bed in the far corner, what looks like a mini fridge against one wall, and a wooden desk piled high with computer equipment. The sheer amount gives the stack of generators way more context. In fact, I doubt they're even enough to fully power the array of monitors—at least four —each one displaying a different view.

The footage on the first monitor is all too familiar—it's this shack. There must be a camera outside, positioned to capture the surrounding area. The second monitor features a grainy image of a small, wooden room. Upstairs? I can even make out Domino, prowling with his back to me.

The view on the third monitor, however, excites me the most—a web browser. Could a place this remote have internet access? Eager to find out, I surge forward, placing my fingers on the keys.

The previous user already had a webpage maximized. A news story, it seems, documenting the urgent case of a missing woman. I barely recognize the smiling image of the creature headlining the article, her smile blinding, her makeup immaculate, her hair perfectly styled in a fresh blowout.

God, I was so pretty—the way a doll is. Artificially beautiful. My father raised this woman to preen brightly before the camera no matter what hell she was experiencing internally.

And, damn, I excelled at it.

Thunk! Domino's footsteps continue to beat against the floor above, snapping me from my pity party. Tearing my gaze from the picture, I read the article itself for any relevant details.

It's sparsely written, mentioning the restaurant, and a shootout, but I scan the entire document twice before I realize one glaring omission—there is no mention of Tristan Lucas, dead or alive. Odd. There's barely any acknowledgment of my father, either. Other than the fact that my abduction is under investigation, this account seems suspiciously sparse. Too clean.

Either Domino's been lying to me about everything from the start, or someone else is pulling the media's strings, tightly controlling what they can and can't reveal. Law enforcement? Obviously, they wouldn't want vital details of an ongoing investigation to leak.

My gut, however, is warning that there's far more to it. Someone with influence is desperately trying to sway the public's perception.

The prime suspect? My father, of course.

Though how much influence he could wield supposedly from a hospital bed is anyone's guess. If he were ever in the hospital, that is.

Now is as good a time as any to find out for myself. With a wary glance at the ceiling, I lash at the keyboard one-handed, typing the most relevant term I can think of.

Roy Pavalos

The first headline to populate confirms his fate: **Local politician Roy Pavalos currently in critical condition.** With bated breath, I skim the opening paragraph only to find that the author included no details as to his status beyond the title.

But I do discover a tidbit of information that Domino never bothered to tell me.

According to sources, the Pavalos couple was ambushed by unknown assailants near the international airport. Though currently under investigation, a judge recently approved the politician's weekend travel plans...

Despite the writer's flare, I know that statement is pure bullshit. Why would—seemingly on the eve of his indictment—law enforcement suddenly grant my father permission to get on a plane?

More importantly, why wouldn't he tell me if that were the case? I was out with Tristan, but I never even got a text or a warning phone call. My father wouldn't leave without me.

Unless…

I suck in a breath as the room begins spinning. Helpless, I grapple for the edge of the desk to right myself. In the process, I knock a stack of loose documents to the floor.

Absently, I stoop to gather them, scanning the topmost pages as I do. Tucked among the pile is a handwritten list composed of words I vaguely recognize. Towns? There are roughly twenty entries, written beside various dates within the past few months.

All but four have been crossed out in black ink.

I don't have the mental capacity to question why that might be as my vision blurs with stinging tears.

Domino was right all along.

And he must be anxious to gloat. I didn't even see him come in. I just know that his hand is the force latching onto my forearm, steering me backward.

"So damn stubborn," he snarls against my ear. "I told you to lie down."

I'm too weak to resist his strength. The second I'm on my feet, he shoves me back, but I land on a surprisingly soft surface that isn't the floor.

The bed, I presume. The ceiling above is blindly white—fresh. My nostrils flare, picking up the stench of wet paint lingering beneath Domino's musk. Unfairly, he still manages to smell enticing while drenched with sweat and after spending hours in the sun.

"What is this place?" I ask, startled by how thready my voice sounds. My entire body aches in varying degrees of agony, bordering on excruciating.

And yet, somehow, it's easy to overlook it all in favor of waiting for his reply. As long as he speaks, nothing beyond this room matters. Just what he breathes into existence.

"This… Is one sliver of territory unclaimed by either Jaguar or Mateo."

He's moving. I can see his form flickering toward the foot of the bed though I don't have the strength to lift my head enough to see him clearly. He grips my ankle, yanking off my shoes one by one. When his palm grazes the sole of my foot, I stiffen.

"W-What are you doing?"

He doesn't respond, seemingly intent on his hands. Persistent, he rubs the sensitive flesh on my heels, and the pain gradually blossoms into something resembling pleasure more.

At the back of my mind, I realize what he's doing—massaging me. The shock of that alone lulls me into a daze so dizzying that keeping up with his words is more strenuous than the walk here.

Territory. Jaguar...

"This is where I've been storing five years of secrets," he continues. His voice floats through my ears as he continues his ministrations. "About your mother. Your father. You. What I have here should be enough to placate any doubts you have. You chose me once. You need to do that again, and again from here on out. Do you hear me, Ada-Maria?"

My eyelids are too heavy to keep open for longer than seconds at a time as my brain sluggishly churns through every word he's said. Something about information. Something…

"Do you hear me?"

"Huh?" My voice comes out too soft. A whisper.

My brain resists any commands I send its way, shutting down my body one sense at a time. Soon my eyes seem closed for good, and the only sensation I'm aware of is the steady pressure of his fingers rubbing both of my feet, gently manipulating the muscle. It kills what little part of me is still alert that he can give me this. A tiny fraction of mercy amid a sea of agony. If I expected to find that sympathy reflected in his voice, I'm sorely mistaken.

"I'll take any mystery out of what I want from you, Ada," he tells me. "I want you on my side, no need for threats, or lies, or deception. I want you to hear the truth for yourself. See it with your own eyes. And when this is all over, I want you to choose me. Only me."

I'm too far gone to process his request accurately. I just know that some part of me reacts to the heat in his tone. And for a second, I think…

I think I almost believe that he means it.

Every single word.

CHAPTER FIVE

It feels like I've barely closed my eyes by the time I reopen them to a pale ceiling and bare cement walls. A blissful confusion lasts for a few seconds before I remember where I am—in a shack in the middle of nowhere, with the very man who plunged my life into chaos…

Domino.

I toy with the possibility that he's locked me here, choosing this place as my new prison. Would that outcome even surprise me?

I don't have long to ponder it. A heavy sigh resonates from somewhere close by, containing a hint of a raspy baritone I'd know anywhere. He hasn't left me yet.

I turn toward the sound, wincing as my muscles ache in protest. This mattress is new, with a hard layer of crinkly plastic beneath the thin sheets that loudly betrays any movement. By the time I haul myself upright, I expect to be greeted with a smirking, smug Domino.

Instead, the room I find is empty, bathed in the glow of artificial light. He's here, though. I can sense it in the primal part of me that quivers, catching his scent in the air. Sure enough, another low sigh draws my attention, and I stand, swaying to find my balance. A few stumbling steps bring me to a section of this place I have yet to explore.

Whoever built this strange bunker managed to include a bathroom. It's smaller than the two at his estate, outfitted with a shower stall large enough for one person. Squeezed in beside a toilet and sink looms a tall figure, his jeans undone, one leg braced against the toilet seat.

I stop, swaying unsteadily as my gaze roves over him with a greedy interest I can't deny. Even his ass is beautiful, composed of rippling muscle trapped beneath tanned skin. Surprisingly, I'm more drawn to what he's holding, poised expertly in one hand. Any previous illusion of his drug use is finally confirmed. I've literally caught him one-handed.

He must sense I'm here before I even inch closer. Loose black hair shrouds his gaze as he cocks his head to find me. In the same smooth motion, he drives the tip of a syringe into his thigh, pressing the plunger down. I flinch in sympathy—though, to his credit, he doesn't even wince as the amber liquid floods his muscles.

Instead, he raises an eyebrow, more surprised by my appearance. "You're awake."

"I'm awake," I manage to croak.

He turns back to his thigh, withdrawing the syringe and capping the needle with the built-in safety cover. The way he manipulates the instrument conveys more confidence than some of the doctors and nurses I'd been subjected to during my stints in and out of the hospital.

He's done this before—many, many times. Still, he manages to project his trademark Domino Valenciaga coolness as he disposes of the syringe with some sleight of hand.

"I thought you'd sleep a little longer," he adds, eyeing me from over his shoulder. I've been out for a while. His appearance reinforces that suspicion; he's changed, switching the denim shirt for a loose black one.

"Don't tell me you were intending to give me a dose next," I counter. Would I welcome another unasked-for high? The sad part is I don't know. Some sick, degenerate part of me might even crave the offer.

Not that he makes one. He lowers his leg, standing at his full height. As he refastens his jeans, those dark eyes rake me over, his head cocked. "Not now," he says cryptically. "We need to talk."

An understatement if there ever was one. "T-Talk?" I don't know how to process that word coming from him. It could honestly mean a milieu of things, ranging from benign to terrifying. To soothe my unease, I just shrug and rattle off the first distraction I think of. "I'm thirsty."

As if prepared for the request, Domino approaches me, his arm outstretched. I jump, before I realize just what he has—a bottle of water.

I grab it, draining the entire thing within seconds. I've barely finished swallowing when he shoves something else toward me—a rag.

"You should clean up, first," he suggests. "Then, I'll explain my terms, and we can go from there."

Terms. It sounds so clinical, a polite explanation for what he really has in mind. Another test. A new mind game.

"You sure are taking your time revealing your evidence," I croak.

Though do I really want to know the truth behind whatever mysteries he has up his sleeve?

"Come here." He crooks a finger for emphasis. When I don't move, he stalks closer and snatches my uninjured wrist, hauling me deeper within this narrow space. The first thing I notice is a blurred, filthy mirror displaying my image over its cracked glass.

No wonder he's being so cautious around me. I look like hell. Admittedly, not as bad as I feel I should, all things considered. The makeshift brace on my right wrist remains intact, though the visible flesh looks mottled and bruised. The sight alone is enough to illustrate just how drastically my life has changed within the past few weeks.

Gone is the beautiful woman featured in that article. In her place is a broken creature composed of wounds and ruined flesh.

But someone did their best to treat me while I was out. The signs are subtle, at first. A Band-Aid here, another there… That same person cleaned the skin around my many scrapes and bruises, taking care to treat every single one.

I swallow hard, forced to admit that Ines isn't here to blame. That leaves only one other suspect…

My eyes dart toward him, but he's already staring back. I bite my lip, caught off guard by the fleeting expression crossing his face. It's pensive. Curiosity makes that elusive green of his irises more unreadable than ever.

"Hold still." Before I can resist, he's behind me, already tugging my jeans down my hips. I hiss as he peels the denim from my sore, sweat-soaked limbs. I've barely stepped out of the legs when he spins me to face him and turns his focus to my sweater.

"Why?" I croak, my gaze on his fingers.

"You stink." His tone is harsh enough to counter the gentleness with which he frees my injured arm from a sleeve. "Once you've showered, I can focus without having to smell you."

He shoves me back, and I stumble into a crudely made wall composed of plastic sheeting.

"What about the brace?" I inspect it again, noting it's sturdy exterior.

"It should be waterproof," Domino explains, still blocking the only exit. "Try not to submerge it though. It should hold long enough to get you to Terra."

"I think I prefer the villa oasis as my prison," I say, facing him again.

His amused grunt comes as a shock, and I miss the moment he turns a dial affixed to the wall, activating the faucet. The water comes out startlingly cold, stealing my breath away. Instinctively, I jump to avoid it—only to run directly into the body that comes to block my path.

I freeze, registering the hard planes of muscle pressed against me. He feels so firm. So goddamn solid. So hot. His heat is a barrier against any chill, and some greedy part of me craves every ounce. My body's needs are separate from my brain, and not even logic can serve as a big enough deterrent. I hate myself for the first coherent observation that comes to mind—I would have given anything to have him this close to me just weeks ago.

To have his hands on my bare back, the thick fingers possessively cupping my spine. I'm delirious enough to seek comfort in his touch, but some aspects of him can never be ignored. Like the roughened callouses that scrape at my skin when he draws me closer. As if realizing what he's done, he pushes me back, meeting my gaze.

The water pelting us gradually heats up, feeding wafts of steam that obscure our surroundings. He seems larger this way, looming above me, blocking any escape.

"God, you can be so fucking convincing." One of his hands nudges my chin disapprovingly, and whatever spell held me captive snaps.

I hate this man. Every inch of him should repulse me to the core of my being. It's sick to fixate on his mouth with sudden longing. Maybe the walk here exhausted me to the point of insanity? Or…

"Did you drug me?" I blurt out, recalling how many times we've shared the same water bottle. Maybe the needle was just for show, an act timed for me to witness.

Jaguar hinted that he had a high tolerance when it came to narcotics. It makes sense. All that wine and now the water. Apparently, he can drink it all and remain unaffected by whatever drug he laced it with—something strong enough to knock me under every time. What the hell has he been through to develop such a high tolerance?

"Would it matter if I *did* drug you?" He's closer, his lips brushing my cheek as he reaches past me, snatching something from a metal rack hung around the showerhead. "You're still alive and able to function—"

"So are you," I rasp. With every passing second, more information is coming back to me. Namely, his whispered conversation with Luis. "You mock me for my past, when you're no better than an addict yourself."

He doesn't deny it outright—and that's the unsettling part. Instead, he cocks his head as if surprised by the comeback. "Even drugged, you're still my mouthy Ada-Maria."

My belly flips at his gritted tone, and another confession rips from my lips. "I used to wonder what it would feel like to be yours."

God, I couldn't fake the genuine pain in my voice if I wanted to.

His eyes narrow, but he recovers quickly enough, reassembling his stoic mask. "You *are* mine," he corrects, smoothing his palm along my lower back for emphasis.

His tone makes it sound far from romantic. To be owned by him is a punishment, a position no woman should desire.

Before I can reply, he palms my shoulder, guiding me beneath the spray, rag in hand. He's soaked within seconds, his damp hair clinging to his forehead, threatening to obscure those haunting eyes.

This twisted intimacy does something to my brain, melting what little common sense remains.

"I wanted you to love me." I'm not sure where the confession comes from. Maybe I was drugged after all, and I'm ascending another high.

I hope so. It would explain the frown tilting his beautiful mouth downward—I'm hallucinating, of course.

"Love," he echoes while dragging the rag across my chest. "I'm curious. What does that term even mean to Ada-Maria Pavalos?"

The dangerously low cadence of his voice, paired with his steady ministrations, lulls me into a daze. I *must* be drugged. It's the only explanation for why I'd find anything but pain lurking within his touch. I almost forget that he posed a question at all.

Until he nips my earlobe.

"Love," he bites out. "Does someone like you measure it in terms of wealth? How much money a man can throw your way? How expensive a car he drives?"

I choke back a laugh. Ironically, the Domino Valenciaga I knew, was none of those things, just a humble man who drove a battered blue truck. Yet, he seemed more appealing than a million Tristan Lucases.

"I never cared that you didn't have money," I admit, closing my eyes to block out his face.

It stings to admit just how little I do know about him. Where his newfound wealth has come from, for instance? An estate like his couldn't be bought overnight. For years, he must have maintained it from a distance, all while working for my family in Terra Rodea.

Not to mention this place. An underground hideout in the desert, powered by a mass of electric generators, isn't a cheap expense, I'm guessing.

"Money means secrets," I tell him, sucking in a breath as his fingers graze my ribcage instead of the cloth. Slowly, he traces a path up between my breasts. When he stops, I realize that he's roughly in the vicinity of my heart.

"Secrets mean lies… I thought you were above it all. That's one of the reasons why I was so drawn to you."

"One of the reasons?" he prompts.

"I thought you were different," I admit. "Not perfect. No knight in shining armor, but someone I could trust. A man who didn't give a damn about money or power. Someone normal. Someone—"

"A fantasy," he warns against my ear. "Can I blame you, though? For being so damn naïve? For a woman who grew up as you did, you sure have an inflated sense of morality."

He's right. All this time, I desired a man more skilled at lying and mind games than my father ever was.

"Don't mock me." I sound like a petulant child, but maybe I am.

He can joke about it now, but in retrospect, my naivety serves to highlight how little access I had to good men in general. I took any hint of kindness and ran with it, despite knowing full well the kind of work Domino did.

He was never a saint.

"At least now I know better," I tell him, squaring my chin. "You hate my father because you want to be him. You sneer at his methods, but you wouldn't mind being in his place, is that it? Money. Women. Influence. You're no better than the rest. A selfish bastard—"

"Selfish…" He mulls over the word choice. Then he cocks his head and… He laughs. The sound raises goosebumps despite the sweltering heat. "Ada, if I were being *selfish*, I would have ripped you to pieces and gladly washed my hands of you to the first monster who came calling next. Anything after—" He inhales, taking his time to decipher my scent. Then he sighs as if the flavor eludes him. "I've done to protect you. Speaking of Don Roy, as horrible as you think I am, I'm sure you've tasted his wrath for yourself. More than once. Tell me something—" His voice deepens in a way that triggers a wave of unease. It's too soft. "He whipped you. Why?"

I bite back the insult that immediately comes to mind. Attacking him won't get me anywhere. If he's offering answers, I'd be a fool to spurn him now.

"He whipped me for the same reasons you did. Because I dared to question him."

I hate this memory. It unfolds swiftly, sucking me under. I can recall the smell of the office he kept on the second floor of the house—a long, narrow room that overlooked the tennis courts and gardens. Bookshelves lined each wall, containing everything from works of Shakespeare to Chinese philosophers. I think he considered himself a great thinker. For a man like him to rise from nothing to a seat of power, I suppose he was.

He could see beyond the limits most men heeded. Kindness. Empathy. Fear.

Ruthlessness was a weapon he honed to perfection, and he wielded it against everyone. My mother, it seemed, had already been drained of everything by him. So he turned to me.

"I asked him one question," I say, seeing that very moment replay like some horror movie—one I don't even recognize the star of. "Why. That's it. Why."

And because of that "insolence," I deserved to be punished. In the world of Roy Pavalos, violence trumped all other forms of communication. Words could be misconstrued, and mercy was a weakness. That wasn't the first time he whipped me—nor was it the last.

But I distinctly remember the shift in him that I never noted before. His eyes had been colder, his upper lip curled from his teeth, his anger unbridled. In his gaze, I saw a darkness that haunts me still—a callous disregard.

As though he could have killed me easily and dumped my body beneath the tennis courts.

It's that man who could have killed Pia Inglecias. It's that man who Domino served so diligently. It's that man I've devoted my adult life to—and not entirely out of fear, either.

Mainly...

I never wanted to see him look at me that way again. His approval was preferable, no matter how I had to debase myself. No matter the cost. I gladly paid it just to feel like I mattered to someone.

Despite the hell my father put me through, I couldn't face his rejection.

I still can't.

Domino exhales sharply, snapping me back to the present. "I didn't have the upbringing you did. My family wasn't rich, and I didn't have the luxury of being shipped off to a boarding school."

He exits the stall completely, and I assume he'll leave, which seems to be his mode of operation whenever the conversation turns to him. Instead, he settles both of his hands on my shoulders, spinning me so that my back is to him.

"I would have given anything for a mundane experience like that. To have a life, even under the purview of an overbearing father. I might have preferred that…"

The pain in his voice is so tangible I can feel it like a noose around my throat, every bit as restricting as his collar was. If I still doubted that he truly is Navid Inglecias, his hoarse retelling offers ironclad proof.

"The pity was one thing," he adds, while dragging the rag down my thighs. All this time, he's continued washing me. "I could handle that. The sympathetic looks. The concern from strangers my mother endured whenever she shuffled me to and from the hospital. It was the pain I found unbearable. Men like your father, they boast about overcoming adversity and hardship to get to where they are. Poverty. Neglect. But they never mention the agony that comes with physical weakness. Tell me, how did Pia describe my condition?"

I stiffen as his hands still against my spine. One by one, he flexes each digit as if testing his strength against me. How easy would it be for him to snap bone the way Jaguar did?

He rakes both hands down to my hips as if to answer my question. *Very* easy.

And I'm powerless against him.

"I want an answer, Ada-Maria."

"That… That you had a heart defect," I say, utilizing the term Pia herself used. She rarely spoke of her brother, but always referred to him with respect. I don't think she ever resented him. Not once.

"Defect," he echoes. "That's one way to put it. My cardiac output was a fraction of what it should have been for a boy my age. I could barely walk a few steps without getting winded. No running for me, and certainly no boarding school. As one of my doctors once remarked, it was a miracle that I functioned to the extent that I did."

His hands settle against my hips as I try to imagine him too weak to walk unassisted. It's almost unthinkable. Was his temper just as volatile then? Or maybe this rage is his way of making up for lost time.

"How did you get your heart?" I ask.

He sighs. "I'm getting there."

A wave of warmth sears my back, and I assume he's stepped forward, filling the mouth of the stall, and blocking out what little light reaches this corner. I'm in my own parallel world of shadow, ruled solely by him.

"I need you to understand what it felt like," he continues, his mouth grazing my earlobe as he speaks. At the same time, his fingers creep up my shoulders, inching toward my throat. "Beyond the weakness. That was just one aspect of it, but the other? It was the *pain*. Though my heart was beating, my organs felt constantly deprived of oxygen. Do you know what that does to your muscles? Your bones? I couldn't take a breath without feeling like I was suffocating."

His thumb nudges my windpipe for chilling emphasis.

"My body was in a perpetual state of agony," he continues. "You are no stranger to pain, Ada-Maria. I want you to picture the worst agony you've ever felt, and multiply that tenfold."

My broken wrist should be the paramount experience—but it isn't. Ironically, only one agony fits that description—*him.* Hearing him claim I meant nothing.

"Not a day went by that I didn't wish for death," he adds. "So I found an escape in whatever I could."

His voice paints a grim picture, and my chest tightens in understanding.

"Tell me," I prod.

"Morphine. Codeine. You name it, and they pumped it into my veins just to give me some semblance of peace—" His fingers leave my skin, only to sink through my hair. As if from miles away, I hear the slap of the rag hitting the floor. Then his breath drowns out everything but the steady spray of the water.

He's closer, entering the stall fully until I'm forced against the far wall. The air in my lungs escapes in a gasp. Helpless, I brace my good hand against the slick plastic shrouding us, painfully aware of every inch of him. From the wet fabric of his shirt against my back to the harshness of his jeans on my thighs. Every scrape rouses an ache inside I can't deny.

"I can't put into words what that feels like. To crave oblivion just to keep your fucking sanity. When even breathing hurts too much. It's an affliction that I always believed you'd need a small fucking heart to understand. So imagine my surprise when, almost a decade later, I looked at the face of a woman and saw that exact same pain."

It's pathetic to be ravaged by jealousy for a woman I've never met. Especially now, alone in his grasp, close enough to feel his heartbeat hammering through flesh and bone. My pulse surges to match his, each beat thundering like a hammer blow.

"This woman," he continues so hoarsely my own throat contracts in sympathy. "I saw myself reflected in her sad, gray eyes…"

He cups my chin, guiding me to look back at him. I don't know what unsettles me more—the heat in his tone? Or the way his free hand comes to graze my belly, palm first.

"You were so damn beautiful. So lost. In so much pain—the kind of agony few can understand. I knew then that I wasn't wrong for seeing you as more than Roy Pavalos' daughter. That you were worthy of…"

He trails off without finishing, and I can barely find the air to speak. "Worthy of what?"

He laughs darkly before confessing, "Of everything. But nothing could ever erase who you are at your core. The daughter of Roy Pavalos, a man who turned deception into an art form. You have no idea as to the depths of his cruelty, do you?"

He wrenches me to face him, swiping my hair back. From this angle, I have a clear view directly into those endless, greenish eyes. They're as unfathomable as ever.

Though wait…

A rare emotion peeks through for an instant—one that stirs painful recognition. I saw it the night I hurt my nose, and again when Ines informed him that Jaguar was on his way.

Of course, the first time was years ago, the night I hit rock bottom, and he came to save me.

"I'll show you if I have to," he warns, his voice low. Enhancing the ominous anticipation building in my belly. "So, you know exactly what you've been up against without even realizing it. Roy Pavalos never gave a damn about you. But I have. From the very start, I've always been focused on little Ada-Maria. I want you by my side willingly. I want you to help me finish what my sister started. And I want you to know why."

He's even closer, his body pressed against mine, his hands sliding downward…in between my thighs. I groan through clenched teeth as fire rips through me, unexpectedly hot. I'll never get over how my body reacts to him. As though he's electric and I'm a live wire greedily leeching from him whatever I can take. Anything to feel pulsing and sensitive.

Alive.

The feeling must be mutual because his mouth greedily feathers over my parted lips, searing them with the heat of his breath.

"I want you to know why I've spent five fucking years at your father's feet. I need you to understand the truth, and I need you to realize that trusting in me is your only choice."

"Why?" I whisper.

His mouth is so close I feel every twitch of his lips as he speaks. "Because, even at my own fucking detriment, I can't seem to stop trying to save you."

His next kiss robs my breath, my senses. All I can do is arch into him, letting him nudge my legs apart, all while taking care not to jar my injured arm. I marvel at the gentleness, though the look in his eyes is anything but. They glow hungrily, as if he wants nothing more than to devour me whole.

Body and soul.

"The things I've thought about doing to you…" He draws in a ragged inhale as what feels like the rugged tip of a nail continues to trace the delicate flesh at his mercy. I gasp, my head spinning.

Somehow, I still manage to choke out, "Like what?"

He uses his fingers to spread me apart, arousing sparks with every harsh brush. I'm on tiptoe, arching into him.

"*Like*, pinning you against the wall until you know who you belong to."

Eyes blazing, he inspects the brace—a glaring reminder of another man who dared to claim ownership of me. My attention, however, drifts beyond it, to the front of his pants, reduced to a bulging mass of strained denim.

My throat dampens, lips parting around a plea I'm not brave enough to voice.

But he knows me too well. One of his hands withdraws, leaving a chill behind as he grasps for the zipper of his fly. Slowly, he lowers it, as if intentionally ratcheting up the tension.

I'm dizzy when he finally wrestles himself free, letting the water christen the taut, angry flesh beneath. I've never seen someone so aroused.

I reach for him, brushing the tip of him with a trembling finger. The sound he makes guts me.

When I meet his gaze, I swear I hear something snap. I'm in his arms within a heartbeat, his body in between my legs. There is no warning, before he slams into me. To the hilt.

It burns. It aches. It's incredible. No man should feel this good, and this violent. His next thrust wrings a cry from my lips that he swallows with a brutal kiss before trailing his lips down to my shoulder.

"I thought I knew what pain was, before you," he murmurs against my throat. There is a coarseness in his voice I'm not used to hearing. My breathing hitches as I contemplate what it might be. Honesty? "But nothing compares to the agony of Ada-Maria Pavalos."

Pointed, his tongue traces the path of my pulse. Then lower, lathing my breast. The heat of his breath paired with the steady sensation of falling water is…

Maddening. It's all I can do to keep breathing as my thoughts scatter. I've had so many men in my lifetime. Too many.

But none have ever felt like this. Touched me like this. Spoken like this.

"You drive me mad; do you realize that?" His heavy lids reduce his eyes to blazing slits. Intense doesn't even begin to describe the feelings he arouses. "Mad—" He punctuates the grated admission with a hard thrust.

And another.

Another…

My orgasm hits like a freight train at full speed. No mercy. No concern for my injuries.

It's painful, drawn out by his still thrusting cock until all noise is wrung from me. Helpless, I sink my teeth into his shoulder and ride out the final, brutal climax.

Wave after wave.

CHAPTER SIX

My descent to earth is swift and brutal. In some ways, it confirms my worst suspicion—Domino Valenciaga is a drug, capable of packing a devastating withdrawal. Rehab won't be enough to escape him.

Perhaps I never will…

It doesn't help that this time feels different. Harsher. Probably because the shower isn't connected to a seemingly endless water supply like those at his estate. At some point, the spray becomes ice-cold before slowing to a mere trickle. Then sensation is a shock, clashing with the fire still burning within my skin. As my awareness of the rest of the room returns, I'm freezing—everywhere but the parts of me engulfed by a consuming heat.

At least, this is one high we both seem susceptible to. His breath scrapes my throat, each exhale ragged, though no such unsteadiness is reflected in his body. Firm, his weight pins me to the wall, his hands on my waist.

I lift my head, finding him staring down at me. Something flits across his gaze, too dangerous to inspect in full. Whatever it is, vanishes as he sighs, withdrawing from me.

"We should get ready to move," he says, shutting off the water before leaving the stall. By the time I follow him out, he's already readjusting his sodden jeans.

Watching him brings back the full brunt of what we've done—what I've been doing with him from the start. Telling myself I hate him, only to be swept under the second he shows a hint of vulnerability. Again, I've proven how easily I fall prey to his manipulation.

Shame floods my cheeks, warring with a fragile hope that the concern I saw in him was real—this time, anyway. To distract from it, I do the only thing I can—focus on the present.

"What is this place?" I ask, paying the bathroom closer attention. The door to the main space has been left open all this time, letting out what little steam managed to accumulate.

At a second glance, the layout is cramped, most likely designed for just one person. Everything, from the mattress to the bathroom, seems less than five years old. Not to mention the faint smell of fresh paint and the electronic equipment.

"This?" He leaves my line of sight only to return seconds later with a handful of fabric he tosses my way—the bedsheets. "Think of it as a safe house. Jaguar and Mateo have dozens between the two of them, on both sides of the border. This one, however, was claimed by Carlos Domingas right before he died. I'm one of a small few who even know its location."

"You've been busy despite role-playing as a bodyguard," I point out, struggling to wrap the makeshift towel around myself one-handed. "Buying an estate in the middle of nowhere. Doing business with Jaguar and Mateo on the side. It's a wonder you even had time to do my father's bidding."

He heads into the main room without giving me a reply. I follow him, noticing the various items strewn throughout the small space. One is a square black case that he stoops to open. After a moment of rummaging, he offers a handful of items to me. The first is a black long-sleeved shirt and another pair of jeans in my size.

I struggle to dress while biting back my questions. By the time I wrestle one foot into a pantleg, I can't hold them back anymore.

"I'm tired of being in the dark."

He goes rigid, still fixated on whatever is inside that case.

"Please…" Blinking rapidly, I eye the ceiling, trying to make sense of the tumult of emotions running through me. Confusion. Fear. Shame. Hope, maybe, mixed in among the rest, dinged and tarnished by everything he's put me through.

"You want my trust?" he asks, shifting to face me. In his hands is a small box and a metal instrument I recognize with a pinch of fear. Scissors. "Then trust *me*."

He stands, prying the scissor blades apart. From this angle, I have a clearer view of the words printed on the box—brown hair dye.

Something Luis said comes back to me. *You think I didn't recognize the face that's plastered all over the news reports? If you want to buy yourself more time, I suggest you cut her hair, at least.*

When Domino reaches toward my face, I have a chilling suspicion as to what he intends.

Maybe I'm just too damn tired to resist.

I DON'T KNOW how much time it takes him to finish. When he does, my hair is still wet, though utterly transformed by the whims of the man behind me. He steers me before the bathroom mirror, and I do a double take.

This woman is a stranger, her hair no longer than her shoulders and several shades darker. My eyes look enormous in contrast, filled with fear.

"Is this part of your plan?" I ask, observing his expression in the mirror. "Do you really think a haircut and dye job is a good enough disguise?"

"Look up." He curls his fingers beneath my chin, tilting it himself. Apparently satisfied by the result, he releases me, turning his attention to the clumps of shorn hair coating the floor.

"How many times do I need to tell you to trust me before you seriously consider it?" he asks.

I don't think he realizes how those words resonate.

"So I'm just supposed to quietly accept everything you've said like a good girl? Question nothing?"

My breathing hitches, heralding the tears that slip free. I swipe at them angrily with my good hand, hating myself for showing weakness in front of him.

Though, for once, he doesn't seem willing to gloat. His heat penetrates my skin like a knife, conveying patience I can't deny. In his shadow, I look so small. Helpless.

"I... I want to trust you," I admit.

Does that make me a fool? If so, it's too late to deny it now when my body still burns with the remnants of him, and his taste lingers on the tip of my tongue.

"I want to know the truth. About Pia. My father. Everything. If you really want my loyalty, then just... Just be the man I thought you were, because looking back? I don't think he was entirely a figment of my imagination, and if there's even a small hope of that, then tell me now. Give me something to cling to."

"Something to cling to." He laughs, and I brace myself for the reality that this is the choice he's made. To lie and obscure. To push me away.

Then he turns, fixing those searching eyes on me. In them, I can see him wrestling with both halves of himself, coming to some grudging agreement. "Fine. Ask away."

There's no mocking in his voice. He means it, and I don't dare hesitate. "Who is Luis? Where are you taking me? What is this place? And what do you want with Pia's body?"

His lip twitches into a shocking cross between a frown and a smirk. Then he sighs. "Like I said before, consider Luis an old family friend. He was your mother's doctor. For a few years before Roy turned against him."

"My mother?" I blink, trying to recall seeing that man before. Then I remember that I rarely accompanied her to those grim medical appointments.

Domino did.

It doesn't slip past me how hard this must be for him to finally lay some of his cards on the table. To let me in, even a fraction. Despite every instinct warning me to remain guarded, I sense some part of me soften anyway.

"Why is he helping you?" I ask.

"Mutual interests. As for where we're going? Back to Terra. I need whatever information Pia stole to use as an insurance policy against your father. But he was never the real reason why I was in Terra Rodea in the first place. Roy Pavalos was the target, but trust me when I say that I could have lived out the rest of my life without thinking of that bastard once."

"So fine," I say, licking my lips. "I'll play along. What was the catalyst, then? You just magically found Pia's diary and decided to go on a revenge crusade?"

"No." He looks down, his jaw clenched. "It's not quite that simple. The 'catalyst' was a person. Someone you know well, actually."

This, I assume, is the revelation he's been preparing me for since the start of the conversation. Am I ready for it? I don't know. An impending sense of dread urges me to reenter the main room. I cross to the bed, perching myself on the edge of it. When I do, he appears before me, and the dread solidifies into terror.

"Your mother," he says, casually confirming my suspicion in the most unexpected of ways. "Years ago, she contacted me out of the blue."

"You're lying," I blurt, but he isn't smirking for once. His expression is too damn stern, revealing a hint of something I don't trust at first. As the seconds tick by, it doesn't vanish —vulnerability?

"I thought it was a trap at first." He starts to pace, raking his hands through his wet hair. "Somehow, she figured out my identity and was doing her husband's dirty work. Roy has a habit of annually tracking down anyone he sees as a loose end and dispatching them before they have the chance to strike. Maybe he learned I was alive and my connection to Carlos Domingas?"

"How do you even know it was her?"

"Because she sent me this." He crosses over to the burlap sack I recognize from our trek here. From it, he takes a small object that he holds up for my inspection.

Pia's diary.

"H-How…" But it makes sense, after all. Who else could retrieve that journal, but someone close to my father?

"I didn't trust her motives," Domino admits, as if reading my mind. "So, I ignored her. I assume she felt desperate enough that she called me directly, and I recorded her. Do you want to hear it?"

"I…"

It's as if someone decided to tell me that the planet I've been living on my entire life isn't earth. In fact, I think I'd believe that over *this*.

That my mother invited a viper into our family, with the hopes of what?

I'm staring into space, but he must take my silence as an answer because when I blink, he's before me again, this time holding a black device in the palm of his hand. Its shape roughly resembles a toy I used to play with as a child—a tape recorder. Grainy and distorted, a soft voice issues from it, filling the room.

"…I know you have no reason to trust me." I recognize that beautiful cadence—and yet, it sounds so different from the soft murmur I know so well. That explains it, though. Domino was tricked. This woman wasn't Lia Pavalos.

But then she sighs, and recognition lances through my gut like a knife.

"I don't even want your trust," she continued. *"I want you to gain Roy's. The only way to stop him is from the inside, and I'm sure that you know firsthand exactly what he's capable of, Navid."*

Domino hits a button, halting the recording mid-stream. He's made his point.

"How… How did she even find you?" I choke out in a rasp.

For what seems like an eternity, he eyes the device in his grasp. Then he shrugs, raising his gaze to mine. "Because she was the one who arranged my heart transplant."

"How?"

He holds my stare for so long that I'm numb by the time he finally speaks. "By sending my mother to Carlos Domingas." He continues to pace, stroking the dark stubble on his chin with one hand, still holding the recorder in the other. "I still don't know the depths of her connection to him. She never told me, even after all this time, and I can't exactly ask him. What I'm sure is that Julian had no idea, which only furthers the mystery."

"Juan." The name springs to my lips before I fully recall how I know it. Juan Domingas, Jaguar's younger brother who supposedly died years ago. Horrified, I remember the taunt Jaguar liked to repeat toward Domino—*Little brother.*

"You have his heart," I croak. At least I've finally stumbled upon the missing piece of that mysterious puzzle.

"Kindly donated by the Domingas family," Domino says darkly. I don't glean much gratitude from his voice. Instead, I distinctly catch a raspy note of something that might be…pain?

"That story is beside the point. I found out later that my mother was sent to Carlos by none other than Lia Pavalos. But as far as I knew, she hated that bitch," he adds bluntly, his gaze fixed somewhere in the distance. After a long while, he shakes his head, eyeing the recorder again. "So I didn't believe Lia at face value. Not until I heard her speak." He raises the device higher and strikes play.

"I know you have no reason to trust me," my mother said. *"But to be frank, you're the only person I have left to turn to, so imagine how I feel."*

A man answered her, his deep baritone unmistakable. *"You have five seconds before I hang up."*

I gape at the current Domino. Hearing his past self when paired with the present, it's obvious how much colder he's become over the years. Back then, his voice still held a flicker of emotion. Anger—more than when he speaks to me.

"Fine, how about learning the truth about what happened to your little sister?" my mother suggested. *"Don't tell me that you believed a fifteen-year-old girl could disappear overnight without a trace?"*

"I mourned my sister a long time ago," the past Domino said. *"And I refuse to let anyone use her name to dredge up the past, especially not a Pavalos. We're done here—"*

"She's dead," my mother said, so quickly that static almost consumed her words. *"Did you come to that realization by now? She's dead. I don't know if Roy is directly responsible, but I'm sure he had a hand in it."*

Domino's silence reveals his answer better than words could.

"Why are you telling me this?"

"Because she was just one in a long line of victims. Victims of my husband and his blind ambition. But I'll spare you the false sympathy. I didn't contact you out of some misplaced sense of guilt, but I need someone with as much of a stake in this race as I have."

Watching Domino's expression now, I think I have a decent mirror into how he must have looked back then, grappling with the revelations my mother told him. Obviously, he came to the decision to trust her, at least within his five-second deadline, because he finally speaks.

"Why the hell would I trust anything you have to say?"

"Because at the end of this, we can both get what we want. An end to the empire of Roy Pavalos. Did you read the diary?"

"You mean the recollections of a schoolgirl you now claim was murdered?"

A pang of guilt shoots through me at the grit in his voice. I can't imagine the pain he must have felt having someone dangle the past over his head.

Though petty vengeance smothers the pity. My mother merely played him the same way he's been playing me— doling out information in snippets at a time.

But this isn't the woman I knew for the past twenty-five years of my life. I don't even recognize her.

"Do you want to know why I'm really calling you?" she asked Domino as the recording continues. *"I'm afraid. I've seen the damage my husband can leave in his wake. No longer can I watch him wreak havoc and pretend I don't see it."*

"Let me guess. You've had an epiphany?" Domino asked.

"Something like that," Lia replied just as coldly.

"You really want me to believe that you would turn against your own husband?"

"No," my mother said. *"I want you to believe that what I've learned is horrifying enough that I can't be a part of this anymore. I can't stay silent, and I can't watch my daughter be roped into this darkness without knowing that I did something to stop it."*

"What the hell are you talking about?" That irritated note is a trademark of the Domino I know, but my mother wasn't intimated by him.

"I'm talking about women—young girls—being sold to the highest bidder. I'm talking about a criminal enterprise in which my husband can kill, beat, or destroy anyone to cross his path simply because he feels like it. I'm talking about his henchmen who do things that would curl your toes—"

"Why would she ask you for help?" I interject.

Domino merely raises a finger to silence me, letting the recording play on.

"Again, why contact me?" he asked.

"Can you honestly tell me that you aren't the least bit curious as to what really happened to your sister?" Lia replied. *"What she might have found on Roy Pavalos to warrant murder? Have you really been able to live in peace all this time without knowing why? I certainly haven't been able to."*

"So then tell me what happened."

"I don't expect you to listen to me without evidence. For now, just know that I have the answers," Lia continued. *"This was the first call. I'll let you think over what I've said before I contact you again."*

"And what if I were to tell your husband about this?"

Her laughter was a shadow of the charming giggle I grew up hearing echo off the walls of our estate. *"He wouldn't believe you, even if you played this recording for him. I assume you were smart enough to capture this conversation, yes? Keep it for your records. I have nothing to hide."*

"Except your evidence," Domino pointed out.

The line must go dead because the next few seconds only contain a staticky silence.

"What evidence did she give you?" I croak, my mind racing.

He tosses the recorder back into the sack, but I can't resist the thought that there might be more on it that he didn't play.

My mind keeps circling back to how my mother phrased my relationship with my father—*I can't watch my daughter be roped into this darkness.* I've never heard that note of horror in her voice before. In fact, I've never heard her speak so openly to anyone. Envy colors my view as I cycle through every interaction I've witnessed between her and Domino Valenciaga. I mistook his concern for her out of kindness, but was there more to it?

"What was the nature of your relationship with her?" I demand outright.

He raises an eyebrow, shifting from guarded to amused in a heartbeat. "She gave me what I needed to join a reckless crusade against Roy Pavalos, if that's what you mean."

"And what was that?"

His eyes take on a faraway look as he says, "I don't know if you're ready to hear it."

"So you lie and obscure." I haul myself upright, aiming for the doorway. "Maybe I should take my chances with rattlesnakes and heat stroke—"

"Wait." His voice…

The rawness in it stops me in my tracks. Regardless, he grips my forearm, but there's no real force in the touch.

"Your mother told me that only one person held the answers. About what happened to Pia. What she stole and why. Everything."

"My father?" I ask, meeting his probing stare.

But the look on his face is anything but smug.

"No," he says carefully. "*You*."

"M-Me?" Every ounce of air leaves my lungs. I somehow manage to croak just two words. "You're lying."

Though why would he? My mother is dead so there's no point in trying to turn me against her. A smarter move would be to convince me to join his crusade against my father by painting him as a murderer. It's what he's done all along, after all.

But did he ever believe that?

Or all this time, was I the one he truly plotted against? I think back to the collar. The whip. Everything he's done since.

Those weren't random acts of violence.

It was retribution.

"You believed her…" I stagger, grasping for anything to keep me upright. I find it in a wall of strength that nearly knocks me off-balance, sturdy and impenetrable. At the same time, I cringe away from him. "Don't—"

"She loved you."

I flinch at his tone. He sounds so damn angry, as if he cares more about my perception of her than of himself.

"You killed her." Angrily, I push against his chest. Unsurprisingly, he doesn't budge.

"She only ever went against your father for *you*, but I'm not here to rehash some family drama. For the longest fucking time, I tried to hate you. I spent every waking moment trying to square the woman I saw with the creature I've had described to me. By Pia. By your mother…"

"And what kind of woman was that?" I ask, even though I already know the answer.

He seems to take his time compiling one, anyway, his lips pursed in concentration. Finally, he meets my gaze again. "The kind of woman who betrays her friends, does her father's dirty work, and sleeps with any man who flashes a bit of money her way."

It's a fair enough impression—but admitting that doesn't make hearing it sting any less.

Especially when I contrast his opinion of me with the one I'd always held of him. This supposed stranger who entered my life, was a blank slate. Someone with a fresh, untainted view of Terra Rodea. How stupid I'd been.

"So you believed them?"

"No," he says, catching me off guard. "But I don't think you can blame them, either."

"Oh really?"

"No. Because of *him*. Roy Pavalos taints everything he touches. You've lived in blissful ignorance of who he really is for twenty-five years. As cruel as you think I've been to you, I haven't even told you the half of it—but maybe I should pull the wool from your eyes—"

"I know exactly who my father is!" I succeed in wrenching from his grasp and continue to back away until my shoulders strike the wall beside the bed. But then I turn around, fumbling with the hem of my shirt, exposing my back to him. "I have the scars, remember? I know who he is…"

But I think I've always stopped myself from understanding just what he's capable of. No more.

"Stop stringing me along and tell me. If you want my trust, then this is your only chance to earn it. So spit it out." I turn to face him, but the look of disgust on his face is the last sight I expect.

"Let's start with your father," he says. "I've seen the cruelty he is capable of firsthand, and I'm telling you now—you don't know the half of it."

I swallow hard at the confidence in his tone. It's a dangerous emotion where he is concerned, typically displayed before he reveals some trick hidden up his sleeve. Like a collar, a whip, or the cruel, cold truth.

"I do know one thing," I admit. "That you killed for him."

"You do?" he counters, cocking an eyebrow. "Because you saw the bodies for yourself? Or because it was simply in my job description?"

Ironically, his "job description" was one of the many things about him that seemed so damn conflicting. As sick as that makes me, I used to obsess over the work he supposedly did for my father. It was puzzling. How could a man, seemingly noble enough to attend to a sick woman, be capable of all manner of horrific acts at my father's behest?

"I never cared," I lie. "But that just puts into perspective how much of a hypocrite you seem to be."

He raises an eyebrow, those lips set quizzically. He isn't angry. More… Curious. "Oh really? Think. Why would your mother seek me out in the first place? Why would she want me so damn close to him?"

I feel my brows furrow. "What are you saying? You deserve brownie points for faking your loyalty to him?"

"Not quite." His voice takes on that low, grated quality that wrings a shiver from me. "I couldn't put a wrench into all of his plans, mind you. But where I could, I carried out Don Roy's orders, just in ways he wouldn't expect."

"Are you claiming you never killed after all?"

"No, I did," he admits, and the look in his eye confirms that grim insinuation. "In self-defense mostly. Typically, I arranged for slightly different fates for his intended targets. I made a note of them all. Meticulously. That was what your mother tasked me with."

My eyes narrow as I recall the list I found earlier. The one that seemed coded with various names and locations. Did he leave that document there specifically for me to stumble upon?

I wouldn't put it past him. God, the man is infuriating. Groaning, I dig at my temple with my trembling left hand, trying to see through the maze of lies and half-truths he's been spinning all this time. In the end, I can't make sense of a damn one.

"He would have found out sooner or later," I counter, exasperated. "Especially if there were no bodies to show for those executions—"

"Oh, there were bodies. All mutilated beyond true recognition—but dental records and DNA could, of course, be faked. After all, I convinced you with a clever arrangement of barbeque and a few persuasive words, didn't I?"

And perhaps I can feel less like a fool for falling for his trick in the first place.

"So you've spent half a decade lying to me and everyone else. What an achievement. And to think, I used to admire you."

What I intend as an insult has a vastly different effect—he smiles in a beautiful display of white teeth. It doesn't reach his eyes, however. They gleam, containing the fragments of his signature fearsome rage. "Do you even know what it is a woman *should* admire in a man? You talk about loyalty, but what about patience? I've wanted the same woman for the past five years."

The intensity in his voice steals the breath from my lungs. Tortuously, he lets the silence linger as if to prove how little power I have when he's like this. Starkly honest, his gaze taking on that distant, impassive shade of green.

"I've studied this woman in and out," he adds, crossing his arms. "I gave her the benefit of the doubt despite every fucking thing pointing to the same conclusion. I don't live in a fantasy land, Ada. I trust only what I can see. What I can taste. What I can feel."

"And what did you feel?" My voice sounds so fragile in comparison to his. "It must not have been strong, because you were still able to hurt this woman. Abuse her in the worst way. Make her doubt everything. Unless you're speaking of Alexi."

"Then you haven't been paying attention." His voice takes on that low, grated quality again, raising goosebumps with every strained syllable. "I've tried to deny it. Believe when I say that I wish more than anything that I didn't give a damn about you."

"So why hurt me? Why lie to me? That's not caring. That's not respect. That's not…"

I shy from voicing this particular word. It sounds so melodramatic to say, all things considered. And yet, I wind up blurting it out anyway. "That's not love."

"I think it's been well established that we both don't know a damn thing about what that word truly means."

As if that makes it any better. As if that excuses what he's done to me and erases the painful past lingering between us. Like hell it does.

"Besides, if hurting someone isn't 'love,' then what does that say for your father?"

The bastard. I hate the way he can do this—how he takes joy in twisting my perceptions and corrupting the world around me.

"Don't bring him into this—"

"Why not?" He uncrosses his arms, keen to take on the challenge—but the look in his eye doesn't inspire the dread I'm used to feeling. It's different, a softer hue of greenish-brown. "My own father was a drunk who ran out on my mother when I was too young to even tie my shoes. He left her pregnant, with a job that could barely pay half of the bills. She was too busy trying to keep a roof over our heads to do much else. I grew up believing that love was expressed in smothered tears and fake smiles. You wallow in your misery as the daughter of a wealthy politician, but I can assure you that growing up in poverty isn't much better. My mother never whipped me, at least." He sighs, his lips pursed. "I might have preferred if she could. If she had some outlet."

"I don't think any parent should look to their child as an outlet of any kind." Horror seeps into my voice, too real to disguise.

The hard line of his jaw softens a fraction—but even that slight change is enough to transform him. For a second, he resembles the man I used to pine over—stoic and unreachable.

"You have a point," he says thickly. His eyes lose their guarded nature for a heartbeat—and I'm frozen, holding my breath. "And a man shouldn't look to the one woman he claims to love as a symbol of everything he hates—*son of a bitch*!"

His tone is whiplash, and I recoil as if struck. Then I realize that his gaze isn't aimed my way, but on the nearby computer screen. One look, and I see exactly what has him on edge.

A sleek black truck pulls into the frame, presumably from one of the cameras tracking movement toward the shack. It skids to a stop in a cloud of dust, and two men climb out, moving swiftly in our direction.

CHAPTER EIGHT

"God damn it, Luis," Domino snaps.

I picture the gray-haired man. Did he betray our location?

"What's going on?" I ask.

Turning to me, Domino jerks his chin toward the floor. "Finish getting dressed. Then stay here and stay quiet. Don't even breathe unless I tell you to."

I stare as he mounts the steps, slamming the trap door behind him. Swallowing hard, I look back at the computer monitor in time to catch the men approaching the door. In the same instant, Domino opens it to greet them.

"Ralph, Mick. This is an unexpected visit." His voice easily reaches through the earth and wood down to me.

"Mateo had a feeling you snuck into his territory unannounced," a male replies, his voice unfamiliar. "He'd like to have a word with you. Clear the air, so to speak."

"Oh, is that so?" Domino's voice deepens to the raspy baritone I know all too well. "Is he keeping tabs on me now?"

"What's a little surveillance, all in the name of friendship, Dom? He would like to 'rehash' the terms of your agreement. Considering that Jaguar's raising hell from here to the border, it's not like you have plenty of places to go. Speaking of Jaguar…are you alone?"

"Why wouldn't I be?"

"Because Jaguar seems to think that you went on the run with someone that you weren't supposed to. How did he put it? His 'merchandise'? Mateo was very interested in that aspect."

"If Mateo is so interested," Domino replies, "why didn't he come here himself?"

"What would the fun in that be?" the second man replies.

I can't make out much of them from the grainy camera footage, but one man is nearly as tall as Domino, while the other looks to be a foot shorter. Both wear loose-fitting shirts and jeans, with the shorter man sporting a backward baseball cap.

As they barge inside, I can't tell from Domino's posture whether he believes them to be friends or foes, but I notice that he stands protectively near the trap door leading to the lower level.

"Mateo doesn't want a fight here, Dom," the first man states. "Why not come quietly?"

"Come quietly," Domino murmurs. "That doesn't sound very 'friendly.'"

"Well, I don't think you have much of a choice, considering that Mateo isn't in the mood to take no for an answer, and Jaguar is out for blood. You think Mateo is the only one who figured out you'd be here? The bastard's crazy as fuck, but he sure ain't stupid. Now… Let's be *friends*."

Silence extends for seconds before Domino's shape flickers in the footage. A heartbeat later, his voice rings out.

"Ada-Maria." I hear the rattle of the trap door opening and the staircase creaking beneath his weight. I stiffen as he appears in the doorway, his expression shadowed.

"Get ready to head out." It seems like he's speaking to me, but I'm already dressed, my boots firmly tied.

When I start toward him, he raises a hand in a silent command. Then he approaches the sack, grabbing something that he slips into his pocket. When he returns to my side, he immediately presses an item against my palm.

"Keep this on you—" Warm, his lips nudge my ear as he whispers, "don't let them see it. Anyone so much as looks at you wrong, be ready to use it."

I swallow hard, registering the weight of the object he's given me. My only reference source is the much smaller utensil that I'd use to slice cucumbers—a knife.

"Hide it." Domino guides the blade into the pocket of my jeans. It's thin, conforming to my hip. I can't even see its shape through the denim.

"Come on." Impatient, he leads the way toward the staircase.

I hesitate, unable to tear my gaze from the computer monitor. Those men hoover near the trap door, and it hits me all at once that, yet again, I'm on another dangerous precipice. With Jaguar, I had at least some small level of buildup to go on.

"Ada Maria—"

"Coming." I step forward, keeping my injured arm to my chest as I mount each step. Days of isolation have made me overly sensitive. I smell these men before I even see them— musk and sweat and the spicy hint of tobacco.

"So this is the little missy causing all of the trouble," one of them growls as I reach the mouth of the trapdoor. For a second, Domino's bulk blocks my view, but when he moves, I'm faced with the two figures I witnessed on the camera footage in stark detail.

The shorter one is blond, his smile crooked, his brown eyes beady. Beside him stands the taller man, his hair a cropped black, his skin tan, and his eyes a rich, unreadable brown.

The taller man inclines his head. "Shall we?" He's the owner of the first voice I heard while down below.

"Lead the way," Domino commands, but he draws even closer to me.

I follow him outside, relieved to find that the setting sun robs the heat of its intensity. A rich, orange slashes the sky just above the horizon, tinging everything in a bloody scarlet.

The truck the men drove is parked just a few feet away, coated in a layer of reddish earth. Apparently, they weren't in the mood to take the scenic walk Domino and I did.

"Looks like you'll have to ride in the ass end, Dom," the shorter man says while the other claims the driver's side. "Though, we could make an exception for your friend. I'm sure I could find a seat for her." His gaze travels up and down my body.

"Not necessary," Domino says, possession radiating through his voice. "She stays with me. Unless Mateo gave you alternative instructions…"

The taller man laughs him off. "Easy, Dom. Have it your way."

Leveraging his weight against me, Domino easily steers me toward the back bed. It's covered in dust, with only a low guardrail and a hatch to keep us from falling out. As we near it, the engine roars to life, revving menacingly.

"Here—" Domino grips my waist, giving me enough of a boost to climb up one-handed.

Swiftly, he settles beside me. At the same moment, the truck lurches over the uneven ground. Somehow, Domino manages to wrench the tailgate shut as the vehicle picks up speed. The only reason I don't go flying is because he slings his arm over my shoulders next, riveting me to his side.

"Buckle up!" one of the men shouts from the front seat.

Domino's expression is rigid, his eyes fixed on the rapidly receding shack.

"Don't trust them." His voice invades my ear, resonating deeper than the roar of the engine. In this case, I'm inclined to take him up on that advice.

We're moving recklessly across the landscape, seemingly with no clear direction. Up ahead, the moon is a faint circle of silver against a darkening sky while the sun still makes its final stand in a vibrant display of color.

In this moment, the inhospitable environment seems beautiful—a lovely contrast to the urgency Domino barely manages to suppress. His pulse is surging, spurring mine on.

Holding his stare, I ask, "Where are they taking us?"

He frowns, processing the question. When he finally lowers his mouth near my jaw, the wooden shack is no longer in sight.

"To Mateo. He controls the drug trade in this region. In terms of temperament, he's cut from the same cloth as Julian, though slightly more reasonable."

I recognize the note of caution in his voice. He speaks of my father the same way.

"What does he want?"

"He'll want to assert himself if he thinks he has my balls in a vice," he adds gruffly. "Just follow my lead and keep a clear head. He feeds off making people squirm."

"How did he find us?"

"Luis," Domino says grimly. "The bastard must have made a deal."

It's addictive, hearing him speak so freely. Amid the uncertainty, I'm reckless enough to push this brief window as far as I can.

"How did you meet him?"

Whether I mean Jaguar or Mateo, I'm not sure. Perhaps both, and I wait anxiously for whatever reply he's willing to offer. He claimed my mother played a role. I need to know more.

Suddenly, the truck picks up speed, sending the wind rushing past my head, whipping my hair into a frenzy. The chaotic noise provides cover for Domino to find my ear again and speak without the risk of being overheard.

"You already know part of the story," he points out. "Your mother meddled in my life to arrange a life-saving transplant. Maybe you should think from *that* perspective. How would she know men like Carlos Domingas?"

He's bringing this up for a reason. Perhaps not just to taunt me.

"You love to speak in riddles. Don't tell me my mother taught you that as well?"

"No." He adjusts his position, spreading out one leg over the dusty flatbed while keeping the other braced against the sidewall.

"As it turns out, you get a taste for various hobbies when you've spent the first half of your life on mandatory bed rest."

A chill washes over me. There's something so murky about his past, even though I knew everything there was to know about his sister.

Almost everything.

To think that there was a whole part of her life—a whole person—that I barely had knowledge of. Someone who, a decade later, has dominated my world in various ways. The shift is karmic in a sense, everything coming full circle.

But where will it finally end?

"Tell me more," I plead. "About your life with the Domingas family."

If it bothers him to continue this tale in the back of a truck, he doesn't show it.

"From what I've heard, Juan wasn't quite as charismatic as Jaguar. Supposedly, he was Carlos' favorite, the one he never believed was cut out to fit in his world. Too soft-hearted. Too weak. He was only nineteen when he died, but the circumstances were cloudy at best. I just know that they found him collapsed one day, and he never regained consciousness."

"So Carlos offered you his heart?"

It sounds odd to me, though I come from a world where men hoard everything from money to women selfishly. If one of my brothers were in the same position, I'm positive my father would rather let him die than relinquish a part of his precious Pavalos bloodline to anyone.

Would my mother do the same?

My memories of Lia feel as fragile as broken glass, far too sharp and numerous to ever put back together.

I picture her, beautiful with a delicate face, wide blue eyes, and gently curling hair in the same blond shade as mine. We were never similar in appearance or personality. I was curvy and cripplingly shy as a teenager, while she seemed born thin, and tall with a breathtaking beauty that didn't require a surgeon and makeup to achieve.

All in all, she was the shining example of my father's warped version of what family should be—meek, quiet fealty.

I always believed her innocent of my father's machinations, the humbling factor to his brash public persona—but I was dead wrong. All along, she was just as cunning.

"Carlos Domingas never offered a damn thing to anyone," Domino says, snapping me back to the present.

This area seems even dustier, and I'm coughing, jerking with every jolting lurch of the truck. From inside the cabin, I can hear the faint pulse of rock music, adding a strange contrast to the intimacy of this conversation.

"Then why?" I ask.

"You need to understand how the Domingases see the world. How they view their family and what it means to them. For Juan and Julian, there was no other reality than their father's empire. No talk of college or getting a job outside of the family business. The Domingas realm was their beginning and their end. Close-knit doesn't even begin to describe it. So, no, Carlos didn't just give me his son's heart. In effect… I merely took Juan's place. I became him."

CHAPTER NINE

He makes it sound more macabre than a symbolic acceptance, but I choke back my horror and listen.

"My mother had no idea what she signed me up for. Not that it would have changed her mind knowing the alternative."

His eyes are stormier than ever, fixed on the darkening horizon. What little sunlight remains is quickly snuffed out by threads of indigo and violet. Darkness rapidly consumes, and the car's taillights ignite the earth with a reddish tint that resembles hellfire.

"What happened?" I ask him.

He inclines his head, gripping me tighter as the truck lurches at an even higher speed.

"What happened is that I made a deal to stay alive. But at what cost? I didn't just accept a donation from Juan Domingas—for all intents and purposes, I became him, with all the same expectations as if I had been born into the Domingas clan. My past identity didn't matter to them. Carlos stripped me of everything I used to be and molded me into who he wanted. Looking back, I can't blame him, not fully. Who would want to lose a son if you could gain another? The only problem was that I was not Juan, not that it mattered to him. Julian, on the other hand…"

He tenses in the way he does only when he speaks of Jaguar. I once suspected that the animosity between them went beyond their little game with me in the middle—and I was right. It's far more personal than that.

"Julian couldn't accept that his brother was dead. To hear him tell it, Juan was a saint, a perfect soul. Innocent. Not a threat to him. But me? I was the opposite of that."

He laughs darkly.

"How?" I ask.

"Let's just say that Julian wasn't used to fighting for his spot. Suddenly, he wasn't the heir apparent, destined to rule after his father. But jealousy is only part of it. That bastard loves owning people, literally and figuratively. And if he thought I wanted you? Not only would you be a useful tool to destroy Roy Pavalos—the bastard he believes killed his father—but you would double as a convenient means through which he could control *me*."

I nearly choke as I remember something Jaguar said.

"If I were to fuck you here and now, plant my seed in that sexy little body. My child would make you mine in a way you could

never escape. Both of you would be my family. Forever and always…"

At the time, I told myself that it was his way of trying to unnerve me. But what if it wasn't a taunt, but a promise.

One big happy family.

"I never planned on selling you to him," Domino adds. "Not once." I feel his arm tense around me as if he expects me to pull away. Maybe I should.

Despite everything he's done, it still stings to hear him discuss my fate so casually. I can't reconcile that with the man who lurked within my line of sight for five years. The stoic figure I used to watch in the dark. The one constant I used as a crutch to get through the hell my life had become.

I can't see him as the monster who pledged me to a future no different than the one I escaped at my father's beck and call. I could glorify that past if I wanted to. Tell myself that I was only doing what any dutiful daughter would. That selling myself was *my* choice.

My mother thought so. The more time passes since hearing that recording, the more it stings, clashing with the part of me aching in mourning for her.

"How did my mother know Carlos Domingas?" I ask, returning to his original dare.

Domino sighs.

"Tell me!" Genuine desperation seeps into my voice. "She led you to a man you describe as a monster. How would she know him? How could she turn on my father like that? And—"

I break off, aware that I'm shouting, but I finish that statement internally anyway.

And how could she just abandon me?

"Your mother loved you."

"Did she?" This is the second time he's insisted that, taking up for her in a way he's never done for anyone else. Not my father. Not me. Not even Pia.

I don't know why it irritates me as much as it does. Doubt sneaks into my skull, arousing a million dangerous thoughts. Like the suspicion that his relationship with Lia Pavalos was far, far closer than he led me to believe.

How ironic would that be? Once my father's trusted right-hand man, he seduced not only his daughter, but his third wife, right under his nose.

"Did she know?" I ask him softly. There's no need to specify what I mean, and my heart tenses up in grim anticipation of the answer.

"Did she know about the plot your father hatched?"

Domino must take joy in spelling it out so clearly, but when I glance up at his expression, smugness isn't what I find. His eyes are narrowed, his jaw thoughtfully tilted. Every bit of the calculating bodyguard he pretended to be is on full display. No wonder my father was fooled by him.

"Yes," he admits, "she did."

My eyes burn. After all the pain I've been through during this nightmare, I would have thought that nothing could hurt more than his torment.

I was wrong.

"Which," Domino adds as my thoughts begin to spiral with betrayal, "is why she begged me to intervene and save your life. That's why she volunteered to lure your father into a trap despite knowing the risk."

A trap…

"The airport?" I ask. "She lured him there?"

"And she didn't hesitate. No matter how hard I tried to talk her out of it. So yes… Ada-Maria, she did love you. More than you will ever know."

The whiplash of these opposing emotions is enough to drive me insane. I think it does, actually. My perception of the universe shatters, and for a split second, I'm almost grateful to Domino Valenciaga.

But therein lies another harsh reality that his words lay bare.

"Why couldn't she tell me any of this herself?"

"Look at me." He brushes his thumb along my lip until I comply. "Put yourself in her shoes. She was married to a monster who corrupted her entire world in his image, even her own child. Don't deny that your father molded you under his thumb. You would have jumped off a cliff if he told you to."

I try to wrench out of his grasp, but he holds fast, forcing me to admit the truth that we both know.

If my father told me to jump in any context, I would only pause long enough to ask him how high. It feels so strange to reconcile that. These past few days alone, I've been able to convince myself that his hold over me wasn't as resolute as it was. That I always had some autonomy in the things I did and said. That I was the same Ada-Maria beneath the sex appeal and carefully cultivated image.

I was lying to myself, of course.

I squeeze my eyes shut against the threat of tears to no avail. They fall regardless as I recall the person I was leading up to my dinner with Tristan.

I wasn't the soulless monster my mother seemed to think I was.

It was worse than that. I was like a bird locked within a cage outfitted with barbed wire. I could tell myself that it wasn't my fault—that I never meant to cause the people around me pain.

Another lie.

After Pia went missing, I was the one who climbed into the prison my father built and gladly locked the door. It wasn't hard molding myself to his influence and becoming the perfect soldier used to further his aims.

It was easy, and his praise outweighed any doubt, comparable to whatever drug I happened to be on at the time. I never had to consciously take the blame for anything I'd done, because deep down, I always knew that I could blame him.

"How did you do it? How did you work for my father all this time? Did you use the drugs to dull your conscience?" I demand, scanning the planes of Domino's face. I want to see it—the same insecurities I feel, chewing at his sense of self-worth, making him feel hollow. I'm not the only one with a bad habit for pills—he's just far better at hiding it.

"Dom-Dom isn't like the rest of us," Jaguar told me on the balcony of Domino's estate. *"He has a much higher tolerance to most benzos, opiates, and the like. It would take a hefty amount to down someone like him. I'm sure he told you all about his tragic backstory."*

"One day, I'll tell you that story," he muses, and the ice in his tone feels like a door slamming shut. Our unfettered conversation is over, and the quiet, cold Domino has returned, glowering at the horizon with a vague expression I can't get a read on. Is it regretful? Or resigned.

"But now, I'll tell you what you need to know to survive. Keep that knife within reach always. Stay as close to me as you possibly can—Mateo will most likely try to separate us. See if you can keep that from happening. If not, the second you can, break away and head for the desert. Keep running no matter what. I'll find you. Do you understand?"

"You always change the subject when the topic turns to you." Rightfully, I'm irritated, but I have enough sense to still pick up on the warning in his tone. This isn't a mind game, I suspect.

Swallowing hard, I eye my injured arm and wonder what else Domino and his associates have in store.

"We're almost there," Domino warns before I can decide on an answer. "Get ready."

I follow the line of his gaze to a ridge jutting from the earth. Even in the semi-darkness, something about it draws attention. Perhaps it's the faint tendrils of light emanating from the base, slightly too bright to be moonlight. Kicking up a cloud of dust in its wake, the truck lurches suddenly to the left, veering toward the natural structure.

"Mateo is reasonable for the most part," Domino adds, continuing my haphazard history lesson on his enemies and allies. "But he's impulsive and prone to outbursts when he feels cornered. Jaguar must be bearing down hard on his ass for him to risk confronting me directly."

I can hear the irritation in his voice. He's on edge, but not for the reason I think I might assume at first glance. He's not afraid of Mateo, as much as he's worried about the lost time.

And he should be. A hospital can only hold a fully conscious and vindictive Roy Pavalos for so long. It's just a matter of time before he comes after any perceived enemy, guns blazing. Whenever I try to picture what he might do to someone like Domino who dared to betray him in such a way…

Domino might find himself being served on a plate, much in the same way he pretended to serve my father to me.

"Don't worry." His voice slips into my ear, and for a second, I wonder if he's truly read my mind. "This little hiccup will only delay my plans for you, nothing more. Whether or not it kills me, I will get you to Terra—"

"Get ready, Dommy Boy!" one of the men calls from upfront. "It looks like Daddy's home!" Raucous laughter gives the statement a sinister tilt.

Domino rises into a crouch, positioning himself near the exit. The closer we come, the easier it is to make out more details of this location. Tucked within the ridge's shadow is a square structure, much larger than the shack he brought me to.

I strain my eyes to make out a line of what looks like barbed wire fencing sealing off a narrow perimeter. Dark shapes flicker in the shadows, and I can finally identify the faint glimmers of light—flashlights.

For all their bravado, the men in the truck fall silent as we near the fortified barrier where a large metal gate bars access to an earthen road.

A man stands behind it, rattling a series of chains that clang menacingly.

"Looks like the boss is feeling feisty tonight," he calls, his voice gruff. "I suggest y'all don't keep him waiting."

"You hear that Dommy Boy?" one of the men upfront shouts. "I don't think Mateo's gonna be very forgiving of the fact that you've left him high and dry after all."

If the taunts affect Domino, I can't tell. He projects the same stoic calm, his eyes fixed on the gate and the figures moving beyond. I count at least six men roaming nearby.

From here, I can only make out the glint of what might be a square, one-story building—one with no windows. As the truck rolls along, we pass one of the men on patrol, flashlight in hand. The brief amount of illumination is more than enough to make out the massive gun slung across his back.

I suck in a breath, inching closer to Domino. I've never seen a weapon like that one up close. It looks military grade, and I suspect that most, if not all, of the men scattered throughout this fenced-in landscape, are carrying something similar.

Suddenly, the truck rolls to a complete stop.

"Well, Dommy, this is where we leave you." The tall man climbs from the driver's seat, leaving us parked in the middle of the fenced-in area.

Behind us, the gate slams shut, and a metallic clang makes me suspect the man we passed is using those chains to bolt it.

What is this place?

I remember what Domino said about his shack and wonder if the same method applies to this area. A stash house for the cartels before they smuggle their illegal goods over the border.

But what kind of smuggled goods would need this level of security or this much space?

I don't think I want to know.

When Domino places his hand on my shoulder, I let him guide me to the back of the truck. Grunting, he climbs out first in a fluid display of grace before reaching up for me. His hands land over my waist, slipping beneath the hem of my shirt to graze the flesh of my belly. I suck in a breath, too startled to resist as he easily lifts me down to him.

"Stay close." His lips nudge my ear as the two men circle around to meet us.

"Oh, one more thing, Dommy," the taller man says as his eyes slither in my direction. "Mateo would like to see you alone. No witnesses." His coarse laugh does little to soften the hostility lurking behind his thin smile. "Don't worry, though. Mick and I will be more than happy to entertain your little friend while you're busy—"

"She stays with me." Domino doesn't even raise his voice, but I feel goosebumps come to life over every inch of my exposed skin.

His stance is electric, his eyes gleaming in the glow of a passing flashlight. The second it darts away, he's a monster composed entirely of shadow, and—despite everything he's done—I never realized how intimidating he can be, based on his sheer size alone. The man is all bulk, and Mick, the shorter of the two, has the sense to take a hasty step back.

"Let's not cause a scene here, Dommy," the taller man warns, still grinning. I don't miss how his right hand falls to the front pocket of his pants though, and I can clearly envision him concealing some kind of weapon there. "Play nice. Boss' rules—no toys inside."

"She stays with me. I suggest you make an exception to the rule, Ralph."

The man's eyes narrow, his smile falling flat. "Listen here, you little bitch—"

"Enough!" A louder voice rings out across the clearing, and I whip my head toward it, finding a man standing in a rectangular doorway cut into the building. Orange light spills out behind him, illuminating his slender build and the rich ebony hue of his skin.

"Let them in," he demands, whirling on his heel to venture deeper inside. Booming, his voice easily reaches us. "I don't have time to clean up a mess, and I'd rather see her for myself. The little bitch who has Julian Domingas breathing down my fucking neck. But I'll tell you this, Domino—you so much as blink in a way I don't like, and I'll give my men the order to shoot you *and* your whore. Understood?"

"Damn," Ralph mutters under his breath. Hissing, he spits onto the earth, inches from Domino's feet. "Looks like you were just saved by the bell, boy."

"Likewise," Domino replies coldly. His grip on me tightens as he heads toward the doorway, and I scramble to catch up.

"We'll be here waiting, just in case Mateo changes his mind," the man with the raspier voice, Mick, calls out. "Or in case we need to clean up a mess after all."

CHAPTER TEN

I suppress a shudder while taking in as much of the building as I can.

Cut into the metal siding is a rigid door swung open to reveal a narrow room with an alarmingly low ceiling. Domino has to bow his head just to clear the doorframe, and he only has a few inches of space remaining once he stands upright.

The floor is dirt-streaked concrete that I highly doubt has ever seen a mop in its lifetime. Naked metal forms the walls, and the slightest noises echo, amplified times a million. I'm mocked by the frantic cadence of my own breathing, along with the steadier, deeper exhalations of the man beside me.

A long folding table cuts the room in half, flanked by an array of rusted metal chairs. At the far end of the table stands a man nowhere near as tall as Domino, but with a slender frame and confident build that gives him a similar allure. He's beautiful too, with large brown eyes set into a face composed of stern features and a chiseled jaw.

I think back to the days my mother would drag me to mass with her, and I'd eye the frescos on the walls out of sheer boredom. Some of them displayed breathtaking images of cherubs with soulless eyes, so real I expected them to blink.

This man looks like he stepped out of one of those paintings, leaving his wings behind.

"Mateo," Domino says, dashing any mystery of his identity. "I can't say I was expecting to pop in for a visit."

"Domino." Mateo smiles. "That's because I didn't expect to have Jaguar up my ass accusing me of betrayal, now did I?"

Whereas Jaguar gave off rough, unpredictable energy much like his feline namesake, Mateo is far harder to read. An animal comparison for him might be a serpentine creature. A sly, cunning snake.

"You weren't supposed to make your move for another three damn days. Should I inform you what that means?" He extends his hand, all five fingers erect. "It means that I didn't have the fucking time to get my men into place—" he lowers a finger, leaving four remaining. "*And,* I didn't finish the fucking passports you asked for. No wonder your little doctor friend came crawling to me, begging for my protection."

His upper lip twitches as if fighting a smile. It's as if he expects Domino to react. When he doesn't, he shrugs, three fingers held high.

"I've lost three days of running my operation in peace. And, finally, Domino? I've lost my patience dealing with you and that psycho at your back. You've caused quite the shitstorm, and my only question now is…"

He palms the table with both hands, leaning over it. The metal squeals in protest of his weight, shifting back and forth on wobbling legs.

"How the hell do you plan to make it up to me?"

Before Domino can even open his mouth, he raises an admonishing finger.

"Trick question—you can't. It's over, Domino. It's all gone to fucking shit. Jaguar is less than twelve hours behind you; did you know that? You'll be lucky if he doesn't send his little gang crashing through the gates any minute. How the hell could you fuck this up?"

"Julian is impulsive," Domino explains, his voice level. "You know that. You also knew that trying to predict him at all was a losing game. I warned you—"

"And I warned you that what you wanted wasn't easy to come by," Mateo spits back. "I can't just conjure false credentials and safe passage overnight, Domino."

"No. But you could have your contacts draft fake papers in less than an hour if you wanted to. You purposefully drew this out in a bid to play the long game and milk Julian before you made your move against him. That was your mistake."

Mateo scoffs, his brows drawn together. "No. I think my *mistake* was getting in the middle of your sibling rivalry in the first fucking place. I had a shipment planned for tonight —a big one. Thanks to you, Jaguar won't let anything leave my compound that isn't your head on a bloody stake. I miss this delivery, I miss my money, and I'm sure you wouldn't want that, would you? Of course not."

"Should I hazard a guess as to what you're transporting that could be that time sensitive?"

"Don't play coy with me." Mateo's voice loses the polished edge. "Don't pretend like you didn't know the nature of my business before you roped me into your plan to circumvent Pavalos."

"And I warned you that I won't ever come near your 'business.' We had an agreement between us, and that didn't include being your errand boy."

Mateo's smile widens. "Ah, I see you've already jumped to a conclusion about how you can graciously solve the problem you created for me. There is another solution, of course—" He turns his eyes on me, and the allegory of devil and angel is starker than ever. "Everyone from the Feds, to Pavalos' proxies, are pissing themselves to get their hands on her, should she happen to be alive. Ada-Maria. Last I heard, the bounty for any information surpassed half a million, and I'm sure it will climb by the day. That's a lovely, tidy sum to more than clear up this misunderstanding between us."

My breath catches at the implication. My father is looking for me.

If he's willing to pay that much money even for information, then there's no way he would throw me to the wolves the way Domino claimed. Right?

I eye the figure in question, but I can't gauge a read on him —though his motives take a back seat to the predatory greed in Mateo's gaze.

"What's stopping me from putting a bullet in your brain and taking her for myself?" Mateo asks.

"I can think of several reasons," Domino replies. "I'll settle with just one, though—within the time it takes me to bleed out, Jaguar will already be at your throat, ready to take over your entire little enterprise. You know it as well, which is why you didn't have Mick and Ralph do your dirty work the second they found me. To go against Jaguar, you need tact, which you frankly don't have."

"You think you're the only one who knows how little Jagger's brain works?" Mateo counters. "Give the bastard a pretty woman to stick his dick into, and he'll be too distracted to give a damn about anything, at least for a few hours. I've been dealing with him long before you came along, Domino. And while you were up Roy Pavalos' ass for the past five years, who do you think had to wrangle Julian's ego on a daily basis?"

"And who do you think still kept him on a leash, despite being up Roy Pavalos' ass for the past five years? Convince yourself that you can take him on alone if you want to. Leave me out of it. As for her..." Domino's upper lip coils back from his teeth for a heartbeat before he reassembles his mask. "Threaten her in front of me again, and you won't have only Jaguar to contend with."

"Brava!" Mateo throws his head back and claps as he circles toward our end of the table. He moves with easy grace, lighter on his feet than Domino could ever be.

Up close, he reminds me of the models I mingled with at social events, beautiful and lithe, bred to be ogled rather than fight.

Most wouldn't consider my father intimidating at first glance, either. He isn't beefy like my uncle Rodrigo, and his charming grin softened the planes of his face. If I didn't know him, I'd see the same fatherly figure most in the city did.

They never witnessed his temper unbridled like wildfire, burning anything within its reach. Or heard the low baritone that could make the insane seem convincing. Doable.

I just need you to get close to him, Ada-Maria. That's it. Close enough to teach the lying bastard a lesson. Prove your loyalty to me. To this family. Don't you give a damn about anything beyond yourself?

My father's unassuming demeanor shielded the monster lurking beneath, capable of any and everything. This Mateo must be cut from the same cloth, just as dangerous.

"Ada-Maria Pavalos in the flesh." I startle from my thoughts as a warm hand captures my chin, lifting it.

My nostrils wrinkle at his scent. I'd expected something delicate, like perfume. Not the acrid stench of cigarettes and beer.

"She's sexy; I will give you that. *Despite* your shitty attempt at a makeover," Mateo adds, raising an eyebrow. "But I've known you long enough to sense that pussy isn't what gets your heart pumping. No, Dom, I don't think it is." He strokes along my jaw and shrugs. "Who knows what secrets lurk inside this pretty skull. That's the real draw for you, I'm sure. Rumor has it Roy kept her close and fed her dirt on allies and enemies alike. Why, Ada-Maria here is a literal fucking encyclopedia on the political intrigue of Terra Rodea. Some men would pay a pretty penny to discover just what those secrets might be."

"And you won't ever get the chance to find out." Domino grips my shoulder, drawing me closer to his side.

Mateo, however, doesn't relinquish his grasp, and I'm trapped between them both.

"You want my help, then you play by my rules," Domino warns. "She isn't even on the fucking table. Understood?"

Smirking, Mateo releases me, raising his hands in a gesture of surrender. "Understood. *Claro.* But I want you to ask yourself who would be a better ally if your chances of getting her into the city turn out to be a pipe dream? Me? I'll just sell her, you know that. Take my money and run. But Jaguar?—especially if the greedy bastard thinks he can get a rise out of you by dangling her body before you in pieces? Oh, Domino. You and I both know that by the time he *does* sell her, there won't be much left. Think about that while you fix the mess you've made."

Domino hisses through clenched teeth. "Where is the drop and when?"

Mateo chuckles, beaming once more. "I'll save the details until you're already in too deep to pull a fast one and decide to make up with Jaguar out of spite. I'm no fool, Domino. Everyone knows that all little Julian Domingas wants is his happy family intact—which is why you have the balls to go against him in the first place. We all can't be so lucky."

I look at Domino, watching how he processes that statement. His eyes narrow imperceptibly, but his expression is otherwise blank.

"I will say, that my little detour isn't too far out of your way," Mateo continues, shrugging. "Two birds with one stone."

"Where?"

A petty realization comes to me—Domino isn't the only one prone to speaking in riddles. I thought he learned it from my mother, but what if it's merely the way Carlos Domingas and his associates interact—via mind games and subtle manipulation.

Mateo must be an expert at this tactic because his eyes gleam with barely concealed excitement. He's enjoying this. "Do you take me for a fool? I know how you operate,

Domino. I'll tell you in good damn time. But first… You can explain what it is you want from little Ada Pavalos, here. As I've stated, the pussy can't be *that* good—" his gaze slithers over my body. "What are you up to?"

"Keep her out of this," Domino snaps. "That's your second warning."

Mateo chuckles. "You think you're far smarter than you are, Dom. Lucky for you, we're on a time crunch. You best get on the road now—" he reaches into his pocket, withdrawing a set of keys that he tosses to Domino, who catches them in a fist. "The job is simple on its face. Nice and clean. You drive to one location. Wait for the goods to be loaded. From there, it's an easy drive to the second checkpoint where you will receive the final cargo. Then you drive it over the border and drop it off at the end destination. Sound easy enough?"

A muscle in Domino's jaw twitches. "It sounds simple," he says softly. "Too simple. What the fuck am I transporting?"

"Ah, but that's the thing." Mateo winks, stroking his chin. "I think it's best if you don't know that little detail. You drive. You leave the truck where you're told, and that's all you have to know. The trip overall will take two days, but I think you can spare the delay given the alternative."

"And if I fulfill your role as an errand boy, what do I get? A participation ribbon and a pat on the head?"

"Yes." All traces of humor leave Mateo's gaze. "And you get my blessing to cross the border. Unless you want to take your chances with Jaguar's men instead?"

He waits for a reply that doesn't come.

"Good," he says with another dazzling grin. "Give my men time to get the truck ready, and you'll leave within the hour. Until then, make yourself right at home, and be sure to play nice. Unlike Jaguar, I don't keep my men on leashes."

Still smiling, he strolls from the room. "Oh, and Domino?" his voice drifts in through the doorway. "You aren't to look at the cargo. Do that, and you forfeit any protection I might otherwise provide you. Just do your job like a good boy, and there won't be any problems."

As he retreats, Domino faces forward, glowering at the far wall. "Stay close to me," he warns. "Something's off."

His hand tightens over my wrist, and I can feel the tension vibrating through his very bones.

"What do you mean?" I croak.

He cocks his head as if listening for something. I do the same, scanning the activity taking place outside. The men are patrolling in the darkness like before, and I don't spy anything abnormal.

Then again, I've never been in a camp of criminals preparing to smuggle something over the border. The tension infects my entire body, leaving me trembling and on edge.

"What do we do?" I whisper to Domino.

"Nothing for now." The words have barely left his mouth when approaching footsteps near our direction.

"Looks like it's your lucky day," Mateo declares with a booming laugh. "We're ready. Remember, you drive to the first checkpoint—and no peeking. You might be in for a surprise if you do. The truck has a tracker embedded in it, of course, along with an *explosive* little surprise should you decide to be naughty and break my one, teensy rule. This way." He beckons us with a curt nod, and I follow Domino out into the darkness.

"There is just one other thing," Mateo says as I pass him. Suddenly, he lunges, snatching my arm.

I barely choke out a scream before Domino is spinning on his heel, tensed to fight. At the same time, Mateo snags a fistful of my hair, wrenching my head back as something jarringly firm encircles my neck. His hand? No, it's too thin, the shape horrifyingly familiar.

Domino's expression only cements the suspicion. "You son of a bitch—"

"A *smart* son of a bitch," Mateo says, releasing me. "Did you really think I'd let you go off with my merchandise and trust that you'd play nice? Think again. These are my terms —a nonnegotiable deadline."

I stagger forward, nearly colliding with Domino—but I'm too focused on my neck to care. With trembling fingers, I trace the contours of the strange, metal device constricting every breath I take.

"A shock collar," Mateo declares. "A brand-new device my boys devised, specifically outfitted with enough juice to kill the wearer instantly, should they step out of line, of course. And don't think of doing something stupid, Dom," he warns as the other man advances, his hands clenching into fists. "I'd be a fool not to have a backup detonator—" He reaches into his pocket and withdraws a small black device that I assume is a remote. "Luckily for you, and your lady friend, you can keep her skull intact as long as you do as I asked. Keep your word, and I'll keep mine. Any questions?"

"You bastard," Domino growls, but he pivots, coming to my side instead. His eyes scan the collar, and I catch that rare glint of emotion I've come to dread—fear.

"Now, we can get down to business. This way." Mateo stalks forward, heading out.

A nudge from Domino is my only cue to follow.

With every step, I'm reminded of the restrictive, constricting pressure on my windpipe. Something Mateo said won't stop replaying in my mind. *You can keep her skull intact...* What the hell did that mean?

"Keep moving," Domino warns grimly, pulling ahead of me.

I can't find enough breath to reply. Instead, I focus on putting one step in front of the other, exiting the structure last. Up above, the sky is a deeper, rich blue that enhances the glimmering moonlight. I can make out the moving shapes of the other men, and as we round the metal building, I finally get a better sense of the scope of this camp.

It's massive, with the barbed fence surrounding the entire perimeter. Yellow floodlights provide an orangish glow that illuminates a walkway beaten into the earth itself, leading to a makeshift parking lot where two massive vehicles sit side by side. One has its headlights on, throwing off a blinding glow.

"This is your baby," Mateo says, gesturing to the truck in question. "The other is a decoy. Mick and Ralph will deploy on a similar route to draw off any suspicion. Your pickup point is a location north of here. That will put you within a day's travel of Terra Rodea. The drop-off is a terminal just outside the city's entrance. You'll go through my route and use the false documents in the glove compartment to escape any unwanted notice. Once you finish the job, you'll be free to go, and we can maintain our friendly relationship. Any questions?"

"The collar?" Domino demands.

"Oh, that comes off at the final checkpoint. As long as you reach it in time with no little hiccups. Mick and Ralph will be my eyes and ears until then."

Without another word, Domino starts for the truck, pulling me behind him.

"Oh, there is one other thing," Mateo adds as we near the passenger's side door. "Since you're filling in for a trip that was already scheduled, the expectation is that you're a driver, returning an empty vehicle after completing a shipment. A female passenger doesn't exactly fit with that cover story, does it?"

"That sounds like your problem," Domino says smoothly. "She stays with me."

"So you say," Mateo replies with a grunt. "But if it comes between you blowing my operation and winding up in federal prison or being a good boy, I think you know which option is preferable. After the pickup, the girl goes with Mick and Ralph, who will cover your rear, and then you can reunite once you cross the border and secure my goods. Everyone is happy." He laughs again, eyeing Domino as if he's preparing for an outburst—a fight I suspect he's itching to have. "Let's keep our *heads* about this, shall we?"

"Fine." Domino nods with a casualness that shocks even me. "Have it your way."

He wrenches open the door and grips my waist, hauling me inside. I scramble onto the seat as he slams the door and circles the truck.

I can't hear whatever words pass between him and Mateo before he opens the driver's side door, but his eyes blaze in a way I can only compare to a handful of moments.

Namely, when I first woke up in his estate and realized the man I'd come to trust only saw me as an enemy.

As the driver's side door closes behind him, he grips the steering wheel before jabbing the key into the ignition.

I open my mouth, prepared with a million different questions—but he shakes his head. "Wait."

I follow his gaze and find Mateo looking on from the edge of the field. Devoid of the spotlight, his real expressions break through his confident façade. He's angry, his teeth gritted. I'm not sure if he can see us through the glass, but I sense his gaze is firmly fixed in Domino's direction.

A hostility that Domino more than reciprocates.

Quiet rage emanates from him as we wait, presumably for a signal to move. In a crackle of static, noise emanates from the console in between Domino's seat and mine. A radio? Another barrage of noise provides a clearer idea of what it is. Voices?

"We'll take the lead, and you follow," a man declares. Judging from the tone, it's Ralph. The other truck revs its engine and then pulls off as two men wrench open another gate on this end of the encampment. "We'll head west, around the main highway for now. First checkpoint in five hours. I assume you won't attempt any unnecessary detours. Until then, we'll be in touch. Safe travels!"

Their laughter echoes ominously before the noise cuts out altogether.

In silence, Domino starts to drive, maneuvering the truck through the gate. The second we clear it, the semblance of civilization once again gives way to the seemingly uninhabitable desert.

"Son of a bitch," Domino hisses through clenched teeth. "I was wrong."

I whip my attention toward him, feeling my heart in my throat. "What? You mean you *didn't* expect him to outfit me with a shock collar?" Despite my terror, my voice comes out barely louder than a whisper.

"Loud noise won't set it off," Domino explains, though that reassurance lessens my unease only a fraction. "I suspect Mateo has it rigged to his discretion. Given that he mentioned the bounty on your head, I doubt he'll be in a rush to detonate it—"

"You don't sound very confident of that," I snap.

But he sighs, almost as if in defeat. "There's something else. Mateo is rarely this reckless. Whatever he wants transported must be hot if he's scrambling to rush it over the border now. The bastard's set us up on a suicide mission."

"So, what now?" I keep dragging the tip of my finger along the edge of my collar, barely touching the cool metal.

Domino takes his eyes from the road long enough to shoot a searching glance my way. "Mateo's hedged his bets, but I am no one's patsy."

"So, what are you planning?"

I'm not familiar with this side of him up close. The calculating man with the intelligence to supposedly outsmart even Roy Pavalos. Someone who could go undetected in the heart of my family for five years. A man that even my mother trusted, though to what aim?

I still don't know.

There's no better time than now to ask, but when I lick my lips in preparation, he sighs.

"Tell me about the night my sister went missing. All of it. Whatever you remember."

"Why?" I blurt out, completely thrown off by the change in subject. "It's hard to remember much with an explosive collar around my neck—"

"Just tell me," he insists. "Call it curiosity, but I need to know."

If possible, I'm even more on edge, my stomach in knots. One reason why he's mentioning this now is driven by pure paranoia. I voice it anyway. "So that you can confirm whatever hate bias you have against me?"

Rather than argue, he faces the road, dead silent.

But I'm not finished. "Was that your plan all along? Toss me to those men and walk away, knowing that you achieved at least one of your aims. You've destroyed another Pavalos—"

"No. I want you to confirm my suspicion that I'm not a fool for risking my neck to keep your ass safe. That I'm not craving a woman who could be a fucking murderer. Don't play coy with me—" he adds before the shock fully sets in.

Murderer. When paired with the topic of Pia, I don't think he'd use that term flippantly. What the hell did my mother tell him?

"Whether it insults you or not, I need to know," Domino insists. "Tell me... Please."

He keeps his gaze on the road as he speaks, and the only indication of emotion is how his eyes blaze.

"I would never hurt Pia." Even I can hear the lie in my own voice.

I may not have hurt her directly, but I played a role. I did my duty as the good daughter, and I didn't let myself think of the consequences. But I never thought those consequences could go beyond a few hurt feelings.

I still can't believe that she's dead. Not really. Domino will take me to Terra Rodea, dig up the lawn of his old home, and we will both realize that he was played for a fool. Pia is still out there. Because…

The alternative is too terrifying to consider.

"Ada…" His voice is so gritty I imagine him shoving each word through clenched teeth. "Please—"

"All I remember is screaming at her," I admit. It's strange to hear him in this role, pleading for answers. "I took her diary, and she confronted me outside our old dorm building. Did my mother tell you that part?" I force a hollow laugh. "She loved me so much that she had me shipped away to a boarding school just twenty minutes from the house. What kind of mother allows that?"

A mother who surrendered her child to the machinations of Roy Pavalos.

"Pia was my friend," I reiterate. "I never wanted to hurt her. She started screaming at me that I was a traitor and a horrible person, and I told her to go to hell." It all unfolds so clearly in my mind, nearing the point in the nightmare where I usually wake up. "I tried to leave. She grabbed my arm. And I pushed her—"

Those words stick in my throat, and I can't find the space to say anything else. In my head, I shoved her away, determined to leave.

The memories after that are a blur. I just remember getting home. Breaking down. Crying so hard it felt like my ribs might break.

"I never saw her again after that." My voice cracks, and for the first time, I let myself fully acknowledge the pain lurking behind the mental wall I've locked all thoughts of Pia behind. I miss her. God, I miss her so much. "I did love her, and I wish I knew what happened to her—"

"You think you don't?" His voice is so cold I jump and peer in the side-view mirror, half-expecting to find Mateo and his men in hot pursuit. But no. Now, at least, I can identify the source of his animosity toward me.

Pia. It's always been Pia.

"I don't think," I rasp, licking my lips to find traction to keep speaking. "I *know* I don't know what happened—"

"Really? Because your mother seemed to think that you did."

It hurts, like a rusty knife sinking deep, to hear him speak of my mother so freely. So intimately. I cringe from imagining how they must have interacted, trading secret glances, and whispered lies. It's so hard to process the idea of her actively working against my father, but Domino's confidence undermines any lingering doubts I may have. He is a man who trusts few and claims to understand only a handful of people. Jaguar. My mother. My father.

He's studied them like a book.

And he wouldn't make a claim like that if he didn't think he could prove it. Knowledge of that suffocates me, and I reach for the handle of the door even though I know jumping out now would be futile. I entertain the thought anyway.

But then I picture the humiliation of having him be the one to rescue me. Again.

All with that hate shining in his eyes.

"What are you saying?" I ask, facing him directly.

"Ada…" He sighs in exasperation, gripping the steering wheel so tightly that his knuckles strain against the skin. "You asked me why your mother would believe you were too much like your father? Think back to the events surrounding Pia's disappearance and honestly ask yourself why that may be."

"Stop speaking in riddles and just tell me!"

"No," he says darkly. "I'll show you." He reaches into his pocket, withdrawing an object that he tosses onto my lap.

I barely manage to catch it, preventing the small device from falling—the recorder.

"Press play," he demands, coldly eyeing the road. "And after this, no more lies."

CHAPTER ELEVEN

I suck in a breath, registering the feel of the device against my palm. It's so light despite containing something so weighty—my mother's voice. The last words I'll ever hear her speak.

Am I ready to listen?

"Press play," Domino commands, making the decision for me.

I stall for a few more seconds, cycling through the potential explanations. Did my mother learn about my father and Pia? Or perhaps she told Domino some trivial story about me as a teenager, and *that's* what's fueled his hate.

I hope he truly is that petty. There is only one way to find out. Finally, I press play.

"…I love my daughter," my mother said, her voice a shadow of the soft murmur I always knew.

"I do. But I never protected her the way a real mother should. I let her be swayed to sin, and I stood by as Roy corrupted her soul. You ask why I would come to you? Because Navid Inglecias died years ago, far too weak to ever prove a threat to him. You are one enemy he will never see coming. I used to be content to wait for God to take action upon Roy, but I'm afraid I can't wait any longer. After what he's done to Ada..."

"What has he done?" Domino's voice is a jarring reminder. I'd been so lost in hearing my mother speak, I'd forgotten this conversation was from the past. *"Frankly, I don't have the time to listen to your heartfelt regrets."*

"I know you don't," Lia insisted. *"I'll cut right to the point, then. Unwittingly, your sister took something she didn't understand the significance of. Something that, even revealed after all these years, will paint him out to be the monster he's always hidden from the world. It's all part of a web more twisted than you can imagine. All this time, the bastard thought I didn't know. That he was that damn good at hiding everything from me. He even kept a file on your family after all these years. I didn't understand why at first. He's afraid."*

"Cut to the point," Domino snapped. *"You said Pia's dead. How do you know that? Prove it, or we're done—"*

"Wait!" Lia inhaled raggedly, her anxiety so palpable I can feel it, tightening my chest with every breath. *"All I know is the morning after your sister went missing, Ada-Maria was so distraught I couldn't get a word out of her. Hysterical. There was blood..."*

My heart pangs. *No.* This is too much—obviously another mind game. My thumb twitches over the stop button.

"Don't." Domino grabs my wrist, taking one hand off the wheel. "Just listen."

"She was covered in it," my mother said matter-of-factly. *"Her back looked like it had been torn to pieces. Shredded... Roy wouldn't tell me what happened, and Ada... It was like she became another person overnight—not that I can blame anyone but myself."*

"What are you saying?" Domino demanded, his anger as electric then as it is now.

Lia sighed. *"I'm saying that you have every right to revenge, but the only reason I'm contacting you at all is Ada. I want my daughter protected when Roy's lies inevitably catch up to him. He has far too many enemies. I can't protect her."*

"Why would I give a damn about your family?"

"Because if you protect my daughter, I will ensure that you have access to resources you could only dream of, and plenty of connections to topple Roy Pavalos from the inside out. It could take years to achieve, but I think if your ordeal has taught you anything, it's that patience can be rewarded."

"But at what cost?" Domino bit back. *"I don't think your 'resources' are quite the gift you believe them to be."*

"Perhaps not, but you don't have any better options. To take down Roy, the most vital piece will be finding your sister's body. Only one person in the world can help you do that."

"Your daughter? I hope you don't think I'm stupid enough not to pick up on what you've been alluding to."

"No, you're not," my mother admitted. *"And I won't insult your intelligence by denying it. I think my daughter might have played a role in your sister's death, but even if she did... She isn't evil—"*

"Stop the car."

I lunge for the door, gasping as pain lances up and down my injured arm. But I don't care. I ram against it until it flies open.

I only catch a glimpse of the dark, uneven landscape below before I jump, throwing myself onto the ground. The collar jolts with the movement, biting into the tender flesh of my throat—but by some miracle, I don't black out instantly, instead landing heavily on my knees, tasting dirt. Belatedly I realize why—he's already stopped the truck.

"Damn it!" I hear the driver's side door fly open, and I scramble to my knees as Domino races to my side. I've only gone a few feet from the vehicle itself, but the earth is jagged and rocky beneath me. Domino almost slips as he comes to a stop.

"Are you fucking insane? You want to break your legs next—"

"Get away from me!" I lash out, one-handed, but the anger toward him is irrational. The real source is already dead and gone. I can't scream at her. I can't slap her. Can I even hate her?

Yes. A sob rips from my throat, and tears fall as everything I thought I knew finally crumbles down around me.

All these years… She knew. Long after I told myself that I was just *that* good at hiding it. The abuse. The pain. The fear. I never went to her directly. No, like the good daughter I strived to be, I merely swallowed it all and smiled through the discomfort.

Meanwhile, she twiddled her thumbs and begged for help from a stranger rather than come to her own daughter and…

What? Apologize?

The wounded little girl in me demands more than that. She should have used whatever resources she promised Domino to cover her own escape. She should have divorced my father like his previous wives did and never looked back. She should have intervened the first night he reached for a belt or a whip.

She should have protected me.

But that would have been too easy, I guess. Instead, she primed a stranger to destroy her own family rather than do the job of a real mother.

I hate her. I hate her so much it hurts, like my chest might explode from the sheer intensity of it all. Ironically, my father never inspired this kind of seething rage despite everything he's done. I never made the excuses for him that I did for her, perfect, precious Lia who always stood faithfully by his side.

"I need you to listen to me." Domino's voice seeps into my skull, inescapable no matter how hard I shout to drown him out.

Because I *am* shouting. Screaming.

"How could she? How?" My throat aches, but I can't stop. "How could she just leave me there if she cared so damn much? How could she ignore what was happening in front of her own goddamn eyes? She should have never reached out to you in the first place. She only had to come to *me*!"

I would have listened. I spent so damn long convincing myself that a good daughter obeyed her parents' demands no matter how demeaning, how cruel, or senseless.

Or how twisted.

I'd been taught that being a Pavalos trumped any other loyalty or moral—but not only by my father. My mother's devotion served as a living example of his twisted standard. God, I used to seethe at how she could stand beside him and smile. If she could do it, then how could I ever dream of breaking away?

Domino should have known that better than anyone. My burning eyes latch onto him, standing paces away without an ounce of visible emotion. He should be smiling. Laughing. Gloating.

This is what he wanted all along, wasn't it? To hurt me.

"You... You believed her. You never even asked me. Had no proof. Nothing. You just took her word, and you think I'm the sick one?"

More tears fall as I recall just how oblivious I was to them both. The times I would pine after him like a cat in heat, or when I took pity on my mother for what her life had become.

"I never did anything to you," I croak as my vision blurs. "I only admired you. You think you've done all of this to destroy my father, but you haven't. You've become worse than he is. You're the same kind of monster! ...Say something!"

I'm unnerved by his silence. It stretches on and on. When I wipe away my tears and see his face clearly, his frown is unexpected.

"Your father was only one of my targets," he admits, sinking into a crouch.

I steel myself against the part of me that lurches at the concern in his voice. The genuine Domino is so elusive that I'm never sure when he's merely putting on an act at my expense. Though...he's rarely composed himself like this, speaking freely on my level, no hands around my throat, no blood spilling between us.

"A mere stepping-stone on a much larger goal. Your mother had her flaws," he tells me. "She was self-righteous to a fault, and prone to underestimating those around her. She used the Bible as a litmus test and refused to acknowledge when it fell short. She loved you more than I think you will ever know."

"And she turned you against me from the very start," I surmise.

"No." He cocks his head, surprising me. "In fact, I think she went through great lengths to ensure I couldn't kill you, even if I wanted to."

Does that upset him? His eyes darken, as unreadable as ever. Desperately, I try to decipher something, but he reaches out, smoothing a stray piece of hair from my face.

The gesture disarms me, and my rage sputters and dies. "What do you mean?"

His mouth tilts into a grim smile. "Think back to what you told me about Pia. Something only you would know—and information conveniently missing from her diary."

His tone conjures one episode in particular—Pia's affair with my father, and her possession of my mother's ring. He's right. Only one person could have deliberately hidden that detail. "My mother... She ripped out the missing pages?"

He nods, removing his hand from me to stroke his chin instead. "I assume she felt that only you could fill in the blanks."

"So you're blaming her for holding me captive? For whipping me?"

"Give me more credit than that, Ada-Maria. I had more voices than your mother's in my ear."

I start to deny that assertion, but then I remember that he had Pia's diary all this time. And there was one other "voice" who had every reason to poison him against me.

"Alexi."

He smiles in a far-off way, devoid of any warmth. "She has no love for you, that's for sure. But even petty gossip isn't enough. I saw what you would do for him without asking any questions. No hesitation. Seemingly no regret. You don't realize the kind of woman you come off as. So goddamn vulnerable one minute…" He extends his hand again, stroking his thumb along my cheek. "And heartless the next. You fuck with men and women for the sheer hell of it. And yet I am supposed to ignore the countless voices telling me the same thing?"

"Yes." I shrug off his touch. "If you ever want to claim that you cared for me in some way, you would have. You wouldn't trust the word of a woman who fucks a man like Jaguar either. Did she help you spy on him too? Or is she just drawn to anyone who sees themselves as an enemy of my family?"

Domino chuckles, inclining his head, his gaze shrouded by shadow. Only the planes of his face, highlighted by moonlight, have any definition, rendering him as impassive as the landscape surrounding us. "Not that it's any of your business, but Alexi's reasons for working with Jaguar have nothing to do with you, though I doubt you can believe that. In your world, everything revolves around Ada Pavalos."

"So what are her reasons, then?"

He shakes his head. "That is for her to tell. Just know that her rationale for supporting Jaguar is no different than yours for supporting your father. Loyalty, however misplaced it may be."

I stiffen at the comparison. "Then why not protect her from him the way you have me?"

Though, has he really? When I think through his actions, they could be merely characterized as him selfishly protecting his asset. My life matters to him until the second I deliver whatever information he's after.

His expression, however, doesn't portray the cold cruelty I expect.

"Do you think what I've done has been to protect you?" Again, he fingers a lock of my hair—only he tugs, triggering a stab of sharp, brief pain. The second I gasp, he relents. "No… Everything I've done has been entirely selfish. When all of this is over, you might find yourself envying Alexi."

I slap his hand away and relish the brief surprise that crosses his face. As much as he claims to know me inside and out, he didn't predict that.

"You always try to distract when I get too close," I croak. "Just tell me the truth. Please."

"The truth…" He appears to mull over the question. Hell, I have to wonder if he even knows why himself. "The truth is that Mateo isn't planning to uphold his little plan. My guess is this 'checkpoint' is really an ambush, and his men will strike at the first opportunity. The bastard knew better than to risk close combat with me. When he strikes, it'll be out in the open or with no warning. Usually, I'd let him play his little game and turn the tables when he least expects it."

"But this time?" I prod, sensing an unspoken *but*.

His mask wavers before finally cracking to reveal the unease lurking beneath. "Things will get messy from here on out. What I need is your trust—"

"Then tell me what you're really after. No more games. No more lies."

"Fine." He moves too quickly to track.

Before I realize it, I'm on my feet as well, pinned to the side of the truck. His breath nuzzles my cheek, his eyes so intense it hurts to meet them head-on—a dazzling green rivaling the moon itself.

"What am I after?" he murmurs, lethally soft. "Everything. All of it. I've waited long enough. I didn't spend five years at your father's beck and call for the hell of it. No one—not Mateo, not Jaguar, and certainly not Ada-Pavalos… No one will stand in my way."

His shoulder jerks—my only warning before he captures a fistful of my hair, twisting the strands through his fingers.

The motion draws my mouth more readily within his reach, and he takes advantage, pressing his lips against mine.

But only *just*.

It's torturous intimacy. Every breath we take is shared despite the pressure on my throat. His scent poisons the air entering my lungs, reinforcing his presence in every way imaginable. Even the threat of my skull exploding any second on a madman's whim can't distract me from him.

"I once believed that I'd be content with destroying everything Roy Pavalos has built with my bare hands. Then taking whatever remains from Jaguar and seeking out the peace those motherfuckers denied me. I thought that was enough…"

He's so angry. I can feel every movement of his lips to punctuate each word. He means this, all of it.

"Along the way, I've changed my mind. I've set my sights beyond the downfall of my enemies. I'm going to take Ada-Maria Pavalos for myself—" His free hand captures the back of my throat.

"W-What?" I inhale greedily just to find the strength to question. "What do you mean?"

"I *mean* that, when this is all over, you'll be begging for me —and it won't be as a ploy to save your life, either. No, I'm adding you to my tally, Ada-Maria, in more ways than you can even begin to comprehend. First, I'll pry loose every secret Roy Pavalos instilled inside that pretty little head. Then, I'll come for your body. Your soul."

His possession is a physical entity I can actually feel settle around my throat, every bit as oppressive as this collar.

"And if I refuse?" My voice shakes so badly in comparison to his. It's laughable that I could ever stand a chance against his might.

And yet, he seems to take pity on me, removing his hand from my neck to stroke my cheek. Roughly. His fingers shake, revealing the sheer level of restraint he's utilizing.

It's like he's constantly battling himself when it comes to me —an unending war between lust.

And hate.

"You won't have a choice," he tells me. "You were mine the second I tasted you. Ever since that first day in your father's office when you strolled up to me in that tight fucking skirt. Mine then. Mine now."

"But for how long?" It's dangerous to provoke him, but it's the only card I have left to play. "If Mateo—"

"You leave Mateo to me."

"Why should I?" I counter, voicing the argument that's been circling my brain, impossible to ignore completely. "I don't owe you a damn thing. If anything, I should be looking for a chance to escape. Who's to say what you'll do with me after you get what you want?"

I've never asserted myself like this to him. I want him to react with shock.

Instead, he looks thoughtful. "I already told you that your mother ensured your safety," he says. "Do you want to know how?"

He raises the recorder he must have had at the ready and presses play. My mother's voice fills the void, and I'm not prepared for the pain I feel all over again.

"I will help you, but know this. My daughter has the answers you're looking for. You keep her alive. No matter what happens, you protect Ada. Do you understand?"

My eyes burn, surprisingly dry. I must have cried every tear I had left.

"Is that why you tortured me?" I ask him. "You knew you couldn't kill me. But I hate to break it to you, Domino. I don't know a damn thing about any of this."

He levels me with a searching gaze. The longer he looks, the more his expression hardens. "I'll make you an offer," he suggests. "One we can mark now in blood to cement in every way that matters. You trust in me, and I will never forsake you. I swear on my life."

He cuts his gaze down to my chest, peering at the spot where my heart frantically beats.

"You stand beside me, and I will always protect you."

"So you keep saying." But my arm, let alone the various scrapes and bruises all along my body, betray that.

"And words mean nothing," he replies in agreement, sliding his thumb beneath my chin, lifting it. "You keep forgetting that I am not your father. I won't rely on threats to get my way. I have my reasons for wanting your help, but if you see this through to the end, you stand to gain your own resources to work with. Your own power. You do realize that should anything happen to your father, everything he owns goes to you."

Shock has me gritting my teeth. It's pathetic that I *didn't* realize it. Of course, my father's possessions would be divided among me and my two brothers, Demelio and Pablo. Not that an inheritance changes a damn thing. I stand to end this nightmare with my family in tatters.

"Lucky me," I hiss. "I might get a few dollars out of it."

"Don't play coy," Domino warns. "You know damn well the difference between being under your family's shadow and the chance at autonomy. You think Jaguar or Mateo will allow you to claim that for yourself? Hell no. I'm offering you more than a chance to stay alive. I am offering you a new life."

"Just under *you* instead of Roy Pavalos?" I snipe.

"Under me." I shiver at his guttural tone. "That is exactly the future I foresee for you."

I recoil, scrambling to brace my good hand against his chest. I'm proud of myself for doing that much—for pushing against him despite his strength. He overpowers me, anyway, brushing his mouth across my lips a second time.

Only he lingers.

Lunges.

Claims.

This kiss is fiery—more dangerous than anything Mateo or Jaguar could offer. I must resist. Otherwise, he'll believe he's won this round.

My first impulse is to bite, clamping down over the tip of his probing tongue. I savor his pained groan, triumphant. Until he growls. *Oh no.* That sound is sharper. Grittier. Excited.

Rather than retreat, he surges, grinding my body against the unyielding metal. He's so big, capable of brutalizing me with little effort—but he doesn't. The gentleness with which he imparts every slow, searching kiss terrifies me more than if he bit me in return. I'm helpless against this form of attack, letting him in further than I should…

Working my jaw to keep up, I kiss him back. Harder. More.

Of all the comparisons for my brain to jump to, Jaguar comes to mind, his cruel intensity and need to devour. For what it's worth, Domino is a different kind of predator. One adept at luring his prey into a false sense of security. Pretending as though, for a second, his aim isn't to kill—he wants something more. Something too vast and elusive to convey in just one kiss. It's evident in the groan that catches in his throat as our chests collide. The way he avoids putting any pressure on my right side.

His touch is invasive, easing between my legs to stroke along my inner thigh. Possession radiates through his fingertips, wringing a shiver from me.

God, I hate him the most when he's like this—so close to the ideal I've built up inside my head. My fantasy Domino would kiss me like this. Hold me like this. Exhale harshly against my skin as though the scent of me mattered more to him than fresh air. Like I mattered.

To someone.

But I was burned by that lie once.

"S-Stop." I rip away, panting.

To my shock, he steps back, swiping his hand over his mouth.

"You're right. We need to move before Mateo decides to show off his new toy." He's cold in an instant, all trace of passion gone.

The ease with which he can change so drastically should be a warning sign. A smart woman would take it as a clear contradiction against whatever he says. Actions speak louder than words.

And right now, he has his back to me, retreating toward the driver's side of the truck. "Come on. Get in."

I follow him warily, but as I reach the passenger's side door, a noise catches my ears. Voices—but too faint to be Domino.

"…you better answer, you son of a bitch. What the fuck is your status?"

Domino sighs, reaching for a radio shoved into the console between his seat and mine. "Road trouble," he snarls into the receiver. "Meet you at the checkpoint. I wouldn't want you to slow your own progress by doubling back."

A reply comes quickly, garbled by more static. "You son of a bitch—"

"See you there, Ralph." Domino must switch off the radio because all noise from it dies completely. In the resulting silence, he sighs again.

"For now, we have no choice but to play along with Mateo's little scheme and look for an opening. I have a few contacts I can try to find more info about this collar—" He reaches out, running his thumb along the edge of it. "Once the truck has the first load of merchandise, I could use it for leverage. Then I'll come for you."

He meets my gaze, drilling in the promise. "Afterward, we get to Terra."

"And what if you can't?" I ask.

"There is no *what if*," he counters. "Failure isn't even an option."

CHAPTER TWELVE

Our destination isn't a random shack in the middle of nowhere this time. Instead, a small town unfolds, seemingly out of thin air, as the dirt road gives way to one more maintained. What few buildings we pass sport colorful exteriors, and stray dogs dart through the alleyways. The glimpse of normalcy is a stark reminder of everything I've lost during this hellish ordeal.

Far too soon, the small town flits by, yielding to more desert and endless road. Above, the sun begins to rise, painting the horizon in shades of pink and amber before igniting the landscape entirely in a soft golden glow. It hits me how beautiful this part of the world is, though ragged and inhospitable.

Much like the man beside me.

It's been hours since we last spoke, but I resist the urge to prod him for more information—like where the hell we're headed exactly. Soon, my questions are answered for me as an industrial complex appears on the horizon.

DELCORP DEPOT reads the black lettering on a rusted sign affixed to a barbed-wire fence lining the road. Three large brick warehouse-style buildings form a row, with an asphalt parking lot full of trucks visible behind them.

Even if Domino wasn't tense beside me, I'd sense something was off with this place. A sinister aura emanates from the property. Every muscle in my body stiffens—especially when I glimpse a familiar vehicle parked alongside the gate.

"Get ready," Domino warns. "Remember what I told you and follow my lead. Trust me."

Trust him. I don't know whether to laugh or take those words at face value, now that the time to put them to the test has come. It isn't like I have much of a choice.

If this really is an ambush, the key players are already in place. Mick and Ralph stand beside another man who motions for us to stop. As Domino complies, rolling down the window, the third man calls, "Bring it around the back for loading."

"As for the little Missy, she can step out and join us," Ralph adds, his smile revealing several missing teeth. "Then we can both get right on our way."

Domino doesn't move for so long that I start to question if he'll drive off entirely. Then, without a word, he leans over me, and shoves open the door on my end.

"Get out." His tone is low, his gaze averted. My belly quivers. Am I pathetic for wanting reassurance? A look. A glance. Anything.

"Can we get a move on?" Mick snaps, his impatience palpable.

I jolt to awareness and realize that all eyes are on me. Cautiously, I descend from my seat. On shaking legs, I approach the three men, feeling the back of my neck prickle with awareness.

I turn to find Domino watching me, and I swear something unspoken passes between us.

Encouragement?

If so, he hides it well. Outwardly, his expression is stone. When the unfamiliar man gestures him onward, he drives, and my stomach sinks. If the worst comes to pass, this might be the last time I ever see him.

"We should get going," Mick warns as the truck rounds the corner. "Before they finish loading."

That must be what the third man intends to oversee as he heads in the same direction, though on foot.

"Relax," Ralph counters, smoothing his hand over the stubble coating his chin. "We have time. More than enough for us all to get acquainted on the road—" he winks at me. "There are about another five hours until the next checkpoint. Go take a piss while we wait."

Frowning, Mick saunters off, leaving Ralph and me alone. Their truck is smaller than the one Domino took, resembling an RV.

"You nervous?" Ralph wonders, coming to stand beside me.

I look over and flinch as his eyes blaze with open lust.

As strange as it feels to admit, Domino inspired a different set of emotions from the start. Hate, yes, and some fear as well, but there was also a familiarity I couldn't deny. I knew him. Sometimes, I could even read him, but this man is a new animal, and it strikes me just how rusty I am.

Less than a month ago, I could smirk coyly and converse with someone like him, all without breaking a sweat. I would relish the glimpses he snuck at my breasts and plot a plan of attack to get what I wanted.

This time should be no different.

Squaring my shoulders, I crane my neck to take him in, utilizing the skills my father taught me. He's tall, holding himself in a cocky way that conveys he's the leader of his little duo. I can't overpower him outright, his bulk evident in muscles that strain his arms.

Licking my lips, I weigh my approach. For now, friendliness seems like the best option.

"Where are we going?" I ask, making my voice soft.

He smiles, stepping even closer. "Just a simple little road trip. A nice long drive through the desert and the back roads. We'll be safe and sound back in Terra Rodea before you know it."

"Are you from there?" Inferring from what little information Domino gave, Mateo must regularly import his "goods" over the border. As a result, these men probably know this landscape in and out, and won't be easy to outrun even if I could.

"No," he admits, his eyes narrowing. "But I've dabbled in the city here and there. I know your daddy from his reputation. And I've certainly heard of you." His tone deepens with double meaning, and my cheeks flame.

Desperate to get my bearings again, I ask a more pointed question. "What kind of stuff are you carrying? These trucks are, um…big."

A hint of suspicion flits across his gaze. "Nothing that you need to concern yourself with."

Damn it. I force a smile and think of parties and alcohol, and the drug-fueled ways I used to spend my time. It wasn't so hard to play dumb back then.

"They look hard to drive," I stammer. "I just hope the stuff isn't too heavy. It could make us slower."

His gaze loses that hard edge. "Don't worry yourself about that—" he fingers a lock of my hair without warning, and I bite my lip, determined not to flinch.

"We'll drive pretty fast, but we'll still have plenty of time to get to know each other better. Let's head out."

Right on cue, the truck we drove in rounds the corner, Domino visible in the driver's seat. If this really is a setup, he excels at disguising any tension.

For now.

"Looks like we're all ready to go," Ralph says, slapping the side of his van. "Mick, hurry up, you son of a bitch. It's time to get on the road." To me, he extends his hand. "You'll ride in the back. We've made it nice and comfortable for you."

Dread builds ominously in my belly, but—despite their obviously predatory intentions—Ralph and Mick aren't the source.

It's *him*. The man who claimed to watch me from the shadows, always. Unaware of his attention, I'd been able to suppress my own emotions time after time. I never had to contend with those dark, watchful eyes on me in the moment. I never had to sense the anger emanating from him.

God, it literally feels like I'm balancing on a wire, trusting Domino Valenciaga not to let me fall.

But I'm past being afraid. Inhaling deeply, I extend my hand toward Ralph and follow him into the truck.

This time, I don't look back.

CHAPTER THIRTEEN

I t's one thing to humor Domino Valenciaga. The true test of my insanity comes in just how far I am willing to actually put his plea to the test. *Trust him.*

The sad part is that I've spent five years doing so implicitly, if only believing that he'd save my life out of loyalty to my father. Now, I'm not sure what is driving him. His heated confessions?

Or the blatant fact that my mother made sure he needed me alive to reach his aims?

Neither reason should matter. He may need me, but what if I don't need him? I've manipulated my fair share of men long before Domino Valenciaga came into my life, and something tells me I'll have to do the same long after.

Still, those weeks of isolation have left me woefully unprepared for just how jarring it is to face the full brunt of one man who sees me as only an object, let alone two.

"Welcome to your palace for the time being," Ralph says as he leads me through the narrow space. It looks like an RV, though one modified to have a single exit near the front and the driver's seat partitioned off from the back section we're in now. Overall, it's relatively clean, consisting of a small kitchenette, a booth with most of the leather seating worn away, and across from it is a raised ledge with a mattress on it and a stained set of white sheets. My stomach crawls at the sight, but I never let my smile so much as flinch.

From the corner of my eye, I sense Ralph in between me and the exit.

"We should get on the road," the other man, Mick, calls, approaching the open doorway. "Mateo will skin us alive if we show up late to the next…*checkpoint.*"

I stiffen at his shift in inflection.

Ralph, however, continues to smile, though it doesn't reach his eyes. "Alright. We'll both take the front for now. You just sit tight, little Missy."

I swallow hard, weighing my question carefully before voicing it. "When will we meet up with Domino again?"

Ralph's grin stretches a little wider. "Don't worry your pretty little head. We'll meet up with him at the final checkpoint once we're in Terra and he's completed his job. Then you can get rid of your little necklace and be on your merry way."

His laugh turns the statement into a joke more than an earnest promise. Regardless, he leaves, closing the door behind him, and I'm sure I hear a lock engage.

Heart racing, I perch myself on the edge of the booth, contemplating a million different options. The first, and the one I'm hoping for the most, is that both Mick and Ralph don't have nefarious motives at all, and I make it back into Terra unscathed.

The more likely option is that Domino was right, and we've sprung their trap. So now what?

I inch closer to the front of the truck, where a wooden partition separates it from the back. I can barely hear the scuffle of the two men settling into their seats before the engine roars to life and the vehicle lurches into motion.

I press myself against the panel, straining my ears for any hint of conversation. I only catch grunted snippets before a barrage of deafening rock music drowns out everything else.

Damn it.

Alone, I'm left to dwell on the inevitable. I turn to one of the small, filthy windows near the bed that offers a view outside. I can't get a good glimpse of the road behind us—or if anyone is on our tail.

Stop. I shake my head to banish the doubt. My sole concern should be keeping myself alive. Should Mick and Ralph deviate from their supposed plan, I can't overpower them physically. Not without the aid of a weapon. Ironically, I still have Domino's knife, and I slide my hand over my pocket, feeling its shape beneath the denim.

Not that I know how to use it. My methods always relied more on manipulation than violence.

Liar, a part of me whispers. The last time I ever saw Pia replays in my mind over and over again. I cursed at her. Shoved her. Then ran.

I tell myself that Domino—or anyone for that matter—is jumping to conclusions by assuming that I had a bigger role to play in her disappearance. I loved her. I would never hurt her.

So then who did?

Could a fifteen-year-old girl really learn information on a man like Roy Pavalos salacious enough to kill her over? It sounds too sordid, even for my family.

The twisted part is I think I'd sooner get a straight response from Domino than my father. The thought of seeing him again makes the air stick to the inside of my chest. It's a cruel form of whiplash to go from believing he was gone for good, to now having to accept that he isn't dead after all. Across the border, in Terra Rodea, Roy Pavalos is alive and well, and maybe I truly am as pathetic as Domino claims I am for hoping that everything he told me was a lie.

No one could blame any woman for being unwilling to accept that both of her parents may have loathed her all along. My mother was one thing, with her lofty ideas and pious catholic upbringing. But my father…

While St. Margaritas was barely a twenty-minute drive from my family's estate, we rarely spent time together in those days. He had his political events to attend, and my mother had her many charity organizations and parties. Even before everything went to hell, I was an afterthought to them of both.

That all changed not long before Pia went missing. Suddenly, my father displayed an interest in my life that he never had. Little did I know that, like always, it wasn't me he was interested in. Just what he could have me do *for* him.

A sudden noise jars me from the memory. I startle to awareness, blinking as the vehicle skids to a stop.

Hope rises in my chest. Is Domino here after all?

My heart pounds as I ease myself to my feet and inch toward one of the windows. The sun blazes, illuminating a landscape that doesn't remotely resemble a checkpoint. Instead, the ruthless desert extends seemingly for miles. From the front of the truck, I hear a door open and close, followed by footsteps approaching this side.

They're too slow to allude to an unwelcome visitor. As the figure appears in the window built into the door, my heart sinks. Mick, his teeth bared in an expression far too gruesome to be considered a grin. He takes his time, toying with the latch before finally opening the door.

"Hey there," he calls to me. "Ralph is gonna take over for a while so that you and I can get better acquainted."

He mounts the steps one by one as an alarm goes off inside my skull.

Regardless, I have enough sense not to let my unease show. I force my tried-and-true smile, keeping my back close to the partition. He's barely closed the door behind him when the truck lurches into motion, and the familiar rift of rock music seeps through the wood again.

I'm painfully aware of how enclosed this space is. The door is the only realistic exit, but he positions himself in front of it and gestures toward the mattress with a wave of his hand. "Have a seat. Let's have a nice talk for a bit."

I follow him woodenly, perching beside him on the stained sheets. The second I do, his hand lands over my thigh, squeezing the flesh. "I'm sure you and Domino got up to plenty of fun."

Damn it. The last thing my brain should be focused on now is how foreign his touch feels. After days of being subjected primarily to just one man, the rough sensation of another's touch is grating on my frayed nerves.

I've forgotten how to preen and primp. How to endure. How to lie so well that I fooled even myself.

It's harder to tap into the muscle memory that made it so easy to submit to unwanted advances.

Snap out of it, Ada!

I smile back and force my hand to twitch toward him. "Are... Are we close to stopping?"

With his gaze on my leg, he begins to stroke up and down, bringing his fingers alarmingly close to my inner thigh with each pass.

"I ain't one to follow the tabloids and shit," he says against my ear. "But I heard of you. Prancing around, spending your daddy's money. Even as fucked up as you look, you're still pretty damn hot." He brings his other hand near my cheek, brushing the tangled hair from my face. "I'm sure Domino has had plenty of fun with you, the bastard. What about you and I have some fun as well? I think you might enjoy this far better."

His hand boldly dips between my legs, and any other time in the previous month, I think I would have spread them willingly—assuming I had a directive from my father. Maybe that's the twisted reason why it's so damn hard now. Why my entire skin threatens to crawl off my body as I register his touch. My thighs twitch before I even realize it, clamping his hand between them.

He laughs, undeterred. "Don't tell me you're a picky little bitch? I think you should play nice. It's a long drive back over the border, and Ralph plans to take a turn at the next rest stop. So let's have our fun while we can—"

He's too fast, shoving me onto my back, easily maneuvering on top of me. Pain lances up my injured arm, and my mind goes blank as blood rushes to my ears. I register the moist heat on my neck first below the collar—his mouth.

Both of his hands claw at my chest, trying to wrench up my shirt, heedless of the brace on my wrist.

I inhale through my nose, biting back the agony to fixate on an immediate course of action. I can't panic. He's too strong, his wiry body seemingly composed of solid muscle. The second I even acknowledge his strength, I feel his knee jab into my hip, blocking the knife from my reach. All I can do is rely on instinct. So I blindly lean in the direction of his mouth.

The bastard doesn't even stop to question my supposed change of heart. His lips lash at mine sloppily as he fights to shove his tongue down my throat. The taste of him is ten times worse than the smell—like licking an ashtray.

Still, he rolls onto his side to give me better access, wrenching me on top of him. In the same course of time, he manages to draw the hem of my shirt up over my breasts, struggling to pull it off completely.

My thoughts are a scattered mess, overpowered by the need to escape. Run. It takes everything I have just to swat the fear aside and think.

With him on his back, I have a clearer view of the window straight ahead. Should I manage to escape from the RV, I wouldn't make it far without being seen over the relatively flat terrain. There's nowhere to hide.

But, if I somehow manage to catch both men off guard, could I even drive the truck?

As if my thoughts were the cue, the entire vehicle suddenly pitches sharply to the right.

"Shit!" Mick shoves me off. Panting, he glowers in the direction of the driver's seat. "Fucking bastard. What the fuck Ralph? Playing around when—"

"No fucking game!" The rock music cuts off, allowing the other man's voice to reach us clearly. "Someone's on our tail!" He grunts, and we're thrown so hard against the side of the truck I taste copper. My ears won't stop ringing as I blink to regain my bearings and find myself sprawled over the far end of the mattress while Mick scrambles to his feet.

"What the fuck?"

Again, the vehicle pitches sideways, but the entire floor vibrates this time, the windows rattling in their frames. It's as if the road switched from asphalt to uneven earth, and we're going fast. Too fast.

Panic surges up my throat—a flavor composed of blood and salty sweat—but I still have the sense of mind to recognize a way out when I hear one. Someone is behind them.

Domino.

My heart swells with a mixture of hope and disbelief. He's here—and I have no better chance to assist in my rescue than now.

I'm already crawling to the edge of the mattress, but Mick doesn't react. He's at the partition, bellowing at the wood.

"What the fuck is going on? Ralph?"

Suddenly, amid the crunch of the tires skidding over earth and gravel, the truck comes to an abrupt stop. My stomach lurches as I lose my balance and nearly careen into him. I barely manage to brace myself against a countertop bordering the kitchenette—but for the first time, I have a clear shot to the door.

At the back of my mind, a part of me warns that there's no way I can outrun these men. But it's not like I have any better options.

I bolt onto my toes and throw myself down the small set of steps. Fumbling for the door, I manage to grip the latch, but the second I try to open it, my hair is tugged viciously from behind.

"What the hell? You little bitch!"

He wrenches so hard I fly back, landing on my hip, feeling the middle step bite into my side. Pain washes over me as my wrist is jarred in its brace, but there isn't time to indulge in the agony. A flicker in my peripheral vision betrays the moment he reaches for me again, clawing at my arm. Frantic, I kick out at the door with both feet, utilizing every ounce of strength I can muster. With a violent pop, it flies fully open.

"Fuck!" Mick succeeds in yanking me back, and I slam into the wooden partition, gasping out as my vision goes black.

It returns in snippets at first. I just see Mick standing over me. His hand curling into a fist. That fist flying through the air.

Then bright spots dance across my vision.

I'm lying on the floor when I can see clearly again, feeling the gritty linoleum against my cheek.

"You stupid bitch!" Mick steps over me, pounding on the partition. "Ralph, what the fuck? How many are on our ass? You don't think it's him? Mateo swore they made a deal—"

"Just get the fuck up here!"

"Shit."

I feel a hand latch onto my ankle, dragging me down the hall. A door opens, and I'm shoved inside a narrow space, too dark to make out clearly.

"You stay here, you fucking bitch!"

The door slams trapping me alone as heavy footsteps rattle the floor. He must leave the vehicle entirely because I hear a far-off shout. Then a louder, sharper noise draws a scream from my throat.

I recognize it, despite only having heard it once before in far more morbid detail.

A gunshot.

CHAPTER FOURTEEN

Two loud pops rip through the air. Then silence falls, one so heavy only the sound of my breathing disrupts it. Scrambling to my knees, I fumble in my surroundings, straining my eyes to get a better view of where exactly I am.

An acrid, putrid stench gives me a grim idea. As I feel out, my hand lands over a firm, round surface that confirms that horrific suspicion. It's a bathroom, barely larger than a closet, consisting of a small toilet and a minuscule sink. I blink as my eyes adjust to a faint sliver of light. It comes from one direction in particular—a small window with a wooden shade partially drawn over it. I lunge to my feet and push it higher, but a thick layer of dust and grime obscures any view.

Shit.

Desperate, I strain my ears for any sign of Domino, hoping against the worst. The sound of those gunshots keeps echoing in my mind, but I can't let myself consider any scenario in which he isn't alive.

Think, Ada! My heart is pounding so fiercely it feels like it might crash out of my chest. A cold sweat coats my back, and my teeth won't stop chattering. I think I'm at the point where my brain has learned to block out the pain, but only for as long as the adrenaline remains high.

Luckily, there seems to be plenty to keep my nerves on red alert. Someone's coming. I can hear their steps approaching from outside, along this end of the RV. They move slowly. Cautiously.

Not Mick or Ralph. The cadence is different, more graceful, and not heavy with bravado. Someone unfazed even by gunshots.

My heart swells with recognition, and I pound on the door as hard as I can. "I'm in here! Domino!"

A sound echoes that I assume is the main door rattling on its hinges. Those slow, steady footsteps continue—belonging to the figure cautiously mounting the stairs one by one until, finally, they slow near my hiding place. The latch jiggles as it's tested, rattling the entire frame.

"It's locked," I call, pushing against the flimsy panel. "Can you open it?"

He's silent—but a subtle click sounds as the door finally gives way. I scramble to push it open...

Only to recoil in the same motion, putting as much distance between myself and the figure on the other end as I can.

"Hello there, little minx," my rescuer growls.

I go cold, registering all the ways this isn't right. His voice is far too deep for one. The cadence alone cements my instinctive fear, but I'm pathetic enough to hope I'm wrong. Pray.

In a swift, controlled motion, he steps forward into the light, and reality grossly contradicts the sight I expect to see. Domino isn't the one standing here, panting with the effort of taking on two armed men alone.

This figure is too broad. His eyes are darker, his smile predatory.

Jaguar.

Alarm belatedly surges through my veins to replace the shock. My free hand is in my pocket before I know it, grasping for the knife.

"Easy," he purrs, raising both hands in a gesture of surrender. They're empty—he's unarmed. Or so he wants me to believe.

His dark pants could certainly disguise the outline of a weapon. As I inspect both pockets, he chuckles.

"Is that any way to show your *gratitude?*" His guttural tone transforms the word into something violent, even as his smile remains intact.

I can't stop myself from scanning the sliver of hallway behind him, hunting for someone. Anyone. The RV itself is empty apart from us. I can't hear the signs of another person.

Did he really come here alone?

"I didn't believe it," he murmurs, shifting to block my view. A whiff of his scent hits me full in the face, heightening the dread building in my stomach. I step back, pressing myself flat against the wall.

It's no use. His widening smile confirms what my own logic tells me—I'm trapped.

"Dom-Dom *really* left you all alone, and in a state such as this—" his eyes trace the contours of my collar, but he doesn't seem alarmed by the sight. "That's a damn shame, darlin'."

Left you. I ignore the word choice, for now, desperate to keep my breathing in check. He leans against the doorframe, his bulk apparent as muscle ripples through his shoulders, down his arms.

"You're lucky I came to rescue you when that bastard didn't." He extends his hand, and a closer view reveals the calloused surface is streaked with reddish dirt. "Come on. Let's get you out of here."

Any other day I wouldn't hesitate. Survival would be my paramount concern, and I wouldn't feel this irrational pang in my throat at the thought of Domino leaving. Some pathetic part of me wouldn't keep wishing for him to show up. Now.

Please…

"Did you hear me?" The shift in Jaguar's tone is so chilling I jump. Sweat slicks my palms, threatening my grip on the knife—and his gaze cuts to it instantly.

"Don't tell me you were hoping for *Domino*," he chuckles out the name, and yet the broken cadence is more unsettling than his previous growl. It's enough to shatter his gallant hero façade. This is no rescue.

"Choosing him has only gotten you that shiny new accessory around your neck to complement that pretty black eye," he adds.

I wince, self-conscious despite everything else demanding my focus. He's too big to overpower. Too heavy to outrun. My only hope at all is to find a way past him and hide.

But how?

The sight of his outstretched hand carries the same damning inevitability as a death sentence. I leave with him now, and I'll never see Domino—let alone Terra—again.

So fight, a tiny voice in my head insists. *Do something!* The plan forming in my mind is desperate. Insane. The Ada Pavalos from a few weeks ago would never consider it.

But she hadn't been beaten and maimed and betrayed twice over.

"Don't tell me you'd rather stay here. We don't have long before Mateo catches wind of this little party. I bet the first thing he'll do is try to set off that pretty little necklace of yours. The bastard never could share his toys."

The threat strengthens what little resolve I feel building within me. Tightening my grip over the leather handle, I look up.

"Where are we going?" I ask, my voice hollow and trembling.

Jaguar's gallant grin twitches, and I recall a lesson I once learned the hard way—he doesn't like to be questioned. "Somewhere safe." He extends his hand again, flexing the fingers impatiently. "Let's go."

I step toward him—only the knife is still in my grasp. Even as I reach out, I seem unable to let go of it. So I don't, twisting my hand so the blade-side faces down. In slow-motion, I watch as the metal bites at the calloused palm in its path with a ferocity I shouldn't even be capable of.

"Shit!" He instinctively rocks back on his heels, snatching his hand away.

A tiny sliver of space opens beside him, and I lunge. There isn't time for shock or horror. I just pivot, sprinting over the peeling linoleum.

Rather than shout, Jaguar just…

Laughs. Slow and leisurely, his chuckles meld with my hammering pulse, creating a twisted melody.

"Oh darlin', if you wanted to play, you only needed to ask."

This narrow hallway is unending. It feels like an eternity before I reach the steps near the door and stagger down them. My ears pick up the sound of footsteps in my wake—but they're too soft.

Too slow.

Too patient.

"I'm going to have so much fun breaking you…"

The taunt chases me out beneath the cripplingly hot sun. My eyes stream, glazed with sweat as I try to find an exit. Something. By chance, I spot the driver-side door of the cab left ajar, and I lunge for it, wrenching on the handle.

I've barely widened the gap when an arm swings out to slam against my chest. Ralph? Choking back a scream, I grapple with the knife, swinging it senselessly before I realize there's no use in fighting.

Ralph isn't attacking me. He's too still. For the first time, my nostrils register the spicy, overwhelming stench of copper as my eyes note the scarlet substance painting nearly every surface. Blood. Puddles of it flood the seat, adding a gruesome backdrop to where this man's head should be.

"Oh God—" Nausea crawls up my throat. Frantic, I stagger back, running straight into another body.

Only this one is standing, pulsing with dangerous virility.

"We'll chalk this little outburst up to shock," Jaguar murmurs against my ear. He snatches my chin in the same instant, easily fighting off my attempts to break free. I can't see him from this position—only feel his unyielding strength easily wrestle me into submission. "A little nap should help you feel all better."

A shadow rushes at me from the corner of my eye, too quickly to dodge. A sickening thud resonates through my skull next.

And the world goes black.

CHAPTER FIFTEEN

I wake up dazed. For a few precious seconds, I float in blissful ignorance, relishing the peace...

Then the pain sets in. Fear comes next, flooding my veins with each frantic beat of my heart. Soon, every nerve in my body burns with desperate energy—it's electric. The air itself contains a warning—a masculine scent infecting my lungs with every breath. *Move. Danger.*

Rustling noises heighten my anxiety before I even hear it—a voice piercing the silence like a knife. "Wakey, wakey, Ada-Maria." Though in a ghoulish singsong, that guttural baritone requires no introduction.

It's as if an invisible hand yanks away the veil of sleep shrouding me. I'm painfully awake. Heart racing, I spring into motion, scrambling to guard my head before I even get my eyes open. When I do, darkness is all that greets me. And pain. I'm lying flat on my stomach, but a pulsing ache stabs through my left side. Paired with the cold, grainy texture of the floor beneath me, I suspect I've been thrown here, unceremoniously.

Judging from the telltale weight on my throat, I'm still wearing the collar as well. That isn't the only unwelcome realization. A groan rips from my lips as I crane my neck back, taking in my surroundings via what little illumination there is. The room isn't entirely dark—a monstrous shadow is blocking most of the light, letting in only a trickle of orangish glow to see by.

"There we go." As the "shadow" looms larger, the scent in my nostrils turns cloying, betraying what it really is. Or who. Someone tall, with handsome features so perfect they could have been chiseled into stone. A name instantly comes to mind, inspiring a wave of terror that leaves me quaking.

Jaguar.

"I have to say," he murmurs, sliding his tongue across his lip. Those predatory brown eyes glitter with malicious intent—too real to be imagined. "Despite looking like hell, you're still damn fine."

Fear paralyzes me as he grips my chin, wrenching it back. The side of my face burns, and a fiery agony near my eye warns that once again, I've met the hard end of a fist. His?

"No wonder little Dom-Dom's chosen you as the star of our little pissing contest."

He leans forward, bringing his face into clearer focus—as well as the room behind him. It's narrow, with plain walls and a low, water-stained ceiling. My fear grows; I don't recognize it.

Confusion makes me dumb enough to speak. "What… Where—"

"Uh-uh." He tightens his grip with a force that mockingly contrasts the false gentleness in his voice. "Don't worry. You and I are going to have a nice little chat about everything. But first? Darlin'!" He gestures with his free hand, and a soft voice greets him, the speaker out of my view.

"Yes, sir?"

"Get little Ms. Ada here all cleaned up. Then show her around. She won't be our guest for long."

"Yes, sir."

He releases me, turning on his heel as a smaller figure appears by his side. She's thin and pale, wearing a black bra and a skirt barely longer than a pair of underwear. Her brown hair has been tied back from a delicate face, every feature accented by dark makeup.

"Bring her to the showroom when you're done," Jaguar calls. "See you then, Ada-Maria."

His chilling laugh echoes as he retreats through a doorway, shrouded by what looks like a curtain of hanging beads. Their sparkly nature contrasts sharply with his darker demeanor, giving our surroundings a more garish edge.

"Come on." The woman steps forward, reaching for my injured wrist before she changes tack, grabbing my other hand. "We don't have long. You don't want to make him angry. Trust me."

"Where are we?" I ask.

"That's not important," the woman whispers. Persistent, she tugs me to my feet, using her slender body to stabilize mine. "Just follow me, and keep your mouth shut."

I'm limping to keep up as she hurries me through the doorway. The hallway beyond is narrow, with no windows and only a naked hanging lightbulb to illuminate the way. With furtive glances, I inspect whatever I can to get my bearings. My feet are bare, scraping against a gritty linoleum flooring. I run my hand over my pocket, unsurprised to find my knife missing.

A few feet down from the room we exited, the woman guides me through another doorway. A small sink sits along the far wall, along with a shower stall.

Shit.

"Over here." Near a filthy mirror, the woman releases me, tugging at my shirt.

I look even worse than before, mirrored over the smeared glass. At least now, I have a clear view of the collar. It's about an inch wide, shiny enough to reflect what little light there is. If I wasn't aware of its sinister nature, I'd assume it was a choker-style necklace.

Just one with no way of opening it.

Intent on her task, the woman doesn't seem to notice my preoccupation with the device. She reaches for the clasp of my jeans next, but I back away, raising my hand defensively. "What are you doing?"

"Just do what I say." She keeps darting her gaze toward the door. "He can't be kept waiting. Please…"

With frantic movements, she continues to undress me. Given that I can barely keep my balance, I have no choice but to relent, craning my neck to take in the rest of the room. There are no windows in here. No indication of what or where this building might be. Apart from the overall grime, the air smells wet and moldy. Are we underground?

"We need to hurry," the woman insists. She scurries away with my clothing in her hands, pausing only to bark over her shoulder, "Wait here."

I follow her anyway, unable to shake the dread building in the pit of my stomach. It's as if an invisible clock is ticking down. When time runs out, who knows what will happen?

Nothing good for me.

Luckily, the woman seems too distracted to notice when I peer into the hall after her. She heads left, disappearing through another doorway. I can see someone moving just beyond the archway. Jaguar?

No, they're too thin. Another woman?

"Please! I told you not to move!" The brunette reappears, frantically ushering me back into the bathroom. In her hands is a strip of black material that catches the light. She unfurls it, revealing a dress only a fraction more conservative than her skimpy ensemble.

"Put this on—"

"Where are we?" I step back, heart in my throat. "Please. Just tell me something."

"P-Please." Her eyes cut fearfully toward the doorway before she steps forward, bringing her mouth near my ear. "You're in hell," she whispers. "And the man who brought you here? He's the devil."

With that admission, she grimly tugs the dress over my head. I'm numb as she tackles my hair next, revealing a pouch she must have carried here as well. Inside it is a brush and a tube of lipstick that she swipes across my lips.

Taken all together, I don't recognize myself. It's a change more drastic than just a haircut and a dye job. There's something in my eyes I don't ever recall seeing there before. A hard, frozen expression.

I shiver before I fully process why—I look like someone.

I look like Domino.

"Come on." The woman takes my uninjured arm, pulling me into the hall.

This time, we head right, venturing further. The hallway itself is plain, borderline decrepit. Any room we pass looks barely furnished. Most contain cots covered with thin blankets and a few chairs. Past them all is an archway opening onto a larger space that vaguely resembles some of the clubs I used to frequent—just not one in the upscale part of Terra Rodea.

The walls are bare concrete, sporting a row of what looks to be windows, each coated in a layer of black paint to block out any view. A bar looms at one end of the space, plastered with posters of half-naked women. Across from it is a round stage with a pole in the center, and seated in a booth beyond it, lurks the room's lone audience member.

He slowly claps as I approach, and my body comes alive with a mixture of pain and unease. There's a predatory quality in his gaze that even Domino lacks. Something violent and insidious.

It's hungry.

"Step right up." He crooks a beckoning finger at me while the woman by my side remains rooted in place.

He's wearing a similar outfit to the one he wore at Domino's estate. A black shirt and dark-wash jeans must be his preferred style. The tattoo on his arm remains bared, etched with such detail it seems to move, the jaguar prowling along his bicep.

When I'm only a few feet away, he leans back, appraising me with another searching glance. As I am about to take another step, he snaps his fingers, and I instinctively stop short. Satisfied, he nods, a smirk playing across his lips.

"Welcome to one small sliver of my domain." He gestures to our surroundings with a wave of his hand. "This lovely place here is a new acquisition. Within a few weeks, it will be the belle of the ball. A star attraction. Not that you'll be here to see it."

My stomach flips as I pick up on the dare he doesn't voice. *Ask me why.*

Licking my lips, I weigh the least dangerous response while simultaneously inspecting the rest of the space. Apart from the windows, I don't see a door—but there must be another entrance.

"Eyes up here," Jaguar snaps. Terrified, I whip my gaze to him, but he's still smiling. "Come closer."

Sucking in a breath, I take a step. His scent worms into my lungs, lethally potent. I swear, the pain in my arm intensifies with every inch gained as if heightened by his mere presence.

Only God knows how I manage to suppress the shiver ripping through me as he captures my uninjured wrist, pulling me the rest of the way—violently. With a startled grunt, I land on his lap. My knee digs into the seat cushion at his side, and his hand on my hip is the only thing to steady me.

Through a heavy-lidded gaze, he inspects me yet again, and I can't even begin to unravel the tumult of emotion lurking behind his eyes. An overarching theme can be assumed, however—rage. "I'm surprised Dom-Dom let you out of his sight, let alone with those two fuckers. Not that he had much of a choice, given your flashy new hardware—" he nods to the collar. "Who knows what naughty things they might have done to you if I didn't happen to swoop in? You're welcome."

He grips my chin, applying a subtle amount of pressure with his thumb. Then more…

Belatedly, I realize what he wants, and I rush to pry my lips apart. "T-Thank you."

"You're welcome." He grins, but his eyes remain flat, coolly observant. "What were you doing so far away from old Dom, anyway? Don't tell me he grew bored of his little Ada."

My cheeks flame at the insinuation, but his malicious tone triggers another concern. I don't see Mick lurking around this room. I contemplate the risks of questioning him again, but the curiosity is too great to smother. "The men I was with, are… Are they—"

"Dead?" He phrases it so casually. As though he's referring to the weather and nothing more. "Yes. It will send a nice warning to Mateo and clean up loose ends. I'm a big fan of neatness. Tidiness." His deepening tone makes my heart stutter, and his smile grows even wider.

"Domino did a bad, bad thing by taking you from me. It wasn't your fault, of course…" As he speaks, he trails his finger up along the curve of my brace, grazing the tender flesh of my shoulder beneath. With every dangerous caress, I jump. "But I think it's best if you learn sooner than later—"

Pain! I scream before I even fully register what he's done—dig his nails into my forearm, jarring the limb. Just as quickly, I choke off the cry, gritting my teeth against any sound. My eyes water at the fiery agony darting through my right arm, but I breathe through it, straining to hear every word he says next.

"Domino has no loyalty," he explains, loosening his grip. "The bastard is cocky enough to think he's always been one step ahead, but he isn't the only one with friends in high places. I know all about his little plan to stab me in the back, then take you and the Pavalos empire for himself. My question is, do *you* know what he's planning?"

He gently strokes the hair from my face, but I've learned my lesson. I don't say a damn thing.

"I'm sure he's filled your head with plenty of silly little lies," he says, unbothered. "You don't want me as an enemy, Ada-Maria. But don't take my word for it. I want us to be friends. I'll even give you a gift, to prove my sincerity."

I brace myself as he reaches into the pocket of his jeans and withdraws a silver, square item that I recognize instantly. It isn't a weapon, but no less dangerous. A remote, much like the one Mateo taunted me with.

"It wasn't hard to find who Mateo used to supply his little toys. I was even able to have this particular collar reprogramed to a different detonator—" Jaguar wiggles the remote while I scramble to keep up. Reprogramed? My puzzled expression must amuse him enough to enlighten me without prompting. "With this, you won't have to worry about Mateo getting trigger happy, as long as I block the signal every twenty-four hours. Removing it completely will take a bit of finesse, though."

He inspects the contraption in question, but disgust isn't what I see flash through his dark eyes. It's glee. Ironically, I once thought that Domino's familiarity with a whip was chilling, the hallmark of a true monster.

I was wrong.

"This baby is a unique design, used primarily by one man who likes to keep his girls under lock and key. Care to guess who?" he asks, an eyebrow raised.

I clamp my lips against replying, and he shrugs.

"No? I'm sure Domino would recognize it."

His tone is deliberately casual, daring me to question him. When I don't, he laughs, fingering the curved bit of metal resting directly over my windpipe.

"Lucky for you, I'm willing to help you remove it. Would you like that?"

His tone is more playful than earnest. He's lying.

I nod anyway, fighting to keep any skepticism from my face. "Y-Yes."

"Good." His smile falls in a way that heralds the sinister nature no doubt lurking behind this "offer." With a flick of his wrist, he returns the remote to its hiding place. "I'll let you be in control for once. Control of who lives and who dies. I bet Domino never gave you that privilege, huh?"

He narrows his eyes when I don't react. Jerkily, I shake my head, but I'm too terrified to question him. *Who lives and who dies…*

"Isn't that right?"

I nod, feeling my pulse hammer in my throat.

"So I'll tell you what your prize will be. I'll continue to jam that pretty little collar's receiver in exchange for a life. Don't worry," he adds as I flinch. "Not your own. In fact, darlin', I think this should be an easy choice to make. Domino or your father. Which one will get blown to pieces?"

His inflection never changes. I can't tell if he's serious, or merely spinning a game of wordplay.

"Pick," he warns, pressing his thumb against my lower lip. "I won't ask twice. Unless you aren't flattered by the honor."

"N-No." I shake my head emphatically, nearly falling off his lap in the process. "No… I-I'm grateful—"

"Then who," he demands, leveling me with a cold stare. Gone is the mocking semblance of warmth. He is all ice. "Who dies first?"

My heart lurches, recalling the last time I heard him utilize this low baritone—right before he broke my wrist with his bare hand.

"I don't understand what—"

"Should I tell you something, to make your choice easier?" His breath prickles over my skin, like the warning sparks before hot embers catch fire. "Let's start with Domino, first. The bastard stole from me, did you know that? He's nothing but a fucking thief. He promised you to me, practically used you as a fucking bargaining chip in his war against Roy Pavalos, and then decides that he doesn't want to share after all. He hasn't told you the real reason he hates the bastard, has he?"

His fingers flex against my thigh before withdrawing. Then he snaps them inches from my head.

"Yes, sir?" a woman calls from beyond my view.

"Whiskey on the rocks," he demands, cutting his gaze up to mine. "Make it two."

A commotion comes from the direction of the bar. I assume the other woman never left and is fulfilling his demand, but I don't dare take my eyes off him. Balancing on a highwire must feel like this—like the slightest twitch of a muscle in the wrong direction could lead to disaster.

"My father used to run with Roy Pavalos." He tilts his head in a seemingly casual motion, but I'm not fooled. His upper lip curls back, his eyes narrow. He's angry— much like Domino when he recounted his past. "He considered him like a brother at one point. Trusted him with his life. Until one day, the bastard decided he didn't want to share his empire anymore. Not that I could blame the motherfucker." He extends his hand again, making me flinch, but he reaches past me, grabbing a shot presumably from a tray. "Here."

He offers me one before draining his own glass. I rush to copy him—but he snatches my wrist before I can take a sip, sloshing liquid from the rim and down onto my fingers.

"A toast first," he grates, his voice low.

He lets the silence build as if daring me to propose a reason of my own to toast to. My lips twitch. I'm ready to blurt the first thing that comes to mind.

Raising his glass higher, he beats me to the punch. "To mercy," he murmurs, mutilating the word into something violent. "Now drink."

I immediately throw my head back, choking down the burning liquid as the collar's edge bites into my windpipe. I've barely swallowed when he takes my glass, handing both to a woman who scurries out of sight.

"Yes, Roy Pavalos wanted it all for himself," he says, continuing his tale. "What he didn't know, was that my father was one step ahead of him." He taps my chin with the tip of a calloused finger. "He thought he had someone on the inside, you see? Someone he could trust. Someone he revealed his whole plot to take down Roy Pavalos once and for all to. Care to take a guess?"

My mind goes blank. According to Domino, Carlos died long before he went to work for my father. Could he be referring to Pia?

No. Something flits across his expression, transforming it for a heartbeat—hatred. Hate so consuming it chills me to the core. If I didn't know better, I'd assume he was referring to *me.*

"You look like her," he murmurs, cupping my cheek while my heart pounds against my ribcage. "Just a little, around your mouth. That sly cunt. She played my father for a fool, but it was his own damn fault for trusting a Pavalos. What she stole from him, though? That I would like returned to me very, very much."

Something in his grated tone emboldens me to brave the risk and ask him outright. "What?"

I cringe in anticipation of a blow.

"A ring," he says simply, lowering his gaze to my twitching hands. "Silver. Ornate. Worth a massive fucking penny in more ways than one."

I can barely keep my expression blank. I knew someone who owned a ring like that...

"My father entrusted it to Lia Pavalos once upon a time," Jaguar explains, returning his attention to my face. "May she rot in hell."

He waits, displaying that predatory intensity once more. He wants a reaction—an opening to pounce.

Defiantly, I make my face blank, constricting every last muscle. My jaw is throbbing by the time he finally sighs in defeat, still stroking the side of my face.

"You have a lot to atone for, Ada-Maria. Dom-Dom's sins, as well as your bitch of a mother's. But first... You can accept your gift now. Who should be punished?"

His tone leaves no room to stall. "I..."

"Sir!"

I whip my head around just as a door opens near the stage. Painted the same color as the walls; I didn't notice it before. Another man stands behind it now, his face bathed in shadow. "You should come to see this—"

"You dare to fucking interrupt me." Jaguar's grated baritone is as startling as a bucket of ice water being dumped over my head. So chilling. Soulless.

But the other man is persistent. "I... Sir, there's something you should see."

Jaguar doesn't reply for a handful of seconds that feel like an eternity. Finally, he shrugs me off, and I barely manage to stand without falling, swaying to find my balance.

"Baby!" He snaps his fingers, and a woman appears in the doorway I came from—but she isn't the slender brunette. Shock rips through me, and I forget to school my expression.

"Take Ada-Maria to her room," Jaguar commands. "We'll continue this later."

"Yes, baby." Her voice a husky purr, the woman stalks forward, grabbing my arm only out of sheer obedience, I suspect. Disgust radiates from her—almost as much as the loathing I'm sure exudes from me.

We make it into the hall before she finally wrenches away, spinning to face me.

"What the hell are you doing here?" she hisses.

"I could ask you the same question," I counter, but disbelief robs some of the hostility from my voice.

She looks like hell, a shadow of the woman who pranced around Domino's estate days ago. Matted, blond hair hangs loosely down her shoulders. Her outfit—a skintight pink mini dress—is less revealing than mine, but it's rumpled, giving the impression that she's worn it multiple times without it being washed.

Stalking ahead, she turns into a room a few doors down from the bathroom. It's small, with a battered leather couch along one wall, two narrow cots, and little else. With a forced yawn, Alexi stretches out her arms and throws herself onto the sofa.

"Ada-Maria, here at last," she says, an eyebrow raised. "Frankly, I'm surprised Domino gave you up after all. He seemed determined to fight over you like a dog with a bone."

I hate the familiarity in her voice. It rouses those nagging suspicions as to her relationship with Domino all over again. Just how close were they?

No. I quash the thought, gritting my teeth. Now isn't the time for petty jealousy. That relentless sensation of seconds counting down returns. *Tick tock.* Paired with the looming threat of Jaguar's "gift," everything in my body is warning me that when time runs out…

This won't end well.

I need to escape.

Or wait for Domino, a tiny voice in my head whispers. God, I hate the part of me that longs for him. It's unexpected. Weak, not to mention just plain pathetic. For all I know, Domino is already at the border and hasn't looked back.

The truth is, he was right—he can find Pia on his own. I'm no longer necessary to his grand plan.

It's time to devise my own strategy for survival.

"Where are we?" I ask, ignoring the bait for now. "Near Terra?"

Any hope I have is dashed by her scoff. "Hell no. Far from it—" her eyes dart warily to the door before returning to me. Sitting upright, she leans forward, lowering her voice to a whisper. "Jaguar won't risk letting you out of his grasp. Not until he knows for sure what Domino wants you for. I bet he'll move out soon and bring you straight to his compound."

"The *Guarida*?" I ask.

If she's surprised by my use of the word, her scoff disguises it. Then she laughs. "That place is paradise in comparison. No, Ada. He's taking you *home*."

A feeling like falling washes over me. I can taste my own fear, welling on my tongue like fresh blood—then I realize it is blood. I've bitten my tongue hard enough to bleed.

"Why?"

Her eyes blaze, as if my perceived ignorance is an insult. "Don't be stupid. He won't let Domino take you anywhere. Not until he knows what he wants you for."

"Domino wants me to settle a score," I say. "Nothing more."

"Oh, bullshit! And you really believed that? God, you were always so goddamn gullible, Ada. This is about far more than revenge. I'm sure you could guess that by now. Though it's not like you could go far with that shit around your neck."

Weighing my options, I decide to play into the narrative. "So tell me what I don't know?"

She stands, coming toe-to-toe with me. Her beauty is as incredible as ever head-on—but undeniably frayed. Her makeup is smeared in places, her breath sweet with the faint hint of alcohol.

"Wake up, Ada. The world doesn't revolve around you. This is all much, much bigger than your surgically enhanced ass. God, I don't even know what would be better. Crushing your fragile worldview by telling you the truth? Or letting you find out the hard way."

Her smile is mean, her lips peeled back from her teeth—but in her eyes lurks an unstable, wild expression I recognize instantly. Fear.

"You can't tell me," I say, taking a shot in the dark. "Can you?"

Bullseye. She flinches, her lips pursed. "You always were too fucking dumb for your own good, pretending to be so sweet and innocent while your father ruined lives. No wonder Pia couldn't stand you."

I wince. I should have expected this line of attack—but that doesn't make the jab sting any less.

"I don't remember you being that close to her, either—"

"Closer than *you* were. You see, we both came from families that valued hard work. We didn't have the benefit of spending our daddies' money with no damn clue as to where it came from." Her confidence repaired, Alexi steps up to me, inclining her head. "She hated you. Little Ada-Maria with more money than brains, too fucking dumb to see that her daddy was a murderer."

"And yet, you always seemed to want my leftovers," I bite back.

"You make it sound like it was hard," she says, raising an eyebrow. "The truth is, Ada, the only reason men like Tristan gave a damn about you in the first place was because of your father. They wanted him, not you. Though hell, at least Roy Pavalos took pride in gloating over the lives he ruined. Did you even know, or are you still playing naïve after all this time?"

"Know what?" I say, genuinely confused.

"You would think the fact we were friends would have made a difference to him," she says coldly. "But it didn't. When he needed my father out of his way politically, he made sure he was ruined for life. That we *all* were. There wasn't even a penny left for me to inherit. Did you even notice? Or were you too busy trying to cover your ass after Pia went missing?"

I couldn't hide my surprise if I wanted to. I didn't know. From what I remember, Alexi's father was a prominent businessman who dabbled in politics, but a bad investment deal became public and ruined his prospects. I never even considered that my father might have been behind it.

In hindsight, I should have.

"I…" Words fail me, though I doubt she'd accept an apology. Something else she hinted at worms into the forefront of my mind, and I latch onto it like a shield against guilt. "What do you know about what happened to Pia?"

"As if you don't know," she spits back.

"It isn't often that you know something I don't," I say coldly. "Why not test your luck?"

Her eyes cut to slits. "You really think Domino gives a damn about you? Think again. In fact, you being here just proves it. The bastard must have been planning to ditch you all this time. Now it all makes sense…"

Her harsh laugh slips beneath my skin, irritating prickling insecurities. I can't resist playing right into her trap.

"What do you mean?"

She places her hands on her slender hips, and I find that the beautiful manicure she sported at Domino's estate is now chipping and cracked. "I mean, Domino told me all about his plans for you. I just didn't realize that he was serious."

Ice water—that's what this sensation is comparable to. Cold, grim fear drips over me in waves, each one more disarming than the last.

"What plans?" I demand.

Her smile tilts into a cruel grimace. "To leave you behind to rot."

Without another word, she saunters past me, slamming the door in her wake.

Chasing her down would be the smart thing to do. Demanding answers—dragging them out of her if I have to. By the time I can form a coherent thought again, I'm leaning against the wall, running over every damn detail of the past few days. Who honestly knows what Domino's true intentions have been at any given moment?

He lies with such chilling ease I can't even blame myself for falling for part of it. I believed him when he claimed he needed me to find Pia, at least. Though he hinted that wasn't the case either.

There isn't time to cry and dwell in despair.

The strange part is…

Despite how my eyes burn, no tears ever fall.

CHAPTER SIXTEEN

Alexi doesn't return after several minutes. By then, I've snapped out of my pity party. Fuck her. A few days ago, I might have played into her little mind game—not now. I don't need her help to find a way out of this. I just need to think.

Cautiously, I stand, taking in the room more carefully than before. It's small and narrow, with no other exit, and no window to peer from. Before I can fully weigh the risks, I creep to the door. It isn't locked, and the corridor beyond is empty, though voices and echoing footsteps betray a hive of activity.

Jaguar claimed this was a "new acquisition," apparently not the *Guarida* Domino threatened me with. Another club? Either way, there has to be an exit.

Cautiously, I reenter the hall, shivering as my bare feet contact the floor. The next room down isn't empty. Two women lounge on a pair of rickety cots. Their eyes rake over me before darting away, but they don't call out.

So, I keep walking, nearing the archway separating this section from the larger space Jaguar dominated. A glance through it reveals that the "showroom" is empty now, but that ominous tension feels heavier than ever. It doesn't help that Alexi's taunt keeps replaying in my mind. *The bastard must have been planning to ditch you all this time…*

I fight to ignore the pain of betrayal. All that matters now is finding a way out. With a glance over my shoulder, I inch forward, my eyes glued to the door beyond the stage. It's unguarded, but the second I take another step, someone grabs my forearm from behind.

"You idiot," that same person hisses against my ear. The soft cadence diminishes some of the fear washing over me—it's not Jaguar. "Risk your life if you want to but act reckless, and everyone will suffer. Then again, you never gave a fuck about anyone but yourself, did you?"

I spin to face Alexi, her eyes slits. "Go be a good girl and wait your turn—" she jerks her chin toward the room she first led me to.

"Don't touch me." I shrug her off, turning back to the door. "Like hell will I listen to you—"

"Fine. Then what about him? Domino left a message for you. Did I forget to mention that?" she taunts in a whisper. Could she be lying?

Possibly.

And yet, she smirks as I whip around to face her. "Even though he's probably back in Terra by now, I'm sure you're pathetic enough to want to hear it."

It hurts to acknowledge the fleeting desire. Shame forms a knot in my chest, making it harder to breathe.

"Good," Alexi hisses. "So, turn around, go back, and *wait*."

Open hatred is written all over her face, but something in her eyes makes me hesitate. That fear I caught a glimpse of is back—just ten times more obvious. A heartbeat later, it's gone, squashed behind a cold glare.

In the end, I don't know what finally makes me retreat. It isn't that I believe her. Maybe it's the gnawing acceptance that waltzing from the front door most likely won't be the way to leave this place.

When I return to the room, I sit on the nearest cot, facing the door. Unease is a blanket, threatening to suffocate me, but Alexi, for all her bravado, doesn't appear.

It wouldn't be the first time she ever failed to follow through. In school, bailing was practically her MO. I think it's one of the reasons Pia was so drawn to me in the first place—as a backup for shallow friends like Alexi who couldn't be counted upon to remain enamored of her twenty-four-seven.

For the first time, I regret that my captivity isn't more thrilling—no whips and chains to distract me. It's too quiet here. My thoughts run rampant, taunting me with a million different realities at once.

The first is Jaguar's cruel insinuation. Domino never intended to keep me safe. From the start, I was only ever a bargaining chip, used at his discretion—but I can't get his words out of my head. Or how he said them…

A man shouldn't look to the one woman he claims to love as a symbol of everything he hates…

But even his betrayal takes the back seat to a growing horror.

Pia. My own mother insinuated I might have something to do with her death. Did I?

God, I can't remember. Nausea constricts my throat, threatening to bring up what little remains in my stomach —but my gagging is a reminder of the discomfort I've ignored up until now. I'm starving, but that gnawing, persistent hunger isn't the comforting friend I've relied on all these years. It merely reinforces how many ways there are to truly suffer. Another method of torture Jaguar can employ.

I can't stay here.

Lurching to my feet, I head for the doorway. I've barely taken a step when a figure strides from the shadows, her hands on her slender hips. "You really don't know how to fucking listen, do you?" Alexi hisses. "No wonder Domino got bored. And Tristan, too, while we're on the subject."

Her cool smile gives no indicator of even a hint of grief.

"You seem heartbroken by the fact that he's dead," I snarl.

"Why would I be?" She waltzes past me, reclaiming her sprawled position on the couch. "Don't tell me you are? Funny, because I don't think Domino would keep this little secret—Tristan was planning to sell you out from day one. Though I doubt that would turn you off. It seems like you have a thing for men who don't give a shit about you."

I shouldn't be so surprised that she knows. After all, Domino named her as his coconspirator, helping him keep tabs on Tristan's whereabouts and motives.

"Apparently, you knew them both better than I did. Fine. But… You said Domino left a message for me?" My voice breaks, and I hate myself.

But Alexi doesn't seem pleased by my curiosity. "Domino must have a thing for damsels in distress, though I shouldn't be so surprised he fell under the spell of Ada Pavalos, like so many other fools."

"I guess that's why he entertained you, then," I snap.

She nods. "We don't all have rich, powerful daddies to clean up our messes and pay for our bad little habits." Her gaze turns distant. "Some of us have no choice but to make a deal with the devil."

Domino or Jaguar in this instance? She doesn't elaborate.

With an exaggerated sigh, she stretches her arms and rises to her feet. "I suggest you stay here," she warns on her way into the hall. "Jaguar doesn't take kindly to disobedience, and don't be fooled by the others. They'll sell your ass out in a heartbeat."

"Wait!" I start after her, seething with irritation. "What did he say?"

I nearly run into her as she stops short. "Apparently, he thinks you're a pathetic bitch who would be better off overdosing than letting Jaguar have you. I think I'm of a different mind, though. I hope you suffer."

She skips off, swaying her hips, but I've lost the urge to follow her. Instead, I sink back onto one of the cots, kicking myself for trusting her in the first place.

Seconds pass, but she doesn't return to gloat. In her absence, the noises of the others nearby take over again. Coughing. Whispering. Crying? The various sounds create a deafening murmur—until a sudden commotion shatters the hush.

"Girls!" a man shouts, but his voice isn't deep enough to be Jaguar. "Everyone out now. Line up! We need to clear out. Now!"

I rise to my feet and peer into the hall. At least ten other girls swarm from various directions, all heading toward the showroom. I join them without thinking, finding myself in the middle of the pack, being herded past the stage, through the door the other man came from.

My pathetic escape plan is revealed for the folly it was the second I cross the threshold. This isn't an exit, at least not outright. Instead, we're led into a small, bare room lit only by a single overhead light.

"You keep your mouths shut," a man demands, guarding a pair of metal doors. "Get into the truck."

He shoves open one of the doors, allowing in a rush of fresh air. I inhale it greedily, sensing the same dryness as the desert Domino and I traversed. So, Alexi was right—we aren't near Terra.

"Head out," the man commands.

One by one, the women hurry past him, onto what looks like a parking lot. Beneath their frantic breathing and the man's shouts, lurks the hum of what could be a truck engine. We're being moved, and dread suffocates me. What did Alexi say? *He's taking you home…*

"Hey!" Someone rams into me from behind, jarring my shoulder. "Get out of my way!"

The voice is Alexi's, and I assume her nails are what I feel digging into my forearm next. I recoil instinctively, only to feel something press against my palm, small and firm. The shape is too familiar to mistake.

"This is for *Domino*—not you," she snarls against my ear before what feels like a bony hand slams into my lower back. "He said you'd know when," she adds before raising her voice to loudly snap, "I said move!"

Head held high, she waltzes past the man and through the doors.

"Hurry up!" Impatient, the man practically shoves the woman ahead of me forward. When his eyes fall over my face, however, he raises his hand. "Not you. You stay with me."

He pulls me aside, and I panic, clenching the object in my grasp. This dress has no pockets. The only space I can think of to hide the syringe is beneath the edge of the brace, against the swollen palm of my right hand. Thank God. It's thin enough to fit, but even the slightest pressure against my wrist is excruciating. White spots speckle my vision as my pulse hammers through my eardrums. Desperate, I suck in air, fighting to breathe.

Focus, Ada! I blink until my vision clears. From this angle, I have a clearer view of the outside. A parking lot was a correct guess, but a narrow one, squeezed behind another brick building. Yellow headlights paint the asphalt, illuminating a slight sheen of rain.

"Next!"

The final three women scurry out, heading left, hugging this building, presumably to be loaded into the back of the truck.

Once they're out of sight, the man takes my arm. "Come with me."

He steers me through the doorway, and the rain is as bracing as a slap, the air heavy with tension. I can practically taste the unease emanating from those nearby. Even Jaguar?

I don't have to assume for long.

As my vision adjusts, I hear his voice first, rough and grated. "She rides with me."

Blinking, I make out a large truck, its headlights blinding, but the man doesn't pull me in that direction. Instead, we head past it, where a van waits. It's black and sleek, resembling one of the luxury vehicles paraded by rich politicians through the heart of Terra Rodea.

The door to the back seat is already open, and the man shoves me toward it. "Get in."

I scramble onto the leather as my spine stiffens with awareness of the predator nearby. His scent fills the space along with the spicy tinge of smoke. A cigarette? I look up to find him watching me, seated on a leather seat before a tinted-glass barrier. Presumably, the driver is behind it, responsible for the van lurching into motion. Overall, the interior has been custom designed, outfitted with leather seating on either end and a minibar placed in between.

"You and I need to finish our little chat," Jaguar says. In one hand, he sports a lit cigar, the burning embers igniting his gaze. "Have you decided yet?"

The rain patters off the windows, adding a chilling backdrop to his question.

"I..."

For whatever reason, something Alexi said comes back to me. *You were always so goddamn gullible.*

That might not be a bad thing? It just means the curiosity in my voice is genuine as I ask, "Who do you think I should pick?"

His eyes narrow, and I nearly choke—before I realize that his expression doesn't contain the volatile anger I'm used to. He's thoughtful. I can only pray that sentiment lasts.

"Your father is a bad man, baby," he says, tilting his head back against the headrest. "But Domino? He's dangerous. Roy Pavalos, from what I've seen, follows a creed. He has loyalty, if only for himself—" he chuckles, and I feel my cheeks flame, as though I'm the butt of his unspoken joke. "He has some honor, more than our little friend Dom, anyway. *That* bastard? He has no loyalty."

The sick part is that I can agree with him in that sense. Domino seems to pledge allegiance only to himself.

But I can't forget what he said to me in the shower. *Even at my own fucking detriment, I can't seem to stop trying to save you...*

"I'm sure you've realized that," Jaguar says, intruding upon the memory. "While you've been here, safe under my care, do you want to know where that bastard has been?" A deep laugh resonates in his chest. "He's at the border, attempting to cross as we speak. So much for his gallant hero streak."

He puffs on his cigar, igniting the end a deeper red. The glow reflects off his irises, mimicking flames.

"Do you even know why he wanted you in the first place? Politics. Our Dom is a very smart lad. He likes to play it safe, and for him to blow his cover as a Pavalos lackey, you must be very special to him. Do you know why?"

Danger. My spine tightens as I sense the double meaning behind his words—suspicion.

"I…"

"No!" He snaps his fingers, sitting forward. "Speak clearly. Do you know what he wanted you for?"

"He hates my father," I croak. "He wanted to hurt me, I guess."

"Hurt you…" Apparently satisfied by that answer, Jaguar sits back, stroking his chin with one hand while the other taps his cigar into an ashtray balanced on top of the bar. "And he did, didn't he? The bastard. I will only treat you how you deserve to be treated. Do you understand that?"

"Y-Yes," I say quickly.

"Good." His smile widens, his teeth glimmering in the dark. "Dom would never give you that kind of assurance. Promises mean nothing to him. Neither does upholding his word. *Loyalty.*"

This time he gives the word a noticeable emphasis. The same way my mother might refer to her prayers and the religious figure they centered around. With utmost reverence.

"He made my family a promise once…" He turns his gaze to the window, scowling at the darkened landscape. I copy him, unable to make out anything definitive. It's pitch black. This road, however, is bumpy, jostling the van almost constantly.

Every movement jars my arm, forcing me to grit my teeth against the pain. Sweat drips down my neck, and I'm sure he'll notice I'm hiding something. Though hell, maybe I should use it now? Domino's "gift" could serve as more than a mocking joke.

It's the only chance I have to escape. Even as the plan unfurls, doubt undercuts any hope I feel. I'm not stupid enough to believe that I could catch Jaguar unguarded. Unless…

"A promise to honor the Domingas name," Jaguar continues. "To remain by my side, family in every way but blood. We gave that motherfucker everything we had to offer. And do you know what he did?" He extends his empty hand, curling the fingers over his palm one by one. "He fucking spit in my face."

His anger is chilling, resonating in my bones.

"I could have killed the bastard a million times over. Do you want to know something? I've offered him chance after chance to make things right. But for you… I'll make an exception. You ask for his head, I'll bring it to you. After I exact an apology from him, of course. Just say the word."

Fighting to keep my face blank, I think back to his twisted "offer." Of course, it was never a real choice at all.

And it should be an easy concession to make. Tell him I want Domino dead and keep myself alive for a while longer.

But with Jaguar, I suspect that nothing is just talk. Every word matters to him. Even a death threat wouldn't be uttered without a consequence to pay down the road.

"So what will it be?" he demands, flicking his cigar again. "I've been patient, but I'd like an answer. Now."

I drag my tongue across my dry lips. "I—"

"Come here." He crooks a finger, and every ounce of air leaves my lungs.

Shit. Even now, I can catch the glint of something peeking beneath the edge of my brace. I can't risk him seeing it as well.

"Ada-Maria." His tone takes on that lethal edge, and I have no choice but to jump out of my seat. By chance, my gaze happens to fall across the mini bar, and I angle myself toward it, keeping my right arm close to my chest.

"I… A toast?" I don't even know what exactly I'm asking for. Maybe I should take Domino's advice literally? For all I know, this could be a lethal dose.

One last high before the inevitable.

"A toast," Jaguar echoes in a tone that makes my entire body go cold. I force myself to keep breathing as the seconds tick by. Finally, he sighs.

"To your decision, I presume?" His laugh raises goosebumps, but I find a small shred of relief in the absence of that volatile anger. For now.

"Yes." I drop to my knees before he can change his mind, forced to stabilize my injured hand against the floor of the van.

As I reach for the bar, Jaguar chuckles again. "Make mine a whiskey."

"Okay." Shaken, I tug on a glossy handle, revealing a mini fridge, complete with multiple selections of liquor. Beside it, is a small cabinet containing an array of shot glasses.

Suddenly, the vehicle jolts, throwing me against the cabinet. I grit my teeth, using the momentum to angle myself away from Jaguar's gaze. At the same time, I wrestle the syringe free and tuck it against a corner of the fridge, out of his sight.

At a glance, I can tell it's full, the amber liquid impossible to identify. I'm reminded of the night I tried drugging Domino—and failed. Perhaps this time, I should take whatever it is myself, and hopefully pass out before Jaguar could make me answer a damn thing. Some pathetic part of me craves that easy exit.

"Is there a problem?" Jaguar asks.

"N-No." I grab the first bottle of whiskey I spy and attempt to open it one-handed, all while using my body to shield any glimpse he might have of the fridge's interior.

"Here—" A shadow comes for me out of the corner of my eye. I barely choke down a scream as I recognize it—his hand.

He easily wrenches off the lid before grabbing the base of the bottle from me. Holding my gaze, he jerks his chin toward the cabinet.

"A glass, baby."

I snatch one—belatedly realizing that the syringe is still in the fridge. If I move even an inch, he'll see it.

Impatient, Jaguar clears his throat. "You need a bit of *home training*, don't you?"

My belly quivers at the malicious emphasis he puts on those two words. I recall how Domino utilized his whip, and I suspect this man has a similar method of "training" in mind.

"H-Here." I nearly drop the cup in my rush to raise it—straining my arm as far as I can—and he delivers a generous shot, seemingly none the wiser.

"Now yours," he prompts.

I set the full shot on a tray built into the top of the cabinet. Shit. There isn't a feasible way I can think of to spike one drink, let alone his.

"I have to wonder if you're stalling," Jaguar says with another coarse laugh. He reaches for me again, raking his thick fingers through my hair. "Hurry up."

I jump into motion, grabbing a fresh glass, but I don't hold it out to him.

"I-I can pour this one," I say, forcing myself to meet his gaze.

He smiles, but I can't read his intentions as he sits forward, offering the bottle to me.

I set the shot on the bottom shelf of the fridge and grab the syringe, sticking it into the cup while praying my body shields the sight. When I reach for the bottle, Jaguar's face is expressionless.

By the grace of God or sheer luck, the van jolts again, throwing me forward a second time.

"God damn!" Jaguar shouts.

He turns his focus on the driver, and I balance the bottle between my knees, grab the syringe, and rip the cap off with my teeth. My fingers shake as I empty the contents into the glass. Just as I sense Jaguar turn back to me, I knock the syringe out of view and pour a generous serving of whisky.

"It's about damn time," he snaps as I add the fresh shot to the tray.

Then I return the bottle to the fridge, knocking the empty syringe further back.

"Good girl." Jaguar's slow smile returns, unfurling over his lips as I shift toward him.

"To Domino," he murmurs, grabbing a drink from the tray.

My heart sinks, and I scramble to disguise my disappointment. Only God knows which one he took.

Looking at the remaining shot, I can't tell if it's tainted or not.

And it's not like I can refuse.

Slowly, I take the glass, bringing it to my mouth.

Jaguar eyes me expectantly, and it's a frantic heartbeat before I realize what he wants.

"To Domino," I croak.

He throws his head back, downing the whiskey in one go. I follow him, only to sputter as the burning liquid sears a path down my throat.

"Damn," he hisses. "That's some good shit."

He slams his glass down onto the bar and sits back, threading his fingers together behind his head. "Now, where were we? Oh, I remember…"

From this angle, his tattoo seems alive, twitching in motion, ready to pounce.

"I'll be honest, it doesn't matter who you pick," he adds, inclining his head thoughtfully. "I just want to hear it from your sweet mouth. I don't think you realize just how special you are. Daughter of Roy Pavalos. Toy of Domino Valenciaga. Our little Dom-Dom rarely pledges his loyalty to anything, but he sure seemed determined to hold onto you."

I can hardly keep up with what he's saying—I'm too busy tuning into every inch of my body, waiting to sense the telltale signs of an impending high. My head feels light, my breathing unsteady. Though hell, it could be due to a drug, or a mere result of being so close to a man like this.

Even his smile seems sinister. "I didn't think anything could distract the bastard from his vendetta. Five years of his life thrown down the drain. And he hasn't even told you why?"

But I know why—because my mother roped him into her own personal war.

It's dangerous to play with him. Dangerous to risk asking him a damn thing.

Still…

"You can tell me," I rasp, steeling myself for violence in return.

Instead, he laughs. "Domino has his own damn ambitions. Don't be fooled by his rodeo cowboy act. He's no better than I am. He stood by your father's side for five years. That's plenty of time to pick up a few things. From the very beginning, the bastard has had his eyes on the top. Me? I don't pretend to be anything other than what I am." He removes his hands from behind his head, extending them on either side of me as if the calloused skin is proof of his words. "I want Domino to return to the fold like a good boy. If not…"

He frowns, his brows wrinkling. The expression casts him in a different light for a split second. Just as quickly, he recovers, wrestling his lips into a shadow of that sly grin.

"We'll see just how badly he wants you." He swipes his thumb along my jawline, lifting my chin for appraisal. "And how far he'll be willing to go—"

Alarm dances up my spine before I even realize why. Then I feel the subtle jolt rocking the vehicle—we've stopped.

"What the hell?" Jaguar reaches back, rapping his fingers on the glass partition. "Why the fuck have we stopped? Andre?"

No reply comes from the other end.

Hissing, Jaguar reaches for a control panel but misses. Only to swipe and miss again. "The hell?"

He shoves me away from him, and I go flying, knocking my shoulder off the paneled wood siding. Panting, I look back to find him sitting upright.

Or trying to. His hands grip the edge of the seat, the knuckles stark white. Suddenly, he slumps forward to his knees.

"Jaguar?" Paralyzed by uncertainty, I don't move, even as he pitches over onto his side. It could be a trick. Hell, is it even possible for a drug to work this fast? Still, when he doesn't so much as twitch, I inch forward, tapping his shoulder. "Jaguar?"

He groans, his head lolling. A pinch of hope grips my chest —but then I see his eyes.

Both remain alert, glowing with rage. I go still, tensing for the moment he'll recompose himself. When the seconds tick by, I risk reaching toward his hip, finding his pocket.

I swallow as I feel through the thick material. The collar suddenly feels heavier, threatening to cut off my breathing with every ragged inhale I manage to drag into my lungs. Then…

I spread out my fingers as far as I can, and despair washes over me. It's empty. Desperate, I lunge for the other, grunting as I struggle with his weight. At the same time, I keep glancing at the partition, expecting it to lower at any minute. By now, the driver must realize something isn't right.

When my fingers strike a cool, metallic object, all thoughts of caution leave my mind. I rip the remote loose and shove it into what little space there is in the brace. It hurts like hell, but I ignore it, focusing on the interior of the vehicle instead. As the adrenaline wears off, a frantic sense of impatience replaces it.

Now what?

The van hasn't moved despite the hum of the still-running engine. For all I know, we could be surrounded by his men.

Even so, I don't think I'll get a better chance than now. Teeth gritted in determination, I reach for the nearest door.

I've not even touched the handle when it's suddenly opened from the outside. The second I inhale, my pulse surges, my chest so tight I can't even breathe fully—but even while suffocating, I'd recognize this scent anywhere.

This man anywhere.

It feels as though the universe slows to a crawl as I turn my head, catching only a glimpse of the figure lurking beyond, his hand outstretched.

One word from him, jolts me back to awareness like an electric shock. "Run!"

Everything is a blur of frantic movement and impenetrable darkness. By the time I regain my bearings, I'm panting, dripping wet, lying on the earth as a stronger force keeps me steady. Jaguar's van is a distant shadow, edged by blood-red taillights. Somehow, I've been transported outside it—but the how isn't a mystery for long. Presumably, it has everything to do with the heavy body pinning me flat.

Maybe I'm dreaming, but never in a million years could I envision this smell so perfectly.

Or this voice.

"Don't move. Not until I tell you to." The guttural baritone triggers a wave of conflicting emotions. Relief? Dread? Fear?

It feels like ages before he finally lessens the pressure, hauling me to my feet. "We need to run. Keep your head down."

I crane my neck instead, fighting to see his face. "How did you—"

"Come on!"

It's raining heavier than before, turning the earth into sludge. Through the chaos, I can still make out the ruby glow of the van's taillights. It's unmoving, the back seat door thrown open…

But Jaguar never appears.

"This way." Domino steers me in the opposite direction, deeper into the darkness. Soon, I can't see the road anymore. Just a turquoise sky and endless black. My only sense of where I am comes from the muddy earth at my feet and the few noises loud enough to break through the downpour.

Raised voices echo in our wake. Shouts. Then a louder, sharper blast rips through my eardrums.

"Get down!" Domino wrenches on my arm, dragging me to my knees, and his weight settles over me once more. Despite the danger, he's steely calm, his breathing steady. It seems like barely a few seconds have passed when he hauls me to my feet again.

"It isn't far," he warns. Is that concern in his voice? If so, he doesn't slow our pace any, dragging me after him. "We don't have long before Jaguar sends out the cavalry."

Blinking through the rain, I realize that we're down a ridge, where, hidden from the road, sits a hill just big enough to hide another truck behind, barely visible in the dark. It's smaller than the one he drove from Mateo's.

Domino hastens to it, wrenching open the door to the passenger's seat. Once I'm inside, he quickly claims the driver's side, starting the vehicle. As the overhead light clicks on, I'm not prepared for the man I'm faced with. If anything, he should appear stone-eyed and impassive, the way he has from the start.

Not now. He looks so…

Furious. Rage vastly different from the anger I'm used to seeing in him. He's not gloating. Hell, he's not even looking at me.

But my eyes are drawn to him, tracing the planes of that stern face. A streak of scarlet along his temple makes me stiffen.

"You're bleeding—"

"What?" He frowns, eyeing himself in the rearview mirror. Sighing, he swipes at the blood and shrugs. "It's nothing."

"I'm beginning to have a new appreciation for your planning," I croak.

He grips the wheel. "I suggest you put your seatbelt on."

I warily glance back, half expecting to see a whiz of flying bullets heading our way.

"He'll be down for a few hours, at least," Domino says, reading my mind. "But his men won't be. I'd rather put as much distance between us as possible."

"How did you know?" I still can't wrap my mind around every little variable he must have accounted for. It puts his entire scheme into a new perspective. "About Alexi, and the drug. How did you even know I would be able to poison him in time—"

"I didn't." His expression is constricted, his mouth tilted into a thoughtful grimace. His obvious confusion is the only reassurance that I didn't imagine his denial.

"What? But you gave Alexi the drug…"

He nods. "And I still had every intention of having to fight my way out of there, tooth and nail."

"Why? You thought I'd take the drug myself? Alexi hinted as much."

"Because I underestimated you," he rasps. "Again."

It's so strange to hear him admit as much out loud—let alone with genuine awe in his voice. If only the circumstances were different, and we weren't on the run for our lives. I think I'd have the energy to gloat. As it stands, all I can do is stare at him.

"One would think I'd have learned my lesson at least." His gaze darts in my direction, settling over my face with an intensity that makes my cheeks flame. Then his attention drifts downward, and his eyes cut back up to mine. I suck in my breath at the hint of relief I see in them.

"How did you get here?"

"I was right," he snarls, turning his attention back to the road. "Mateo set me up, but not how I expected—I wasn't his target, *you* were. The bastard made a deal with Jaguar to hand you over. Though, I'm guessing things didn't turn out how he planned—" he nods toward my neck. "But he left you with a fucking souvenir."

"Jaguar claimed he reprogramed it at least," I say weakly, lifting the detonator. Only God knows how I managed to hold onto it. For something so damn small, it feels incredibly heavy. "As long as I press it once a day, supposedly Mateo won't be able to set it off."

And hopefully, Jaguar didn't keep another remote for himself.

"That sounds like him," Domino says coldly. "What the hell happened back on the road. You were only out of my sight for five damn minutes."

"We were attacked. Mick and Ralph are dead."

"Shit. I knew something was off," Domino admits. "I was stupid enough to think that neither one would act before the next checkpoint. My mistake. Given that the truck hasn't blown up yet, I assume Mateo is hoping to reclaim his merchandise."

"How did you get here?" I demand. "How did you even know where I was?"

"Because I know Jaguar. There were only a handful of places he could head to. Luckily, I still have some friends in low places. One thing I don't understand, though, is that he wasn't moving you toward the border. If anything, he was bringing you deeper into his territory. It isn't like Jaguar to hide his toys."

"Alexi was there. She said he was bringing me 'home,'" I say, shuddering at the prospect.

Domino scowls, his knuckles white against the wheel.

"What's wrong?"

He risks taking his eyes off the road long enough to send a searching look my way. Then he sighs. "Rumor has it that your father is awake. Even on his deathbed, Roy Pavalos will have a plan B in mind. Jaguar must have been planning to use you as leverage to buy more time."

I'm in too much pain, and far too exhausted, to even process those words properly. I close my eyes instead, resting my forehead against the glass of the nearest window. If Domino intends to deliver any more unwelcome surprises, he holds off. Finally, I lift my head and face him again.

"Where are we going?"

His jaw remains clenched, and I recognize his trademark suspicion.

"I've trusted you this far, haven't I?" I softly point out.

His eyes narrow as if he wasn't prepared for that argument. Finally, he grates an answer through clenched teeth, "To Terra—via any means necessary. The most important thing is finding Pia's body. And," he adds, eyeing my throat. "Getting that damn thing off you."

Something in his tone reminds me of an accusation Jaguar made. *I'm sure Domino would recognize it…*

"You know who made this—or one like it at least—don't you?"

I'm holding my breath as I watch him process the question. I don't know what to expect, in all honesty. A lie?

Instead, he sighs. "Your father," he says. "He used a similar form of collar. I shouldn't have to explain in what context."

"And you copied him," I say thickly, envisioning the leather version he put on me at his estate. "Should I thank you that it wasn't explosive, at least?"

He frowns—that insult hit its mark. "A collar like that needs a specific charge to be released," he says, choosing not to address my accusation directly. "It's a small device. Your father would have one."

He doesn't explore just what that means. For now, I ignore it in favor of another pressing issue.

"So what now? We just drive through the gates and hope that Mateo doesn't detonate the truck?"

He scoffs at the suggestion. "No. Like your father, I also have a plan B."

"Which is?"

He hesitates a second time, but I don't have to prompt him to speak. "I don't think Mateo is in any position to turn down assistance with his merchandise. Not with two of his men dead. Securing his transport will ensure our way over the border—and fast. No explosions necessary."

I can't disguise my shock. "You'll still go along with his plan, after all this?"

As the seconds stretch into minutes, he doesn't reply. I could write it off as him being concerned about a pursuit, but there isn't a sign of another vehicle in sight, let alone one of Jaguar's. This must be a back road, far from the main highway leading to the border.

Which means no better time than the present to goad him into a conversation.

"You think Mateo will still even *want* your help?"

"Mateo would accept help from the Devil himself to secure his shipment. He won't have a choice," he adds, squaring his shoulders. "You should worry about what's next. We'll pass one town before we reach the border. We'll resupply there, get new clothes, and buy time to make the crossing."

"And what exactly are you shipping?"

His eyes cut to mine, narrowed in warning. "Don't ask questions you don't really want to know the answer to. When we get into Terra, you help me find Pia. Do that, and I'll keep my end of the bargain. Understood?"

"Tell me what I'm risking my life to help you smuggle, and we'll have a deal."

It's dangerous to make bargains with him. It's even more dangerous to test the limits of his patience. But hell, after tonight, I'm willing to gamble. Despite all odds, he came for me.

He hisses, gripping the wheel more tightly. I can see the gears turning in his mind. Trust me? Or keep pushing me away.

"Tell me you'll hear me out," he demands. "No fucking temper tantrums. No outburst. No whining. You listen."

"I will," I rasp. "Just tell me."

I shiver as he inclines his head my way. His smile is terrifying, tilted, and cold. "I haven't checked, but I assume the cargo holds drugs for now," he explains. "Once we reach the border town, it won't be anywhere near that tame."

My heart sinks, but I choke back my disgust. I'm done running from the truth.

"I want to hear you say it," I croak while meeting his gaze. After all, he's already hinted at what men like Jaguar and Mateo traffic in. "No more word games. No more double-talk."

"Women," he says. "Is that what you wanted to hear? Mateo wants me to smuggle a group of women, twenty at least, into Terra Rodea. From there, he can transport them throughout the country. I won't say what he plans to use them for, but I think you can figure that out on your own."

And I can.

I try to push my horror aside, fighting to get a grasp on the inner workings of his twisted world. Mateo. Jaguar. He claimed that they were all connected.

"I thought Jaguar trafficked in women."

"He does," he says carefully. "But more and more Mateo's been encroaching on his territory. A confrontation has been brewing between them both for a while. I suspect Jaguar hasn't helped things any."

"And you?" I question.

"What about me?" He inclines his head, and I realize that the shadows along his face are deeper than before—an observation that triggers a tendril of alarm down my spine.

"How did you get roped into their feud? After all, you claimed to hate my father because of his crimes, but this doesn't sound any better."

"I just want to get across the border," he insists, returning his focus to the road. "Spare me your comparisons until then."

This is one of those rare moments when I can sense more than just anger or annoyance from him. Something that prickles beyond the barriers of his apparent control, straining that nonplussed demeanor. He's uneasy.

That feeling grows more potent with every passing second. I can sense that he's not saying something. Something important.

CHAPTER EIGHTEEN

He parked Mateo's truck about an hour from where he found me. Cautiously, he takes time to inspect the sliding door to the cargo hold without ever testing the latch. Apparently satisfied that it hasn't blown up—yet—he steps back, heading for the driver's side. "Get in," he calls back to me.

I'm not so easily convinced. "And what if Mateo decides to hit his little detonator button while we're on the road?"

He shrugs and wrenches the driver's-side door open. "Then he kills me, loses the bounty on you as well as millions in merchandise. I think I'll take the risk."

I choke down my apprehension and follow him inside. Despite my doubt, we make it the first few miles without incident. Only then do I release the breath I wasn't aware I'd been holding. The further we make it without incident, the less tense I become. Soon, pockets of light pierce the darkness beyond the windshield, providing a newer worry to focus on. A town?

A small one, but I assume it's our destination because Domino veers left, venturing down a road so narrow the truck threatens to scrape the sides of either building. We travel at least three blocks before finally he turns into a gap in a barbed-wire fence, surrounding a structure made of gray cement bricks. A garage of some sort. One of the metal sliding doors is raised enough to reveal a modest workshop where two men mill about. The taller of the two has a rag dangling from his hip streaked with what looks like oil. He wipes his hands off on it, craning his neck curiously as Domino climbs from the truck.

"We're closed," he shouts in slightly accented English.

I watch Domino fearlessly circle around to my end, and I roll the window down in time to catch him say, "Change of plans. Get Mateo on the line. I need to talk to him. Now."

"The fuck?" The man's eyes narrow as he tosses his rag aside, rising to his full height. His right hand lowers to his pants pocket. From the peripheries of the property, at least three other men converge on the garage. "This ain't no office, and I certainly ain't a damn secretary."

"And if Mateo wants his merchandise over the border in time, he doesn't have a choice," Domino insists. His confidence is breathtaking, once again reinforcing just how easily he could fool not only my father, but everyone else with his bodyguard ruse. "Get him on the line."

The man's eyes cut to slits, but he jerks his chin, beckoning us inside. "It's your funeral."

"Let's go," Domino says to me.

I climb from the truck, only to feel a heavy hand land over my shoulder, providing enough stability to get my bearings.

"Stay close," he warns near my ear. This tone is different from the one he used just seconds ago, revealing a glimpse of his true unease. "If I tell you to, you run."

I don't need to be told twice. I lean into his touch, scanning the garage with every step we take. Two more men lurk in the background, carrying various boxes and items. They eye us guardedly, keeping their distance, while the man we're following leans against a counter strewn with tools. Head cocked, he inspects us, scowling. "You don't look like the usual team Mateo sends. How the fuck do I know you're not setting me up?"

"Call him," Domino commands.

The man fishes a cell phone from his pocket, dialing a number. He must put it on speaker, because I can clearly hear a gruff voice rasp from the other end, "This better be important."

"There's a bastard here who demands to speak with you—"

"I think your supply problems have doubled since the last time we spoke, Mateo," Domino says, stepping forward. "I've heard it's not polite to say, 'I told you so,' but I'll make an exception."

"You son of a bitch," Mateo growls, his voice broken by static. "Where the fuck are my men?"

"You should be worried about your merchandise," Domino counters. "I don't think Jaguar is content to let you keep your little sliver of the border after all. He'll make a move on you soon. Looks like you need a volunteer to secure your final shipment—and here I am. Lucky you."

"You think I'm that fucking stupid?" Mateo bites back.

"I don't think you have a choice. Tell your men to stand down, and I'll take your last shipment. For old time's sake."

"I should put a bullet through your skull—"

"But you haven't," Domino points out. "Tell your men to load the truck, and we'll be on our way."

Silence extends before Mateo finally barks out something in another language the man holding the phone must understand. Then the line goes dead.

"He says to let you through." The man cuts his gaze to me in a way that makes me feel stripped to the bone. "She doesn't look like the type to be in this line of work, though. If anything, she looks more like she should be on the other end of this little trip, if you know what I mean." His tone is anything but friendly, and Domino stiffens, his grip on me tightening.

"Yeah, I know what you mean. This one is for a special client."

"A client who likes his girls fucked up?" The man laughs but turns, shoving the phone into a drawer. "Though it's not my place to ask questions."

"No. It's not," Domino says. "She's not your concern. You can tell me about the other merchandise, though."

"You don't do this often, do you," the man replies, but his tone is harder. Suspicious? "No details worth knowing. You move the shipment over the border and bring it straight to the destination in Terra. No detours, and I shouldn't have to tell you that there is no peeking either. You keep your nose in your own fucking business. The truck is sealed for the crossing, so any tampering will draw attention from the agents. Though again, I shouldn't have to tell you this, should I?"

"Damn right you don't," Domino replies, releasing my arm. "But I guess you'll be wanting us to get a move on soon. What's the ETA on the loading?"

"You brought the first shipment?"

Domino nods.

"Then you leave it here, and—"

"Leo," a newer man calls from the doorway. "All clear. Everything's intact."

"Good." Leo, the man before us, sighs, though not all the suspicion leaves his gaze. "You won't be able to cross until tomorrow morning. Mateo forgot to mention that part."

"He did," Domino says, and that rare note of anger returns, disrupting the calm. "What happened to this being time sensitive?"

"It is," Leo replies. "But you happened to come at an unlucky time. The guards have changed out, and this new bastard is a stickler for a stricter, more orderly system when it comes to breaking the rules. He insists that he'll only ferry over Mateo's goods in the daytime, when you can slip in with the rest of the usual foot traffic and go unnoticed."

"So, what are we supposed to do until then?" Domino asks.

The man smiles, revealing a missing tooth near his back molars. "There's a motel up the street where you can stay, free of charge. You'll head out bright and early with the merchandise and just an hour or two until you're over on the other side. My man Marcos here will show you the way."

I can't tell what Domino thinks or if he feels the same increasing anxiety I do. Rather than argue, he nods and heads out toward the front of the garage, where Marcos stands, waiting.

"Lead the way."

He doesn't reach back for me this time, and I nearly run in my rush to catch up. By his side, I don't feel any safer. The noises of the quaint town echo loudly, seeming ten times more sinister than they had before. Every footfall, and barking dog serves to send my already heightened nerves skyrocketing. It's another harsh contrast to how sheltered my world was before. A carefully crafted cage of gilded mansions and social events. The few times I ventured beyond that beautiful illusion were in the backs of luxury vehicles parked alongside a random alleyway or back road.

But I've never been up close and personal to the grim reality that lies beyond Terra Rodea. Unsurprisingly, Domino doesn't seem as out of place here. He stands tall, cautiously surveying our surroundings. He's on edge, though it's barely noticeable. Still, I watch his hand near his pocket and wait for any outbreak of violence.

"This is it," the man leading us says, nodding toward a modest two-story building with neon lights spelling out the motel's name in glaring red font. It looks like the kind of place I wouldn't accept a one-night stand in.

"*Gracias*," Domino says as the man retreats. Then he grabs my hand, pulling me after him.

The interior turns out to be not much more appealing than the exterior. The walls are lime green, the floor a faded wood with peeling varnish. A lone woman stands behind the counter, scanning a magazine.

"One room," Domino says, flashing a wad of cash. "A tip if you can provide one with a view of the street."

With barely a glance from her magazine, the woman fishes a key from a hook on the wall behind her and tosses it to Domino. "To the left." She jerks her chin toward a nearby staircase.

Domino follows, dragging me after him and down a narrow hall.

Various noises seep through the walls—moaning, the hum of a television, and a shouted conversation between a man and a woman. In fact, judging from a giggling twosome we pass, most of these occupants seem to be couples.

When Domino finally slows near a room at the end of the hall, he unlocks the door and shoves me inside. "Wait here," he says before slamming the door—but with him on the other end.

"Wait!" By the time I wrestle the door open again, he's gone, and unease goes to war with my common sense. I've trusted him this far, haven't I?

Reluctantly, I reenter the room and lock the door behind me. Now, without the aid of adrenaline, the pain chooses to throb at full force. I spy a bathroom and enter it, grimacing as I finally face myself in the mirror above a small sink. Dried blood coats the side of my face, and the tender skin beneath promises a bruise.

Using a washcloth, I clean myself as best as I can. What I'm left with in the end, is a stranger I barely recognize, watching me with my father's gray eyes. It hits me now that Domino is right—I haven't stopped to assess what life I'd lead outside of being a Pavalos.

If I survive that long, anyway.

When I reenter the main room, Domino hasn't returned. All I can do is sit and wait, listening to the noises seeping through the thin walls. Finally, the doorknob turns, and I lurch to my feet.

"It's me," the intruder warns before slipping inside. Domino. In his arms, is a black plastic bag, the contents of which he dumps out onto the bed—a pair of women's tennis shoes, a pair of gray sweats that might fit me, and a white shirt. There are also a few energy bars and a bag of chips that I assume constitute the closest thing he could come to regarding a meal.

Rather than explain, he pushes past me, turning his attention to the room's lone window. He draws the blinds down, securing a pair of blue and yellow floral curtains over it next.

"I give it an hour, two tops," he says in that hard, grim tone I know so well. The same he uses whenever he references Jaguar or my father. "Before reinforcements come. You noticed it too, didn't you? The bastard was merely stalling. Should we make it through the night, we won't be able to step foot near that garage without being ambushed."

"How can you be so sure?" I ask.

"Because I know Mateo," he declares gruffly. "Daytime only, my ass. He moves his merchandise at night." He cranes his neck to eye an alarm clock on a nearby nightstand, conveying the time in blaring red numbers. "I bet they'll wait until after midnight. That gives us some time, at least. You should eat—" He nods to the assortment of snack foods. "From here, we can see the road and know when they'll head out. My guess is he knows better than to delay the shipment, and he'll have one of his men take the truck, while calling in backup to deal with us."

"If you knew that, why come here in the first place?" I'm floored once again by his convoluted thought process.

His amused chuckle, however, fully tips my mind into turmoil. "Because this is exactly what I counted on."

I sink onto the mattress, too exhausted to keep up with him. My feet are throbbing, my throat on fire. On top of the various aches and pains, hunger gnaws relentlessly at my belly. At random, I snatch an energy bar from the pile and devour it. Only as I set the wrapper aside do I realize what I've done.

I didn't stop to use my hunger as a weapon.

When I look up, he's watching me, dark eyes as alert as ever. I suspect he's aware of every petty thought in my head. All he does, though, is advance to grab another bar that he tosses toward me.

"Have this one too. You'll need the strength."

"I have an explosive collar around my neck, and you think eating is the most important thing right now?" I don't know if I'm joking or serious.

Either way. I'm caught off guard by the rich laugh escaping from him. It lasts only a heartbeat—just long enough to melt any doubts I might still harbor.

"Eat," he commands, his expression rigid despite the chuckle still edging his words. "Considering what I have in mind for you after we remove that damn collar, you'll be grateful you practiced swallowing."

He could have punched me, and I doubt my shock would be any less. His humor is as strange and twisted as every other aspect of him. Terrifying on the one hand. Irresistible, on the other.

Rather than counter him, I sigh, fiddling with the edge of the wrapper. I'm a coward for ignoring the obvious innuendo, but this moment feels too raw. Too delicate to risk ruining.

When I finally sneak a glance at him, he's looking away from me. "So, what do we do now?"

He returns to the window, scanning the street again. Looking over his shoulder, he smiles, and it's the most chillingly beautiful thing I've ever seen. "We wait," he says simply. He moves toward me only to snatch something from the mattress I didn't notice before—it must have come out of the same bag as the clothing.

He lifts it, and I recognize the shape—a cell phone, very basic in model compared to the previous ones I've seen him use. A burner?

He dials a number and sends me a searching glance as if debating whether or not to let me overhear. That fragile, burgeoning trust in me must win out.

He stays.

"It's me," he says gruffly into the receiver. "I'll be at the rendezvous point by daybreak for the handoff. Remember our agreement—no questions."

He hangs up and powers off the phone completely before removing the battery. Both he tosses into a wastebasket in the corner of the room.

"Are you going to tell me who that was?" I ask, not expecting an answer.

He surprises me with words rather than tense silence. "Soon. For now, get some sleep. You'll need it."

He stalks past the bed, returning to the window. Peeling up a sliver of the curtain, he peeks beyond, scouring for any hint of movement.

"I need you to tell me more," I say.

He inclines his head curiously, but doesn't even glance my way. "Do you think so?"

"Yes. *Please.*"

I can't see how he processes the plea initially. His back remains rigid, his gaze on the window. Suddenly, he lets the curtain fall from his grasp. Then he turns to face me, but I'm unprepared for the intensity of his expression. It's steely and impassive, like stone.

"You should wash up before we go," he says, jerking his chin toward the bathroom door.

"Wait," I start. "Can't we have one honest conversation—"

"Come on." Ruthlessly, he advances, herding me into the bathroom, where he strips the sodden remains of the dress Jaguar gave me. Naked, I step into the shower while he manipulates the faucet, much like he had at his bunker.

This time, he strips himself from the outset, squeezing into the narrow stall beside me. Gripping my chin, he tilts my head beneath the spray, watching me with those impassive dark eyes.

"I want you with me," he says gruffly. "Is that what you want to hear?"

"You want me to help you find Pia," I clarify, but I don't sound as sure of that as I thought I was.

"I've always wanted *you*. Ada-Maria Pavalos." He steps forward, moving slowly, his hands by his sides. One by one, he flexes them, extending the fingers before bending them so sharply the knuckles crack. "By my side. On my arm. In my bed. Whichever way I could get you. Because I knew the very first day I saw you, that you were the key to everything I desire. You once asked me what life I envision for myself. I'll tell you now. I want the life that was denied me. A beautiful woman. A beautiful home. A beautiful life."

His smile adds a cruel, mocking edge to his statement, but the hoarseness of his voice erases any doubt he isn't telling the truth. These words he means—every single one.

And I can see that, looking back. The beautiful, sprawling estate he maintained in the middle of the desert. All of the cryptic, guarded speech when it comes to me.

And right off the top of my head, I can think of several facts that prove his assertion for the lie it is.

"You have a funny way of proving your devotion to a woman you claim to…"

"Love?" he finishes—but that's too tame a word. Whatever he feels for me is something far more ominous, warped, and tainted by possession and perhaps some desire. I can't deny his lust—after all, I've experienced it firsthand. "Is that the word you were fishing for? The one you don't even know the meaning of, yet you seem to love throwing around in relation to what I couldn't possibly feel for you. Though I think we both established…" He hooks his hand loosely around the collar on my throat, forcing my chin into the air.

Defiantly, I hold his gaze, but the joke's on me. His eyes are practically on fire. The intensity takes my breath away. Literally. I'm left gasping as he flexes his grasp, tugging me against him.

"Neither of us know what love is. But if I had to describe it, I don't think it would resemble what you imagined that night, when you saw me as your savior, come to rescue Ada-Maria from herself. I'm not someone you should crave. If anything—" His breath fans my cheeks, his lips a hairsbreadth from mine. "You should fear what you do to me."

Something in his soft tone makes me bold enough to question. "And what is that?"

"You make me reckless," he declares without missing a beat. "Foolish enough to risk taking my attention from a potential target to play word games with you. You make me question everything. You always have."

"And yet, I can't seem to make you open up to me. Or tell me the truth. Or—"

"The truth is that I never intended to let you go. Though, I think you know that. You've always known it. From the day we met, you sensed what I couldn't even admit to myself until you were crouching at my feet, those beautiful eyes fixed on me. You were always mine, Ada-Maria."

Were these words uttered by any other man, I think they would come across as sweet. Some passionate, romantic confession. Voiced by Domino Valenciaga in his guttural rumble, the terse statement is anything but charming. It's a death sentence. A promised voice by a madman who truly has no intention of letting me go.

I think he enjoys watching that understanding wash over me. The same way he must enjoy running his finger along my pulse point, sensing how my heart races. Then stutters completely when I feel his lips graze mine.

The kiss is mesmerizing in its brutality. So sharp, aided by the grating scrape of his teeth. Then shockingly gentle as his tongue comes to swipe the sting away.

I'm in his arms before I know it, crushed against the wall of the stall, his heat insurmountable.

Large, his hands settle over my waist, snatching me to him. I suck in a breath, my heart racing. I've barely filled my lungs when he steps from the shower, still holding me captive.

The shift in temperature is a shock, but he seems unaffected, backing me into the bedroom.

"Should I demonstrate just what you do to me?" His voice is so guttural I don't just hear it—I *feel* it vibrating through my bones.

The promise of destruction glitters in those dark eyes as he inclines his head, taking my mouth with another kiss. The second I tilt my chin to match his savoring strokes, he pulls back, just enough to let me catch my breath. The look in his eye terrifies me. It's piercing enough to bolster every word he's said. And yet, no man could possibly claim to care for a woman, and yet look at her the way he's looking at me.

Like he only wants to devour me, body, and soul.

His lips settle over mine more firmly this time, easing them apart for his tongue to claim and devour. This should be painful with all my injuries taken into account.

But pain is merely a whisper in the face of him. His touch smothers it, his heat intoxicating enough to distract from everything else.

Even as his fingers ghost down my forearm, I'm powerless, swept away by the tide that is Domino Valenciaga. He lifts me by my waist, pivoting toward the bed. I land on the mattress face up as he looms above, flexing his fingers menacingly.

My breath catches as he crouches, cupping my calf in one hand before seizing the other. He spreads my legs slowly, moving to fill the space between them.

Images of the last time he was in this position flash through my mind. I feel my back arching in anticipation as his nails scratch along my skin.

"You are so beautiful." As he speaks, he runs his lips along my inner thigh, inching higher until…

I groan as what feels like his tongue lathes over me. This isn't like before—he's taking his time, tasting me with savoring laps.

Pleasure mounts ruthlessly, building with every groan he smothers into my skin. Every scrape of his nails on my flesh as he tightens his grip. His assault is maddening. Like a hot poker, I feel his tongue jab deep, wringing a cry from my throat.

"I want to hear you say it…" His voice echoes off the inside of my skull before I even see his lips move, repeating the request. "Tell me you trust me."

My heart lurches. I can't. After everything he's done, it's a bridge too far.

Or so I think until his teeth catch the edge of sensitive flesh and my thoughts go blank.

"Say it," he demands, verging on a growl. "You trust me."

"I…"

His fingers fan out, raking up the length of my leg to join the pressure of his tongue. I can't breathe as he eases the thick ridge of a knuckle inside me. Another. There's a daring edge to his motions—he's driving a little deeper than before, applying more pressure. More.

It's too much. My knees twitch, fighting to draw together, but his bulk prevents them from closing.

I'm at his mercy, a slave to his whims. Drawing in a ragged breath, he adds another finger, sinking both deep with a crooked motion that has me jerking over the mattress.

"Dom!" I clench my teeth over the rest of his name.

As if in punishment, he shoves those digits inside me again, grinding against my inner walls to sow friction.

"Please…"

"Say it."

He voices the words into me, churning my insides into an inferno. Even if I wanted to speak, I can't find the breath to.

Abruptly, he pulls away, letting the cool air baste the flesh he'd ravished a heartbeat ago. I barely shiver before he's on top of me, pinning me to the mattress. I can feel him, pulsing between my legs. One thrust, and he's inside me…

But only just. The tip? And yet, the fullness is damn near unbearable. Too much, and yet nowhere near enough. I never knew torture could be this cruel.

"Dom—"

He bucks his hip, sinking deeper—still only a fraction.

"Do you trust me?"

My eyelids flutter, fighting to keep him in view.

"Ada—" He thrusts again. Harder. Again. "Say it."

"I trust you." It's like he rips the words from my throat against my will, dragging out a confession I wasn't even aware of.

Yet, he still isn't satisfied. Teeth flashing, he growls, "Again."

This time, I physically push the words out. "I trust you."

He grunts, dragging his teeth across my collar bone. "More."

My mind reels. What more could he want? Then it clicks.

"I trust you, Domi—"

"No," he groans.

"Navid."

He bucks, driving himself so deep it hurts—but in the best way possible. The kind of pain only he has ever inspired within me.

A cruel, addictive agony.

CHAPTER NINETEEN

Our twisted peace doesn't last long. A sudden noise draws his notice and, within seconds, he's by the window, peering out through that sliver in the curtain. Whatever he sees makes him turn toward the bed and snatch his clothing from the floor.

"We need to leave." In a deft display of muscle, he tugs on his pants. "Get dressed."

He inclines his head toward a pile of fabric strewn over the floor—the sweatpants and shirt from earlier. I manage to pull the pants on one-handed, and Domino appears by my side to assist me with the shirt. I've barely shoved my feet into the shoes when I sense his mouth near my ear.

"We can't go out the front."

I don't know what that means. Not until he starts dragging me near the window.

It doesn't open fully—just wide enough for him to wedge his arm through the gap—apparently, that's all he needs. He jerks his wrist, and a wrenching squeal sounds from the hinges before the window flies open entirely.

Below is a loose grouping of trash cans, overflowing with rubbish and a narrow alley. From here, it's obvious that activity is happening at the garage, namely a bright yellow glow igniting the darkness. Headlights.

Domino positions himself behind me, palming my waist. I can sense his intentions even before he guides me to the windowsill. How exactly he intends for me to jump with only the use of one arm?

Apparently, by going first as an example. Lithe on his feet, he mounts the sill before I can. In a single leap, he lands hard in a crouch, one hand braced over the pavement. Just as quickly, he's upright again.

Low and gruff, his voice reaches up to me. "Jump."

I want to refuse. Then I see a flicker of movement beyond him—a flash of red light. Taillights. If there really is a truck of "merchandise" being loaded at the junkyard, it's on the move.

There isn't time to think. I just scramble onto the ledge and jump, bracing myself for the impact. The pain.

But it never comes.

He catches me with a grunt, cradling my right side against his chest to avoid jarring my shoulder. By the time I turn to see his face, he's set me down, nudging me toward the mouth of the alley.

"Let's go."

I pant, racing to keep up with him until, without warning, he stops short. "Get back."

We're near the garage now, but from a different angle, peering into the yard from behind a metal fence. In the darkness, I can see men moving about, as well as the glowing red taillights of Domino's truck.

"Stay here."

He inches closer, moving along the fence, then out of sight.

Not even a few seconds later, I hear a man cry out. Then a gunshot.

I go numb, my thoughts a frantic whirl—I can't move. Then another sound pierces the quiet. A shout, guttural and insistent. "Ada now!"

I lurch toward the sound of his voice, only to find him standing near the truck beside a man—a man whose head he has a gun against. "Get in the truck," he says to me.

I don't hesitate, scrambling into the cabin. My eyes, however, remain glued to him. He takes his gun, slamming the butt of it against the man's skull with a sickening thud. The thug goes down, and Domino rushes to claim the driver's seat.

It all barely lasted seconds, but plenty of time, apparently, for the other men at the garage to notice. A shout goes up, and someone rushes from the shadows.

"Get down," Domino warns. "Don't look up."

He must slam his foot on the gas, because the truck jerks forward, and I barely manage to lower my head before a monstrous crack echoes, so loud my eardrums throb in the aftermath. Another gunshot?

"Shit! Keep your head down!"

The vehicle swerves, so suddenly I lurch out of my seat and smack my head off the dashboard. The floor shakes beneath me as a monstrous crash resonates, followed by more shouts. I can sense the speed picking up, winding through the narrow streets.

"Mateo's crossing won't be open, after all," Domino says once I assume we're clear of the garage.

When I finally raise my head, we've gone beyond the town, tearing through the back roads of the desert.

His eyes aren't cold with defeat, but glittering with a cruel, devious gleam, I know well. "Luckily, I arranged for a contingency plan—"

"This is what you've wanted," I blurt out. It's an insane suspicion, but it only grows the more I see his face. "Whatever Mateo was transporting. You never intended to go along with him. You just wanted this…"

But judging from his past comments, whatever we're transporting in this truck isn't typical commercial merchandise.

"Do you plan to sell them to Jaguar?" I ask bluntly. Though if he is, would I even take offense to that?

Yes. The anger comes from nowhere, but I feel it more intensely than I think I've ever felt this kind of disgust. Hearing him claim my father participated in this trade was one thing. But I never saw it up close.

Not like this.

"Answer me—"

"If you even have to ask that fucking question, then you never knew me." He doesn't even take his eyes off the road, and yet I have no trouble picturing the full venom in his gaze. That cold glare.

"Fine," I say quickly, settling back into my seat. He told me that most of his "work" was a front. He always had an ulterior motive, but what could that be in this case? "You aren't planning to sell them," I say cautiously.

He's silent, still maneuvering through the open desert.

"Okay," I add warily. "So, you'll let them go? Won't Mateo's men come after us?"

"Mateo's been laying low," he replies. It isn't a direct answer either way, but his voice has lost that harsh edge. "The local authorities haven't taken too kindly to his business lately. Thanks to bribes from Jaguar, they won't do his bidding so easily, and he can't risk them finding any opening to probe deeper."

"And what about Jaguar?"

"He'll come, and soon," Domino says confidently. "I'm counting on it."

Suddenly, he brings the truck to a stop, kicking up a cloud of dust in our wake. As he climbs out, I scramble to follow.

He heads for the back, inspecting the lock on the bottom of the grate. He must take Mateo's threat seriously enough that he doesn't open the cargo hold.

But he doesn't have to.

I hear them anyway—soft, muffled cries emanating through the metal that twist my stomach into knots. A wave of emotion hits me all at once, and I turn away, gulping at the fresh air.

My father did this—or so Domino would have me believe. He facilitated this and cultivated a business that thrives on young women being brought into Terra for God knows what.

I want to deny it. God, I do.

As Domino has insinuated over and over, I know my father better than anyone. I know what he values above all, even his family. His own life.

Power, no matter the cost of maintaining it.

"What are you going to do now?" I croak, eyeing the wilderness stretching beyond. "Turn them over to Jaguar to make amends?"

"Get back in the truck—"

"No." I start walking, refusing to look back.

"We need to move. Before Jaguar's men catch our trail—"

"I won't be your accomplice." The words stick in my throat, because deep down, I know how shallow they are. I have no right to turn my nose up at any crime, after what I've done.

But maybe I've grown a new moral fiber in the time since I left Terra. I won't be a part of this. He'll have to lock me back there with the rest of his casualties of war.

"Ada-Maria." His voice sounds bitten out, a sign that he's at his limit. "Get in the truck—"

"I suggest you put me in the back, because that is the only way I'm going anywhere with you—"

"So that I can explain."

Curiosity robs my anger of its intensity. Dejected, I turn to find him watching me, but there is no smug grin to discern a lie from. Instead, his eyes meet mine coldly despite the distance, and I know in my gut that every word he'll utter next will be the truth.

"We're too close," he warns. "Don't let it fall apart now."

My throat tightens as I force down a hard swallow.

Slowly, I take a step toward him. Another—but in the same amount of time, he surges forward several, grabbing my arm to haul me back inside the front cabin.

"Speak," I demand, as he takes the wheel. "Now, or I swear to God!"

"I've arranged a meeting with another contact who can get us border access—and disable whatever bullshit bomb Mateo rigged to the back—but we need to move fast. Before Mateo realizes and sends us all sky high."

"Jaguar?" That pinching sense of unease returns, but I can't discern a single emotion from him. Not even guilt.

He remains fixated on the uneven terrain, navigating quickly. Almost too quickly. With every lurch and jerking of the wheel, my stomach dips.

If Mateo doesn't set off an explosion, Domino's driving might.

Finally, he sighs. "When we get over the border, you help me find Pia, and then you're free to go wherever the hell you want. Roy Pavalos or the moon. I only ask that you hear me out before then."

"Tell me who you're meeting with first."

"We're nearly there," he says gruffly. "You'll see for yourself. All I ask is that you trust me. Keep your head down and stay by my side. Afterward, you come with me to Terra. Can you do that? Can you promise me that?"

"I don't know," I admit, picking up on the tension wafting from him. It's different from his volatile anger when confronting Jaguar or Mateo. Whoever we're meeting is a new form of monster. "Why can't you just tell me…"

But as we crest the next ridge, the answer becomes obvious enough.

Three vans are parked in a line near what I assume to be a wall-less section of the border; their colors and insignia make their designation clear—federal agents.

"Oh my God," I croak.

Domino just drives, parking paces from them.

My heart races as he wrenches the keys from the ignition and raises his hands in a gesture of surrender.

"Remember what I said," he warns before climbing out. "Trust me."

"Keep your hands visible," one of the officers shouts.

Maybe they aren't who we're meant to meet. Could Domino's meeting have been hijacked?

But Domino approaches them fearlessly, and one of them steps forward to speak to him. The subtle familiarity betrays that they must have met before. Enough that Domino's posture, while tense, isn't anywhere near the state he enters when he's near Jaguar or Mateo.

Eventually, he nods toward the truck, and the men circle around to the back. Presumably, they work to disable whatever explosive Mateo rigged it with because, within seconds, a parade of women streams out one by one, visible in the side-view mirror.

My heart sinks at the grim confirmation. Maybe, some tiny part of me still clung to the faint hope that he might be wrong about all of it. Instead, the early morning glow illuminates the women in stark relief, undeniably real. They're pale, stick thin, each wearing a variation of plain clothing.

Kidnapped, a voice in my head whispers. They must have been taken from various locations without warning and packed into a truck like animals.

Ironically, much like how Domino stole me.

The officers approach them, seeming to take down their names while Domino slowly returns to the truck.

"We'll serve as a diversion," he explains. "They've left the tracker intact. We only need to drop it off at the checkpoint. Mateo won't realize for a while at least, that he's been set up."

He waits, but it's seconds before I understand what he's really doing—offering me the chance to refuse. Scream. Make a scene to draw notice and announce who I am.

But I don't—and not because of him. He's brought me all this way, and after everything I've been through, I deserve to see this through to the very end. The only way to find out for sure what exactly he's been after is to be there and witness the unveiling myself. I'm done being his willfully blind victim.

It's time to take my blinders off and face the reality awaiting me, no matter where it leads…

Or what I discover in the end.

"How long?" I ask instead.

Domino hides his shock expertly behind a guarded tilt of his head. "We should make it into the city around sundown. Then somehow get to the old Inglecias residence without arousing suspicion."

"And these agents will just let you prance off into the sunset?" I ask, eyeing the men warily.

"Like I said, they'll let us go. For now."

"So that is what you were doing all this time. Working for the very people trying to put my father in prison?"

He doesn't even dignify that with a response. His silence, however, speaks for itself.

"That's what you meant when you claimed that you were undermining him all along."

In reality, all those people he claimed to kill were instead ushered into protective custody.

"It's not a fairy tale, Ada-Maria," he warns. "There are no good sides in this story. Just sides. Theirs, your father's, and mine."

"You make it sound so hopeless."

He doesn't reply to that. Instead, he turns his attention to the windshield as one of the men advances, gesturing the truck forward. Rather than relieved, I feel even more uneasy.

Something has been left unsaid, and yet it lingers in the air regardless.

"I suggest you hold your questions for now," Domino advises as he takes off, down the seemingly abandoned road. "I can promise that you'll have far more by the time this is all over."

CHAPTER TWENTY

It's dark when I startle awake again—all while choking down a wave of guilt. Only a true monster, desensitized to the brutality around her, could find the capacity to sleep at a time like this.

Apart from a few minutes to utilize the bushes as a makeshift restroom, we haven't stopped. At least now, the vast landscape looks a lot more familiar. A view of rolling hills and manicured countryside sends a pang through my chest, and I sit straighter, scanning the road for a glimpse of the city.

"We're about an hour out," Domino says, explaining the absence of the skyscrapers I grew up surrounded by. "Once we enter Terra proper, I won't have a shot in hell at hiding you for longer than a day at most."

Which is as much of a warning as it is a blanket statement —*don't waste my time.*

I'm too tired to reassure him now. Instead, I watch the

world around us slowly morph into a familiar cage of concrete. The sight inspires an ache in my chest. Whether Domino realizes it or not, his secluded estate was much like a tiny piece of upscale Terra Rodea, planted in the middle of nowhere. Can he even make that connection himself?

All along, he's been building a miniature version of everything he claims to hate.

"So, what now?" I ask him.

"We need to drop this truck somewhere. I know a place. We'll get a smaller vehicle to navigate through the city in and buy more time."

"And then what?"

"Then?" He inclines his head as if he never had the question presented to him so directly before. "I finally enact my version of justice."

The promise doesn't conjure any of the warm, fuzzy feelings my father liked to inspire during his campaign speeches. In Domino Valenciaga's world, justice carries the same connotation as blood.

I WOULD HAVE THOUGHT that after weeks of captivity, I'd be relieved to return to Terra Rodea. That I would enter the city confines stronger, and with a sense of triumph over having survived my ordeal. In reality, I barely look up from the road as the rural desert gives way to crisp asphalt.

Something my mother said won't stop niggling at the back of my mind—*I want my daughter protected when Roy's lies inevitably catch up to him. He has far too many enemies. I can't protect her.*

She was afraid of more than just my father. Once Domino claims whatever information he's after, how much danger will I truly be in?

"We won't have long," Domino warns as if reading my mind. As suggested, we've left Mateo's semi in an abandoned industrial complex just outside the city, in favor of a smaller truck with a flatbed and a crew cab. "By now, Mateo must realize that the GPS location isn't where it should be. He'll attempt some attack out of revenge, I suspect—but Jaguar will be watching, if he isn't back in the city already."

"And then what?" I say, shifting my focus back to the present. "You get Pia's body, but my father is still alive, and Jaguar is angrier than ever. What do you even stand to gain?"

"Everything," he growls. That dangerous gleam ignites his gaze again, drawing a shiver from me.

"And then what?" Will he return to his estate?

His jaw clenches in that telltale way. Question time is over.

"We're almost there," he says, eyeing the road intently.

Sure enough, when I follow his line of sight beyond the windshield, I'm hit with a chilling nostalgia.

Ten years later, and somehow this sleepy neighborhood looks exactly the same now as it had then. My palms sweat as I note the small, square-shaped dwellings squeezed in beside each other. Until finally…

The brown house on the left-hand corner of this street comes into view. My throat tightens the second we pull into the driveway.

My palms are slick with sweat, my stomach in knots—but I can only imagine how Domino feels. He stares straight ahead, his expression stone. His eyes, however, are distant, gazing at something far beyond this narrow space. He's miles from me in a heartbeat, trapped somewhere I will never be able to follow.

"What do we do now?" I ask, hating myself for bothering him.

His jaw tenses as if he remembers I'm even here. Without a word, he exits the truck first, heading toward the flatbed. Unlike the one Mick and Ralph drove, this one has a covering over the bed, obscuring whatever might be on it. Like a rusted metal shovel, that Domino grabs one-handed. Where he found it, I can't even begin to guess—and I don't have the heart to ask as he approaches the house with slow, deliberate steps.

It's nearing sundown already, and the fading rays of sunlight bathe his body in a golden glow. I watch him, trying to reconcile this hulking figure with a sickly boy too weak to leave this very house. Soon though, my thoughts turn to my own sordid history with this dwelling. Being here in person is far different from pulling a potential burial spot out of nowhere. For the first time, the implications of what I've insinuated sink in—as well as the consequences if I'm wrong.

Left with no choice, I follow Domino out, skirting past the brown dwelling entirely until we reach a rusted gate barring the entrance to a minuscule backyard. In my few visits to the Inglecias house, I rarely set foot back here.

All these years later, it's surprisingly small. A lone tree guards the back of the space beside a weather-worn swing set.

"So, where should we start?" Domino asks as I draw even with him near the yard's entrance. His eyes blaze, raking over every inch of earth. "Under the flower beds? The swing set?"

"I..." My voice trails off as the folly of what I've done hits me like a punch to the chest. Seeing this place in person, it feels laughable that Domino could fit within the yard comfortably, let alone a body. "I'm sorry."

He doesn't react. Doesn't move. An irrational need to keep speaking infects me. I'm a broken record at this point, capable of repeating just one phrase. "I'm sorry."

"I couldn't protect her," he says softly. At the same time, he grips the top of the gate, wrenching it open. "She needed me, and I couldn't even lift a finger to help her. And now? I'm still failing her."

"I don't know what to do."

"Tell me what happened." He crosses over to that lone tree at the back of the property, bracing his hand against the bark. "From the start. Just the truth. That's all I want."

"I… I just know that, I never wanted to hurt her."

It feels pathetic to admit, yet it's probably the most genuine thing I've ever said to him. There's no defensive hate. No excuses. Just guilt.

"I'm sorry—"

"We came all this way," he adds gruffly, turning his focus to the ground. "Just pick somewhere to dig, and we'll see if your 'hunch' is right. We can consider that your apology."

I can't tell if he's serious or not. Still, I choke down any reservations and copy him, eyeing the damp earth at our feet.

"Take your time," he says, his tone a fraction softer. "Where should we start?"

I inhale shakily while scanning the minuscule lot. There aren't many places to hide a body in retrospect. For some reason…

I can't take my eyes off the tree.

From the corner of my eye, I see Domino follow my gaze. Without any explanation, he hefts the shovel and starts digging, grunting with the effort. After the first few chunks of soil are removed, I crouch down, assisting with my bare hands.

We work mindlessly, in an eerie tandem. That inexplicable countdown I sensed while in Jaguar's domain returns with a vengeance—only this time, I suspect only seconds remain.

Ten.

Nine.

Six.

Four.

Two…

I hear it before I feel it—a clunk as the shovel strikes something too firm to be dirt. Whatever it is feels smooth beneath my probing fingers. Cylindrical…

"Let me." Domino crouches by my side, using his larger hands to brush the stray dirt away. The sun has fully set now, leaving the newborn moonlight as the only illumination. I have to blink several times just to make out anything against the dark earth. Then…

A flash of color. Fabric? I paw at it until I'm able to discern a hue, at least. Something pink. Or at least it used to be.

Pink like the clothing Pia Inglecias used to wear.

Including the last day I ever saw her alive.

I THINK I FALL. My knees buckle, and I'm kneeling over the cool, loose earth—but an unmistakable presence shrouds me from behind.

"It's alright. Don't look."

He moves to cover the hole we dug, presumably with the very shirt he was wearing. His bare back ripples as he stands, his head bowed, shoulders tense.

I choke down a hard swallow. "Is it—"

"You've done enough," he says, helping me to my feet. "Go wait for me in the truck. I'll finish up here."

There's genuine grit in his voice. As much as it pains me to revisit these memories, I can only imagine what he feels. Hate? Relief? Grief?

I look up, faced with his rigid back, and I can't discern a single emotion other than determination. With the reverence of a man in a church, he gently kneels over the disrupted earth, running his hands over the black cotton crumpled there. His head lowers, and I feel like a voyeur, spying on a private moment I have no right to witness.

Somehow, I manage to stagger back toward the truck unassisted. When I reach for the handle, however, I lack the strength to tug on it. It's as if everything I've been through decides to hit me all at once. The pain. The exhaustion. The guilt.

I wallow in it all, and I don't even react as someone approaches me from behind. For all I know, it could be Jaguar.

But no…

I smell him before I sense him round the back of the truck. In his arms, is a wad of fabric that he sets down gingerly beneath the cover. My stomach churns as I realize what might be wrapped inside the makeshift bundle.

"Is that—"

"I didn't want it to be her." His tone alone confirms the question I didn't finish asking. "Not like this. At least… I know she's finally safe."

"What will you do now?" I ask softly.

He faces me as stray strands of dark hair obscure his eyes. The green in them is sharper than ever, glowing in the semi-darkness. "Bury her," he says simply. "Someplace far nicer than here. It's what she deserves…"

He trails off, and I swallow down a reply. Now isn't the time to prod him for more answers. He needs this silence, so I let him have it for as long as possible. The only disturbances are the quiet chirping of insects in the background and the growing wail of police sirens in the distance.

"We should move," Domino says finally, glancing at the sky. "Something's off. I don't think we've been spotted yet, but I'd rather not stick around to find out. But you know what this means." He fixes me with the full brunt of that piercing stare. "*Who* is responsible," he adds ominously.

But do I? My conflicting memories keep replaying in my mind. Even my mother hinted at who she suspected might have played a role in whatever befell Pia—and not just my father. My thoughts race as I look down and spy something else, glinting in his palm.

"My mother's ring," I say softly.

Alarmed by my recognition of it, he curls his fist around the delicate piece of jewelry before securing the door to the back. When he faces me again, his expression is thoughtful rather than defensive.

"You see a ring. In reality, this is a blood diamond, taken years ago from a mine Don Roy and Carlos Domingas used to fund. Not only is it worth a fortune—" He uncurls his fingers one by one, revealing the item resting on his palm. Years buried in the earth haven't been kind to it. Its beautiful details caked in muck, the brilliant gemstone in the center dulled with grime. "But its origin would unearth a wealth of both Domingas and Pavalos secrets should anyone with power dare to look. Julian no doubt came to the same realization."

"Why didn't my father take it back?" I ask, musing out loud.

"He probably didn't realize. It's a clever trick, to conceal a weapon right beneath your enemy's nose. I'm sure Carlos thought your mother would slip it to a reporter or political rival who could bring the scandal to light. Instead…"

"Pia got a hold of it," I say grimly. "So, this is what my mother wanted you to find?"

It feels so foolish to say. All of this trouble for a stupid ring?

"You sound disappointed." Domino holds my gaze with a seriousness I don't expect. "You'll learn that power is mostly symbolic—and fragile. In the hands of a teenage girl, this ring is just a silly trinket. If Julian, on the other hand, can reclaim it? There's no telling just how he'll use it." He eyes the ring as he speaks. It looks so minuscule on his massive palm, too tiny to ever be of significance. "Your mother thought it was worth dying to find. I'm inclined to take her word on that."

Deep down, some part of me cringes at his faith in her. It's far more than he's ever been willing to have in me.

"Now you have what you're after," I say thickly. "What next?"

"This was only part of it." He comes closer, reaching out. Slowly, he fingers a lock of my shorn hair, frowning at the colored strands. For a heartbeat, I swear I see a glimpse of the man I used to watch from the shadows. "I wanted my sister's body," he says thickly. "But now I need to know the truth." His voice is the deepest I've heard it. For once, the cadence isn't cold—it's rippling with far too many emotions to decipher. "Tell me what happened."

The truth.

"What if I hurt her?" I demand. "Could you live with knowing that? If I was the one—"

"I know *you*," he insists. "Whatever you tell me, I'll believe."

My breath catches. I'm so caught off guard by the statement that I just blurt the first thing to come to mind without worrying about the consequences.

"I pushed her." My voice breaks over the confession. It's so surreal to hear it stated out loud with no excuse to soften the blow. "I pushed her. I don't remember much after that."

Luckily, my mother filled in the blanks. According to her, I became a different person afterward. A murderer?

"What if... What if I killed her?"

I can barely look at him, but he grips my chin, forcing me to.

"I can feel a part of me trying to remember," I admit. "But being here made me realize one thing. I was angry with her. So fucking angry. I—"

"Killed her?"

His voice... It's harsh, and yet at the same time devoid of the anger I'd expect. The hate.

"Before this mess?" He gestures wordlessly with his hands as if the concept is too damn vast to ever explain. "I would have believed that in a heartbeat. But now?"

He lashes out, cupping my chin again with a harsh gentleness that makes my stomach clench. Those ruthless eyes cut down to mine, piercing through me with a single searching glance.

"I don't believe you have it in you," he tells me.

I lick my lips, mustering enough air to reply. "To kill?"

"No. To lie." He releases me, frowning up at the sky, but I'm struck dumb by that simple admission.

He believes me.

"But what if—"

He raises a hand, and I finally notice what has him on edge. A noise, growing louder by the second. It's persistent, a mechanical whirl coming from above. A helicopter? I follow his gaze and realize I'm right. At least three circle the air not far away, nearing the city's downtown.

Could they be looking for me?

"We need to go," Domino warns, ushering me inside the truck.

When he joins me, he flips on the radio, hunting through the various stations until he finds one broadcasting what sounds like a news report. *"…civilians near West and Maple are to be on red alert. Defer to any police vehicles and follow all detour instructions."*

"Shit," Domino hisses. "You know where that is, don't you?"

"The hospital?" I don't grasp the significance at first. Not until I catch him eyeing my collar in a way that churns my stomach. "My father," I rasp. "Could something have happened?"

"I don't know." Taking the wheel, he pulls into the street, navigating through the neighborhood. "But we need to get that collar off your neck, and fast."

"How?" I ease the remote from my pocket, eyeing its metallic surface. In all the chaos, I'd almost forgotten my own dilemma. Perhaps this is karma for whatever happened to Pia.

I'm destined to have my life end in a similar violent way.

"Your father would know how," Domino admits. "But I always have a plan B."

His gaze warns me not to question him—but not out of secrecy like the previous times he kept me in the dark. I sense his motives this time are purely out of mercy.

Because whatever this "plan B" is, he knows I won't like it.

Not one damn bit.

CHAPTER TWENTY-ONE

With no resources to enter the hospital undetected, no allies, and, most importantly, no time, Domino's plan must be just a desperate way to console me before we both accept the inevitable.

I'm fucked.

The weight of the collar feels insurmountable—countered only by the strength in Domino's grip as he takes my hand, still driving with the other. Watching him, I don't even think he realizes he's doing it, giving me this one small shred of reassurance.

Maybe it's pathetic to cling to him so fiercely, tracing the contours of his knuckles beneath shaking fingertips. Even so, a part of me must feed off his stability because, with every passing second, I feel less…

Insane? In the resulting clarity, I don't find much bravery, however. Just resolve.

The issue of the collar aside, I'm ready to face my father and demand the truth I'm owed. No matter where the answers may lead...

But preparing myself mentally is a whole lot different than acknowledging the reality. As it stands, we won't make it within a mile of the hospital, let alone close enough to demand a damn thing from Roy Pavalos.

Domino, of course, knows as much. This drive through the winding city streets is merely for show, nothing more. Presumably, with a manhunt on my trail, it won't be long before we're discovered anyway.

Perhaps killing time is one last mercy he's willing to give me.

Which makes me an even bigger bitch for intruding on the silence by clearing my throat. "We don't even know which hospital he's in," I point out—one logistical flaw among many. "Or which room. Which floor. And if this commotion has something to do with him—" I gesture in the direction of the helicopters, though by now, they're barely audible in the distance. "We have no way of circumventing the security—"

"I know that." Domino's voice is eerily level, displaying the unnerving confidence he had when confronting Mick and Ralph in the desert, and again with Mateo. That patient, predatory calm. "I also know we're being followed. Don't forget that Mateo's truck still has its tracker intact. If Jaguar isn't already here waiting, then the bastard isn't half as intelligent as I give him credit for."

Here being a rundown industrial complex that resembles the place we left Mateo's truck initially. Unease grips my chest as my pulse begins to surge. Paranoia gnaws at the fragile part of me willing to trust him. Within seconds, that hope is battered beyond all recognition.

"Then why are we heading *toward* it?" I croak.

His fingers twitch in my grasp, and I loosen mine in anticipation of him pulling away—instead, he bears down harder, almost to the point of pain. His eyes gleam in the glow of a passing streetlight, fiercely determined.

"I need you to trust me," he grates, but it isn't a command or harsh order. It's a plea, coated in raw earnest. "No matter what. Can you promise me that?"

Can I? I eye our clasped hands, my throat so tight it hurts to breathe. "Tell me what your plan is."

"No." He didn't even hesitate. "You'd refuse outright on principle alone. But this could work. Just put your faith in me again."

His voice is deep enough to convey passion in that request despite everything in my logical mind warning me against it. Damn. It almost sounds romantic.

Putting my life in his hands for the umpteenth time.

Romantic, or insane.

"I need you to say it," he prompts, navigating around a wide, decrepit building with broken windows. "If you can't, we'll find another way."

From his steely gaze alone, I can sense for myself that there isn't another one. Not one he believes will work. Grim anticipation heightens every single second. I can almost hear the time counting down.

Ten.

Nine.

Three.

Two…

"Yes," I whisper, recalling the way he risked taking on Jaguar's convoy alone just to find me. As much as it chills me to admit, by that point, he didn't need me anymore. Not really. "I trust you."

He parks so suddenly the vehicle jolts—and in the same instant, everything goes to hell. Chaos is the only word that comes to mind as at least two dozen men race from the shadows, swarming the vehicle before Domino can even reach for his gun.

My hand aches in the absence of his touch, but that craving takes a back seat to terror as one figure steps forward, recognizable even in the dark.

"Speak of the devil." With that grim statement, Domino rolls down the window on his end, enough for the figure's guttural words to reach us.

"You both have been very, very naughty," Jaguar growls, still advancing. I figure few would notice the slight wobble in his steps; he carries himself so well otherwise. Warily, I look from him to Domino. Both must be cut from the same indestructible cloth.

Or perhaps Jaguar has his own secret vices that help him withstand a shitload of drugs.

"I'm surprised you've come crawling to face your punishment so eagerly," he adds. "I was hoping to savor the fun of tracking you down like rabid animals—"

"We came to make a deal," Domino cuts over him. "I suggest we cut through the bullshit and hash out the terms."

I'm stunned by the lack of inflection in his voice despite the numerous guns trained in our direction. Even so, he withdraws his own weapon, keeping it below Jaguar's view.

"No deal," Jaguar says, now close enough to make out the same dark outfit he wore in the van. His hair is mussed, his overall appearance less crisp, even in the glow of the vehicle's headlights. Rather than diminish him any, the fact just reinforces the suspicion that, from the very second he regained his senses, he's been hunting us down with the same zeal as his feline namesake. "I think I'd prefer to see your brains paint my walls instead. After we have an emergency family meeting on the importance of loyalty." He raises his hand, revealing the dark glint of his own pistol. "Now get the fuck out. Both of you. Preferably on your knees."

"Oh, I think you'll want to take me up on this offer—" Domino raises his weapon, twisting his body toward me in a fluid display of muscle. "Consider it non-negotiable."

The coldness I feel against my temple a heartbeat later could just be a stray gust of wind blowing in through the window. At least, if it weren't for the cruel promise dripping into my ear next. "She's no use to me with this collar on, and supposedly Roy Pavalos is the only one with the knowledge to open it. You get her free, then you get what you're after."

Jaguar's laugh is raucous and booming, clashing harshly with the tense atmosphere.

"You aren't in any position to be making threats, Dom-Dom—"

"You're the one who needs her alive," Domino counters. "Not me. I blow her brains out; you lose the only leverage you could ever hope to have over Roy Pavalos. Don't pretend like he isn't the real reason why you're here. What better time to strike than now when the bastard is wounded?"

"Confident of you to think you could even pull that trigger before my men have you in pieces," Jaguar points out.

"They fire on me, they fire on her," Domino replies coldly. "Which is why you haven't given them the order to. She dies, and it's nothing to me. But you'll risk losing your pesky bit of leverage."

"Wrong." Jaguar shrugs. "I could blow you both to pieces and take my sweet time picking through the mess to find the ring."

"You could. If it's even here, that is. You could always torture the answer from us," Domino adds, presumably suspecting Jaguar's next threat. "But that would take time. With Roy Pavalos regaining his strength by the minute, how long do you think you'll have?"

Jaguar's face is unreadable—apart from an almost imperceptible flicker of emotion across those dark, fathomless eyes.

"So, what would you have me do, Dom-Dom? Let you skip away merrily into the sunset?"

"No. Take us to Pavalos and get him to remove the collar. Then present him with the ring your damn self. That's my trade."

Jaguar barks out another coarse laugh, but this one is devoid of any mirth. "Always with the tricks," he scolds, waggling a finger. "That doesn't sound like a very fair exchange."

"I could always kill her now," Domino suggests, and the pressure on my temple increases.

I want to believe that he wouldn't. That it's all a lie. A lie…

That the conviction in his voice is merely for show—he's *that* damn good of an actor. The doubt barely has time to sink in when I swear I see his head jerk from the corner of my eye, though his gaze remains fixed on Jaguar. A message to me?

Don't worry.

But then he adjusts his grip on the gun. "Maybe I should—"

"It's your lucky day, Dom-Dom," Jaguar says, but happiness isn't the emotion I'd ascribe to the grit in his voice. "We were already on our way to a little tea party with Don Roy as the guest of honor. He even decided to leave his hospital bed for the occasion."

I frown. My father arranged to meet with Jaguar? Considering the swarm of legal trouble he's in, I doubt he'd be allowed to leave the hospital so easily. Without explanation, Jaguar reaches for the door to the back seat, opening it before the shock of his words can even set in.

"Roy," Domino says gruffly. "You know where he is?"

"You can drive," Jaguar tells Domino while climbing into the back. "Maybe I'll change my mind on the way there. Maybe not."

"You're too shrewd to give into the reckless impulse, Julian." With apparent confidence, Domino lowers his gun from my head and reclaims the wheel. Finally, I exhale but watching him, I don't sense the same relief. The set of his shoulders remains rigid, conveying an unease he can't hide. There might as well be a real jaguar crouched on the back seat. "At least not until you get what you're after."

"Enough chatter," Jaguar declares, keeping his gun trained on the back of Domino's skull. "It's time for a tearful family reunion, hosted by Don Roy himself. He's already waiting for us at his family's estate. *Vámonos!*"

His words chill me to my core. I don't doubt this reunion will be tearful.

And terrifying.

"YOU BROUGHT HIM HERE." Domino's incredulity matches mine as I eye the gates of my family's estate, barring the road before us.

"Are you insane? I'm assuming the helicopters are your doing? You took Roy Pavalos from the hospital?"

Jaguar's grated chuckle must serve as confirmation because Domino hisses, slamming his fist against the wheel. "Fuck, Julian! You didn't stop to consider that the police would check here first?"

"They won't be looking here," Jaguar says with a chilling laugh. "At least, not now. Thanks to a friendly tip, they believe Don Roy might have been taken hostage by one of his many enemies, heading outside of Terra in the hopes of a ransom. We have a few hours at least. The men I have planted within the Pavalos guard will see to that."

His breath sears my ear, startlingly hot. I don't have to turn to see why—he's directly behind me, ensuring I hear every word.

"What, Dom-Dom? Don't tell me you thought you were the only one who managed to embed yourself within the bosom of Don Roy?"

If Domino is surprised, I can't tell. That steely calm is impossible to crack, obscuring any real emotion lurking beneath.

With a cool tilt of his head, he addresses the man behind him. "I suppose you can have them let us in, then?"

From the corner of my eye, I see Jaguar roll down the back window and extend the arm sporting his tattoo.

Not even a second later, the gates up ahead begin to part. Usually, my father keeps at least two men staffed in the station manning the entrance, and a few more around the perimeter. Despite the supposed calamity taking place downtown, that arrangement seems unchanged as Domino pulls ahead through the outskirts of the property.

God. I can't describe what it feels like to be back here again. It's more visceral than emotional, resonating like a kick to the stomach as one by one the different aspects of the Pavalos Estate flash by. The tennis courts. The manicured lawns my mother spent so much of her time cultivating.

The house, with its winding balconies and the Spanish influence my father insisted the architecture have. Viewed now, with a gun to the back of my head, it all resembles nothing more than a glamorous cage. A façade in which I've lived most of my life under the shadow of violence and lies.

Looking back, it's hard to square those memories with the dwelling I see now. My father's influence is evident everywhere, infecting the beautiful landscape in a way that transcends even the sinister aura of Domino's estate.

"Home sweet home," Jaguar singsongs as we pull up to the front of the house. "You ready to say hello to your Daddy after all your time away?"

He exits the vehicle, supposedly while keeping his gun on Domino.

When I look at the man beside me, his blank mask hasn't faded any. "Let's go." His voice offers no hint of softness either, but when he reaches for my hand, his fingers give mine a firm squeeze that I feel down to my toes. I didn't realize until now just how much I needed that sign. Craved it.

Just as quickly, he releases me to reclaim his gun before joining Jaguar outside of the truck.

Together they perform a strange, almost graceful dance of pointed weapons and fluid movement as Domino moves to my end and helps me out.

I've barely stood upright before Jaguar is already closing in. "Inside," he commands.

Domino takes my uninjured arm, and I'm herded between both up the front steps leading to the home I grew up in.

It smells the same. How strange is that? Like the faint hint of flowers, the impeccable trace of lemon-scented cleaner, and cigar smoke.

My heart races, even though I know it shouldn't be possible. I've been gone several weeks, but so has my father, according to Domino.

Still, as we mount the winding staircase, I'm flashed back to ten years ago when I did the same as a dazed teenager. God, it's so real. Realer than the scattered nightmares I've had since.

Trembling, I rounded this very corner and saw him...

It could be the shock of just being back here. Maybe it's a delusion conjured by dread. Whatever it is, more of that memory comes back to me.

I saw him. But he wasn't alone.

I don't know how I could have forgotten it. Or perhaps I just suppressed it...

Her voice. A low whimpering sound that didn't match the same fearless girl I knew.

"Did you think you could steal from me?" My father's voice was so cold, even the memory chills me to the core. "Did you think I wouldn't know it was you?"

A sound echoed, driving me onto the tips of my toes. From the hall, all I could see was his back, and a shadow flicker over the floor before a sharp crack resonated. Regardless, my cheek stung in sympathy as I recognized the sound.

A slap.

"You parade that damn ring around. Did you want her to see, was that it? You think you can threaten me? You can keep it."

Another sound came, but it was too loud. Too heavy.

Then a thud.

I don't know what drew me closer then, but when I crossed the threshold of his office, all I saw was red…

"Ada?" Domino's voice in my ear draws me back to the present.

I blink rapidly, struggling to adjust to the current reality. I'm shaking. Cold sweat drips down my neck, gluing the shirt to my skin. Ironically, I'm still lingering at the mouth of my father's office—but the vast difference between then and now is the only reason why I know I'm not hallucinating. In those days, my father stood tall, cigar in hand, his gray eyes indiscernible. Booming, his voice would reach me before I even set foot in the room.

Ada-Maria…

This time, there is no bellowed greeting. The man facing me now sits in the leather seat behind his desk, flanked by four armed men who don't seem alarmed by Jaguar's presence. They surround my father warily, their weapons poised at the ready.

To his credit, Roy Pavalos doesn't seem alarmed by the show of force—though a few glaring signs allude to whatever injury landed him in the hospital for so long. His right eye is slightly swollen, and a healing scratch mars his lip. From what Domino told me, my mother lured him into a "trap" that wound up with them both in a car accident. He must be injured enough that he can't stand.

And yet, he holds himself with every ounce of command I'm used to. With one look, I'm reduced to a fifteen-year-old girl again, and everyone else in this room fades away.

He says nothing. I don't know why I find that so strange. Silence, like violence, is only another weapon in his arsenal.

I feel it jabbing deep with every step I'm forced to take as Jaguar commands us forward. Then he stalks past us, leaning against a corner of the desk.

"Wonderful," he declares, clapping his hands. "What a beautiful, heartwarming reunion between father and daughter. Makes your fucking heart bleed, doesn't it, Dom-Dom? We'll cut to the chase, and I'll admit that I've already told Don Roy here all about your little betrayal. Though I'm sure we can let bygones be bygones. After all, Dom-Dom, you've just made my position ten times stronger by offering yourself up on a pretty little platter. Along with little Ada-Maria, here."

I barely hear him. I just watch, hating the mix of emotions that wash through me. Relief. Regret. Hope. Hope. Hope…

Domino was lying, after all. My father wouldn't do that to me. He wouldn't.

But I watch his eyes dart around the room—everywhere but at me. Domino is who he seems drawn to. Furious at.

Domino is the only one deemed worthy of his focus.

"Did you do it?" I don't know where the strength to speak even comes from. I must silence Jaguar mid-rant because I see his eyes cut to me, cold and narrowed.

Instantaneously, I sense Domino draw closer, radiating possession. His nearness alone gives me the strength to keep speaking.

"Did you tell him to kill me?"

Finally, my father shifts his attention to me, and I shudder. Shock isn't what I find in his gaze, nor alarm at the collar around my throat. No. In his eyes, I see the shadow of the girl I've always been. Worthless. Soulless. Desperate.

To him, I'm barely worth that wasted second of his time before he turns to Jaguar.

"You bother me for this?" he demands, and I flinch, shocked by how much softer his voice sounds, though still commanding. "You think to barter me down? Bring me something worth waging my life over—"

"Pia." A shiver runs through me as I hear my own voice echo. Never before would I ever interrupt my father. "Just tell me. Did you kill her?"

Or did I?

It's so damn pathetic to crave an answer from him after all this time, let alone expect one. And yet… He looks my way, and I suck in a breath.

"Interesting—" That voice isn't my father's. Jaguar instead, slinks around his desk to stand in front of him, his lips contorted into a chilling rendition of his usual grin. His eyes are ruthlessly cold, however. Merciless. "It looks like we've unearthed a bit of familial drama here," he drawls with a low chuckle. "Don't mind us. Continue—" Still smirking, he steps aside and gestures toward my father with a wave of his hand.

It's easier than it should be to ignore him. Instead, I focus on the pair of gray eyes identical to my own, blazing with every ounce of the cruel confidence I remember.

"I must have forgotten it," I say hoarsely. "But I saw you here that night. With her."

From the corner of my eye, I see Domino stiffen. Remarkably, he doesn't say a thing, though I know he's listening to every word.

"She was here, wasn't she?" My voice loses strength the longer I meet his gaze. It's as if the past ten years wash over me all at once. The fear he used to inspire in me with a single glance. The sting of his whip.

The pain of disobeying him.

My heart pounds as more sweat drips down my back. I'm swaying, rocking back and forth as my knees threaten to buckle. He doesn't have to say a single word for me to sense the danger building with every second I continue to face him like this.

But I'm not a scared teenager anymore. The memories in my head don't fade away beneath his glare—if anything, they feel more real by the second.

"You confronted her," I add, narrating the fragmented recollections as I recall them. "She had stolen the ring, and you were angry—"

"You look like hell, Ada-Maria." My father's voice rings out with all the authoritative clarity I remember. "You need rest —" He cuts his gaze to Jaguar. "Send her away."

"Oh, I don't think I will," Jaguar says, shaking his head. "In fact, it sounds like Ada-Maria here wants answers. I'm inclined to help her."

He crosses over to one of his guards and extends his hand. Obediently, the man withdraws a gun from his pocket and hands it over.

"Let's make things a little more interesting," Jaguar says, advancing toward me.

"What are you doing?" Domino pivots to block his path, but Jaguar laughs again.

"Relax." He nudges Domino aside and presents the gun to me on the flat of his palm. "I'm going to help the beautiful Ada get the answers she seeks. Don Roy speaks only one language," he tells me with mock seriousness. "Take it."

His tone leaves no room for argument. With trembling fingers, I grip the handle of the weapon one-handed. Its weight comes as a shock. It's almost too heavy for me to wield the way Jaguar and his men do, keeping their guns always trained on their targets.

I let my hand fall instead, taking care to avoid the trigger.

"Ah, that's no way to carry on a proper conversation," Jaguar scolds. "*This* is."

He aims his own gun squarely over my father's head. "I was hoping to remain civil here, but I'll try a question of my own. I would like to broaden my territory and expand into lovely Terra. To do that, I require 'cooperation' with whoever controls said territory. In this case, it happens to be you."

He lets that statement hang for a second before he chuckles. "I guess that isn't much of a question after all."

"You think this display is enough to rattle me?" my father asks. His tone is unaffected, his gaze harder than steel. "I've heard the rumors, but it seems you don't have much of your father in you after all. No balls to negotiate like a man on equal footing."

"We all know what 'negotiating' got my father," Jaguar counters, raising a dark eyebrow. "But how rude of me to interject. I cede the floor back to Ada-Maria."

He shifts his focus to me, and I swallow. The aches and pains battering my body choose now to assault me at full intensity. I hurt all over, and this childish voice in my head won't stop warning me to shut up. *Run. Hide. Don't make him angry.*

"I thought I might have done it," I say instead. "That I pushed her and hurt her. But it was you. Wasn't it?"

This time, my father's eyes narrow imperceptibly. I don't understand why at first—not until I register discomfort in my left hand. I've raised the gun without realizing it. Now the mouth of it is pointed somewhere over his chest. I flinch at the sight, but I can't seem to make myself lower the weapon.

"Just tell me. Please…" I've never begged him like this before, and yet he doesn't so much as flinch. As the seconds tick by, a demand wells within me, and I can't choke it down. "Answer me!"

"This isn't the time for your childish little tantrums," my father snaps.

There he is. This is the man I remember from that night—and nearly every day since whenever I dared to question him.

Faced with this fearsome glare, the person I used to be would have dropped her weapon and fled. Pleaded. Groveled.

I don't. "Just tell me," I croak, but despite how weak my voice sounds, I can't deny the strength in my tone that wasn't there before. "Just tell me the truth—"

"If you don't mind, let me interrupt again," Jaguar declares. He approaches my left side, ignoring Domino's warning hiss. "I'll be even more helpful. Don't forget our unfinished business, little minx," he adds.

It's a heartbeat before his meaning sinks in.

"You have a choice to make," he taunts, fingering a piece of my hair. "How convenient that both options are in this very room."

Domino or my father.

Despite his voice in my ear, I ignore him. This isn't about revenge, or hate, or even genuine curiosity. All along, I think I've known the real answer to this riddle anyway.

I just need to finally face it for myself.

"You killed her," I say, holding my father's gaze. "Why?"

He scoffs, but as it turns out, a verbal confession isn't even necessary. Written across his gaze is an answer more blatant than if he said it out loud. *What the hell do you think?*

"I want to hear you say it." I've never heard my voice this cold. Ice. My grip feels firmer, and the gun doesn't waver anymore. It feels dangerously light in my grasp, easier than ever to aim. "Why?"

"Why?" Suddenly, my father sits forward, slamming both hands onto the desk before him. "Because she thought she could get in my way. The little bitch thought she could blackmail me." His eyes slide to Jaguar before meeting mine again. "Don't make the same mistake." That command carries all the power I'm used to—but it rings hollow. In the next breath, he looks away, and I know in my soul this is all I will ever receive from him.

Silence and disdain.

Anger rises in me, more violent and twisted than anything I've ever felt. I swear, I see red, and the gun is even higher now. My wrist aches with the effort of holding it steady, but —without prompting from my brain—I can see my fingers adjust to find the trigger.

"Easy there," Jaguar interjects. His hand lands over my wrist. "I have my own loose ends to tie up," he adds, addressing my father and resuming whatever conversation they must have been in the middle of. "All I'm asking for is a few little territories—and all of Terra Rodea. A small piece of what you owe my family."

My father's lips curl back from his teeth as he spits. "You won't get shit from me."

"Oh?" Jaguar inclines his head, and a jolt of grim familiarity shoots through me. "Fair enough. I guess we don't have a deal after all. Not that it matters to me. After all, my father taught me the creed you two used to share—" He brandishes the gun with deceptive grace, finding the trigger without hesitation. "Always have a plan B."

It happens so fast I can't even cry out. All I see is the gun brandished in his hand before the sound rips through my eardrums.

"Don't look!" I'm in Domino's grasp, or so I assume, my face pressed to his chest. This time, I resist his touch and force myself to watch the scene unfolding before me.

Maybe it's the threat to my own life by way of the collar. Maybe I've already cried all the tears I had left.

Either way, even as the truth resonates through me, I don't feel a single tear fall. Instead, I find myself spinning to point the gun in my hand—only now, it isn't hard to aim it firmly over my target.

"Naughty, naughty," Jaguar murmurs. In his eyes, I don't find an ounce of fear. If anything… Excitement glimmers within their dark depths. He's enjoying this. "I shouldn't have to remind you that it's five against two, do I?"

"Don't—" The voice in my ear is grittier than I'm used to. With uncanny ease, Domino palms my wrist, easing the gun from my grasp. Rather than brandish it for himself, he tosses it onto the floor at my feet.

"Good boy," Jaguar taunts, his eyes narrowing. "Now that the pesky housekeeping is out of the way. You give me what you fucking owe, or you can join good old Roy in hell."

"The collar—" Domino spins me around, ensuring that I only see Jaguar and not the lifeless shape slumped behind my father's desk. "Then we trade."

"Dom, Dom, Dom. Always so damn bossy." Jaguar seems to play with the gun, fiddling with it idly before he finally aims it squarely over Domino's chest. "Give me the goddamn ring."

"Shoot me," Domino counters. "But then you won't have shit."

"I'll have the lovely Ada-Maria," Jaguar says with a chuckle. "And you can imagine all of the things I'll do to her before sending her soul to join yours."

"You could," Domino counters. "But not before you hear my offer."

"And what offer would that be? Another lie?"

"Take the collar off Ada, and you get the ring."

Jaguar shakes his head. "Not good enough—"

"And you get me. One favor. One chance to have me at your beck and call. That's what you've wanted from the fucking start, isn't it?"

Jaguar raises an eyebrow. "Why the hell would I believe even for a second that you would be so kind?"

"You can't take on Mateo alone," Domino counters. "Neither can you navigate the shitstorm you've just brought down on all our heads by killing Roy Pavalos in cold blood. But you put the word out that I killed him, I'll be indebted to you for protection."

"Like a good brother," Jaguar says, his smile callous. "But how can I be sure you won't change your mind?"

"You can't. But if it's between working with you or a murder charge, for now, I'll hedge my bets."

"Good old Dom," Jaguar snarls. "Always so damn honest."

He stalks forward, grabbing my chin with one hand while brandishing the gun in the other.

"Don't get impatient," he warns as Domino wavers in my peripheral vision.

I shudder as his thumb slides over the collar. I can't see what he does, but with a subtle click, the pressure relents.

"Why look at that," Jaguar says with a mocking bit of laughter. "I'll think about your little offer Dom-Dom,"

Jaguar says. "But you're right. Since *you* killed Roy Pavalos, you'll have a lot bigger problems on your ass than little old me."

"What are you playing at?" Domino demands in a coarse tone. "You're impulsive, but not stupid. You wouldn't accept using me as a patsy unless you don't have any other choice. You mentioned a plan B."

"Ah, that." Jaguar strokes his chin, smearing droplets of blood that must have splattered there. "Poor Don Roy was just a formality. There are several other promising candidates who can serve in his place as the Pavalos figurehead."

"Rodrigo," Domino says coldly. "You made a deal with him."

My uncle? I swivel my head toward him, but he remains fixated on the man across from us.

"Bingo," Jaguar says, but he isn't gloating anymore. "The bastard was tired of standing in the shadows, but aren't we all? Still, our arrangements might be a bit more amicable if he doesn't know I killed his brother directly."

"But with me serving as your so-called assassin, you get to use me as a scapegoat, but still keep Rodrigo in check."

Jaguar lifts his free hand in a mock salute. "Everybody wins, and you get to stay alive despite my better judgment. As a bonus, I think a few days on the run will give you plenty of time to reconsider stabbing me in the back again. But first… Where the fuck is the ring?"

Domino holds his gaze for a dangerous few seconds. Then slowly, he slips his hand into my pocket, withdrawing the tiny piece of jewelry. Without a word, he tosses it to Jaguar, who snatches it in his fist.

"I could kill you now," Jaguar says, drawing out the threat. "But I think I'd prefer to give you one last chance. After all, you'll be dead by sundown tomorrow without me. It seems as if you have no choice but to return to the fold, baby brother."

"You give me time to get underground," Domino reiterates. "Then I'm yours."

"Like you have a choice," Jaguar hisses. "By now, I'm sure some timid little maid has alerted the police. The bastards will be here soon, and I don't think the little game you played by ratting out Mateo will work a second time. Go."

He snaps his fingers, and Domino doesn't hesitate, snatching my wrist. His speed is impossible to keep pace with. Within seconds, we're outside, and he's shoving me into the passenger's side of the "borrowed" truck.

"What does this mean? What's happening?"

"Jaguar got his wish," Domino growls, claiming the driver's seat. "I'll return to the Domingas' fold. For now. I don't have much of a fucking choice."

"You did," I point out. "I could have shot him."

"No, you couldn't have. This is my fight. Not yours. I don't want that for you." The grit in his tone guts me. Paired with the dark, stormy look in his eye, I can see that this hurts him. It's more than just a simple setback.

This is his worst nightmare.

"And what about my uncle?" My voice comes out so soft. "Does that mean he was always working with Jaguar?"

It churns my stomach to consider it. Is anyone with the name Pavalos not scheming by nature? Even my mother seemed infected by my father's secretive nature.

"Probably." Domino stiffens as if remembering I'm even here. Then he sighs and faces forward, stoic once more. "The bastard just hedged his bets once he saw there might be an opening to claim your father's empire for himself. Either way, my original plan still stands," he continues while palming the wheel. A second later, we take off down the driveway. "Even if the timeline has been pushed back, Jaguar won't stand in my way for long. As for you… You could come with me. I'll need to regroup. Find Ines. Reclaim my territory and *our* villa."

His tone alludes to more than just an unknown future on the run.

This is a plea—one of the few he's ever voiced to me. It lurks beneath the gruff baritone, simple in essence—*come with me?* I'm so focused on his tone that it takes me a moment to notice his deliberate word choice.

"Our?"

"Yes, the villa has been in your mother's family for generations. That's why I thought you may remember it."

"Oh," I croak. It's all I can say.

Does it sting that he's revealed yet another snippet of my mother that I wasn't aware of? Yes. At the same time, it's another layer of honesty that I can't fault him for sharing. This revelation only proves there is so much I still don't know about the past. So many fucking questions that my brain hurts at the prospect of counting them all. I haven't even had the time to acknowledge my father's death, let alone decide what to do next.

But as I look into the eyes of the man beside me, I realize that I never had a choice.

From the start, I was always his, but in a way that differs from my father's brutal ownership. Domino Valenciaga doesn't require a collar to keep me close.

He never did.

From the start, I always *chose* to tether myself to him.

Even if it kills me.

~ The world continues in Blood Diamond Jaguar's first book ~

A WORD FROM THE AUTHOR

Hey there!

Thank you so much for reading! If you enjoyed the story, please leave a review and recommend the book to any friend you think would love this twisted world. You'd have my eternal gratitude. Even a short sentence goes a long way!

Then, come join the rest of us dark romance lovers in my Facebook Group where you can get snippets, sneak peeks of upcoming books and even help vote on aspects of future novels.

Come to the dark side:
https://www.facebook.com/groups/lanasbeautifulmonsters/

WANT MORE STUFF TO READ?
Join my newsletter and get a **free book**! Plus, you get to stay updated with any new releases, random giveaways and exclusive sneak peeks!
https://www.lanaskybooks.com/newsletter

Other Novels: https://lanaskybooks.com/

FREE BOOK - JOIN MY NEWSLETTER

DARK, TWISTED ROMANCE

Join my newsletter and get a **free book**! Plus, you get to stay updated with any new releases, random giveaways and exclusive sneak peeks!

https://www.lanaskybooks.com/newsletter

ABOUT THE AUTHOR

Lana Sky is a reclusive writer in the United States who spends most of her time daydreaming about complex male characters and parenting her Cockapoo Joey. She writes dark, twisted romance across several genres. Her titles include everything from mafia romance to vampires.

facebook.com/AuthorLanaSky

twitter.com/lanasky101

amazon.com/author/lanasky

pinterest.com/lanasky101

goodreads.com/lanasky

instagram.com/lanasky101

bookbub.com/authors/lana-sky

tiktok.com/@author_lana_sky